'A spectacular literary achievement' Ann Patchett

'A grand and stirring love story, written in exquisite
prose . . . [a] sheer delight!' Namwali Serpell

'Kiran Desai reveals the breadth and depth of time,
how it weighs on families and nations caught within
the drama of history. She captures this with a rare
and astute sensitivity that, no matter her subject,
casts a light on our present' Hisham Matar

'*The Loneliness of Sonia and Sunny* is both epic and intimate.
This is a story of two young people, and a story of families
and belonging. That Kiran Desai also finds a way to deftly
thread unflinching questions about the imagination and
creativity through these immersive pages is brilliant
evidence of her formidable and incomparable gifts
as a writer. What a magnificent achievement, made
all the more rare for its compulsive readability.
I could not put this book down' Maaza Mengiste

'A novel so wonderful, when I got to the last page,
I turned to the first and began again' Sandra Cisneros

'I had been dying to read a gorgeously written, sweeping
novel like this. Desai's tale – devastating, lyrical and deeply
romantic – grapples with the complexities of artistic ambition,
migration, loss, love and confronts a central question: What
does it mean to belong? How does one reach ever toward
the future when haunted by the past?' Khaled Hosseini

'A masterpiece . . . Desai's trust in her own process pays off,
as vignettes of just a page or two intersect with the novel's
central obsessions – love, family, writing, the role of the
US in the Indian imagination, the dangers faced by a
woman on her own – and come to a perfectly satisfying
close . . . magnificent' *Kirkus* (starred review)

The Loneliness of Sonia and Sunny

Kiran Desai

HAMISH HAMILTON
an imprint of
PENGUIN BOOKS

HAMISH HAMILTON

UK | USA | Canada | Ireland | Australia
India | New Zealand | South Africa

Hamish Hamilton is part of the Penguin Random House group of companies
whose addresses can be found at global.penguinrandomhouse.com.

Penguin Random House UK,
One Embassy Gardens, 8 Viaduct Gardens, London sw11 7bw

penguin.co.uk

Penguin
Random House
UK

First published in the United States of America by Hogarth, an imprint of
Random House, a division of Penguin Random House LLC 2025
First published in Great Britain by Hamish Hamilton 2025
001

Printed and bound in Great Britain by Clays Ltd, Elcograf S.p.A.

The authorized representative in the EEA is Penguin Random House Ireland,
Morrison Chambers, 32 Nassau Street, Dublin D02 YH68

A CIP catalogue record for this book is available from the British Library

HARDBACK ISBN: 978-0-241-77082-5
TRADE PAPERBACK ISBN: 978-0-241-77084-9

Penguin Random House is committed to a sustainable future
for our business, our readers and our planet. This book is made from
Forest Stewardship Council® certified paper.

In memory of my father

Family *of* Sonia Shah

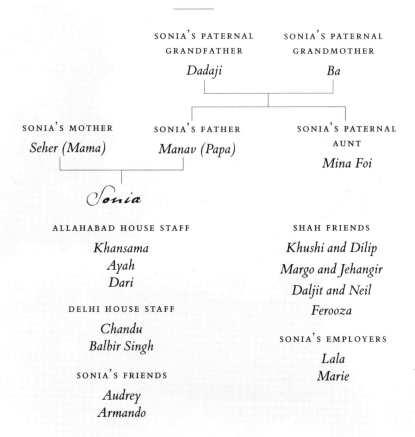

SONIA'S PATERNAL GRANDFATHER
Dadaji

SONIA'S PATERNAL GRANDMOTHER
Ba

SONIA'S MOTHER
Seher (Mama)

SONIA'S FATHER
Manav (Papa)

SONIA'S PATERNAL AUNT
Mina Foi

Sonia

ALLAHABAD HOUSE STAFF
Khansama
Ayah
Dari

DELHI HOUSE STAFF
Chandu
Balbir Singh

SONIA'S FRIENDS
Audrey
Armando

SHAH FRIENDS
Khushi and Dilip
Margo and Jehangir
Daljit and Neil
Ferooza

SONIA'S EMPLOYERS
Lala
Marie

Illan de Toorjen Foss

Family *of* Barbier

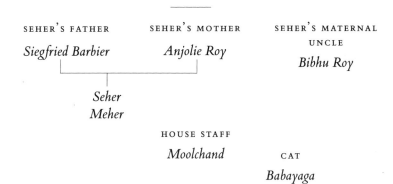

SEHER'S FATHER
Siegfried Barbier

SEHER'S MOTHER
Anjolie Roy

SEHER'S MATERNAL UNCLE
Bibhu Roy

Seher
Meher

HOUSE STAFF
Moolchand

CAT
Babayaga

Family *of* Sunny Bhatia

SUNNY'S MATERNAL GRANDFATHER	SUNNY'S MATERNAL GRANDMOTHER	SUNNY'S PATERNAL GRANDMOTHER
Nana (the Colonel)	*Nani*	*Minnie Bhatia*

SUNNY'S MOTHER   SUNNY'S FATHER

Babita   *Ratan*

SUNNY'S PATERNAL UNCLES

Rana
Ravi

Sunny

BABITA'S FRIENDS

Sara and Murad Habib

Vanya
Umberto

UNCLE RANA'S SONS

Chiki and Chika

DELHI HOUSE STAFF

Vinita and Punita
Gunja
Allahabad driver
Bahadur

SUNNY'S GIRLFRIEND

Ulla

SUNNY'S FRIENDS

Satya and Pooja

GOA HOUSE STAFF

Olinda
Naresh

DOG

Pasha

Lonely? *Lonely?*

1

....

THE SUN WAS STILL SUBMERGED IN THE WINTRY MURK OF
dawn when Ba, Dadaji, and their daughter, Mina Foi, wrapping shawls
closely about themselves, emerged upon the veranda to sip their tea
and decide, through vigorous process of elimination, their meals for
the rest of the day. Orders must be given to the cook at breakfast so
that he could go directly to market. It was Mina's fifty-fifth birthday,
the first of December in the year 1996, and the mutton for the dinner
kebabs had been marinating overnight in the kitchen.

"Rice?" Ba shouted. "Roti?" She was growing deaf, but she knew
she must raise her voice over the morning traffic thundering past the
front gate and the cawing of hundreds of crows—their racket and the
sun's struggle so closely linked, it was as if each morning the crows
gave birth to the light. "Pilau?" she suggested. "Paratha?"

Perched above them, at the entrance portico, sat a plaster bust of a
portly gentleman in a cravat, perhaps inspired by a drawing made by
the bungalow's original owner, who had toured Europe, sketchbook in
hand, in the same manner he'd observed foreigners doing in India. And
perhaps it was the fault of the artist's rendering, or the dissonant surroundings of Allahabad, or a splattering of bird droppings, but the
bust resembled less a dignified nobleman than a foolish snob with an
interest in the sky overhead, which had not turned vivid for a quarter
of a century. Not since the national highway had been widened to accommodate the lorries that trawled cabbages, cement, goats, wheat,
and—if one was to believe the newspapers or the gossip—prostitutes
and venereal disease.

Unperturbed by the fancy gentleman, or the polluting lorries, or the family upon the veranda, the crows' *kava kaw* rose to crescendo.

"Cauliflower?" Ba urged. "Spinach?"

"Potato?" Dadaji said, lifting his feet off the ground. He rubbed them together as lovingly and extravagantly as if they were soft, velvet hands. "The Gujarati loves a potato more than most," he said, as if explaining themselves to an absent anthropologist. They were a displaced family, Gujaratis marooned in the state of Uttar Pradesh. Years ago Dadaji's law practice had brought him to the Allahabad court.

Two squat phones—one in the living room corner, one on Dadaji's desk—rang out like toads in a swamp, *trr trr trr,* and they knew it would be a birthday call from Mina Foi's brother, Manav, Dadaji and Ba's second child. Dadaji picked up the phone on his desk and Mina Foi the extension in the living room. Ba never spoke on the phone for she had not the habit, even if she'd had the hearing.

"Long life, Mina," Manav wished his sister.

"It's been too long already," said Mina Foi. She wanted to tell her brother that she hoped the missionary couple would stop by as they had last year with cookies made with chocolate chips brought from Iowa—but then they may not remember it was her birthday, and she could not remind them. She was forbidden to make telephone calls on her own because they were a useless luxury.

Dadaji discussed the rising value of one of his investments, and then, at the end of the conversation, he inquired about the health of his daughter-in-law, Seher, and his granddaughter, Sonia.

"We are worried about Sonia," Manav answered. Sonia attended college in Vermont. "She's fallen into a depression. She weeps on the telephone, then when we call her back a day later, the same."

"But why?" asked Dadaji. "She's been there three years already. Why is she suddenly crying?"

"She says she is lonely." The last time Sonia had traveled home was two years ago.

"Lonely? *Lonely?*"

In Allahabad they had no patience with loneliness. They might have felt the loneliness of being misunderstood; they might know the sucked-dead feeling of Allahabad afternoons, a tide drawn out perhaps never to return, which was a kind of loneliness; but they had never slept in a house alone, never eaten a meal alone, never lived in a place where they were unknown, never woken without a cook bringing tea or wishing good morning to several individuals:

Namaste, Khansama.

Good morning, Mummy.

Good morning, Daddy.

Mina, good morning.

Ayah, namaste—

Whenever Dadaji thought of the Wordsworth poem he had been taught in school—*I wandered lonely as a cloud / that floats on high o'er vales and hills*—the line struck him as so ridiculous, it made him throw back his head and guffaw so hard his upper dentures fell down with a smash. But feeling unusually generous because of the growing value of his shares, Dadaji directed Mina Foi to telephone Sonia. Because vision problems afflicted him—a detached retina, glaucoma, cataracts—he put a magnifying glass to his rheumy red eye and bent over so his nose touched the address book as he read out the number for the Hewitt College dormitory in North Hewitt. Mina Foi put her finger into the holes of the telephone dial and tried for nearly an hour to call until her finger numbed. Finally the phone rang distantly, and someone with what she assumed was a cowboy drawl answered.

Luckily Dadaji picked up the extension line. Mina Foi did not trust herself to speak to a cowboy. Her finger remained stuck up in the air with a crick.

"Hallo, hallo, please connect us to Sonia Shah, who is in room number five," shouted Dadaji. Then when Sonia arrived at the phone booth, "What is the matter? Why is your father saying you are un-happy? Your studies are all right?"

"Yes," said Sonia in a measly voice.

"Then? What is the problem?"

"What do you get to eat there?" Mina Foi inquired.

"Macaroni!" answered her grandfather on the phone extension.

"No, Dadaji," answered Sonia, "the menu is very international. We have Chinese night, Mexican night."

Mina Foi ventured, "Indian night?"

"Lunch is sometimes Tomato Tigers, which are tomatoes and cheese on a toasted English muffin with curry powder on top."

"Never heard of such a thing!" Outrage.

"Pudding?" Mina Foi whispered.

"Brownies with ice cream, pecan pie, and blueberry pie."

Just to contemplate such lavish mysteries made Mina Foi faint with heartbreak.

"Pie is a very American food," Dadaji confirmed. "Well, what are you crying for, you lucky girl?"

Sonia tried to explain. "I've ballooned in my own head. I cannot stop thinking about myself and my problems. I'm dreading the winter. In the dark and cold, it will get worse—"

"Do some jumping jacks, get your spirits up, and then pick up your books. You have to persevere through hardship. If I hadn't left the life I was born to, you would be in Nadiad, married at sixteen, not studying in America."

Mina Foi's hands strangled each other in her lap when she remembered her childhood visits to their ancestral home, where the women scrounged what was left after the men had eaten. When the girls menstruated they were banished—even from this marginal existence—to a hut at the bottom of the property, where they ate from clay dishes that were later broken upon the rubbish heap so they would not pollute the world.

Dadaji had single-handedly extracted them from such backwardness. He may be iron-willed and furious-tempered, but these were precisely the qualities that had given Ba a place at the polished mahogany dining table every day of the year. When he had retired, he'd taken her on a round-the-world trip along with his younger brother, Amal Kaka, and Amal Kaka's wife, because Amal Kaka had not yet stolen the ancestral property and the brothers were still close.

All these years later, Ba and Dadaji could not remember a single sight, not a monument, not a museum, but they never forgot the green muffler lost on the way to Machu Picchu or the machine that promised to deliver a recorded history of the Vatican through headphones, but when they put in the coins, it didn't, and when they went to complain, the counter was closed for lunch. "Should we return in twenty minutes?" they had asked the guard. "Does lunch happen in twenty minutes?!" the guard had replied angrily. They remembered this, then they remembered how they had suffered constipation in Vienna and spent a day searching for reasonably priced fruit but found none. In London, at a hotel called The Buckingham, where you assumed people would be honest, they had been told breakfast would be included in the rate, but it was not. They'd saved a small fortune in Paris by cooking rice and lentils in the electric kettle for their dinners, Dadaji climbing on a chair and dismantling the hotel room's fire alarm. They'd been disappointed by French cooking—what was all the fuss about? They found the same three sandwiches and two sauces everywhere they went. With these two sauces, the French had terrorized the world.

Then, in most foreign lands, they'd observed that the denizens had no respect for Indian tourists, whereas they pursued and flattered the white ones. Therefore it was best to reside among your own people and keep to your own meticulous standards. Having made the big world small, Ba and Dadaji returned home satisfied.

"Why lonely?" said Dadaji to Sonia. "We found Americans most friendly. When we went to the Grand Canyon, we left our bananas on the bus, and a lady got off and chased us down to give them to us. She had to wait for the next bus."

"They are friendly," agreed Sonia's tiny voice.

"And a beautiful country," said Dadaji.

"It is," said Sonia.

"And so much empty space!"

"Yes." They heard Sonia begin to weep, and then the line went dead.

They reemerged upon the veranda; it would be too extravagant to call again. The sun was now glinting blearily above the haze; the crows had quieted; and the hunchbacked ayah had arrived to sweep, lugging

a twig broom several times her size. With her head and face covered
with her sari, which was the color of dust, she swept the dust from the
house to the veranda, then down each wide, shallow step out into the
guava orchard—which in season produced the famous pink guavas of
Allahabad—fanning the dust into the dust upon the dust, to make a
final pattern of dust scallops all the way to the outskirts of the compound.

By evening, the dust would have flown back and clogged the little
wire squares in the insect screens, covered the philodendrons, shad-
owed the name on the gate that read *M. L. Shah, Advocate, High Court,*
sanded the papers and files, imparted a crunch to the typewriter keys.
When Sonia had been a little girl, Mina Foi had shown her—with a
certain pride in her misfortune—that when she spat into the sink, she
spat out lorry dust beige.

Ba and Dadaji hadn't taken Mina Foi on their round-the-world
tour, for by then, she had proved herself unlucky, and when someone
is born unlucky, you don't have to make an effort with them. Thirty-
three years ago Dadaji had greeted his daughter's return from a six-
month marriage with silence suffused with blame, although he was the
one who had brokered the engagement. It had felt like Mina Foi's fault
because she was unfortunate.

"Nothing ever works for Mina," Ba had announced, and it was as if
her tragedy had been washed, folded, and snapped into one of those
black tin trunks filled with trousseau saris and mothballed woolens
that outlasted generations. On her birthday each year, though, to make
it an occasion, the Ambassador was soaped and washed by the driver in
as intimate and friendly a manner as if the car were a buffalo, then
driven to the front portico for mother and daughter to visit Mina Foi's
patrimony, the ancestral jewelry secured in a locker at the State Bank
of Baroda. On the way, they dropped Dadaji off at the Colonel's home
on Thornton Lane to keep his weekly chess-playing appointment.
Clad in a navy blazer and red tie, for he always dressed formally when
he left the house, Dadaji joined the Colonel, also clad in jacket and tie,
waiting with the chessboard on his front lawn and he reminded the
women to return for him in two hours' time.

Mina Foi was wearing her new birthday sari of flowery purple. Her mother wore one in a green wavy pattern. Both women had switched from cotton to polyester, which they found more durable, glamorous, and easier to care for. On her feet, Mina Foi wore her usual blue Hawaii chappals. Her soles were chapped. She had a wart on her nose, a slight mustache, and soft, hairy legs, which she lavished against each other under her sari when she was pleased, or sometimes in bed, in the predawn when she was peaceful, holding on to her sleeping breasts. When she held her breasts and caressed her legs in this early hour, it was for a little gentleness and kindness at the beginning of the day.

Mina Foi and her mother arrived at the bank and descended from the daylight into the morgue-like basement, where a security guard with a curly mustache and a rifle that belonged to the past age of weaponry guarded the metal lockers that held sleeping treasures. A clerk recorded the time of their arrival and held the shaky ladder so Mina Foi could clamber to their family safe at the topmost row, from which she handed down faded boxes and plastic bags, noticing meanwhile the clerk's bobby-pinned henna toupee and feeling a pang for his vanity. The boxes and bags bore the names of establishments long shuttered, names that came from a past age of grandeur: Jewellers Gopaldas Chandraprakash & Sons, Bhagatram Jainarain Jewellers, Haji Rafique Jewellers, KG Sultania Calcutta Walla Jewellers. The plastic bags were discolored and crispy with age, secured with rubber bands that had melted in the summer heat and hardened into wormy encrustations. The cotton wool that wrapped the jewels was also gray, but inside the gleam of the gems had been concentrated by age. Mina Foi and her mother admired the cloudy rubies and emeralds, the knobby pearls with a clotted buttermilk sheen that were mixed with glass and simple beads in the gay Gujarati style. There were kundun diamonds in large, clumsy chandeliers, part of Mina Foi's dowry that Ba had worried Mina Foi's in-laws would keep after Mina Foi's divorce. When they didn't, the better to establish they were the blameless party, Ba experienced not happiness, of course, given the circumstance, but a resettling of her gut. The State Bank locker had been decimated, then it was restored. Her spirit had been assaulted, now it was sanguine.

There was, however, a deeper sense of loss that haunted her, one she had inherited from her mother, who lamented, over and over, a precious Burmese ruby the size of a pigeon's egg that had vanished when the family was forced to leave their business in Rangoon and return to Nadiad. The loss of the ruby and the downfall of her father's wealth meant that something had shifted in Ba's sense of self.

When Sonia had last visited her grandparents in Allahabad, the summer before she left for college in the States, Ba and Mina Foi had taken her to the bank to visit the family gems. After reciting the story of the lost ruby from Burma, Ba had dutifully said, "The most beautiful set of all will be for you, Sonia, when you marry." She'd masked the pain of uttering this sentence by looking serious, as if discussing illness, and she had turned away in case Sonia brazenly accepted, "Thank you, Ba."

Mina Foi had helped Sonia try on a pearl bracelet with a tricky emerald clasp, remembering how she'd worn it on her wedding day with—and this is what still wrung Mina Foi—a giddy hope. She had been so innocent, and when her innocence was destroyed, she'd felt so ashamed. It had suddenly occurred to her that she was fastening her ill luck upon Sonia: "Take it off!"

Ba, unable to stand her plummeting heart, had said, "Come on, now, put it carefully back!"

But the clasp would not unclasp, and Mina Foi had to wrest the bracelet off Sonia's hand, scraping her skin.

"They don't wear jewelry in America, just small trinkets," Ba had said.

Now, on Mina Foi's fifty-fifth birthday, Ba made sure that the gems were not frivolously tried on, only admired and counted to make sure no piece was missing. She mopped the sweat from her upper lip with her hankie. "Fortunately you've never been one for dressing up!"

Did Ba mean that had Mina a taste for dressing up, her divorce at age twenty-two and the fact she no longer had an occasion to adorn herself would have been intolerable? That she was fortunate in this regard? Or did her mother mean it was fortunate she'd been divorced and that her wedding jewelry had been returned to her mother's bank locker?

She felt an unusual stab of hate for Ba. If her life had been different, Mina Foi might have been a different person as well—one who might have enjoyed sitting before her reflection at a dressing table mirror, dabbing perfume behind her ears, donning earrings, a necklace, rings, bracelets.

She said, "But how would I know if I'm one for dressing up or not?"

Her mother did not answer, not seeing how this question could be answered, and they bundled the pearls, emeralds, rubies, diamonds, and gold back into the dingy cotton wool, back into their secret boxes, back into the crispy, disintegrating plastic bags. They swept away the broken, wormy rubber bands and asked the clerk for new ones.

"I don't have any," he said grumpily. "Why did you not bring your own?" Then he opened a drawer and gave them two, glaring.

Mina Foi locked the safe again and handed back the spindly key. "Why don't you make a stronger key?" she asked. Mother and daughter climbed back up into the late afternoon, unsettled by how this excursion hadn't reiterated and deepened their bond, which they considered unassailable, but had instead taught them that it could be vanquished by a pearl.

"Do you think Betsy and Brett will come by with chocolate chip cookies the way they did last year?" asked Mina Foi.

"I don't know. They may not remember."

"Should we stop by their house?"

"Stop by their house? But it is far out of the way." Betsy and Brett lived in a poor neighborhood at the outskirts to emphasize their missionary devotion. "And we are already late collecting Daddy."

Exactly on time, Ba and Mina Foi retrieved Dadaji, who was waiting amidst the Colonel's petunias in a deflated mood because he had lost the game, and they returned home feeling the relief of approaching sundown, anticipating the dinner that would bring their deliberations at the hour of dawn to a culmination.

"The galawati is a damn tricky kebab," reminded Dadaji. "It must be smooth as silk."

Ba said, "Khansama uses no egg or any kind of binding agent, and then it is an exceedingly delicate task to turn the kebab. But you can only eat such rich food occasionally or you will develop gout."

Ba supervised Khansama delicately turning the kebabs, and she counted so no piece went missing before it was served. She inserted her nose deep into every dish to sniff closely and suspiciously, making sure all was as it should be. She checked the storeroom and the fridge to be certain every jar and canister was depleted only in exact proportion to their meal. The cockroaches that lived inside the warm laboring fridge didn't bother her—in fact, she couldn't see them, the voltage was so low. Neither did she notice that atop the greasy jars, daddy longlegs had got their long legs stuck and died. Nor that at the top of the door almost as tall as the wall, a lizard had been squashed, and the squashed leather of its torso and empty face still dangled from the high door-frame.

Then she bathed. In Allahabad they took their baths before dinner and dined formally about the table in their pajamas, nightgowns, and robes.

"It's Daddy's, it's Daddy's," shouted Ba when Mina Foi reached for the last bit of potato. Ba never addressed her husband directly, disrespectfully, and she rescued the delectable morsel to deposit on her husband's plate. This delivery of a potato to her husband linked back to the loss of the Burmese ruby. Dadaji ate it with a spoon and a fork and the disgruntled expression of having to be the person dealing with a problem as usual. "Everyone likes a potato," he said, "except for our daughter-in-law, Seher. She is the only person I have ever met who does not like a potato."

Mina Foi's finger zipped out and collected a stray sliver of fried onion that lay upon the tablecloth, and she put the sliver in her mouth with an absent-minded expression, not glancing about to see if anyone had spotted her because if nobody sees you, you didn't do what you did. She was brimful of sadness for no particular reason, just a poignancy, a melancholy that comes from eating such royal food when your life is so very empty, when there is austerity in all matters save dinner. Or was it the phone call to Sonia that had unsettled her, bringing in the big world and the knowledge that other people out there lived lives in fresh snow hills eating blueberry pie? Or she was brimful of sadness because the missionaries had indeed forgotten her birthday. Her niece, too, she remembered, had not thought of wishing her aunt.

Ba's flower-shaped diamond earrings, which she never removed, not even when she slept, caught the glum light in the dining room as she licked the last dal off the ladle with housewifely efficiency. She began to count the number of kebabs to make sure that none disappeared before the leftovers were presented at another meal.

"But Khansama may not have served all the pieces in the first place," Dadaji said. "Or even cooked them."

Here Mina Foi said loyally, "Mummy knows exactly what a kilo of mutton looks like." There was no point harboring anger against the only person who had tried to give you a birthday treat.

When the knives and spoons had been licked, the size of leftovers memorized, and the melamine dishes removed, Dadaji held up his hand.

When he did this, Ba upturned her surprisingly small palm, the paleness of which had indicated caste superiority, so it was considered at the time Ba and Dadaji's marriage was arranged. When Ba upturned her palm, Mina Foi repeated the gesture with her large brown hand that resembled her father's. Khansama came out with a tray laden with bottles of pills and handed the bottles to Mina Foi, who counted the pills into the palm of Ba, who in turn passed them one by one to her husband, who conceded to lift his own water glass to his mouth. Vitamins, papaya enzyme, cod liver oil, Dabur Chyawanprash.

"The date has gone on the Seven Seas garlic capsules." Mina Foi scrutinized one of the bottles.

"You take them then," Dadaji ordered Khansama. "Don't waste them. Give them to your children—perfectly fine for another year or two."

Mina Foi noticed that the yellowed newspaper that lined the tray read: *Boy Brought Up by Wolves Is Found in Tribal Area.*

After all the practical matters had been taken care of, Dadaji said, "Look here!"

They looked at him.

"When I was playing chess with the Colonel, he happened to mention his grandson in America—I'd completely forgotten about the boy. I asked if he was married—he has finished his master's degree—and they said he was not. I asked what he was waiting for. They said he had his own ideas and those ideas did not amount to anything. Meanwhile the Colonel's wife told me she could smell a royal aroma when she drove past our house. She said, 'I thought if they didn't send us any kebabs, then there must be some reason. At least give us the recipe, I've been begging for years.'"

"Why should we hand over the secrets of our kitchen for no reason?" asked Ba. In any case, why would the Colonel's wife make such a request when everyone knew a person must always render a sly omission when pressured for a recipe—subtract an ingredient, jiggle a quantity to leave the recipient tormented: *Something isn't right!*

Dadaji said, "Let's take the remaining galawati over tomorrow."

"But why?" asked Mina Foi. "We could eat them for lunch."

"If Sonia is lonely, the problem is easily solved. Let us make an introduction between Sonia and their grandson."

Dadaji, Ba, and Mina Foi each privately recalled an incident from a decade ago that nobody had forgotten, when the Colonel had encouraged Dadaji to invest in a woolen mill started by an army colleague to whom the Colonel believed he owed his life—they had fought in Kashmir together. The business failed, and the considerable investment in military blankets, socks, balaclavas, and sweaters had resulted in a financial loss to Dadaji, who had been as upset, naturally, as the Colonel had been apologetic. While the incident had interjected a new undertow of regret and falsity into their former neighborliness, by the magnanimity of continuing to dispense free legal advice on the subject of the Colonel's court case seeking compensation for the family land in Lahore that was lost during Partition, by continuing to send across kebabs and other dishes from their kitchen as unstintingly as always, by continuing their games of chess and gallantly losing, Dadaji had been unconsciously biding time until he might call the debt home.

It was essential to remain close to those who had caused you harm so that the ghost of guilt might breathe through their dreams, that their guilt might slowly mature to its fullest potential. Not that Dadaji had thought it through—it never worked to consciously plot, to crudely calculate—and he himself was astonished at the possibility of what was unfolding. Even now it would never do to name this liability. The Colonel would not allow his grandson to bear the burden of his grandfather's mistake. Dadaji and Ba may simply suggest a desirable match between the grandchildren, two America-educated individuals, two equals, two people who naturally belonged together because of where they came from and where they were going. Without either of them mentioning it, the obligation might be beautifully unraveled.

Ba and Mina Foi were once again witness to the brilliance of Dadaji. He might have lost the afternoon game, but he'd played a consummate match of chess. Said Ba, "And they will not have the face to ask for a dowry!"

Again the driver soaped and washed the rotundity of the Ambassador and drove the family to the Colonel's residence. They carried a ceremonial scalloped silver platter of kebabs.

Dadaji said, "We recently heard from our granddaughter. It seems loneliness is a big problem over there in America."

Mina Foi noticed on the side table of inlaid ivory that along with the Colonel's wife's ikebana arrangement, there was a photograph of their grandson. Haughty with the nose of a nawab but the lips of a cherub, he was reading a newspaper. She found him handsome.

"Lonely? *Lonely?*" said the Colonel's wife.

"Without people one is nothing," said Mina Foi. "Especially in wintertime. It snows nonstop over there." Betsy and Brett had lent her *Little House on the Prairie,* which had become Mina Foi's favorite book. She must have read it a hundred times, although her parents considered novels as much a useless luxury as telephone calls to missionaries.

PART

II

Winter Vast
and Forlorn

2

....

WHILE VERMONT IS SMALL AND FRIENDLY IN SUMMER, with every sweet thing—farmer in the farmers market, child in the pond, bee in the foxglove, fox in the chicken coop, bear in the beehive— in its own sweet place, in winter distances expand, the sky looms with weather, the hills turn to mountains, become vast and forlorn. For two months following their Christmas break, the students of Hewitt College were expected to scatter like migratory birds to intern in establishments that represented their future professions: a puppet theater, an investment bank, the Numismatic Society, a rainforest institute. But foreign students were on a visa that did not allow them such employment, and those who couldn't afford to return home, or labor for free, took up jobs on campus and were tutored in the assorted moods of being solitary in the wintertime.

Sonia was employed in the library, and this last year of her degree, she trudged uphill every weekday morning from the Gerstein Chen House, a dormitory at the foot of a hill in the hamlet of North Hewitt that stayed open for students who had nowhere to go. Entering through a gap in the stone wall that ringed the college property, Sonia walked past the mansion that housed the music department, patterned all over with the caterpillar feet of ivy, and from a window just below the chimneys, she glimpsed a greenish lamp glowing and knew that Lazlo had been playing the piano all night.

She walked past the red barns that housed the alumni office where Armando was employed. He didn't live in the Gerstein Chen House; he was pug-sitting for Dany, the drama teacher, on the other side of North Hewitt. She unlocked the door to the modern white cube of the library where she spent the day mostly alone; the only other person there over the winter term was Marie, who came in during the mornings and supervised Sonia. Too often Marie found Sonia reading the books she was supposed to be transferring from the Dewey Decimal system of cataloging to the Library of Congress. But who could resist a whole library to oneself? Sonia read Eudora Welty and Katherine Mansfield. She read Isak Dinesen and Jean Rhys. When it was dark, Sonia returned to the Gerstein Chen House and boiled ramen noodles atop an electric coil in a kitchen perpetually lit by fluorescence. For a treat she dipped into a carton of Chacharoni that her friend Audrey Hong had left her. Audrey's original name was Jung-hee, but when her family emigrated from Seoul, her father had renamed her in honor of Audrey Hepburn; her sisters were Greta and Marilyn.

After ramen, Sonia settled to writing stories for her senior thesis in literature and creative writing. Missing her family made her strongly conjure India. She began a childhood fable about a boy who climbed into a tree and lived like a monkey until he became one, a process complicated by his being mistaken for a holy hermit.

On Sunday mornings at exactly ten A.M., Mama and Papa called the phone that rang in a booth in the hall. "Be quick, be quick!" Papa fretted over the cost.

But Sonia talked at length despite the paltry amount she had to convey. She told them about a particular squirrel who had targeted her, hammering boldly on the window demanding to be let in before clambering peevishly through a hole he'd gnawed in the roof and sleeping in the attic exactly above her head. In the early morning she would hear him stumble down the green shutters, bound into the candelabra firs using the trampoline effect of the telephone wires, and make his way to the deli at the crossroads, from which he fetched stale baguettes out of the dumpster. These he tried to store in accordance with his natural instinct, but the ground being too frozen to bury anything, he stuck the bread into Sonia's boots on the porch or threw hard dinner rolls down the chimney. Sonia also told her parents about Marie, her supervisor. She had ginger hair to which Marie attributed her sassy attitude. She was married to Cole.

"*Coal?*" asked Papa.

"C-O-L-E."

"But why a name that sounds no different from C-O-A-L? Everyone will laugh and say *Blaaaack as Coaaaal.*"

"Nobody laughs." Her father's Delhi party humor and pretend American accent annoyed her.

It was Marie who spotted a yellow coat in her church charity drive and fished it from the bottom of the bin for Sonia. It was sharp against the season, trimmed in forest green, the wool thick and good, and Sonia had grown very fond of her tawny, curried lion coat.

"Let me take a photograph of you to send to your family—have they ever seen snow? Go stand over there by the firs. Goodness, that really is an awful coat," said Marie, fascinated by the lurid shade of her gift. "But I guess you can never be lost."

Marie was proved wrong. Somewhere in the midst of those weeks and months, with storms barreling down from Canada or gaining momentum buffeting east across the Great Plains, Sonia fell headlong into the polar chill. Her spirits altered for no reason, just a whim of their own register, the accumulation of one note of solitude shifting weight to another. She could be overcome with panic and weep until the weeping became diarrheal; she may then be unexpectedly delivered to a raft of calm and transfixed by the snow's companionship as it lost the urgency of arrival, lingered, luxuriated, unraveled in slow motion— seducing itself, that lucky snow. Then her mood might switch. She might sit by the window feeling as if she were a lonely grandma and watch the flakes gathering speed again, flying by until she felt she were flying herself, drawn into the snow-salted wilderness. Eventually loneliness and snow became the same thing in her mind, lighter than air, made of nothing; only upon tackling the stuff did you realize it had piled too heavy to yield.

From her bedside drawer, she took out the curious amulet her mother had given her and that had originally belonged to her grandfather Siegfried. It was a gau box from Tibet, a portable altar for a deity or a talisman, fashioned from tarnished, battered silver that was carved intricately with curly clouds swirling into dragons. It could be worn about the neck as a heavy pendant, or attached to a belt, or carried in a mountain pack over the high Himalayan passes where travelers would need a supernatural guide through the wilderness. Sonia unhooked the amulet's latch to reveal a miniature painting of a blood-red and leopard-black figure. It pranced forth, gesturing, poised like a scorpion holding its sting. The creature's arms flowered into what looked like claws; its heart was ebony and slung with necklaces of gold leaf, luminescent painted rubies, and pearls. It had a maimed leg whittled like a sadhu's wooden staff. This creature's face—but it had no face! In its place was a cracked void, a broken visage, a skeleton's porthole eyes.

In case Sonia needed a demon deity to keep other demons away, to keep her safe upon her journey, Mama had given the amulet to her daughter upon the eve of her departure to America. Sonia kept it open by her desk when she worked; sometimes she put a pebble or an acorn before it as if it were a writing god, terrorizing her, inspiring her. The demon's name was Badal Baba, Hermit of the Clouds. But could Badal Baba protect her? He was even more a foreigner than Sonia was.

*

SONIA WOULD ALWAYS BE ABLE to precisely recall the afternoon when another snowbird swooped over the granite cliffs—leaving feathery drifts that obliterated the shape of the library steps—and a tall man in a brindled fur coat and an imposing, mothy karakul hat climbed the steps to the library.

Sonia came out with the shovel.

"I didn't bother with the steps because I didn't think anyone would come."

"There are a few people in these hills," he said, almost sternly, in an accent she could not place, "who need a library."

He took the shovel from her and made a narrow path, then he turned and smiled, although his gaze didn't focus upon her but remained internal. He had a greyhound face, distinguished and lean, and when he took off his hat, Sonia noticed that his dark hair held a streak of gray. Later while Sonia worked quietly at the computer, he took volumes of art books off the shelves, made a sea of open books upon the table, fished many colored pencils and pens from his coat pockets, sketched, hummed. He wrote in the books and underlined passages.

"You can't do that!" exclaimed Sonia. He was writing in *The Letters of Vincent van Gogh*.

"Oh, I forgot, I always forget!"

He went out and paced. He came back. Outside the temperature had dropped, the snowfall had slowed, the snow now roosting, the forest gathering flakes.

Three days later, the stranger returned.

When Sonia walked by to water the plants by the window, he said, "Listen," and lifted his headphones onto her head. And there passed between them, inappropriately for their disparate ages, an awkwardness.

The headphones were warm. She heard a harrowing cry.

"What is that?"

"An owl. I have the calls of over two hundred owls," he said. "The Sokoke, the Ryukyu, the Torotoroka, the Oaxaca screech, the laughing, burrowing, the Chaco, Ural, Sichuan, the boobook, the winking, Tasmanian masked, the fearful, bare-legged, the Stygian, the northern saw-whet, the pearl-spotted owlet, the Ookpik, also known as the tundra ghost, also known as the Great Terror of the North."

Sonia looked at her hands with their long twig fingers on the oak table. They looked unfamiliar and exaggerated.

"Here are some Indian owls—the Bubo bengalensis, the Athene brama." The *chirrur-chirrur* of a spotted owlet calling out was overlaid by the sounds of traffic, automobile horns, people.

"It screeches just like the owl that lived behind my grandparents' house. It would watch me so solemnly when I brushed my teeth, I would begin to laugh."

"Is that when you were happiest?"

"Yes." She felt surprised by the question, so simple, and her answer, so simple. An ordinary evening in a house full of people is what a child loves best.

"What did that bathroom look like?" The far, penumbral land of the Allahabad bathroom that Sonia shared with Mina Foi was as large as the bedroom they also shared and situated on the gloomy side of her grandparents' house. A tribe of vicious black-and-white-striped mosquitoes prospered by a shallow bay of slime where the water never drained. There were buckets under the taps and a wooden platform of soft, rotting wood upon which to stand as you bathed, slapping your bare behind when mosquitoes attacked. The soap in a pink plastic soap dish set upon a matching plastic stool, scenting the whole bathroom with a deep leafy smell, was green Margo. The brown laundry soap, the same color as the lizards that hunted the mosquitoes and with which each morning Mina Foi washed her knickers, had melted into a clay lump in a corner of the windowsill that was never dusted and was hung lavishly with layers of cobwebs made by spiders long deceased.

On the other side sailed a lofty sink below an almost postage stamp–size mirror cemented into the wall, and at another corner, the pot was marooned. Above it, all the way at the high ceiling for the sake of momentum, lodged a tank of water dangling a long chain. If you hung upon it, the water began a sluggish churn like a serpent turning about the cracked, discolored ceramic bowl before it vanished with a muffled rainy-season gutter-thunder down the aged gullet.

The hunchbacked ayah came in, even as you shouted at her that you were bathing. She moved slowly, as if burrowing a tunnel, to collect the discarded clothes and crept slowly out again, always following the same path along the wall.

Outside the bathroom window was a mulberry tree in which lived the owl that swiveled his head and looked in, astonished, its gaze like a lamp from the fog of its feathers. Its feathers, Sonia remembered now, looked as if they were specked with snow; to look upon the owlet made one feel cool even in the heat of summer.

The man listened attentively, although he had taken a clementine out of his pocket. He made a neat ribbon of the peel, gave Sonia a segment, and ate one himself. "Do you know a book about shadows by the Japanese writer Tanizaki? No? He argued that shadows and shadowy old bathrooms were a doorway to the past and that shadows make life theatrical and mysterious, earthy and natural. I remember those Indian bathrooms."

"You were in India?"

He gave her another section of clementine. "The bathrooms in the palaces and forts of Rajasthan were melancholic spaces with marble troughs that could never be filled in such a water-starved landscape. Pigeons shuttled through, monkeys reached in and stole our clothes while we were bathing—I had never seen so many animals about. It was as if we were the creatures in the zoo and they were free; the monkeys, the peacocks, the cows would come by and look at us through the windows."

The man got up and did a sideways bird movement, then he did a mean-eyed bandit monkey. He said, "I can do many more just like that! I practiced these movements when I was a child, and I never forgot them."

He took another clementine out of his pocket. "May I ask why you are here?"

"The college is shut for two months through the winter."

"Why?"

"It's too expensive to heat, and during this time we are supposed to find internships, but foreign students can work only on campus. That means Armando, Lazlo, and myself—but I hardly ever see them."

"You're alone all winter?" he asked.

"Yes."

"I'm alone, too!" he said.

"My only company is a squirrel who hammers on my window when there is a blizzard."

"Then why don't I invite you to dinner this weekend? We shouldn't have to eat alone when all the rest of humanity is out enjoying themselves." His name, he said, was Ilan de Toorjen Foss.

CHAPTER

3

·····························

THE SEATS WERE HARD CARAMEL LEATHER THAT CREAKED
when she sat down. The car was lacquered the same mustard color as
Sonia's coat.

"I appreciate your coat," he said.

They drove satelliting past snowbanks, the car headlamps catching
the eyes of deer. Sonia could see past the leafless trees to previously
hidden moonlit cliffs and ranges. An exquisite, high feeling rose within
her, but again she felt a fateful awkwardness, and to quell it, she asked
why Ilan was here in Vermont.

"The snow light and the quiet are like a secret doorway. My paintings become stranger."

"You're a painter?"

"Is there another way to live?"

"My grandfather, my mother's father, was also a painter," said
Sonia. "He was a theosophist from Germany named Siegfried Barbier
who went searching for the occult in the high Himalayas, riding on a
mule. Isn't this a coincidence?"

"Ah, that explains your height. There is no such thing as coincidence. Did he find it?"

"He vanished while mountaineering, long before I was born."

"I knew when I saw you the story would not be simple. I have an
intuition."

Why did she tell him such a private detail immediately? Because her
condition of winter loneliness had grown acute, and she felt compelled
to tell her most compelling stories so she would be attractive and they

could know each other quickly, profoundly, so she could relieve her solitude.

They drove to a Japanese restaurant on a cliff overlooking a half-frozen creek.

"What do you paint?" Sonia asked before she wondered if this was a foolish question.

"I paint seemingly good things as evil and seemingly evil things as good. I put together what does not go together. That is all I will say. There is nothing more horrible than an artist who begins talking nonsensical art theory when asked what he is painting. Most artists talk like this now. That is why I don't have any artist friends. I learned from Van Gogh—you should think about your painting absolutely simply, like a traveler describing a landscape or a scene. If you do that, then you live inside your paintings—and all I want is to live inside my paintings."

Sonia was distracted by the sushi in front of her. "I've never been to a Japanese restaurant before," she admitted. Audrey Hong had shown her how to mix a button of wasabi into the soy sauce and how to hold chopsticks, the upper one as you would hold a pen, but she worried about mishandling them.

"Never? Don't tell anyone! What have you been doing your whole life, you poor one?" Ilan lifted up a piece of nigiri that smelled of the sea and popped it into her mouth. One of Sonia's cheeks was singed by cold from the pane of glass on one side of the table, and the other cheek felt almost liquid in the heat of the nearby fireplace. The heat melted and curled like molten oil into her ear, and she was seduced by the golden phoenix sparking and hissing up the chimney, the grove of bamboo beyond the window—little leaves each covered with a slip of snow—bowing deep to the hush.

"Tell me," he said. "Who are your parents? Does your mummy love you?"

This was a strange question, but it also seemed like a kind question because it was one she might answer: What could she say to a stranger older than her by . . . how many years? Very many years.

"Yes. Doesn't your mother love you?"

"No, she does not. That is why I'm interested."

"Are you sure, she may without showing it?"

"No," he sounded cross, as if this was the wrong response. "She never loved me."

"Why?"

"Is there a reason for such things? I don't know. I know it is true, that's all. Can you imagine what it is to have a mummy who hates you?"

"No."

"Why do you say that? It makes me feel more unloved."

What a strange turn! Sonia compensated: "But my mother is remote, and she does not love my father."

"Ah, remoteness can be intelligence, it can be selfishness, unhappiness, or superiority and judgment, or she is listening to some internal music."

"Her remoteness goads my father. He cannot stop spying on her, and she's always trying to get away."

"She must be beautiful."

Sonia was proud of her mother's beauty. "Yes," said Sonia, "but she becomes angry if anyone says so."

"Hmm, that is unusual. Most women begin to purr when they are told they are beautiful."

"She says Indians are obsessed by who is beautiful and who is not, that they have no imagination in how they perceive beauty, they take the easy way out, they imprison people, those considered ugly and those considered beautiful. Evil people flock to the ones who are perceived to be beautiful, and the ones who are considered plain are condemned to suffer and fail."

"Why is that? Beauty is beyond good and evil. Good people are also attracted to beauty," said Ilan.

"But they are pushed out of the way by the evil ones. Men follow my mother in the park; there is one man who has been going to Lodhi Gardens every single day for twenty years to stare at her, and we have no idea who he is. My father won't let her go to the market without questioning the driver to find out exactly where she went. One day she cried and said she couldn't even shampoo her hair in peace, she felt his impatience outside the door. And he said that my mother read so deeply on their honeymoon, that when she emerged from the pages, she had nothing to say. The book was more interesting to her than even Dal Lake, let alone her new husband." Sonia had inherited her love of books from her mother, who had inherited it from her father, Siegfried Barbier.

"What was she reading?"

"Kafka's *The Castle*."

"An interesting choice for a honeymoon—an acute estrangement that foresaw what overcame Germany."

As Sonia spoke Ilan sketched her in a notebook; he wrote what she said above: *My grandfather went searching for the occult in the high Himalayas, riding on a mule.* He took a photograph of her with a tiny Leica. He said, "You have an interesting family and expressive hands." This flattered her, and in the days and months that followed, Sonia continued to betray her family and herself.

They finished the bottle of sake, and Ilan reached under the table and placed one hand on each of Sonia's knees. When she clamped her legs together, he smiled, reached up, and placed a hand into her shirt. Nobody observed him, the staff was either discreet or inattentive, and there were no other diners. Looking at their reflection in the window amidst the bamboo, feeling a hand about her breast, Sonia felt her life divide into two—her normal life and this reflection—and she felt her breast transform under his palm into a dove.

"Why don't we go back to my house?" asked Ilan, but when they were in the car, Sonia was nervous. "I'm tired," she said. "I should go home."

"I see." He became formal and polite. He dropped her back. "Thank you for this evening." He bowed.

When Sonia was back in her dormitory room, she lay down on her narrow bed and realized she was intolerably drunk. She raised herself up to stop the feeling of falling into a fathomless depth, paced the harshly lit hallway, sweated a sour stench, shivered yet found her clothes unbearable and pulled them off. She went to the bathroom and drank from the faucet—the more water she drank, the more sloshed she became. She knelt at the toilet, retched up the expensive meal, the cost of feeding herself for a month or more. She returned to her room, lay back down, and dissected the cost of not having gone along with Ilan—which was to remain uncomforted and alone—until she heard the squirrel in the attic begin to shift around, making a great noise as if he were wearing boots and rolling his stored kernels across the attic floor. She shouted at him when he was on his way to the dumpster to collect stale baguettes: "You're supposed to be a tree dweller!"

The squirrel glared at her. If he was meant to be a tree dweller, she was meant to be a cave dweller.

In the library the next morning, she watered the jade plants roughly and shelved the books carelessly. She told Marie, "I had dinner with that man who has been coming into the library."

Marie said: "That old man? Can't he pick on someone his own age?"

Sonia felt savage. "He's a painter," she snapped. An artist may have a different reason to engage with her.

"Has anyone ever heard of him?"

Sonia had searched the card catalogs in the library, the newspaper archives stored on microfiche. She had found only one notice of his name, as part of a private collection in Switzerland, a painting called *The Dictator's Wife*.

"He's not old," said Sonia.

"He must be thirty years older than you."

"I don't think age is the problem."

"It most certainly is," said Marie. "What youth means to these old men, it's disgusting."

Not long ago, Marie had said to her: "You never seem interested in a boyfriend. In three years since you've been working in the library, you haven't had a single one. Well, I think it is wise of you. You should find out who you are yourself before getting mixed up with somebody else."

Some weeks went by, and when Mama and Papa phoned, Sonia was sobbing again.

"What's the matter?"

She could not answer.

"Aren't you writing your stories?" asked Mama. "Or reading?" To read a particular novel in a particular place could be exquisite. Sonia was unable to read. She had checked out *Anna Karenina* from the library, but even a love story in deep snow country did not hold her attention.

Twelve hours later they called again, and she was still weeping, now in a gasping hysterical way, as if barely keeping her head above the flood.

"Tell Marie if you're lonely," said Mama, taking the phone. "She's a kind lady, isn't she? Or give me Marie's number and I will phone her myself."

"No!" She imagined the phone ringing in the dollhouse-size home by Route 9 where Marie and her husband, Cole, lived. She imagined it being Mama informing them all the way from teeming New Delhi— a city of more than ten million souls, each of whose lives could not be emptied of people no matter how they might try—that her daughter was too ashamed to let Marie know she was lonely.

Sonia replied to her mother, "I spend all my time trying to pretend I am not lonely!" If you are lonely, you feel ashamed, and the only relief to your shame is being alone, which is what makes you lonely in the first place.

"What about the boy from Bulgaria, or the one from the Philippines? They're probably feeling the same way as you."

Sonia waved at Lazlo when she saw him on the path by the pond. He waved back, turned, and retreated along the same path, as if he'd forgotten something. Part of Lazlo's mystery was linked to his expression of aristocratic sadness that nobody could approach—he froze in response to any human acknowledgment. When nobody paid him any attention, he returned to life. Once, Sonia heard him singing light and high in the library stacks. She called, "Lazlo," and he stopped. Then when he thought she had moved away, he piped up again as if to pipe himself over the hills. Armando, when she telephoned, invited her to dinner. Armando wasn't lonesome. He was beloved by the alumni office ladies for his stories about his mother's collection of handbags, his sister's several suitors, his father's birthday parties in Manila, where there were always as many dishes as he was years old.

"Sonia!" Armando opened the door to the drama teacher Dany's home with a lavish gesture, clasped her to him, and waltzed her into the entrance hall. "I have to tell you something."

"What?"

"I'm gay!" he said, making a beautiful curtsy with his arms extended.

"I'm Filipino and I'm gay! I'm a double minority." In America these facts had depth and value. "I think I always knew," he told her, "and that is why I said I wanted to become a priest."

Armando was a senior like Sonia, and he considered it would be wise to stay on in America because it would be easier to be gay here than to be gay at home. But how to get a job that would allow him to switch his student visa to a work visa?

"Do your parents expect you to stay in the States?" asked Armando.

"They want me to stay because the world would open up and life would be freer for a woman, but they say they will be proudest if I return."

They were silent, thinking for a bit. After they graduated, they would be allowed one year of work experience in the States, but by the end of that year, they would either have to find a sponsor, or someone to marry, or return to their native countries. Armando put on Dany's apron and stirred a codfish stew with tomatoes that rumbled and spat red and orange upon the stovetop. He had followed a recipe from Dany's Spanish cookbook.

"Well, you can't tell anyone this," said Armando as they sat down to eat whatever hadn't splattered out of the pot. "Promise?"

"Promise," Sonia confirmed, making a mental note not to tell secrets to one who gave away secrets while swearing others to secrecy.

"Well," he said, "last weekend I was so bored, I was just looking about—and I came across a folder of letters."

He couldn't help but read them, and he'd learned that Dany had a lover from Yemen named Ali, whom he'd met when Ali was a waiter in London and who was now a married man with children in Sanaa. For twenty years the two men rendezvoused for two weeks in Istanbul, the ticket paid for by Dany, the excuse to a wife wrangled by Ali. Armando's eyes spangled wet. "Isn't it beautiful and *so* sad?"

"And so lucky and so unlucky—poor wife, poor Dany, poor Ali, poor dog." She noticed that the curl in the pug's tail had come uncurled as she sat at the window, staring fixedly at the driveway, awaiting Dany's return.

"You know who I like?"

"Who?"

"Lazlo! I can't stop thinking about him. I wrote him a love letter."

....

WHEN SONIA RETURNED TO THE GERSTEIN CHEN HOUSE, she attempted to distract herself. She drew a bath, submerging herself in the bright, hot water, the eggshell smell. Yet she could not prevent herself from what she was about to do. A certain stage in life was passing, and she needed to wrangle a romantic experience soon—wasn't this why she was in America in the first place, to experiment with love anonymously in the company of someone as unknown to her as she was to them, an experience that could prove an embarrassment or mishap, yet never follow her, remaining within the discreet pages of winter?

Dripping water, she phoned Ilan from the phone booth.

He sounded delighted. "Oh, I thought you didn't like me. Come immediately! I'm here working all night."

The house was farther away than she had surmised when she set out walking. She trudged up one slope and down another between dunes of plowed snow, the air so frozen that it burned her face and hands. Entering a driveway without a gate, she proceeded up a country road that wended through a forest. Beyond, she saw a valley under the moon and a fleet of deer, soundless black shadows moving across the silver. She saw also the shadows of the snow-covered hemlocks and black walnuts, the maples, the winged wahoo, and the hills. She saw two enormous urns holding high soufflés of snow, and up ahead, a shape of a house, grooved pillars two stories high, the lights glowing in one set of rooms.

Ilan opened the door into an entryway dominated by a beaked totem figure that Sonia would learn was carved out of a petrified fern

tree and came from the island of Malekula. The room leading from the
entryway was mostly empty save several trestle tables piled with books
and objects; a distinguished divan upholstered in yellow velvet; and
two Japanese screens that were stretched out twelve feet each, painted
in ink brush on grayed, worm-eaten paper, one with a scene of mountains and waterfalls, the other a scene of islands and ocean. A ceramic
bowl of marijuana, smelling richly, was drying on the windowsill by
the radiator. Ilan was standing at a table of photographs, dressed in
tweed wool robes.

"Look, Sonia, here is my mother!" He handed her a photograph of
a young woman, her dark hair waved elegantly to the side, a gloved
hand elegantly reaching out, an elegant foot clad in an elegant low-
heeled shoe kicked up in the air as she was being helped out of a shiny
wood-paneled boat resembling a water beetle and onto the jetty of a
hotel. Rugged mountains high above, whittled like arrowheads, contrasted with a lake that you could tell was dreamy and voluptuous.

"Where is that?"

"The Grand Hotel Villa Serbelloni on Lago Como. In summer you
can swim in Lago Lecco on the other side where there is less boat traffic, along with thin, shy black water snakes. The water is so soft, it feels
milky, and as you swim in the barely sun-warmed lake—you should
not be so foolish as to lower your legs into the freezing deep but keep
your toes splashing at the sun-warmed surface—you can look upon
the snows up high. When you get out, you shiver and shake gold snakes
of water, which slip into the olive trees that also shine and shake, so
they are like leaves of lake water, then gradually the sun warms you
and you stop shaking to become a gecko or a stone—completely still."
He surveyed the photograph with interest as if he were looking at it for
the first time. "But look at the number of waiters and porters to the
side: How I hate rich people!"

"But you must have been rich if you stayed in such a hotel?"

"That is why I know that everyone should hate the rich."

"But here you are, enjoying being rich, too!" Sonia could see that
his distaste was equal to his pleasure.

"Yes," he said. "Look at how glamorous my mummy was. It was

on the afternoon of this day—the day this photograph was taken—
that I saw her reflection in the lake and thought, *I am in love with my
mother!*"

"I thought you said she doesn't love you."

"Yes, she does not."

"Where is she from?"

"Her father's ancestors were bankers for the Ottomans; they left for
Vienna and Paris. Her mother's family were colonial officials in India."

"India?"

"I told you I had a connection to India—I already know something
about you, you see."

He went over to examine the marijuana and chopped at it with a
palette knife like a housewife with a spatula. He screwed together a
travel marijuana pipe, filled it, lit it with a match, inhaled, and exhaled
two puffs through his nose.

"And this is where I live now, when I am not here." The next picture he picked up was taken from a distance, and it showed a very different landscape: a scattering of ruins in what appeared to be a cactus
jungle. In the center, a wall painted a deep earth red stood with a fireplace hewn from a single square of volcanic stone. The windows of this
ruined wall opened onto valleys and canyons far below through which
grazed shoals of clouds.

"Where is this?"

"Mexico."

He had been unhappy all his life until he defected to Mexico to
become an artist like so many artists before him—where many people
from many parts of the world went to escape. Some had escaped the
wars or poverty in Europe, some had been exiled from other parts of
the continent, some had gone for the Revolution, some in search of a
primitive ideal inspired by artifacts they'd seen in the museums of Berlin and New York. Some went on the G.I. Bill and passed their time
drinking hard to torch the past from their memories.

"Why did you go?"

"For the ecstatic moment: *There will never be blue without yellow, without orange!* That was written by Van Gogh in a letter to his

brother. Everything I saw I wanted to paint. I suffered from Stendhal syndrome—do you know what that is? No?

"I sat my first evening in the plaza of a small town built on a slope of a smoking volcano. It smelled of copal from a religious festival and of sulphur from festival fireworks. I heard a brass band. The sound came invisibly from here and then suddenly from the opposite direction, then from far up the hill. I saw gigantic skeleton puppets from behind the convent, from above the trees—and then, abruptly, the music cut off mid-tune, as if the band members had received a premonition and dropped their instruments to run.

"I painted in a hacienda of umber, cold even in summer when the light was too bright to see anything outside. The clay pots that held quince trees were so old they were turning back into mud and streaking the walls upon which they stood—and in the cupboard there were Silesian coffee cups, pink and gold, the color rubbing off, handles too tiny to hold.

"In a mountain church, I saw a bride dressed in black, weeping on the arm of an ancient man. There was no bridegroom. As in India, I couldn't understand what was happening or why—no book could explain it to satisfaction, and everyone you asked said something completely different. I realized that while I was looking for the surreal, I had found something else—the idea of the surreal was European. Europeans came at the truth upside down. I painted a lake fisherman whose feet had actually turned to hyacinth roots; he'd never owned shoes.

"I thought Mexico was a country where I could be happy and it wouldn't be a tawdry happiness. I could be miserable and I could assume a noble misery. The tragic is elevated in a way it isn't over here, and happiness must necessarily include a whisper of sadness.

"Barragán was responsible for the restoration of this ruin. You know Barragán? You don't know? What are they teaching you in college?

"Never mind." He took her hand and drew her up the stairs that rose to a landing with a mirror set into the carved woodwork. "Look," he said, putting her before the mirror. "Your body has intelligence.

You're like a leopard. You must never grow fat." From this landing, stairs branched right and left to separate wings of the house. Ilan took her up the right set of steps to another sparse room with a brass bed and a fireplace of white tiles with blue ships. She said, "But it's freezing."

He said, "Yes, get under the covers quick!"

Then he dove in himself and pulled off his clothes from under the quilt, throwing them out in a playful way, tweed robes to the right, pants to the left, socks to the lamp, underwear straight to the moon. He turned to her and stuck his warm tongue into her warm mouth in a manner so frank that it was surprising and humorous.

Sonia looked at the pocked moon, felt the mechanics of sex at a remove, and the first sex was over before it properly began. She looked at Ilan and herself as they lay back away from each other at disjunct angles. She went to the bathroom and washed the rust-colored slime from between her legs, relieved by her body's discretion. Poor body, it had done its best to stand by her and not behave independently of her will; it had not unleashed a melodramatic run of scarlet; it had not called out in fear, nor made a theater. When Sonia returned, she moved up to lie neat and straight upon the bed, with her head on the pillow and her hands upon her slim belly. She felt lighter, thinner, slightly hysterical. She was certain she was behaving incorrectly—she didn't know how a woman should behave or what a woman should say at such a time. "We forgot to draw the curtains," she said.

Ilan seemed surprised. "It is beautiful to look at snow."

Then he laughed. "You're a middle-class housewife!"

"No." She was insulted. "It's that the moonlight makes us look spooky."

Eventually Ilan came up to the moonlit pillow himself. They both slept, Sonia fitfully, until, in the middle of the night, a freakish wind hurtled over the mountains, sliced under the doors, and wailed in the voice of a witch through cracks in the windows that were shaky in their grooves and began to rattle.

"Wake up, wake up!" When Sonia jumped awake, Ilan was racing in a panic, stark naked, turning on lights, throwing clothes on. "Wake up, I'm catching a cold, I'm catching a cold! Help me!"

Although part of her was observing him with interest—she had never seen an adult man flapping naked before—she felt panic as well. She reached down to where her clothes lay on the floorboards by the bed and threw her own sweater at Ilan.

When he was dressed in two layers of warmth, he returned to bed, holding her tight with relief. Her heart was still thumping when she began laughing, feeling a camaraderie in the fact that Ilan had embarrassed himself just as much as she had perhaps embarrassed herself. "That was a performance!" she said.

"I get sick in ten minutes!"

Once a man is saved by a beautiful young woman and snuggled under goose down, found charming, and gently teased, a man is happy. Ilan took Sonia's feet between his.

"You're heating your feet with my feet!"

"Let's make love again?"

"But then you'll have to take off your clothes again." There was a raw ache between her legs.

The next morning when Sonia woke, Ilan was looking out of the window, his fingers splayed against the light that suffused the room even though the sun was on the other side of the house, because it reflected off the snow and caught the ice needles scattering from the pines. He made his fingers into warring batons. Sonia worried about getting out of bed naked in such stripped sunshine. She understood why a painter would travel a long way for this clarity purified by snow.

Ilan turned and said, "What if I paint a picture and the picture becomes your fate? It can work that way." He watched her with an expression she could not read.

"Which way?"

"Well, if you are a good artist, which I narcissistically think I am, and you work every day of your life, gradually you give more of your life to art, you begin to subtract your life so it becomes such an emptiness you dare not look upon it. Slowly, every day and every hour, every month and year, you continue like this, gathering material like a magpie or a bee, moving it laboriously like an ant, consuming and crumbling it like an earthworm. Like a magpie, an ant, an earthworm, a bee, collecting and gathering, moving one more crumb of your life into art, one crumb of ordinary life into dream life, one crumb of reality into unreality, your intuition develops so you have a finger on the pulse."

"On the pulse of what?"

"Just on the pulse. You seize upon the undercurrent; you paint what happens before it happens. Sometimes you paint a portrait and someone falls in love with it, it makes them sensual, or finally content, or it gives them courage, ambition, and they live an expansive life once they have an image of themselves that encourages this. Other times you can paint a picture that unsettles someone, that reveals their inner shame, or that contradicts who they themselves think they are, that trails them, that forecasts their future and entraps them—maybe I will paint a picture that the whole world will know and you'll become angry and feel you don't exist outside the painting."

"But you wouldn't do that?" she asked.

"Who knows what I will do? You know you've become a true artist when even the death of the person you love most in the world is another opportunity to paint, another way to acquire depth."

Sonia felt a seed of narcissistic hope that she would indeed be painted; surely an artist chooses only a woman with an unusual face to be his bedmate. She thought of her grandfather, the painter who had hunted the occult, and her grandmother who Sonia resembled. The intensity of her grandfather's life, the tragedy of his vanishing, had made it so that afterward, his two daughters, Sonia's mother and her aunt Meher, could not tolerate ordinary life.

Ilan leaned over and found his camera by the bed and took a picture of her. "Don't worry," he said, "you are only long black hair and one obsidian eye."

He opened his eyes wide to look directly into hers. "Your eyes are gray," she observed.

"Dark gray, but ringed with amber, can you tell?" He opened them wider so they became the eyes of an owl.

"Yes."

"And I'm vain about my eyes. And I am a painter. What if this means I will become blind?"

"That doesn't make sense."

"Yes, that doesn't make sense," he said. "Should we get up and eat strawberry jam for happiness?"

*

A WEEK LATER SHE accepted his invitation again, and they fell into the habit of meeting every weekend; each time they met, they did the same thing exactly. They drove out, feeling exalted by the landscape, hungry for dinner at the Japanese restaurant, where they no longer had to order. The waiter brought them a parade of dishes: a mineral-smelling broth, a barely set delicate custard perfumed with chrysanthemum, bright roe that burst marine between their teeth, pickled autumn roots. They were almost always the only guests, but once in a while, an aged lady in a long mink coat—so black that it shone silver and gave not the impression of warmth but of chill—was helped in by a chauffeur and a middle-aged caretaker clad in a baby-blue parka. In the ladies' room one day, the caretaker told Sonia she was from Malawi and that she lived in a mansion in the hills, part of a staff of five, all from Malawi. When Sonia told Ilan this, he said, "I should paint their portraits, mistress and staff in a row against Whale Mountain."

After dinner they returned to Ilan's home, tooling by the two urns that held the extravagant snow soufflés, which trembled and let bits of snow fly and join the wilder, formless flakes fleeing the conifers. Every time Ilan passed the urns, he poop-pooped his automobile horn to let his house know he was returning. "What a pompous house," said Ilan, "built with shipping money by my great-grandfather. Rumor goes he brought a maid here and she killed herself to escape his assaults. Perhaps that is why the light has this unsettling presence. The light remembers. I am using it to paint."

"May I see your paintings one day?" asked Sonia. She thought about *The Dictator's Wife,* the reference to which she had found in the library, but she didn't want to admit to Ilan that she had researched him.

"No. They are incomplete. I have to protect them."

"Tell me what you are painting, then—like a traveler's account?"

"No, I won't tell you, or my painting will lose its power, but know I am painting a good painting. When I am painting beautifully, my saliva feels *holy* and my ears feel dusted with pepper. But if I lose my energy, or my painting loses its secret mystery, I will retaliate. And I like you, I want you here, I want to take your nipple and pull it into my mouth!"

In the mornings, Sonia flipped the pages of art books before Ilan left for his studio in the barn, at which time she would need to leave, she had been advised. She paused at a painting of people enjoying an excursion in the Alps. A black shadow cut across the canvas, and Sonia knew from her mother's home in the Himalayas that this was exactly how nighttime and daylight arrive in the mountains, in stripes and behemoths cast by mountains upon mountains. The more she dwelt on the painting, which at first appeared to be a pleasant scene in nature, the more it affected her as something else—a pretend natural scene, figures preoccupied each with their own reenactment of a bucolic tableau. Real life was fake life. Something else was occurring, and it felt—

"*Uncanny?*" she said, and Ilan came over to look at the painting as well.

He then went over to the divan and lay back—his face altered.

He said, "Sonia, can you stop looking at that? Why did you show me that picture? It upset me."

"I didn't show it to you, you came over."

He looked at her straight and defiant: "You showed it to me. You opened to the page and said, '*Uncanny?*'"

"Why does it upset you?" She thought perhaps this painting, which was virtually one of happiness, left a person feeling forlorn.

Over the two months that followed, Sonia learned the indolent pleasure of walking about naked under someone's gaze, she learned that the more sex you have, the more you want, and that to wake up having sex and be almost asleep while having sex was delicious. She learned the pleasures of sideways intimacies—the reaching over to someone's plate to get a section of their sushi or clementine, letting go of formalities—and singing tunelessly and happily so another will listen and laugh. And she learned the most profound pleasure of all: having someone to talk to as you fell asleep or in the middle of the night should you wake, which returned her to the memory of the high hard bed that she shared with Mina Foi whenever she had visited Allahabad as a child. They would tuck the mosquito netting under the thin cotton mattress, working all the way around, but inevitably one mosquito found its way in, and just when they felt safe, it came helicoptering. "Oof baba, oof baba," Mina Foi would say, dressed in her rose-patterned nightie that was still bold in those days and smelling sweetly of coconut hair oil as she tried to clap it between her hands.

In many ways, Sonia felt as if she had returned to being a child, a more playful child than she had ever been. She thought that this was what people spoke of when they spoke about love: You were outwardly more adult and treated with greater consideration, but secretly you were more childlike, more free, more full of laughter. When you were alone, you felt and lived like a serious, curbed adult, but meanwhile you were treated like a child. If you remained solitary all your life and were not well-off—again she recalled Mina Foi—you were considered an imbecile.

It was Mina Foi who had first whispered warning that men might be wolves concealed behind quite normal exteriors. "Even though you are too young, I'm telling you so you beware and learn."

It was Mina Foi who had encouraged Sonia: "You go and be lucky, my dear. Don't be like me."

....

ONE DAWN HOUR, AFTER THE TEMPERATURE HAD SUD-
denly risen and Sonia could hear the snow outside Ilan's house growing sudsy and retreating, the forest dripping, the drip percolating
through the moss into the earth, she set out as if for an early morning
walk. She would leave no incriminating footsteps. Ilan was still asleep
as she made a quick detour to his painting studio in the carriage barn,
which she found secured by an iron bar that in turn was secured by a
padlock. Where did Ilan keep the key? She peeped through the window, but it was blocked by a canvas. She went around to the other side,
and here, too, something blocked her view, but she noticed there was
a gap in a corner higher up. She went to the garden shed and fetched a
crate, and when she climbed up, straining on tiptoes to look through
the gap no bigger than her eye—the thump of her heart telling her to
be-quick-be-quick—another eye locked onto her eye so swiftly that
for a moment she thought there was a living person trapped there. The
eye was dilated by urgency. An internal voice sounded, as if the trapped
person spoke inside her head: *Happiness is for other people.*

Sonia climbed back down and ran to replace the wooden crate. She
had trespassed. The eye in the studio had noted her. Who was *not* happiness for? A raven tipped its head and watched. The windows of the
house seemed to be watching her as well. She wondered if there were
security cameras that Ilan had never told her about. What if he was
awake looking out?

And, in fact, he was awake and at the window. "Where were you?"
he asked.

"I went for a walk." She pretended she was busy blowing her nose. Her heart thumped louder. She felt Ilan's eyes on her.

"That's not true."

"Why wouldn't it be true?"

"Don't lie."

"I won't."

But she stank of her lie. She was afraid of her lie. She hated her lie. Her face, guilty as a guilty dog's, gave her away. Why had she spied? Ilan had trusted her. She had betrayed his trust. Was she afraid of the mystery of Ilan? Who was he? Whose eye had fastened upon her own?

After a pause, Ilan looked up with an opaque stare and said: "There is no future for us beyond sex. If you observe, our conversations are nonsense."

"Are they? Why do you think that?" Sonia was shaking in shame but also for an unnameable terror beyond shame, as if she were learning that she would never be able to talk, in fact, to anyone.

"Who knows? Different countries, different upbringings, different ages."

But then his mood switched. "I need to find energy to work." He put on Harry Belafonte and sang the song about the banana boat. Ilan had told Sonia that his family had owned cargo ships that transported fruit from Chile, from Cuba. One of their ships was named *Prospero*. Sometimes they transported other goods, like a lifetime's worth of lemon soap purchased as his grandfather's kindness to a beautiful widow soapmaker. In exchange for what favors, who knew.

"That's why you smell of lemons!"

"And so do you when you use my soap."

"It smells lovely."

"Yes, darling, you are lovely."

*

"WHO IS THIS PERSON and why did he come?" asked Marie.

"He's working on his paintings. He says his imagination is pure because the snow light is so clear and his focus is sharp."

"Then why is he preying on you if he's supposed to be focusing on his work?"

"He isn't preying."

"I don't trust this."

"Why not?"

"I trust a bashful man, a man who takes things slowly."

Obviously it wasn't Marie's thinking that Sonia was irresistible and that being swooped up was a thrilling indication of this. Or even that it may be true love, and true love can happen as swiftly as a glance chancing across a room. As swiftly as a whiff of lemon soap that made one think of a clement climate.

"He's going to invite me to New York City," she said. "He has an apartment there."

"I still don't understand who this person is and why he is here in the dead of winter. It doesn't add up. Where is his family?"

"He hates his family."

"Or maybe it's that his family hates him," said Marie. She left sniffing for her Weight Watchers group, which had awarded her two gold stars for dropping two pounds.

Armando said, "Don't listen to Marie. Who is anyone to question another person's desire? Even a single night of happiness is better than not having happiness at all."

This was the same Armando Fritz Baltazar who had wished to become a priest, who had, out of all the one hundred and fifty students slumbering late on Sunday mornings, woken early, donned a suit and tie, and taken the college van that ran especially for him to church. Sonia began to see Lazlo and Armando together now. Always Armando ahead, Lazlo following. Always Armando talking and Lazlo hesitantly, quizzically, smiling. Armando spoke for Lazlo as if he knew his thoughts: "Lazlo will like the mint tea." "Lazlo is scared of the dark."

*

ONE EVENING, AS THEY were leaving for dinner, Ilan paused and looked at Sonia. "Come," he said, taking her by the hand to a room that was lined with closets and opening one that was packed tight with finery. He plucked out an evening gown. "This might fit you, put it on! You either make yourself into a person worth knowing or not."

When she was dressed in golden green silk that rose high at her neck but dipped to the base of her spine, leaving her arms and back bare, Ilan put on a robe of a deeper bronzed green. He took her to the mirror on the landing: "Now you will see!"

They had thirty-two years between them, but dressed in this way, they were a match. Their eyes glittered, as did their dark hair, parted and combed smooth; their noses were strong, their cheekbones high, they were tall and mysterious.

Said Sonia, "I'm more beautiful now than I was when I met you. We look like the Raja and Rani of Indore photographed by Man Ray."

"You better stick by me." He took a picture of them in the mirror with his little camera.

*

SONIA WASHED HER HAIR on a Sunday, and she used the travel hair dryer that was plugged into an outlet by the indistinct priestly figure from Malekula in the entryway. Why the hair dryer was by the imposing creature, she couldn't tell, so she put it away.

She heard Ilan: "Sonia! My hair is wet, my hair is wet. I'm going to catch a cold. Where is the hair dryer? I can't find it. Sonia, come and find it. Were you using it? *Where did you put it?*"

"It's in the bathroom."

"I'm catching cold. I'm catching *cold. Why did you move it?*"

"Because it was in the hallway."

"You come here right now," he said, hopping and leaping, "and put it back where you found it! My hair is wet. I'm going to get sick. I'm going to fall sick."

"But everyone dries their hair in the bathroom—"

"Don't argue with me, you stupid!" He ran to the bedroom and got into bed with his wet hair. "I will *not* go to dinner with you."

Sonia came to the door. He put the sheet and pillow over his head and refused to talk. The longer he lay in bed, curled in the pose of an injured child, the more Sonia felt the wrenching guilt of seeing an adult so unhappy that the sheets were over his head.

While he continued to fail to rise, she sat in the chair wondering whether to leave or stay. "Look, I'm sorry. I'll never move it again."

She rubbed his back. He didn't squiggle away. This was someone who had saved her from the silence of the Gerstein Chen House. She went on rubbing in scallop moves, then in gentle raking moves such as the Allahabad ayah made sweeping the dust, slow and even, all the way out.

Eventually, after a long while—during which time the sun fell behind the mountains and the scene went abruptly dark, an ashen tragedy, a household with no lamp on and no cheer—wary sadness showed in Ilan's eye that opened from under the pillow. Gradually he roused himself. He'd aged; he was no longer vibrant or handsome. He was a defeated person staring unhappily at his feet.

Still looking down, he said, "I'm okay now, but don't do that again."

"I won't," said Sonia.

"I hate my feet." He looked up at her beseechingly.

She said, "They have character!" They were large and gnarled.

"I am ashamed of my nose."

The days were longer now by the end of February, and on the first day of March, watching a line of ravens flying low through the mizzle to attack a hawk in a hemlock, Ilan noticed the unusual sight of a car climbing the hill and parking between the two oversize urns. He recognized the proprietor of the Floating World restaurant who had been away in Japan. It was from him Ilan had purchased his Kyoto screens painted in ink made from the soot of whale oil. Years of living in the hills beyond Kyoto had convinced his friend that countryside Vermont and countryside Japan were naturally compatible. Here, as there, were snow mountains, hermit poets, twisted pines growing out of rock, silence married to shadow, shadow twinned to gaunt winter light, to skeleton light, to light subtracted upon faded floorboards, to evening light red as a fox that curled for a moment in the white porcelain on the sideboard. Here, too, was a cricket by the woodstove.

But Ilan did not introduce Sonia to his friend. "Quick," Ilan said, ordering her to go upstairs and hide under the bed. Under the bed were dust bunnies and a dead wasp. What if she sneezed?

When the man left, Ilan came laughing. "Is there someone hiding under the bed by any chance?" He had his camera and took a picture.

Sonia began to weep.

"What is it?"

"Why are you hiding me under the bed?"

"I don't know," he said, looking stricken. "I imagined you would want to hide."

"Why did you think I'd want to hide?"

"I didn't think. It was an instinct to protect our private happiness. When you let other people in, that is when trouble begins."

She continued to weep.

"You're making me the bad guy. I'm not the bad guy. What did I do? Why don't you go if you are unhappy. Am I holding you?" He was chopping his marijuana.

"You're right," he said later, looking stricken. He pulled her to him and tickled her under the chin. "Probably I am nervous because I am leaving."

"You are?"

"Yes."

"When?"

"In two days."

"Two days? Why didn't you tell me earlier?"

"I don't know—I am scared I will miss you."

"You don't know me enough to miss me. You don't know me for more than a short time."

"Oh, I can miss someone after a day. Let's meet somewhere—"

"Where?"

"Anywhere—let me think. Portofino!" He was delighted by his proposal. "Where the film stars go. Everyone must go to Italy—do you know why? Because there you learn that religion depends on the human artist or else it wouldn't exist."

"I don't have a visa to travel to Europe," she said. In a few days Hewitt College would open and Sonia would return for her last semester. "I'll need to find a job and transfer from a student visa to a work visa—that is going to be almost impossible." Visa concerns were foremost in her mind. If she tried to stay on in the States, how would she ever find a sponsor? If she returned to India, would a door shut behind her, never to open again?

"I see." His face fell. "I should be thinking of my painting and instead I'm thinking about your visa. That's the trouble. You take in a stray cat and then your whole life turns to worrying about it."

"I should have applied to a graduate program in writing." Sonia hadn't been determined enough, perhaps because she wasn't confident enough. "I am not convinced by my story."

"What is it about?"

"A boy who becomes a monkey."

"Ahhh—don't write orientalist nonsense! Don't cheapen your country or people will think that this is actually India—it's dangerous. Indians may not be Protestants, but neither are Indians monkeys."

She brought her story for him to read the next day. He read half of it, frowning, then he put it down and said, "I don't like it, to be honest. I will respect you by saying that. It doesn't feel true."

"You said you learned that surrealism is realism in Mexico?"

"I said that there is no such thing as surrealism in Mexico. This is the Great Indian Rope Trick. What Westerners did to you, you are doing to yourself. Why don't you write about your aunt? The one you said still lives with her parents and isn't allowed to make a phone call."

"You mean her arranged marriage?"

"No! That's even worse. Don't write about arranged marriages."

"Her divorce?"

"That's better. You have a good mind, I have observed it—don't degrade yourself.

"Look," he offered, "I will help you." He made a phone call and said, "Lala, I have a friend. She is a foreign student who needs a job after she finishes college. Maybe you can find something in your gallery? She is not your typical spoiled, rich Third-Worlder, and that is why I like her."

Ilan handed Sonia an address and a phone number. "Go immediately to Lala before she forgets this conversation. She is a bit crazy; don't pay too much attention. Take advantage of being in New York to educate yourself. Do you remember I was angry when you looked at Balthus and said '*Uncanny*'? I became angry because I see how he did it. He was a fake war hero, a fake count, he had a fake name, a wife who may or may not have come from a samurai family, a disingenuous way of speaking about his work. The shameless lies made the art true; the true art made the lies real. Everyone thinks the mystery is the little girls showing their panties, but the mystery lies elsewhere. Do you understand? Always tell a big lie, darling, to swallow the truth—with the small ones, you'll get found out and be thrown in prison."

In the moment of leaving a day later, he was jolly. His suitcase was by the door. "Hey, you're sweet." He kissed her. He kissed her again. "What do you want with me? Why are you after me? All women want to own me, they want to possess me." He licked her neck, a quick small lick.

Ilan locked the door of his house behind himself and Sonia. The taxi he had called drove up; he got in and waved wildly from the window as it drove away. He took out a camera and took a picture of Sonia standing there.

And he was gone.

In a few minutes the taxi came back. Ilan jumped out. "Darling, you are my dear," he said, clasping her. Then he was gone again.

By evening, Sonia felt a drastic draining. She waited for Ilan to telephone. You cannot miss anyone after so short a time—but, yes, you could. She waited, and as the days drew on to weeks, she continued in a perpetual nausea of waiting, but still the telephone did not ring for her in the hallway of the Gerstein Chen House.

She tried to edit her story about the boy who climbed into a tree and was mistaken for a holy hermit because of idle statements that could as easily be silly as profound: *Emptiness is form, and form is emptiness.* Ilan was right. It felt like nonsense.

*

THE ART GALLERY OWNER, Leone "Lala" Leloup, surprisingly answered the phone and suggested they meet in person. Hoping she may learn something about Ilan's whereabouts, Sonia traveled to New York City on an early Peter Pan bus, which trundled past lilac snowbanks, past black rivers carrying silver on their scales, past sodden woods, ochre and scarlet bushes. She watched the reflection of the gray sky in the ditches and furrows of stubbly fields filled with snow melt. She imagined putting an ink pen into the black bloom of a watercolor cloud in the wet sky. It was a sharp desire that surprised her.

They passed small towns, a shuttered motel with a wooden Indian figure outside, a Wok n' Roll, a Sudsy, and a Mobil. When she got off the bus at Port Authority five hours later, a man standing just where passengers disembarked hissed, "Taxi? Taxi?"

She said, "Thank you," taking him for a cabdriver soliciting passengers. He took her bag and walked briskly away. She ran after him. They walked down the main avenue and into a side street. "Where are you going?"

"I'm getting you a taxi."

He kept walking, Sonia gasping behind. The man stopped at a taxi parked by a curb where garbage was being hauled from the dungeon of a skyscraper. He opened the door and swung in her bag, saying, "That will be forty dollars."

Sonia said, "But why do I have to pay you?"

He pointed at himself. "Because I'm——" he said, "and nobody messes with me."

She missed who he said he was and felt deeply ashamed to be conned the very minute she'd set foot in New York City; she'd been adequately warned by Marie to stay alert. The taxi driver who had been taking a lunch break in his parked cab was from Pakistan. "Why you gave him money? Why you gave him your bag? You should be careful of these people. Why weren't you careful? You should be careful!" He finished his lunch.

Harried and humiliated, Sonia missed her first sight of the Midtown crowds—women in business suits and sneakers, halal lunch carts, tourists, a man with a billboard that read *Abortion Kills Babies*. And she missed her first sight of the Upper East Side—the couture fashion, the restaurants of forbidding wealth. By noon, she entered a marble lobby on a street near the Metropolitan Museum of Art and traveled in a polished oak and brass elevator to a living room that was hung with bright abstract paintings and lined with sculptures. "Twombly, Hodgkin, Albers, Hepworth, Clemente, Frankenthaler, Basquiat," said Lala, studying Sonia to see if she recognized the names. She did, some of them.

"Ah." Lala surveyed Sonia with a canny gaze that zipped from her toes to her face. Lala's hair was a cascade of gray ringlets; she was dressed in a below knee–length triangular wool skirt and jacket that looked eccentric. Taking hold of Sonia's elbow, she drew her to the window and held her at arm's length as if examining her for purchase. She took her chin and moved her face about in sharp directions.

"I see," she said. "Ilan has an eye. Well, it is true that in an art gallery the receptionist must be beautiful. Or else, exactly the opposite: ugly enough to be a collector's object."

"I haven't heard from him since he left."

The woman looked at her and said almost kindly, although she was not a kind woman except when she was being deceitful, "Ilan is a complicated person, but maybe he tried to help you."

She owned a gallery in SoHo, but she was experimenting with a space in Brooklyn in a district of warehouses and disused factory buildings on the waterfront. The many artists who resided there had named the neighborhood Dumbo—for Down Under the Manhattan Bridge Overpass—to dissuade the bankers, but Lala was betting on the bankers arriving.

"I go to India often," she said. "Do you know my friends Bubbly and Ronny Mirchandani who own the textile museum in Mumbai?

No? They flew me to Hampi, to Ladakh, to Great Nicobar in their private plane."

She asked Sonia, "How many languages do you have?"

"English. Hindi. A little German."

"I don't care for the Germans, and the Germans don't care for me. No French?"

Sonia contested bravely, "Spanish is more useful in the States, isn't it?"

Lala sighed. "French is the language of the salon, and if you don't know it, you cannot join in a certain conversation that is unachievable in another tongue. This conversation has a history. Sophistication doesn't come free. If you're not born to it, it takes determined effort. Well." She sighed. "I will employ you. My office will process your temporary visa, and little money, eh? This is a favor to a friend. But you cannot adopt that expression in the gallery; you have to be person-able. Attempt to dress with some flair. Never wear jeans, not even at home on the weekend." She went into another room, presumably her dressing room, and brought forth some clothes. "Try this. Startling orange is a good color against your skin.

"Look, I know everything, my dear. I know why Ilan sent you." She managed a thin smile that was half a grimace. "You don't have to pretend." Sonia felt a countering of the shame she had hiding herself away when the proprietor of the Floating World had come to visit and Ilan had told her to hide under the bed.

She was back in Vermont by night, boiling Chacharoni in the kitchen when Armando came blustering in, stamping the slush off his boots.

"I can't find Lazlo."

"He's never here."

"He's not anywhere else."

Sonia followed Armando to Lazlo's room on the second floor, and when there was no answer, they pushed the door open and found Lazlo lying on his bed with his arms and legs sticking straight up, quite fro-zen, and his eyes open wide. His belongings had been neatly packed into a cardboard box by the side of the bed. Each time they gingerly touched him, he screamed.

The ambulance came to the Gerstein Chen House, and two days later, they heard that Lazlo's parents had arrived and flown him back to Sofia. When Armando phoned a number he'd ferreted through his work in the alumni office, which gave him access to student files, a voice answered in Bulgarian and the line was crisply disconnected. He tried again. The same thing happened. Some of Armando's bravado went limp, and a complication entered his personality. During the days before term began, he came to the library to sit with Sonia. "I am his only friend," he kept repeating. She thought of the sultry photograph she had seen by Armando's bed, of Armando himself. "Lazlo took it," he had said.

Sonia remembered: Armando talking, Lazlo listening; Armando striding ahead, Lazlo following; one growing larger, the other smaller. But of course this may not have anything to do with what was amiss with Lazlo.

One day, Sonia took the college van into town, bought a phone card, and late that night phoned the number in Mexico that Ilan had scribbled down when he left, although he had said, "Wait for me to call you. I am hardly ever there, and nobody will speak English."

She phoned and there was no answer. She phoned again. When she phoned for the third time, a woman picked up and screamed furiously in Spanish, then hung up as if Sonia had woken her. She thought she might have the wrong number but didn't want to take the risk of disturbing the woman again. One week later, she tried one more time at a morning hour. She remained incredulous that you could sleep heart-to-heart with another person, your nose reaching for air by his neck, spend mornings looking out of the window together at falling needles of shining snow, that you could share so many stories, but the person may care nothing for you and vanish overnight.

There was no answer, and Sonia telephoned her parents instead, imagining the drawing room in Delhi, each parent on either side of the living room sofa, her mother reading intently, her father looking searchingly with a lighthouse sweep every now and again at her mother, as if he was a man observing a woman he does not know, simply with a male gaze, one without a marital history, with a touch of amazement— then getting up to blare the television, feeling resentful of the way she continued to read.

Their cook, Chandu, would be folded over at his middle and asleep on the kitchen stool because her parents must follow protocol and wait for eight P.M., when they could finally call out to him so he could un- fold himself, light the gas with the rolled-up bit of checked waxed paper in which the sliced bread came wrapped, and warm the food he had prepared earlier, the vegetables though, irretrievably soggy. On the back burner would be his own meal of rice and dal, which he would consume after Mama and Papa had eaten, sitting on the floor under the lightbulb with his thali on the day's newspaper that by now both Mama and Papa would have read. After his meal the newspaper would be rel- egated to the old newspaper heap.

But nobody answered the phone. It rang and rang.

6

....

THERE WERE NO CHILDREN AT THE DINNER PARTY MAMA
and Papa were attending at the home of their friends Neil and Daljit
Singh because there were no children in India anymore in the homes of
successful parents of a successful class. The children were in Geneva,
Hong Kong, Sydney, London, New York, and Vermont. They were at
Harvard, Oxford, Siemens, the United Nations, Microsoft, Amnesty,
Seagram, McKinsey, the World Bank, Sloan Kettering, and Hewitt
College. The men were drinking hard, and after a few single malts,
they were roused. They laughed *haha hoho* and inquired of Neil, who
had studied with Papa in Doon School and had just returned from a
business trip to Moscow, whether Russian women were as beautiful as
rumored.

"Well, it is true that until twenty-five you see some beauties," declared Neil, "but after twenty-five, as if overnight, they become the
exact opposite—like potatoes in a sack."

"Same with Punjabis," said Papa. "After a certain age, the women
begin to spread."

They weighed the qualities of women of various nationalities about
the globe: Were Brazilians truly so stunning? "On the beach of Ipanema,
yes, but everywhere else they are just like us—only they don't care what
they look like in a bathing costume."

Dilip, who had a paunch upon which to rest his whiskey glass, ruled
on the entire Middle East: "No matter the elegance of the face, when
you see the bulbous quality of what comes below, you want to run for
your life."

China, Korea, and Japan: "There they have the opposite trouble," said mischievous Jehangir, "instead of being too round, they are too flat."

Americans: "Hefty dames, they'd wallop anyone."

They didn't even mention the continent of Africa. But they concurred: "Italian and French women, my goodness!"

As they talked, Mama noticed their expressions became rabid. There they were, half chewing, half salivating, those balding fathers. They discussed film stars and news readers. They went all the way around the globe and back, to where the women in the room, in handloom kurtas over turtlenecks, flesh-colored socks slipping out of stiff arts-and-crafts bazaar jootis, failed to rise to any wit. Instead, they began to attack the women the men praised: "Indian women are the most stunning!"

Mama switched subjects. She indicated the painting of horses that hung above the sofa. She didn't like the cubist forms, but this was beside the point. "Terrible what the goons are doing to him," she said of the artist, Husain. Recently, Hindu religious sensibilities had been offended by a delicate sketch by him of a bare-breasted goddess Saraswati as she sat with her vina, a fish, a river, a lotus flower. He had sketched it out of love, but now it inspired hate. A mob had broken into an art gallery and destroyed his paintings. The conversation of the dinner party moved inevitably to the unending violence between Hindus and Muslims, the destruction of the Babri mosque in Ayodhya four years ago that had once again ensured the hate would forever reignite.

Neil's wife, Daljit, and Jehangir's wife, Margo, glad to be leaving the previous conversation behind, turned passionately to each other: "Thank goodness the children are out of India. The bachchas must never return."

Ferooza was Mama's closest friend. She had no children of her own, but she agreed: "This country is going to get more intolerant. Anyone might be in the wrong place at the wrong moment."

They finished with gooseberry tart and custard. The mood of the evening had not returned to lightness and Papa felt thwarted. He'd wanted to have a silly-billy time. He wanted to *haha hoho* because he was amongst friends and nothing indicated friendship better than saying any reckless, off-color thing. What is more, some unpleasant memories had risen as the women commiserated on the tedious subject of fraying secularism.

When the centuries-old Babri mosque had been rubbled, Papa had tossed out the sweets being distributed by his celebrating colleagues at Gupta Brothers, where he was a managing director, and he called out like an orator, "*The British have won!*" This was according to his philosophy that the British policy of divide and rule, pitting one religious community against the other, was triumphantly playing out beyond independence. When in 1984 there were Hindu–Sikh riots, Papa had also posited, "*The British have won!*" but he had stayed home while many Hindus ignored the curfew and drove heroically forth to save their Sikh friends before their homes went up in flames.

Mama had urged, "Shouldn't you make sure Neil and Daljit are all right?"

Papa had replied, "There is nothing one man can do against a mob."

Neil had, in fact, been caught by a murderous mob driving home as fast as he could. Seeing that cars were being stopped and checked for Sikhs, who would be pulled out and burnt alive, he had wrested the kara that identified him from his wrist, thrown it out of the car, and managed to take another route home. Had he been a turban-wearing Sikh, he would not have been spared.

Mama and Papa careened home, Papa driving drunk through the winter fog like the other men at the dinner party. "Those women are too bloody sensitive for their own good. They get overwrought and overreact. By their own hysteria, they are going to bring disaster upon themselves."

Mama said that Margo, Daljit, and Ferooza were making a rational assessment, because each time the familiar Indian darkness revealed itself, it was more potent because memory of violence builds upon memory of violence. And it was the men who had struck her as hysterical when they compared women of various nationalities. "You spent half the evening talking about women like cattle. Why don't you look in the mirror before you judge people on their looks?"

"People don't judge cattle on the basis of their looks."

"Don't you all tire," Mama continued, "of going on and on, this one is beautiful, this one is ugly, on and on and on—it's a disease!" She added, "You don't know your own mind or heart, Manav. It's a mess and muddle."

Papa sped up as if he wished to force an accident, skidding about corners, and when they arrived home and Mama got out to open the front gate for him to drive through, Papa accelerated straight at her. If she hadn't leapt aside, she would have been injured if not killed. She looked at him through the glow of the car headlights, and he looked steadily back at her. Mama learned that despite his mess and muddle, his inebriation, he was clear on one thing: He *did* wish to hurt his wife.

Terrible things happen in the heat of an argument between a married couple. Mama ventured into the icy bathroom to take a shower so as to force herself to disengage and bring down the register of rage between them. The bathroom pipes wavered vertically and horizontally across the walls—the plumber had sawed, reset, angled them, tried every kinky direction and fitted in valves to cure the chronic low pressure and repetitive air locks. This had not worked. When Mama turned on the taps, she heard a distant sound of water blocked by its own steam. She shivered and fiddled the knobs—cautious, small exertions—trying to wind down the hot water to the smallest piddle, mingled with the right measure of cold to calm the vapor. The pipes gasped and whooped in a crisis of emptiness, and there was a fruitless borborygmus of water in the geyser. She hopped in and out until, finally, with operatic suddenness, the frustrated water gathered momentum, the whole system vibrated and strained, hiccupped and spat, and the silted shower spout shook and roared and spent its entire scorching bellyful of angry water and untidy steam upon her.

Scalded, she exited and heard Papa say on the telephone: "Sonia? What is it?"

Mama hurried to take the receiver from him. This was not their usual time to call.

Sonia said, "Lazlo had a nervous breakdown some weeks ago. We found him completely frozen with his arms up in the air."

"The Bulgarian boy? Have you been alone in the house?"

"Yes. The ambulance came and took him away."

"Don't stay there by yourself. Go to Marie."

Sonia said, "I don't want to end up like Lazlo. I've had enough."

Mama stood later that night with her forehead against the cold headache-imparting windowpane, looking out to where a madman slept in the ruins of an idgah in the municipal park behind the flat, steps to a pulpit climbing into the dark. The idgah was older than the Babri mosque—when had it crumbled and succumbed to a new version of the city? She didn't know. And she couldn't feel anything but exhaustion right now, although to be a mother meant you should have empathy for your child, worry about your child.

Evil whiskey vapor came out of his every pore, and Papa felt sickeningly guilty—he might have murdered his wife had she not jumped aside. Because Papa felt guilty, he felt resentful. Because he felt resentful, he wanted his wife to soften this feeling of his, to agree it was an ordinary drunken disagreement, to which they should pay no attention. Instead, Mama slept in Sonia's room, refused to speak to him at breakfast, and made it known that she would not forgive or forget, because certain matters belong in the category of matters that can never be forgiven or forgotten.

When he was at work in his Connaught Place office, where Mama would not overhear, Papa telephoned Sonia: "Look, Sonu, do you remember when you were crying all the time and saying you were lonely?"

"I feel even more lonely now."

"Well, Dadaji recently asked me if you would like to be introduced to the Colonel's grandson. Remember that greedy family, the ones who are always asking for soup to be sent when they are sick and kebabs when they are well?"

"Oh yes!" This was Allahabadi custom, she remembered; dishes were always being exchanged, and one saw them paraded through the neighborhood in tiffin carriers, in thermos flasks, upon plates covered in napkins tied in rabbit ears.

"Dadaji told me that he and Ba made an informal visit to the family to assess the boy's situation. Apparently he is living in New York, and you might at least make a friend from home when you go to work there." He was certain now he hadn't been about to kill his wife. Mama's mind was in a heightened state after macabre dinner-party talk about murderous mobs. He was simply driving the car abruptly forward. He was a good husband and father who believed his daughter could be anything she wished, but even if she became prime minister, he wanted her to have the support of love and family, not only to excel in her career. "Should I tell them to go ahead?"

Filled with a despair and desire for revenge against Ilan, who promised, "*Darling, you are my dear,*" Sonia said, "Yes. It's good to meet a man whom your family knows, or you are only someone to be made use of."

"But take it lightly? If it works out, it does. If it doesn't work out, it isn't meant to be. Just don't say a word to Mama; she will be angry that I brought this up. She is a most unnatural mother."

I T WAS STILL FRIGID WHEN HEWITT COLLEGE OPENED FOR spring term in March, the cars of returning students and teachers wending up the hills, reversing the journey they had made in December. Audrey Hong in her giant SUV, a silver capsule that traveled soundless and climate controlled; Isla Tewksbury, who had been born in a rainbow bus; Orlando Machado, who was Spanish via Havana and Miami; a gentle professor of Italian lyric poetry who drove so slowly—making sure he didn't startle the mating foxes, in case there were any—that he was fined by the cops for being a traffic hazard.

By April, the wind carried a tender swell, shoots peeking through the bracken. By May, Vermont had entered its fragile season, the transparent speckled time of honeysuckle and cloudberries, of spring rain falling in polka dots, which triggered and spun the scent of lilacs and hatched them into clusters of stars. Frog spawn dripped down stems; the birds' calls turned so honeyed, those disappointed in love found the trills difficult to listen to: "Will you? *Will you?*"

Sonia, completing her senior thesis—part literature and part creative writing—wrote a fictional version of her aunt's story:

Upon a midnight hour, twenty-five years after his mother had made him swear on her deathbed to forsake Mina Foi, Mina Foi's true love, Ernest, returned. He crept outside Mina Foi's window and made the chirrur-chirrur of the owl Mina Foi herself had taught him when they had been sweethearts. Mina Foi cracked open the window. "Forgive me, Mina. I made a terrible mistake."

But there was no longer an owl living in the tree outside, and the unfamiliar hoot alerted the dogs from the servants' barracks. They began to bark, a light switched on from another window and spilled upon Ernest, now balding and stout, straddling the rain gutter. "You?" Dadaji thundered. "Cut a straight line from my property!"

"The bugger!" he said at breakfast the next morning. "Thinks he can drop you and run, then saunter back decades on!"

"When someone says they are sorry, shouldn't one accept it?" said Mina Foi. "Maybe he had a weak moment. Maybe it was his mother forbidding her son to marry me because she was so damaged by her own cruel fate that she wished to destroy the happiness of everyone else."

"A man who is weak once, will be weak again. A man who betrays once, will betray again."

Seeing his forty-six-year-old daughter still unconvinced, Dadaji threatened, "Everyone will laugh themselves silly, a pair of gormless ninnies gadding."

"Who is there to laugh?"

Dadaji had refused to eat his dinner, his lips pursed, staring out, lifting his hand, then letting it fall uselessly to the table. He refused to take his medicines. "I have become obsolete." He showed the betrayed eyes of a man with a wrinkle in his retina who might soon be completely blind.

Mina Foi summoned all her strength: "Daddy, I'm scared to grow old alone."

"Well, what of it? Your mother and I are alone," he replied.

"What are you talking about? Here I am every moment, day and night, looking after you."

"You're only here because you have nowhere else to go. Children watch out for themselves, that is what one learns as a parent."

Mina Foi, her fingers buttoning and unbuttoning her cardigan, blurted out: "Your! Very! Existence! Depends! On! My! Unhappiness!"

Sick to her stomach after having said this, and full of the fear she might not have her parents beside her if something went wrong again as it had so reliably gone wrong in the past, she sent a note to Ernest that said: It's too late; our time has passed. My parents need me.

The next morning, seeing by her misery that she had succumbed,
Dadaji was jolly. As a treat, Ba ordered his favorite jam roly-poly, and
Mina Foi was permitted to enjoy his jokes once again, to be quizzed:
"What is the smallest nation in the world?"

She refused to say "the Vatican," although this was an easy one
she'd been asked before.

"Why that expression?" he said. "Good heavens, anyone would
think you'd swallowed a cow."

Sonia writing this story felt guilty. Wasn't she betraying her aunt, who couldn't withstand another betrayal? She wondered also whether she was not damning herself. What you write, don't you become? While Ilan had suggested she write about Mina Foi, he had also suggested that Sonia not write about the marriage arranged for Mina Foi after Ernest had kept the vow made to his mother, because arranged-marriage stories were not dissimilar to orientalist stories about monkeys. An arranged-marriage story, even one that ended six months later in divorce, felt true and false. True because it happened. False because it was feeding the West what it wanted to consume about the East. The audience made it false. Lifting this one story out of all the others made it false. Careful not to orientalize, Sonia wrote that Mina Foi ate pears, not pink guavas from the guava orchard beyond which the highway thundered.

Professor Conti loved this story so much he fell in love with Mina Foi. The character who is an afterthought in everyone's lives can take center stage. This was also fiction—the unloved attract love and understanding.

For the critical part of her thesis, Sonia wrote a treatise on the subject of magic realism as it graded into orientalism. Was it that her monkey story wasn't well written, or, as Ilan suggested, was there a fatal flaw?

Sonia argued that Latin American, Asian, and African cultures possessed a great deal of homegrown magic. Rumors of ghosts came bursting out of folk societies, especially those without electricity. Superstition possessed the richness of art. A fantastic tale was another kind of mirror, another kind of metaphor, a way to expose larger-than-life brutalities, a rot beyond rational understanding, a way to say things about a dictator you could never say outright. Also, there was the practical purpose of being able to leap between times and places, to reveal patterns and connections beyond the reach of a realistic book in realistic time. Sonia referenced Bulgakov and Dinesen, Calvino and Rushdie, Morrison and Márquez.

The term "magic realism," invented by an obsolete German scholar in the 1920s, had been seized upon by the Western world and used to circumscribe the non-Western world, but then the non-Western world, as was its inevitable downfall, became persuaded and ashamed by what the Western world thought. It refused its own myths, its own premonition dreams. It began writing in ways that were dislocated from itself. How, in fact, did magic realism relate to myth, fairy tale, science fiction, fantasy, fable, religion?

Sonia considered the enticement of white people by route of peacocks, monsoons, exotic-spice bazaars—exotic to whom? you might ask—but there was legitimate concern over how India would be perceived in the larger world, the fear that stories cheapened by proliferation, decorative outside and hollow inside, would reduce the seriousness of the nation, demean its soul, deflect attention from the compelling necessity to report on a vast unreported landscape, on millions of people with middle-class aspirations, the ordinariness of poverty. Would the dilemma vanish if the abundance of stories grew as abundant as life itself?

Did You Get That Very Silly Letter?

CHAPTER

8

....

As SHE DID EACH MORNING, BA SET OFF TO INSPECT THE household, a magpie of darting attention: her diamond earrings and gold bangles glinting, her glance sewing a quick seam, the keys to all the doors and cabinets attached to a jingling ring tucked into her petticoat. She counted the sheets brought back by the washerman; she resettled the almonds into a jar appropriate for their depleted size, pleased not to waste space; she made two smaller containers of cornflakes from one big one—division made things last longer.

This motto of austerity by which they operated meant Ba and Dadaji didn't heed the pleas of the owner of their bungalow, Mrs. Luna Pant, when she made a formal visit each Diwali. Over the exchange of dried fruit and nuts, she implored Ba, Dadaji, and Mina Foi to at last cede the lease to Number 10 Cadell Road. Fifty years had passed, and all this time, Dadaji had continued to pay a rent of the past, so greatly did the law favor the tenant over the landlady.

Mrs. Pant's pleas made Dadaji all the more convinced they'd be wise to stay. "Two hundred and fifty rupees and fifty paise a month!" he would chortle, and while Mrs. Pant was of the opinion one should never do anything for a tenant who paid a rent so insulting, Dadaji believed one should not squander extravagance upon a leased property. He refused his family electric generators, inverters, and stabilizers, let alone air conditioners. There was no pump to pump water to a water tank and no water tank to store water—instead Ayah, at two P.M. or two A.M., whenever the municipal supply trickled in, filled the buckets that filled so slowly, she had to stand by them for an hour or more. Savings led to triumphant savings. Savings had impoverished their existence.

Ba apportioned Delite biscuits—one and a half—for Dari, Dadaji's former secretary from his law practice. Now that they were both retired, he came Monday mornings to assist with Dadaji's personal paperwork. Together they operated under the same philosophy as Ba inspecting the storeroom: The more rigorously you divide small and humble, the greater your eventual gain. They invested the tiniest possible amount in the largest possible number of companies, stocks, and pension schemes.

Dadaji, awaiting Dari, made notes at the veranda worktable, his rheumy orb at the saucer-sized magnifying glass he held to the numbers. Mina Foi, wearing black, square-frame spectacles, sat at a smaller table with scissors to trim extra paper from the bottom of old letters, which would be later used to make labels for new addresses to be glued over the old addresses of envelopes being reused. She cut large envelopes to make two envelopes from one. She was thinking how she was worse off than a servant—a servant at least received a salary and a half day off on Sunday. She was thinking about her true love, Ernest, whom she had met in college when she was wearing fashionable cat-eye glasses and bell-bottoms—Mina Foi had been fashionable once—and when he was wearing fashionable cat-eye glasses and bell-bottoms, too. But Ba and Dadaji dismissed Ernest as an unsuitable Christian, saying he came from a family of untouchables, that his family had converted in order to escape the caste system. The darkness of Ernest's skin revealed this, according to Dadaji, who happened to be equally dark although not a Christian (which told him that their family wasn't so low as to have to convert), and also the fact that Ernest relished offal—marrow, brains, kidneys, trotters, tripe—which Mina Foi had unfortunately divulged, never thinking it would be used against Ernest and herself. But before Dadaji could refuse permission for this marriage to a casteless consumer of tripe, the Christian family was the one that said they would never allow Ernest to marry a "Hindoo." Ernest was preparing to rebel when, as if in a soap opera, Ernest's mother contracted blood poisoning, lingering precisely long enough to make her son swear upon her last breath that he would never marry Mina Foi. In the urge to break all things that comes with grief, Ernest gave his word—and

Mina Foi had *sympathized*. And so Ernest, murdering one sadness with another, went straight to the train station from the thorny English cemetery where they buried his mother. Before the scandal traveled far, Dadaji made inquiries, and within a month, he brokered an engagement for Mina Foi to a man they had never met. This was the man whose family had returned Mina Foi to the Allahabad veranda.

*

"BEAUTIFUL OLD-TIME MUSLIM MANNERS!" Dadaji, Ba, and Mina Foi chorused as they did each time Dari came cycling through the gate, his figure absolutely erect and his hand raised in salaam. He disrobed the dinosaur typewriter and looked to Dadaji for the day's directive. When he was told that today they would not be dividing shares and subtracting numbers but composing a marriage proposal for Sonia, Dari confirmed: "Sonia Baby is right, it isn't good for a girl to live alone so far away. Someone nearby should be looking after her interests."

And succumbing to the pleasure and responsibility of this unusual task, Ba forgot her skinflint budget, Mina Foi her oppression, Dadaji his shares, Dari his biscuits.

"*Dear Colonel,*" Dadaji dictated, "*I am writing to you about my granddaughter, Sonia. Age twenty-two years. School matriculation, Model School. B.A. from Hewitt College, town of North Hewitt, Vermont, United States of America.*"

Dari typed until a *ping!* went off at the end of the line. Then he stopped. "Huzoor," he respectfully admonished, "it is not a business letter. You have to sweetly tell her good qualities while also being honest so they do not later complain that they have been cheated."

They looked out to the ayah sweeping dust. Pigeons skimmed low with twigs plucked from her broom, headed to the nests they were building lodged in the rolled-up veranda blinds. They looked upon the eternal lorry traffic from which irritation they were saved somewhat, Dadaji because of his eyes, Ba because of her hearing, Mina Foi because she had other troubles.

After working for an hour, they had composed:

My dear Colonel,

If my accounting is correct, we have been chess partners and neighbors for forty-three years now, addressing each other as Colonel Sahib and Lawyer Sahib. Side by side, we have gone through life with all of its ups and downs. Today I am raising a delicate matter. My granddaughter is feeling lonely in America, and she has entrusted us with the task of finding her a life companion from a family in which we place the highest trust. We come from different communities, but that is of no importance to us. We believe that compatibility and integrity is all that matters, and from our long acquaintance, I feel confident, my dear Colonel Sahib, that you agree.

If Sonia is not of a studious nature, she has done relatively well in her exams.

If she sometimes gives in to low spirits, she can be counted on through trials and travails.

If she is stubborn, she does not chase after every whim and fancy.

If she has inherited the family temper, she never holds a grudge.

If she is a little over tall and a little over dark, she has fine features—

"Where is the photograph?" asked Ba.

"We don't have one—now what?" And they telephoned their son at the offices of Gupta Brothers in Connaught Place.

Papa had been employed for his Westernized veneer, his ability to give orders with aplomb and investigate the sort of venture that would be needed to make India more modern. Papa broke ground with notions that inevitably failed, but the ghost of failed endeavors lingered, and, inevitably, three or five or ten years later, another company came along, executed the same plan for modernity—and brilliantly succeeded: *Two Minute Masala Noodles!* You could argue he was unsuccessful precisely because he was over-successful, able to glimpse the future before the rest of the nation.

He was irritated to receive the phone call from Ba and Dadaji at his workplace. His thoughts had moved on since the day he'd spoken to Sonia about this prospective introduction.

"We cannot marry her into a family that is focused on her looks," Papa exclaimed. This was strange for a man who never missed an occasion to comment on a woman's appearance, Mama would have said, but Papa saw no contradiction.

"In a love marriage, everything can be mismatched," said Dadaji. "The person might be rich, poor, high caste, low caste, ugly, or beautiful. But in an arranged marriage, it is the family's duty to align each matter."

Nobody mentioned how he had failed Mina Foi with the man in Brussels, who, succumbing to family pressure to marry, had told his parents, "Your choice is my choice. I don't need to meet the girl." He had flown in for the wedding with the understanding that Mina Foi would join him when her immigration papers were processed. In the meantime, she would serve her in-laws. Because this family, too, was poorer and lower down on the caste ladder (although not as poor or as low as Ernest), Dadaji surmised they were eager to have a hasty marriage, notwithstanding that the repetitive mention of their son's Belgian address suggested that they believed this would undo any disadvantage. Two months after the wedding, the postman delivered an anonymous letter to Number 10 Cadell Road. When they opened the envelope on the veranda upon which Mina Foi was destined to spend many more years than she ever expected, they found a blank sheet of paper, within which there was a photograph. The photograph showed a man and woman before a Christmas tree with two children in their pajamas, obviously the progeny of the foreign woman and the Indian man pinning a star to the fir, and the man was obviously Mina Foi's new husband, except he was laughing joyously in a way they did not recognize.

"I don't have a photograph of Sonia," said Papa on the phone.

A photograph was essential proof, but they made up for the lack of a photograph by including the entire sheet of letter paper and a previously unused envelope upon which Dari wrote in an exquisite, formal hand. And they bolstered Sonia's case with an offering of kakori kebabs laid upon the scalloped silver salver, covered by a starched white napkin.

"But my grandson is in New York," the Colonel told Dadaji, the salver between them.

"Sonia will be there as well."

"He is very picky."

"So is she."

"He spends all his time reading news."

"She spends all her time reading novels! He is not the outgoing type?"

"No, the brooding type."

"With a name like Sunny?"

"Yes, they called him that pet name to change his nature, but it had no effect." The Colonel peeped under the starched napkin.

From her bed that night in their home on Thornton Lane, the Colonel's wife said to the Colonel in his bed on the other side of the nightstand: "You and I have been foolishly bowing and saying thank you, thank you—and they have been plotting to purchase Sunny with a kebab. No mention of a dowry, you noticed!"

The Colonel replied, "Let's forward the letter to Babi. She can decide whether to send it to Sunny or not." Babita, their daughter, Sunny's widowed mother, lived in Delhi. Her approval would be necessary.

The Colonel's wife wanted to bring up the money Dadaji had lost in the military woolen mill. She opened her lips to say that rupees lost in blankets and balaclavas was no reason to barter their grandson away, that these were not medieval times when you offered a male child up for sacrifice, that the Colonel's idea of morality was so unyielding that it was immoral. But a long marriage had taught husband and wife that sleeping is better than fighting, so they closed their eyes as tightly as their mouths and turned to face away from each other.

While upon the same night, in the house on Cadell Road where the highway noise had drowned out the chirrup of owls and the subtle leaf

sounds that had once turned the sullen summer nights delicate and rustling, highway lorries sent unsettling fingers of light into Ba and Dadaji's bedroom. Ba woke and peeled off the sheets from which the starch
had been leached by the damp of Dadaji's night sweats. She extended
her arm from the darned mosquito netting upon which yellow stains
bloomed to turn on the brass lamp, one of a pair transferred from her
husband's office when he retired, under which he'd composed his legal
arguments during monsoon days of shadow, winter days of fog. In the
dim voltage that imparted about as much light as a candle flame, she
swung down her feet, holding on to the spindle bedpost—the beds in
Allahabad were planked high as the windowsills for any errant breeze
that might come wandering. Opening her wardrobe, she began to pack
a small duffel bag with a petticoat, panties, a handkerchief.

"Where are you going?" said Dadaji, sitting up, trying to see
through his wavy vision.

"To Rangoon." She went to collect her toothbrush and her tongue
scraper.

"Rangoon?"

"I must."

"But why?"

"The ruby," she said.

"What ruby?"

"The ruby from Rangoon, size of a pigeon's egg. Or there won't be
anything in the bank locker."

"Why won't there be anything?"

"When Sonia gets married, there won't be anything left." Mina
Foi's dowry had been repatriated, but if Sonia successfully married, the
jewels would once again be exiled. Jewels to which she belonged, just
as much as they belonged to her.

Dadaji considered what bird brains women had, such basic greeds
and jealousies. At the end of their long lives, all they thought about
was a bauble and who should have it: not so-and-so, not so-and-so, and
definitely *not* so-and-so.

AND SO IT WAS, ONE GUSTY DAY IN MAY OF 1997, A MAILMAN trudged down the streets of Fort Greene in Brooklyn and plucked the letter detailing Sonia's shortcomings from his bag. It almost flew from his hands, but it didn't, and he dropped it through the stiff brass mail slot of a sober, liver-colored brownstone, where it lay on the dulled parquet until Lou Orsini, who'd lived forever on the second floor, scooped it up, almost tossed it out with the Panda Garden delivery menus, but didn't. He saw it in time and propped it on the stairs. When Ulla and Sunny returned from the Korean deli with toilet paper, tofu, sprouts, and six assorted artisan ales, Ulla almost trod on it but didn't. She made pincers of her fingers and brought it up despite her hands being full. Ulla was the girlfriend Sunny had never happened to mention to his family, although for over a year now, they had shared a lease, a bed, a Con Ed utility bill, a laundry basket, and on some absent-minded occasions, a toothbrush.

"What does your mother say?" asked Ulla, unlacing her sneakers.

Sunny would forever regret not bundling the letter away, but it was so astonishing that his guard was down. "Look," he exclaimed, "I have a marriage proposal!"

Oh, how could he have forgotten that love, when it arrives, arrives always twinned to its destructive force, as inevitably as God and devil, life and death, home and the leaving of it; that information collected during sweeter moments will be turned to ammunition and dispelled during war; that what is innocent in the morning will not remain so by nightfall.

Ulla took the letter from Sunny.

"*My dear boy*," Babita Bhatia had penned in her customary envy-green ink.

I am writing to give you the news that we are the target of an intrigue—your grandfather has sent me this unashamed proposal of marriage for you from his neighbour on behalf of his grand-daughter, who is studying in some flyspeck of a college that I have never heard of. Like the one Sara Habib's son attended, where he received a degree for inventing a frisbee that flies 0.1% faster than other frisbees. Incredibly, the letter lists all her faults and says she wishes to get married because she is lonely. Anyway, I thought you'd have a hearty laugh, and now I can tell your grandfather, who doesn't wish to offend his friend, that I have dutifully forwarded the letter to you.

It was delivered by the Allahabad padre, who was on his way to a faith convention. He brought along some marvelous kebabs made by the Shahs' cook, who originally came from Lucknow— filthy as can be, but it's the dirt under the fingernails that imparts the flavour. In the morning, two of the kakori had vanished. I called Vinita and Punita, who professed ignorance. "Who ate them then? A ghost?" When I told their mother, she said, "Beat them with a broom, make them sleep under the stairs, starve them. Teach them how to behave."

"You are overestimating me," I told Gunja. Am I the kind of person to go beating children with a broom? Although now I think it was a ploy of hers, to attack the girls so I had to save them—one cannot outsmart these people.

Meanwhile, how I wish I could teach Vini-Puni to make a meal worth eating. Their attention is on everything but their du-ties. Each month brings fresh trouble. I drove by the market the other day and spotted Vini with the Afghan students who are al-ways loitering by the comics lending library. I half suspect she took

> the kebabs to give to one of those loiterers, because no doubt the
> path to an Afghan's heart is via a kebab.

Sunny used to put his fingers in his ears and shout, "Mummy, please stop this gossip!" But because these letters held grotesque fascination for Ulla, who found them as riveting as *Masterpiece Theatre,* Sunny was in the habit of handing his mother's letters to her after he'd skimmed through.

Sunny had explained that Vinita and Punita were his mother's servant girls, daughters of his mother's cleaning maid, Gunja, who had eight living children—three had died in infancy (Babita used the phrase "popped off"); and Gunja's husband was a drunk who sold chicken and mutton bones for a living, collecting them from dhaba eating places, then transporting them to a bone meal fertilizer factory. They occupied two rooms in Begumpur, but Gunja could not afford to have six daughters at home; she'd have to marry the elder one, although she was only fifteen. To give the child a little more time, she begged Babita to keep two of them in exchange for housework. Vinita had already been taught how to make pigs in blankets and a chicken liver pâté with brandy; the younger one, Punita, was enrolled in a neighborhood charity school but helped her elder sister in the evenings. Even though she had two servant girls for free, Babita was to her mind involved in a social experiment to uplift society.

The gray modernist house in which the Bhatia family lived had been designed by a disciple of Le Corbusier and built by Sunny's paternal grandfather, a former finance minister who had swiftly acquired several palatial properties in a manner that could only be explained by corruption, although by the time Sunny was born, the properties had been lost to further corruption, save the Panchsheel Park house that had been sectioned into three, one third for each of the minister's sons, Ravi, Ratan, and Rana. When Sunny was eight, his father, Ratan, died of a heart attack, and nobody in his father's family had spoken to Babita since—they accused her of driving Ratan to despair with her harangue. Sunny's widowed grandmother, Minnie, had composed a will leaving the property, which was in her name, to Ravi and Rana, compensating her daughter-in-law Babita with a slim portfolio of investments and a set of Spode egg cups in a woodland rabbit design, which she had always coveted.

The value of the investments had fallen, so Babita contested the will in court, but because the courts were overwhelmed and usually resolved such cases well after everyone involved was dead, she expected to stay on in Panchsheel Park until her own demise.

When Babita exited her front door, she turned her nose up and to the right if she saw elder brother-in-law Ravi to her left, and she turned her nose up and to the left if she saw younger brother-in-law Rana to her right. The egg cups, held ransom, resided in brother-in-law Ravi's glass display cabinet, and once in a while, to annoy his sister-in-law, he lingered over breakfast in his garden where she might espy him in his paisley dressing gown: "My-oh-my, what a cunning egg cup, and is this little Peter Rabbit under the blackberry bush?"

*

WHEN ULLA LAUGHED, "CRAZY!" Sunny saw an ageless Ulla, all the way from what she must have been as a pixie baby to what she would be when she was a pixie ancient.

Ulla opened the second letter enclosed within Sunny's mother's letter and, "What's this?" she pounced. And there—because Mina Foi had harked to the lament that Sonia's chances might be ruined without the compelling case made by her face, and had clandestinely plucked a photograph of Sonia to slip into the envelope she had been entrusted with sealing—was Sonia. Tall, slender, a braid down to her waist, standing against snow-laden firs in a disconcerting, curry-colored coat.

"It's the custom to send photographs, of course," yelped Sunny, but he dared not peek. The switch in Ulla's voice made him adopt an impenetrable expression as he began to collect some documents into his satchel, which held his precious first laptop computer that resembled a tub-shaped flying saucer. Just another half hour and he could exit with the righteous haste of someone on his way to work. Sunny worked the night shift at the Associated Press, where he had been employed straight out of his graduate program at Columbia University in an entry-level position, learning the rules of the AP Stylebook, editing, and sending out on the wire the news that came winging in at all hours. His part in the enterprise was small, but it felt crucial because the stories were urgent: thirty black churches in the South burned to the ground in eighteen months; there was violence between Israel and Hezbollah; an earthquake hit China; the Chemical Weapons Convention treaty entered into force; the comet Hale–Bopp approached Earth; Osama bin Laden declared war on the United States; and Charles and Diana divorced. Sunny longed for the day he might see his byline in a print newspaper and considered pitching a story to the news desk; it was permissible to do so.

Ulla, annoyed by his vague expression and his desire to flee, said: "Are you sure this letter is innocent?" If he hadn't been behaving guiltily, Ulla wouldn't be suspicious. If she was not suspicious, he wouldn't be behaving guiltily. To have kept Ulla hidden from his mother, as he had, or to remember his Indian life, made Sunny turn from Ulla sometimes. It was his remoteness then that made Ulla long for him even when he was in the room, which made her love him *more* despite their arguments and be provoked by him *more,* which increased their arguments.

"There's nothing sinister about the letter," he said. "Everyone gets these at my age, forwarded by relatives, friends, people who've never set eyes on you—a great pile arrives when you finish college, and the flood continues until everyone is settled. Then there is a lull before they begin marrying off the progeny of these mishaps, each generation lesser than what came before, because what hope can you have from such a process?"

At this moment Sunny's phone rang. Sunny and Ulla maintained two phone lines so that Sunny could give his mother his private number and tell her that he lived with a housemate. Both Sunny and Ulla knew it would either be his mother or Satya, his closest friend, who telephoned him daily.

Sunny didn't answer the phone. "I am an ineligible, poor journalist— only one such letter has arrived," he placated Ulla a little more. "Satya, who is going to be a doctor, must have a hundred. Whenever he gets depressed, he orders takeout from Punjab Hut, locks himself in, listens to old film songs while rereading his marriage proposals, and he cheers up."

This didn't cheer Ulla, however. She had first thought Sunny was shy, if a bit childish in his inability to admit openly to a relationship. But now she understood the consequences and perhaps the true purpose of this secrecy: Sunny was keeping his options open. "Surely," she said, "surely your family in India realizes that it is disrespectful to me?"

Silence.

Ulla yelled: "*They don't realize it is disrespectful to me, because they don't know I exist!*"

Sunny kept his gaze averted. "Look, however progressive my mother is, she is an Indian woman from another generation. Do you really think I can tell her that we sleep in the same bed? If I was taking this proposal seriously, wouldn't I have hidden the letter instead of saying, 'Look, Ulla'?"

Ulla sighed. "I should be feeling angry, and I *am* so angry, yet I also feel bad for this poor girl who is being marketed. It's a scandal that they treat women like this."

"Well, they treat men the same way and you're not showing *me* sympathy."

At nine P.M., Sunny fled for the subway wishing he were as uncoupled as the purple wind that blew through the city. Even in this country, where he'd assumed love was different from the Indian version, it was not a private endeavor, but all about being a public event. If you didn't stamp and stamp love with legitimacy and acknowledgment, and stamp it some more, silver and gold, with further legalities and recognitions, the ghost of future lost love infiltrated and your love became irrevocably unformed, the lack folded into its substance.

In the elevator of the Associated Press Building at Rockefeller Plaza, Sunny's brows trembled. He observed his clay-colored shoes, the geometric print of his navy shirt. He remembered the story about a Chinese philosopher who had dreamt he was a butterfly. The dream had inspired the question: Was he a man dreaming he was a butterfly or a butterfly dreaming he was a man?

He couldn't articulate to Ulla, lest she claim to be the victim of his ambivalence, that his life now seemed at a remove, that it was sometimes unrecognizable to himself. Whenever he walked up the creaking mast of stairs to their seagull's nest apartment, he was surprised anew by Ulla's elfin beauty, by the pine floors, by the white Ikea couch, by the Western lightness and comfort that was, apparently, his. He often couldn't determine how he felt exactly about his new life, and it was how he happened to behave then that elucidated his emotions. But he was also unsure whether he was behaving from honest impulse or from playing a part, taking his cues from the people, the weather, the food, even the objects around him: The bowl from a North Carolina potter filled with farmers market heirloom tomatoes; the deceptively simple cut and calm gray of his first coat that was not a parka; snow and darkness in the afternoon; an omelet filled with smoked salmon and dill cream cheese.

One thing seemed certain: If India existed, then America could not, for they were too drastically different not to cancel each other out. Yet despite this fact, they refused to remain apart. India invaded his life all the way from the other side of the world, and then life here became instantly artificial, a taunt. He became an impostor, a spy, a liar, and a ghost.

By ten P.M., Sunny had settled into his cubicle in the deserted newsroom, save for Dan, a journalist who was a veteran of the Vietnam War and always worked the night shift at the sports desk. Sunny was editing a story on Dolly the cloned sheep when his phone rang. He knew it would be his mother. He had thought he would be able to love her better from New York.

....

SUNNY AND ULLA HAD FIRST MET BY RIVERSIDE PARK IN the cafeteria line of a hostel for international students and American students interested in an international experience. This hostel may have had an academic purpose, and it may have looked staid from the outside, but in actuality, it was a hysterical airport of love affairs as students from around the world—menaced by perpetually expiring visas and the panic of limited time—romanced each other in fast-forward, having but two or four years to trick their native fate, leapfrog into another nation, another class, another skin, to sample all the world offered. It was a wonder anyone managed to achieve a degree.

A Danish dancer chased a Senegalese student of engineering; a Hungarian communist teacher's son stalked an American soy sauce baron's granddaughter; a girl from the Midwest tracked the lone Scotsman. There was a slapstick randomness to these loves conducted in dozens of languages during movie nights or ballroom dancing lessons, or in the cafeteria, where everyone went despite the dullest food in the city in case a potential romance awaited by the steamed vegetable medley.

For Sunny and Ulla, these were their most joyful days: when he had first found himself vulnerable to her hedgehog hairstyle and the way she swayed so freely at ballroom dancing; when she had first been stirred by the old-fashioned grandeur of his hawk nose and his hawk eyes, his formal bearing and correct manner as he waited with his food tray and his folded *New York Times,* reminding her a little of her Kansas grandfather who had emigrated from Sweden. This was when they had first begun to tweak their calendars, hoping to run into each other as if by accident, and began to suspect similar intent in the other—when they both knew and didn't know at the same time.

Ulla lived in a part of the hostel divided into mini apartments—three students sharing a kitchenette and a bathroom—and one of the young women in Ulla's apartment, Mala, came from Delhi, just like Sunny. He'd been considering asking Mala to broker a formal introduction to Ulla, when one night in the cafeteria, as if she had deduced his interest, Sunny overheard Mala begin to denounce the disheartening and repetitive occurrence of Indian boys running after white American women, always picking the most pallid, androgynous ones, the kind who withdrew to spend moody hours scribbling in diaries. This was what attracted them, said Mala, because no Indian woman was bequeathed enough privacy to thus indulge herself with a solipsistic obsession over her own psychology—encouraged to chart the fluctuations of her temperament in response to deep crises that were inevitably banal. These women, meanwhile, realized they could snag a Third World man far higher up the ladder of class and money than any fellow white American, where their prospects were dim, simply by using the bargaining power of their citizenship and their pale complexion.

"You're Mala's friend."

"I wouldn't put it quite like that."

"Why not?"

They built their first bond, Sunny and Ulla, on their mutual resentment of Indian women in general and Mala in particular, tumbling into this conversation because they had no other. No matter what Ulla was doing, Mala had to be doing that *and* something better. "If I say I'm working at a summer camp in Maine, she says she'll be working at an orphanage associated with the Dalai Lama. *And* she is applying for a Fulbright. If there are two peaches, Mala has to eat the best peach, or both peaches. She would never in a million years eat only the lesser peach."

"It is exhausting to be near such greed." Sunny gave a little bow of acknowledgment both externally to Ulla and, secretly, internally, for he had identified similar embarrassing hungers in himself but was determined to evade them and loathed them in others. Something about arriving in America, he'd observed, made one want to grab enough for past, present, and future all at once. He wanted to protect America from those like himself, but then, if others were gobbling and grabbing, he should, too, or he'd be left behind. Then the next instant he felt sickened by self-disgust.

"And you won't have any luck reforming her," he warned Ulla. "These instincts go deep. Even if friendly on the surface, they'll wobble your confidence in as many underground ways as they can, so that one day, you'll be so little threat that they'll get all the peaches and all the fellowships."

That was why he ran from Indian women, he told himself.

"Why do they do it?" asked Ulla.

"Well," said Sunny, "in India there are too many people and men control everything, so they have to get what they want in primitive ways, with fake friendliness. Here there is much less opposition and much more to gain—so here, my God, these women become monsters."

Thus Sunny adopted an expert's role on the unfortunate qualities of Indian women, oblivious of the fact that before Mala and Ulla's friendship had been tattered over peaches, Mala had educated Ulla on the miserable personalities of Indian men: Indian men and their controlling attitudes, Indian men and their mummies, their jealousies, their pride, their rages and entitlements—the way they became lecturing gurus telling everyone everything about everything before the first gray hairs fringed their ears, the way a disproportionate number were driven by the ambition of finding a white woman—all the better to escape India.

"Why?" Ulla had asked.

Well, Mala had said, they might then reclaim India with dignity once they had a safety raft and finally manage to be nice to fellow Indians so they could make use of India in earnest now that they had lost the fear of being swallowed back. Or they might go in quite the other direction and pretend they were not Indian at all. Say all the bad things about the country so white people didn't have to.

Either way, they no longer lived an *honest* life, said Mala.

Did you have to be with your own kind in your own country to be honest? Ulla wondered. *Wasn't it laudable to search outside yourself?* Ulla had found Mala both prejudiced and dishonest. She had left India after all, hadn't she? Also, she suspected that if a white man were to present himself as an option, Mala wouldn't turn him down.

Sunny was touched by how Ulla's dislike for Mala hadn't translated to dislike for all Indians. Or perhaps he was flattering himself into thinking he was therefore utterly unlike other Indians.

And Mala had made one severe misjudgment: Ulla wasn't outraged by Indian men chasing American women. She loved to be desired, and if being American or freckle-skinned or a pixie blonde delivered her to the top of the heap, well, would any woman turn away her natural advantage?

Only later did Sunny wonder if Mala had both made their relationship possible (Indians were not foreign or unknowable to Ulla any longer) and also impossible (she had provided Ulla with all the avenues of complaint). Certainly, together Sunny and Mala had bequeathed Ulla a complete lexicon of arguments against Indians, male and female. As if each gender of a certain class, the Westernized class, hoped to make it in America by waging mutual war. It was because of Indian men that Indian women were forced to run. It was because of Indian women that Indian men would do anything to get away.

FOR THE FIRST DAYS OF LIVING WITH A GIRLFRIEND, EVERY-thing had been surprising—the fact, for example, that Ulla and Sunny had different ideas of privacy. Astonished to find no lock on the bathroom door of their new home, Sunny rushed, expecting Ulla to come in at any moment, which she often did, wandering in to chat about trivial matters while Sunny was in the shower, even to nonchalantly pee. When he went to the hardware store to buy a latch, she collapsed into giggles: "How can you be so shy!"

She would throw off all her clothes and wander about the apartment, delighting in the Brooklyn sunshine spangling through the leaves of a maple.

"It's far easier," said Ulla, however, "for you to say you're from Delhi than for me to say I'm from Prairie Hill, Kansas. New York favors foreigners."

Sunny had been startled to discover that Ulla's real name was Mary but that she had decided in high school to go by Ulla. Frequently, when asked where she was from, she said New York City, not Prairie Hill, betraying the place she loved and could enchant Sunny with by recalling a land so flat and empty you could see your friends arrive from hours away, where stars blossomed at your feet at nightfall, where the wind never stopped gusting.

Ulla showed Sunny how to snip open cartons, buy fabric softeners and drying sheets, telephone for a gas connection, order a hamburger (how lucky she was to be with a Hindu who ate beef, she had no idea). She gave him all the information on American life you couldn't get from having read "A Perfect Day for Bananafish" or *Slaughterhouse-Five* or *Two Serious Ladies*. These books had not been practically useful, but it was the eccentricity of America and Americans as conveyed by them that had first powerfully drawn Sunny to this country. His calling was journalism, but his love was fiction because only fiction could thus dwell on quirkiness.

If Ulla enjoyed her role too much to be discreet about it, she was nevertheless kind and painstaking. "Say *A*," she said. "Say *P*." She tutored Sunny to pronounce words so he would be understood: "Parrot" not "Barrot," "Vegetable" not "Wedgtable." She taught him to say "Good!" when asked how he was instead of "Terrible," because nobody likes a cynic.

"I do," said Sunny.

By then Ulla had gathered momentum and was collecting proof he avoided words like "bra" or "pantyhose."

"Say it!" she would insist. It was presented as a game, but he experienced it as a taunt, and as he more intractably refused and nurtured the beginnings of resentment, Ulla began to feel oppressed in turn.

"If you tried to dance," she said with some bitterness, "you might like to dance."

"Why don't you eat fish?" responded Sunny.

"We only ate fish once or twice a year, that's why, and every mouthful my mom would warn, 'Watch out for bones!'—because it is true, you do keep getting bones!"

And when Sunny returned from the supermarket with a proud jar of Grey Poupon Dijon mustard, she said, "I don't like silly mustard. I like plain old Heinz."

"She eats only salad for lunch, and when she orders pizza, it's always a plain cheese pizza," Sunny reported to his friend Satya.

Not only did Ulla prefer a pizza pie without anything but a tomato base and mozzarella, Sunny had discovered she considered a simmering complexity of sauces or a mix of spices as barbarous inventions. Should a puddle of yellow begin to race across the plate to join with a puddle of brown, she felt *fear*. When they went out to eat, she prayed with all her concentrated might the restaurant would be Italian.

They began to notice that while they could each be stung at various times by inadequate cosmopolitan flair, they rested their pride on their vulnerabilities—on refusing to give up what, perhaps, they most hoped to lose. And what they most hoped to lose, then, was what they fought most for and what most defined them. At a certain point it became a tragedy. A tragedy when you took the wider perspective and considered the fact that Sunny belonged to the first generation of men of his class in India who actually cooked and didn't direct women and servants while grabbing the praise.

"Whatever I eat, I find he's slipped curry in there," Ulla announced in the indulgent tones of the owner of a weird foreigner to a group gathered at a tapas restaurant to celebrate the birthday of Ulla's friend Natalina, who used the occasion of having an Indian at the table to recount her recent trip across Rajasthan to teach women to use solar ovens: "My God, being a blond woman traveling alone in India, they just go mad—they cannot conceive of you as a person. A man on the platform reached through the train window and grabbed my breasts, and as the train began to leave the station, he ran along with the train, still holding on."

Sunny steadied a slight tremble in his hands by very precisely slicing a bacalao croquette using knife and fork. Wasn't there a suggestion that he was in some way responsible, in a long series of associations? He felt insulted and guilty, then annoyed at having to feel guilty or insulted, especially while eating at a restaurant in the West Village that would gouge his bank account. He delivered a triangle of frittata neatly to his mouth and chewed with his lips firmly closed, to place himself at a far civility from his nation, to prove with his table manners, familiarity with the foods of Spain, and sympathy for female travelers that he was not like those men to be found on every street corner in India, staring lustfully, bestially, as if they were no longer human, at women they didn't consider to be human.

"Did you get sick?" asked someone. "I hear everyone gets sick in India."

"When I went to the doctor, he was like, 'You have everything!' But," Natalina assured Sunny, "after Equatorial Guinea, India was similar to Chicago."

Sunny sipped his Basque wine. Secretly he was thinking that this woman had some nerve to go from her New York City apartment—no doubt equipped with a stove, microwave, toaster, fridge, blender, coffee maker, hair dryer, vacuum cleaner, television, computer, music system, heater, fan, air conditioner, boiler, furnace, if not also a bicycle or car—to tell women in India to cook their rice in a cardboard box covered with silver reflective paper so as to prevent deforestation and climate change.

At home Sunny said: "Ulla, why did you say I put curry in everything? I put spices in everything, not curry in everything. There's no such thing as curry, in fact. It's a fake word invented by the British."

He distinctly heard his mother's voice in his ear say, *Who is this stupid person?*

Ulla said, "Well, then all of India must have been conned by a British mistake. In every Indian restaurant I've been to, I see curry written all over the menu." Later, she thought Sunny had left for work when she telephoned her father: "He says he doesn't put curry in everything, yet he does. It drowns out all flavor in a burning inferno of pain."

As Sunny moved closer to listen, as gingerly as possible, the floorboard made an equivalently slow toothache moan and Ulla hastily hung up.

"I heard what you said." Jig of brows. "Curry doesn't equal chilies! You're even getting what you have wrong, *wrong*!"

"You were eavesdropping!"

"Maligning people is a worse crime."

"It's awful to be a snoop."

Why was it that in the Western world, snooping to uncover a crime was a worse crime than the actual crime! Ulla's civilization was built upon not snooping and wandering about naked. Sunny's civilization was based on donning your clothes and listening to every conversation.

How on earth had it come to pass that, in this Brooklyn idyll of triumphant multiracial calm, they'd reached such distrust? They reconciled this time at a bar on Lafayette, and from their reflection in the salvaged salon-station mirror behind the counter, they saw they had reason to reconcile, for they were simply so beautiful together. As beautiful, more beautiful, than any of the mixed-race couples in this neighborhood renowned for the beauty of its mixed-race inhabitants. The owner of this establishment had once asked if they were looking for work.

"Doing what?"

"Waitressing, bartending. I'm opening a restaurant on DeKalb called Urbane, and I want it to reflect how cool this neighborhood is."

Sometimes they fell to wondering if there was a joke being played, if the joke was on them. A joke like that of an Indian paying a lot of money to eat at a restaurant named Le Colonial.

"Should we leave for another neighborhood?" they sometimes asked each other. But then, seeing the new arrivals—Icelandic-Peruvian, Rwandan-Vietnamese, Dutch-Japanese, Cuban-Kazakh-Irish—beginning to produce children that had never before been seen on Spaceship Earth, Sunny and Ulla couldn't bear to leave this compelling scene they themselves had helped to create, all these couples, two by two, who had begun to shove out the original residents, uniformly poor and black. In a few years nobody would remember this. But now when they hurried home, Sunny and Ulla couldn't avoid the anger that gathered in the shadows. They were wary of being mugged by residents of the projects just beyond.

Once, Sunny *had* been mugged as he walked home from his night shift at five in the morning by a boy who appeared to have a gun, but it might have been a stick held under his shirt. When he woke Ulla, she insisted that a reluctant Sunny report the incident. The cops arrived and drove Sunny about in their patrol car to see if he could spot the boy again. But when Sunny saw the boy, he looked away.

"No?" the detective asked, lean, alert, chewing nicotine gum.

"No."

"Why did you do that?" Ulla was upset when Sunny told her. "They get away with a small thing, then another small thing, then they do a big thing."

But she knew that if Sunny had identified the boy, she'd have taken the opposite side of the argument.

"We are *more* guilty," said Sunny, "in the scheme of things."

"Get out of our neighborhood, you bourgeois white mother-fucker!" a man had shouted across at a new neighbor moving in next door. And although Sunny's sympathy lay with the man who yelled out of the window, he knew it was a hypocritical sympathy. He hoped, in fact, to get a free pass, that as a dark-skinned person he'd be seen to have more legitimacy in this neighborhood than a white person. But his smiling at black people on the street felt lying and condescending, rooted in a wish to be accepted into this neighborhood of elegant brownstones and a quick subway line to Manhattan, while also cohabiting with Ulla, who was essential to his self-respect. He wondered if Ulla felt less guilty to be invading this neighborhood because she was with Sunny. Both of them, in conversation with others like themselves, made certain to mention the well-off African Americans buying homes here, to shift the conversation from race to class.

Sunny registered himself hypocritical, too, when he looked away from other Indians he saw on the street—Indians who were also avidly ignoring him, trying to make it in America by avoiding one another, as if it was better to be one Indian than two Indians, better to be two Indians than three Indians. And better an Indian in New York than an Indian in India. Even more so an Indian in a village in France that was empty of other Indians entirely, especially Indians of the same class who would undo your poise, shine a light upon your shames, your lies.

And then there was Satya. Satya was Sunny's childhood friend who would never in a million years comprehend that it may be better to be one Indian instead of two Indians or two Indians instead of twenty Indians. They'd attended Tiny Tots in Delhi together in miniature blue shorts and miniature ties already knotted onto elastic bands that fit under their collars. They'd gone to Mount St. Mary's in Delhi together, they'd had mumps together, they'd taken a delightful trip together when Sunny was a bachelor's student following a story in Mysore about the government's curtailment of subsidies for traditional weavers. In a case of mistaken importance, he'd been assigned to a scheme encouraging journalists to promote tourism and invited to stay at the Lalitha Mahal Palace Hotel. They had gone swimming in the maharaja's pool at sunset, a warm wind carrying the aroma of the sere hills and stirring the papery bougainvillea. Satya—black hairs on his chest so extravagant they whorled and formed black roses upon him—couldn't swim, but he pawed with such wild energy that his splashing carried him from one end of the pool to the other.

When they had dined in a romantic alcove of enamel and gold mirror work, it had seemed a little peculiar, Sunny registered, to have Satya opposite him sharing a mango kheer and later to have Satya snoring by his side in bed, the pillows lavished with sandalwood perfume and rose petals. Their friendship had begun to take on the attributes that should have been assigned to a romantic partner, and perhaps they had each begun to wonder if their formative moments would take place not with wives or children but with each other. Together they had decided to apply to study in the United States, Satya for medicine, Sunny for a master's degree in journalism; the Mysore article was the centerpiece of his application to Columbia University. But here their paths had diverged—Sunny's to New York City, Satya's to Rochester. They missed each other, and one weekend, when Sunny and Ulla were still residing in the international students' hostel, Satya had taken a Greyhound bus all the way down.

Ulla had claimed a deadline for a class, and Sunny had felt ashamed at his girlfriend's departure, as if she did not love him. Then, trying to look at Satya through Ulla's gaze, he thought Ulla was disdainful of Satya's roly-polyness encased tightly within a home-knitted pullover and his ardent and frank conversation. Keenly aware of Satya's lack of sophistication, and feeling exposed by it, it was as if he'd cheated Ulla.

Satya didn't mention Ulla as they walked about Union Square and Washington Square Park, and neither did he show the slightest tourist interest in Manhattan on this his very first visit. He noticed neither the skyscrapers nor the homeless people on the subway grates, neither the Buddhist monk on a skateboard nor a gaggle of models with poodles in booties. Interspersed by some aimless humming, he told Sunny about his running battle over the television in the residents' lounge, where only Satya wished to watch *Golden Girls*. And why was it against the rules to dry his underwear out of the window? And why couldn't the shuttle pick him up even if there wasn't a designated stop outside his condo complex? "You think I am your private chauffeur?" the driver asked.

"What about me?" said Satya. "You think I am some sort of prostitute that I enjoy to keep standing on the road?"

Back in Sunny's hostel room, Satya made a phone call: "Double the dose of amlodipine, test for uric acid and glucose, check the potassium level, prescribe gabapentin for the nerve pain." He was being asked to give his opinion on a patient for whom he had been part of the monitoring team. How the different parts of Satya melded was a mystery.

Satya began to tuck sheets about the inflatable mattress on the floor. He got plumply into bed, folding both hands under his cheek as in a child's picture of godly sleeping people. Sunny got into his bed as well and burst out: "So, what did you think?" For Satya to not have an opinion on the first occasion either of them had met a proper girlfriend was impossible.

"About what?"

"Ulla, of course."

Deep soul sigh. "Ulla sees you as an Indian, and you see her as an American. The whole thing is based on a misunderstanding."

"She isn't only an American to me."

"How can she not be an American to you?"

"I said *only*."

"The main reason you want her is that she is American. You will get very angry at me for saying so, but when you fight, you won't be able to tell the real fight behind the fight."

"A person is not only their nationality and race, Satya," Sunny persisted. "After a bit you no longer notice you're a different color. At least inside the house you don't notice it anymore."

This had been a revelation to Sunny and Ulla, this mystical lightness.

*

WHEN ULLA HAD HEARD Sunny with Satya, she'd said: "How chatty Indian men are!"

"Quarrelsome Bong!" she'd said of a Bengali she'd met at the gym. "Tambram snob!" she'd said of a colleague. She'd pointed to a woman skipping the line "in her Indian manner."

"I can say 'Bong' and 'Indian manner,'" Sunny had said, "but you cannot." But where could she have learned to brandish local prejudice with insider's pride but from Sunny himself, or from Mala, her old nemesis?

"But you criticize America all the time!" she'd retorted.

"God, you Protestants, don't you ever talk openly?" he had said. And then, when he didn't receive an answer, "Why don't Americans have passports? Weren't your parents curious about the world?"

"They had other priorities—like saving for my college fund. They weren't rich."

"With a big house and two big cars?"

"Two cars is a necessity where we live. And, in fact, my parents did go to Mexico."

Ulla's parents had exulted in Cancun because of the exchange rate; Sunny remembered a previous conversation about how they'd been excited to eat four tacos for $1.25 and how her mother had procured a mani-pedi for seven dollars in a nice salon.

"Why do Americans endlessly talk about the best deal?"

"All travelers talk about the best deal."

"No, the British still exchange the weather: Today a spot of sun, such fun; tomorrow rain, such a shame."

"And what do Indians say?"

"Indians come up close and stare: 'What, you are bald and still not married?'"

They'd laughed then.

"My hot samosa," she'd called him.

"Ulla, you are not to say that!"

Almost choking with laughter: "Okay, okay, my bad-tempered Bengal tiger."

There was no hope all over again.

"Flaky blonde!"

"Bossy Indian patriarch!"

They were failing to keep their arguments personal, or unique and respectful to their individual beings, or even to the situation. Was it true, then, that there had been something to Satya's warning? Should you live with an American to beat the American over the head for being one? Should you find an Indian to complain about Indians?

In the apartment below, through the gap near his shower pipe where there were some missing tiles, Lou Orsini could hear them fighting in their bathroom. If he were ever regretful he was divorced, by the time he'd flossed his teeth, he was inspired to compose a new song for the band he played in called the Love Handles: *Thank the Lord I am divorced / You could not drag me back by force!*

And returning home one spring evening from the Korean deli, Ulla and Sunny unlocked their brownstone's front door to find the letter from Babita propped on the stairs by the great carved mirror, oriental in its decorative details and its crown of colored glass glimmering in the dark of the entryway.

12

....

B ABITA BHATIA HAD LEFT THE HOUSE WITH HER BUL-
bul nose pointed sharply to the right, as Uncle Ravi, exiting his door,
turned his squat nose to the right. And she turned her bulbul nose
sharply to the left as Uncle Rana, looking from his window, turned
his philandering nose to the left. After collecting her mail at the gate
and bringing it into her living room, Babita picked up her silver inlay
letter opener and sliced open the envelope sent by the Colonel. She
read the missive and studied the photograph of Sonia, then snorted and
considered throwing the letter away. She spoke silently to the ghost of
her husband: "*Ratty, when Sunny marries,*" she said, "*I will be more alone
than I am now. You didn't take care of me! Is this a country where women can
manage on their own?*"

She got up and surveyed herself in her three-paneled dressing table
mirror. Did her sari's pink run too garish for someone her age? She was
forty-nine years old, her skin was still as plush as a magnolia petal, her
profile still pert. She was certain one of the reasons Ratan had married
her was for the haughty elegance of this profile. And Babita—what
had she wanted from Ratan?

She had wanted Ratan's father. She had admired the patriarch's
wealth and prestige. Her first gifts—a silk tie, Brut cologne—had been
gifts to her father-in-law, not her husband. Her father-in-law, who had
reveled in Babita's spirit. Their unconcealable affection teased a boundary, enraged her mother-in-law, broke her husband. But this was
hardly an uncommon occurrence in an extended family—one kind of
love graded into another, a girl married a boy to join the household of
the boy's father, a father-in-law secretly fell in love with his daughter-

in-law, a wife with her brother-in-law, an adolescent with his aunty, a widow with her son.

Angry at feeling old when she was yet young and to defuse a threat by ridiculing it, Babita sat down at her desk and composed a forwarding note to the marriage proposal for Sunny. As she wrote, though, her malaise worsened. How desolate it was to have to hoard one's thoughts and jokes for future company, how tedious to translate them into a letter. How sweet it was when one could undo the lethargy of time by chatting with someone about the little things. You could always find a person to converse with over the larger matters—a government scandal, the delayed monsoon—but it was the tiny concerns, the moment's observations, that you couldn't save up to tell, for you didn't even recognize their full potential to add meaning to life unless you articulated their humor, tragedy, menace, or charm. The sight of an ant, say, who appeared to be valiantly carrying his slain fellow soldier on his back; whether it was safe to take a bath despite the fact that rogue monkeys who were fed in the temple nearby had taken a dip in the water tank; whether a sari's pink tipped too pink.

Again she addressed her deceased husband: *"Ratty, I was wrong not to love you. I was wrong before you were wrong to die, I can admit that."*

People die of a heart attack when they may secretly be dying of heartbreak. But life is made of seasons, seasons change, emotions change. During the brief time Ratan had been in the hospital, the doctors trying to save him, Babita, the atheist, had prayed: *Dear God, just let him live and I promise I will love him and believe in you.* But he had died.

Ratty, don't die. If you die, so will I. If you live, I will love you—after all!

Babita walked out upon her bedroom terrace draped with bougainvillea and looked out upon the building site across the street. In the early years of one-story bungalows in Delhi being built up into flats, the taller residences had been divided into three flats, but now they were a level higher and being divided into eight.

Babita watched the laborers' children astride a tunnel drainpipe made steady on a heap of sand as their parents worked. Swaying from side to side, they sang a song in a language Babita could not identify. Where did they come from? Their hair was reddish and rough, their bellies swollen with malnourishment. She found she was surprised, then dismayed by her own thinking that poor, malnourished children did not have songs to sing. When they saw her looking, ten mischievous faces sparkled at her; they were too young to know their lives offended.

By the side of the site, on a washing line of rags drying, she saw a withered grayish bra like a snakeskin. Just as with the children's song, she felt surprise, and then, again: What did she think? Women so poor would not have a bra? Neither did she know if they donned the same type of panties she wore or the antiquated undergarments worn by her grandmother that peasants presumably still donned in the countryside. She did not know how they washed. She did not know where they went to the bathroom. Where *did* they go?

She thought they were beautiful women if she looked past their poverty; it had become generally true that the richer you were, the uglier and more unmannered you became. It was the corruption and aggression—eventually you received the face you deserved. She considered Uncle Rana, his toad stature, his jowls and wattles, his squinty eyes, his florid nose. Just because she turned *her* nose in the opposite direction when she passed him didn't mean she did not register *his* nose.

She went inside, applied deodorant to her underarms, and called, "Vini-Puni, gym shoes!" Then, hitching her sari higher, she laced her gym shoes, leashed her dog, Pasha, and prepared to set off on her evening constitutional, picking up the letter she'd just sealed. She paused. Why needlessly upset Sunny with a girl who would not interest him?

But to reiterate her good character to herself—she had been asked to forward it after all—she gave the envelope to Vini-Puni to post.

"And don't go making eyes at the drivers," she warned.

Vinita glowered because the drivers were making eyes at *her,* not she at them.

In Lodhi Gardens, Babita walked briskly and competitively, accelerating to overtake others, shouting "Right" to alert people that she was approaching them to their right, or "Left" if she planned to triumph to their left. They inevitably became confused for they had never heard of this protocol and scattered like brainless fowl as she sped about the paths that circled the turbaned tombs dating from the fifteenth century. When Pasha tried with all his might to pull her toward the pond filled with barely treated sewage water, people stopped and laughed at a rich woman being humiliated by her expensive dog. As she dragged unwilling Pasha along—she knew if he managed to get in, he'd sit obstinately in the opaque sludge crawling with mosquito larvae until nightfall—she caught a gentleman pissing into a rosebush and pounced: "For shame! Because of people like you our nation won't improve."

He hurriedly zipped up, but this evening, the usually life-affirming activity of overtaking other walkers and having altercations with men pissing in public depressed her. Perhaps it was the weather that disheartened: muggy, spore-ridden, and nether-ish. Perhaps it was the tossed picnic plates that lay upon the scummy pond surface without sinking, or the irritating fact that from the bushes, the legs of lovers protruded, their upper bodies entwined and shrouded by foliage, the better to hide their kisses. She felt like chasing them out, too, just as she had the pissing man. Perhaps she was wearied by the long drive to the park in office traffic—whatever health benefits she'd accrue by a loop and a half about Lodhi Gardens would be undone by breathing petrol fumes.

When she was home, Babita showered. The water spurted momentarily hot from the roof tank pipes that had been heated by the sun all day, but eventually they disgorged cooler depths. She powdered herself with Pond's Dreamflower talc, and when she sat down to dinner, she maintained the protocol she'd set, alternately praising and criticizing to instruct yet encourage the staff: "The fish is fried crispy, but the pudding is too tight."

The girls would never be excellent cooks, no matter how meticulously she trained them—what it took was a thoughtless measure of spice, a certain nonchalance about the kitchen. Vinita's eyes burned.

Babita felt her temper rise. "Why are you looking at me like that? Didn't you hear what I said?"

"Haa."

"What 'haa'?"

"Ji haa."

"And what did I say? Repeat what you heard so I know you've understood me correctly."

"Ji haa, Auntyji, the pudding should be less tight," said Vinita.

Babita sensed a mocking tone.

"Don't put that hair oil in your hair, you are overwhelming the house like an attar shop near Jama Masjid."

The younger one, Punita, was the beauty. Babita watched her fill the dog's water bowl.

The last time her neighbor, Sara Habib's husband, Murad, had come to the house, he'd noticed Punita. Asking to see her English homework, he'd pulled her to sit upon his knee. She had been required to name four kinds of boats, and had completed the exercise perfectly: *ship, canoe, kayak, yacht.* She had written a story called *Miss Cat and Miss Mouse.* She had been on a camping trip to Corbett National Park, where she'd seen the print of a tiger's paw on the sand by the river. An actual tiger you would only see if you were an important person like an American president or a Bollywood actor. So she had learned and informed Babita.

Babita had observed something unsavory in the manner Mr. Habib clasped Punita. He had said, "Dear little girl, dear, dear little girl, don't be afraid of Uncle, sweetheart."

She had said, "Please don't bring the child into the living room and seat her on your lap. She will begin to look down on her own family in the kitchen."

At night Babita tossed so much that her nightgown wound around her and she suffered indigestion. She listened to the watchman bringing down his wooden staff and blowing his whistle on his rounds. She thought this kept only the watchman safe: Thieves learned they might rob on the other side of the neighborhood from where he was. On the other hand, if he hadn't been instructed to march and whistle, he'd feel free to nod off. She switched on her lamp. After her husband's death, which had occurred when she was thirty-three years old, for a span of time, she and Sunny had shared a bed. One day Sunny had returned to his own room without a word. This had upset her profoundly, but she had no way to articulate her upset. Her response was irrational. They hadn't spoken for a week, and neither of them had ever made mention of this episode. Years later Sunny had burst out with: "*I am not your spouse. You have to let me be. It isn't fair!*"

It had been necessary to send him to New York to make his own life.

Babita sought her water glass. She confronted the fact that it was not Vini-Puni's insolence or the too-tight pudding. It was not the people at the building site with their close-up poverty. Not her precarious position as a widow in a household united against her. Not the ammoniacal fumes of men pissing in the park. Nor the legs of kissing couples protruding from the bushes.

What curdled was the photograph she had enclosed in the letter to Sunny. It was Sonia's face planed like a panther: thick eyebrows and blazing eyes, sad and defiant, angry and accusing, a magnificent mouth of downturned reproach.

Two weeks later, at dawn, when in Delhi and across the nation, widows and widowers made their phone calls to reassure themselves they were not alone although night had informed them otherwise, Babita telephoned Sunny from the phone on her bedside table. "Sunny," she said. "Sunny, did you receive that very silly letter?"

The crows outside her window raised their wings of doom and cawed. Soon the sun would wrest control, everything set by then in stone.

Sunny heard his mother's voice enmeshed in a thicket of *kava kava kaw* that transported him to his home city and made him remember that each waking moment of a crow's life is aggressive: Their voices warned, their wings sliced like swords, they robbed and killed all day.

"I should let you work," Babita began, "work comes first." She feigned indifference, but her armpits itched. "Do you remember that family in Allahabad?"

"No, and less do I care," said Sunny. "Don't meddle, Ma. You think it's harmless, but it is harmful."

Leap of heart. "Who is meddling?" she exclaimed. "You'll find someone on your own when you are ready." She hurried this sentence to prove it wasn't that she didn't want Sunny to find someone, just not *this* person *now*.

"Well, I did find someone!" It came bursting out, stimulated by Ulla's bitterness.

"What do you mean?"

"I have a girlfriend!" he shouted, as if he'd been afflicted with one. *"Who?"*

"It doesn't matter who! Anyway, it's not going to last."

"It isn't?"

"No! Not with all the nonsense you've been dragging into my life."

Babita immediately telephoned the Colonel, raising her voice above the crows on both sides of the line now. She reported, "Sunny is not interested. He will need somebody more modern."

The Colonel said, "Right-o!" in a delighted tone because this meant an end to the feud with his wife, who believed they had been tricked into exchanging Sunny for kebabs. And now that Babita had dismissed Sonia, Babita turned her mind to the staggering news of an American girlfriend.

At 7:30 A.M., Vinita came in with the tea tray and newspaper. Babita turned to the travel page first and found an account of an Alaskan cruise. It had become something of a fad for Indian children who'd achieved an American life to treat their parents to an Alaskan cruise, to allow them to experience for a week what they'd bequeathed their children for a lifetime—the bliss of being able to pretend they were not Indians and that India didn't exist. Where they might see enough white people and empty white landscapes to convince them this was so. What was so odd, Babita reflected, was that this striving to escape India felt patriotic: If you were a worthy Indian, you became an American.

It's All Love

....

LALA TOLD SONIA THAT WHEN SHE FIRST OPENED SOHO Leloup in 1969, SoHo looked the way Dumbo did now. Six days a week, Sonia walked fifteen minutes down streets of derelict warehouses from the studio she was subletting to Dumbo Leloup, once just avoiding a homicide outside the Chinese takeout where boys and men with gold teeth gathered and many drugged-out people jigged, slumped, tripped, and begged down the road to the subway. She took the route by the Good Fortune Trading Company and the mysterious, deserted Buddhist monastery slung with barbed wire. The Farragut Projects were to the left; a low buzz from the Con Ed station emitted from the right. Rats competed with pigeons over stale discarded pita in the dumpster outside the pita factory, and a smell of bilge water rose from the Navy Yard, which was overrun by a band of feral cats that suffered from feline leukemia. She passed by the empty lot where trucks were hosed down, the place that made industrial metal sinks, past Los Papi's, past the oversize parking lot drenched with chemical waste owned by Jehovah's Witnesses. She walked down toward the river away from a luxury high-rise, a middle finger to the poor. She came to a warren of office spaces rented by Hasidic landlords and a deli with a perpetually sticky floor owned by a mild bespectacled Syrian. A Nepali stood at the cash counter; Ecuadorian and Colombian men unpacked crates of spotty fruit and limp vegetables onto synthetic green grass and made sandwiches from piles of breaded chicken, salamis, cheeses, and mayonnaise salads covered in Saran Wrap. Here, where the rats knew every gap and cranny in the broken walls and pavements, there were daily model shoots pitching glamour against dereliction, bling against poverty. By the waterfront where they planned a new park, immaculate Korean brides were photographed against the Brooklyn Bridge. A lot of money was going to be made here; the sound of jackhammers never ceased.

Sonia unlocked and lifted the metal grille and opened the gallery that was almost directly under the flashing subway tracks. She listened to the rattle of cars and trains, to helicopters farther overhead that were for tourists or wealthy people flying to summer homes on Long Island, occasionally NYPD helicopters bombinating. Was New York City fast and exciting? Or noisy and desperate?

Sonia had been hired to sit in this gallery and be so fashionable that she did her part to flip the neighborhood into a millionaire's haunt. It was boring—she yawned and yawned again. She decided to read *Anna Karenina,* the book she had tried and failed to read in Vermont because she had been too distressed. Anna had been unable to read her English novel on the train home to her dull husband because she so thirsted to live the life described in the book. Now Sonia could barely read *Anna Karenina* because when she read, a tingling overcame her, she so wished to be writing it herself. What a tingle, an almost unbearable, sublime tingle, from head to toe. How many millions of observations and moments it had taken to compose this book! Sonia began to make notes, she wrote descriptions of landscapes, snatches of conversations. She wrote down everything Lala said because Lala was given to such startling statements that Sonia was drawn to listen to her exactly as much as she was repelled.

Lala opined: "You are lucky—you inherited the long legs and the height of a German. But the best mixture is in fact the quadroon, one-quarter black."

She said, "Never marry with the Japanese because they snore all night, even the women, because of the nose. And if you have children with them, they will turn out bowlegged."

"How do you know?"

"A friend of mine who goes only with the Japanese told me. If you marry with the Chinese, the legs turn out okay, but not with the Japanese. Who knows why, it is one of the mysteries."

She said, "Mexicans are constructed for physical labor, and they are not good in studies. They are unsuccessful immigrants in America because they are not good-looking and will always be the working class."

She said, "One of the reasons one's sympathy is on the side of Palestinians is that they are beautiful people, and somehow it just makes it worse when good-looking people are maltreated. It's the same with the Kurds, who are better looking than Turks."

She said, "Albanians are all thieves. But you can trust a Lebanese. I've never found that to be untrue."

She said, "Who are the most intelligent people? Jews, it's obvious. We've known that from the beginning."

She said, "Frankly all of you Indians are a bit strange. You court favor like a mania!"

She said, "I confess I don't care for the Arab, but I admire the Persian and the Ottoman. The fall of the Ottomans was one of the world tragedies."

She said, "I told my friend who has an art foundation in Marseilles that if you invite the Russians, you'll find they drink like mad and do pee-pee in the bed."

She said, "I met a man from Haiti, very black—we became great friends. He was extremely cultivated, always wearing an excellent jacket and an excellent cologne."

This old vocabulary of race lingered on improbably in the drawing rooms of the wealthy along with a nostalgia for the past so strong that it could reinvigorate. Lala's father had been a colonial official in the French colonies, just as Ilan's mother's father had been one in the British colonies. She said, "Colonialism originated and prospered because of attraction. It was love, first and foremost. The Orientals cannot have enough of white skin, as you know. That is how the British conquered India with a handful of people. My father had a taste for brown-skinned women; he wasn't satisfied with the boring girls he grew up with. Oh, he married appropriately, of course, but he had his adventures!"

One late-summer day she arrived with an art collector. "Sonia, I have a request," she instructed merrily. "Take down your hair."

She turned to the gentleman and said: "What do you think of her?" And then: "Come by the window, Sonia, why are you skulking?"

The man had a wedding band, a boxer's build, and a forbidding face that looked as if it had been punched out of natural alignment, yet he winked kindly at Sonia to let her know that he understood this was not agreeable to her.

"She is the protégée of de Toorjen Foss. You know him?"

"I know of him. He guards his privacy. I respect that. *The Dictator's Wife* is a masterpiece—the dictator is portrayed as a sympathetic figure. There was a notice about him recently in *Le Monde,* and it's just a matter of time before his fame detonates."

"What do you think of this exhibit?" the man asked Sonia, gesturing at the show that took the garbage problem for its inspiration and featured strings attached to mirrors reflecting dangling bits of garbage the artist had unearthed from garbage mountains around the world, including one in Mumbai that dated to British Victorian times.

Sonia had felt proud at the mention of Ilan, and she knew she should not. She was further upset she had been asked to take down her hair and furthermore that she had done so, uncoiling it from the two looped braids she had made. Lala appeared to be flirting with the man through Sonia.

Sonia said: "It's a garbage show about garbage."

The man chuckled. He said, "I like this girl."

"Art for the sake of politics may as well be politics," said Sonia.

Lala telephoned Sonia later the same afternoon and spoke sharply. "For shame! That was a disgraceful way to speak, and if you don't transform your attitude, I must ask you to leave. It is your job to promote the art in the gallery and to cultivate an amusing manner. I am surprised Ilan would suggest anybody so surly and impertinent. You came to me with no experience. You have absolutely no idea how to comport yourself."

A few hours later, the collector telephoned Sonia at home. Lala must have passed on the number. "I will be frank—it's always the best way—if you want to spend a night in the arms of a friend, I stay at the

Romare in Room 313. Or there is a restaurant in the hotel and we could meet there. For me, such matters are never only about sex."

Sonia looked out of the window of the studio she was subletting from a yoga instructor who had strung together several appointments at wellness retreats. This woman had kept her suitcase by the door, but she had taken a minute to point out that the building opposite was painted white, so it felt light inside her apartment, even if the room didn't get direct sun. And that the fireplace obviously didn't work, but the female figures carved into the mantel were iconic for a feminist, which she was sure Sonia was, just as she was herself, it being only rational. She reminded Sonia it was illegal for her to be subletting this studio, so Sonia must say she was a relative by marriage. After she left, Sonia had registered the loud silence, the skyless view trimmed in Christmas lights without which one might just die of sadness. She had taken out the amulet of Badal Baba, the faceless imp, held it to her forehead, to her heart.

Lala called Sonia again. "Will you meet Mathias?"

"I don't want to go," Sonia said. "I want to read my *Anna Karenina*." Wasn't Tolstoy overcome by the sublime tingle even as he wrote? How could he combine that with the practical necessity of putting words on paper? What experiences he must have pursued—wouldn't Sonia need to live a life to tell a tale? Yet to write meant stepping out of life, isolating yourself. If you tried to balance the two, wouldn't you be living a life for the sole purpose of creating a fictional life, not one that would take its natural course, but one that you would be bending and shaping toward a secret purpose? You wouldn't make a choice for happiness, but for an escapade you might relate. Yet Sonia didn't want to sleep with Mathias.

Lala said, "It's useful for a young girl—and you already learned this—to have a dalliance with an older man, let alone a man who is one of the top three collectors in Europe. Don't be childish. A cultivated man can teach you and help you. And it will make Ilan jealous. It will be a good thing for you, I cannot help but think."

"Ilan isn't *here* to be jealous."

"Maybe he will come back if you give him a reason."

"Doesn't this collector have a wife?"

"Nobody cares about the wife. You must know that by now. To have an affair in a European manner is something light, not something heavy and guilty. But one of the girls I recently hired in SoHo is very sympathetic. She is Croatian, eyes of Adriatic blue, raven hair—the girls of Croatia are especially beautiful, quite distinct from Serbs and Bosnians. I saw her watching Mathias. He is ugly, of course, but with a savage ugliness that compels women."

The SoHo branch operated quite obviously as a geisha house, for here Lala kept several ingenues for the pleasure of her male artists and collectors, for them to gain in optimism. If you are buoyed by the young woman in your bed, you claim the big stage the next morning, become expansive and generous, make an expensive purchase, put your work forward in a way that everyone believes it's worth something.

A clever recruit would exploit this situation, and once a youthful Lala had played this game herself, gaining the knowledge and influence to acquire a valuable collection of art; now she initiated her employees, professing she was helping them, but Sonia often felt hard eyes upon her, often caught an expression of distaste tightening Lala's lips in the guise of a smile.

Opening a can of soup later that evening, it occurred to Sonia that the collector might wish to sleep with her simply because Ilan had. And in the proposition she had received, in what Mathias had said about Ilan, she had been given an inkling of Ilan's imminent fame. To sleep with a girlfriend of a secretive genius may give the collector an edge over Ilan, some useful knowledge of him. Or perhaps it was nothing but primitive male instinct: He'd smelled a competitor and wished to piss in the same place.

*

IT WAS SUMMER'S END when one afternoon, the phone rang in the gallery.

"Sonia! It's me! I'm here! I'm in New York—when can you come? Come immediately! I'm in my apartment," said Ilan.

"Why didn't you phone me all this time?"

"Don't scold! Let's be happy to see each other. I went on a painting trip—believe me, I missed you so much! But I was clever, wasn't I? I knew where to find you, I knew Lala would keep you safe!"

Why did Sonia believe him? She believed him so their playful and private life, their innocent and spooky life, their magic island existence, as if within a painting, as if within a book, may begin anew.

She left the gallery early and took the subway to where New York was a settled and wealthy city: wide stretches of clean pavement pale as sand, uniformed doormen sitting at high desks in marbled vestibules. She arrived at a slim limestone building decorated with a fanciful castle turret that overlooked the Hudson River; pressed the small ivory button in a brass panel that read *de T. Foss;* and when it made a waspish buzz, she pushed open the heavy door of glass encased in a wrought-iron design of Madonna lilies and stepped into a dim gold entryway. When the elevator got to the top, it opened directly into Ilan's apartment—and she was in his arms, the feel of him and the place between his ear and his neck where her nose exactly fit, the lemon soap smell of him, instantly familiar.

"I thought you had vanished!" Her eyes brimmed.

"I'm here, why aren't you happy?"

"I *am* happy."

"I see that—I'm happy, too!" He was throwing off his clothes. He threw his shirt to the right, his trousers to the left, his socks atop the lamps, and his underwear to the setting sun. Sonia threw her dress up and over her head. Everything was as festive as when they first met. They made love in the living room, in a bedroom wallpapered in an unusual design of fruit bats, and finally in the shower. Later she walked about, saw that the apartment had floors of parquet, a maid's room, a pantry— and when she looked out, she could see the river and a tugboat with a star in its nose and a star in its tail and the George Washington Bridge in the distance, as wistful as a Hokusai print. When Ilan opened the window to dislodge the stuffy, milty smell of sex, they heard the roar of the city, a combination of sounds gathering and rising.

"Listen to that! When I was in Bombay, staying at the top of the Taj, I opened my window and heard this: the lion roar of a great metropolis. The same in Mexico City. I love it. It gives me energy."

Hand in hand, they walked to dinner. The air was warm and slightly malarial by the Hudson.

"I am scared it will be different in New York. Not the private world we had in Vermont," he said.

"No, it will be the same," she said.

"Why?"

"Because we are the same."

"Yes. When I saw you, my first thought was, *Ah, this is my Sonia!*"

"Where were you all this time?" she asked.

"Most recently I was in Zurich visiting my family."

"Zurich!"

"Yes. What do you think? That I don't have things to see to, that I have only a barefoot little Indian in my life?"

Someone came out of a building with her bulldog, paused while her dog put its entire face into a smell, for it had no snout, and said to them, "You make a handsome couple!"

Again they occupied a private universe. Ilan stayed away from other people, intuiting his success, just as Mathias had observed; the stratospheric success he was planning would lie in remaining apart from the crowd. Occasionally he went alone to meet an acquaintance or someone from the art world. When he did so, he came back upset to the point of sickness. "Why did I drink? I was nervous, I was unhappy, I thought, 'Let me have some fun for once, maybe it will make me more easygoing'—but they are all stupid. This is a banker's town, it's a provincial place. Why didn't you warn me not to go, why didn't you remind me?"

It took a long while of soothing with his photographs, his books, his film reels and his recordings of sounds, his cutout pages from magazines to make collages, his boxes of flea market finds—a toy music box, a spinning top—to return him to the mood of whatever he was painting. He mulled his lists of art supplies with names that intensely conjured places, emotions: Madder Brown, Seneca, Terra Rosa, Japanese White, Caput Mortuum Purple. Some he had named himself: Yucatan Hurricane, Grandmother's Handkerchief, Father's Violet Death. He painted in a studio in the former Meatpacking District, where he said a freight elevator traveled up to a space that looked onto the cityscape that never stopped moving. From this vista, it was still the New York of Edward Hopper, who was as much a connoisseur of holy light as any Old Master. Sun on a redbrick chimney made the same unbearable tingling as the light upon Madonna and child. A tingling like a reader longing to write.

"Why is everyone alone and desolate in Hopper's work?"

"Because that is how he felt. That's the only explanation."

Sonia's heart was a Hopper painting. She was yet to be invited into Ilan's studio.

She remembered not to lavishly praise another artist when on Friday and Saturday evenings they went to the museums, where Ilan sketched and stalked the paintings as if he wished to occupy the quiet of Vermeer's kitchen pierced by a letter, Goya's nightmare of decrepitude and war, Van Gogh's bed that made a person burst into tears— a grown man with a modest bed like that! They surveyed Kiefer's forest suffused with Nazi terror—the forest remembers—and Cornell's velvet box with the story of a dancer dancing upon a panther's skin laid over the snow, under the stars, for a highwayman. Imagine him living at Utopia Parkway in Flushing, Queens, with his mother; artists who are poor and live with their mummies—again one wants to cry. It's hard for an artist to grow up; it's stacked against you. There was Magritte's dream of a house dreaming of a home and the empty square of de Chirico—after the long journey, when you finally arrive, there is nowhere to put your heart. There was Rembrandt's lace and Hodgkin's Malabar rain—he had traveled to India in the same way Ilan had gone to Mexico, and he found emotion so big that it dwarfed form. There was Rothko's depression greater than any cathedral and O'Keeffe's Black Place that suggested life was something to be worked out between you and mountains. When you gazed upon these paintings, you wanted no other life. In the Impressionist room—remnants of breakfast upon a sun-splashed cloth, wife in the bath, Sunday in the park— again the voice of someone outside the window, looking in, sounded inside Sonia's head: *Happiness is for other people.*

Hours went by, and when her feet throbbed, when her toes went dead in the high heels Ilan preferred she wear, she dared not suggest they leave until the guards ushered them out into the chill of a fall night that felt so alert, so feral. They were the very last museum-goers to leave the museum always.

They drank martinis at the Algonquin, and Sonia said *Light Coming on the Plains* was a tantric painting. A rational hierarchy had broken down, as if O'Keeffe had gone under a wave, and when she came back up, she saw small as big and big as small. She viewed the world through the sockets of a skull beached upon a desert. Sonia said she had read O'Keeffe's letter: *When I traveled to India, I learned to trust my dreams. I knew anything could be true.* Ilan didn't seem to be listening while he drew Sonia in his notebook, but he wrote what she was saying: *After such a long journey, there is nowhere to put your heart.*

They ate at a restaurant where the food was from another time and place: caviar and oysters, artichokes dismantled and reconstructed for delicate eating, salmon bathed in chanterelles and cream. Quite often, in this world conservatively luxurious, Sonia saw other couples similarly disparate. She saw creepy old men on stiff legs, dressed in expensive coats and cashmere scarves, accompanied by women or men two or three or four decades younger. She saw white men with Asian women, dark men with blond women. She observed the old men paying for the young women and the young men, the dark men paying for the blond women, the white men paying for the Asian women, but these were not like the Asian women on the subway line to Sunset Park or Flushing. These had pearl skin and silk hair, and they dressed in pleated origami. They spoke in such subtracted, dulcet tones that the clink of the heavy silverware on porcelain chimed louder than their voices.

The waiters said, "Good evening, sir. Good evening, madame." In the stores on Madison Avenue, the doormen said, "Good day, sir. Good day, ma'am." In Bergdorf Goodman, Sonia stood on a little round podium and the staff arrived with dresses and coats. They offered to hem a skirt or tuck in shoulders. They bent down on one knee and fitted shoes on her feet. Ilan bought Sonia a ruffled, turquoise-green bikini in an old-fashioned style, in case they went to Portofino; an old-fashioned plum silk brassiere with panties that looked like shorts and fit up to her navel; a fitted raspberry wool dress that came below her knees and low boots in rabbit-soft mauve suede, a matching handbag, an antique garnet brooch, and a pale lilac long-haired coat in a slim cut to replace the mustard coat from Marie's charity church drive. The coat looked like a living creature; it slinked about Sonia's length. The shop assistants congratulated Ilan: "The lady looks beautiful."

Sonia appraised herself and saw she had become Ilan's young mother, this time lavishing him with praise and affection. Ilan said, "Don't move, darling," and took a photograph with his Leica.

The store was empty on the day they bought the lilac coat, for it happened to be a day of economic collapse. While the shop assistants were carrying on as if nothing was amiss, like butlers in a fallen mansion, the small news screen in the elevator indicated panic about the world, stock traders covering their mouths, the markets in apocalyptic free fall, savings and pension funds wiped out in a matter of hours. But the collapse did not affect Ilan, for he was too rich, and it did not affect Sonia, for she was too poor. The department store had a café on the top floor with a view from so high above Central Park that it became an illustration of the city, not the city. They drank champagne looking down upon the lambent foliage, and Sonia, confident of her unusual beauty highlighted by her new dress, said to Ilan, "Do you know how lucky you are that I am here? When you didn't telephone all these past months, I might have married the Allahabad colonel's grandson."

"Who is that?"

"My grandfather's friend's grandson. He asked my father, my father said why not, something may come of it, and they began to investigate the boy."

Ilan laughed so hard that he raised his feet and kicked them about: "Oh, I have to be careful. I've heard these stories. This is what happens if you have an Indian girlfriend—she goes home to see her family for one week and comes back married."

What had happened to the proposal? Sonia realized that she had never been told, she had never asked. She didn't want to know, she didn't care. Her life had returned to being interesting. She said, "Remember you warned me never to write about arranged marriages? So I knew I had better not accept one—or I'd end up writing about one."

"Are you still writing?"

"I don't have the focus, nor yet the subject, but I am making notes."

"Didn't I tell you that you have an unusual mind? I know you will not write what everyone else writes. You will make me proud to be with you."

*

THE OVERHEAD LIGHT TURNED on in the middle of the night. "Sonia, please wake up. I am lonely."

"I'm asleep," she said.

"Sonia, I hate to wake in the middle of the night. It's scary and I need your company."

"I can't work my way up. I'm deep in the well."

"Oho, but you're talking!"

"I'm talking but I'm far away."

"Let me ask you just one thing: I am worried about my project."

"What is your project?"

"I cannot tell you. You will steal my idea or you will talk to somebody in your gallery and they will steal my idea. Sonia, I'm getting angry now about those paintings we saw at the museum. Why did you keep on talking about Georgia O'Keeffe? Her flowers are sentimental calendar art—anyone can tell she is a phony."

*

"SONIA, CAN YOU WAKE UP, please? Tell me one thing: Do you think I will be famous?" A question, a threat, an insistence, a plea.

"I heard *Le Monde* wrote a piece about you."

"Ha ha, yes. I have the aura of a person that only those in the know, know. The journalist, she loved me! I could tell this woman believed she will one day boast she discovered me—you have to flatter someone like that, no matter how ugly; the ones who praise you most are always the ugliest, I had to close my eyes—but more famous than *Le Monde*!" Sternly like a dictator child.

"Well, why wouldn't you be?"

Ilan laughed. "You're a funny person. There is a simplicity in you that I like, that I admire. Yes, why wouldn't I be?"

"Because when there is no choice, there can be no other outcome."

Wriggling his backside into her softness, he said, "Hold me!"

*

WAKING: "SONIA, WILL I be famous?"

For variety's sake: "Hmm, well, maybe with a certain select community."

"Oh—which community?" Recognizing a joke, lurking laughter.

"Third-Worlders and liberals."

"But I want everyone to like me. Even First-Worlders, fascists, and the pope—then I will work and work, I will tear my arse." Clutching her tight, he was a person fierce in laudable intent. "In this world, you are famous or else you are nobody."

"Why nobody?"

"Well, yes, that is interesting to consider. Many of us don't live in communities any longer, where you are cherished just for your family having been known for generations, where everyone stays in the same place. Then if you are religious, that alters everything because you are part of a people with a history and faith that allows you to belong not only in the present but also in the past and future. But if you have no home, no faith, no community, and a scattered, inattentive, or resentful family, you are alone in the big world. If you are not famous, you don't exist.

"Even in the Old Testament, God created man because he was lonely. A profound point—you see? And in the Hadith of the Hidden Treasure, God says: 'I was a hidden treasure. I loved to be known.' Concealed in the 'I loved to be known' is 'I want to be acknowledged. I want an admiring friend. I want to be famous.'"

They had overcome their early difficulty of having nothing to say by settling upon an inexhaustible subject of conversation—the subject of Ilan. In exchange for her bad-luck passport and her inexpertness and youth, for the rewards of indulging him endlessly, Sonia endlessly in-

dulged him. The more Ilan talked, the bigger he became; the bigger he
became, the happier he was; the happier he was, the more secure and
safe she felt, like a mouse in someone's pocket. He may lose his temper
and fling the mouse out of his pocket, but then he always tucked the
mouse back in because he needed someone to talk to all of the time.
There could be no fame, no existence, without calling out and receiving an answer. If you wish to be known, you must conjure the audience that loves you.

*

"SONIA, SHOULD I PAINT a painting called *Mother Swimming*?"
Said Sonia, "Certainly." *Mother Swimming*! He'd consented to tell
her the subject of a painting for the first time!
"Is it a good idea, do you think?"
"Of course."
"Why of course?"
"Even the name is lovely."
"But I don't think it is a good idea after all to paint *Mother Swim-
ming*."
While he tested the idea, Sonia understood she must hold on to it
tight. The more he attacked, the tighter she must hold, so the finer, the
more whittled the idea became. Finally when it was fully viable, Ilan
might begin to work. It would encompass worlds, *Mother Swimming*.

*

"SONIA?"
Sonia burst into tears.
"Too much narcissism?" He said this ruefully.
"You talk about yourself so much that I cannot think, not even in
my sleep."
"But I need it!"
Ilan paced and regurgitated his ideas with a concentrated internal
gaze. He ate the last plum and the last nectarine. He consumed quanti-
ties of nuts, olives, and bread torn raggedly from a loaf. He spat out
pits and rinds as if they were the skin and bones of enemies. He opened

the window and rained pistachio shells outside. He made lists of famous people and wrote dates when famous artists did famous things, so that a kabbalah-like magic might be unlocked, scooping him up into its spell of fateful numbers. These he showed to Sonia.

He showed her the maroon and green notebooks he ordered from Cairo, from a store behind the Al-Azhar mosque, the leather spines embossed with his initials in gold. He showed her that he saved all his used tubes of paint, his brushes—when he was famous, they would be important. He saved all his pairs of worn-out shoes. Every day he photographed his worktable and his face in the mirror. With another camera kept in his studio, every day he photographed the paintings he was working on that Sonia never saw. He kept every sketch made on a napkin. He kept every barbershop receipt, every list of groceries, every visiting card, invoices of painting materials procured from special shops in Florence, in Kyoto. If you gather enough to put into a museum, you may one day achieve one. He was planning for eternity.

This was his work life. His domestic life was that of an impoverished, eccentric, miserly aristocrat who always has plenty of money in the end. A miserly, eccentric, impoverished, wealthy aristocrat who is full of superstitions—for how else to explain his family's uncanny luck through the ages, or to trust in retaining it?

Ilan swallowed a raw clove of garlic each night to keep the vampires away. He believed that eating pumpkin seeds would rid you of worms. He was terrified of drafts, preferred to shut the windows and perspire indoors, believed it was unhealthy to take too many showers. He threw salt over his shoulder to keep away the bad spirits. He never walked under a ladder. He thought a hat on a bed, a scavenger bird on a withered branch, or an umbrella opened inside the house were intimations of bad news. He was a thief and believed he gained in energy this way. He stole a book of Max Ernst collages from a library, a porcelain asparagus from the home of a financier, engraved hotel silver from the Metropole, a child's marble, a clay acrobat from an unguarded provincial museum in Mandalay.

After her days in the gallery, Sonia no longer returned to her room by the Navy Yard. "Look," Ilan said into her ear. He undressed her and put her on a chair in front of the mirror. He laid her upon the table, bent her over the desk. He made her sit on him with her clothes on and her underpants off.

They made love in front of the mirror, against the mirror, sometimes they made love for a few hasty minutes, sometimes for hours, sometimes their mouths searched each other in the dark, sometimes their lovemaking was intense and serious, sometimes childlike and innocent, sometimes they were like two machines working smoothly against each other, stretching their limbs and undoing their workday tension and the NYC strain of subways and crowded streets, sometimes they were careless as if the other might have been anyone at all, sometimes it was a failed playacting that made them laugh. He made her unashamed. He took a photograph of her. Naked in the mirror, she was always beautiful. "You're like a leopard," he said again. "Absolutely dark, a glimmer of light in your eyes and your hair, not an extra pound, the tip of your nose twitching. I will paint *Sonia as Leopard*."

It was much nicer to imagine oneself a leopard than a person. Her human shame went.

One day Ilan found her reading *Anna Karenina*. She saw the ember come alive in his eye. "Every scene of that book is a painting," he said. "Don't read that or it may become a mirror to our own fate. You'll live your life to follow the book—and that book has many victims, by the way."

Sonia remembered she must never provoke him with beauty created by others.

14

....

ILAN WENT TO SEE A CHIROPRACTOR FOR A SUDDEN SHARP pain in his knee, and while he was gone, Sonia made a pot of lentil soup—which she knew Ilan liked because his nanny used to make it, although his mother called it peasant soup—so that they could stay home in the evening, so that he could rest his leg and eat something comforting. Dismissing a small, nagging fear, she proceeded optimistically. She added ginger, a sprinkle of chili flakes, and fresh coriander.

When Ilan walked in, hobbling with a cane, which annoyed him—when he didn't feel well, he felt angry; illness was a harbinger of old age and old age was impotence—his brow wrinkled and his nose. "What is that smell?"

"I made soup!"

"Oh?" He sat at his desk.

"Sonia," he said after a bit, "come here."

"What is it?"

"I cannot work. The smell bothers me. It upsets me."

"Just try." She brought out a spoon. "You have to try it before you say you don't like it."

He shut his eyes and swallowed. "Aah." He opened his eyes and leapt up, dropping the spoon. "*What is this?* There is something I don't recognize and I don't like it. I don't know *what is in this. What is it? I can't eat it!*"

"There is almost nothing in it. Salt, ginger."

"*Ginger? But I hate ginger.* Look, don't do this. Why are you doing this? You're spoiling things."

"But you eat ginger. You had some the other day." He'd ordered black cod poached in a ginger broth.

"Not twenty pounds!"

"Well, look at it this way," she said, trying to recover the situation. "Nobody wants to poison you."

"How do you know?"

"There is nobody here."

"You are."

She left the room.

"Sonia? You can come out. I threw your Indian dish out of the window."

"Onto the pavement?"

"Onto the ginkgo tree. That tree always stinks, so I paid it back."

Ilan clasped her close and kissed her messily all over her face. "I'm over it. I was upset, but because I love you so much, I was able to dismiss it." This was the first time he mentioned the word "love," and it filled her with joy.

She in turn thought: *I did not react or get angry, so I must love this person, too.*

"You see," he said, "if you obey me during the first few minutes of crisis, then I can also calm down. Look, now everything is fine. We're getting along, we're learning, you didn't start arguing, so I could also be generous."

*

ILAN WATCHED FILMS FROM boxes of reels he had spread out. His parents had taken turns with the new film camera his father had bought. Sonia saw Ilan's mother in a ruffled bikini, smiling, waving, jumping with a bomb-splash into the Mediterranean.

"Wouldn't your mother like to meet your girlfriend?" Sonia ventured one day.

"Don't ask me that."

"Why?"

"You know my relationship with my mummy."

"But you do visit her?"

"Yes, she is my mother, but I also see that she is small-minded and a racist. She won't think you're a charming, educated girl. She will think you are a poor Third-Worlder and look to see your dress, your hair, your makeup, your shoes—and to all this, darling, by the way, you pay no attention. And women should pay attention. A groomed woman is beguiling and mysterious."

"She's a racist?"

"Well, if you were a Parisienne, she would want to meet you. She is a snob, I told you. She buys cheap tabloids that follow the royal families. Anyway, she is in Zurich, so it doesn't matter. She plays bridge and considers herself enlightened because one of her maids is a Muslim in a headscarf. If anyone says anything about Muslims, she says, 'But Fatima is a wonderful woman, reliable and honest. I would trust her with my life.'"

His mother in turn filmed Ilan's father, who drove a Porsche with the top down. They were in Capri, they were in the Hollywood Hills. He had a pencil mustache and a cigar; he poop-pooped the automobile horn.

"What was your father like?"

"A playboy. He had no discipline, he never denied himself a good time, he thought of himself as a bon vivant and had an endless stream of mistresses. My grandfather was the same."

"How did they have the time if they ran a shipping empire?" asked Sonia.

"Time expands for a person like this, darling; they live double and triple lives simultaneously. They eat two dinners every evening—one with the wife and one with the mistress—yet they remain trim. Meanwhile they have great clarity of thought from walking a tightrope. Their daring makes them nimble, their eyes shine, they are secretly saying, '*I won! I won!*'"

"Weren't your mother and grandmother angry?"

"Mm?" He was puffing on a small marijuana pipe he'd bought at a store on West Fourth Street that looked like a glass turd.

"They behaved like all the women I knew in my childhood. They counseled each other to take it philosophically; it was to be expected that rich husbands would have affairs. Out in the world they pretended nonchalance for the sake of their self-respect—some of them even went so far as to express pride in the virility of their husbands. Meanwhile they coached each other on how to turn these times to their advantage. They understood they had to look after themselves financially and swiftly extract property, move bank accounts, before it was too late. Men are guilty for just a moment, only at the discovery of a hurtful affair when the wife, grandmother, children, kitchen maids, cooks, dogs, and cats are crying—you read *Anna Karenina*?—by week's end they find reasons to deny their guilt and become defiant. The brief time to seize advantage vanishes. When my father had transferred one apartment too many to my mother's name, this very apartment in New York, in fact, he grew resentful and left her permanently."

"You must have been angry at him?"

"The more I missed him, the more I loved him."

"Didn't you feel sorry for your mother?"

"She grew bitter, impatient—she flew into rages, she associated me with my father. I loved her less."

"My father never cheats," said Sonia proudly.

"You think he went alone to the Greek islands?"

Sonia told him Papa's solitary travels were a cause of marital strife. "My mother accused him of not taking us along and of spending all the money on himself. He said he earned the money and couldn't afford to take three of us, so it was only fair he gave himself an occasional selfish treat."

"Is it possible to go to the Greek islands alone? To Santorini, Rhodes? To Naxos, Paxos?"

"Why not?"

"It isn't fun to go by yourself to a holiday place, hobbling across pebbles to enter the sea, swatting away the wasps excavating holes in your grilled fish, searching for shade when there is none. Only if you are with a lover can you forget such grotesqueries and see the colors— green, purple, red—unraveling in the water. The underwater colors of the Mediterranean are different from any other sea."

"My father went alone to Italy, too."

Ilan made a resigned face like one deciding not to ruin someone's innocence.

"Not everyone is like your father!" she said.

Papa considered Sonia so precious that he did not cheat on Mama because that in turn would harm Sonia. Although this may not really be the reason her father was not a cheat. Perhaps he simply couldn't loosen his death grip upon her mother, but that is how it made Sonia feel. Because when someone betrays their spouse, they also betray their daughter and the small life of the house: the trustful dog, the cat with the attitude of a movie star, the houseplant venturing a new leaf, the leftover vegetable soup, the worn socks, the sliver of soap stuck upon the new bar of soap. They betray all these creatures and all these objects that have no idea they've been made into a joke, that their lives are actually something other than what they understand them to be. In the end, the betrayer can only scorn such naïveté.

"But what if you are like your father?" said Sonia.

"Do you think I would throw you away so cheaply? I love all of you." He gnashed on an apple. "Even your strange fingers, even your crooked little toe. I even love your temper."

"My temper!"

"Yes, darling, you have a temper. Don't think I don't notice it."

He went to the fridge. "Aren't there any more apples?"

"I didn't eat them," she said shortly, upset by their conversation.

"Then where are they?"

"You must have eaten the last one."

"What did you say?"

"I said I don't eat apples, so you must have eaten them. You know you don't notice yourself eating them."

"Don't contradict me," he said.

"I'm not. I'm stating a fact. When you are working and smoking pot, you eat everything in the cupboards and everything in the fridge."

"Don't deny me. I'll get angry," he said and went into the back room and shut the door.

Twenty minutes later he opened the door and said: "All I ask for is some apples. Is that so difficult?"

Sonia persisted: "I *do* buy apples."

It was her pride to spend her small income on groceries. She stopped at one or another of the expensive markets in the neighborhood that were like boutiques, showcasing each fruit clad individually in a netted cradle lit by hallowed light. She bought cave-aged hard European cheeses of the kind Ilan liked and rustic loaves of the kind he liked. She bought apples, carrots, cherry tomatoes ripened on the vine and bitter salad greens, just as Ilan liked, and crisp white wine and laundry soap, toilet paper, almond wood oil, and garbage bags. He refused an intrusive maid, so she washed the dishes, mopped the floor, changed their sheets, washed their clothes. She ignored the fact that Ilan didn't brush his teeth much, ignored the fact that Ilan's clothes were stained and that she had to soak the underwear in a solution of bleach before she washed it, ignored the fact that he left the toilet filthy and she was the one who cleaned it with a brush. Because the dirt and disorder did not make her revolt, again she had suspected she had found love.

*

A MONTH LATER ILAN ate the last carrot. He got into bed. He got out of bed. He left the bedroom.

He shouted from the living room at Sonia in bed, "Don't take a hot shower again, do you hear? The vapor creates a psychological anxiety in me. The air is too high and rarefied, too full of tiny particles to breathe."

Sonia remained silent. How to take a cold shower in winter?

"You come and sleep out here on the sofa," said Ilan, "and let me sleep in the bed. You are the one who behaved badly."

"Let's talk," said Sonia.

"Come out."

"I'll talk from here."

"I'm unhappy."

"Me too."

"Okay, let us part."

"Okay."

She feigned sleep.

A groan of anguish and anger. He leapt up and switched on all the lights. "You come out here and apologize."

After a bit she said, "I'm afraid if I do, you'll run into the bedroom, lock the door shut, jump into bed, and go to sleep."

Silence. Then she could hear him begin to laugh a bit. Eventually he came in, got into bed under the feather comforter, and slept by her side. The next morning when she came out he was already up, drinking coffee.

"Did you hear the tigers last night?"

He showed her what he had drawn as they fought. It was an island, a parenthesis of tropical green in a dream of blue. A picture of happiness.

"Why are we fighting? I want to be here with you."

Outside a squall blew upriver and encased the trees of Riverside Park in ice.

*

THEN ILAN ATE THE last pistachios.

He went to the bedroom and shut the door. Sonia sat on a chair.

He opened the door. "Who takes you out to fancy dinners every night? Who found you a job in New York? You moved in here uninvited; what do you do in return? I'm the only person around working and striving and tearing my arse apart. All I ask is that there are apples, carrots, and pistachios. Is that too much?"

Had she moved in here uninvited? It was true that he helped her. She would not have a job or a visa to stay in the United States had it not been for him. Yet her rage surged. She thought Ilan was correct in saying that she had a temper.

He shut the door again, he opened the door again. "Sonia? Do you hear you have to obey me?" He repeated "o . . . b . . . e . . . y" in a slow, sinister voice. "Or I will be angry and we won't get along." Two horns of marijuana smoke came out of his nostrils. "You come here, get down on your knees now, and swear you will o . . . b . . . e . . . y me."

Then Sonia, despite her attempt to quash her rage, despite her fear, erupted: "You shitty bastard!"

"What did you say?"

"You shitty bastard! That is what I said."

He switched to extreme madness. He smashed the teapot and the coffeepot, he smashed a row of glasses, he smashed a row of cups, he smashed a pile of plates, he ripped her silk scarf, he broke the little bowl showing Mount Fuji she kept her earrings in, swept all her belongings that were in the apartment into the garbage outside the kitchen door. "Sonia, you clean all this up, then get down on your knees and apologize, or you fuck out of here."

Frozen, Sonia continued to sit, astonished she was accepting such humiliation, angry at herself and at him, scared of staying—but also scared of leaving. The walls were pocked and stained with tea, and the floor tiles were chipped; there was broken china everywhere. Outside the window, the spider-legged water tanks on neighboring buildings seemed to look in on her like familiar friends who were on her side, as if they belonged to an old-fashioned science fiction. A tugboat—like the little duck that could—went upriver between jagged frozen banks. It believed in sturdiness of honor and industry. One couldn't help but cry at its ignorant, brave heart.

Ilan opened the bedroom door. "Why are you still sitting here?"

"It's three A.M. How can I go?"

"Why can't you? Someone tells you to leave their house and you don't go? Don't you have any shame, you shameless person? Don't you know to go fuck off when someone tells you to go fuck off? Do you not understand such simple language? Fuck out of here . . . Now go fuck off, fuck out of here! GET OUT! And I'm going to fuck other girls, do you hear me? GET OUT FUCK OFF! I'm going to fuck other girls from now on!"

She got up, exited the apartment, took the extravagant elevator down, walked to Broadway in her absurd, tight tailored dress and her absurd high-heeled shoes. The wind whittled sharp by skyscrapers sliced right at her neck and the street was empty and silent but for a resilient family of rats moving inside the garbage bags. A single taxi came inching down the bleak avenue, the driver clenching the wheel, leaning forward over it. "Dirty Dumbo?"

Back in her studio, Sonia felt too weighted by sadness, too light from emptiness. The heaviness made it impossible for her to move; the emptiness made her nauseated. She retched, but nothing came up except a poisonous froth that looked like frog spawn. She looked at herself in the mirror but was unable to register her reflection as it related to herself. Her unhappiness and argument with Ilan was lodged between herself and herself.

She remembered the amulet belonging to her grandfather, took it out of her drawer, unfastened the clasp, and inside found its empty, broken face looking into her broken, empty face; at least another creature acknowledged her. The thought of an eternal void was comforting to her right now. "Badal Baba, Bhoot Baba, Bhoot Baba, Bhoot Bibi," she prayed. "Make me into a ghost." Badal Baba sometimes took the form of a ghost, sometimes the form of a woman, a beast, a cloud. She slept with the amulet under her bed. Badal Baba's power was also in his maiming.

Three days later Ilan telephoned.

"Oh, I'm grateful you answered. I'm lonely and miserable," he said.

"So am I," she said. "I feel sick."

"Then why don't you come?" He half wept. "Oh, it's so sad. You're always saying you need this, you want that. All women begin demanding things and become gold diggers—"

"Did you ever miss a dollar from the change bowl?"

"You have higher ambition. Everyone wants something from me. Nobody loves me. Nobody helps me."

"But it was you who was not fair to me," she said.

"What does that mean? *Aaargh*. I already said I'm sorry, but you were also provoking me. Do you want to punish me now?"

"No. I won't punish you. I lost my temper, too, after all."

"Some temper from you I can take, darling."

And thus after his almost-apology for his false accusation of her not buying enough apples, carrots, and pistachios and his true accusation of her taking hot showers and cooking lentil soup, they had reconciled, and after their reconciliation, Sonia had apologized for her protest. When she had done so, she felt two contradictory emotions: upset that she had claimed some responsibility for their altercation and relieved they were no longer arguing. They watched a documentary about Edvard Munch, who appeared to have every misfortune, which cheered them. Brilliant art and deep life most certainly derive from unhappiness, no matter that psychologists tell you the opposite can be equally true, that mental stability and contentment can create valuable art just as successfully. While they watched, sitting on two separate chairs, Ilan and Sonia held hands. "Why is it that all movies about artists are bad? Every single one. Nobody gets it right."

Ilan clasped her tightly through the night when they finally fell into an exhausted sleep, and Sonia's barnacle toes splayed about his ankle, his fingers held on to hers.

Art is how you climb out of the abyss after you've made yourselves into beasts. You have to hook on and rebuild yourself from outside in. This is why it is essential to live in a civilization offering theaters, opera houses, philharmonics, film festivals, cafés, and parks with magazine kiosks and benches upon which to read a newspaper. A city where you can go to a museum of a country that no longer exists, or a lecture on the vibrant culture of tenements, or the 92nd Street Y to hear a great pianist who is still miraculously alive, with a repertoire of expressions of anguished intensity, or a film about an Iranian road worker having an existential crisis. It is important to live where you can turn on public radio and listen to a quick roundup of crimes of war around the world followed by an hour-long conversation with an Irish poet about the consequence of his faith upon his meter. This reassigns you to the calm and rational side of things.

And it is important to look at paintings. They went to a show of the artist Morandi, who had been rediscovered. His shells and his bottles were solemn, austere, and moral. They were the opposite of money and war, of time tearing ahead without concern. How could so much be conveyed by an empty bottle; how could an empty bottle be the keeper of one's conscience?

Said Ilan, "I'll tell you a secret if you don't tell anyone; there is a humanity, a democracy—and this I copied! One day I will be more famous than Morandi and I will appear modest, even when I am completely shameless."

Sonia read the little plaque that said Morandi, a bachelor, lived modestly until he died with his three unmarried sisters—Anna, Dina, and Maria Teresa—in an apartment on Via Fondazza in Bologna. This made Sonia like him. The quiet of the paintings reminded her of Cloud Cottage, her mother's family home in the deodars, rotting so naturally that nobody thought to fix anything. She said, "My mother is like a Morandi bottle. When I look at her, I feel the same emotion."

She missed her mother. Mama didn't trust wealth; she didn't respect fame. She knew that an artist was a slippery person and that art could be a slippery endeavor, that an artist may follow the darkness until eventually the darkness followed him. Where had her own father, Siegfried Barbier, gone? Mama still didn't know, and she certainly wouldn't want Sonia to find out.

*

IT WAS IN FEBRUARY that Sonia heard from Marie, her former boss at the Hewitt College library, who told Sonia she would be coming to New York with Cole to attend Alice Wu's wedding.

"Marie is coming to New York," Sonia told Ilan. Sonia had worked with Alice in the library when Alice had been a senior and Sonia a freshman, and Alice had generously invited Sonia to her wedding as well, perhaps so Sonia could chaperone Marie and Cole, who were terrified of the city, which was a place where anything could happen at any time. Alice was marrying a fellow student from her PhD research lab, where working together they'd bred a bacterium that was resistant to every antibiotic, this being useful in developing the next generation of antibiotics.

"She is not beautiful, your Marie." Ilan remembered her from Hewitt.

"She is. In her own way."

"That means ugly, darling." Ilan chuckled. In an older woman, he could take unattractiveness humorously.

"She's just her age. What if you had a girlfriend your own age?"

A lettuce leaf fell from his mouth. He looked stunned, as if she'd shot him.

"Eek—scary!"

"You are much older than I am."

"You're trying to make me feel bad. You are trying to lower me so you have more power. I've had much younger girls than you!"

Sonia was startled by this but tried to ignore it because they could not afford another altercation. "Anyway, Marie's looks are not her fault."

"Yes," he said, with sadness. "And it doesn't matter what the parents look like, there is never a guarantee. My uncle and his wife are good-looking, but my cousin is so ugly."

"Isn't that the person you said looks like a Roma while the rest of the family looks European?"

After a shower, Ilan came out and said, "Sonia?"

"Yes?"

"You are simplifying matters and lumping them together, and everyone listens to simple lumped-together stupidities, so if you say this you have power. Because I said my uncle's daughter looks dark Roma and my mother looks European, and my mother is beautiful and my cousin is ugly, that does not mean I think the Roma are ugly and Europeans are beautiful. You stupid! A person can be an ugly Roma or a beautiful Roma."

"You said yourself that your mother is a racist and wouldn't want to meet me because I am Indian, that if I were a Parisienne she would be pleased."

Ilan went back into the bathroom to brush his teeth and, midway, his mouth full of toothpaste foam, he came out and spat upon Sonia's face.

Back down in the elevator, waiting for a taxi, Sonia knew Ilan would take sleeping pills and sleep like the dead, then wake up and continue painting. She knew she would not sleep for days, her stomach and heart would heave with grieving, she would not be able to eat, she would not be able to think.

15

....

ALICE WU'S WEDDING WAS HELD IN THE AFTERNOON AT
a church in Cobble Hill, followed by a banquet in Chinatown at the
Golden Unicorn. Sonia scrubbed the apartment all day to make it less
dismal, for when Ilan was alone even for an evening, his surroundings
became lifeless and the apartment took on a mood of filth and abandonment. She told Ilan that she would surely be home by nine P.M. to
spend an hour or two with him before they slept.

"Should I come, it may be interesting?"

"But then you'll have to talk to Marie, you will say the people are
unsophisticated, and you'll start shouting in the middle of the wedding
that your tomorrow will be fucked."

"I see." He looked wistful.

When Sonia arrived at the pretty redbrick church, she was happy to
be reunited with Marie and Cole, but the service unfolded slowly and
the banquet in Chinatown began almost two hours late. The couple
and their guests wished to draw out the celebration, while Sonia prayed
they would wrap it up quickly. She tried to keep calm. She began to
panic. She twisted about and picked at the skin about her nails. Marie
said, "What's the matter? You're so fidgety."

"I'll be late. Ilan is waiting."

"You're allowed to go out with your friends for an evening, right?"

"Yes," she said, although this was not true.

What was true was what she could not tell Marie: that as their fights
had grown more primitive and fiercer, Ilan and Sonia had become
more secretive, more dependent. When someone has seen you as less
than human and may at any time betray this information and inform

others that you are actually a ghoul, it means you have to be more solicitous of the other, more closely a pair. And after you've gouged one
another, your missing parts belong to your fighting partner; you need
to be constantly with the keeper, the consumer of your vital organs,
your mind, your heart, or you no longer exist.

Up on the stage Alice was in a red qipao, and the guests were beating their chopsticks against their glasses, clamoring for the bride and
groom to kiss. They played a hilarious fertility game with an egg that
was passed up and down and around the groom's trousers. How odd it
was that people married; she would certainly never be married to Ilan
with a crowd of friends to cheer them on. This evening had nothing to
do with her life. "I have to go!" she exclaimed. Marie said, "Stay,
Sonia, we haven't seen you in so long and we've only had two courses.
I think there are nine or ten more including the Peking duck."

Sonia stayed, but she visibly fell apart. She found she could not lift
her chopsticks; they were trembling so violently she could not eat.
Finally she said she was going to the restroom, and then she fled and
called Ilan from a pay phone. He said in his softest, most beaten-down
voice that he had eaten at a falafel cart because he didn't have the spirit
to be in a fancy restaurant alone.

Where was she? he asked tenderly.

"Everything is late, they started late and—"

"Why didn't you invite me, then? I could have come and sat quietly
by your side. I love you so much."

"I'll only be a little longer."

"Aah, don't say that you're going to be longer." His tone switched.
"You promised me and I'm waiting for you!"

She was shaking when she returned to the table. "I have to go,
Marie. I can't delay." She dropped her Benaras stole without noticing
and ran out. There were several floors to the restaurant, and on each
floor a different celebration banquet was taking place. At each floor the
elevator opened and crowds of people left and got on, holding the elevator open, waiting for lingering guests to catch up. *Hurry up,* Sonia
thought. *Hurry, hurry.* But nobody hurried.

Marie, in her long skirt and low heels, jogged coatless down the street after Sonia waving Sonia's silver stole. Cole, in his uncomfortable suit, chugged after Marie. Sonia noticed that when Marie had tried to find the ladies' room, Cole had followed her with his eyes to make sure she found her way.

"I'll see you into a cab," called Marie.

"I'm all right, go back, go back." Sonia tried to shoo them away. Chinatown is confusing even to New Yorkers; she found herself at the wide entrance to the Manhattan Bridge where traffic from many roads converged.

Marie caught up with her, said "Stop," and put her arms around her. "Does this man know what he's doing to you?" said Marie. "If he does, it is unforgivable."

Marie's arms did not feel right. Sonia hated Marie because Marie saw Sonia's terror. Sonia said, "I think he is mentally unwell." Marie said, "Well, quite obviously, but why isn't he taking medication, then?"

Finally a taxi came. Sonia jumped in. She was crying in fear. The driver watched her in the mirror.

"You are the same age as my daughter. What are you crying for?"

"I'm late and my boyfriend is angry. I'm too scared to go, and I'm too scared not to go."

"If he's making you scared like that you should never return. You should go to your family or to a friend. Should I drive you somewhere else?"

She continued to cry.

"Look, I can take you home to my wife and daughter. They'll look after you."

This made her cry harder.

She turned the key and opened the door into the dark apartment. The lights were off and Ilan wore his eye mask. He had taken sleeping pills and was as good as dead, except he was breathing heavily. When she shook him, he said slurring, "I have become dependent on you for my happiness. That may be scary for you to know, but when you were not here, I thought let me just end the day. I missed you too much."

She sat in the darkened room with Ilan heavy and drugged, filth and chaos all around, the smell of weed and tapes of porn. She listened to Ilan breathing, time passing in and out, in and out, as disinterested and sinister as a clock.

*

"YOU DON'T LOOK WELL, habibti," said Sami, who had been a pharmacist in Aleppo and now owned the deli near Dumbo Leloup.

"You are not concentrating on your work," said Lala. "You are late and distracted. What's wrong?"

"Why isn't she leaving Ilan?" Sonia had heard Cole whisper to Marie. "Shouldn't we say something to her?"

"Why are you staying on?" Marie had asked Sonia before Sonia shut the taxi door in Marie's face.

Why? Because you have to be a person to be able to leave, and hadn't they noticed that Sonia was no longer a person, that she was made of fear? She could not think any one of her thoughts through. Nor could she call upon her parents, because she had told them nothing of Ilan and every phone call now involved her deceit and interrupted and threatened the world she was in. Ba, Dadaji, and Mina Foi were so far away upon their Allahabad veranda, so beside the point of her life in New York, she had forgotten them, as if they were figments of her imagination. And—how ruthless her unhappy love was—when one evening Papa told her of Ba's death, she didn't even register shock. She didn't try to picture the scene of Ba's demise, or to feel it. Nor did she pause to honor Ba's person. She did not light a candle in the gloaming, chant a prayer for her spirit to be free—little magpie of darting attention, shining and jinglejangling keys in her petticoat, sparkling diamonds in her ears and in her nose. She couldn't feel any emotion for Ba, because Ilan was between her and the rest of the world. However, when she spoke to her father, she wept heartrendingly, and he had no idea that her grief was not for Ba, but for herself.

16

....

O NCE AGAIN, AS SHE HAD DONE MANY NIGHTS NOW FOR many years, Ba had risen from the sour sheets that had leached their starch to Dadaji's night sweats, extracted her arm from the darned mosquito netting to turn on the brass lamp, and in the dim voltage that imparted about as much light as a candle flame, swung down her feet while holding on to the spindle bedpost on her side of the high bed. She had opened her wardrobe to pack a small duffel bag with her petticoat, panties, handkerchief, toothbrush, and tongue scraper.

"Where are you going?" Dadaji had once again asked, sitting up, seeing the scene in stripes through the wrinkle in his retina.

"To Rangoon."

"Why?"

"I must."

"But why?"

"To die!"

"Why die there?"

"It's my home."

"*This* is your home."

"Get me my shoes, then. I will go outside and check to see that, no, this is *not* my home."

Dadaji had held on to the bedpost spindle on his side of the bed and, swinging down, tried to put the bag away and persuade her to come back, but she became distraught, exhibiting a physical strength she did not actually have.

"Your house isn't there anymore." He had raised his voice so she might hear. "The country has a different name. The city has a different name. You need a passport and a visa."

These loud, simple sentences sounded brutal. She was confused. She could no longer remember the present; she could only remember the past, and she was in a rush to get there.

"But I was born in Rangoon."

"It is still dark. You won't find the road. You will be robbed. Wait until morning and make an early start."

This logic persuaded her. This was how the ruby from Burma was lost, in the chaos of leaving, in a journey made in the night through brigand country. She wished to be reunited with her missing treasure that lay over the horizon of this life. She had climbed back into bed and hastily turned off the lamp when she saw a furry moth approaching, noisy with the mechanics of flying. This moth had been chasing lamps all evening; it had followed Ba and Dadaji from living room to dining room to bedroom. They'd hurried to close the door against it, but they were slowed by age, and before they managed, it was diving about their bed and they knew it would be their companion all night, aroused periodically by lorry light or bathroom light or moonlight, perhaps drowning in one or another's water glass before dawn. There were so many insects about that you never took a sip of water in the dark for fear of what little beetle was scrabbling the surface or trolling the depths.

Just before dawn, Dadaji had been awoken again, this time by the severity of stillness by his side, and switching on the twin lamp, he saw that his bird-wife of sixty-seven years had indeed flown the coop of Cadell Road. He made certain her breathing and heartbeat had stopped. Again he held on to the spindle bedpost and swung down. He flung open the long, thin prayerful doors that led directly from one room into another, for the house was without hallways and you could startle another's privacy abruptly. He went through to the kitchen where Ba would never again satisfy both her dread and secret hope of catching the cook fishing a bit of mutton into his mouth or find her daughter making SOS calls to the missionaries.

Dadaji reached the final door that opened toward the servants' barracks and, unlatching it, caterwauled: "Young man! Young man!"

A bent figure approached the steps, slowly moving into Dadaji's smudged vision. "Young man," he said to their cook, who had first been employed when he was eleven years old. "All that cream and sugar, all that ghee and salt you put in the food—it has finally killed your memsahib."

*

PAPA STARED OUT AT the ruin of the mosque behind the Hauz Khas flat. The buffalo of the Sikh family displaced by riots was grazing at the corner of the municipal park where a leaky tap had turned a patch of the brown grass green. He held the phone to his ear and heard his daughter's weeping from a distance that was compiled not only of the distance between New York and New Delhi. He had been trying to cry over his mother the way Sonia was crying but found that he could not. Something stood between him and his grief. Was he worried he would be unable to rescue himself if he allowed himself to grieve deeply? Or did this occasion of death reveal how shallow their relationship had been?

His mother had never truly felt like his mother. They had been friendly, mother and son, but friendly does not equate the kind of love that devastates when it departs. They never spoke on the phone longer than a sentence or two, and these brief sentences served only to highlight the fact they had nothing to say. They'd never lingered on the Allahabad veranda, never discussed anything other than meals or weather. In fact, they didn't have a language to speak in, for he spoke no good Gujarati, she spoke no good English, they communicated in Hindi, and Papa's Hindi wasn't good enough to tackle a complexity. When he returned during holidays from the Doon School, it was as if he were a visiting person from higher up the class ladder, his mother an uneducated village girl from a landscape he had never seen. Who she was, what she thought to herself during quiet times, he had no idea. Perhaps that her son did not feel like her son? Perhaps that her husband did not feel like her husband, but more like a deity who possessed all the elements within which she existed? But surely Mina Foi, bad luck daughter, had felt exactly like what she was: Mina Foi, *bad luck daughter!*

When Mama had touched Papa's shoulder upon hearing the news of Ba's death, he shrugged off her hand in a careless way and made it known to her that she had no right to comfort him or even to mourn. He reflected that she'd never shown her in-laws a modicum of traditional respect, never invited them to Delhi to spend a month or two. She had observed them from a distance as if they were characters from a humorous provincial theater, and what broke his heart now was how they had never complained. They had never said to him, "What a mistake you made in your marriage." They were in surprising ways utterly modern. Or was it lack of caring? Or was it the same thing?

At the most they mildly remarked that it was a strange matter indeed to be married to a person who did not enjoy a potato. But that was to them the difference between being a human being and not being a human being. If you were a person, you would like a potato; if you were a hollowed-out masquerade, it would be thus revealed. Their daughter-in-law was not a daughter-in-law.

Mama did not feel like Papa's wife. In Deer Park, Papa strode ahead to escape the growing void between them and the silence that neither wished to discuss, saying he needed to walk faster to get proper exercise. Mama was embarrassed at this because only inadequately enlightened men walked ahead of their wives in a park, and a passerby might interpret her as a backward woman.

Finally, during an interminable meal, she said, "With Sonia gone, it makes sense I find some occupation. I've spent years wasting my life."

Papa allowed internal sardonic laughter to show upon his face: Here was his wife enjoying a comfortable home, a cook, a maid, a car and driver, a gardener for the roof garden, a washerman, an ironing man—entirely at his cost—and now all of a sudden, at age forty-seven, she complained she'd been frittering her intellect.

She registered his expression. "What?" she asked.

"Nothing," he said getting up, his expression again making it clear.

She set about searching for a job. She applied for the position of program coordinator at the India International Centre. This position would require her to present a calendar of concerts, lectures, film showings, and exhibitions. Mama's degree was in history and she spoke about her focus on early civilizations of the Indus Valley. She discussed how the center could present a lecture on Gandhi in South Africa that included sensitive material about the mahatma's racial intolerance. They talked about what they could do about the fact that art is art, but dinner is dinner—no matter how talented or renowned the artist, there was always an exodus of the audience at intermission.

She must have impressed the committee, and when she received notice of her appointment, Mama looked suddenly so youthful that Papa relented and took her out for a celebration dosa at the Ambassador hotel's Dasaprakash restaurant. They had a chuckle watching extended families rinsing their hands and mouths in the hotel fountain after their meal and Papa raised his glass of thick purple grape juice: "To my brilliant wife!" But he couldn't help himself from losing his temper at the waiter who was slow and the dosa filling that was skimpy. They returned home in familiar hostile silence, Papa blaming the waiter, Mama thinking that this was supposed to have been her celebration treat, Papa thinking that he must thank his friend on the board of the India International Centre—he must have surely put in a word on his wife's behalf.

He said, "The Ambassador has gone downhill," attempting to bridge the rift and undo his urge to sabotage the afternoon, but seeing his wife still punishing him, Papa remembered her irredeemable attitude toward Ba, who was now dead, and voiced his previous thought out loud: "We must thank Chibu; he must have had something to do with your getting the job."

Later that same week Mama visited a hair salon and directed the hairdresser to cut her hair into a bob. "Shorter," she urged.

"What happened to your hair?" Papa almost screamed. Her long hair, when the sun caught it, would burn a glowing mahogany. For many days he huffed, "You've willfully destroyed your looks to hurt me," but then his friend Neil remarked, "I say, your wife is looking tremendously glamorous," and Papa, looking across the room, saw all of a sudden that it was true. The cut highlighted the bone structure of her face. It angled at her chin. She was a modern-day Nefertiti.

He privately forgave her. Despite himself he'd become a progressive, forward-thinking man, one with a professional wife with bobbed hair, who had a driver's license and might drive their car were the driver not required to spy on her. She earned enough to pay for the household groceries now, for her own clothes and shampoo, which elated Papa—he enjoyed many aspects of her working. He told people he himself had encouraged her to work.

But one evening she mentioned having lunch with a Dutch human rights worker who was working with local women's groups to halt the sex trafficking of underage girls, and Papa grew leery. "Prevent sex trafficking? Ha! He'll be part of the problem! You have to watch out for these firangs; they still come to India to find a native girl, leaving their pasty-faced wives behind, whom they will never divorce, by the way. They think they can have their fun for free."

Another morning she took a scholar from Tehran to see Humayun's Tomb, pointing out the weaverbirds' grass nests dangling from the palms, the wasps' paper nests in the alcoves, a parrot perched on the remaining crimson glazed tiles, the chirps of bats interred within the crumbling graves of princes and princesses. They discussed whether ruins should be restored entirely or partially—keeping the patina of age. They spoke of how beautiful it must have been when the Jamuna River had flowed by and before it had receded into a drain. The blue dome of the royal barber's grave was familiar to the Persian scholar—it was Persian blue!

Papa said, "I thought you said you were working; instead you are gallivanting."

She said, "I was instructed to be hospitable to international artists and scholars."

"*Hospitable?* What the heck is that supposed to mean?"

He believed there existed a natural attraction between Persian and Indian—there was a history that had been interrupted and an undercurrent doubtless remained.

He drove across from his office in Connaught Place, walked around to the India International Centre cafe veranda, and saw Mama eating mango ice cream while she interviewed a Finnish musician who studied the sitar and was introducing Mama to a composition by Arvo Pärt, to which Mama responded. The quiet of this piece made you feel as if you were in a primeval forest, alone yet with invisible, elvish company.

Papa could understand a work coffee, but mango ice cream in a frosted silvery dish with a frosted silvery spoon suggested flirtation.

That evening he put the security chain across the front door, and when Mama returned and encountered it, he came to the chink and said, "Why come back here? I thought you were off to the Finnish boondocks?"

She said, "You're going to be embarrassed tomorrow."

"You are the one who is going to be embarrassed. Everyone saw you—the librarians will be tittering."

The library had a wall of glass that looked out upon the inner courtyard through which everyone passed on their way to the café. He imagined the scene: The librarians who often came to work with their long hair newly washed, making it up right at the front desk when it had dried; the unfinished PhDs who spent shortsighted decades at *India and the Cold War* or *The History of Tamil Migration to Singapore;* the retirees nodding over the foreign newspapers that arrived long after the news they held had passed into oblivion, which made these newspapers a soporific—he imagined all of them looking up in unison and seeing his wife in her stylish bob, in her graceful sari, on her way past beds of springtime seedlings to eat mango ice cream with the scarecrow foreigner.

He unlatched the door because the cook, Chandu, came running, and there might be a greater scandal if Chandu should waggle his tongue to tell the servants up and down the street that the wife had been shut out of the house by the husband—and if these servants in turn told their employers.

If you had a cook, you behaved better than if you had none. If you had a dog, you behaved better than if you had none to save it from having to crawl under the bed with its tail between its legs. Even if you had a mynah bird, it would grow prim upon hearing a rude argument, and to see your bird nervously treading on its perch, well, it shamed you into behaving better. They had no bird and no dog but a cook who noted everything because he had no other life at hand. However, at night when Chandu had gone to bed, Papa's rage had not abated. He looked up from his newspaper and announced, "I'm going to tell that twit from the boondocks to keep away from my wife."

"Please don't," she said tiredly.

"You may not care about your reputation, and to hell with it, I agree. But what about mine?"

On his way to work, Papa stopped at the India International Centre. As ill luck would have it, he found the musician immediately, listening to the birds in the Lodhi Gardens trees and making musical notations.

"Stay away from my wife, do you hear?"

Mama, who had always spent much of each day reading, began to read incessantly when she was home. With desperation she read through all of Dickens, all of Woolf; she read Austen and Chughtai; Ginzburg, Borges, and Mulk Raj Anand's account of a day in the life of a toilet cleaner. Reading so much emphasized in her the aura of stillness and refinement that had attracted Papa to her in the first place, but more than ever this quiet and refinement did not allow anyone else in. She mostly refused now to go to dinner parties with their group of friends, claiming a headache. When each person individually made certain to concernedly inquire, with lowered voice, leaning in, "But where is Seher?" Papa had to say over and over, "Migraine."

But on the eve of Papa's birthday on the first of March, he protested, "We keep going to everyone else's home and we're not inviting anyone back." Mama felt she couldn't make an excuse, and they sent out dinner invitations. Mama and Chandu decided the menu should be ample yet not ostentatious—parties in Delhi had become obscene.

Papa came home from the office early and said, "Only one non-veg? When we go to Neil's or Dilip's or Jehangir's, they have chicken and fish or prawns and mutton, if not prawns, mutton, *and* chicken!" Holding his shaving mirror up before the bathroom mirror that morning, he'd discerned at the crown of his head the first swirl of balding he couldn't imagine away. When Sonia telephoned to wish him many happy returns, he could scarcely speak.

Mama was wearing no jewelry save small silver earrings, as if she were married to a poor man, a mean man, or were a widow. She was wearing her usual cotton; he wanted her to wear silk. He said, "Can't you dress up a little?"

Mama had bought him a gift of an anthology of Urdu poets in translation. It was a small volume from an antiquarian bookseller encased in a carapace of caramel leather, shaped like a lozenge that may be slipped into a pocket. Papa tossed it into a corner. He felt it was actually a present to herself. "Where are the flowers?" Their floor was covered with a dhurrie; he wanted a Kashmir carpet.

"If you're going to invite people, invite them in style!" All of a sudden Papa went wild, peeling off rupee notes in a manner Mama had never observed in him before, sending Chandu with the driver, Balbir Singh, to INA market for prawns. He phoned Chocolate Wheel, where rumor had it the Gandhi family procured their brown bread. "Long life, Uncle, bless you," said the proprietor's daughter when he went to collect the marble fudge cake. Papa noticed she was more affectionate and enthusiastic about his birthday than his wife was.

It was difficult to throw a party in a household that was a bog of resentment, but Papa brought forth the single malt. They were all there—Neil and Daljit, Khushi and Dilip, Jehangir and Margo, and Ferooza—and eventually the cake was carried out with five candles.

"Isn't there ice cream?"

"I don't believe so," said Mama.

The party conversation had been centered on their respective attempts to master the new art of Hotmail, which was essential for them to keep in touch with their children abroad, when Papa, looking down and his jaw working so his cheek twitched, loudly said, "*Bitch!*"

There was silence.

Then Neil said, "What's got into you, chum?"

Said Jehangir, "Age is a bitch."

Margo said, "Time to turn up the music—"

"We need more whiskey."

"Or less whiskey."

"It's too late for less whiskey."

"Then one for the road?"

"We already had one for the road."

"One for the ditch?"

But Mama would not be diverted. She had a daughter, and she must stand up to men who used language that demeaned women.

"Please tell us," Mama asked with icy elegance, extending her delicate neck as a stem holds a flower. "Who is the bitch? Do you mean Khushi, Ferooza, Margo, Daljit, or myself?"

Papa didn't answer. He worked his jaw.

She held her glass aloft a little too long. She set it down. She looked calm; inside she was quaking. But she was glad everyone had heard. It gave her permission to proceed with a plan she had not yet articulated to herself.

In an effort not to leave obviously early, their guests left too late, when they were all dropping with exhaustion. Her closest friend, Ferooza, kissed Mama—not cheek to cheek but a warm, wet smack. "Let's do something special soon, go somewhere new," said Ferooza. "To Ladakh or to the Valley of Flowers—the Himalayan Institute has a ladies-only trek."

A weeks-long trek to the Valley of Flowers was impossible. Mama and Ferooza were both working women with not even enough time to train for a mountaineering expedition, and so they settled on a picnic in Mehrauli at the city outskirts. Balbir Singh, Papa's spy, parked by the charred black rock of Balban's tomb, and they walked past Jamali Kamali and the ruin into which Metcalfe had built a fireplace, and climbed to sit at the top of the step well. They could see the spire of a brightly painted new temple in Mehrauli village and hear the sound of boys playing cricket, but around them it was still full of thorn bushes. A caravan of ants flowed past holding white eggs aloft—an empire was on the move.

Ferooza opened a bottle of wine she'd brought in a cooler.

"Ferooza—"

"Yes?"

"I think I must leave."

"Leave?"

"You saw how he was the other night. I can't live with him anymore."

Ferooza and Mama sat quietly. Ferooza poured the Grover white in a big dollop into the stainless steel tumblers, almost causing them to topple.

She said, "Where would you go?"

"There is still our family house, Cloud Cottage, in the hills."

Cloud Cottage—consisting of Big Cloud, Middle Cloud, and Little Cloud—had been left to Mama and her sister, Meher, by their parents. But Meher had left to study at the Royal Academy of Music in London, and at the start of a promising concert career, she played in the Salzburg Festival, where a music aficionado in the audience had watched her in her periwinkle chiffon sari execute one of Beethoven's last sonatas with a psychological depth startling in one so young. He married her, and wealth had removed her from their lives, Meher's excuse being that she could not find a proper piano to practice on, not in the entire tone-distorting country. She had relinquished her share in Cloud Cottage to Mama. This generosity had felt like a betrayal. A betrayal of what? Of her childhood, of India, of their father, who had chosen India over Europe, of the poverty the family had experienced when both parents had lost their childhood landscapes, one to the Partition, one to the war in Germany. The family had turned Cloud Cottage into a boardinghouse style of inn, and eccentric lodgers had come to stay for a week or for the season, individuals jettisoned by history and empire, supping on potato frankfurter soup (doubtless the source of Mama's antipathy to the potato).

"I remember meeting your delightful mother once," said Ferooza. She didn't say she remembered a baleful energy bearing down inside, although outside it was resplendent, sun-warmed hills, slow purring bees weighed by pollen, cabbage butterflies making ribbons and bows in the horse chestnuts. "I wish I had known your father. What an improbable marriage your parents made—a romantic epic."

"Well, in a romantic epic, it would have played out as the triumph of love over racial divide and the brutalities of war, but in real life it was as if their marriage had been based on a catastrophic misunderstanding. My father would set out hiking alone, for longer and longer periods of time; we often didn't hear from him for months at a stretch." Mama studied the river of ants and took a swallow of wine, enjoying the fact that it tasted so astringent. "The year I turned sixteen, he did not come back. We found no clue except he had left behind the amulet of a supernatural creature he called his Badal Baba, which he always took with him on his treks, as if he didn't need its protection any longer. I still imagine he must be alive out there in the mountains and that if I go to live in Cloud Cottage, he might return. It's ridiculous to think this way, yet this is how I think."

Ferooza filled up the tumblers again. "You are a remarkable woman, Seher."

Mama closed her eyes. "Hardly."

"No, it's true. You are a most unusual woman; you must know and believe that. Your life will have another chapter, even if you can't foresee it. One thing I have learned by middle age is this: The people who are strong are the ones who appear weak, and the ones who appear strong, well, the confidence usually rests on luck and money—or stupidity. I watch women who are certain of their security, and therefore of themselves, lecturing the room on the subject of feminism, ordering their servants to slave from before dawn until after dark—and I know they wouldn't be able to manage two days of my life, which happens to be the kind of feminism you fight for until you're raw and bleeding, which saves you only just a little more than it devastates you, just enough to keep your head above water."

"Is it that difficult to manage alone?" Mama asked.

"Terribly difficult," said Ferooza, "but if it is necessary, then how hard it is or isn't is beside the point. And—this is interesting—when you come through, without any of what others expected of you or you expected of yourself, you find yourself magically afloat. You don't fall! One day you are *simply yourself*."

Ferooza had never imagined the hardships that would come her way despite having been born into a wealthy, progressive clan. Her mother, Yasmina Sofia Zebunissa, was a descendant of the Nawab of

Akbarpur, and while most of the family had left for Pakistan, Ferooza's branch had stayed, publicly proclaiming they could imagine no home but their ancestral home, but privately at each wave of sectarian violence fearing they had made a fatal mistake.

And sometimes Ferooza could not manage bills, taxes, gas connections, phone lines, tricky water supply, a cheating scooter wallah, alongside her job of running a nonprofit for women's advancement. She had to ask her friends for help, aware that single women with no family around were a nuisance. The friends petitioned their husbands, waiting until they were delving deep in their whiskey-and-roasted-cashew moods, but these husbands soon tired of helping the tribe of single women and took their annoyance out upon their wives in turn. What irritated the men most about Ferooza was not just the need. They bristled at her refined accent. They laughed about how often she dropped mention of the year she had spent in Paris. They didn't like the fact that she could converse on the Khilafat movement or the similarities between Topkapi Palace and Fatehpur Sikri or bring up Rembrandt's Mughal paintings.

A single woman was expected to be grateful for any scrap that fell her way. Someone who belonged to a religious minority had to appear meek and patriotic. On the surface Ferooza was meek, grateful, and patriotic; inside she suppressed an anger so deep nobody had ever glimpsed it.

*

THE SETTING SUN SANK into the ocherous haze about the tombs. Ants and bats exchanged the strength of their numbers. By the time Mama and Ferooza finished talking and thinking their private thoughts, the atmosphere had turned threatening with streams of twilight creatures flapping from the subterranean tombs. They walked back fast to where the watchman and driver were standing by the Peugeot worrying over what might have happened to the picnicking ladies.

WHEN THE TAXI COULD GO NO FARTHER, MAMA GOT OUT. The journey from Delhi had taken eight grueling hours. It was an April evening in the Landour hills. The light upon the close wooded hills was furred and soft; the light upon the far denuded mountains was clear, divine. Floating in ether were the ghost snows, from Bandarpunch to Nanda Devi. Into the deodar dark, Mama descended the steep slope to the house that was perched like a toadstool on a rock midway down the mountainside, and she walked into Big Cloud Cottage, where crusty, cracked oil paintings by her father, Siegfried Barbier, still hung upon the walls. Clouds hatched by mountains, mountains by clouds—ominous, in the colors of deep emotion, they depicted the cragginess of an interior landscape.

Mama discovered Moolchand, the manservant, asleep in Meher's brass bed, Babayaga the cat perched atop his head like a Russian hat. Babayaga jumped up, showing bellicose yellow eyes from the black of her fur, and ran toward Mama yowling as if in complaint, not greeting. Babayaga was half feral. Her father was the wild *bagarbilla* who'd eaten the chickens, when Moolchand kept chickens. He had fed them marigolds, so their yolks were pure gold, and he mourned them.

Old Moolchand woke. "I was keeping the house safe," is how he explained sleeping in his employer's bed. His manner was laconic. He was allowed to do exactly as he pleased because he'd lived here longer than Mama; he'd looked after Mama's mother until she died. She had summoned him when she needed him by ringing a cowbell, and Moolchand had helped her to the bathroom and even bathed her, it not occurring to either mistress or manservant that this was un-seemly.

Moolchand retreated to the kitchen and eventually, with catarrhal cough and spit out of the window as he walked past it, brought Mama the meal of her childhood upon a tray. She sipped potato soup. Across from her, keeping her company, were family photographs: herself and Meher, tiny figures on a lawn that was carved out of the wilderness, and in striped Bengali cotton saris at a table with a Rosenthal teapot. Her parents' wedding photograph hung alongside, showing two star-tlingly different-looking people: her mother in scarlet silk, with the serene smile of someone in on the cosmic joke, and her father with a ruby stud in his ear and with eyes that revealed the person they looked upon but never reciprocated to reveal himself. Another showed the family of four on horseback, dressed in Bavarian felt trousers, riding at an elevation above the tree line.

These photographs, even at the moment they had been taken, were nostalgic. They had longed for the place even when they were in the place; they had longed for the moment as they lived it; they had longed for themselves. They had been right to feel this way. It could not last.

Mama sat out with Babayaga until late, looking upon the enchant-ment of the forest. A scops owl came out to hunt a squirrel. The owl was disrupted by the branches and found it difficult to land; the squir-rel ran from branch to branch; the bird followed but still couldn't catch the squirrel. The squirrel was silent, the owl was silent. Briefly, before they vanished, the squirrel running, the bird gliding, the owl swiveled and looked at Mama. The woods filled with cool moonlight.

The next morning, Mama posted a letter to the India International Centre tendering her resignation. Middle Cloud, at the bottom of the mountain on Tehri Road, had been rented to a boarding school founded by missionaries for their teachers to stay in. The rent would be enough for Mama to live on in Big Cloud at the top of the slope, if she pared her expenses. Little Cloud, which was her father's former studio, was a converted garden shed. A forest enveloped Big Cloud, Middle Cloud, and Little Cloud.

*

WHEN PAPA WENT TO Mahesh Stores, they said: "We haven't seen your wife recently; normally she comes every week."

"She's repairing the roof of her family home."

The neighbors: "But where is your wife?"

"She is redoing the bathrooms. Nothing more uncomfortable than the bathrooms in that house."

He went to a concert where concertgoers inquired: "Where is Seher? You've been coming alone to everything."

"It isn't safe to leave the house empty. The *lalas* and *dadas* have been prowling about with a measuring tape, taking stock of the property, which has become valuable."

The librarians: "We received *The Tagore Omnibus*. Tell your wife we are keeping it on reserve."

"Don't keep it—Tagore was a pompous idiot number one!"

The retirees who had survived the news, snorted awake over the tops of their newspapers. The reading room of forever unfinished PhDs raised their prematurely gray beards from *Trade Between Ancient Rome and the Malabar Coast* and *The Matriarchal Societies of the Kalavan-thulu Courtesan Caste in Eastern Andhra Pradesh*.

Jehangir and Margo's wedding anniversary at the Gymkhana: "Surely she will come down from the mountain to join us?"

"If she doesn't let the cat in at night, it will be lifted by a leopard."

Dr. Pamela Lalwani, who operated the neighborhood clinic: "She may be looking after the cat, but who looks after you?"

"I don't need looking after. I'm a grown man."

Behind his back, they agreed: "That wife of his has run off."

In the evenings, Papa drank alone, and as he drank, he drummed his fingers and chewed upon his pain. He said, "*Damn her!*" out loud on his evening walks in the more-deserted Panchsheel Park maidan. He said, "*Bitch! Bitch! Bitch!*" in the shower. He threw her birthday present book onto the junk pile. Seeding Papa's anger was his shame. He remembered the Finnish sitarist. That encounter had made him feel as if he was a backward, stereotypical Indian male, controlled by jealousy. A

possessive person always seems illiberal. He fished the poetry book out
of the junk pile and hid it behind the row of other volumes on the
shelf—so he didn't have to see it but wasn't proving himself to be a
philistine. The book had a knobby vertebra, the endpapers were marbled marine blue, and the pages were edged in gold, flimsy in comparison to the binding.

A day will come for sure when I will see the truth
My beautiful beloved is behind a veil, that is all

He told Chandu he was going on a business trip. He told his secretary, Tandon, that he was taking a short leave to take care of family
matters. Balbir Singh drove him to the airport, and a half hour later
when he was sure Balbir Singh would have left, he exited the airport
and hired a car to take him to Landour. When they arrived at the Landour bazaar, they got stuck in the market as always, in a jam of cars
blowing horns because the vehicles surging up the steep incline and the
vehicles inching down negotiated the same narrow bottleneck. Slowly
they inched by Modern Bread, Modern Computer Shop, Modern Bazaar, Modern School, Victory Eggs, Sabri's Antiques. *Sabri's!*

Papa had once upon a time seized his advantage by helping Mama's
mother as part of his courtship of her daughter. He took care of the gas
connection and the phone lines, and when they fell to poverty and sent
Moolchand to Sabri's—ferrying one object after another to be sold—
they did not know the owner had been instructed to call Papa whenever a dispatch from Cloud Cottage arrived. On the day Papa proposed
to Mama, he sent the objects back in a celebratory parade, including
the precious Rosenthal teapot, white with pink rosebuds. Mama's
mother was moved to tears; Mama was humiliated to the point of
tears. She could not explain to her future husband why she felt she'd
been sold-bought-sold with a teapot.

She happened to look through the window and saw Papa descending the hill. Stomp! Stomp! Stomping to keep the dust and dirt off his
shoes and heeding inside himself a demented stamp of his foot, even
here in the susurrating forest. Without thinking, she opened the back
door and ran out the other way. When she came back about fifteen
minutes later, realizing that she couldn't continue to evade a confron-

tation, she found Papa sitting on the veranda, with the cat watching him steadily from under the geraniums, the tip of her tail going like a metronome.

"How long will you stay away?" he said when they were inside.

She answered in the annoying manner of a Zen monk, "Until the mountain once again becomes a mountain."

"What is that supposed to mean?"

"Everything in my life has become false. I am no longer capable of the hypocrisy."

He took out his scuffed brown leather wallet, threw it down on the table, and circled the room. Clouds of rain and mold stains spread on the walls, the tablecloth, a watercolor that was the inverse of what it purported to be, not a pine bough, but the space revealed by it.

He said, "Look, I know I have not been fair, but don't you love me anymore?"

To say the word "love," the one they'd avoided for years, was so ridiculous that it just sat there.

Finally Mama said, "I want to be alone, that's all."

"But why?" They looked at each other. It was terrible.

"Leave it," she said, "it doesn't matter anymore."

"How can it not matter?"

"There is no point in pretending," she said. "I can tell that you feel the same way. I can see it in your eyes."

He knew the truth of her statement. So many angers and resentments had been added into the mix that the love was gone, or resided only in memory. But if you remember love so powerfully, surely this means you still feel it. And even if he acknowledged it was gone, the trouble was that he still wanted the love and he still wanted her in Delhi because she was still his pride. It was such absurd stubbornness, he'd be the first to agree.

He wanted to say something sarcastic, but instead he asked to use the bathroom and walked through the house he had first entered as a young man accompanying a friend who was a friend of Meher's. He passed by the photograph of Siegfried Barbier's psychotic eyes, which were the eyes of a Himalayan bathroom spider. When a woman has no family of her own left, doesn't she normally cleave closer to her husband? The opposite had happened with Mama.

In the bathroom there was still the same bucket as always under a tap. The copper tumbler oxidized green on the narrow shelf over the sink held a single worn toothbrush. Papa was glad to see there were not two toothbrushes, that the Finnish musician was not a resident, nor the Persian scholar telling true tales about the blue of Persia. Behind the door that inadequately closed because the wood had swollen hung a faded nightdress that smelled light and floral, the way his wife always miraculously smelled even in the heat of a Delhi summer. He put his wandering nose in its folds and thought of alpine flowers.

He came out, and as he sat down, he dropped and broke his water glass.

"It doesn't matter," she said for the second time that afternoon. "Let me stay here." She turned swiftly to practical details. "I won't ask for a divorce, and I won't ask for money."

In exchange for letting her go, she would allow him his honor by not legalizing their separation. She understood that this was the necessary bargain. The terms were to his advantage.

"What about Sonia?"

"It seems she is happily settled in New York. In any case, she will have two homes, the Delhi home and this home."

Papa looked out of the window; the deodar dark invaded his eyes and for a moment he thought he'd gone blind. The pain was too great. Papa wanted to subtract it. He wanted to say, "Well, pay me back then for all that you took, all the money I spent on you all these past years." But he managed to remain silent. They had not attacked each other, they had behaved for the first time in a long while with civility, but this just made a worse sorrow. If he left now, it would be the end of their marriage forever—but he had no choice.

He got up and walked out. The huntress metronome of Babayaga's tail stopped moving when he shut the gate, but the hillside dogs all along the way barked at him as if he were a stranger, and the forest monkeys made obscene gestures.

....

ARIE VOLUNTEERED AT A COMMUNITY CENTER RUN BY
Catholic Charities that held mental health seminars. She knew mental
illness could use a person, but sometimes some people used the mental
illness. "Why isn't Ilan seeing a doctor?" Marie had confronted Sonia.

"Shouldn't you see a psychiatrist?" Sonia had dared suggest to him.
"My grandfather had similar compulsions—he said the darkness followed him long before he followed the darkness. And wouldn't it be
fascinating and fashionable to be analyzed?"

"I understand your grandfather. When I feel the darkness approaching, I dread it, but the truth is that *I also love it*. I need it to work. In any
case, you go to one of these phony psychiatrists and say, 'Hey, I'm
Napoleon, by the way,' and they say, 'Well, you have a point.' Instead
of saying, 'Well, where is your carriage then, if you are Napoleon?'"

Besides, Ilan had Sonia instead of a doctor. "Sonia, what's the matter with me do you think? Why am I this way?"

"If Mummy does not love you, then the world is upside down. It's
the wrong story."

"Yes, you are right. I have everything else, more than anyone, so
why am I so unhappy?"

"Because you have an artistic loneliness."

"Yes."

*

"SONIA? ARE YOU AT work? Can you immediately come? I am not
well."

"What happened?"

"A bad thing. Come fast! Tell Lala I need you."

"A really bad thing?"

"Why would I call you otherwise? *Come now.* I'm scared. Someone keeps calling me and hanging up."

"Who?"

"You don't care about me—you're like all the others, all those horrible people who attack me."

"Who attacks you?"

"Everyone attacks me."

Sonia didn't bother asking Lala; she knew Lala had appointed her to look after Ilan. She locked the gallery, posted a sign on the door, and ran to the subway. Cherry blossom season had arrived, and puffs of candy petals carried by mild breezes detached noiselessly from the trees, broke softly about her heart. She went in and found Ilan at his worktable. "What bad thing?"

"There," said Ilan, and pointed at the shelf over the fireplace.

"What is that?"

"My hat with a bullet hole through it."

"Are you sure it's your hat? Where was it?"

"I left it in Mexico. It's my Mexican hat."

"Strange."

"It came in an anonymous box."

"Who could have sent it?"

"Someone who wants something. Someone is angry that I painted them and sold the painting, or someone is saying I have a stolen painting. Or it is a warning, someone wants to take my property. Maybe the cartels want my land to build condos or hide their dirty business. Maybe it's because my father and grandfather cheated people. Or someone had a bastard child and is angry."

"Couldn't this simply be a prank?"

"*What kind of prank?* What if I am killed? What if someone is waiting and watching? *I am scared.*"

Sonia was also scared, his fear infecting her, but she did not say so because one couldn't abandon a person whose life was threatened.

"Should we leave?"

"And go where?"

"Vermont?"

"Why do you think Solzhenitsyn lived barricaded there? Or Trotsky in Mexico City? He was terrified someone would hunt him down with a gun—and then came Ramón Mercader del Río carrying an ice pick."

"Should you tell someone?" Sonia asked, imagining voodoo in the woods, assassins crawling under the granny-scented lilacs of the Hewitt hills.

"I cannot trust anyone. Only you."

"Why *me*?"

"Why did you say *that* and sow a doubt?"

*

FRIGHTENED ON HIS BEHALF, and half deranged, Sonia brought from under her mattress the demon amulet she trusted to frighten other demons away. She knew the miniature painting would appeal to Ilan's superstitious side. "It'll scare away the other demons. That's why it's important to have a demon. My grandfather called it his Cloud Baba."

"You said he never became famous."

"He had no ordinary life. He painted clouds, he became a cloud." She wanted Ilan to know that she was not a person who did not have mysteries of her own, a person who had nothing to give and everything to gain. She wanted to rebalance the power a little in her favor before it entirely slipped away. There was a growing sense she had run out of time, for matters—what matters? she couldn't have said—were closing in, and things—what things?—were crowding upon her.

Ilan unhooked the clasp and opened the little door, instantly cheering up. He enjoyed games and curiosities—and he started back as if he'd put his head into a hermit's cave and instead of seeing the beatific smile of a meditating sadhu, he had been confronted by a leopard-black, blood-red tantric fright. Demon or god—one could not tell. Beast or leper—one could not say.

He looked at it hard and long. "But this is extraordinary." He showed Sonia his arm: Every hair on it stood on end. "It comes from a forest that no longer exists. It's a relative to my spirit from Malekula. People have forgotten that painting is not a decorative enterprise to please and flatter, nor is it about illustrating the events of the time—it has a sorcerer's purpose. It plays messenger between an unknowable darkness and a person's fears. But can one trust the messenger? You end up praying before what you yourself created. Where did this figure come from?"

"We don't know exactly." Sonia told Ilan the story her mother had related about her grandfather Barbier, who had spent months each year trekking. In the forests of Sikkim, where Buddhism was older than the Buddha, close to animism and tantra, her grandfather had noticed by the light of flickering oil lamps, upon the walls of a monastery, sooty murals of long-tailed and winged beasts. When he asked, "What are those?" the caretaker monk said, "Oh, you know, in the rainy season they come out of the ground and fly about."

"Where?"

"Everywhere," he said, gesturing outward as if to ask, *Can't you see them through the fog and the downpour?*

The monk wasn't simpleminded. Sonia's grandfather had observed that he lived in a world where dragons were real. Intuiting that the traveler who had journeyed alone was in torment, the monk said, "You are a man who has lost his face. You need a god who can understand you."

"A god or a demon?"

"No difference." And he must have dropped the amulet carved with clouds and dragons into his hand.

"It isn't possible that the monk gave it to him," said Ilan. "If you are going to give such a work of art away, you have to do so within the first hours it is in your possession. A day later you don't own it, *it* owns *you*. It turns you into a robber, it turns you into a liar, it can even turn you into a murderer."

He began painting harder. During bouts of insomnia he sometimes left to work in the middle of the night. As the weeks and months passed, he became deeply attached to Badal Baba. He called it "*my* demon."

When a short notice about Ilan appeared in the glossy magazine *Artforum,* Sonia noticed his expression alter. "What does it say?" she ventured.

"It says, *'An intriguing and brilliant artist has matured in the shadows. His world is intensely personal and imaginative. It addresses different worlds colliding and contradictions that only art can reconcile. It is scorchingly political, but yet adamantly art for art's sake, the historical to honor the personal. History is always someone's story.* Mother Swimming—*the first sexual awakening comes through the mother, a violation, but so beautiful*—*is a canvas that belongs in a cathedral.'*"

Ilan could not contain his joy. He danced folk dances, *hop ta daha ha.* He played Sonia like a tabla. He pretended to be a train, a ship's foghorn down a foggy strait, a clopping horse, an airplane. He imitated fearsome sharks and nibbling squirrels. He became a monkey leaping sideways for three round orbs: olives, tomatoes, and cherries. He became a dirty pervert behind the door, waggling his member, sticking out his tongue.

"This is wonderful news," said Sonia.

"*Miauw meow,*" he said.

"Can I see?"

And Sonia saw printed in the magazine *Mother Swimming, the Lake Remembers.* The water dissolved Mother into a dream. She swam out as if it were the last swim before the war. A shadow sliced across the surface.

Buoyed, Ilan invited a most important curator of international exhibitions to see some of his work. He would show this individual his paintings and then return to the apartment for lunch. Sonia should please prepare the table, the food, the plates—and then remain absent. She must not cook and make a sloppy Indian stink, she should not leave her cheap Indian things lying about, which would lower the value of his art.

In the morning, Sonia, in a recurrence of fear, wondered what to do: If she left the prepared food procured from a delicatessen— a poached wild salmon of deep orange pink with a fennel and preserved lemon compote, a sparkling green salad with pine nuts and parsley, luscious olive oil–roasted peppers—in the refrigerator, it would be too chilled; Ilan's teeth couldn't take cold, and he believed the flavors and aroma would not be properly released unless the food was served at room temperature. But if she left the food on the counter, it could grow germs, and he believed food must not be left out for more than fifteen minutes or it would be dangerous to eat.

Sonia put the food in, she took the food out. Out and back, out and back. For half an hour with panic in her heart, she simply could not decide. Food in, food out. And at what time did she need to remove herself from the apartment, leaving no trace?

In the end, the curator wasn't hungry. When Sonia returned to the apartment after sitting a long while in a café, Ilan was home and told Sonia that the gentleman was so impressed by Ilan's work, he didn't spare a moment being distracted. The paintings would be shown in several exhibitions and biennales: London, Seoul, Basel, Rio de Janeiro, Venice. Soon after, they received news that the director of the MoMA had purchased *Mother Swimming, the Lake Remembers* to put into a museum vault designed to survive fire, earthquake, terrorist and nuclear attack.

Ilan danced the Highland Fling he'd been taught at his boarding school in Scotland. He hopped Sonia in a rustic frog hop, a country wedding dance, about the room. He danced Bollywood style, bumping bottom against bottom with energy and happiness. He became Batman, a submarine, a happy warthog scratching his behind upon a tree in the sun, utterly unconcerned about fame.

Sonia felt she was part of it—she was, she had helped. She was his good luck charm. Her Badal Baba was bringing him luck. He enveloped her. "I want to swallow you. I am making a vow: I will never act to part us. I never want us to be apart."

They went to see the goopy river of Frans Post in the Metropolitan Museum of Art; to eat at the fancy restaurant full of creepy rich people; to see a film about a charming pickpocket; to visit the Chelsea Flea Market, where Ilan bought a toy car for himself and for Sonia a kitschy figurine of two dogs, a larger one standing behind the smaller. "See, I am the bigger dog looking after you. I promise I won't harm you, not even your funny crooked toe. And I won't let any harm come to you. If anyone dares to attack you, I will *woof woof* and drive them off."

They walked home in a shaggy, drenching rain, sharing an umbrella, and when they put the key in the apartment door, they found it unlocked. When they turned the knob and flung it open, they found a woman, auburn hair shorn close, reclining on the couch. She didn't blink her amber eyes. She said, "Well, wouldn't I be a fool to be surprised."

Who cried?

Ilan cried.

He fell to the ground in an instant, began to drag himself about. "*I'm scared, I'm scared, I'm scared!*" He howled and kicked his legs so there was no way of conversing with him. Or of properly thinking. "*Booo hooo hooo hooo!*" He covered his face, tears streaming down. "*Forgive me. Don't leave me!*" he wept. "*I will grow old alone,*" he howled louder. "*Don't leave me! I told her nothing about us, I promise.*"

Sonia was startled to discover that he was not saying this to Sonia, as she had initially thought, but he was saying this to the woman who had just arrived. She had a startling face, all in angles.

To Ilan, the woman said, "You might have spared me when I've been so ill." Then she turned to Sonia. "Good evening," she said coolly. "Are you one of the secret girlfriends?"

"No." Sonia was dizzy. She was a child; here was a woman. A woman whose race, class, wealth, dress, nose, lips, cheekbones, manner, voice, and accent keeled toward an expression of high elegance and turned Sonia into a cockroach.

"Am I?" she asked.

The woman got up and beckoned Sonia out into the hallway and shut the door on Ilan. She lit a slender cigarette. "Pack carefully and make sure you don't leave anything behind. It's vulgar to find panties in a drawer. And please don't take any souvenirs with you. We have had unsavory experiences in the past—the last girl is still blackmailing us."

"Blackmailing you?"

"She has a baby and will blackmail us for the rest of our lives."

"He has a child?"

"He has a few bastards. The most recent is a year old."

"With whom?" Sonia was moronic.

"A student like you."

Wailed Ilan from the floor: "She cheated me. She wounded me. She raped me. I'm not going to pay for that bastard."

"I won't blackmail you," said Sonia to Ilan's wife.

The woman looked at her as if she did not believe it, and under her unswerving gaze, Sonia felt worse humiliation than any she'd felt with Ilan.

She moved swiftly and practically to demonstrate her scrupulous honesty. She had no claim on this home, but she had more belongings to pack than she would have expected. There was the makeup she had never learned to apply. There was the expensive French perfume Ilan had given her to commemorate the evening of their reunion, reminiscent of the musk of Vermont woods, but that she had only once or twice used. There were the suede boots, the lilac coat, and raspberry dress he had bought for her. There were brocade slippers, a silk dressing gown. There was *Anna Karenina,* but no case for her to pack her things into, so she stuffed grocery bags from the kitchen.

"You can't carry those down the street in the rain," said Ilan's wife.

"I'll call a taxi," said Sonia. She remembered she had no right to be using the phone and asked if she could use it. When she received permission, she telephoned Carmel Car Service.

Ilan was lying flat on the floor now, on his stomach, with his eyes shut and his ears wide open. For a moment there was an aspect of camaraderie between the women as they carried the bags down to the lobby to wait by the door. It was midnight. The taxi did not come. On a rainy Saturday night, cabs were in short supply.

The atmosphere became tense again.

Ilan's wife didn't look at Sonia; she turned herself into her distinguished profile and lit another cigarette. "He cannot be alone. If he is alone, he ceases to exist—you didn't guess?"

"No," Sonia said to her. Why hadn't she? Ilan had told her so many stories of betrayal and deceit, she had trusted the stories were *not* stories that were true of him, because surely you would not tell someone a damning true story about yourself. But that was the trick. He *had* been telling her about himself—drip, drip, drip, paralyzing her, tiny drips of poison habituating her to the story of betrayal and lies, so that her life, too, would drip-drip transfer to a story not quite real. She would live a false life.

"It's a pathology with him. There will be a woman right now waiting for him to arrive in Portofino."

"Portofino?"

"Or wherever he is planning to travel. You had a practical purpose. You kept his illness at bay. I hope you weren't reading emotion into it. To undo his madness, he needs a daily dose of marijuana, sex, and adulation—am I right?"

"Yes," said Sonia, seeing clearly now.

Ilan's wife's left finger had a ring—a storm of gold fossil that matched her eyes, an unusual ring of the kind you would procure for someone you unusually loved. She saw Sonia's glance.

"When I met him, I was seventeen, he was twenty-three. He was scrawny and misanthropic. He didn't get along with his mother and I did not get along with mine, yet they were delighted by the marriage because both families were wealthy, and so we escaped together. About seven years later, he changed. He became extroverted. His face broadened and relaxed, he began to shine, to look intelligent and handsome. I thought perhaps it was the beginning of success, but then I understood that he had found that you can use betrayal to unearth confidence—it was the cheating that had led to the success. The more he lies, the greater his confidence, the more successful he becomes— and he is determined to continue to do whatever results in his ascent, because nothing, absolutely nothing, is going to stand in his way. Fame, as you have gathered, is the way to take revenge on those who did not recognize him for so long, and on Mummy. He will burn down the whole world because Mummy doesn't love him, and Mummy, as you probably learned, is a monster." Ilan's wife spoke in fierce, frank tones. She stubbed the cigarette out on the pavement under the heel of her boot.

"I know he has a madness," said Sonia.

"He exploits his madness."

"Why?"

"To terrorize and control, my dear, for a paranoid and psychotic sixth sense, for canny insight that delivers a closely and wickedly plotted world. You don't develop an artistic talent by being sweet and kind, you know."

She arched her back. "He didn't take you into my bedroom that has the Joseph Cornell box with an angel and a cloud, did he?"

When Sonia didn't answer, Ilan's wife lit another cigarette. It was past one A.M.

"So shabby," she said, quietly shaking her head. "Didn't your mother tell you to stay away from old goats?" Despite her foreign intonation, she sounded very familiar to Sonia now.

And Sonia was in the taxi halfway to Dirty Dumbo when she remembered Badal Baba. *She had left Badal Baba behind!* He was under the mattress on Ilan's side of the bed so that he might stalk Ilan's dreams. Each night before he slept, Ilan unclasped the tarnished case and started back when Badal Baba leapt forth. "When it comes to a painting like this, your spirit shifts, your mood shifts, you get to the other side of pain, you become determined your life will not be ordinary. You go to sleep thinking: *Tomorrow I will see my painting!*"

Sonia must turn back! She couldn't turn back! She paced her studio until dawn, burning as if she were covered in boils. Boils of shame, fear, grief, and rage. If she had not given Badal Baba away, he would have protected her.

The next morning, despite her terror at having to face Ilan and Ilan's forbidding wife, Sonia took the subway back to Ilan's building. The janitor who was mopping the lobby refused to let her in.

"Don't you recognize me?"

He wrung out the mop. "I recognize nobody. I know *nothing* about *nothing.*"

She left a wretched note and asked him to at least drop it into Ilan's mailbox. *Please return my grandfather's amulet. It is a family heirloom. You cannot keep it. It isn't fair.*

"Fairness" was not a word in Ilan's vocabulary.

....

ULLA INVITED SUNNY HOME WITH HER TO KANSAS FOR Labor Day weekend for the simple reason that it was unnatural to be with a boyfriend for a length of time and not to introduce him to her family—and also to reiterate that he, meanwhile, had not even informed his family of her existence. She warned him: "My parents are normal, okay? They aren't reading *The New York Times* and watching BBC." She told her parents: "He's moody. Don't pay him any attention." These remarks made her parents nervous.

"What if they don't like me?" asked Sunny. It wasn't as if *he* wasn't nervous.

"They love me so much that they'll welcome anyone I bring home."

While Sunny understood that Ulla was emphasizing that he had never invited her to join him on a trip to India, he was intrigued to be traveling to a part of the country that was unreachable to a foreigner, an America he could never see on his own. A mythic land imbued with memories of Dust Bowl poverty, of fields worked by migrant labor, of proms, sports heroes, and cheerleaders; six hours to the nearest mall; real cowboys swearing genuine curses on cattle farms; a black-sheep uncle covered in tattoos in a trailer park; an ancestor whose diary from the Civil War indicated he didn't know which side he was fighting for, although he had carefully recorded each time he ate bacon.

Already on the way to the airport Ulla regretted her generosity and her passive-aggressive point-making. She knew this by the vehement extent to which she hoped her father would *not* make Sunny his special beans with a ham hock simmered for a day in a Crock-Pot in the garage, to be eaten with corn bread. As they were checking in for their flight, she wished Sunny were not checking in alongside and hoped her mother wouldn't take him to see the Native American artifacts displayed at the Rotary Club. She didn't want Sunny to find her father's *Consumer Reports* in the basket by his reclining chair. She didn't want her father to tell Sunny that he'd found an excellent deal on his own tombstone. She didn't want Sunny to see that her father was so overweight he couldn't bend to cut his toenails and that her mother had to cut them for him. She didn't want her mother to sing the Betty Boop song while fluttering her lashes. She remembered all the nasty things Sunny had said about Americans being provincial and fat, all the hateful things he'd said about Republicans that he somehow linked to the lack of fresh herbs and spices in cooking, which he linked to having no passports, which he linked to killing innocent civilians in Hiroshima and to the United Fruit Company, which operated rapaciously in Latin America the way the East India Company had in India.

She would not be able to stomach him shamelessly accepting her parents' hospitality, pretending he'd never uttered such calumnies. In truth, Sunny *was* ashamed, but he pretended he was not; to pretend he was not, he sat quietly at the boarding gate as if mulling over some diverting subject. He didn't dare tell Ulla that he had brought along a little black reporter's notebook. He thought of Satya, who had said, "Didn't I tell you long ago—forget those goras. I have never had a good experience with them."

When they were skimming across the prairie—the huge middle of the nation, so vast and uniform that you felt you could travel forever and it would still hold you in the peace of its belly—Sunny smiled guiltily over at Ulla manning the wheel of their sporty red rental. Ulla pointed out a former one-room schoolhouse, a dugout home. She detoured through the ghost town of Nicodemus, which had been settled by former slaves during Abolition times. Once visiting there as a child, Ulla had shrieked when a rusted jalopy came crawling down the street with no driver—until she spotted an old lady at the wheel as it passed by, one of the last residents, her face too low to look through the windshield. Sunny saw tumbleweed and prairie chickens. They escaped his camera, but he captured with his recently purchased Nikon the aban-

doned oil pumps creaking and the graveyard where the wind sucked so
strong the graves were scoured clean. He photographed a wild turkey
that couldn't get over its own reflection in a new, polished gravestone.
It was infatuated with the bird looking at it from the other side of the
false divide that was yet so familiar. It walked to the back of the grave
and found the beloved there as well.

Sunny and Ulla continued on until the coppery light of sunset
complicated the landscape, revealing dips and crannies in the fields and
dirt roads that the midday sun had undone. "Don't take photographs
of my parents," said Ulla.

Ulla's parents may not have passports, but they had always especially welcomed and enjoyed the foreign students Ulla had introduced
them to during her undergraduate time in Lawrence. They enjoyed
gloomy Christopher from Ghana, who cultivated his misery by lying
upon an unmade bed staring at a bare lightbulb. They enjoyed Elena,
who claimed to be a good witch from Romania and bathed among the
sunflowers with a hose pipe.

The house was centrally air-conditioned, and when they shut the
doors and windows against the relentless wind, it was quiet enough in
the floral-wallpapered dining room for the grandfather clock's ticktock
to exert itself, exposing the uncomfortable fact that Ulla's parents and
Sunny knew so little about their respective landscapes that they struggled to find things to say that could not be misinterpreted or did not
reveal their ignorance.

Ulla had told Sunny he was not to say anything complimentary
about socialism or Jimmy Carter or even Bill Clinton. He should not
praise the healthcare system in Cuba or Sweden. He should not express
wonder at women voting Republican. He shouldn't venture—not at
all—to the subject of guns.

She had warned her parents not to divulge they owned five guns
kept locked in the basement. That Ulla herself had hunted wild turkeys
when she was a child, that she was a better shot than her father. They
must not ask if cows were sacred or whether Indians still lived in mud
huts.

Ulla, vigilant to both sides, saw that Sunny was not able to perform to his eccentric self, that her parents' bawdy humor was oppressed. They were subdued and courteous. Ulla had never heard her mother not swear for whole hours at a time. They passed the beans and the corn bread. The ticktock asserted itself while her mother wondered if it was safe to say she had enjoyed the movie *Gandhi*. Maybe "enjoyed" was not the word.

The nicer her parents were to Sunny, and the nicer Sunny was to them (although he was certainly hoarding spiteful observations), the more enraged Ulla became at his shamming, at her parents being conned.

Finally they found a topic of conversation: Dr. Jaishankar Reddy and Dr. Premshankar Reddy, two unrelated Dr. Reddys who had taken jobs under the same United States government program that brought doctors to underserved rural areas in exchange for their immigration papers. Together they ran the local health practice.

Ulla's father said, "We're grateful to them."

Ulla's mother said that younger Dr. Reddy had recently returned to India to marry in an arranged marriage. "He'd never met his wife before—she still dresses in traditional costume, and she mostly stays home. Padma, older Dr. Reddy's wife, is part of the community—she's been here for ten years and is very outgoing."

Ulla worried about her mother's innocent use of the word "costume." She worried she had forgotten to tell her parents not to bring up arranged marriages—not at all—because Indians are asked all the time about the subject and it's just too tedious and stereotypical.

She was relieved that Sunny merely remarked that he would like to meet Doctors Reddy and Reddy. She was glad she had already warned her father not to ask about the large red dot that he described to Ulla as resembling a gunshot wound between younger Mrs. Reddy's eyes.

That night, in the bed oversized for her childhood room, Sunny turned to Ulla like a friendly bear. "What are you thinking?" She did not relent. She imagined the conversation her parents must have had before they replaced her single bed with a double bed for this visit. Seeing her unresponsive face, Sunny felt annoyed that she had chosen to remember all the nasty things he'd said instead of allowing a change of heart. He began to taint his thinking.

Over the following week, Ulla's parents took him to the school where Ulla had studied and the swimming pool where she had learned to swim, showed him the photograph of her in an unrecognizable incarnation at her high school prom: curled hair, makeup, pantyhose, and high heels. A boyfriend on the wrestling team. Sunny's expression made Ulla want to kill him.

They took Sunny to see the Native American pottery shards and stone arrowheads displayed at the Rotary Club, drove him to the buffalo farm to see hulking raggedy creatures whose very breathing raised dust clouds, and accompanied him to the World's Largest Ball of Twine, which had been mounted in a display hut under a sign at a forlorn crossroads. They took him to a museum built by a man who'd spent his life creating objects out of scrap metal, broken crockery, and yard junk; the last exhibit of this home museum was the preserved mummy of the man himself. Sunny was moved—here was a person making his life into art in a place where he had no artistic company and few supplies, so few he eventually had to use himself. He may have been a simple man from the Midwest, but there was an affinity between him and the Egyptian pharaohs, wasn't there? Sunny took out his camera again but put it away when he and Ulla visited the home of the older Dr. Reddy.

Although Dr. Reddy was away at a conference in St. Louis, his wife opened the door. Padma Reddy was dressed in jeans and sneakers, hair in a bun, twenty-four-karat gold in her ears and nose. She regarded Sunny with a suspicion that was familiar to him from India—her look telling him she was not persuaded. Not persuaded about what? *Just. Not. Persuaded.*

The Reddy home was a museum of the homeland preserved: heavy, dark, carved furniture, brassware, silk carpets. An enormous blown-up picture of their son, Shiva, occupied the wall above a black leatherette couch. Sunny and Ulla were startled by screams in Telugu from a back room. In that back room, Mrs. Reddy explained, was her bedridden mother-in-law calling out for attention.

Mrs. Reddy served Sunny and Ulla a homemade mango yogurt sorbet made with frozen mango pulp from the Indian store all the way in Kansas City. She said she'd recently been hired to teach Spanish in the local school; she'd taken an online course and qualified. Sunny found this intriguing, imagining her students learning Spanish with a desi accent. He dared to take out his little reporter's notebook. Might he pitch this story to the Associated Press? On Cinco de Mayo, she had cooked Mexican food for her students. It was easy because a kachumber was basically a pico de gallo, rajma was no different from frijoles, a makki ki roti was a corn tortilla.

On the evening before they flew back to New York, Ulla and Sunny sat out on the back porch with Ulla's mother, who looked wistful. She said, "We never imagined we'd stay on here. But John had a good job at the farm insurance bureau, and I had a good job at the school, and it was a good place to raise kids."

She liked living in a small place because you could see up ahead. Your right hand knew what your left hand was doing. It meant innocence in a world that was no longer innocent. From where they sat, at the end of the street, Sunny could glimpse the empty grasslands blowing to eternity. "But nobody can live here who doesn't love the wind."

"I really liked meeting your parents," said Sunny after they had dropped off the sporty red car at the rental place and were at the airport awaiting their return flight.

Ulla said, "You didn't meet them."

"What do you mean?"

"They were so not themselves that you did not actually meet my parents. My poor dad, when it's this hot he likes to sit in his underwear, guzzle a beer, and yell at the television. And because you were there, he couldn't. My mother couldn't even swear, she was so scared of you."

She marched ahead of him in the airport, and when Sunny said, "Our gate is on the right," she turned to the left. "You have no sense of direction," he exclaimed.

"Yes, I do. The opposite of where you are going is the right direction."

Sunny did not reply, although he dove his brows hither and thither to keep some self-respect.

Everything in her house had felt fake, he reflected now—the walls were hollow; the plumbing and the electric wiring seemed inserted into a cardboard house; the shower stall felt false; the carpeting synthetic; the lawn as unnatural as the microwaved and canned food—as if they had been in an artificial capsule set upon the true Earth. And if he was fighting with Ulla, it would be unethical to pitch a story about the Reddy family on the prairie to the AP. And he and Ulla would have to love each other again for her to agree to correct what he had managed to get wrong. .

*

ON THE EIGHTH OF September 1998, Sunny telephoned Satya to wish him a happy birthday and to tell him about his Kansas holiday. Satya answered the phone sounding tearful and said he couldn't speak because he was depressed being alone, the years passing him by.

On the day before Thanksgiving he telephoned Sunny, sounding sprightly despite being exhausted from a rotation in the radiology department. He'd decided to take matters in hand. He'd telephoned his mother in Delhi and requested her to find him a wife.

"The head resident here went back to marry a girl from Firozpur where his grandparents are from, and he told me it was the best decision of his life. The whole world became home—present, past, and future were connected."

"Why don't you join a matchmaking service? You can't depend on your mother."

"I did. It wasn't for me. This one person sent me a Hotmail and wrote, *I see you will be too high-maintenance.* Even in small towns, they have picked up an American vocabulary. Another one from Vizag was sending me nonstop messages: *Miss ya even if I haven't met ya! I cried all day on Valentine's 'coz I was hopin' for a card at least!*

"Sunny, I just want to come home and chat in the kitchen with another person whom I can understand and who understands me—say this stupid thing happened today, that stupid thing happened."

But when you lived with someone who didn't understand you, it kept the situation malleable, thought Sunny. *In being unknown, you might yet transform into something more interesting.*

"And then, don't be offended," Satya said, "but I find that you are so depressed, that speaking to you, I become depressed. When you and Ulla fight, it affects my relationships."

"What *relationships?*"

"The truth is that I've been too scared to even enter into a relationship because of you."

Now Sunny was riled. "That's upside down, Satya! That's inside out, man. *You* are the one who phones me to complain all the time. *I'm* the one who listens to *you* for hours, and then *I'm* influenced by what you say, and *I'm* the one who gets depressed!"

It had crossed Sunny's mind that he might be sensationalizing his fights with Ulla, making a greater devilish conflagration, transposing the highlighted version to cheer his loveless friend—that he might be making his own situation more miserable to keep his miserable friend company and to assure him coupled people were no happier than the uncoupled.

"Ah, don't be angry, Sunny," said Satya, conciliatory. "I was going to ask you to come with me to meet the girls my parents find. They don't know America, they won't understand what kind of person would fit into my life, but my cousin told me it has become acceptable to go with a close friend. It will take a few months to research the right families, but by April or May next year my mother will be ready and each of these families will provide a feast to hook a doctor son-in-law—we can eat like kings. You can forget your fights with Ulla and her plain cheese pizza!"

....

Funny Flat Smell of Home

....

....

Babita went to the mirror and asked her reflection: *"Now is there a girlfriend? Or no girlfriend?"*

Sunny had telephoned to let his mother know he was returning to Delhi for a long-overdue visit—he hadn't been home in two years, and, coincidentally, while visiting his mother, he would also be helping Satya choose a wife. He said in addition, he hoped to find a story to pitch to the international desk at the Associated Press because he needed to find a way to exit from the lowest entry-level rung of learning the rules of The Associated Press Stylebook, to becoming a reporter. He didn't feel competent writing about the United States and wouldn't be deemed competent (unless Ulla corrected his mistakes), but perhaps he could claim expertise in India or find a compelling story that straddled boundaries.

Sunny had not mentioned Ulla to Babita. Babita had not asked.

"What do you think, husband?" She cocked her head and pretended to hear a response from an Ideal Husband: *You're asking me? Well, I will be happy to have Sunny to myself, of course—it would be awkward to have a stranger in the house.*

She realized she could not admit even to herself and her ghost husband an opposing, persistent other thought: *But I would be proud to shepherd my son's American girlfriend about Delhi.* Have everyone stare when they were presented with indisputable proof of Sunny having conquered the powerful White World. Wouldn't this elevate Babita? Subtract her pain at losing her son and allow her to sally forth like someone with global reach, a safety net, a person apart from the masses?

This line of thinking made her remember the time she had holidayed in England. She already knew the names of streets and buildings in London, the towns and countryside, as well as any anglicized Indian did. She knew Trafalgar Square, Harrods, Marks & Spencer, Paddington station, Charing Cross, Tintagel, the temperamental Brontë moors, the Lake District. She knew the weather she had never experienced.

But then the toilet cleaners in Heathrow had been Indian—Punjabi farm women, heavy-hipped and elderly, waddling and rocking stiffly from right to left as they pushed their cleaning carts. They might have disembarked from an Air India flight and never left the airport. Although Babita knew she should proclaim the dignity of toilet cleaners and proclaim pride in Indians who had working-class jobs in Britain, she didn't feel pride; she was dying of shame. She hadn't quite recovered when she took a tour of London and the tour bus driver turned out to be Indian, too. She had sat in the front for the best view, but that meant the bus driver could easily speak to her. He said to her familiarly: "Chori, chori, chori. This is a nation of thieves." He made a dismissive gesture as they passed any building of note. British Museum: "Chori, chori, chori." Buckingham Palace: "Chori, chori, chori." She hated the bus driver who suggested she and he had been robbed. She wanted to belong in the drawing rooms of those who had plundered, those who would never even think of having to admit this, so comfortable in the environs of their stolen wealth were they.

When she saw Tipu Sultan's sword in the British Museum and scraps of his kingdom scattered about London—his chair in the Sir John Soane's Museum along with a motley oriental collection—she felt the same way she did when she'd seen the Punjabi toilet cleaners in Heathrow. Luckily there was a show at the V&A on the maharajas. Here she went and recovered her self-regard by looking upon their decadence during the time of Raj: their Rolls-Royces and Bentleys, their art deco furniture, their gem-encrusted cigarette lighters, their lipstick and compact cases, their evening bags and decorative gewgaws.

A black-and-white film of Gandhi in his thin dhoti arriving in the freezing rain for the Round Table Conference in London in 1931 played in a corner, and this did not alter her pride in the rajas but suffused her with an entirely new emotion of honorable self-worth. But when a pimply, shabbily dressed Indian student next to her exclaimed "Bapu!" and burst into tears, she moved hastily away from him.

Her mind returned to Sunny's American girlfriend. Thriving in the United States was a way to stick it to England. If you ever deigned to visit Britain with an American passport, you'd visit looking amusedly down upon them from a more powerful nation. Through a different lens, Britain would be rendered quaint.

....

"ILAN IS A VERY COMPLICATED PERSON—YOU COULD NOT have imagined otherwise?" Lala had looked past Sonia into the horizonless distance when she told her that they would be letting her go. Sonia would receive three months' salary, but in a week Lala planned to give another young woman a chance in Dumbo Leloup. "You should consider returning to India—believe me, that is where you can put your education to best use. It may seem like harsh advice, but later on in your life and career, you will thank me. The scope of your life will broaden in your own landscape, however counterintuitive this may seem now."

How would Sonia ever tell her mother that she had lost Badal Baba, that she was no longer safe, that maybe Mama was no longer safe in the forest, either, without their protective deity? She locked the door to her sublet studio and dropped the key into the mailbox. She took the subway to Penn Station, the train to Newark. At the moment the plane parted from the runway, she felt the relief of escaping the endless waiting for a person who has abandoned you. But when the flight landed in Delhi, penetrating its cocoon of gloom, she was overcome by terror at being so far away from where Ilan might find her again. When she emerged from the baggage claim at five A.M. and sought her father in the enormous crowd that at first sight seemed to consist of only men, he was startled to find that the light had died in his daughter's face and she was so emaciated, it was as if she had been starved.

And when Sonia looked at her father, she noticed that two sets of eyes had lost their fire: father's and daughter's. He said, "Mama is in the hills."

It was usual for Mama to spend time at Cloud Cottage, but wasn't it peculiar that she hadn't returned to greet Sonia?

"She's become like Greta Garbo: *I want to be alone!*"

They settled themselves into Papa's comical little Peugeot, their faces each filling an entire window, and putt-putted back to Hauz Khas. Papa had decided against calling in Balbir Singh; his noting Mama's absence would be unbearable—of course he would notice nevertheless and gossip with Chandu and the maid, Alpa, but airports made the lack of love more painful, just as did the observant eyes of servants, friends, dogs, cats, and mynah birds, if you had any.

And thank goodness for the dawn streets of Delhi. The unhatched sun remained distant in its cloaca of smog, the city showed its centuries, the color leached from the sky, trees, buildings. On the singed fringes of grass along the road and on the traffic circles, Sonia saw homeless people deeply asleep. Delhi was an exhausted city. Delhi looked as if it, too, had been abandoned by love.

This would be the time Sonia and Papa would grow close, not merely father and daughter, but two wounded individuals negotiating life together—careful not to ask prying questions, in case they would be asked questions in turn, glad to have each other even if Papa often wished she were not there to see his indignity and even if she often worried her father would intuit her shame. The shame that segued to fear to grief to anger. She didn't want her father to notice that when she broke away from shame-fear-grief-anger, berating herself for being unable to let go of Ilan's betrayals, she experienced a more drastic terror: Searching for herself, besides these formidable emotions, she was missing. She was simply not there.

They climbed to their top-floor flat, and at the head of the dim stairway, Chandu was smiling, holding out her favorite lemon cake with *Hallo Sonia Baby!* in pink icing. And in her childhood room, there was a card purchased at the deaf school's annual bazaar that read, *Welcome home, my dearest Sonu. Love, Papa.* On the dressing table, there were roses from the Hauz Khas market where the flower seller outside the shrine plucked the petals to pretend the roses were buds that would open in the morning, not flowers that had bloomed the day before.

Here, too, was a letter from Mama, Papa having heroically left it unopened. Mama had written: *Come to me as quickly as you can, once you are rested from the journey. Your bedroom at Cloud Cottage is ready. I am waiting along with Babayaga and Moolchand.*

Ilan hadn't cared for Sonia enough to consider her well-being, while in Delhi there were people who had been loyal to her all the years she had been away.

She noticed that while the flat looked the same as it always had from the outside, just older, inside it had been transformed into a bachelor's home. Papa had moved into the guest room and remade his former bedroom with Mama into a study. Sunlight filtered through the mulberry and silver oak her parents had planted when they first moved in; the tree light merged with the iodine light filtering through the woven cane blinds. The tincture of light deepened the rose of the faded armchairs; the diverse colors of the books that had once been as tawny as lions, pink as Jaipur, marmalade as wasps, blue as sky without so much as a speck of pollution, had now faded into harmony.

In the corner was Papa's new computer covered with a madras plaid tablecloth. He had hired a computer technician to put it together. Large as a pig, oinking and beeping, a monitor from a company dealing in surplus Chinese parts, a hard drive from a resale shop, a salvaged keyboard, a mouse from a discount store—it had taken weeks of coaxing to get it to function.

Each day, at the time of his morning tea, Papa began the slow process of switching on a voltage stabilizer, then turning each part of the system on so it warmed up slowly and didn't explode from effort before he dialed the internet.

The psyche can sometimes expand after a trauma, and the changes in Papa's life were transforming him in many ways, so pastimes and philosophies once closed to him now magically allowed him in. He was beginning to read the history and religions of the subcontinent as written by various obsolete scholars and pundits, and to make notes on the computer. Avoiding Western concerts where he might meet the *haha hoho* dinner-party friends with whom he no longer wished to convene, he was frequenting concerts of Hindustani music—of raga, bhajan, thumri, qawwali. The length of a raga that had once made him impatient, now soothed him. Raga Yaman, for example, played by Sultan Khan on the sarangi, was a contemplative piece of music longer than time, longer than sorrow. After he attended a concert of Abida Parveen singing the songs of sufis, wild with abandon, he returned home and removed the volume of Urdu poets that Mama had gifted him from its hiding place behind the books on the bookshelf. He wondered if he should teach himself the Urdu script so that he didn't need to rely on a translation.

While Papa thus simultaneously explored both the computers of the West and the music of his own country, in the mint-painted, tube light–lit kitchen that stank with gas emanating from the grimy, red gas tank, Chandu laboriously beat morsels of lamb before he softened them in raw papaya according to the instructions of Khansama, who had, when he and Chandu were both relatively young, been sent on the train from Allahabad to stay in Delhi for a month and impart his recipes.

So this sad couple, abandoned by love, father and daughter, ate like the nawabs of old on folding picnic chairs outside the kitchen where the television was. Papa no longer wanted to dine in the formal dining room, and it was easier to watch the evening news as he ate and to inform Chandu, "*The British have won!*" when after peeping through the porthole glass in the kitchen door to get his timing exactly right, Chandu rushed out another puffed chapati.

Playing the role of mother as well as of housewife, Papa took Sonia to the doctor, the dentist, and the optometrist. When the optician at Bonny Eyewear discovered Sonia needed glasses, it occurred to Sonia that perhaps shortsightedness, not psychological distress, made her world blurry. But while she could now detect the details of faraway faces and landscapes through new lenses, she remained enveloped within the blurriness of her mental state. She seemed disconnected when she made the requisite telephone call to Dadaji and Mina Foi. Dadaji had broken his pelvis.

"But why did you return?" Dadaji reproached. "Oh well, now try to make the best of it, what else to do."

Mina Foi told Papa that Dadaji could not tolerate being bedridden. "You must pay a visit. I cannot manage him. He made Khansama sieve the soup of vegetables and cut the carrots into sticks instead of rounds, then into squares instead of sticks. He shouted: 'Call yourself a cook? You're a charlatan!' And at the gardener and driver: 'Idlers! All of my life I've been one man feeding a hundred.' He barred Dari from the house: 'Don't bring your germs!' He makes Ayah clap her hands on the veranda for hours to chase away the crows."

Mina Foi said to Sonia, "When are you coming to see your old aunt, naughty girl, always khee, khee, khee. But life is no joke, let me tell you."

How to socialize when you don't want anyone to ask you questions? Yet Papa and Sonia made one necessary round of visits to friends, because it was essential that a child pay her respects upon returning from abroad, proffering a gift to those who had helped raise her: After Eight chocolates, an impressionist calendar, a scented lotion in the exotic fragrance of honeysuckle. Sonia had brought no gifts, but they forgave her, having heard rumor of mysterious malaise.

"How wonderful you are back to keep your father company. He's been moping since your Ma ran off. Men can't manage alone," said Margo.

"Boyfriend? Boyfriend?" asked Neil. "You can confide in me."

Khushi said, "Not a trace of a Yankee accent! Why not? How disappointing."

"Bless you, beti," said Uncle Dilip. While his face was that of an uncle, his hand found the curve of Sonia's waist.

Ferooza said, "You know I think of you as a daughter, Sonu. It's a joy to have you back."

Sonia admired Ferooza's skill in masking her converted servant's quarters residence on the rooftop of a house: the walls painted her favorite Parisian blue-gray; objects selected with precision, coming together like a bowerbird's bower; thimble-size coffee cups rimmed in gold; a carved silver box that held stamps. And she recognized with a pang the string of festive lights to transform a drab view. Ferooza's cat yawned from her cushion throne.

"Moti Bibi has grown fatter!" Sonia complimented Ferooza.

"She's very fat," said Ferooza proudly, as if it were she herself who was sated. "Meri Moti Moti, my fat pearl!" When the silence of the night woke Ferooza, she calmed herself by stroking her cat, who twisted and purred under her hand. Thus they churned a little richness, a little butter and cream, between them.

In Paris, Ferooza had lived in similarly cramped rooms, in the attic of a large, divided residence made of honey-hued stone near Notre-Dame, where the toilet for number two had been down the hallway; she had to take a large, heavy key and walk to an icy cabinet that was situated up a few wooden steps to unlock the commode. But this is where Ferooza had learned several life skills from the occupants of the other tiny attic apartments, including women from various parts of the Islamic world: from Iran and Turkey, Morocco and Egypt. They granted Ferooza an expansive sense of self. She remembered Niloufer, Zeynep, and Tagreid. They taught her how to be stylish even if she had little money, to indulge in shoes and handbags in surprising colors, in a blue bowl from Samarkand unearthed at a flea market; how to buy good bread; how to decant herself a drink from a crystal decanter; how to perhaps color her hair flame red and smoke a cigarette. "It's so important for a woman to experience having her own home," said Ferooza to Sonia, "to be her own woman. I think that's why your mother decided to leave for Cloud Cottage."

A photograph of young Ferooza stood on her desk, as if to remind herself of herself. It showed a girl with an oval face that belonged in a lover's locket. Ferooza turned her gentle, wise eyes upon Sonia. "You don't look well, my darling."

After these necessary forays, Sonia and Papa kept to themselves. Papa unlocked the liquor cabinet, taking the key hidden under the third and fourth layers of the newspaper lining his wardrobe, and brought forth the Laphroaig. "Life is too short to be stingy!"

Up on the roof they played Papa's newly purchased tapes of Noor Jehan and Begum Akhtar. They played Iqbal Bano singing "Hum Dekhenge." The picture on the cassette cover showed the singer wearing a black sari to protest the dictatorship of Zia that had banned the poetry of Faiz. She had performed before a crowd of fifty thousand, and this crowd was going mad in the background. As Papa and Sonia listened to the song, they were covered in goosebumps. To be a citizen of a troubled postcolonial nation gave a person gravitas. To be holding out against the crass new world gave a man gravitas. To be wounded yet fighting on against the barbarians gave one gravitas. To be exiled, abandoned by love and luck, gave them gravitas. What happened within a family, what happened between a couple, was no different from that which happened in a nation under dictatorship, running on fear. Far above, planes blinked across the sky, and below, the madman in the ruins of the idgah came out and shouted, "India Pakistan Arrrrrgah." A monster bat with the wingspan of a kite flew from the Hauz Khas tombs to drink nectar from night flowers, to hunt under the bright hot moon.

....

WHEN MAMA TELEPHONED SONIA AND ASKED, "WILL YOU visit soon?" Sonia answered, "Yes, I promise I will."

"When?"

"I am not sure."

"Are you looking around for something to do, then?"

"Not yet."

"How about working for an art gallery like you did in New York?"

"*No!* I've had enough of art galleries! You may as well sell me into the sex trade. It's a filthy, corrupt business."

Mama, startled by her daughter's outburst, worried she had been brusque and harsh. Perhaps it was too soon after Sonia had returned for her to begin job seeking, although a month had passed. But if her daughter became independent, Mama would be free to stay in the hills. This was no way to think. Yet she did think this, and she also observed that while it was true there were some ambitious daughters in this generation of educated, well-off young women encouraged to stretch their wings to the limit, the majority seemed not to wish to stretch their wings very far but still expected parents or husbands to provide for them. They were languid and charming, the way only pampered women could be. Their hair rippled down their backs the way it never could if they had to cook and clean, take public transport to a job.

Meanwhile an American degree was so frivolous that it was sheer madness. "In her time in college," Mama fretted to Ferooza, "she studied Leopardi, the Yanomami Amazon tribe, Coltrane and Chekhov, Iran and the West, the philosophy of Hannah Arendt, ecology, creative writing, pottery, animal behavior, Dryden, Pope, and Swift."

Ferooza reported that Sonia looked exceedingly unwell and that her only company was her father, who spent hours on the rooftop garden, drinking whiskey and talking nonsense about subjects he knew nothing about. Ferooza's family had held all-night mehfils, gatherings of poetry and music on the watered summer lawns of their home; she had actually experienced the culture of loss Papa was trying to co-opt. But when she had last seen Papa, he had presumed to lecture her on Ghalib. He had said, "You know, Ferooza," then adopted a sudden interior look after a series of serious coughs and declaimed in gravelly voice to send a line of poetry forth, recall it, send it forth again, tentatively, ironically, in a flash of abrupt temper, and finally philosophically, indistinguishable from the night breeze. *Why did you go on alone? Now remain alone some days longer.* He had educated Ferooza about *herself,* lectured her on *herself!*

"Are you writing your stories at least?" Mama asked Sonia. Mama remembered the beautiful one about the boy who sat up in a tree with his beloved langur monkeys.

"It was oriental nonsense," proclaimed Sonia. "And it feels childish and absurd to make things up. After a while you want to write the truth, plain and simple."

"How about a publishing house, then? Or if you worked for a magazine, it would feed your own writing."

It was Ferooza, in touch with all kinds of people through her women's nonprofit Saheli, who eventually heard about a cultural magazine, *Kala,* that would be published quarterly by the wife of a cabinet minister who had previously been in the foreign service. Srimati Shakuntala Mithal, a madam ambassadress for culture, had taken inspiration from a Mexican art magazine called *Artes de México* that she had admired during her husband's tenure in Central America. It was both glossy and scholarly enough to be placed in a five-star hotel, or upon a diplomat's coffee table, or in a university library. A wealthy boutique hotelier, coincidentally her son-in-law, would provide the funding, and they planned to include articles on the heritage of arts and crafts, architecture, textiles, dance, literature, music, and cuisine. Sonia had been employed at a legendary art gallery in New York, a branch of one of the first in SoHo. She had studied in a liberal arts college renowned for dispensing an education so sophisticated as to be useless save for the cultivation of an eye divorced from need, and this would be in tune with their target audience. Perhaps she might write for them?

Papa insisted on driving Sonia to her appointment at the address on Prithviraj Road, and when Sonia requested that her father wait outside, her request didn't make logical sense to him. Srimati Mithal would surely wish to ascertain Sonia came from a good family, a distinguished father who had dressed, for a certain je ne sais quoi, in a mothy poncho from Dadaji's round-the-world tour. Papa was curious to see the dwelling of this suave diplomat, and secretly, maybe, he wished to ambush Mama and Ferooza's plans. He was upset they had conspired to find Sonia a job, as if he wasn't an adequate father.

"You can't come with me." Sonia had an inkling of her mother's suffocation, and they had an argument standing outside the gate, which was watched interestedly by the security guards. Finally Papa said: "Go on your own, then! I'll make a round of the gardens." At the edge of the lawn was a venerable pillared banyan under which the philosopher Krishnamurti had given talks against the notion of gurus— although he maintained the demeanor of one, spoke like one, dressed like one, had the following of one. Srimati Mithal had compiled a sari-clothbound edition of the wisdom he had imparted: *Under the Banyan Tree.*

At the portal to the bungalow, roses floated in a shallow antique brass basin from Kerala filled with water. Two antique temple oil lamps from Orissa stood on either side, and beyond was the drawing room in earthen shades, magnificent with Chola bronzes and sculptures of celestial Khajuraho women that had been indiscreetly hacked from temple panels. The drawing room held various seating areas, and there were many people waiting here: the minister's petitioners on low stools, a group of unfashionable village relatives who had come to see a doctor in the city, a Madhubani painter who had won the presidential medal looking uncomfortable. A beige uniformed bearer served each guest a plate with a half samosa and a half barfi.

Outside, Papa craned to see how many water tanks a cabinet minister had on his roof. He decided to go by the kitchen to sniff what a minister may be having for dinner when the security guards came chasing after him to say he couldn't sniff a minister's dinner, what was he thinking? There were four guards with guns on the roof—north, south, east, west—as well as three watchmen with guns in an entrance booth, another three at the back gate, and sandbags piled here and there in case of terrorist siege. This kerfuffle resulted in Papa refusing to leave the property because his daughter was still inside the residence.

"But then why are you outside?"

He explained to the guards that she was an America-returned daughter who wanted to make her own way and meet her prospective employer without her father in attendance. The guards felt sorry for Papa having such an ungrateful child. They delivered him into the gold-earth interior. Papa said to Sonia: "They wouldn't let me stay outside! I tried, mind you. I told them I had an independent daughter who was embarrassed by her father."

Now he began studying the sculptures, his spectacles low on the nib of his nose. "In the old days," he said loudly to nobody in particular, "you could buy these by the kilo. I remember when I was sent to tour petrol pumps in Khajuraho, sculptures quite as impressive were lying about unguarded everywhere. You could simply pick them up and walk off with them."

"Papa, you're suggesting they are stolen," Sonia hissed.

"How am I saying they are stolen?"

When the bearer brought him the same plate assigned to everyone, he exclaimed, "Half a samosa! By golly! I'll have a whole one, if you can afford it, thank you very much."

Sonia said, "I'm not going to get this job." All of a sudden she wanted it. If you didn't have love, if you didn't have reliable parents, you had better find work.

Madam cultural ambassadress was magnificent and severe in rustling muga silk, shahtoosh shawl, heavy tribal silver, and kohl-lined eyes. She addressed Papa and Sonia sideways, to speak musingly: "I don't know why it is that I'm endlessly being sent daughters for internships. It gets in the way of my work, looking after all these daughters for whom some occupation has to be found, so that they may get into an American university—they have to show their social commitment—or to pass time until they get married—to make them more marriageable. But it's also our duty to educate the young, no matter how false their interest, so I take it on.

"I will give you the number of my daughter, Maya, who is editor in chief. She graduated from Smith College in the United States, where she studied cultural anthropology. You know Smith?"

Sonia noted that she was taking care of her own child while complaining about other parents taking care of *their* children.

When the next day Sonia telephoned Maya Mithal, who had kept her name when she married, she said: "Ya, ya, Mum told me about you. I am a feminist and so is Mum—we are looking for talented, young women writers. I am sorry I can't meet you. Actually I am expecting a baby, and my due date is almost here, but why don't you send us something so we have an idea of your style?"

Sonia could write anything she pleased that fit within the realm of culture. Their next issue was conveniently on Delhi; she should try to find a local story.

The idea for a story came to Sonia and Papa on an excursion to Old Delhi. Papa had parked the Peugeot at the outskirts to avoid it getting scraped and scratched, as was inevitable in the scrum. While it was past nine o'clock at night, when the streets of New Delhi were emptying, here there was whirling life about the wizard green-lit minarets and domes of Jama Masjid. Women rushed hennaed feet under their black burkas; an elegant, bathed bearded man in starched white accompanied an elegant, bathed bearded goat in a rickshaw; the attar shop was open for Papa to buy little flasks of perfume containing the essence of first rain, so he may proffer the gift of fragrance—dabbing a little on the wrists of the people he met in New Delhi, who had forgotten such courtesies. In food stalls, proprietors sat with wide-girthed ease amidst their wide-girthed pots, ladling biryani, and a psychedelic mess of color spilled from the sweet shops. Rotis flew overhead tossed from roti makers to waiters who rushed in fast-forward. There was a feeling of a great river, of the momentum of thousands of meals served to hundreds of thousands over ages.

"Bade Mia!" Papa insisted on greeting the proprietor of Karim's. *By the grace of Allah,* said the menu, and *Good food makes good mood.* Sonia was conscious she was at the crossroads of myriad stories. She caught a glimpse of a woman's smile before she vanished down a back lane.

They ate pasanda and ishtew, burra kebabs and sheermal rotis. Sonia said, "It's very strange that no writer or filmmaker has set a scene here, isn't it?"

"Sonia, why don't you write about kebabs!" pounced Papa.

And so the next week Sonia went out with a notebook to document the rivalry between Aseem Chacha and Nadeem Uncle at either end of the back lane in Khan Market. She researched the tabak maaz of Kashmir; the Afghan reshmi; the chapli, peshawari, and kastoori of the North-West Frontier; the kebabs from the royal kitchens of Palanpur and Patiala. The Hyderabadi royals were famous for their mad luxury—the last nizam had scooped the jewels of the Russian tsars and sent his laundry all the way to Paris. The pathar kebab was invented here, cooked on a hot stone to absorb the flavor of the minerals, and the shikampuri was made with roasted cashews and a sliver of egg in the center. Food sleuths and historians had resurrected the recipes of the royal banquets and claimed to have revived the dorra kebab from the Salar Jung archives. This kebab resembled an orientalist fantasy: Thirty-two rare spices rendered it soft as marrow and the kebab was steamed in silk over low coals that had been smoked with sandalwood. The silk must not burn, and the kebab should be revealed by a single pull of a thread, like a nautch girl.

Sonia began to feel vertiginously ill—she could not believe in such stories. She thought of Ilan; his voice said, *Don't write this nonsense.* She thought he was right.

But she continued and researched the kebabs of the princely state of Awadh, the origin of the shammi, the galawati, the kakori, invented in the village of Kakori when the nawab lost his teeth. It was ground anew with each addition of the fifty-two spices—actually, some said fifteen spices, some eight, but all vowed secrecy. These were the kebabs Ba and Dadaji's cook had excelled in making.

Papa devoted himself to assisting Sonia. He thought that the Indian kebab was Persian in origin, from kam-aab, less water, but looking up the word in a weighty dictionary, he decided the kebab's roots lay in Dari and Pashto, making the kebab Afghan in origin: "Just like Rumi. Now they keep saying uncivilized country—they forget."

Whatever its origins, the Indian kebab—massaged, marinated, oiled, spoiled, pampered, pompous, romantic, a perfumed aristocrat—had become a different creature from the Turkic, the Persian, or the Afghan.

Sonia attempted to work at Papa's computer. There were so many kebabs they fell right out of the article. When she tried to write about the culture of each one, the material ballooned. *This was India,* she thought. *You might try to write a slender story, but it inevitably connected to a larger one.* The sense could never be contained.

She shut the door of the study, but her father came bursting in on her—after all it was *his* door to *his* study nook, which contained *his* oinking computer. He tried to read over her shoulder. He wished he had been hired to write the article. Papa had become interested in art and literature after meeting Mama's family. They proclaimed art was democratic, open to anyone, but they didn't behave as if this was true, and he felt he had been barred from being an artist, an intellectual, by them as well.

Chandu brought a midmorning Nescafé. He said to Sonia, "You are thin as a worm and writing about food! You'd better fatten up or nobody will take what you write seriously."

Alpa, the maid, came in; no matter how Mama had tried, she had never succeeded in teaching Alpa how to knock on a closed door and wait for a reply before admitting herself. Alpa began to sweep over Sonia's feet, announcing meanwhile that she, Alpa, was putting on too much weight.

"Do some exercise, then," admonished Papa.

"I clean houses all day; how much more exercise can I do?"

"That's a different kind of exercise," said Chandu. "The kind you do makes a person old. The other kind makes a person young."

It was now that Sonia decided to go to Cloud Cottage to write in the quiet of the mountains. She would have the seriousness of her new employment within which to hide her gouged self, and perhaps Mama wouldn't notice the emptiness at her core.

"Yes, go," Papa said, agreeing. But he promptly felt the hypocrisy of his agreeable statement and lost his temper. "Maybe you can tell your mother to stop self-dramatizing."

"She's self-dramatizing?"

"Yes, she has all these romantic notions of being a hermit from her mad father. Probably he came from a Nazi clan; that is the only explanation for his going off into the mountains instead of returning to Germany. They say they have no relatives anymore—how is that possible?

"Anyway, when you live with a person who is mad, you also become mad," said Papa, "which explains your aunt Meher, your mother, and myself."

The next day he said: "Just inform your mother that Chandu's wife needs back surgery—tell her to kindly contribute half the funds. And by the way," he added, "while you're asking, can you tell your mother to lend me money to buy a new car? My Peugeot is falling apart."

And then, as Sonia left for the station, Papa said, "Look, just tell your mother, 'Return to Delhi. You can live your own life, and Papa will live his own life. Nobody is going to bother you.'"

Sonia was filled with pity for the childishness to which we are all condemned when love comes to an end, filled with rage because it wasn't right to make a child the arbiter of her parents' battles, and filled with fear. One evening she had listened to her father howl under the hiccupping shower pipe and there is no worse fright than to hear your father despair.

*

IT WAS AFTER SONIA had departed, after some days of depression, that Papa roused himself and made a dramatic petition to his boss— eldest and vaguest of the five Gupta brothers of Gupta Brothers— proposing a business trip to Japan to investigate ways in which the East had successfully adapted modernity unto its own purpose. He had read in the travel pages of *The Times of India* about a bewitching toilet with a toasty seat that disguised bathroom noises within a recording of the water warbles of springtime thrushes. The toilet could also shoot water out at different speeds, temperatures, and directions and dry the person enthroned upon it with gusts from behind. Papa wondered if the upper classes in India would invest in such a toilet.

Whenever Papa devised an overseas business trip, it was to detour to a part of the world he wished to see. Considering investment in a zipper factory in Hungary, he had conjured his Greek and Italian holidays, where without wife and daughter he had traveled like a jolly tramp without a care in the world. Thinking ahead to Hindi computer programming, he had flown to Seattle; on the way back he had seen Borobudur. A warehouse business in Saskatchewan had allowed him to meet Sonia in D.C. during her first year in college. Now he thought he might take the bullet train from Tokyo to Kyoto and experience contrasting currents of old and new. He might identify Mount Fuji by the preciseness of its shape as he blew past—vision peeled—not to be left wondering if all he'd detected was a cloud amidst cloud, a hallucination he wished to be real. The glamour of this journey would allow him to triumph over his wife, and if the news of his abandonment by wife, now also by daughter, were broadcast all over again in Delhi, he would be in a place so wondrous the news wouldn't reach him. He would not invite Mama along so that she could not refuse to come; he would leave no number with anyone so it might not happen that she would not call. He read about the geisha district of Gion—he might condescend to tell the *haha hoho* dinner-party crowd that he'd found a Japanese girlfriend to teach him to use chopsticks. He might say, "I found two. When one sulks, I go to the other; when the other one begins to sulk, by that time the first is delighted to see me again!"

When he heard about the singing toilets of Japan, the octogenarian Gupta, pale as if leeches had sucked his color, clapped his feeble hands soundlessly. He was the brother most devoted to the customs of the past, yet the most tolerant concerning dreams of the future. The world was already so changed from his childhood, he knew anything was possible. "Excellent, excellent."

But then Mr. Gupta asked Papa if, before his proposed trip to Tokyo was considered at a board meeting, Papa might kindly accompany him to a cement bag factory in rural Orissa. The primary business of one branch of the Guptas was cement, and it would be lucrative to purchase a cement bag business in which to pack their cement. Cement bags were not different from singing toilets because romantic notions were not different from plebeian: All were expressions of the same oblivion.

As Papa paced on his roof garden, a crow tried to land on his head. "It thinks you are a cow," said Chandu to Papa. "They can't tell the difference." He meant to be comforting. Chandu, too, had once heard Papa cry under the hiccupping shower and felt himself freeze. There is no worse fright than to know the vulnerability of the man who employs you, whom you need to remain strong because you yourself are powerless.

....

Sonia walked through the wisteria-draped front door of Cloud Cottage into the dank odorous house where time had been cultivated to be as slow and unconcerned as a turtle. An oil painting by her grandfather hung in the entryway above the shoes and umbrellas. Initially abstract in appearance, it was of a finger of white cloud touching the retreating snow on a black mountain slope. "Mama?" she called and received no answer. She walked out onto the ledge of unkempt garden and saw her mother weeding the pumpkins. Embracing her, Sonia burst into tears.

They sat together on the mossy stone garden bench. Mama had cropped her hair into what the barber called a boy cut, and she had become as skinny as her daughter. She wore a faded baggy dress, as if she were a forsaken missionary. Babayaga, with a heavy, purposeful tread, came meowing complainingly, and when she leapt onto Sonia's lap, she sneezed a wet spray upon Sonia's face and dug her claws into her leg. "If she were a human with her personality," said Mama proudly, "she would be unbearable. But because she is a cat, we love her."

"She remembers me!" exclaimed Sonia. How had she stayed away so long? She had forgotten what home meant. Home means mother. Home means one's own bad-tempered cat.

Mama suspected that love might have reduced her daughter. She could think of no other explanation for Sonia's bereft expression and her weeping in her mother's arms, and there was no other apparent problem for which you could not recruit help, that you refrained from articulating. But Mama did not voice this concern. "Love" was now a beside-the-point word to her, a nonsense word she treated cynically. Better to be done with it.

A sweet, smoky smell filled the air. Sonia said, "I smell tobacco." Mama said, "That's your grandfather. Every evening at this hour, he would smoke his pipe sitting here looking out at Bandarpunch."

Sonia looked toward the peak that shone a frangible snow gold.

"Now and again," said Mama, "I still smell cherry tobacco and I know he's with me. He must have come to see you."

Sonia felt a precipitous drop. Had her grandfather come for his missing amulet? The dead cannot rest if some unsettled matter keeps them among the living. She had not told her mother. She felt ill.

"Aren't you scared of his ghost?" Sonia asked.

"No, I am comforted. He longed to climb Bandarpunch. He tried three times and three times a storm forced him back. I think of his disappearance as him finally climbing the mountain."

Sonia dreamt that night she was in a house she had never been, in a landscape she had never visited, searching for Badal Baba. She felt pure, unadulterated fear. The ordinary world that she saw about her, that she was trying to trust in, to live in, scared her because it had been proved untrue. When she found Ilan, he was waiting. He pulled her to him. "Darling, you are here at last! I missed you so much, I wore that shirt of mine you wore to bed to keep your smell." But she had never worn his shirt. "You know, I missed the lentil soup you used to make." He was a phantom; it wasn't Ilan inside Ilan's body!

*

THE NIGHTS WERE SO black they purified the mornings, and when these mornings drew gold from the nocturnal cistern, Babayaga was waiting. She climbed to the top of the rock and drew herself tall for the first ray to touch her head in benediction, for the forest to fill with glinting sunlight like yellow butterflies, with yellow butterflies like glinting sunlight. And in these high, clean mornings, Sonia also felt holy, as if the mountain light might one day absolve the coagulated pitch inside her.

The bandy-legged milkman came climbing from Jabarkhet; he must be over seventy now, a rope net on his back holding the milk cans. Sometimes he had a bunch of radishes to sell, or some plums. He was so bent, he didn't look up, nor did he spare a breath on words. He grunted, poured out the milk, washed his little ladle at the garden tap, and went on his way. Mama put on the kettle. Lazy Moolchand rose when the sun was already high, and for a half hour he aired his bedding, flapping his sheets in case he'd shared his sleep with centipedes and spiders. Then he dressed and slowly began his day; he picked every fallen flower and leaf, individually shredding them and depositing them in a heap. He stepped on Babayaga's tail and didn't notice her outraged yowl. Then he squatted, doing absolutely nothing, his chin in his hand. He possessed two shirts. One was his ragged gardening kurta, one a bright red shirt he wore to go to the market. When he put on his special shirt, your heart broke.

Sonia was grateful that she might settle her loneliness between her mother's and Moolchand's, just as she had settled her loneliness between that of her father's and Chandu's. She began to write her article, and as she worked she found that the quiet of her mother's home and the rhythm of life here gave a secret structure, a calm magnitude to her work. She could work patiently. She could unsnarl her thinking.

While Sonia linked the development of the kebab to the history of the country, Mama read *David Copperfield* again. She had become one of those characters in the novels that she loved, the people who read Dickens in the jungle over and over. Why? Because when Dickens is better than your life, then why live your life? It would be foolishness not to read Dickens instead. She told her daughter, "If you keep your existence inside art, you will live wonderfully. Just don't put your nose out."

Sonia did not say, "How can you trust that the art isn't made from the bones and ashes of innocent people?" Was this why she had stayed away so long? Had she intuited that Cloud Cottage, the home of an artist, would return her to thinking incessantly about Ilan? The uncanny presence of her grandfather's paintings was upon her. *Migrating*

Geese portrayed no geese but a ripple on the water evoking the emotion of a landscape from which the geese have flown. The colors were sepia, viridian, midnight, sentimental pink. One, instead of bearing a signature and date, was inscribed *I flew.* It was a cloud in an eye. Sonia thought about the paintings of Ilan that she had never seen in person, save for an eye latching on to her eye. That eye hated Sonia, and to be the object of hate meant one could never be free. There had obviously been secrets in Ilan's life all along. Why had she been subservient to them?

When Mama had asked her why she had stopped writing stories, Sonia had not answered that a person cannot write a story if she looks at the world through someone else's eyes, if his voice still speaks from inside her brain, if she doesn't know if her thoughts are her thoughts, if she can't tell what is true and what is not.

One afternoon she climbed into the attic. In a black tin trunk that read *S.S. Ranchi,* the liner upon which Siegfried Barbier had sailed to India, she found her grandfather's passport, *Subject of the British Empire,* which contained the stamps of countries that no longer existed.

Packed in mothballs lay his greatcoat. Wool outside, lined with fox fur, its pockets were velvet. It was relative to Ilan's coat. Is this why she had allowed herself to be swooped up? Had she recognized the figure or had the darkness recognized her? In one velvet pocket was a small diary over which Barbier had painted weather—rain on a sea, an ocean on fire, a volcano—so it was virtually impossible to read. In any case, it was written in German.

Sonia looked up, and from the deodar forest, through the small diamond-paned attic window, she thought she saw an eye. An accusing eye. Was it her grandfather's eye? Searching for his demon with a cloud face? Or was it a stray leopard or jackal crossing the forest? An owl? A bubble in the glass? Or was it a reflection of her own eye watching her watch herself? She blinked, and the eye disappeared as Ilan's voice sounded: *Sonia, don't make me feel guilty now!* Was Ilan's eye migrating to see if she was betraying him? She stared at a watercolor of dissolving rainclouds where the medium and the subject came together, just as presumably the painter and the painting became the same thing. She spotted the eye in the painting of the rain. A raincloud moved over.

She took the little diary from the greatcoat pocket down to Mama, who said that she thought she had removed all the books from the attic where they were vulnerable to monsoon leaks. One rainy season, a trove of them had been irretrievably damaged. She translated a line for Sonia that read, *To learn about pine trees, said Basho, go to the pine tree.*

"Wasn't your father an engineer?" asked Sonia.

While in the past Mama had maintained a consummate silence when asked about her parents, perhaps she glimpsed a family resemblance in Sonia now, and she spoke more openly than she had before. "Yes, he was employed by Siemens to build canals in India. Like many well-off European men of that time, my father in his youth considered himself an adventurer-explorer. He arrived in his hiking boots with a tent and a Kodak camera—but even before he left Germany, he had been enticed by the romantic notion of East and West coming together under the guiding wisdom of Himalayan sages. He had been interested in theosophy, in Gandhi and Tagore. At that time he painted as a hobby.

"He met my mother, Anjolie, in 1927. She was the sister of his friend Bibhu Roy, with whom he had studied at the Charlottenburg Technische Hochschule and who came from a family of revolutionaries, communists fighting for freedom from the British. Unlike most Indians sent to England to study, because of their antipathy to British rule, he was sent to Berlin. Together my father and Uncle Bibhu went to hear Tagore speak. They frequented the atelier of a sculptor named Kolbe, a family friend of my father's who cast a bronze head of Bibhu. A cast of the head, a gift from the sculptor, was transported by my father when he sailed to India in 1928 and stayed for some months with Bibhu's family in the riverine landscape that Tagore describes in his diaries, which is where my mother grew up. My father and mother fell in love when he walked into that family house and woke my mother, who had been asleep on the sofa. When the family discovered letters between them revealing a nascent romance, they threw my father 'out on his backside,' my mother said. Friendship between races and religions was accepted, but love was forbidden. My parents were not dissuaded; the opposite—it was the catalyst. My mother was educated and spirited. They eloped and were each disowned by their families.

"When the Second World War broke out in Europe, German companies operating in India abruptly shut down, just as they had during the First World War. My father lost his job, and almost overnight my parents were penniless, although he had switched his citizenship, which meant he was not interred in a POW camp with other Germans—Nazis alongside fleeing Jews, missionaries, and pacifists who happened to be in India at that time and were swept up in the chaos. It was also the time the Indian independence movement was at a pitch. When it was all over, my father's apartment in Charlottenburg had been bombed by Allied forces, and my mother's home was now situated in East Pakistan. The Delhi we knew was decimated by Partition. We retreated to Cloud Cottage, our summer home, and accepted lodgers. My mother had a cheerful nature, and, in fact, she enjoyed being poorer because she enjoyed bustling about, being practical and busy. She tucked in her sari pallu, wore walking shoes, rose at dawn to make sure buckets of hot water were delivered to each room, and steamed the Christmas pudding herself—she was famous for her Christmas pudding, the recipe for which came from the mother-in-law she never met.

"When my father wasn't painting in Little Cloud, he was studying maps and deciding upon his next hiking route. Each year after the winter and before the monsoons, he went trekking; each time he stayed longer, carrying his own tent and supplies. Once when my mother asked him what he thought of during those solitary hours, he said he wasn't thinking so much as trying to return to a place where he could trust what he saw again. That while he didn't feel entitled to any such relief, he was trying to return a tree to a tree, a mountain to a mountain, a cloud to a cloud.

"Then one day—"

"He became the cloud," said Sonia softly. To paint bamboo, you went to the bamboo; to paint a mountain, you went to the mountain. To paint clouds, Barbier went to the clouds. What a choice of subject matter. He had vanished.

When she perused her grandfather's library, she found his child-hood *Max und Moritz,* also his copy of Ernest Shackleton's diary, in which he had underlined the sentence *We all have our own White South.* He'd underlined another passage where Shackleton had confessed he could no longer tell whether he was alive; he walked on in unending whiteness—he might just have crossed the border between the living and the dead. Opening volumes by Roerich, Madame Blavatsky, Alex-andra David-Néel, and Annie Besant, books on theosophy, tantra, the esoteric knowledge of lamas, the pages as musky rich and honey-colored as halvah, Sonia found the writing gobbledygook. She agreed with Ilan all over again. Why was it that she had never met these won-drous creatures, flying lamas and soothsayers who could look into past and future? She felt the racial divide between herself and Siegfried Bar-bier. Miracle-performing gurus and levitating lamas would favor white people. Perhaps to be lavished with the devotion of Westerners eager to bow and venerate at their feet convinced these gurus they had over-come the colonial narrative. But if you feel it is better to be admired by white people than to be admired by brown people, then you haven't overcome the colonial narrative. But like her grandfather, Sonia, too, wished the magic were true, that despite all that had occurred, a beau-tiful mingling of cultures might obliterate the divide. For if the divide was not to be bridged by beauty, it would be bridged most certainly by devilry.

While Sonia continued to work at her grandfather's desk, Mama now decided to translate her father's diaries, which could be the key to his mysterious silence. Her German was rusty, and she used a diction-ary. One morning as they worked—the moss glowing splendiferous through the open windows along with the ferns of many dainty kinds; the woodpeckers, crow pheasants, and even parakeets calling out; the smell of resin enriching the air—the phone rang. They jumped. The phone hardly ever rang at Cloud Cottage.

Sonia got up to answer. It was Mina Foi. Mina Foi never made a phone call for the useless luxury of it.

"You sound croaky," said Sonia.

"Daddy has died, and I cannot find your papa."

Sonia telephoned Papa's secretary, Tandon, who informed her that Papa and the eldest Mr. Gupta had traveled to survey a cement bag factory in Orissa, and while Mr. Gupta had returned, Papa had taken some days to travel in the region.

"But where is he exactly? How can you not know? This is very remiss of you, Tandonji."

It was two days before Papa received the news and rushed back to Delhi, where Sonia was awaiting him.

"Why didn't you tell me you were going to Orissa?"

"I needed a few days to myself." It had felt like humiliation, cement bags. To overcome that humiliation, Papa had traveled to see the sun temple at Konark, where he'd encountered the erotic stone sculptures of enormously buxom women with hourglass waists and full moon hips. Their breasts were shiny, and the guard had explained to Papa that male visitors couldn't help but reach out to fondle these stone women. Some were so aroused by the sexual contortions on display, they stepped back and fell splat off the elevated rampart constructed for tourists. Papa had thought that just the way he had embarked upon a wrong path at some point in his life, all of India had taken the wrong fork in the road during an earlier incarnation of its existence. Shyly, waiting until the guard had left, Papa, too, had reached out his hands.

....

VINITA AND PUNITA SQUATTED ON THE KITCHEN FLOOR AND inscribed in English: *Sunny Welcome!* on a piece of board hammered onto a stick for the driver to hold up at the airport.

Babita said, "It should say: *Sunny* comma *Welcome Home.*"

So *Home* was squashed alongside. They wanted to go to the airport to hold their own sign up. Babita thought of the flight arriving in the pre-dawn, the deserted stretch of road between the airport and city, where there had been a spate of robberies with taxi drivers and dacoits conspiring to target travelers transporting expensive items from overseas. She considered the chaos of the airport and its overwhelmingly male presence—and her eye settled on Punita, her lithe figure, her hair in a ponytail, her flowered skirt and T-shirt. The other day Mr. Habib had put his arm about her sparrow shoulders, clutched her close, and said, "Little darling! Who is your only boyfriend—Murad Uncle, right? I'm your only boyfriend. Say 'Murad Uncle is my only boyfriend.'"

Babita decided. "No, the driver and I can't look after you and find Sunny at the same time. You girls stay home, and when we get back, we'll blow the horn at the gate for you to come down and unlock it—so don't fall asleep, understand?"

"Should we keep the light on? If we turn it off, we'll fall asleep." They'd been harshly warned of the cost of electricity, but Babita generously said, "Yes, keep the light on. One light."

Babita had telephoned Sunny to ask him: "What do you want to eat on your first day home?"

Tickled by the question, considering it carefully, Sunny had replied, "Karela fried crisp and blackened, and fish in mustard."

"That fish in mustard Vinita always mucks up. No matter how many times I've instructed her."

"Maybe Kashmiri koftas?"

"All right, first night Kashmiri koftas and karela fried crisp. And should I get train tickets for us to visit your grandparents?"

"I'm not sure when I can go. I told you I'm supposed to help Satya decide on a wife."

There was at this moment an uncomfortable silence on the phone. "Well, you can let me know later; see how you feel when you get here," said Babita.

She put down the phone and spoke to her Ideal Husband, "*He never mentioned the girlfriend, Ratty. What do you think?*"

*

SO IT WAS ONE night in May, Sunny and Satya met at the airport to catch the Air India flight to New Delhi.

"First night I'm having Kashmiri koftas. You?"

"Butter chicken."

They found themselves in a crowd of fellow travelers camped by the gate.

"Going home for a holiday?" a man asked companionably.

"Actually, I'm going to meet some girls," said Satya. This was a lovely life, being talkative while journeying alongside talkative individuals on your way to meet your future wife—hopefully a lady with such a spilling-over family, you may disagree over everything, but at the end of the evening who even cared, you'd join a chorus of snores.

Satya took off his shoes, sat cross-legged on a seat in the waiting area, and wriggled his toes inside his socks. This finding a girl in a traditional way was encouraging Satya to behave in an emphatically Indian manner that Sunny found dishonest. But several travelers responded enthusiastically to Satya. To search for a spouse was to arouse in others their own respective memories of love, danger, deceit, hope, lasting good fortune, or everlasting misery.

"Don't get tricked. After my uncle married, he found he had married a kleptomaniac. The wedding guests found their jewels missing."

"My friend made an unusual choice—he married a girl in a wheel-chair. The minute he saw her, although the whole family turned against him, he insisted: 'My search is over.' He said that no other girl had her spiritual depth."

"What about your friend? Also a doctor?"

"No," said Sunny stiffly from behind his *Chronicle of a Death Fore-told*. "I am a poor journalist, and I cannot even support myself."

A stern response: "You must persevere, or how will you marry?"

"I am happy being a bachelor."

"Sooner or later you will have to succumb."

"Why?"

The man turned to Satya. "Your friend will not be successful in life. His take is wrong."

García Márquez believed fiction and reportage were two wings of the same bird, and in his tale of murder, he was suggesting that a jour-nalist, too, should be considered suspicious and held within the falcon's gaze of fiction. Sunny liked this idea.

When the flight was finally ready for boarding, he joined the line, and a granny pressed upon him from behind.

"You must stand behind me with a little space," said Sunny, upset by such physical proximity. "You cannot stand exactly where I am standing." He took in the sweet country husk smell of her sari.

Life had taught her otherwise. Battles were won millimeter by milli-meter.

"Look," Sunny said, giving up, "just stand in front of me."

She moved in front with the same expressionless face, without a thank-you.

"*Rude person, rude person!*" Sunny said out loud into the air and didn't look to see if anyone sniggered.

He longed for Ulla. He drowned the thought. To recoil from his fellow citizens was a moral failure. By announcing "*Rude person, rude person!*" he only upset his own being. If you were easygoing, you'd be fine in India. It was when you lost your temper and were intolerant that the door shut in your face. He himself had given this advice to so many travelers while assuring them that India was even more chaotic and corrupt than their most hellish visions. Then somewhere in the years with Ulla, he'd moved from giving this advice earnestly to doing so facetiously. No wonder these changing currents had begun to unsettle Ulla, leaving her bewildered and betrayed.

"Hindu vegetarian or omelet? Omelet or Hindu vegetarian?" The flight attendants went about with the morning service trolley.

Satya, who never dithered over his food choices, woke and asked for the omelet.

"I want an omelet, too. May I change my order?" asked Sunny, who had asked for the Hindu vegetarian, pegging it the more righteous choice, one in accordance with his resolution to be peaceable. But before they could make the switch, the flight arrived unexpectedly early, and in the bumpy moment of descent, Satya, gobbling his lucky omelet, was overcome by the realization that this may be his last flight as a bachelor. He was already moved by the approaching end of the search he'd barely begun, teary to be back among a billion souls, each one with a striving, a story. Soon, he, too, would make his singular destiny.

*

WHEN BABITA AND THE driver, Bahadur, reached the arrivals area, she urged him to hold Vini-Puni's sign high. It turned out, he'd left it in the car.

"How can you have forgotten?"

He'd done so on purpose. He found the sign insulting: Hadn't he known Sunny since he was a small boy in half pants? He would recognize him without a sign.

Babita stood at one exit, and Bahadur went to the other. Sunny and Satya exited into the sea of men under a night bright with dust, loud with the irate horns of maneuvering cars. Satya's extended family had gathered in numbers, and Satya, the man with a mission, greeted them with grandeur, but Sunny appeared to have nobody waiting for him. He walked up and down, eyes straining into the crowd. Satya refused to leave in case something had gone wrong. "Aren't they here? Did you give the correct information?"

When the crowd thinned, Babita and Bahadur spotted Sunny.

"I was waiting *there*."

"We were waiting *right there* as well."

"I stood in front."

"But *in front* was where Bahadur was."

"Anyway, anyway . . ." They blamed Bahadur for leaving the sign in the car; he was, after all, paid to take blame assigned him.

Satya said, "Aunty, please give me your blessings."

"I certainly will, Satya. I heard you are on the hunt for a wife."

"Yes, Aunty." Satya grinned over at Sunny in a way that amounted to a betrayal of the intelligence they'd accrued through bitter experience, of the evasive nature of love.

"Finally he has accepted," said Satya's mother.

"Why don't you persuade my son to do the same?" said Babita, although she couldn't have meant anything less—where *was* the American girlfriend? She was happy, she was unhappy.

At home in Panchsheel Park, Babita and Vini-Puni stood about Sunny's suitcase, and Sunny felt his American privacy stripped away. This was love and curiosity so observant, nothing would be too inconsequential for its notice. They would anticipate a freckle appearing on his earlobe. Again he missed Ulla, who never examined him this closely. Why didn't she? Because to examine someone closely didn't allow that person their dignity—or was it that she didn't care?

Sunny unpacked the chocolates filled with kirsch, marzipan, a hazelnut creme; the smoked Gouda, the Camembert, and the Gorgonzola, Babita's taste for which confirmed her sophistication to herself—even extremely Westernized people like the Habibs were not Westernized enough to abide a reeky Gorgonzola.

"Without cheese," he had told Ulla intrigued by the gifts he was purchasing, "my welcome will be half. Once I forgot the smoked Gouda and my mother could scarcely speak to me for disappointment." He unpacked the smoked salmon as well, the trout pâté, the cans of smoked mussels and packaged Knorr soups, the duty-free Talisker and the Cointreau, the Marmite from a British outpost in Brooklyn.

Babita directed Vini-Puni to place certain gifts immediately in the fridge, others in the freezer, others into airtight containers, but they had a difficult time following orders as they were too busy collapsing against each other in gales of giggles. Practically anyone of the male gender between the ages of sixteen and thirty reduced them to this, let alone an America-returned one, let alone one they were, in a manner of speaking, related to.

"Ma, those girls are unbearable."

"Yes, but no one else can be persuaded to take them off my hands now that I've told everyone what lousy cooks they are."

The liquor and the cans of pâté and mussels were locked away in the walk-in closet, and Babita showed Sunny that the key to the closet was hidden in a small papier-mâché box in the desk drawer. In the walk-in closet was another key in the pocket of his father's Burberry raincoat, which unlocked a trunk that led to another key in an airline toilet case dating to the days when Pan Am flew the skies, which opened the steel Godrej almirah, which led to another key in an Aeroflot pouch, which opened the safe inside the almirah where he should lock away his passport and his camera.

No, he'd need his camera.

"What about your D-O-L-L-A-R-S?" Babita spelled out certain words because she believed that while all servants listened outside doors and knew English when they pretended not to, they would have trouble understanding the spelling out of English. Except Punita. With Punita being educated to rise above her class, Babita couldn't trust herself to spell anything around her.

After Sunny took an afternoon nap, they went to Lodhi Gardens to walk Pasha, who had forgotten Sunny but saw that he was supposed to remember him and had sneakily played the part. "He's a real bhondu dog, poor fellow," said Babita affectionately. "But you'll never find a more good-natured, harmless idiot."

"These things go together, isn't that right, Pasha?" said Sunny, scratching the dog's chest so Pasha's leg strummed silly.

"Not in human beings," said Babita. "Most stupid people are not harmless."

She paused to point out two more houses on the street that would soon be rubbled to be built into apartment blocks. "The khatpat never stops. I almost ran away to visit Vanya—my friend who moved to her husband's ancestral property in Goa."

Mr. Habib was at his gate. "Well, well, hello, hello! Home for a visit? Tell me, Sunny, why did you Yanks elect such a character for a president? Can't speak English clearly. Any servant's child could do better. Ask little Punita. She can correctly spell 'Y-A-C-H-T.'"

"You know, there is something wrong with Mr. Habib," Babita said to Sunny when they were out of earshot. "He keeps trying to pull Punita onto his lap. The other day he said to her, 'I'm your only boyfriend, isn't that so? Repeat after me, 'Murad Uncle is my only boyfriend!' I wonder whether to say something to Sara?"

"You must!"

"But it'll blow up. They'll say I'm insinuating a grave offense."

"Do you think he's going any further?"

"No, I never let her out of my sight. I told her, 'Stay away from Habib Sahib.' I try to reinsert some class difference, but her silly progressive school keeps undoing such notions."

In Lodhi Gardens, Babita usually walked fast to get her heartbeat up, but this evening she slowed to savor the reassuring presence of a grown son by her side. Sunny smelled a little overripe, though, from the Gorgonzola packed amidst his clothing.

"Whatever got into Satya?" Babita asked. "Wouldn't it be better for him to finish his residency before getting married?"

"He had a fit of self-pity and told his mother he wanted an arranged marriage."

"Now that you're back from the States," warned Babita, "the girls will be out to get you. They'll see you as their ticket to New York. Just say you have an American girlfriend so they leave you alone."

She had never used the word "girlfriend" to him, and there was an awkwardness to it that they both felt—Babita because the word felt false, Sunny because the word was true, even if it applied to a girlfriend he had recently been unable to kiss, this was how rancorous things had turned.

They fell into silence, but many people stopped to greet Sunny, to say to Babita how wonderful it must be to have her son with her again, to examine the America-returned boy.

Mr. Khanna slowed. "You look just like your father now, Sunny; for a moment I thought it was him."

This was his father's former employer who had instructed his father to bribe a minister for a mining license in protected forest land. When his father refused, this man directed him to bribe a general in the army for a project in a military cantonment area. When his father again refused, Mr. Khanna had sacked him, precipitating the grave family crisis that had perhaps resulted in the heart attack that killed his father. Sunny's grandmother had blamed Babita for not going along with what was practical, which was entirely unfair. She had, in fact, admonished him, "Just don't be foolish!"

When she had proven herself by unearthing a document written to her by her husband in which he had put down in writing why he was unable to perform the corruptions she had encouraged—despite the rewards that would come his way—Sunny's grandmother blamed Babita for *not* taking his father's side in *not* being corrupt.

When he was eleven, Sunny had riffled through his mother's papers and read what his father had written:

They cleared the forest and seven men were killed, scores of villagers were made destitute. There were accusations of rape by the police.

I understand your point: If the system is corrupt, and everyone else is corrupt, it is a death wish to be the only honest one. A man must overcome his resistance to what he cannot change for the sake of his family and his community which will prosper because of his practical nature. A man can only change a system when he is in a position of power, and to get to a position of power, he must perpetuate exactly what he wishes to transform.

Yet, despite these truths, I cannot perform the corruptions that are being asked of me. I cannot tell a lie, I cannot stretch the truth, make it baggy or vague. I would be incapable of tolerating myself. Perhaps it has something to do with my own father. I know that a first inconsequential corruption becomes an empire of corruption. My father has blood on his hands. A son inherits his father's corruption. Corruption rots a family. Rana is matching my father in misdeeds. When he set a fire in his factory for the insurance money, three men lost their lives. Look at Ravi, who has never lifted a finger to work but thinks it is perfectly acceptable to live off his father's ill-gotten gains.

Perhaps I want Sunny to know that his father, amongst all the men of his class, is not corrupt. I want him to be free from this family history. I want him to be free to be honorable.

When his father was unemployed and became dependent on a family allowance grudgingly dispensed, it had made Babita scared, and it had made her cruel. She began to scoff at and counter everything Ratan said and did, as thoughtlessly as swatting a fly—and so accustomed she became to scoffing, countering, swatting, she had ignored the fatigue, the vertigo, the pressure in his chest, the pain in his jaw, as nothing but manifestations of psychological weakness.

When Sunny saw Mr. Khanna in his white shorts, white polo shirt, white socks, white gym shoes, walking at a clip, hearkening to the days of Englishmen in India, deceiving people into believing uprightness proceeded from orderliness and clean clothes—he felt a resurgence of grief for the little boy he had been, age eight, when his father had died. Mr. Khanna had continued to prosper in the intervening years, in his sandstone office complex behind a high fortress that incorporated Delhi's historic walls dating to the thirteenth century. Peacocks with lush tails launched from the trees, calling operatically, pia piu. In winter, roses of nine varieties, Mr. Khanna's lucky number, bloomed in a rose garden.

"Doesn't it make you angry to see Mr. Khanna?"

"I don't let it bother me," Babita answered her son. *But, Ratty, you made yourself ill by not being corrupt. That is the sad truth of this country. You fall sick when you are not corrupt.* "Everyone is corrupt. Mr. Khanna was, in fact, gentlemanly about it. He told your father that if he didn't wish to perform a corruption, he was welcome to leave, and so long as he was quiet, he'd face no retribution. The anticipation of something terrible happening was what made your father ill—he would jump at a leaf falling—but nothing ever happened. Another employer would have delivered a message to keep him silent."

"What kind of message?"

"Someone would have poisoned the dog or tied up the watchman. At the very least we'd receive threatening phone calls in the middle of the night: 'Your husband will be transferred *very . . . far . . . away,*' the voice turning fainter to indicate a possible crossing from the earthly sphere. This is the underworld's idea of a joke."

"How do you know?"

"Everyone knows."

There had been a spell of Delhi afternoons after Sunny's father had died when during his mother's siesta hour, Sunny had called over and over an unknown number, and the same woman's voice answered: "Hello? Hello? Who is this? *Who is this?*" Sunny did not speak, and her urgent bewilderment, his tiny exerted power, had soothed him.

Other times their own phone was shrill, and when he lifted the receiver, there was the breath of intimacy, a telltale jumbly background sound, but nobody said anything, which gave him to understand that the overwhelmed city was full of thousands of empty-hearted people helplessly dialing strangers, mesmerized by the irritated bafflement on the other side: "*Who? Hello? What? Speak or I'll hang up— Who?*"

Of course there were also lewd people making lewd calls, such as the man who, whenever Babita answered, asked, "Aunty, what is your bra size?" He looked at his mother now, hitched sari and gym shoes, bulbul profile. Did she find grim humor in her husband's death? Her expression didn't betray mirth, but determination.

Babita segued into the news she had waited to tell Sunny. "The other day your uncles came to visit me. I was surprised to see them up close after a long time. Uncle Ravi's gums are black from smoking. Uncle Rana's forehead and cheeks are carpeted with boils. When I asked what had caused the boils, he said, 'Torment!' and laughed in a slow, threatening way. '*ToRRmenT, ToRRmenT, Babita Bhabhi!*'

"He is indebted to the underworld and can't pay up. How foolish to borrow from such people. He's out of his depth.

"He began by saying to me, 'Look at what is happening—our

sleepy mohalla has become hell on earth. This small lane can't hold more people and cars.'

"Uncle Ravi then chimed in, 'Better sell, divide, and lead our lives independently instead of being tied unhappily to each other here in a neighborhood that has gone to the dogs, in a city whose fate is irretrievable.' You know how he postures. 'We are growing older, Babi Bhabhi, let's call off the war. If you drop the court case against us, we can divide the property equally and peaceably go our own ways. You can have the rabbit egg cups.'

"Rana then said he knows of a developer interested in buying our house."

Sunny said, "They do have a point."

She said, "Yes, there's money to be made—but where would I go?"

He suspected his mother was planting the seed of a plan to join him in New York.

"Anyway," said Babita, "best stay away from Ravi-Rana. There's no need for you to get involved in their racket."

Sunny had remained fond of his uncles despite his mother's warring. It was Uncle Ravi who had introduced him to Hitchcock and Bergman, who had made him a Buñuel martini when he turned eighteen. It was Uncle Rana who had introduced Sunny to Abba and Boney M., who had taken him to the racecourse in Bombay. Were it not for his stuffy sister-in-law, Rana would have swept his nephew up into his world of gambling, *Playboy* magazines, and Anglo-Indian girlfriends. He favored Anglo-Indian women, who were forced, in order to make a living, to cater to the stereotype men had been brought up to believe regarding themselves.

Sunny had been leaving for his journalism program at Columbia when Uncle Rana leaned out his bathroom window. "Psst, Sunny?"

"Yes, Uncle Rana?"

"*Run, bhago, flee!*"

His uncle Ravi had opened his bathroom window and beckoned him close. "Sunny, a word of advice."

"Yes, Uncle Ravi?"

"Your father never escaped—*you escape!*"

The tombs darkened and the trees turned into shaggy mammoths, the birds made a shrieking noise as if to tell one another about a murder. Babita, Sunny, and Pasha completed their walk and returned home to koftas and karela, then retired to their respective bedrooms on either side of the staircase landing—both bedrooms also opening onto the same wide terrace lavished with bougainvillea in the magenta of passion that deepened just before night fell.

The Delhi house, even though it was divided into three for three brothers, felt spacious and open after a New York City apartment. The floor was of mosaic stone, which cooled Sunny's feet as he walked about barefoot. He felt the current from the fan waft through the cotton sheet when he was in bed, and he wondered why it was that the denser the weave, the more prized a sheet was in the States. It was this that was luxurious, a breeze moving uninhibited through gossamer fabric. Yet he couldn't sleep. He listened to the scuffle of pigeons copulating on the air conditioner outside the window even at this hour, and he remembered, following the conversation with his mother, another story he had failed to divulge to Ulla: the involvement of his cousins, Chiki-Chika, in a scandal associated with a nightclub bar on the Mehrauli road. The nightclub bar, in which they were investors, was named Olive. Why was it named Olive? Perhaps because there were no olives to be had in India, unless you transported them back in the manner Sunny had the Gorgonzola. You couldn't be a non-Westernized, wealthy Indian and attain Olive; nor could you achieve Olive if you were Westernized and honest. Olive was unattainable, save for the Westernized and corrupt.

Chiki-Chika had contracted thugs using Uncle Rana's connection to an underworld don, to evict a man who owned the adjoining property that the nightclub wished to acquire and who had refused to sell. The man, who was a respected cardiologist, was more severely beaten than they had planned, and he died. Uncle Rana's sons were implicated in corruption and in murder.

Uncle Rana raced to the police station to plead and bargain with the police to remove any record of his sons being involved, whereupon the police, to demonstrate what could happen to Chiki-Chika if Uncle

Rana did not conjure an adequate bribe, had tortured a stranger in an adjoining cell. They asked for one crore and one rupee only.

Uncle Rana tried to negotiate the amount down. The stranger in the neighboring room screamed as they extinguished cigarettes on his back. Uncle Rana persisted in his negotiations, but the howls of the stranger became unbearable.

Uncle Rana was divorced and estranged from Chiki-Chika's mother, and he was responsible for his sons. He gave in. Not so long afterward, the factory Uncle Rana owned had mysteriously gone up in flames, the three watchmen died, their families were compensated with a lakh each, and the affair was hushed up so quickly, Babita knew the fire had been purposely set for Uncle Rana to collect insurance. It wasn't enough. Indebted, Uncle Rana took out further loans upon loans against loans from the underworld to pay for Chiki-Chika to flee to New Zealand, a country so bucolic they might reinvent themselves to live as innocently as bunny rabbits in a hedgerow. Now Uncle Rana needed to tidy his affairs so he could join them in Auckland, but so much money was sunk into this Panchsheel Park house that Uncle Rana couldn't leave it behind. It was imperative he persuade Babita to sell.

Sunny gulped a bitter, blue sleeping pill and remembered the slightly flat, slightly old taste of Delhi water and the slightly flat, slightly stale odor of the Delhi night that smelled as if it had been shut away in a cupboard. Sunny may have left India, but despite this he didn't want his mother to sell his childhood home; he wanted it to remain, ready to greet him. Once something was relinquished—like this funny flat smell that lurked deep in his psyche—it might never be recovered.

....

SUNNY AND SATYA DROVE OUT IN BABITA'S CAR TO VISIT
the homes of prospective brides, Babita exhorting Sunny to be home as
quickly as possible, although the first address was hours away in a new
chapter of the city unfolding in skyscraper blocks. As they drove they
considered how changed Delhi was from their childhood metropolis.
Satya, uncomfortable in a stiff long-sleeved shirt, had a moment of
foreboding. "Do you think I did the right thing?" he asked Sunny.

"It's too late to ask that now."

Sunny had brought along his Nikon. He was treating this day as an
anthropological or journalistic exercise, and he asked the driver to stop
along the way so he could photograph a buffalo carcass being eaten by
stray dogs. The driver was humiliated, and Satya, too, felt badly. Now
that he was marrying, Satya was linking himself back to India in a real
way, while Sunny was emphasizing he had left and become a foreigner
who pounced upon the monstrosities India still churned out for the
consumption of foreigners: lepers with no arms, a cow with an extra
leg protruding from its hump.

Satya said, "Sunny, why are you photographing these things? You
are so critical."

"To take pictures is critical?"

When they reached the Garden Estate Towers, a guard lifted the
metal bar to allow them into a parking lot and pointed out the correct
building. Sunny and Satya went up in a lift with concertina doors and
down a hallway spattered with cement. It was dark even in bright day,
lit with spaced tube lights. They rang the bell and were invited into a
similarly dark apartment—curtains drawn against the sun—by a small

father, a small mother in a careful sari, and a daughter named Manjula, much larger than her parents, in a pale green and silver salwar kameez. Satya was not brave enough to look at Manjula, although he felt he liked her. This is why he had brought Sunny, to corroborate his instinctive opinion. Sunny found it difficult to look at her, too, but managed to take in a zestful gleam.

The kitchen door briefly swung open, allowing a sound of mighty chopping and pressure-cooker steam to escape along with a maid holding a tray of cold sugarcane juice.

"Thank you," said Satya. "It's so hot outside."

"It's summer," said Manjula, "so it will be hot." This made him feel foolish.

"This year summer is worse," she said kindly.

"Do you plan to settle in Rochester itself?" asked her mother.

"It depends on where I will get a job, Aunty."

"So many doctors from India are going all over the world," said Manjula.

Her mother said, "We brought up our daughter to be confident. When she was born we celebrated the same way as for her brother."

Sunny saw how terrified Manjula's mother was that her daughter might marry a man who would silence her.

"In fact, it isn't that we treated our children equally," her father said. "We favored our daughter, we encouraged our daughter more because it is harder for girls."

Satya said, "By now everyone knows girls are better than boys."

There was a span of silence. The silence intensified.

Sunny remembered this feeling of death in a Delhi drawing room: the world shut out because of the heat; the ritual of conversation, with nothing to say at the center of the ritual; conversation faltering until everyone was overcome by communal stupor as if contemplating an eternal cosmic egg of nothingness.

Desperate to unearth a topic upon which they might recover the momentum of a social occasion, Sunny asked, "How old is this building?"

"Three years old."

"When will they finish it?"

"It's finished. Only some of the flats have not been set up," the father said. "There was a dispute about the allotment."

"It doesn't look finished," Sunny observed and received a warning flash from Satya.

Their daughter said, "Many Indians settled abroad have bought apartments in this complex. Above us there is an airline pilot for Lufthansa, and across is a woman who was married to a man in Poland. He was fatally ill, and through willpower, he starved himself to death. When he died, she returned to Delhi; they planned it this way."

"Oh?" Sunny became interested, but the father said: "Don't bring up such depressing subjects!"

"We," said Sunny—returning to the subject of this housing estate, saying "we" as a concession so as not to present himself as a condescending outsider—"are putting up these high-rises, and there is already a water shortage and the desert is encroaching. What is the city plan for the future?"

"The government will have to take care," said the father airily.

"But do they have a plan?"

Again the warning flash from Satya.

They turned to Sunny. "Your father was working for which company? What is your last name?" Trying to pin him: caste, class, money, value. "Where do you stay?"

"Panchsheel Park," said Sunny unwillingly.

"You must come from an illustrious family. The people who live there are the most wealthy in the city."

Satya felt a twinge.

"Illustriousness does not equal wealth," said Sunny.

"One does not acquire wealth by chance."

"Corruption," said Sunny, trying to downgrade himself, help Satya thereby.

"No, no. No-no-no-no," the father said soothingly.

Sunny said, "I'm afraid so," and took another sip of sugarcane juice, the glass now in a puddle of condensation that dripped embarrassingly onto his pants when he lifted it to his lips.

Another glowering from Satya, but Sunny continued. "My grandfather on my father's side was corrupt. He was a government minister and acquired at least half a dozen properties, which is why we live in Panchsheel Park."

Manjula said, her eyes brightening, "Your accent is not Indian, but it is also not American. It sounds more British." It was as if she was exhilarated by what Sunny had confessed.

Luckily at this moment, her grandfather, dressed in a pajama kurta, was brought out in a wheelchair by the maid. Sunny could tell straightaway that the old man was an eccentric. To the side was a urine catheter bag covered with a small, brown towel that fell off and had to be repositioned, not that the old man cared. He cleared his throat, stroked his brush mustache, and said, "You are residing in New York City?"

"He is in New York City."

"He is in Rochester."

"There is one place between America and Canada, it is called the Niagara Falls—do you know it? That place is famous."

"Yes, Uncle," said Satya politely.

"You see, one of the longest rivers is in that country."

"Yes, Uncle."

"Which is it?"

"Mississippi, Uncle."

"Correct."

"Do you know which one is the biggest canyon?"

"Grand Canyon," said Sunny.

"One and all make that mistake. The largest canyon in America, that is the continent of America, is Copper Canyon."

"He knows all—*all*—of geography," said his daughter-in-law.

"Geography is my hobby," he said.

"Also Manjula knows. Why don't you let your granddaughter tell something?"

"What is New York like?" Manjula asked.

"She is excited," her mother said. "Rochester she doesn't know yet, but everybody is familiar with New York City."

For a while there was no conversation. The kitchen door opened, and fourteen dishes proceeded in a stately manner. Sunny remembered that in summertime it was always a conundrum whether to turn on the fan and feel pleasantly cool eating unpleasantly cooling food or turn off the fan and be unpleasantly hot eating pleasantly hot food. While in Babita's home, they preferred the former experience; here they had decided upon the latter. They turned the fan so low it barely paddled and loudly buzzed. They put two eggs surrounded by spiced potato, crumbed and fried—their specialty—on Satya's plate and then fished the most tender morsel of mutton and allotted it the thickest portion of mutton gravy that had sunk beneath the layer of orange oil. They topped the mutton and the gravy with the orange oil, which flooded the crumbed eggs.

When Satya contrasted this with his lonely takeout in Rochester, it made his eyes mist to think anyone should hold him in such regard. Across the table, Sunny's eyes said: *You're being tricked by orange oil? It's what they give all the prospective sons-in-law.*

Satya's eyes said: *So what? It shows a habit of caring.*

Sunny's silent response said: *Caring or oppression?* He was drenched in perspiration.

"You are a poor eater," the mother said to Sunny. "As you grow older, you will need more weight." She lifted a spoon. "Here, take—"

"No! I'll be sick," shouted Sunny, covering his plate, and then they were offended.

"Your friend has a ready temper," said the grandfather.

After lunch, they were shown a room, one of the three bedrooms in this flat, that was being utilized as a storeroom in preparation for their daughter's marriage. "These days, of course, there is no such thing as dowry, but it is our pride to make sure our daughter will be well-settled."

They caught sight of a blender, an electric tandoor oven, a washing machine, winter blankets, an air conditioner, an electric heater. The father showed them a lamp that switched on just by a touch to the shade, a Japanese rice cooker, even a stuffed tiger that roared—red light spinning from its eyes. Sunny wanted to take a photograph, but he restrained himself.

"You know, one gentleman, his name was Woodrow Wilson? Do you know his invention?" the grandfather called out as they left.

In the lift, Satya said, "She was intelligent."

"Let's dissect that," said Sunny when they were in the car again, the seats so hot they could barely sit. The driver had been unable to find a shady spot to park. "In the end, she said only obvious things."

"I didn't say anything interesting, either."

"True. She at least mentioned the Polish man who was starving himself to death. Unfortunately her father stopped that conversation."

Satya felt Sunny's disdain as a comment upon himself. After his initial good impression, he hadn't liked Manjula, either, not after the excitement she expressed regarding New York City over Rochester. But he wanted Sunny to say something pleasant about her so he might switch to liking her again and not feeling resentment toward Sunny.

Next they visited another unfamiliar neighborhood, a gated community that advertised London townhouses, twenty-four-hour security, a central clubhouse, a gym, and a meditation center that had been inaugurated by a famous gurudev. The home of this prospective bride had a marble driveway and a koi pond with water lilies guarded by a drooly mastiff whose back had been broken by a fall when he was a puppy. The mastiff dragged himself about on his knees, booming at the guests with a bark of thunder.

"What will you drink? Whiskey, wine, beer?"

Satya didn't drink alcohol, but Sunny accepted a Kingfisher with gratefulness. With a drink he became a more generous person with a sense of humor. He talked to the mastiff: "What a magnificent creature you are, aren't you?"

"He's of the same breed once owned by Julius Caesar," said the gentleman of the manor.

How had Satya's mother found such a family? She had, in fact, made the connection through a successful uncle who had described his nephew as a brilliant American surgeon. "Beautiful dog," said Satya, but this house was intimidating to him, and he was terrified of dogs, which he knew was a sign of somebody who would be identified as non-Westernized. People who did not love dogs, thought dogs were dirty—the way he had been brought up to think—were not urbane.

The father of the prospective bride was dressed in a green Lacoste T-shirt, and after a sip of single malt, he said to the two young men, "My firm keeps pressing me to relocate to the United States, but I reply, 'I am king of my domain here; why would I choose to be a second-class citizen somewhere else?' We have a full-time domestic staff of five, two cars, two drivers. My children went to the best schools, they play tennis and swim at the club. We holiday in Phuket, in London, in Vienna, in Cape Town."

Payal, the girl they were here to meet, wore jeans and a pink Lacoste T-shirt. Her hair was in a pert, hennaed ponytail. Diamond chips glinted in her ears. When a servant brought out a plate, she indicated him toward the guests, saying, "Have some chikki!" The servant bent toward Sunny, mistaking him for the prospective bridegroom.

There were chicken nuggets on the plate, each with a toothpick with which to dip the nugget into a small bowl of honey mustard.

"Tell me one thing: Why do they make the sandwiches so big in America?" asked Payal's father. "You can't fit them inside your mouth—half the filling falls to the ground, creates a bloody mess, and goes to waste."

"I'm an absolute foodie," said Payal.

The mastiff was dragged off by the servant when he tried to slobber up the chicken nuggets.

"What is your favorite food?" asked Satya, relieved to see the dog go.

"I like steak," she said. "Grills and steak."

"You don't like Indian food?"

"No." She giggled with pouty cuteness.

"She's like her father," said the mother. "I like my simple dal-sabzi, but Payal and her father cannot eat a meal without meat. Sausages, lamb chops, pork chops, steak, mixed grills, hamburgers, barbecue."

Payal obviously regarded Satya in the same way she regarded dal-sabzi; she eyed Sunny.

"Where do you live?"

"New York."

"It's my favorite city. We went there in . . . when was it, Mummy? Four years ago? We went to Sloan Kettering and stayed at the Windsor Plaza Hotel, where two Bollywood stars with cancer in their family were also staying. My grandmother had pancreatic cancer."

And then Satya didn't hear anything for a while. He felt such venomous hatred of Sunny, such a feeling of being excluded from the conversation, that he went dizzy. Yet again Sunny had been identified as a more desirable match because his manner-clothes-address-accent fit the profile of a particular Delhi elite.

Sunny felt Satya's withdrawal. He said, "Well, New York was once beautiful, you can see it in the old movies, but it is no longer. And if you are poor in New York City, you don't stand a chance."

"I like you," said the father. "You are speaking the truth, which nobody does. It's a Third World city. We saw packs of rats running in front of the hospital and stinking piles of garbage on the pavement. We saw a man defecating on the subway platform. The blacks are more debased than the Indian poor—I'm not saying they are more poor, you understand, I'm saying they are more debased by society. If you are a journalist, why don't you write about *this*?"

He had established Sunny as a worthy adversary and was challenging him to win his daughter by overcoming the barriers of American failure. In fact, the confidence of this family was intimidating even to Sunny. They were simultaneously more nationalistically Indian and more American in their tastes. They seemed not to suffer a tinge of self-doubt. Sunny needed to complain about New York to give himself confidence in New Delhi. Would he ever admit he'd powered the initial success of his American life on complaining about India or that whatever confidence he had—staked on Ulla, his Brooklyn apartment, his lack of Indian friends—was rooted in his shame?

As he complained about New York and as they agreed with him and grew even ruder, he felt a sting.

"New York City is a shithole city!" Payal's father triumphantly demonstrated his skill in American lingo.

*

BAHADUR SPED HOME BECAUSE they were far later than the dinner
hour by which Babita had expected them. They dropped off Satya, and
when they returned to Panchsheel, Sunny lifted the half-moon iron
latch of the gate, noticing the light from his uncles' windows falling
upon the foliage of the gulmohar trees, which meant Uncle Rana was
home totting his debts and Uncle Ravi was watching Hitchcock or
Fellini. He wished he could visit them. That morning, Uncle Rana had
happened to be at his door when Sunny walked by. He waved. "Come
over?" Sunny bravely waved back and shook his head. Uncle Ravi
popped out as well. "Imprisoned by Mother?" he called.

"Sunny Sanyal"—Babita came to the door in her white cheesecloth
nightie—"is that you at last? Whatever happened?" She poured him a
Cointreau, and Sunny spread his bare toes to the fan's tickle and said, "I
feel as if everyone in this city has gone mad."

"They have," said Babita. "Money flooded in, and now this is a city
of people who can no longer tell their front side from their backside."

The lamplight cast from a tussar silk lampshade over a celadon pottery base made an intimate tableau. On the walls were a series of Daniell lithographs: the ruins of Mandu, the ramparts of the Rohtasgarh
fort looking to a pale blue and beige river. Sunny took a sip of the re-
storative liqueur.

The two girls came to say good night with a half bow–namaste
as they had been taught. "Good night, Aunty. Good night, Sunny
Bhaiya."

"Is the kitchen scrubbed clean?"

"Everything is clean."

"Are the air conditioners on?"

"They are on."

Babita said, "I knew you would be exhausted, so I told them to cool
down the bedrooms."

The girls were aware, as Babita was aware, that they were performing for Sunny—she was showing him she was teaching them and up-
lifting the poor; they were showing that they were learning. Earlier

they had questioned him: "What are the buildings like in America? Do they have buses like us? Do they have shops like us?"

They left—giggling only a little now, the greater hilarity having passed—to climb the outside spiral staircase to their rooftop quarters. Sunny noticed that when Punita turned, she stepped forth like a deer.

"How old is Punita?"

"Thirteen."

After a while Babita and Sunny, too, said good night to each other and retired to their cooled rooms. The girls had switched on Sunny's lamp, turned down his bedsheet, and placed a water glass and an old lemon squash bottle filled with filtered water on coasters imprinted with botanical illustrations of Dutch tulips, a souvenir from Babita's last trip to Europe. Sunny sat up in bed to record in his diary the conversations of the day. Keeping a diary was conducive to a habit of meticulous observation necessary to a career in journalism—or one forgot the details that might illuminate the whole. Could he be like García Márquez, whose work teased the border between literature and journalism? Or like Kapuściński, the great Polish reporter out of Africa? Yet Sunny knew that it was inevitable that Kapuściński would be labeled a racist, as was the fate of Forster, Orwell, and Conrad. Were writers who embodied and illuminated their times eventually condemned by the more enlightened future they themselves helped bring into being?

When the phone rang, Babita picked it up—there was a phone in almost every room in the house, including the bathrooms, and the house had three phone lines in case one or two went dead. She opened the bedroom door, called to Sunny to pick up the connection in his room. She listened.

Satya blurted: "Sunny, it is better you don't go with me."

"What do you mean?"

"I will never find a wife. You dominate the conversation, and you keep on showing off about New York and Panchsheel Park. Instead of being my friend, you are acting like my enemy."

Now Sunny was hurt. After buying a plane ticket. After being knocked out by jet lag, summer heat, and orange oil.

"I can't help it if they keep asking about New York! I told them it was a horrible city. I told them my family was corrupt."

"In a way that means the opposite. You're constantly looking down on everyone," Satya continued. "Your Hindi is terrible; people laugh to hear it. You can't even eat with your hands. It is as if you are ashamed of being Indian. You've become a joke of an American desi."

He hung up before Sunny could respond.

When in the morning Sunny confessed, "Satya told me to stop looking for a wife with him," Babita said, "Good idea. He may one day blame you and say he married the wrong person."

After a bit she said, "It's more important that you see your grandparents. Why don't we visit Nana and Nani in Allahabad?"

Sunny felt himself ease into the comfort of his mother's taking charge; nothing but family worked in India, one may as well not try to escape this fact. But before they left, during his mother's siesta hour, Sunny slipped out and walked to the Panchsheel market at the end of the street to telephone Ulla from a phone booth. He had told her, "Don't call the house; there isn't any privacy. I'll telephone you when I can." It was risky because it would be the middle of the night for Ulla. Were they a loving couple, this wouldn't have mattered—she would sleepily murmur words of longing; the conversation might have an erotic charge—but she did not pick up.

CHAPTER

26

....

SUNNY PUT A FEW CLOTHES AND *THE HOUND OF THE Baskervilles* into a small duffel bag in accordance with his childhood habit of reading Sherlock Holmes on the train to Allahabad. He thought among the best reasons to emigrate was to pack one's own bag and carry it oneself, to have no servants, to clean one's own house. Gandhi had managed to eject the British from India but had failed in his exhortations to get Indians to scour their own toilets and thereby fathom the basic meaning of human rights. Following the repercussions of this lack of understanding of human rights in a logical manner, Sunny thought it explained why Indians would never make good readers of novels: a reader of novels comprehends the notion of individual rights by the simple act of identifying with a person's—any person's—trials and joys. When you considered another person's feelings, another person's dignity, you actually wished to scrub your own toilet. A good novel reader was a toilet cleaner, and so Indians didn't wish to be readers of novels as this would undo caste hierarchies and divides that made their world go around properly.

He wondered if this philosophizing made good sense and if the publishing world would be interested in it as an explanation for the dismal sales of fiction on the subcontinent.

Babita was not a reader of novels, she had never once in her entire life cleaned her own toilet, and she always traveled with a monstrous pile of luggage packed by her staff. Dressed in a caftan for the overnight trip, she directed a swarm of panting porters. Part of what Sunny had brought from New York was being conveyed to his grandparents. They wouldn't like the malodorous Gorgonzola or canned mussels, but they would appreciate the hazelnut milk chocolate, the mild Gouda. Then they always looked forward to Pigpo sausages from the Pigpo pork store in Jor Bagh.

There had been only one space available in a first-class compartment for four, and so Sunny had been appointed to a curtained berth in a lesser carriage. As they drew out of the city smog, he smelled such putrefaction, saw such sights—a shadow puppet of a dead cow in a pool of sewage and shadow-puppet people living in the sewage—as would suggest to him that it would be inappropriate to read Sherlock Holmes. But he opened *The Hound of the Baskervilles* and remembered the saving disconnect of his childhood: this succumbing to pleasure, this understanding oneself to be a figure of fun meanwhile.

Gradually the view switched to extended stretches of farmland and countryside. When he looked up from his book to the more peaceful scene, he reflected on Satya. It didn't matter if Satya agreed with Sunny about Payal and Manjula—a friend never wants you to give them bad news.

He thought Satya had been right about his Hindi. It was so wobbly, he was embarrassed. Yet when he was a child, he had been proud of his bad Hindi, of being so Westernized that he couldn't speak his own language. His thoughts also turned to the news story he'd hoped to find. You can't report on your country if you can't speak your own language. He took out his notebook. Was he keeping notes because he'd transformed into a man who planned to make use of his birth country toward the purpose of being successful in America?

Sunny fell asleep, and when he woke at dawn to a whoosh and a clatter, he inched the curtain open on its wire and saw some chapatis and crows flying forward in a gale, then the same chapatis and crows wheeling backward. He got out of his berth and walked up and down the stalled train feeling elated—it was going to rain and rain so hard it would sluice away his irritations. He passed some students returning to the university; members of an international youth choir playing Snap!; two curmudgeonly judges arguing over Enron's investment in Maharashtra; and three Jehovah's Witnesses with razzle-dazzle smiles and

Hindi-English-Hindi dictionaries. They tried to cultivate him straightaway. "We've come to India for atma seva."

"You're going to serve souls?"

"Exactly."

"With what?"

"Love."

"But we are suffering a surfeit of love in India! We need less love!" The other side of love was guilt and curtailment. "Without love we'd be free to progress."

Further along he passed a compartment full of mustachioed men with rifles.

"Why are those men traveling with guns?"

Whisper. "Shhh, they are protecting their boss."

"Who is their boss?"

"A liquor baron from Rajasthan."

He passed a young woman sitting cross-legged staring at the rain. By her side was a book. Because Sunny couldn't abide passing a book whose title he could not read, he walked by again and saw she had a face planed like a leopard, long lips, and watchful eyes, hair in a single oiled braid, but he still couldn't see the title. So he passed by again. And one more time before he detected it: *Snow Country* by Kawabata.

Sunny wanted to be a journalist who would follow the fortunes of the Enron energy company as they progressed. He wanted to know the life of a liquor baron. Maybe he also wanted to follow the case of the young woman reading a Japanese novelist.

Eventually he ran into his mother. "The trouble with this train," she said, "is that you inevitably meet someone from your past whom you don't want to see."

"Who did you meet?" asked Sunny.

She said, "This irritating Allahabad neighbor's son. And at dawn in your nightie, it is positively gruesome."

They arrived at the station by late evening. "Ghambir Bhai, you're looking very smart," said Babita to her parents' driver, who had been waiting for them the whole day. "What a fancy shirt you have on!"

"Yes," he said, nodding, "it is the Lawyer Sahib's shirt. Now that he's dead, his daughter gave everything away. The tailor altered it—the sleeves were too wide."

"Shah Sahib died?" asked Babita. "Are you sure? I met his son on the train, and he never mentioned it."

"This morning they emptied the house." The driver's glasses were Scotch-taped all around.

If Sunny had not been thinking whether someone with cracked glasses could see well enough to drive—they narrowly avoided hitting a bicyclist—and how someone so wizened had vanity enough to alter sleeves too wide, he would have seen the devilish idea arrive upon his mother's face. It flickered only a moment, and it had vanished by the time Babita responded: "Very foolish. They shouldn't give up the house. People make the most serious mistakes immediately after a death."

"They have no choice. The lawyer's daughter spent her whole life there, but now she is being forced to leave." Fate was playing out in a way that was terrible, predictable, correct, and satisfying to itself.

Babita thought of her own father's foolishness—like his friend the lawyer, he had failed to buy a bungalow when the prices were low. *Ratty, don't die. If you don't die—just don't die!—I will love you—after all!*

They found Sunny's grandmother fussing over their cook, who was frying fish cutlets. "I'm making extra for the Shah family—the cook can take them over before we eat."

Babita said, "I'll walk the cutlets over. I need fresh air after being cooped up, and I should offer my condolences."

Moving swiftly after the cutlets had been drained on newspaper and packed into a tiffin carrier, she set off and left Sunny with his nana-nani, who had been delighted by the way he had inadvertently shouted "Hi!" when he jumped out of the car. They examined him for further Americanisms and questioned him about any American habits they should be aware of. Would he insist upon cornflakes for breakfast? Had he become allergic to everything? They knew of someone who had studied in the States and had returned allergic to dust.

When soon after the electricity failed, a major breakdown, even the streetlamps, Sunny's grandmother sent him with a torch to meet his mother and light her way home. He traversed the murky back lane that had been used only by servants until the highway traffic past the front gates made it common for the owners and tenants of these bungalows to use as well. Perspiring a little, he enjoyed the wild scent of the scratchy lantana brushing against him and the sweet fragrance of rice cooking, the lantern light and candlelight shimmying in windows. He arrived at Number 10 Cadell Road, circled to enter at the front gate and climbed up the portico stairs. But there was nobody on the veranda. He saw a book lying on a vacated chair, picked it up, and shone his torchlight upon it. His eyebrows rose and dove like gulls—it was the same book he had seen on the train. A runny purple stamp on the title page read *Hobson Jobson Second Hand Books, Mussoorie 1961*. The pages were thick, slightly ribbed, the edges like shale. It contained a reproduction of a woodcut of travelers on a train mired in snow. An eye reflected in the window—or was it floating in the hills?

Many Thoughts Came
from My Heart

"WHY DIDN'T YOU PUT HIM ON ICE?" PAPA WAS STARTLED to learn that Dadaji had been cremated two mornings ago. "How could you proceed without me?"

Mina Foi assumed the theater of speaking to someone far away on the telephone. "Huh? What?" she bellowed. "They told us we could not wait. Amal Kaka was here."

Ever since Dadaji's brother, Amal Kaka, had usurped the ancestral property, he'd treated the family he had betrayed as the enemy. After you've cheated someone, you have no option but to turn that person into an ogre so as to justify your own misdeeds. Had he rushed the ceremony and taken Papa's role in the rituals to incinerate his guilt once and for all? To establish his innocence by exposing his nephew's absence for everyone to condemn? Strangely, Dadaji, a lawyer specializing in property disputes, had never pursued a legal case against his brother.

"*I'm dismantling the household now!*" yelled Mina Foi as if she were already as deaf as Ba, as if to tell them she would be unable to hear their reply.

"Hold on," said Papa. "Just hold on. We have tickets for the night express."

Sonia and Papa pushed past the station platform crowds, stepped over the many people who lay asleep—bundled head to toe in sheets like corpses—and found their compartment piled high with the trussed trunks of a whiskered couple who were being settled in for the journey by their son. "Please look after my parents, Uncle," he said to Papa.

Sonia felt the twinge she saw upon her father's face: This man still had his parents, while Papa had now lost both Dadaji and Ba. The whistle shrilled, and the son touched his parents' feet, accepted their blessings, and left. The train began to clop to a tabla beat; the red-jacketed, white-dhotied, brass-badged, turbaned porters hopped off nimbly. The elderly woman lay down and covered her face with her sari, but the old man continued to ogle Sonia and Papa. He believed you were best served by not distinguishing between friendliness and aggression when you encountered strangers.

"From?"

"Delhi," Papa answered.

He pointed at Sonia.

"My daughter."

A panicked look began to overtake Sonia's eyes. She knew what was coming. They were a family betrayed by the first questions.

"Married?" he barked.

Papa jumped up and began to test the various light switches in the compartment.

"Not married!" The old man focused on Sonia with horror. "Wife? Where is your wife?" He turned to Papa for reassurance.

"Don't tell your mother to come to Allahabad," Papa had warned Sonia. "Don't bother her."

Sonia didn't say she had already asked Mama: "Aren't you coming to the funeral?"

Guilt is like yeast. Mama's guilt festered and ballooned. She had risen at dawn when the mist swam low and the clawed, twisted shapes of the mossy, bunioned trees showed through the vapor, as did the silhouette of Babayaga awaiting the sun and the milkman from the village of milkmen. She packed her case and silently accompanied Sonia down the mountain in the taxi, as if she were angry at Sonia, which she unfairly was. She sat absolutely rigid. When they reached Dehradun, Mama got out of the taxi. Her fingers scrabbled at her throat as if politely loosening a noose. "Sonia, I am worried that Moolchand will move into the house and sleep in the beds to claim squatter's rights, or that Babayaga may be lifted by a leopard if there is nobody to make sure she is in at night."

"People will expect you."

"He was eighty-eight," she said. "Monsters live long lives."

"Everyone will talk. You could leave for a few days."

"The way he treated Mina Foi!"

She had taken another taxi back up to the forest that was always on her side. To leave a marriage, a community that upholds a marriage, she would have to be like a ruthless warrior or she'd be sucked back. It had taken such resolve to get this far.

*

PAPA FLED FROM THE old man's questions to change into his pajamas, remembering the example of Dadaji, who had always emerged tip-top in fastidious night attire striped navy and white—as if ready for a bedchamber at the Ritz of London, the Strand of Rangoon, the Raffles of Singapore. He conjured this change in the closet latrine that didn't even offer a handle to hold yourself steady over the toilet hole through which you saw the void blurring and racing below. He would forever now be accompanied by his parents' deaths, for this was the inevitable middle point of life, when all that was vivid would gradually be situated in the past, the present becoming more unsubstantial, ghosts more real than reality. He felt fear rather than grief, or else grief was not distinguishable from fear. He let his breath out in a heaving exhalation. He recalled that he must try to control his emotions before his daughter, for when you are a father, you have to reassure your child when her grandfather dies. You have to demonstrate that life goes on, you have to pretend death is an ordinary event, so she in turn will manage one day to overcome your own death.

Papa remembered his father had taken all matters as if they were ordinary events. He had slumbered soundly through wars, the partition of the nation, communal riots. He never suffered a doubt, never longed, it appeared, for paths not taken. It wasn't religion that made him serene—he'd relinquished religion with his secular education. Was it then his military determination to take a day for a day, never considering past or future? Was it hubris or modesty? Or simply that Dadaji had never embarked on even elementary questioning because never had he asked for so much as a spoon with the call remaining unanswered. How had he managed to make the journey from the certainties of his life into the formless infinite? One of the most vital lessons a parent could give a child—how to leave life—was never imparted. Like the mystic's path, Papa reflected, once the journey had been completed, it was rendered indescribable.

For a moment Papa felt resentful of this father who had jettisoned faith. Without religion one would always ache with not knowing. On his trip to the cement bag factory, Papa had learned that there was an insurmountable difference between himself and his boss on these matters, because despite his wealth, the industrialist believed in the sensible frugality of sharing hotel rooms. Thus, at Hotel Cinderella, Papa had discovered his boss's suitcase opened to a portable altar at which he prayed each morning, rising before the sun to take a vigorous bath, loudly blowing his nose and clearing his throat. Then he began ting-a-linging a bell and extending the vowels of his prayers from the base of his belly as if from a prehistoric cave. At nightfall, moved by the intimacy of brushing their teeth together and settling into beds side by side, Papa, age fifty, had asked his boss, age eighty-one: "Tell me, can't your god excuse you when you are traveling? Why does he demand so much attention?"

"Is this a matter of a joke?" said Mr. Gupta sharply. "When you are traveling, should you leave your heart and soul behind?"

Perhaps there was a direct connection between the gods in the suitcase and the fact that his boss never was tormented when business ventures failed. He knew he and Papa were performing their assigned roles according to a celestial plan that might unfold well after they themselves were gone.

Dadaji may have died, but he hadn't vanished; he had simply changed form. He came through every unoccupied chink in Papa's mind, even more present now that he did not reside within his own body. He accompanied Papa, dictating: *Maintain your standards!* Papa returned to the compartment to brush his teeth in the washbasin by the window with a bottle of water, and he was glad to find their fellow traveler had decided to retire from the shock of journeying with an unmarried girl beyond a certain age and a husband without a wife. He was lying on his back with his eyes closed and his mouth open.

Sonia in the upper berth was awake thinking that the erosion had begun; there was nobody between Papa and the abyss any longer, although luckily for him, he had Sonia to anchor him. One day there would be nobody between Sonia and the vastness. She was unprepared for the simple reason she hadn't found a trustworthy love. Once more she remembered Ilan. He was no longer exactly himself. Like Dadaji, he was taking another form, her memories becoming chiseled and polished by repetition, distilling him into a man with the creative talents of a devil, or the devil himself. The devil knows how to seduce you, trick you, blackmail you. She remembered *Mother Swimming, the Lake Remembers*. Sonia had wanted that shuffling of life and dream, even if a shadow were instilled upon the water.

They proceeded, worming slowly along the tracks between Delhi and Allahabad, the train almost as asleep as the passengers inside, when a gale came gusting over and shocked it still. From the lower bunk, Papa inched the grubby curtain back on its wire, and Sonia saw the silhouette of his inquiring nose.

"Where are we?" she murmured so as not to wake their fellow travelers who continued to slumber opposite, grisly groans and haunted sighs adding to the storm outside.

He looked into the wilderness of wind and rain walloping the sides of what now felt little more substantial than a tin box. Papa could see no light, no habitation. "The middle of nowhere."

He left the compartment and restlessly paced the corridor in his pajamas. As he paced, a short, plump woman in a Mughal poppy-print caftan and gym shoes, her hair brushed up like a bulbul's crest, approached him from the other end of the corridor. He recognized her as Babita Bhatia, the widowed daughter of Dadaji's chess partner, the Allahabad Colonel, and he tried to compose his expression into that of a person too immured within himself to notice anyone. But she stopped. "Manav! It is you, is it? Almost couldn't tell—haven't seen you in so long. What a coincidence. On your way home?"

"Yes."

"Where have you been all these years? Still traipsing around the world?"

Papa's pride got the better of his distress.

"I'm planning a trip to Kyoto," he said.

"My last trip abroad was to Stockholm—my, what a jewel of a place. I felt I was entering a fairy tale."

Travel stories made a person competitive, even about the places he had already also seen, let alone the ones he hadn't.

"I almost went, but decided on Greece instead," said Papa.

"Greece?" she scoffed. "Dour lot. No fun in them since B.C. The only time they become jolly is when they get drunk and throw the plates about. There's nothing to see but a heap of stones."

"It's not a place to go unprepared. You have to learn the history, and you have to have an imagination."

"You might as well imagine at home without coughing up a fortune. I climbed up a hill to an archaeological site, and when I got to the crest, I found a goat on a broken wall, and on the other side were two Pakistanis who said, 'We thought it was a tourist place, but there is nothing!'

"Can you imagine, all that distance, all that money, for an Indian, two Pakistanis, and a broken wall with a burping animal? And then that dry 'kabob!' I kept begging, 'I need a sauce, I need a sauce, or it just doesn't go down.' Thousands of years of civilization and that's all they've managed—crude hunks of meat, dry bread, raw vegetables coarsely chopped."

The train still wasn't moving, but others were getting up and hefting open their doors for air, and bearers with sleep-blunt expressions were bringing thermos flasks wheezing milky beige tea from their tops. The three Jehovah's Witnesses had teamed up with the international youth choir, and they were singing "Glory-glory-glory-glory-glory!" Their travel companion opened his eyes: "*Mother? Mother?*" he began, picking up from the night before. "*Wife? Wife?*" He put two and two together: The poor girl's mother was dead, and therefore she couldn't marry, but had to give up her own life to look after her father. "We don't know what God will give us," he began to cluck, waking up properly at the thought of someone's misfortune. Sonia climbed down from the upper berth and sat reading by the window. She felt a tingle and put the book down. The central mystery of *Snow Country* was never revealed yet expressed in every aspect, uniting the narrative while also tearing it apart.

Outside, the rain was blowing together into different shapes; it made eels, it made paisley. Someone walked past. A little while later he walked by again, craning to see what Sonia was reading. The rain blossomed up. The boy came by again. Sonia sympathized with anyone who craned to look at book titles, so she angled the book. As she did, she noticed the person who walked by had the haughty nose and handsome bearing of an eagle or a nawab, wore a shirt with a tiny pattern like that of a shell's tracks.

Papa came back, saw an interloper gawking at his daughter, and shut the compartment door: "Nosy parker!"

Several times the storm circled as if chasing its tail, before it walked into the distance, still growling, and the train began to move. It was evening by the time they reached the sodden bungalow on Cadell Road.

....

THE HOUSE APPEARED DESERTED, THE PORTLY GENTLEMAN over the entrance with his nose in the air more deluded than ever. "Mina? Mina Foi?" Sonia and Papa opened the long, thin, prayerful doors—and walked smack into Dadaji. He was wearing the quizzical expression he always adopted just as he was about to triumph with the answer to the question he himself had earlier posed. *What is the world's smallest nation?*

Don't know? Come on! Can't guess? He waited. *One . . . two . . . three . . . the Vatican, of course!*

It took a moment for them to adjust to the fact that it was not him but a garlanded photograph hung prominently on the wall following the custom after death. Each creature shows something by its eyes— the elephant, the toucan—and Dadaji's eyes said the joke was on them.

"Papa, the whole house is empty." Sonia drew attention to the fact that the rooms were stark below the fans that dangled from the far ceiling. Only the shadows of objects remained, shadows that had lived so long, they were perhaps more substantial than the aged objects had been in the end.

"Mina?" Papa bellowed for his sister.

"Mina Foi?" Sonia called to her aunt.

"Here." Her voice came crossly from the next room, and reclining in coffin pose—hands crossed over her chest, her feet together, neat and tidy in the bed in which her mother and, three days ago, her father had died—was Mina Foi.

"Mina Foi, what happened?"

She poked her nose through the mosquito netting with the stains spreading like urine across it and regarded them fiercely through her black, square frames. "Daddy died, and when I protested about the cremation—'What about Manav, we have to wait for him'—they insisted, 'You cannot wait to cremate according to Hindu law.' It was done in a very shabby way, no grace to the occasion. The pandit was in trousers. He said he had just returned from another appointment and didn't have time to put on a dhoti. The body was not even properly burned—there were hunks of bone in the ashes."

"The dead are unaware." Papa tried to comfort Mina Foi, sitting at the edge of the bed. A father cremated without his son? It was unheard of except in times of plague.

"When I said to Amal Kaka, 'Let's go back and have some tea,' I thought he would stay for a bit and help, but he said, 'Well, Manav is coming, and he can do his part now,' and he rushed out of the house as fast as he could. The ashes are in the Godrej cupboard along with Daddy's papers."

"Where is the furniture?" Papa asked.

"Oh," she said, kicking her feet about dismissively from under her nightie with its pattern of roses now faded into ghost roses. "I have to leave the house. So they came and carted it away."

"Did the landlady threaten you?"

"She came the minute she heard Daddy died."

Mrs. Luna Pant had tripped up the veranda steps so hastily she left a slipper behind. Mina Foi, uncertain as to how to behave, had proceeded methodically. When the cook cleared away the teapot, eager for Mina Foi to step out and meet her fate, because her fate would be his fate and he wanted to know it—the suspense was too great—Mina Foi called for the teapot's return. She called for the return of the milk and sugar. She scraped the smear of mixed fruit jam left on the plate in vertical stripes and then horizontally until every tiny scarlet check was gone. She stuck out her tongue and wiped the jam knife upon it. She moistened her finger to collect the crumbs.

When there was nothing left on her plate, not even the merest sheen, and nothing in her cup but the bracken of the last dregs, Mina Foi emerged.

"I came as fast as I could, Mina. No matter how old one is when one's parents die, one feels orphaned," Mrs. Pant said. "As you know, we lost a fortune renting to your father, it ruined us, but we never evacuated this property, we never threatened you with goons. We have acted against our best interests—life and fortune have passed us by."

Mina Foi didn't say life and fortune had passed her by as well.

"Now we have a responsibility to our daughter, who is unmarried because we can't provide her with a decent dowry."

Mina Foi didn't say a dowry was not decent. She didn't say that she was also unmarried. She buttoned and unbuttoned the top button of her nightie.

"We old people shouldn't stand in the way of the happiness of the young," said Mrs. Pant.

Mina Foi didn't bother to ask why the happiness of the young should be allowed to prevent the happiness of the old.

"I am certain your father must have made arrangements for you, but take your time packing," Mrs. Pant assured her and went down the stairs to collect her slipper. "We can hold off a day or two."

*

WHILE PAPA AND SONIA were making their way to Allahabad on the overnight train, Mina Foi had woken to the doorbell chiming and a flurry of indigo drops blowing through the insect netting on the windows. She turned on her lamp, which she had loved since she was a little girl—it resembled an upturned translucent soup dish painted with pink flowers—and she knew the train from Delhi would be late. She opened the door, peppery breeze blooming under her nightie, and saw that a drenched crowd had amassed, lit by storm light against the trees shifting as if underwater. She saw the ironing man, the washerman, the electrician, the plumber, the padre, and Dari the secretary, who had put on his only suit, which came from the death of his uncle, who had received it from the death of his employer. She saw the servants hastening from the servants' barracks. Nobody in the main house knew how many generations lived there or even who was who: the nephew of the maid's son-in-law, the many widows with nowhere to go, the descendants of the landlady's servants, the servants' tenants, a servant's servant.

When Mina Foi invited them in, their slippers made putty-colored tracks across the red, polished floors. She led the men to her father's belongings and felt her heart somersault with pity for the pile that remained—items no longer upheld by the powerful character of their owner.

Meek at first, the men tried the clothes on for size. They took the seven pairs of dim but fastidiously ironed underwear. They distributed seven sad, dovish handkerchiefs; five work shirts and two holiday shirts; five pairs of cotton trousers and two of wool gabardine. They regarded, with pious regret, Dadaji's magnificent black coat from London, purchased on his round-the-world tour. Tried on his shoes with formal, disciple-like respect. Fell silent before the enduring weave of three suits made by the Hong Kong tailors of Calcutta. Lamented his navy striped pajamas and his pashmina. Held vigil for his ties, his college badges, his school medals, his lawyer's robes and swallow-tail neckbands, his copy of the Indian constitution. They took the medicine bottles in case they might suffer similar illnesses in the future and the last of the Old Spice shaving cream. The padre's eyes filled with tears at the modesty of the comb with a few teeth missing, the elemental razor, the worn toothbrush. All of us, even the domineering, are human beings. The shaving brush with its bristles still in the direction of its last lathering seemed to be making a humble plea for Dadaji.

Mina Foi had locked Dadaji's ashes into the steel, ark-like Godrej cupboard before—in a crescendo of leave-taking—the mourners removed the rusted cooler, pocketed the screwdriver and tweezers, and rushed the beds through the trees. "I've never slept in a bed," said the cook's wife. She had forgotten to look sad. Neighbors came to watch in case there was something for them as well; their talk strayed to ordinary matters, dengue fever, the water supply. They carried away the dolls in a glass case, dressed in the native costumes of different countries; the stamp album; the binoculars through which Papa and Mina Foi had hoped to see a leopard in Dalhousie but had caught only the intimacies of monkeys; the slide projector through which you could view slides in tawny light of Dadaji and Ba at Machu Picchu and Trafalgar Square; of Mina Foi performing a Bharatanatyam dance pose in bell-bottoms, before she'd been labeled terminally unlucky.

"Take everything," Mina Foi urged, learning that once you began to let go of belongings, it was excruciating to keep a few to highlight the loss. But when they came to the kitchen, Khansama sprang into action and stopped the rapacity. Wielding a broom so filthy nobody wished to be swatted by it, he drove the mob from his beloved margarine tin and his laboring fridge, warm enough for cockroaches to flourish. "The cockroaches haven't left as yet."

Last of all, after the crowd had been dispersed, came the ragpickers, whose community relayed news of death from one end of town to another and had a honed instinct of when precisely to swoop for the detritus.

"So they came, so they came, too," Mina Foi said, recounting the scene, "smelling like ripe potatoes."

They had hauled away the rusted pipes, the broken panes of glass. A mentally disabled child was made to carry the defunct hot-water geyser on his head. Mina Foi was shaken by how fast, how cruelly, an empire falls. Within a few hours all she had considered insurmountable was dismantled, rubbished, looted, gone.

The very same evening, a rat appeared in her bedroom, the first rat they had ever seen inside the house. When she looked at it, it raised its chin to look back at her, and she knew that even the rats of Allahabad had heard the news of Dadaji's death and that its boldness heralded her weakened status. She was now a woman without a father, a husband, a child, a home, a profession. She was nearly fifty-eight years old.

"You must ask for the beds back!" said Papa, going to the liquor cabinet. "Where will we sleep?"

"There is this bed. Daddy and Mummy died in it. That is why nobody would take it."

"There are three of us."

"Sonia can share with me."

"Where do I sleep?" His fingers seized upon a shadow. "Mina!"

"The padre took the bottles."

"That's a sin!"

"Not at all. He is not forbidden to drink. To be drunk is another matter."

Mina Foi was sweet on the church because the church reminded her of her true love, Ernest. While the padre had not dared invite Mina Foi to Bible study in case vigilante mobs accused him of converting Hindus, he always invited her to the annual charity gala, whereupon she had learned that men in church are taught to open a door for a lady to go first, pull a chair out for a lady to sit, insist ladies stand first in the buffet line. The opposite of Hindu and Muslim men, who strode in first, sat down first, ate first, all the tenderest, all the oiliest, all the crunchiest, all the sweetest.

And at this moment, as if in response to Papa's anger, the electricity failed. Although she was reluctant to hurt the padre's feelings, Mina Foi went to the kitchen to collect a candle and to tell the cook to retrieve the whiskey. When she approached, mincing carefully in the dark, she heard a secretive murmur in a voice of treacle. She flattened herself against the wall, her eye by a chink to look into the kitchen where a knob of candle burned on a tin-can lid and illuminated the walls and fan furred thick with smoky grease and grime. "So Mina must leave?" a woman cheeped. "Oh, very sad. Then what will you do? You must be worried, after all these years, so much service to the family—and they didn't leave you anything? No pension, no bonus, no post office account?"

Stunned, Mina Foi continued to listen.

"Well, you know the way we regard you in my house, Khansama," the voice wended on. "We are practically family, we have been neighbors so long. . . ."

Through the crack, Mina Foi could see that the cook's single brown tooth protruded. Then a flicker of wariness crossed his expression and the tooth retreated, but then the flicker passed, he and his tooth again succumbing to the glisten of being courted.

"Khansama, you know how you are famous all over Allahabad, you're the finest cook in town. My son dreams of your kakori and galawati all the way in America."

And then the voice lowered further. A funeral was a time when a person might nab a household servant with a lifetime of training and a treasure trove of recipes. Mina Foi had neglected to remember during the exodus of objects from their home that their staff, too, might be plucked and rushed away—

Mina Foi stepped forth—

And the woman turned around.

"Babita Bhatia!"

The cook realized that what had happened to him all his life was happening to him again—just as he reached out, fate snatched the promise away.

Mina Foi said to Babita, "What nonsense is this? You try to steal our cook the minute Daddy dies?"

"Whoever steals a cook! Would I so carelessly jeopardize our family friendship? You are unhinged by your father's passing."

"Why did you enter from the back door, then?"

"To deliver cutlets without disturbing you."

Papa came calling down the corridor: "And inform Khansama he must bring back a bed— Oh!" His face fell seeing Babita Bhatia.

"Very remiss of you not to tell me on the train, Manav," the visitor exclaimed. "There I was nattering on about Greece—"

"She is trying to steal Khansama," accused Mina Foi.

Sonia made her way to the raised voices. "My daughter," Papa introduced Sonia.

"I didn't see you on the train." Babita tried to smile, but her smile flipped. "You're the one who studied . . . where was it?"

"Vermont," said Sonia.

"Are you here on holiday?"

"No, I've returned to India."

"Why would you give up such an opportunity?"

"Without people one is nothing," said Mina Foi. "It's lonely over there—it doesn't stop snowing."

Carrying each a candle on a sticky tin-can lid, they exited to the veranda. Mina Foi dropped her candle. "We have another intruder!"

Said the shape in the dark: "I'm only Sunny Bhatia. Here to escort my mother home."

"*Sunny? Now why did you come?*"

"Nana-Nani sent me with a torch."

"Well, then, we must hurry back."

"Tell the Colonel that your mummy came to steal Khansama right after Daddy's death," interjected Mina Foi.

"How can one steal a human being?" said Babita. She turned to Sunny. "Mr. Shah's family is in mourning; we must leave them to rest."

Sunny suspected the owner of *Snow Country* was somewhere in this house. He walked reluctantly to the gate; he turned and said, "May I ask for a glass of water. I have a prickle in my throat."

"Wait until we get home."

Sunny purported to cough, and just then—oh wondrous life!—another candle proceeded from the dark of the house. The air was still; the flame stood reverent. It lit only the candle-bearer's magnificent lips of downturned reproach.

"I saw you reading this book on the train," he managed.

"In fact, I cannot read it." The voice that came from those disembodied lips was clear and mellifluous. "I keep trying to but I cannot because I love it too much. I pick it up and drop it, pick it up and drop it."

Sonia put the candle down on the veranda table and her lips vanished.

"This is Sonia. She returned from America because it's lonely," said Babita.

"It wasn't simply loneliness," said Sonia, understanding that this woman she did not know wanted to embarrass her. "It was all the things I'd have to do alone."

"Why would you have to do anything alone?" asked Babita.

"It's the premise of being American: You are an individual, therefore you are alone. Therefore you must be able to do everything by yourself. Rent a car at an airport, drive yourself cross-country to a job in a place you've never heard of, defeat your enemies, trap a rat, make money to pay bills to look after yourself even when you are dying—"

There was a tremble in the hand Sunny gave to Sonia and a tremble in the hand Sonia gave to Sunny. Beyond them evening drowned in the whistles, caws, the shehnai and sarangi of birds and traffic horns, the roar that rises in any metropolis when millions are making their way home. Each hoped their own trembling was disguised by the tremble of the other, by the reverberation of the world at the hour of dusk.

Babita and Sunny strove homeward, as if swimming a breaststroke in a pond of hot spinach, and after a long while, Khansama came clanking up the driveway of Number 10 Cadell Road, tilted unnaturally by a heavy bag of bottles regretfully returned by the padre.

"We should send you packing, lousy fellow; overnight you've shown your true character!" said Mina Foi, gaining strength now that she had staked her claim upon Khansama. "Since Daddy passed, no loyalty to the family." Humiliated, ill-treated, with only one tooth he may be, but he was still their priceless possession, a walking treasure trove of recipes from the lineage of the Kayasths and from the Lucknow begums.

Papa said, "It isn't his fault. It's that sly woman. By all reports, she ran her husband into the grave. Quiet chap. They called him Ratty."

"Was he ratty?"

"Ratan was an elegant man. He once turned in his own wife for stealing cheese at the French embassy. He telephoned the ambassador's residence and said, 'I am honor bound to tell you that at the reception for the French-Iranian string quartet last Saturday, my wife, Babita Bhatia, filched a round of Camembert. She wrapped it in a napkin and put it in her evening bag.'"

"He ratted on his thieving wife!"

"First the cheese, now the cook."

They sat out on the veranda in the Allahabad dark of no electricity. They picked the cutlets of their enemy up with their fingers, dipped them into ketchup, and relaxed into the lovely, careless feeling that sometimes comes after a death, of a picnic among the ruins. Papa tried to telephone the electricity department to find out how bad the breakdown was, and they said, "We are also sitting in darkness!" He tried again and found they'd taken the phone off the hook.

Sonia bathed by candlelight, standing upon the softly rotting patri, pouring feverish water from the bucket over herself, missing the owl that had once watched from the tree outside, and thinking both about Ilan telling her that a Japanese writer had proposed shadowy bathrooms were a conduit to the past, and about the boy she had seen on the train and met on the veranda with a nose like a nawab and eyebrows that dove hither and thither. He had an old-fashioned nose—why did a grand nose seem old-fashioned?

When Mina Foi had bathed as well, aunt and niece climbed side by side into the bed in which Ba and Dadaji had died. Mina Foi, neat and tidy within the shallow grave fashioned by Dadaji's body into the mattress, said to Sonia, who was shifting about her grandmother's bird indentation: "What a lucky miss you had, Sonia. Imagine if you had Babita as your mother-in-law!"

"My mother-in-law?" said Sonia, soothed by the sweet coconut smell of her aunt's hair oil.

"Don't you remember, you goose, when you were crying in Vermont?"

"Yes?"

"*That* is the boy they planned for you to marry." Mina Foi began to snore.

"Too hot to sleep?" Babita asked when Sunny stepped out to join her on the Colonel's veranda past the midnight hour. It was no cooler, but there was more stuffy air to breathe. She was pacing, wishing she hadn't mentioned Stockholm to Sonia's papa because her memory persisted in retaining the silliest of everything, dredging up the scene of her arrival at Stockholm airport when she'd been over-taken by crowds of women in burkas rushing to the passport check for citizens. She had felt outraged on behalf of Sweden! And she recalled breakfast at her hotel, how she had despaired when a Middle Eastern family settled at the adjoining table, five daughters in headscarves, a mother in top-to-toe black, even her mouth covered by a flap she had to lift to eat. Babita did not want them there because without them she considered everything perfect.

She had unfolded the *International Herald Tribune* and searched for the Associated Press byline, felt proud of Sunny when she spotted it. After all, he was employed by the Associated Press, if only to edit. Per-haps it was more elegant to be an editor, anyway; a journalist meant venturing into soiled, dangerous streets. Babita tried to align her ac-cent to British when she asked for tea but was almost offended by her own dark hand—like a monkey's paw—when she lifted her cup. Even though she was moved by the bounty of smoked salmon and salamis, she ate restrainedly because the Middle Eastern family was eating unre-strainedly, jubilantly fetching sugared buns, pancakes, chicken sau-sages. They had the certitude of religious people who never felt ashamed no matter the number of children they produced. She could not admit, meanwhile, that she shared their mania of harassing servants at every given moment. The family asked for little spoons to stir their tea, then a small plate to put the used little spoons on; they asked for hot water, they asked for hotter water. Babita complained the scrambled eggs were stiff; she asked for toast, then fresher toast, then fluffier eggs. The hotel staff did everything they could to accommodate their exacting guests, to demonstrate they were not racist, so as to not be accused of being racist.

Babita had stepped out into air so clear it purified her vision. She was at her most elegant in starched raw silk of taupe with a mulberry trim and discreet amethyst earrings. She stopped at a kiosk for a map and noticed an Indian at the counter.

"From?"

"Bihar." With a slow, insolent smile and a slow, disdainful handing over of the city map she was purchasing, he indicated he was aware there was a battle between her type and his type. He wiped his nose with the palm of his hand and slithered his hand dry on the side of the counter. While she may have won every skirmish, he had won the war by residing here in a virtually unpopulated country where problems could be tackled, which was why the natives believed you could make human connection with anyone, a mother from Tunisia, a kiosk owner from India.

How naïve, Babita was thinking when an African migrant approached her abruptly from the shadows. She jumped, he chuckled, came threateningly close as she tried to scurry by, said something rude in a language she did not recognize. These encounters with an Arab family, a fellow Indian, an African refugee had marred Babita's delight in learning that the royal family was in residence. You could tell that they were, the guidebook read, when the flag was flying. The flag was flying, the king and queen were perhaps glancing out of a window admiring Babita's elegant sari, and she had been irritatingly thinking about the kiosk operator from Bihar.

Babita paused. Why on earth was she here upon an Allahabad night unearthing silly memories? *Ratty, don't die. The bad time will pass, just like a season changing. I can love you—after all.*

The blocked answer came popping forth: No, it wasn't the heat or the delayed journey; it wasn't being derailed in her plot to steal Khan-sama; it wasn't Manav goading her with his upcoming trip to Kyoto; it wasn't meeting brown and black people in Sweden; it wasn't the run of sweat like a squiggly beetle down her back; it wasn't the mosquito in-side her ear. What she was trying to evade and what had filled her with dread was the unacceptable change in her son's expression she had caught by fleeting candlelight when Sonia walked out upon the ve-randa.

"But, Mummy," said Sunny, who appeared now as if summoned by her fears, "surely you were not trying to steal the lawyer's cook?"

"How can you think that of your mother? The cook was out of his mind with anxiety—what is he going to do now that the family is leaving? People never consider the staff."

"Why did you go to the back door?"

"Well," she said, "perhaps I was embarrassed about your saying no to their daughter."

"To *whom* did I say no?"

"To that girl! Don't you remember? Her grandfather sent us a letter elaborating her faults. He was right; she has a screw loose. If she loves a book so much that she cannot read it, then she has not read it, and if she has not read it, how can she love it?"

"What happened to her, then?"

"You can see what happened. She'll be one of those spinsters stay-ing on in their parents' home until the parents die, then carrying on alone with the domestics—Delhi is full of girls like that now. Can't unearth a husband with all of their education and up-to-date ideas." She deftly changed the subject. "I wonder if Satya found a wife."

*

SUNNY HAD WOKEN UNDER the high wing of the roof of his grand-father's house and thought that Ulla was exactly one of the astonishing Americans Sonia had spoken about—who myriad times in her young life had hopped into an unfamiliar rental car, twiddled knobs, tuned in to the Blue Sky Boys or Sir Douglas Quintet, demonstrated her skill at shelling sunflower seeds with her teeth to spit out the husks as she drove, venturing to where she knew not a soul. She might, on a whim, make a turn to another state, settle in New Orleans or Glacier National Park. Stop at a Dunkin' Donuts, strike up a conversation to find out where she might get a waitressing job.

Should something go wrong with Ulla's car or with the unfolding of events, she could regain her poise with a dirty mouth so impressive fate might think twice trying anything on her again. Ulla cussed like a grizzled cowboy on a cattle farm, as far as Sunny could tell. "Goddamn prick! Asshole! Shit! Fuck! Goddamn fucking piece of shit. Crap!" She bent her head, swore, circled, and kicked. She was proud of this ability, emphasizing it before Sunny, who could not yet authentically swear, no matter Ulla's efforts to teach him on their better days together.

"Midwestern women," Sunny had told Satya, awed, "have the dirtiest mouths."

"Punjabi women also have dirty mouths," Satya had said.

He missed Satya. Had Satya found a wife?

Babita and Sunny didn't need to wonder long. Later that very morning, Satya phoned the Colonel's house and Sunny was summoned to the phone. Satya said in a formal tone, "Dear brother, I have found the girl I am destined to marry."

"After accusing me, you're calling me?"

"Who else would I tell? It was a mistake to meet those Delhi girls. You were right all along—I don't want a big-city girl!"

How strange it was that Sunny should feel what he felt—and he couldn't easily define it—in his teeth. It was a combination of curiosity, disappointment, joy, suspicion, sadness, pity, envy.

Satya had been brave. He had been adventurous. Satya's life was becoming a true story.

....

SONIA STAYED HOME BECAUSE PAPA DID NOT WISH HIS
daughter to witness the immersion of Dadaji's ashes at the sangam
where the Ganga, the Jamuna, and the mythical Saraswati Rivers meet.
He was glad she wasn't there to see the irreligious sight of swamis and
boatmen clamoring for more money, more money—who, in the midst
of the ritual, had held his father's ashes ransom, nipping, "Daan, daan,"
in the name of this and that. When Papa stopped paying, they wrapped
up the prayers so swiftly, he felt he'd dishonored his deceased father at
the moment he held him in his hands for the last time. Dadaji might
not cross the river from this world to eternity for the lack of a few
rupees.

Papa and Mina Foi were still shaken the next morning when Dadaji's secretary, Dari, arrived to help tackle the remaining accounts contained in the locked Godrej almirah. Each time Dari and Papa added
and subtracted the infinity of numbers—attempting to make sense of
Dadaji's papers that abounded with fake and faded signatures in their
names and in the names of relatives they had never heard of—the numbers came out differently but never to an amount that would be sufficient to support Mina Foi. They blamed the tricky solar calculator and
summoned the Ambassador, its rotundity washed as lovingly as a buffalo before it was driven around to the front portico for them to venture forth to the several banks in which Dadaji held accounts. They
followed their inquiry through dingy rooms and corridors in which
scowling clerks worked at desks dwarfed under mountainous stacks of
fraying documents. Their job was to make information impossible to
retrieve. They demanded signatures, which they deemed never matched

originals; they said their photographs didn't match their faces; they insisted upon notarized copies of death notices, affidavits on one-rupee, fifteen-rupee, or fifty-rupee stamped paper. Papa and Dari traveled on to cubbyhole notaries—a man and a typewriter under a sign hammered to a tree—or a man asleep under the stairs. Finally they came to a clean Formica desk behind which sat a calm, elephantine presence: The man who occupied it was a pandit as well as an accountant; his hair was shaved save for a single strand, and he wore an orange lungi and kurta and a prayer mala. Behind him a cove of gods was being venerated with incense and mini winking electric lights. He shut his Bhagavad Gita, which lay alongside financial documents; folded his hands on top of the cover that showed Krishna and Arjuna on the battlefield; and announced in a measured voice that Dadaji had no money other than a pension, which would now be discontinued.

"Mina," Papa said, breaking the news, "all there is, is a sum so piddling it won't keep you in petticoats for a year, let alone in mutton and shampoo, or whiskey for when the padre comes calling."

Far from the honest and thrifty man they thought they'd known, Dadaji had been an incurable two-rupee, three-rupee gambler. With the air of staid work, with the respectable veneer of a lawyer, he had squandered his retirement investing in wild schemes, hole-in-the-wall companies, many long shuttered, leaving behind hundreds of thousands of useless shares. Dadaji the lawyer specializing in property matters had never bought property. Dadaji the scrupulous gentleman had assured them there was a registered will. There was no will because there was nothing to bequeath. Yet whenever Papa had asked Dadaji, "Have you provided for Mina?" he had scoffed, "She'll live like a queen."

Mina Foi picked up the paper that recorded the amount of her predicted monthly income.

"Fifty thousand a month," she said. "That's more than plenty."

"There is a dot there."

"So?"

"The zeros come after the dot."

"What are they for, then?"

"Don't you know?" Papa was staggered. "To show nothing."

"Why is there something to show nothing!"

She became dizzy, ran to bed, retired in her customary coffin pose, hands crossed over her chest, her feet together, neat and tidy. It had been Mina Foi's role to look after her parents in their old age, but hadn't they looked after her in turn? Was she not a beloved daughter taken in after a divorce and given a new sari and toothbrush once a year, a rose-flowered nightgown, vitamins, hair oil, and Zenith toilet paper, mutton several nights a week, a patrimony of jewels in the bank safe? A daughter who had the security of knowing each day would be exactly the same as the day before, ending with the same *chk-chking* tribe of lizards watching her from her father's roof, her beloved pink lamp casting its strawberry glow upon her?

You yourself feel like a cheat when you discover your father has cheated you. The whole world becomes a lie.

Dari came to the door with an undone expression. He couldn't see the catastrophe even when it was laid before him. There had been an eternal quality to their lives in the manner of the traffic flowing by the gate. Why couldn't things continue as they always had? "My job was to follow my instructions."

"Thank you, Dari, for all you have done for our family."

He had hoped for a retirement bonus, he had hoped there was a secret pension account. Was he not a respected secretary who had worked a lifetime for a high-court advocate? He felt he embodied a lie. He had lied to his family and community in turn, making them believe he was a valuable employee.

"Beautiful, old-time Muslim manners," whispered Mina Foi faintly when for the last time Dari rode his bicycle upright through the gate and salaamed.

*

THE AMBASSADOR'S CURVES WERE polished again, and Sonia, Mina, and Papa drove to the family safe in the bank that was guarded by the glaring clerk and the thin-as-a-bean security guard, who was holding a rifle so antique it was doubtful he or his weapon might hinder a robbery—but maybe his mustache was fierce enough. Papa and

Mina Foi held each side of the shaky metal ladder and sent Sonia clambering to the locker in the topmost row. They transported the faded boxes and plastic bags to Ba's jeweler, Gopaldas Chandraprakash & Sons. The great-grandson of the original Gopaldas Chandraprakash emptied the contents onto trays lined with velvet and sorted through the cloudy rubies, pearls, and emeralds as if sorting rice for weevils. He examined a pile of cutlery. He lifted a knife—and said, sharp as a knife: "But this is not silver!"

Mina Foi drew herself up straight. "It is German silver from Daddy and Mummy's round-the-world tour."

"German silver is not silver."

"What is it, then?"

Papa said, "Another German lie?"

Germans were considered rational and law-abiding, yet they had perpetuated the Holocaust. His wife was honest and upright but had betrayed him. The silver was masquerading as one thing, it was another. There were connections to be made here. His father-in-law's cloud paintings were nothing but obfuscation.

"The value is not in the gemstones," said the young man. "The value is in keeping them within the family. If you sell, the small sum you receive will quickly be spent on the electricity bill, the grocery bill. If you don't sell, the family heritage value will grow in accordance with time."

Papa looked at Mina Foi's worried face. He remembered Ba's pride in her jewelry; every night she banked her peace on knowing her gemstones, save for the Burmese ruby, were snuggled in the safe-deposit box, ready to protect her should anything go wrong. Like Dadaji, she, too, had remained stable through wars, the Partition, communal riots. Now they felt her distraught presence in the room. Ba's ghost did not know what to think with her most private self having been transported through town and examined.

Papa could not go through with his plan. "It's Sonia's patrimony," he said grandly. "The monetary value is of no importance."

"You should take the knives and forks back to your house with you. No point keeping them in the bank."

But they bundled it all back to indicate what they thought of the jeweler's judgment upon their inheritance and therefore upon them.

"What is this lunch?" they shouted at Khansama—to take it all out on him—when they returned.

"Chinese noodles. Why?" he answered rudely back.

"Taste and see! Needs more soya sauce, needs more carrots, needs more French beans! Overnight you've squandered your talent." He'd used the occasion of death to become lazy. He'd been sad toward the purpose of using his sadness to become slothful.

Was Khansama not the treasured khansama of a grand household that would continue to employ his family generation after generation? Had he staked his dignity on a fake contract? Were the kebabs he made not the kebabs belonging to a culture that extended from past nobility into the future? Had he become a fraud? It was no wonder he could no longer cook. His food had told him so before he knew himself.

"A cook needs a strong master," opined Mina Foi. "He doesn't have respect for me, so he has stopped being careful in his food preparation."

When servants were held to harsh standards, it made them fearful; simultaneously, in contradiction, they felt safe, as if someone was watching over them, so Mina Foi's thinking went. And when they didn't feel safe, watched, and simultaneously held to fearful standards, they could not perform their duties.

"Oh, Mina Foi," said Sonia, "it's like saying God is also the devil!" She thought of Ilan and how she had assumed she was being looked after while she was, in fact, being betrayed.

"Maybe we should let Khansama retire after all?" Khansama heard them say. "But then again, better the devil you know than the devil you don't."

*

IN THE MIDDLE OF the night, Mina Foi and Sonia found themselves on the floor, ejected from the bed by an invisible force.

"Did you kick me?" gasped Sonia.

"No," said Mina Foi. "It is Daddy's spirit."

There was a feeling in the sheets of an emotion straining mightily against them.

Mina Foi had never articulated her feelings about Dadaji, even to herself. She had stifled her resentments. As a child, she had banged the saltshaker in frustration: "The salt is damp!"

As a teenager, she had shaken the curtains in unhappiness: "A cockroach!"

As a young woman, she had whisked Dadaji's leg: "*A mosquito!*"

"*Your! Very! Existence! Depends! On! My! Unhappiness!*" she had said when she was forty.

When she was fifty, Mina bent her head and closed her eyes, but before she could pray, her prayer prayed itself: *May my father die, so wish I.*

She was guilty. Christianity, the religion she hankered after, was about forgiveness. She could *not* forgive—*May my father die, so wish I!*—so she would not be forgiven in turn. She would be banished from her home—where would she go? Every morning Mina Foi washed her own knickers and dried them on the washing line between her window and the tree upon which the spotted owlet had once lived. By the time she finished taking dictation from Dadaji, her underpants were dry and ready for ironing. How could she move to a place where such modest habits would become unattainable luxuries?

"We live in a small flat in Delhi, Mina," her brother had told her abruptly. She understood that her brother was telling her he could not take her to Delhi to live with Sonia and himself in Hauz Khas. He loved his sister, but he loved her in Allahabad. She was not the beloved sister of a successful brother because he had discovered he was not the successful son of a successful lawyer brought up never to tolerate falsehood.

Conned by his own father, not the man he thought he was, Papa paced outside all night. Bitten by the vicious zebra-striped mosquitoes that bred in the bathroom slime, lumps formed upon his forehead, his arms—even his elbows, toes, and ears cauliflowered. Would he now have to support his sister the rest of her life? As well as Sonia, who showed no sign of gaining independence? Two cooks, two drivers, two maids, two gardeners, two washermen, two ironing men, three bottles of shampoo, three visits to the dentist, three helpings of pudding . . . Mercifully he no longer supported his wife and so not *four* helpings of pudding, *four* Sunday shampoos.

He heard a woman's raised voice. Then a man's. Then another woman's. The voices escalated. He heard a scream. He walked over. "What is going on here?"

"A lorry driver has fallen in love with Ayah's daughter—he sits outside her door and cries all night, so she is shouting at him to go because he is spoiling her business."

"What business?"

"Sex business."

"Sex business?"

"Ayah's daughter's husband left her, so she entertains the lorry drivers to make a living. They stay here to rest under the fan. They bring the McDowell's whiskey, but we make kebabs for them."

"You make kebabs for the lorry drivers?"

The man laughed in Papa's face. He no longer had to show the family deference.

"Isn't she quite old, Ayah's daughter?" asked Papa.

"Some of the younger men prefer to have sex with aunties. It comforts them."

"What if I call the police now that you have told me this?"

"When they feel like it, the police come for free sex."

Mina Foi came out, and by the light of passing lorries, Papa asked, "Mina Foi, do you even know what is happening behind the house?"

"What?"

"Who are all those people?"

"The servants. They've multiplied like rabbits."

"Don't you hear the shouting?"

"There is always shouting."

"Don't you see the trucks parked along the road?"

"Ah yes, they are always there at night. Daddy tried to call the police but to no effect."

*

PAPA DECIDED NOT TO investigate her innocence further, but began to consider it may be wise for Mina Foi to leave. Perhaps after enough time in one place things turned to rot and it was necessary to begin afresh.

It was the padre's brilliant idea: At the Jesus and Mary Convent School for girls, the Mother Superior was seeking a dormitory matron. Mina Foi had an impeccable background when it came to table manners and etiquette, orderly habits, hygiene. She may not wish to work, it was unsavory perhaps for a woman of her background—

But—

But—

It was respectable for everyone to work these days, and it wasn't only that times had changed, it was sensible for even a lady to be occupied beyond a bit of knickknack dusting, if she took that over from the maid who was always breaking things.

Just outside the door, listening, was the cook. "Oi, Khansama," Papa and Mina Foi called, catching sight of him. They thought when Mina Foi took the job at the convent Khansama might bicycle over to the matron's quarters to cook for her so she might not be deprived of the food of her childhood.

Sonia said, "At his age? What if a new tenant evicts him? And what if this property is sold, and built into flats?"

"Maybe he had better discuss employment with that Bhatia woman after all," said Papa.

Mina Foi said, "Let me try things out for a month, and then we'll make a decision about Khansama. I may need him."

They drove Mina Foi to the convent after one of the Ambassador's last polishings, for it would soon be sold. Mina Foi held on to her purse tightly and looked down. In her valise were her knickers and her nightie, her good birthday saris. In another bag was her pink lamp saved from the raving mob. The padre patted her on the arm. "Better to be in the company of other ladies."

Sonia rushed, "You can leave, Mina Foi, if you don't like it."

Leave and go where?

"Welcome." A nun from Tamil Nadu in a blue dress and veil came out to meet them and took Mina Foi inside. She would be living amongst people whose habits and customs were unfamiliar, who came from a different class from herself.

Papa thought of his wife, who had said, "Your mind and your heart, Manav, are a mess and a muddle." He was a good man; he was acting like a bad man.

Padre said, "I will check on her, not to worry."

Sonia said, "Why couldn't she have come to Delhi?" Although she knew she didn't want to share her Delhi bedroom with her aunt. She, too, loved Mina Foi in Allahabad and not in Delhi. Still less would she have loved her aunt in New York City.

None of them knew in that aching moment of watching Mina Foi's woebegone face as they drove away that this was to be the happiest time in her life. A convent, like a good kitchen, ran on a combination of fear, guilt, and, in contradiction, feeling safe; the terrifying Mother Superior also looks after you. While at first Mina Foi was ashamed to be employed, she quickly discovered the security of belonging to a religion that upheld the elemental fight between God and devil so intensely that neither could live without the other.

Outside her matron's quarters was a hibiscus bush, and on this bush, Mina Foi might discreetly dry her knickers. Each night after prayers, lights out strictly by nine P.M., she might pace up and down making sure her charges were tucked into bed, broadcasting to them dire warnings of men who were wolves in disguise: "You're too young to know, but I'm telling you so you beware," thus ensuring they would one day swerve straight to the wolves.

Why? Because a fairy tale compels, that's why. You love the beauty, but secretly you also love the darkness.

....

SUNNY AND HIS GRANDFATHER THE COLONEL HAD AN argument about Kashmir at teatime. Sunny said that if Kashmiris didn't wish to be part of India, they had the right to break away; there was a basic flaw in how they had been included in the union of states. On the contrary, said the Colonel, it was the right of every Indian to live in Kashmir, if they so wished—Kashmir shouldn't have special rules—and then it wouldn't be a Muslim-majority state and would become properly part of India.

Sunny said, "What, you want that beautiful place to become a filthy, overcrowded mess like the rest of the country?" And then he realized he'd gone and criticized India, which he had no right to do as someone who lived in the United States.

"Don't argue with your grandfather," warned Babita.

"He fought in Kashmir," said Sunny's grandmother. "What was he fighting for? Your disrespect?"

You can't force people to love you, thought Sunny. *If somebody doesn't love you, it's the higher calling to let them go.* He said he felt like a jog—"Good, blow off your steam," said Babita—and, donning shorts and sneakers, looking like a cartoon "Amreekan," which made everyone chuckle and restored the peace somewhat, he set out. He jogged one way down the back lane. Then he turned around and jogged the other way. He arrived at the house on Cadell Road. Then he jogged away again, but before he knew it, he'd arrived back. He told himself to keep jogging on through the scritchy-scratchy wild lantana bushes, but he stopped and smoothed down his hair.

He walked from the back of the house to the front and saw soapsuds washing to the outside drain in a sparkling heap of rainbow bubbles that quietly pop-popped. Someone was bathing inside. He found Papa on the veranda sipping the Royal Salute Scotch that the padre had been pressured to return. Sunny told himself he should retreat before he was seen, or if he was seen, to pretend he'd made a gaffe and was immediately leaving. But instead, drawn by a mystery he didn't want to name, he walked up the veranda steps.

Papa was feeling melancholy thinking that his father had never found an occasion worthy enough of opening this special whiskey, yet he was also experiencing the relief of learning his sister had been returned to the bliss of her convent school days. He picked ice cubes with his fingers—wishing he had kept the German-silver ice tongs that had been restored in the moment of pique to the bank locker—and was plopping the cubes into his glass when he saw Sunny entering the gate in puffy sneakers.

Sunny said, bowing, "I want to apologize for my mother."

Papa looked up out of the top of his bifocals. "Apologize for what about your mother?"

"I told her she is absolutely not to steal your cook."

"Khansama is a free man." An ice cube adhered to Papa's finger, and he kept his finger in the whiskey until it disengaged. He was thinking they must release Khansama. He was also thinking it would be unbearable for Babita of all people to win the prize of Khansama's cooking. He was thinking, *Manav, you are a mess and a muddle.*

"It wasn't right to come secretly through the back door and lure him immediately after the funeral," said Sunny.

"Look," said Papa, examining the young man—why did they make such fat sneakers in America; they would trip you up—and he held up the little volume encased in a carapace of caramel leather that Mama had given him on his birthday, once part of a library owned by a family who had left for Lahore at the time of Partition.

He scrutinized Sunny's face. "What do you read in America? T. S. Eliot?"

Sunny recited: "*Let us go then, you and I / When the evening is spread out against the sky—*"

"Rubbish!" said Papa, revealing to Sunny that this had been a trap. "*Do I dare to eat a peach?* What nonsense is that? Listen instead to this: *It was also evening dhuan dhuan / Husn bhi tha udaas udaas / The smoke of dusk, the sad beauty— / Husn bhi tha udaas udaas / Many stories, recollected, came to linger in my heart.*"

Papa recited, half reading, half translating. He made his fingers, hand, and arm turn from a flower into an ocean wave into sky.

"You see, your own experience locks onto these verses, not like Western poets where you are shut out—the lines are so damn specific, they are important only for the poet himself. Here, within these words, you begin to think of your own lost love, your own far home, your own father's death."

Papa's wife's leaving lay within the loss of his father, which lay within the impending loss of this landscape. Departure and transformation were inevitable. Fleetingness was an essential component of beauty.

He felt the pain of remorse. He was stealing Mama's sensibility. He put the book away and looked out onto the traffic trawling cabbages and cement, bricks and wheat, goats and—

He remembered the lorries parked by the side of the road. He poured Sunny a whiskey and proffered the bowl of peanuts.

Sunny took a handful of peanuts, sat there, and waited—and his waiting segued into the mood of the poem. Was he waiting for the girl with the leopard face who might emerge once again from the shadows? His bent pose and silent mulling encouraged Papa and endeared Sunny to him. "You know," he said, shifting his feet around in his slippery Kolhapuris, "my life's work has been in business firms that invest in the future—in microwaves, in Hindi computer word processing, in cement and cement sacks—but midway through life, I've discovered that it's only by the past that a man can be profoundly moved."

He took a sip. On the other hand, he reflected, to lecture the young made him optimistic and sentimental about the future. Oh, the contradiction. "The minute you say one thing, the damn trouble is that the opposite becomes manifestly true. That is why I can tell you right now, don't waste your time—go straight to the mystics."

An aberrant ice cube harboring a bubble of air began to squeal in the glass and spin around like a dervish. The sky turned pink, and a sickle moon rose above the traffic.

Sunny looked at his watch and realized his mother and Nana-Nani would be wondering how Sunny could be jogging so long, no matter how furious he and his grandfather were with each other. He leapt up with a hasty farewell, vaulted strangely over a bush, and did not know that Sonia had seen him from the window while she was bathing and had continued to watch from another window. She had not read Dada-ji's marriage proposal on her behalf, but how humiliating it was to think she had agreed to an arranged introduction, as if she was unable to find a man on her own. Which she wasn't able to do, of course, not a man who wouldn't destroy her. What excuse did she have in the United States, where all things were possible? She might have shed the shackles of family, nation, centuries.

When she emerged, her wet hair spread upon a towel across her shoulders, Papa said, "That Sunny Bhatia was here. Nice chap, but he's not a Hindustani. He's a foreigner."

Sonia saw, by the side of Sunny's glass, peanuts laid out in a circular pattern of a snail's shell. She remembered what Marie had told her, that she knew Cole was in love with her when he flipped a pancake before her nose and then jumped over the garbage can. His ebullience had been thus expressed.

"Why did he come?"

"To apologize for his mother trying to steal Khansama. But now Khansama *does* need a new job. But how to pass him on to that horrible woman?"

The next evening the boy returned at the same hour. Papa understood he'd made an impression. He continued, "Sunny, you know when I was growing up in Allahabad, as in Lucknow and Delhi, you'd see these legendary poets out and about before they departed for Pakistan. If you appreciated their verse, they took to you, and if you could trade verse for verse, you were accepted into their circle, king or pauper, they didn't care.

"Yet I didn't know how to appreciate them. I couldn't join in. I didn't have the necessary culture.

"You understand, Sunny, I'd been brought up in British-style boarding schools since I was four years old—yes, I was sent to Miss Oliphant's at age four. While touring for my work, I realized I didn't know my own nation. I couldn't properly read, write, or even speak Hindustani. I said to myself, 'I am not going to die without knowing my country, my language, and learning who I am.' All of us Indians who are educated to be Westernized are fated to make the same journey. If we have any intelligence or any heart, we have to search for ourselves backward. This was true of Gandhi, it was true of Nehru, it is true of me, and it will be true of your generation. You may think it a fine thing to be in America, and when you're young, making your way, there's enough reason to be anywhere in the world—but eventually you begin to wonder who you should have become instead of the person that you are."

Papa ignored what he'd thought while he was surveying the cement bag factory, which was how he wished he had gotten the hell out of India when he was still a young man with an open path.

He called for the whiskey, called for the kebabs. "Sunny, here, have a kakori with your drink—it may be our last kakori."

Sunny took a bite. Oh! He understood why his mother wanted to steal the Allahabad cook! Sonia's cook! So he didn't want his mother to steal her cook? Ah, the contradiction. But where was Sonia? Again, she was nowhere to be seen.

"You see, Sunny, exile and love both undo your sense of self," said Papa. "Look at Rumi. His banishment from Balkh and his infatuation with Shams of Tabriz, these are what shook Rumi and were at the heart of his spiritual quest."

Papa raised his Royal Salute: "The mystics. Don't bother with the other stuff, Sunny." Papa might have learned from his wife's books, but it was Papa's discovery that these poets were relevant to modernity. They had something to say about rootlessness, migration, the loss of love and country. He recited Khusrau: "*The river of love runs in strange directions. The one who loves, drowns—the one who drowns, gets across.*"

The tide was sweeping Sunny away when he happened to look up at the moon over the highway. Again he ran down the steps with barely a goodbye and into the scritchy-scratchy lantana in the back lane.

Upon the last day of Sonia and Papa's stay in Allahabad, Sunny managed to get away earlier and found Sonia on the veranda by herself. She half jumped up to retreat into the house. Sunny almost succumbed to trepidation and turned back. But he continued to climb the steps, and Sonia sat back down—it would be impolite and absurd to hide away. Again she thought of the marriage proposal Dadaji had sent Sunny's grandfather. She had told Ilan that she might have married the grandson of the Allahabad Colonel, and Ilan had laughed so hard he'd kicked up his legs and paddled his feet.

It was easier not to look at Sonia. Sunny moved the cane chair around so he and Sonia were facing the same view of the orchard and the highway beyond. He was conscious of the fact that he had turned her down once upon a time. He had shouted at his mother: "*You think it's harmless, but it is harmful!*" Ulla had said, "*They don't realize it is disrespectful to me because they don't know I exist!*" Maybe his response had been conveyed to Sonia; maybe news of Ulla had reached Sonia as well. Now his mother had tried to steal Khansama. Sunny's expression came across as preoccupied, even unfriendly. The fact that they were both sitting silently side by side, looking out, thinking their embarrassed thoughts, increased the intimacy between them—and the awkwardness of having no conversation. It became unbearable not to find anything to say.

There were peanuts in a bowl again. Sunny again began making a pattern. He said, "Do you agree the peanut is an underrated nut? It's only because it's less expensive that it's considered lower than the cashew."

"The peanut is a significant nut."

Silence again. More silence.

Spotting a bird, Sunny burst out, "What bird is that? A coucal?"

"A koel," said Sonia.

"It's the same color as your hair," he said, although Sonia's hair was the same color as his hair and the hair of everyone passing by. As with the peanut mandala, Sonia had an inkling.

Again the awkward silence grew, as did the intimacy of sitting together.

Ayah crept past them into the empty house to fill the bathroom buckets with the municipal water supply. She turned and gave them a long, expressionless stare. Khansama came back from the market and stopped. He stood in the shade of a tree and stared as well. All the servants in the servants' barracks were aware of the letter sent by Dadaji to the Colonel because Khansama and Ayah had listened to it being composed and then had conferred with the servants of the Colonel and learned also how it had been received. Sunny had not married. Neither had Sonia. Now they had met. But they were not dressed properly, their hair wasn't even properly parted—but never mind, these days anything was all right, wasn't it?

"What bird is that?" The koel flew by again. "A crow pheasant?" asked Sunny.

Sonia was startled that Sunny hadn't remembered that he had already asked, that she had already said, "A koel." Two times she knew. Three times she knew.

The lorries and cars rolled on, eternal. Eternal were the stares of Ayah and Khansama. Sonia had an impression she and Sunny were displaced from time, that they might have been Dadaji and Ba on their veranda, weighted by years together and a culture so deep that they themselves didn't need to strive; they were borne along by its currents, all arguments and options having passed under the bridge. These eternal waters would one day carry them from this life into the next. She turned to him. "My grandfather sent you a marriage proposal on my behalf."

Said Sunny, "We were fated to meet."

"How embarrassing."

Sunny turned to look at Sonia, at the tip of her nose that twitched, her thick eyebrows over black eyes with a central golden flame that roved behind tortoiseshell frames a little too large, the braid that traveled over her shoulder down the side of her white kurta, her lips of elegant reproach. Why had he not thought such beauty desirable in the past?

He said, "Not *so* embarrassing!"

"What did the letter say?"

"It said you were lonely in New York."

"That *is* embarrassing."

"All the best people are lonely. Or you belong to the herd. You suffer no doubt. I don't like those people who belong to the herd and suffer no doubt. Is that why you returned to India?"

"I returned because, ironically, given all the things I had already learned to do alone, including live alone, it was as if there was a hole in my life, and instead of life growing bigger, it began emptying out. The longer I stayed in the States, the smaller my life was becoming." Sonia remembered the months after Ilan's wife had arrived when she was a phantom making her way through the city, nobody noticing her. And if they had, they'd have quickly turned away. She had become one of New York's disturbed souls, stuck on a single thought, muttering, foul, looking inward, terrible things having happened that made it best for others to stay away. If you're treated like a cockroach, why would you not become one? If nobody knows you, won't you become a ghost?

"Did you try to grow your life bigger?"

"Yes, I tried to find a way to define myself from outside in, because I had lost a sense of myself from inside out. I tried to be a vegetarian, for example. But that made me more lonely."

"I can see that. It would be very lonely, just yourself and some vegetables."

"After I passionately claimed to be an animal rights crusader, I stopped being one for no reason and asked for the spaghetti Bolognese instead of the pasta primavera. It turned out I could just as easily care about animal rights as not."

"It would make one lonely, realizing that."

"I went to see a therapist, but that made my life emptier."

"If you empty your life of all that they tell you has caused your problems, what's left?"

"They tell you that makes space for a new life—"

"Nothing sticks to nothing—"

"I joined a Zen center. That made me *even* more lonely—to sit in silent meditation and watch my thoughts flitting by like clouds."

"If even your thoughts leave you."

She checked to see if he was making fun of her, but he was in earnest.

"In the wealthiest country in the world, wealth scared me; I became mean. I counted out potatoes, I measured soup by half a can, I went to bed early. I looked after myself carefully as if I were a fragile crone because nobody else was going to look after me. I suffered a sort of vertigo of my soul. I was unsettled by open views and endless vistas, by dawn. My heart grew small. I gave the evil eye to cute toddlers making a nuisance on the subway, to Orthodox clans throwing celebration picnics in Central Park, to tourists who seemed to make themselves deliberately unattractive, because if you have a big, sticky family, you don't pay a price for being ugly. Finally I thought: What is all this about? Why am I making this selfish life? Why is it supposed to be a good thing to manage on one's own? Why am I not returning to India? For water and electricity? Because other people are poor? Because there are too many people? Although I am also as much comforted by the number of people around as made anxious."

She stopped. Why had she told Sunny these humiliating details?

Sunny didn't mind. He wanted to continue sitting by Sonia's side. He thought how after a day when everything was at odds—full of obstacles and irritations—dusk in India felt always settled, ancient, a civilization that had come to fullness.

32

....

WHEN THE MORNING PAPER ARRIVED, SUNNY, BEING THE
first one awake, collected it and read: *TTIM files complaint against MSL
at JM Rastra. MP(LTTK) holds GL Mukti strike to blame for Vasudev de-
bacle. BORS reverberates in KLM(U) case. SSP Category 5 recipients not eligible for repatriation to FR Lokta.* He understood nothing. How could he
become a journalist in India where he understood nothing? The same
way he felt he couldn't become a journalist in the United States because
he understood nothing.

All he could comprehend in this morass of news was the story of a
journalist who had bought a woman at a cattle fair in Rajasthan. Cam-
els, cows, goats, and buffaloes were the legitimate reason for the fair,
but secretly it was also a place where women were sold. She was in her
sixties, the journalist gauged, but she had no idea how old she was herself. She had been sold from owner to owner, her price less with each
passing year. She had no name but a tattoo on her wrist they could not
decipher. The psychiatrist at the shelter where she had been admitted
said she had no sense of personhood; she regarded herself the way an
animal might. One night, she had run away—the way an abused creature never stops running, is sure of imminent attack, hears silent sig-
nals, is always burrowing to escape.

And Sunny understood a story about a retired railway clerk in Mysore who had grown his fingernails so long they extended across his
room. This feat had granted him entry into the *Guinness Book of World
Records.* Sunny remembered the World's Largest Ball of Twine that sat
in a wooden hut at a crossroads upon the Kansas prairie. What were

these calls out to the universe made by small men in small places? Could he perhaps interview the clerk? He brought up this subject at breakfast.

The Colonel did not believe in free speech, especially not for journalists. The rights of an individual and a news service should be subservient to the rights of the nation, he thought. Yet this was a harmless story, and to mend his relationship with his grandson after their argument over Kashmir, he called his friend Wing Commander Belliappa in Mysore, who looked in the Mysore telephone directory and found the number of the man with the record-long fingernails.

In the afternoon, when the rest of the household were in their respective rooms for the siesta hour, Sunny made a call, and to his surprise, he got through straightaway to the gentleman's daughter-in-law, who said her father-in-law would be happy to speak to a journalist from the Associated Press in New York City. She would rouse him—he never slept in the afternoon, just dozed and flipped through copies of *Ripley's Believe It or Not!*

"Good afternoon," the gentleman spoke crisply on the line, "are you Sunny Bhatia of the Associated Press in New York City?"

"I am. You made an unusual choice. I read the newspaper this morning and thought it should be in the international news. What inspired you?"

"I thought, 'Let me do something nobody else has done.'"

"Are you proud of your achievement?"

"I have made my family proud. That is enough for me."

"How do you cope with the physical problems of growing fingernails so long? You cannot walk; how do you conduct your life?"

"When you have a goal, the problems are lesser in importance. I have the help of my wife, my children, my daughter-in-law, grandchildren, and a full-time servant boy."

"Don't they lose their tempers and say that you have made their lives more difficult?"

"Lose their tempers? What is there for them to lose their tempers about? My wife says never would she have imagined she'd marry a man who has achieved worldwide fame. Visitors attend us from every corner of the world. Like yourself, they cannot imagine a man who lives such a life. But you have to sacrifice if you want to achieve."

"How do you take a bath?"

"My servant gives me a bath. Earlier, I had no patience; now I must sit still. It has made me a more spiritual, contemplative person."

"What did you feel when you learned you had been included in the *Guinness Book of World Records*?"

"In itself the *Guinness Book* is not important. The point is not about having longer fingernails than anyone; what is important is that I am firing up the younger generation to be ambitious. If I can do it, I tell them, I who used to have no discipline, then you can also reach your dream of fame."

When the bell rang, Sunny opened the front door and found Khansama waiting in the sun.

"Your mother asked me to come and see her," he said. Sweat was running into his eyes.

"She is resting."

"It is important."

Babita was in her petticoat, thinking of their return to Delhi in two days' time, of Sunny's return to New York a week later. She put her sari sloppily back on and hurried out to meet Khansama, whose single tooth stuck warily out.

Sunny stood inside the door and heard Khansama say, "I would like to accept your offer to work for you in Delhi."

Virtuous and generous as the triumphant are, Babita softened her victory. "Don't say anything now—I will give you the money for a ticket and send for you in a few weeks. You quietly make your preparations while I find somewhere for my maidservants to relocate." Just as she was counting the money, Sunny came leaping out. "You absolutely cannot do this!"

"Do what?"

"You cannot rob them of their cook. It's unethical!"

Babita's instincts switched on. "Nobody owns a person."

Sunny said, "I promised the family you would not!"

"You promised the family?"

And she *knew,* alas, she knew—like fate playing out in a way that was terrible, predictable, correct, and satisfying to itself—that her son had fallen under the spell of that witchy leopard face. "And when did you have the occasion to promise the family this?"

Sunny was silent. Again Babita knew. "Have you really been going for a jog every evening?"

"It's messed up," said Sunny, "in the deepest way—you can't even get to the bottom of how it's messed up because of all the messed-up convolutions."

"Sunny has not been going jogging," Babita said, accosting her parents.

"Good," said Nani. "It's bad to exercise in the heat. The people who exercise suffer the most injuries."

"But why was he pretending, then?" asked the Colonel. His grandson was profoundly disloyal—to nation, to family.

"He's been making the acquaintance of Sonia Shah, for whom you once received a proposal of marriage. They are still plotting to grab Sunny. During the daytime he cannot take India, he loses his temper, but drink time—cashew-peanut time—he becomes sentimental. That's when they nabbed him."

"But he has already declined her!"

"He can change his mind. Why did you send me that proposal in the first place? I was forced to forward it so as not to offend your friendship."

"It wasn't that we were careless. Your father innocently gave the lawyer some bad financial advice, and they behaved as if we owed them Sunny in compensation." Nani revealed the story about the military woolen mill.

"It's blackmail!" Babita hadn't suspected anything more than the most ordinary ploy of a wily parent sending a comely daughter forth with a platter of kebabs to entice an eligible America-based boy.

"I told your father that if they hook Sunny, we'll be supporting the girl forever, and we'll be looking after the mentally retarded aunt, too, just wait and see. The complication is that the girl is very beautiful."

"*No she is not! She looks like Kali!*" Babita felt like Kali herself, a de-moness goddess burning up and erupting.

And then Babita did something outrageous. She rolled up the news-paper and smacked her son on the behind as he walked by, as if he were the dog.

Furious, Sunny refused to speak to his mother. Babita did not speak to her son. They left Allahabad in silence. In silence they took the train. Sunny knew that Babita was skilled at the abandoned-widow face, that she had greater stamina when it came to their altercations, that she had trained him from childhood to instantly assuage her disappointment in him so that he might be reinstated as the beloved. All he needed to say was, *Talking to Sonia, I realized she is exactly as idiotic as her grandfather told us she was.*

Their compartment mates, a pair of seed breeder brothers who traveled to market seeds to small farmers all over the north, didn't even realize Sunny and Babita were related until they reached into the same bag for a cheese sandwich. "You don't speak to each other? Mother and son?"

Sunny wanted to interview them. Monsanto-patented seeds and farmer suicides were in the news. What would this do to local varieties of carrots, capsicum, and chilies? What would this do to an individual who nurtured seeds in a family farm in the hills? But to be a journalist you have to win over the people you meet, and were they going to trust a man who did not speak to his mother? This violated the laws of the animal-vegetable-mineral kingdoms.

Sunny broke the silence between himself and Babita by accusing Babita of bringing him up in such a Westernized manner that he'd al-ways be a foreigner in his own country, unable to reach important sto-ries. He'd lost his natural sense of identity to one of T. S. Eliot and cheese sandwiches. Sunny said every other student at school had brought roti and sabzi in their tiffin boxes, watched Bollywood movies on the weekends. He'd barely touched his nation. He'd never taken a bus, never eaten in a dhaba. It was in the States where for the first time he had lunched at street vendor carts, caught public transport, used toilets in bus stations.

"So regain your identity then, who is stopping you?" snapped Babita. "You're the one who refused to eat almost all Indian food when you were growing up. You would take a jar of peanut butter everywhere! Now learn Hindi properly and hunt down a true story."

If Sunny could recover the meals of lost years, couldn't he also recover the stories? "In India," an envious Norwegian journalist had told him, "stories grow on trees." But Sunny had no right to them, hundreds of thousands ripening and dropping like fruit before they could be picked. Stories on the confluence of corruption in politics, business, the military; stories about weapons deals, the eviction of Adivasis from their forest homes, AIDS. He might broach these only if he agreed to lose his privilege. To lose his privilege, he would have to live in America, because in India his privilege was tied to his mother, and he could not lose his mother—his mother would refuse to lose him no matter how angry she was.

It was only when they were congratulating Satya on his engagement, allowing their felicitations to mingle, that Babita and Sunny managed to broker indirect peace.

Satya was shining when he entered the house, as if he was already a bridegroom, already a doctor, already an American citizen, already everything. "I was frustrated, and you were also not there," he said, indicating Sunny with a perfunctory gesture, as if Sunny were a lower being.

"But _you_ told me not to come!"

"Yes, but therefore I needed help. I was tearing my hair, and my cousin said, 'You're putting too much pressure on yourself.' He took me to see our family astrologer."

"But, Satya, you're going to be a doctor!" Babita and Sunny exclaimed together.

"So what?" Satya believed in astrology; he believed in spells, mantras, and black magic curses, in cures wrought through prayer and pilgrimage, and in coincidence that was _not_ coincidence.

The astrologer had hummed as he examined Satya's birth chart, a complex scroll in Sanskrit. He gave Satya a piece of paper and a pencil and told him to write as he dictated: "_Fatalistic life._"

"What does that mean?"

"It means your life is fate-directed."

The astrologer sneezed "Hare Krishan!" and said, "Yesterday there was a family here. Their daughter is a perfect match for you. The planets are unusually auspicious. They are traveling with a red-color suitcase."

"Really?" Satya had squeaked. He wanted to believe in his fateful life.

"Her father is employed at the agricultural research institute in Karnal."

Well, Satya and his cousin immediately traveled to the agricultural institute in Karnal a few hours away. They were not allowed into the institute, which maintained a sanitary and secure laboratory, but they questioned everyone coming and going through the gate. Did any employee have a marriageable daughter and a red suitcase? Obviously a lot of people guffawed.

Finally his cousin suggested they take a break. A former college friend of his lived in Karnal; they could wash and eat there. So off they went to a home on the outskirts of town where you could see the fields beyond and where grandmothers still kept buffaloes and planted front gardens with cabbages—even though some of the farmers had become so wealthy because of relatives who had emigrated that their homes, where buffaloes were tethered and cabbages were planted at front gates, were made of marble, even the driveways.

This was not one of these homes. It was a small kothi. They rang the bell. A slender girl came out. She wore a faded salwar kameez. Her lips made a perfect heart. "My sister, Pooja," said the cousin's friend.

Satya knew at first look: He who had imagined that he wanted someone to look after him now understood what he'd really desired was to look after someone else. This person, specifically. He wanted to go back to where he understood things. He wanted to marry in the way his grandparents had, so innocent they didn't know there were people in the world who were alone. Because they couldn't imagine loneliness, they were emotionally whole. So it seemed to Satya.

Widowed mother, sister, and brother lived together. There was no banquet, only a carrot and cabbage vegetable, dal, chapatis. Moderation made Satya feel like a good person. To feel like a good person made him feel safe. To feel safe made him feel calm. To feel calm made him feel like a grown-up man.

"And you won't believe what I am going to tell you next, Aunty," Satya said to Babita. "When the family came to Delhi to discuss matters with my parents *they were also carrying a red suitcase!*" A doctor Satya may one day be, but he'd received a sublime message that was especially thrilling to a scientific man.

Babita cautioned: "Satya, are you sure? An arranged marriage is thoroughly checked out by parents; in a love marriage you know the person well yourself. But here you are marrying someone entirely unknown."

A love marriage found accidentally during the pursuit of an arranged marriage was the most delightful thing. "Aunty, her brother is my cousin's college friend."

"Don't your parents mind?"

"They said, 'Your choice is our choice.'"

Sunny remembered how gentle Satya's parents were. Once, he had stayed with them for a few nights, and he remembered ashamedly how he'd taken his trusted peanut butter jar along to eat peanut butter on puris. During this visit, he had watched Satya's mother massaging Satya's scalp and had seen how Satya leaned against her bulk in a way Sunny had never rested against his own mother.

"Will Pooja manage in the States?" asked Sunny.

Her beauty and her delicacy, her innocence, would inspire others, principally Satya, to make sure she would.

"Where should we go for a honeymoon?" Satya said, stretching out his legs.

"Everyone is going to Goa these days," said Babita. "My friend Vanya has a Portuguese mansion on an island in the Mandovi. I keep meaning to visit her."

"You are right, Aunty. A hill station is nice for a summer honeymoon, the beach for a winter honeymoon." They would marry in January the following year. The partially accurate astrologer had determined the date.

Again Sunny felt—and again he couldn't easily define what he felt; it included envy, scorn, happiness, amusement—in his teeth. "Except you can't swim and surely she cannot?"

Said Satya, "You don't have to know swimming to enjoy the sea." You could wade in the shallows and watch the sun set into the ocean, becoming a little runny at the last moment when its belly rested on the water. You could feel aroused by bare sand and naked water, the scary but exciting fact that there was nowhere to hide.

33

....

WHILE SUNNY HAD NOT MADE ANOTHER ATTEMPT TO reach Ulla—nor had she made an attempt to reach him—and even if there had been an unspoken pact to pause their relationship, he knew he must not return to New York without a gift. He'd heard his mother mention a shop in Aurobindo Market where they sold pure pashminas, not the usual fake mix, and he instructed Bahadur to drive him there after collecting some shirts from the tailor and making the requisite trip to the dentist that every Indian who lived abroad made on a visit home.

"What is your friend's complexion?" asked the salesman.

"That is a ridiculous question," barked Sunny, gums sore, spirit sore. While he was under the drill, the dentist had gloated: "In America, a normal man cannot afford to go to a dentist! He has to come to India!"

Said a fellow shopper to Sunny, "A biscuit shade like that one you are holding would suit dark skin."

"Why wouldn't it suit a pale girl?"

"Tsk, no, it won't look good on a pale girl; she will be the same color as the stole."

"My friend is an American," Sunny consented, even more disgruntled.

"Then go with a medium shade," said the woman, who wouldn't have considered anyone other than a white American when the word "American" was mentioned. "She won't be able to stand up to a shade that is too strong."

The salesman unfolded and threw a dozen weightless stoles at Sunny. "Please don't open every one," Sunny implored, but the salesman unfurled dozens more.

"Take the mauve," said the busybody.

"All-over embroidery?" asked the salesman.

"If it is a gift," said the busybody, "let it be a proper gift."

Turning from Sunny, the salesman congratulated her: "You, madam, with your complexion, you can carry any shade!"

She said, "Actually gold suits me best. It brings out the natural golden tints in my skin."

Babita was quiet at their last supper. Bahadur, the driver, had slipped into the store and understood that an unfair bounty existed in the Western world, not only materially, but also with regard to love. Unable to overcome his jealousy, he had divulged to Babita the fact that they had made an unplanned stop so Sunny could shop for a stole to give to a pale American. Babita felt euphoria—there was still the American girlfriend! Her rage was eviscerated in an instant. She had misread the signs, she had jumped to conclusions. Sunny was simply reserved.

She waited for Sunny to mention the pashmina. He did not. She waited for him to say Babita must come and visit him in New York. He did not. Finally, on the way to the airport at midnight, she broke forth, "I was thinking I'd come to New York before the end of the year."

Sunny thought: *I'll have to tell Ulla to leave the apartment; how will that work?* He said, "But I'll be back in seven months for Satya's wedding."

She said, "I haven't been abroad in so long. Mohini offered me her place in Manhattan. She and her husband will be on sabbatical." Mohini was the daughter of Sunny's father's closest friend. Pitying widowed Babita, she had said Babita would be welcome to stay whenever she and her husband happened to be away, which was often. They were professors at Columbia University and had almost four months off in the summer, two in the winter. Let alone their upcoming sabbatical.

"And if the opportunity comes to pursue a green card, be practical," said Babita to Sunny as they arrived at the airport. Finding it unbearable to be without her son, yet bringing him up to successfully leave for America, meant they'd always live within the strain of her martyrdom. The melodrama and guilt felt Indian even while they tried to escape being Indian, tried to behave not only outwardly but inwardly with what they identified as a Western restraint, thereby creating another tension. What they felt was heartbreak and confusion.

Crowds were trying to squeeze into the doorway past which a few chosen individuals were allowed to catch their flights, the rest of their family left ever farther behind. Sunny, swept up in the multitude, turned and waved and saw that his mother was finally unable to hold back her tears. Then he was pushed on by the bearing weight of people behind him, feeling their desperation concentrated upon his shoulders, his back. He carried the terror and ambition of thousands for the span of time it took to get through the eye of the needle.

Cheating Outsider!

34

....

AND SO IT WAS, AT NOON ON A SATURDAY, THAT SUNNY
climbed the creaking stairs to his anonymous, free, American life, to
Ulla with a mauve stole embroidered with spring green vines. He
knocked before he used his key as was their mutually respectful habit.
He unlocked the door and saw she wasn't home, then he noticed a
cushion was missing from the couch and so was Ulla's shelf of early
childhood education books. He went into the bedroom, and there was
only one pillow on his side of the bed. The drawers on her side of the
dresser were empty. In the bathroom, her toothbrush and her sea algae
shampoo, her rosemary mint soap, her almond goat milk lotion, were
gone.

She had scrupulously left the cooking pans and knives he had
bought in Chinatown, half the Ikea plates and half the Ikea glasses, two
of the four folding chairs. She had left the duvet but had taken the
wool blanket. She'd left the Darjeeling tea and taken the Kansas City
barbecue sauce.

She had been so efficient at dividing fairly, it indicated that their
bills and possessions had been kept starkly and accurately separate in
her mind, so much so that they had perhaps never really been a couple.
It was the meticulous departure of those accustomed to partings, those
who didn't have the money to start over each time, those who knew
that after a while objects intimately shared shed their emotional pain:
sheets became just sheets again, coffee mugs became just coffee mugs.
It was the leaving of those who brought the skill of leaving into the
very beginning of a relationship—so what hope could they have had in
the first place? It was also the goodbye of someone who did not love

the person she left, otherwise anger or wretchedness would have flared up somewhere. It would have been a matter of pride for Sunny to spot a torn document or register a stolen item. She hadn't even left a note.

Sunny sat still for hours. It wasn't his heart that hurt, it was his throat, as if his heart were trying to clamber out of his wounded windpipe. And by evening, he silently wept, noticing that to be abandoned produced a contradictory feeling: a huge emptiness and a tiny trap. Had he offered Ulla India in exchange for America—palace hotels in Rajasthan, a boat down the Kerala backwaters—would she have stayed? But he had not; he had demanded the United States and kept India for himself out of an inherited racial rage, unwilling to share even with his own girlfriend—loyal instead, in some inarticulate way, to whichever side was opposite to her. But he knew that he himself had been resented in India in the exact same way he resented Ulla. Payal's father, who called New York a "shithole city," was deliberately overturning the unfair power balance.

Ulla had been right to leave, but the fact that she had been the one to make the decision humiliated Sunny, and he knew that he felt this humiliation more acutely because she was a white person leaving. Sunny remembered his pride when he was first together with Ulla—it was in great part because she was a white American, but he was ashamed to be proud that she was white. Therein had lain the problem. He had attacked her because he was angered by this pride and because having a white person in such close proximity meant he could heap all his previously unexamined rage—about the difference between a white person's life and a brown person's life, between life in a rich country and life in a poor country—upon her. It had proved an irresistible temptation to destroy what had given him his first taste of being safe in the big world, his first feeling of home in the intimidating nation.

And when was it that Sunny had learned the United States was about only one thing? In the morning when he turned on public radio it began: *race, race, race.* When he unfolded the newspaper: *race, race, race.* The economy, the environment, the journalism, the art, the sport, the war, the water, the wealth gap, the class divide, the summer camp, the prison, the school, the homeless person, the adoption, the birding, the diabetes, the real estate, the mortality rate, the election, the Starbucks restroom, the seat on the plane, the police, the murder, the judge—the conversation came down, in a hammer blow: *Race!*

When exactly had Sunny switched from believing that calling himself *"a person of color"* would mean allowing himself to be boxed in by a term he could not abide and had begun to believe that *not* calling himself *"a person of color"* was letting white people swallow him whole? Yet to emigrate and end up *"a person of color,"* Indians in India (again, he remembered Payal's father), died laughing to think of your downfall from *king or queen of your domain*!

Sunny could not speak. Sunny could not eat. He sat before his meals with clenched fists. "Goddammit." The more he concentrated on swallowing, the less he could swallow. One day he felt such panic on the subway, he couldn't down his saliva. He exited and burst out to sit on the curb, spitting, soaked with perspiration, his heart hammering, wishing to flee its owner.

*

BEGINNERS WERE GIVEN THE night shift, Hindus and Jews were given the Christmas shift, foreigners were given the Thanksgiving, Presidents' Day, Memorial Day, and Fourth of July shifts. Sunny asked to continue to work the holiday and night shifts so his panic attacks and clenched, silent throat would remain private—and so he may blur the fact that he now had no real life besides his job. He embarked upon an existence largely unobserved by anyone, and to have no one observing you, to have no love, felt like living an unlawful, unethical life a person must stifle away.

On his days off, he fled the apartment that was so filled with Ulla's absence. He jogged to the less-frequented areas of Prospect Park, where homeless men had set up camp with a trampoline and baby Smirnoff bottles cast about. He went to movies on his own and to the Strand to buy another Isaac Bashevis Singer book, unfairly on the one-dollar cart. *Off to get dinner,* he typed to the AP reporter in Mexico City with whom he had been working to edit an article on the heroic mothers of vanished daughters in Ciudad Juárez. All by herself, one by one, a woman had hunted down the killers of her daughter.

Just ended things with my girlfriend, not least for the fact she couldn't take spice.

Amigo, came the response, *who doesn't love heat? When I was in Spain, I missed Mexican food so much, I would eat at the Pakistani places.*

Although Sunny could barely swallow, he sought a fuller experience of moroseness than what was on offer in diners and taquerias, where it was cheerful to sit solo. He took the subway to Jackson Heights and was overwhelmed by a powerful aroma of curry as the train pulled into Seventy-fourth Street and Roosevelt Avenue—there was no other word for the smell but the word "curry" he had berated Ulla for using. Here was India awaiting him, along with Pakistan, Bangladesh, Nepal, and Tibet. The waiters weaving between the too-many gilt chairs of restaurants may be from Dhaka and Kathmandu, the manager from Karachi. Their grins of extravagant courtesy made Sunny understand he was the target of an elaborate theater of hostility. He thought their hostility had a point—succumbed and choked down lurid little mouthfuls. He walked farther east to where it was Peruvian, Colombian, and Uruguayan; young women standing on the curb in miniskirts and high heels, soliciting men even in the afternoon.

Sunny went also to Red Hook, where the Fung Wah vehicles that drove to Chinatowns in Boston, New York, and D.C. were parked; to the Bronx, where people lived in kingdoms of junk that looked across at the bejeweled city. He went to Staten Island and watched a cricket match between a Caribbean and a Sri Lankan team; and to the Coney Island boardwalk, past Russian restaurants called Tatiana's and Winter Garden; past seagulls with ketchup on their beaks eating diapers and French fries, all the way to Ruby's, where an old black man dispatched clams and cocktails to Puerto Rican kids. You learn your city when you lose your love and cannot bear to go home to an empty bed.

And after the long subway rides back, still putting off returning to the apartment he'd shared with Ulla, Sunny stopped at a bar in a former apothecary in Clinton Hill. He sat down and sighed deeply.

The bartender shook a cocktail shaker like a maraca. "What is it?"

"I'm alienated." He realized as he spoke that despite his overall sadness, he felt comfort in this term.

"Why?"

"My girlfriend left me."

"Why?"

"I kept accusing her that her parents were Republican."

"Her parents are not her fault."

"Yes," he said, "now I'm unhappy."

"Then change your life."

"Not possible."

"Why not?"

"If I stay in New York, I will have to survive my loneliness, but if I return to India, where there is actually a girl I like"—recklessly mentioning Sonia, surprising himself—"then I will have to survive my mother."

"Then you don't really like that girl."

"But I do."

"Why?"

"Seeing her in her grandfather's bungalow—with her eccentric father lecturing me on mystic poetry and her divorced aunt in a nightgown up to her neck and down to her toes, the bad-tempered cook chopping onions on the floor of a black kitchen lit by a candle—it was like walking into a book from the past. I don't want to live in the present anymore, and I certainly don't want to live in the future—it hurts my eyes just to look at what the world is becoming. So that only leaves the past, no matter its obscenities."

He remembered the Allahabad dusk with Papa declaiming—as if he were a leonine poet reciting in the twilight of an age—about love for a traveler based on a glimpse, of a glimpse that becomes the eternal journey. He had wished to learn the culture that so excelled in the art of loss and sweet-and-sour memory that it had foretold its departure: Only its own vanishing could complete its yearning.

The bartender was named Albana. Albana was from Albania. She had a snowy complexion, extravagantly curly black hair, and the sort of humor where the joke always remained encased in a shell of ice. Her family had lived through the dictatorship of Enver Hoxha. To Sunny, the name sounded like an evil comic-book character, but she had known Hoxha as a real-life monster who had deprived his people of heating, meat, sugar, history, philosophy, Dickens, lipstick, and, most of all, privacy. Neighbor spied on neighbor—they knew the loneliness of constant surveillance that denied you your private thoughts. Unwatched solitude was not loneliness, according to Albana's thinking, but a state of being that was rich and nourishing, naturally sustaining and as precious as sunlight dangling in a quiet room after the war is over.

"You don't know what you're talking about when you say you are alienated," said Albana.

Piquant treatment and a stiff cocktail dispensed by Albana made Sunny feel better, but one night, there was a new bartender at the counter. "Albana? She left to be with her husband in Atlanta."

She had never mentioned her husband. Sunny was just another tedious single man on a barstool with whom she had to converse because it was her job.

Two months passed before Sunny worked up the courage to ask for a meeting with his boss. While he had practiced a concise, collected speech, when he was in her office, his eyes welled and he blurted out wet, muddled words. Ruth Kaminski had reported from El Salvador and Liberia. She contemplated Sunny, noticed that he had lost much of his weight, that he was trembling uncontrollably, and he looked humpy, scaly, red-eyed, poxed. A week later he received a message from the Human Resources Department to say they were proceeding with an application for U.S. residency. He returned to thank her with warm grape tears of gratitude. She said: "Now you will have to prove yourself. And a word of advice: No crying in the newsroom!"

Feeling the pressure of Ruth's dictate, Sunny looked through the notes he'd made and—despite his earlier mulling upon the impossibility of his being able to tell a true story about India—composed a profile of the Fingernail Man. It was sent out on the AP wire and reproduced in several newspapers around the world. He was certain the story had been accepted because it was attractive to editors: *Eccentric India! Only in India!*

Now that he had a few successes to balance his failures, Sunny finally confessed to Satya, "Ulla and I parted company. It happened some time ago, and it's definitely for the best."

"I don't understand. I don't understand. I just don't understand." Instead of Satya consoling Sunny, Sunny had to console Satya.

"We were unhappy; she was right to go. I would have left myself, but as an immigrant on your own, it is harder to leave because you don't have anything to leave for, you have nowhere to go to. The person you have been with has become your home in this new country, so losing one is losing the other. Then Indians are not taught how to leave, nor how to be left. It isn't in our vocabulary. We're only taught how to stay despite absolutely everything. That's partly why we *don't* behave well. We think there won't be any consequence to behaving badly."

To hear Sunny say this wounded Satya, the thought that his friend had been loyal although he was miserable. Sunny was not quite sure how or when in the conversation he agreed to go with Satya on his Goa honeymoon. It had something to do with Satya elaborating upon Sunny's remark that Indians couldn't leave or be left, and that extended not only to romantic attachments but to family. It was traumatic for his fiancée to part from her mother and brother, and she wanted to bring them along on the honeymoon. Pooja had said, "Wouldn't it be better for us to go together?" But if her family came, he'd have to bring his parents, too. He and Pooja could take Sunny instead. "In case," said Satya.

"In case of what?"

"A third person makes it easier when two people don't know each other well." Also, they would be celebrating Pooja's birthday during this time; it would be forlorn not to celebrate with at least one friend. For a moment, as Satya spoke, the specter of his former jealousy resurrected. He batted it down. Satya was the stronger one now. He must be the kinder one.

While at first it seemed peculiar to be asked along on a honeymoon, it became less peculiar the more Sunny considered it. It was a honey-moon that was artificial. He remembered that the Arabian Sea sloshed warm and clumsy. It was the sea in which he had learned to swim dur-ing the holidays they spent at a company guesthouse that was owned by Mr. Khanna, the same gentleman who had pressed his father to commit corruption upon corruption. His father held Sunny's middle as he cheerfully flailed and they sang, "Fishy, fishy, *splish*! Fishy, fishy, *splash*!"

It was just when Sunny was thus climbing to recovery after Ulla's departure that a new employee at the Associated Press named Darko brought Sunny an envelope addressed to him that had been delivered by expedited DHL. The envelope had been thoroughly taped all about, and a return address took up the entire back, reading *Ratna Apartments, number 306B, Sector II, N Block, opposite Krishna Temple, Ramnagar Road Extension.*

It was from the railway clerk in Mysore with the long fingernails. *How dare you write about me in such a disrespectful way?* he had written in large block letters. The letter continued:

I gave you my time and attention. You did not even have the courtesy to thank me. Instead you made fun of me. Even the smallest detail you have managed to get wrong. For example, my daughter-in-law is Madhulekha, not Cherry. Cherry is her pet name. It was she who discovered your article had been pub-lished. My reputation has been destroyed by you in a single stroke. Because of you the whole world will be laughing at me. You think you are so smart and you are so rich living in America, but let me tell you that I am one thousand times more blessed than you are. I have greater riches than you will ever have because I have my HONOR, my SELF-RESPECT, and the REGARD of my community. You are an Outsider pretending to be an Insider. I will be writing to the Associ-ated Press to tell them that they should immediately fire CHEATING OUT-SIDER journalist, Mr. Sunny Bhatia, who writes lies to destroy the life of an innocent man! SHAME ON YOU!

Was it a kind of sadism that made Sunny take the subway back to Seventy-fourth and Roosevelt when his Fort Greene lease was up? Here where the stale curry smell awaited him at the crux of the South Asian section of Jackson Heights and the Hispanic, Sunny rented a stu-

dio. In the adjoining apartments lived Colombian, Bangladeshi, Vene-
zuelan, Irish, Korean, Lebanese, and Dominican families. There were
all-night taco stands close by, halal and arepa carts, momo trucks. At Al
Naimat, they projected Bollywood films on a screen, and Sunny remembered that a rain scene in Bollywood was equivalent to a sex
scene—it was raining in the movies and the tired workingmen were
eating kebabs and being aroused to their most sensual memories. In the
hardware store the Dominican men spoke not a word of English. At La
Elegancia the menu was only in Spanish. In the twenty-four-hour
laundromats people did laundry at all hours. The barbershop was open
at midnight. Sunny found that a visa-procuring service and Pandit
Ram Dyal, an astrologer from Trinidad, shared the same office cubby,
dividing the hours they offered their services. Next to them was a
money transfer to Bhutan and a halal butcher with a freezer full of
forbidding, hoary hunks of goat. A hijab shop sold the latest designs,
cinched-waist gowns, sparkly head coverings adorned with crystals,
and also plain hijabs for going on umrah to Mecca.

He felt far enough that his previous life couldn't reach out to cause
him pain, and because he'd decided that a good journalist undoes his
privilege, while he was just as alone as before, he was pleased to feel
part of a humanity that included tens of thousands of brown working-
class men who had left their families behind and were on their own.
These denizens kept New York City up and running, the United States
up and running, the countries left behind from Guatemala to Nepal up
and running. They were heroic.

Sunny was not heroic. Sunny was a hypocrite. If it hadn't been for
his green card sponsorship, he would still be hankering after Ulla—
after fancy brownstone Brooklyn—but he could hide his hypocrisy,
join the neighborhood as an all-night coolie reporter, and experience
the relief of knowing that never again would he have to put in volunteer hours stocking bulk, non-GMO, unprocessed, organic heritage
whole grains at the co-op, exchanging awkward one-line quips with
white people, attempting a baseball metaphor. What simplicity it was
to walk unselfconsciously to La Gran Uruguaya and order a café con
leche with the retired men in their chapeaus watching soccer, and the

middle-aged daughters eating dulce de leche treats with their elderly mothers, to be among people who accepted him as yet another "person of color" on his own, someone who came to America to make a necessary living.

He cultivated a friendship with Uncle Karma and Aunty Pempa, a Tibetan family that lived in a little brick house behind his apartment block. Uncle Karma said, "When will Mummy come? Mummy must come! Nobody should stay alone. I had to leave Tibet. We opened a shop in Kashmir; then the terrorists came, and I had to leave. Then I went to Nainital and opened a shop there. Then a synagogue sponsored one hundred Tibetan families, and that is how we came to America. I brought my mummy." His mummy walked each morning in a circle about the block, dressed in bakhu and colorful striped apron, murmuring over prayer beads.

Sunny wrote down everything he heard and saw in his reporter's notebook. There was something hard about the denizens here, and something sensual—so much finding of love, tending to love, pride in love, amidst rough lives that wrecked love.

Five months had passed since Sunny had met Sonia, and it was on one Saturday night, from this new stage in his existence, that he composed an email to her and, on impulse, sent it: *I will be back in India next month and in Goa for some of the time. I thought I might write an article for the Associated Press about the men who work on cruise ships, or the women at the Vasco port, or the environmental impact of mining. Perhaps we can meet?*

It had taken him a few revisions to get the nonchalance nonchalant. He didn't mention he would be accompanying Satya and Pooja on their honeymoon. He didn't mention Babita.

EXACTLY ON TIME AND EAGER TO INVESTIGATE SUNNY'S New York life, Babita landed at JFK.

Her face was powdered, her brows combed with the mini comb she always carried in her handbag, and she wore a camel-hair coat over a silk sari in a slim olive and ivory stripe that was arranged about her neck and tucked into her coat like a scarf, with small, mango-shaped gold earrings in her ears. Sunny, waiting in the arrivals area and seeing her emerge before anyone else—her suitcase encased in a canvas cover to protect it from dirt and rough handling—couldn't help an internal chortle.

Riding into the city, Babita remarked that while the pilot had welcomed them to "the city that never sleeps," the outskirts of New York looked as if it had never woken up. But New York became the New York a traveler expected when they drove down Riverside Drive with its frieze of prewar buildings, faintly gold in the wan November light. Because Sunny had only a studio, and because this studio was not in Manhattan where Babita would naturally like to be, Babita had indeed taken up Mohini's offer of her home while Mohini and her husband were in Budapest on sabbatical. Mohini—Mo—had surpassed anything anyone expected of her when she married her thesis adviser, Larry Fuchs, now the dean of social sciences. Fusty, bespectacled scholar of Walter Benjamin he may be, but this was the perfect disguise for his true vocation of fundraising millions for the university from murderous sheikhs and tycoons around the world.

Sunny fretted in the taxi. How would he introduce his mother to Jackson Heights when she had expected him to achieve the address they were arriving at now, at a corner of West End Avenue, close to where he had first met Ulla as a student at Columbia? They got out, and Babita looked approvingly at the building and the African American doorman in livery. However, he didn't treat Babita like a respectful doorman would a respected guest. Instead he cocked his head.

"Mrs. Fuchs said they'd let you know I would be visiting."

He continued to regard them from an angle.

"You see?" said Sunny to his mother after she had proved her identity with her passport and they were in the elevator.

"See what?"

"They are still suspicious that Indians may be living in such a building, and Mohini, after all, lives here only because of whom she married."

Babita didn't view this as a problem. She wished Sunny would live in a building where he'd be the only Indian. Meanwhile she was shaken by the hostile manner of the doorman. Babita thought she was upper class and he was lower class. She thought black people were lower than brown people. She remembered that Sunny had informed her upon her last visit that if she dared make racist remarks in the United States, he would never, ever concede to meet her here again. This was after she had been jostled in a sweaty street fair celebrating Cinco de Mayo and exclaimed, "Can you imagine what will happen when this bunch takes over?" The comment revealed that she also thought Hispanic brown people were lower than Indian brown people. She'd had to listen to Sunny go on for hours about U.S. support for Latin American dictators, military coups that opened the market to American companies and caused corruption, human rights abuses, and environmental disaster. She had thought that Sunny in his earnest American incarnation was a bore—even while he was criticizing the U.S. of A., he was revealing himself as having become American.

On that same trip, when he had played Cesária Évora, Babita had said, "She sounds like a man." And there had been a terrible fight.

They had gone to the Strand, and she had picked up a book of photographs and essays, exclaiming, "Sunny, look how ridiculous! The author's biography says *Paul Costandi is the life partner of Oliver James,* and in the photographer's biography, it says, *Oliver James is the life partner of Paul Costandi!*" And there had been a terrible fight.

She had said, "The Chinese run in a very funny way; just look at that woman running after the bus." And there had been a terrible fight.

She had said, "She's very beautiful, the wife; she doesn't look at all Jewish." And there had been a terrible fight.

But this was how Babita maintained her sense of superiority out in the big world. Sunny had learned the opposite trick: He maintained his sense of superiority by saying horrible things about white people.

Babita privately thought this was the trade-off when one traveled to the West: One could not be one's Big Bad Free Self, but on the other hand, there were significant pleasures to be had—for example, grilled salmon in a French bistro in the exotic season of autumn.

Sunny and Babita walked to Chez Henri. The lamps were golden nuggets nestled in pear-yellow, pear-scented, fog-scarfed trees, dotted minutely with slow-falling specks of moisture. Once they were seated at a green leather banquette, the scarlet Beaujolais relaxed them.

Now that her nose was blooming subtly from the wine and pleased with herself for not having veered into an argument about race, Babita felt able to take pleasure in Sunny's company and tell him what had transpired with the Allahabad kebab cook. It had thoroughly vexed her at the time, but thank goodness that while she had planned to let Vini-Puni go before Khansama arrived, she had reconsidered, knowing that Vinita would be immediately married and Punita wouldn't be able to continue in the charity school. Besides, as Vini-Puni worked for nothing more than pocket money, it didn't make much of a dent in her finances— despite the dwindling return on her portfolio of investments—to keep the girls as well as the new cook. She had renovated the rooftop store-room so that Khansama might occupy it. They would all three share the latrine and bathing tap. But when the doorbell rang on the day of the cook's promised arrival, she opened the door and found that it wasn't Khansama with his hopeful, brown tooth but a young man in tight trousers with a glittering range of shark teeth.

"Now who are you?"

"I am Khansama's son."

"I'm expecting your father."

"My father is too old to make a change to the big city. He is having dizzy spells—he fell in the market. He sent me instead."

"I hired him for his cooking not because I needed just anyone! I have a surfeit of servants."

"My father taught me his kakori, galawati, shammi, seekh and boti, his rara, mince chops, egg chops, his gassi, parda pulao, pasanda, and murgh musallam."

"But how can I put a young man up on the roof with Vini-Puni?" She had conferred with neighbor Sara Habib. "He says he is married, but that's no guarantee there won't be trouble. I had to bring the girls down to sleep in the pantry, but I can't stand hearing them snore. Then when I sent this young man to cook, it turned out he could not even mince an onion."

"What is *your* name?" she had shouted at an aubergine dish. "I have never seen you before. I never want to see you again. *You are hopeless!*"

The young man had said, "I could be your driver instead. I can drive very well."

Babita had replied, "Bahadur has been loyal for twenty years."

Next thing Babita knew, Sara Habib had hired the young man to be *her* driver, saying, "Well, at least the family is known to your family in Allahabad, and that is as much security as one can get these days."

Sara never missed an opportunity. A driver's job was higher up in the hierarchy of jobs, and the Habib household was wealthier than the Bhatia. The young man smiled his smarmy smile at Babita whenever she passed by him polishing the Habibs' imported sedan, paid for by their San Francisco son as a way to placate his parents into tolerating India instead of agitating to join him atop Russian Hill.

"You know," Babita said to Sunny, the memory of Sonia poisoning her speech, "you forbade me to hire the Allahabad cook right when he was petitioning me, so my guess is he didn't dare take the risk of coming."

Sunny said, "If Khansama is tumbling down in the street from dizziness, imagine what an expense his medical bills will run up as he ages!" He knew how his mother's mind worked.

The thought of having escaped a mounting expense comforted Babita. She did not tell Sunny that later that week she had tried to distract herself from lost kebabs by picking up a magazine Sara had lent her—a shiny new cultural magazine—and it had fallen open to an article on kebabs. She forgot she was reading words, and instead she smelled, tasted, the very kakori that had evaded her. When she flipped to see who had written it: *Sonia Shah!* This was the day she had booked her ticket to New York City.

Instead, Babita told Sunny about an incident soon after Khansama's son's arrival and dismissal—as if it was linked, although there was no reason to think so, except for an undercurrent of resentment and threat. Vini-Puni had climbed down the external spiral stairs from their rooftop quarters at dawn as usual and found a giant turd outside the kitchen door, attracting bluebottles despite the early hour. Then they noticed the lock had been expertly picked and the door was ajar. A thief had scraped out the entire fridge, even the entire package of butter; presumably one man had eaten enough for ten. Then, fascinatingly, the thief had washed the dishes and left them neatly in the draining rack.

Perhaps he was simply a starving man from one of the many building sites around. What must it be like for a laborer to witness the lives of the wealthy at such close quarters, to smell the rich steam from pressure cookers whistling in homes all around? To watch blond Pasha drinking filtered water, eating slices of watermelon, being administered deworming pills?

But the food thief had done the enormous tatti exactly outside the back door where you might step in it—which indicated wolfish intent. Anyway, how on earth can you plop your business on demand like that in the middle of the night? Babita had slept deeply; the girls had heard nothing.

"Pasha didn't wake?" asked Sunny.

Pasha had answered their inquiries with a questioning look. He fetched his tinkly ball in case it was the correct answer.

But if Pasha did not bark, had he been given a sleeping potion? Or perhaps he knew the intruder, which would make sense given the girls had not been harmed. Could it have been the Allahabad driver with whom Pasha was now familiar? But why would he do such a thing? And if the girls had not been harmed, they were suspect—they might have tipped off someone—but then nothing had been stolen.

When the police came they said that a thief might have been scoping the place and would return to rob. But why plan on returning instead of robbing then and there? Mr. Habib had been on his way to ride his horse on the Delhi Ridge in cravat and jodhpurs, his driver carrying a bucket of carrots. He presented himself as an authority on crime and said defecation was the code used by certain tribes that ransacked the city. This was how they identified themselves and left a potent message. And these tribes had a way with dogs; dogs never barked at them.

"But wouldn't it be wiser not to identify themselves with a turd?"

"It is a primitive marking of territory. It comes from animal instinct. The aggressive mammal defecates in someone else's territory and announces, 'I'm taking over.'"

"Then why did he wash the dishes?"

And where was the neighborhood watchman? Asleep or on the other side of the neighborhood—or maybe he was the hungry intruder? Babita had saved the girls from police questioning because the story might unspool out of Babita's sight, the police might assault the girls, threaten their mother, Gunja, and her husband, the drunk who sold bones for a living.

Sunny, who would have been dismayed to hear such Indian nonsense had there been Americans listening in, was feeling relieved Khansama had been allowed to retire. He missed India, for although he understood nothing, he felt at home in the story; he enjoyed the arguments presented, the conundrum that might conspire to be threatening or merely silly.

They finished their dinner and Babita said to the waiter, "We have had a most enjoyable meal. May I pay my compliments to the chef?"

"Oh, Mummy, must you?" groaned Sunny.

"Sunny Bhatia, I'll tell you one thing: Always give praise where praise is due."

The chef came out.

"I would like to commend you. The béarnaise sauce is far better than the béarnaise I had in Paris. The salmon is better than in Scotland!"

"Let's go back to Mo's now"—she turned to Sunny—"and have some tea. No point paying a fortune for tea here."

They exited, and the specks of moisture that were slow-falling in the golden eggs of the lamps felt precise and tingly upon their wine-flushed noses. While Larry and Mohini's apartment was not spacious by the standards of India's moneyed class, it was opulent with Afghan silk and wool carpets, miniature paintings from the Kangra School, a priceless stone Shiva and Parvati, god and goddess gracefully enthroned and inclined toward each other, lit with special angled lights as if in a museum.

In the kitchen, they surveyed a chaotic larder that showed careless wealth. There were jars of pesto with expiration dates long passed, three opened bottles of vitamin C, two of Fair Trade cinnamon— "Fair Trade actually pays its farmers less," said Babita. "It's a hoax; it was in *The Times of India*"—and there was only tea-bag tea.

An Indian household without proper tea! They examined every cabinet, and Sunny unearthed an unopened tin of Harrods Christmas tea.

"But there isn't a teapot or a strainer. Better just use tea bags."

So they drank tea-bag green tea, Babita making a face, although she sampled the Pepperidge Farm Milano cookies they found with pleasure: "The Yanks always overdo the sugar!"

When Sunny left, Babita found bread in the freezer—were they so parsimonious they were saving bread? On the bookshelves in the hallway were travel guides to Iceland, Botswana, and the Galápagos Islands alongside *The Historical Roots of the Rwandan Genocide; Apartheid and the Caste System; AIDS in the Developing World*. Armani, Chanel, and Louis Vuitton hung in the closets. She perused Mohini's bathroom cabinets: revitalizing serums, masks, scrubs, and creams for hands, feet, eyes, neck; foundations, lipsticks, perfumes. Yet she still looked like plain-old Mo in the photographs! Only a foreigner could find her attractive.

Babita took a hot shower, and the water came out frothy gold from an enormous showerhead fitted with a massage spout. The soap was soap-free Organic Satin Apricot; the towel was too large to handle comfortably and of plush pale gray to match the gray stone floor that appeared to be embedded with fossilized trilobites. She climbed into a high bed so luxurious that she immediately climbed right out to examine the layers underneath the flax linen sheets: a hypoallergenic mattress protector; a mattress topper of temperature-regulating, sustainably harvested wool; a breathable, Rainforest Alliance–certified, latex hybrid mattress.

"This is mad!" she said out loud.

The bed was too luxurious, in fact, to sleep in comfortably, and the night was not dark the way a Delhi night was. In the never-ending twilight of a New York City night, she heard ambulances, fire trucks, police sirens, street cleaners, and garbage and recycling trucks that made the terrifying sound of thousands of glass bottles being crushed.

*

"ARE YOU SURE YOU want to hike out all the way?" Sunny had asked his mother. "It'll take you two hours almost from Mo's, and there is nothing here, no tourist sights."

"I've come all the way from Delhi, and I want to see where you live." She had secretly brought a silver pendant on a chain for the mysterious American girlfriend, a filigree floral orb. She didn't ask about her, though, because a woman dearer to him than herself, another person joining them in Chez Henri, someone else invited in to explore the decadence of Mo's cabinets? She did not even understand *how*.

She caught the 7 train, and about halfway through her journey, she realized something was wrong. The subway train came up out of the ground, the people left on the train were almost all brown and covered in construction dust, and the train was making stop after sad stop at which working-class folk disembarked. Presumably they lived in the gray tenement blocks beyond. She got off at Ninetieth Street as Sunny had instructed, walked down filthy stairs and found herself in a caked, chaotic avenue under the subway tracks surrounded by factory outlets and discount stores advertising cheap suitcases and shoes in Spanish jingles, grimy groceries proffering overripe papayas, vendors hawking gold chains and religious charms. She saw no white people save a few who looked suspicious—like fake white people. She saw women in hijabs with many babies and Hispanic women in tights and T-shirts that revealed every curve of their bottoms and breasts, also with many babies. They smiled at Babita because they thought they belonged naturally together.

"I thought Brooklyn was fashionable!" she said to Sunny, who was waiting for her in the panadería by the subway stop.

"It isn't Brooklyn!"

"It isn't? Where are we, then?"

"Jackson Heights."

"You told me you lived in Brooklyn!"

"I used to live in Brooklyn. I moved to Queens. I told you!"

"You did not."

"I did so!"

"Where is your girlfriend, then?" So shocked was Babita she could no longer wait for the answer she yearned for and dreaded.

"It ended. Long ago. I told you."

"You did not!"

She absorbed this news. She was overjoyed. She was furious.

"Why leave India, then?" she asked. "You could have had this with no effort at all by moving from Panchsheel to Paharganj."

Her son did not answer her. Her expression was flustered, and he felt as if he had harmed his mother willfully.

They walked past the home of Uncle Karma and Aunty Pempa: "*Mummy has come!*" When they entered the elevator to Sunny's apartment, his next-door neighbor Mr. Rahman joined them with his grocery bags from Apna Bazar. "Ma is here at last!" he exclaimed. "We said to your son, 'When is Ma coming?'"

Sunny unlocked his front door, which opened directly into the kitchen—and the kitchen was in the living room, and the dining room, too, was in the living room, and so was the garbage can and so was the bedroom. He had painted his walls green, and this color looked Muslim to her. A pair of pants hung on two hooks on the wall, as if they were a work of art. They were very wide and very short.

"Why are there pants on the wall?"

"They are Frank's pants."

"Who is Frank?"

"The original tenant. This neighborhood used to be Irish and Italian. I was told he was a mafia member of the meat business and that he had a big bed in the center of the room where he cavorted with a woman from Kyrgyzstan named Varvara."

"You come from a good family." She broke down and wept. "You can't spend your life with vagrants." While in India, Sunny would never wish to live among the poor; in the States, it allowed for a picaresque bravura, this pretense of being a man of the people. Try mounting such fakery in Delhi! She refused to sit down.

"Should we go eat? There is a Peruvian place where you can get cream shrimp soup with a quail egg."

"I'm not up to eating. If you don't mind, I'll be getting back. Why don't you call me a taxi? I cannot face the subway again."

Sunny telephoned for a Mexicana cab, and when it arrived, it happened to be a particularly battered and smelly cab blasting cumbia music. And the road back to Manhattan included a bleak stretch of Northern Boulevard that looked to Babita like no-man's-land. She was unsettled—the way she was when she glimpsed the outskirts of Delhi—to see how precarious her world was. The more blocks of identical apartments she observed, the more forlorn she felt. The more people, the more alone.

She thought of how Sunny might have married Mo; her mother at one time had shyly suggested it, but Babita had batted down the idea because at that time Sunny was naturally too good for Mo. That night in the mirror: "*Ratty, don't die. If you die, so will I! Ratty, he has taken after you! He has taken after you!*" She sat on the toilet, her face in her hands.

During her last weeks, she glutted herself on New York City. She went to the Whitney and to a costume show at the Guggenheim, to Tiffany, Bloomingdale's, to Little Italy and Katz's Delicatessen, to *The Lion King* on Broadway.

She had a special lunch of fresh crab ravioli at a restaurant she had noticed on Columbus Avenue. "May I pay my compliments to the chef? I am a visitor from India, and I would like to tell you I have never had ravioli like this anywhere in the world!"

The ravioli maker was a young man from Maine. "Oh," he said, "you are from India? In fact, I'm going to India soon. I'm going to travel through Asia."

"Here is my number; call me when you are in Delhi," said Babita. "Why don't you stay with me for a few days? I'll show you the city, and you can teach my girls how to make a few dishes—is that a deal?"

"Your daughters want to learn Italian cuisine?"

"No, my maidservants."

He said, "Why not? That will be fun. I'll show them how to make ravioli, risotto, and pizza."

"Pizza? *No!* Pizza we have very good already in the local market, much better than what you get here, where there is almost nothing in the toppings—they skimp even on the vegetables, which must be cheap enough that they don't need to cheat."

On the way back, she stopped in a jewelry store and asked the owner if they'd be interested in displaying some pieces from India that she could send via her son on an annual basis, delicate pieces such as this silver filigree pendant she had here in her handbag, which would be compatible with Western clothing. "I don't like to be dependent on my son for money when I visit, you see!"

She stopped at an antiques dealer near the Metropolitan Museum of Art that she noticed had Asian scrolls in their window and asked if they might be interested in antiquities from India to sell. She stopped at a cosmetics store and asked if they would consider presenting some Ayurvedic herbal products.

In the evening she told Sunny what she had been up to, blustering over any embarrassment, indicating to him that it was scary to grow older without a son who could support her, who could not afford to give her a holiday. She had to depend on Mohini Fuchs.

"People immigrate to America to make good, not fall under the poverty line," she accused.

"I've never seen the States as a place to make myself rich. How is that different from attempting to marry a rich person?" Sunny fought back.

It felt as if he were murdering her with this brutal confession. "Don't romanticize failure and poverty, Sunny," warned Babita. To drive the point home, on the eve of her departure she put on her exhausted widow face. Sunny brought down the palm of his hand upon the priceless Shiva-Parvati statue that was certainly too antique to take legally out of India and gave in: "My boss is going to sponsor me for my green card!"

Then something happened. The god and goddess fell over. Babita and Sunny rushed to pick them up. A chip of Parvati's ear was missing. Had it been missing before?

They found the chip. "Just stick it back on!" Sunny went out to the store for Krazy Glue, and they stuck it back on. For a moment he kept his finger in the goddess's ear. They looked at each other, faces bare: Babita's trip to America had terrified them.

Before Babita zipped up her suitcase ready to leave for the airport, she hesitated a moment then slipped into her toilet bag one of the magnificent little guest soaps in hexagonal design stamped with a royal bee from a box she had found containing guest soaps. On the flight home she kept returning to her tiny theft. It marred her conscience. Why had she wanted it? After causing harm to a priceless antique, she had stolen a bar of soap. It revealed her sad, small state of being to herself.

....

Where Is
Your Favorite Place
to Be Tickled?

....

CHAPTER

36

....

S AFFRON HAZE ABOUT THE MARIGOLDS ON THE ROOF GAR-
den. A chemical sun making her eyes water. The feel of a burr woven
into her wool phiran. Delhi winter afternoon!

Sonia opened the letter sent by Mama. It enclosed her most recent
translations of Siegfried Barbier's diary.

> *Today marks the fifth anniversary of my arrival in India on Diwali
> night of 1927. I am staying at the PWD bungalow in Tajewala after su-
> pervising the canal in Hathnikund. By the house is a peepul tree full of
> monkeys. Under it lives a hermit who tends the slippers and the white-
> washed grave of the hermit who lived there before him. Long steps de-
> scend to the Jamuna River, where a stork stands still, waiting for the
> glint of a fish. The hermit, equally still, waits for a mystical fish. In the
> contemplative traditions, patience has spiritual and artistic reward.
> Waiting. Bhakti. Nothing happens—good!*

> *Eyes looking into eyes. Darshan. Lay your eyes at the feet of the divine.*

> *An object moves from one color to another, drifting into and out of sight.
> I am painting a flower's passage through light upon a single day—a way
> to reflect upon life; one briefly comes into vision.*

> *I am using watercolors for the patterns of afternoon torpor, when one is
> neither awake nor asleep, captive to the images and memories that float
> and combine in the mind, on the screen of closed eyelids like clouds. Two*

figures in sexual congress become surreal creatures; one breaks out in spots and one in stripes.

I am tired of potato soup. When it rains, it becomes potato rainwater soup by the time Moolchand carries it to me through the forest. Why can't we have mushroom soup? Anjolie says it is because mushrooms are too expensive.

Like myself, many seekers come to India and don't know what they are searching for. They became a mirror to the country they have arrived in, and in the eyes of the people they meet, they find a mirror to themselves. Sometimes they realize they've been living entirely wrong versions of who they might be. We speak of displaced identity in relation to traumatic histories, but people have always urgently sought out displacement: in art, religion, travel, sex, love, mirrors, metaphor, dream.

Lila is Maya, Maya is Lila. Illusion is pleasure, pleasure is illusion, wealth is illusion, life is illusion, the center is oblivion, but it's not the void of the West, but the void of the East. It does not signify emptiness, it doesn't mean we don't exist, it suggests we are relative, fleeting, unstable. We change form depending on who looks at whom which way.

How can a devotee attract the mysterious divine? Become what the divinity finds attractive. A painter must paint by becoming his subject's desire.

Painting, longing, waiting. Waiting for what? Searching for what? I must develop my skill, nevertheless.

Does the mountain create the music? Or the music create the mountain? When I tilt my head, high above the bamboo, I can see the mountain the invisible flute conjures. It is here in the forests of Sikkim that I have come by a beautiful gau amulet case carved with clouds—

Maybe Siegfried Barbier would make a good subject for an article in *Kala* magazine, thought Sonia. When she mentioned this to Papa, Papa said, "But he was a failure."

Maybe Papa was also nurturing an antagonistic response to *Kala*. Or his daughter. When her article on kebabs was published, he made photocopies to drop at the door of everyone he could think of, saying, "*I* was the one who came up with the idea! *I* helped Sonia research it."

Sonia begged, "Please stop focusing on kebabs." She wanted to write about other things. What other things?

Papa ignored his daughter. He took her article to Bade Mia at Karim's, to the public relations lady at the Oberoi Hotel, to Aseem Chacha in the back lane of Khan Market, who drew himself up, stroked his exquisitely trimmed beard, and complained he didn't look good in the photograph, nor did his succulent kebabs look nice. "I have never seen a worse photograph! It would have been better if they didn't take one at all."

Papa agreed. "I told my daughter, 'Call up Srimati Mithal, who publishes the magazine, and say, "Is this any way of doing things?" ' "

Kala had hired a well-known Polish photographer friend of the family through their diplomatic connections. He'd shot the photographs in a flat style with a sepia cast, as if he was trying to capture Poland of the past, not India of the present, because in India of the present, he claimed he saw Poland of the past.

Sonia and her father finally had an argument, during which Sonia said, "Why do you keep on telling the whole world what a disastrous article it is?" and Papa had said, "Well, maybe you are grown up now and don't want your father running your life, so perhaps you should find your own place to live, just like Ferooza and your mother. You're an adult; you shouldn't be lingering with your papa."

Chandu was listening. Chandu lived in quarters that had been illegally built on the lower ledge from the roof garden in such a manner as to remain hidden from anyone looking up from below. There was no room in this suffocating closet for his family to stay with him, and he hadn't seen his own children, save for one vacation month a year, ever

since they were born. The servant of the Bhargavas in the apartment
below theirs lived in a cabin balanced atop the tube well on a ledge at
the end of the driveway. The servant of the Joshis on the ground floor
lived in a room excavated under their patch of lawn. If a family had
money enough to live together and didn't, wouldn't it be insulting to
those who were separated from their families by poverty? Never would
they by choice force their children to live separately—let alone an unmarried girl!

Chandu marched—left, right, left, right—and stood ramrod straight
before his employer. He had earned the right to say what he thought
after decades of service: "It isn't safe for Sonia Baby to live by herself!"

Papa and Sonia knew their tempers were on edge. When they returned from Allahabad, Papa's fury had been renewed because his wife
had remained aloof in the mountains. Sonia was restless because she
had anticipated Sunny would have sent her a message—he had hastily
scribbled her Hotmail address into his notebook upon their last meeting. But now she wondered whether his visits to the Allahabad veranda, the peanuts laid out in an ammonite mandala—may not have
been about Sonia but because Sunny was indeed enamored of the wisdom Papa was imparting. *You see, Sunny, beauty is the motivating force of
the universe, said Ibn Arabi.*

With a mood for revenge on Sunny, Sonia had accepted two invitations: one from a mathematician who approached her in the India International Centre reading room and another through their family
doctor, Dr. Pamela Lalwani, who was seeking a match for her nephew,
a divorced divorce lawyer who lived in Atlanta. Sonia had no choice
but to set upon the path of a new life that might one day annul the old.
As her father had informed her, it was unsavory for a loveless adult
daughter to linger with her father and get into bed at 9:30 P.M. with a
nightie up to her neck, down to her toes.

Good night, Chandu Bhai!
Good night, Papa!
Good night, madman shouting, "India Pakistan Arrrrgh!"
Good night, stray dog sleeping in the construction cement!

Good night, family displaced during the riots!
Good night, tired old moon!

*

IN THE COFFEE SHOP off the lobby of the Taj Hotel, a stream of foreigners and holidaying American desis in T-shirts and shorts, businessmen in suits, and women in heavy silks bordered in gold traversed the air-conditioned expanse of marble.

The lawyer from Atlanta, dressed in a Hawaiian shirt, made a cock-and-shoot gesture at the waiter when he gave the order for himself and Sonia: "Two cappuccinos, okay? *Done!* One chocolate eclair, one lemon tart, okay? *Done!*"

Finished with ordering on her behalf, he pounced: "You're Gujarati, am I correct? Shah—your name is Gujarati!" He appraised Sonia.

"My father is Gujarati but not truly so because we've never lived in Gujarat. My grandparents lived in Allahabad, so they had Allahabadi customs. My mother's mother was from East Bengal; her father was German."

He frowned, as if the answer was fishy. "Where in Delhi do you live?"

Sonia felt embarrassed to admit she was still living with her father, so she said she was considering moving out of the family home although her family was worried about her safety. She didn't specify that only their cook had brought up the subject of her security.

The lawyer said automatically, "Gujaratis are totally focused on security, obsessed with grilles and security cameras. There are many Gujaratis," he proclaimed, "in Atlanta. You'll feel at home. A lot of money they have accumulated. One guy, he was so poor when they came, he married in his friend's backyard, lighting the wedding fire in a barbecue grill. Just now he married his daughter in an estate where billionaire sheikhs auction racehorses."

Sonia thought of Dadaji and Ba. Their thriftiness and habit of division was unfortunately stereotypically Gujarati, and so maybe she, too, was stereotypically Gujarati. A Gujarati had to be more generous than others to escape their stereotype, but this snarled with her situation as a single woman, which made her nervous and austere.

The lawyer sensed his advantage. "I must tell you about this crazy Guju I met in Atlanta who was smuggling Freon in his underwear."

"Freon?"

"The substance used in air conditioners."

Still later, he said, "My cousin arrived at the restaurant with his Guju friend, who of course suggested we order two bowls of soup divided into three."

"What is the matter with you?" Sonia lost her temper. "I don't even think of myself as Gujarati. I never went to Gujarat, I never went to Bangladesh, I never went to Germany."

"Sorry, Sonia, that is not good enough, hee-hee," the lawyer said.

"Imagine if you were a white man," Sonia continued, "from Aberdeen or Adelaide, and I ran up to you and said, 'Hey, I have a crazy story about a racist white man I met in Johannesburg for you!' Or what if you were Jewish in New York and I said, 'Remind me to tell you about the stingy Jew I met in Baghdad.' "

"Don't be touchy." He grinned. "All I wanted to say was that I *happen* to know people who have so many locks, alarms, and grilles, and the people of this community—I won't mention the *name* of the community or you will go ballistic, hee-hee—are known to be obsessed with money."

Sonia looked at him, and he looked at her, daring her with his smile, which she now saw held an undercurrent of hate.

"You despise Gujaratis, and you insist upon my being stereotypically one because of my last name," said Sonia, "so what exactly is the point of this meeting?"

"No, but it's true," he said. "I don't like Gujaratis, but I may like you." He winked and produced a printed paper with questions, which he handed to Sonia. "Just have fun with them."

Sonia read through the numbered list:

1. *What is your height and what is your weight?*
2. *Education and marks?*

3. *Top five hobbies?*
4. *Top five movies?*
5. *Top five music groups?*
6. *Favorite color?*
7. *Top five foods? Best dish that you can cook?*
8. *Religion and spirituality? How often do you pray?*
9. *Top three characteristics you are proud of?*
10. *Top three characteristics that you wish to correct?*
11. *Describe the life you want to be living ten years from now and thirty years from now.*
12. *Where is your favorite place to be tickled?*

His knee jigged, his face bobbed, the table shook. Sonia remembered her first dinner with Ilan. The snow bowing down the bamboo, the bamboo bowing to the moon, Ilan sketching her profile. He had said to her: "I knew when I saw you the story would not be simple."

When the lawyer from Atlanta dropped her home, Sonia was contrite. He wouldn't save her. She needed her father. She found Papa contrite, too. He needed his daughter. His wife wasn't going to save him. He had spent the empty Sunday at his computer; even Chandu was away on his day off. He had a strange metallic taste in his mouth. His appetite had vanished, and he hadn't eaten. "He asked you where you wanted to be tickled?" he said to Sonia. "I hope you gave the bugger a kick to his behind!"

*

THE MATHEMATICIAN SUGGESTED A walk in the Hauz Khas Deer Park. "I can drop you at the entrance, Sonu," offered Papa. "I'll turn left if you go right, so as not to bother you." Papa would make sure that no man would ever again dare ask his daughter where she preferred to be tickled.

They parked at Hauz Khas Village, where there were still village families reclining, smoking hookahs outside on charpais in the midst of the rubble, for there was a lot of rubble in this village that was being encircled and invaded by the city; boutique stores, and cafés proliferating. Papa glowered at the mathematician and said, "Take good care of my daughter!" and then he turned left. Sonia and the mathematician turned right, passing a billboard advertising a computer course at the entrance gate, and the gentleman said something surprising: "Tell me, does that girl in the advertisement look Muslim?"

"She looks Bengali," Sonia replied without thinking and immediately felt she'd said something beyond silly.

"A very good answer," he remarked. "A very good answer indeed." Although he was young, he strode in a myopic, academic manner, head bent, considering, hands behind his back.

She understood he meant she did not instinctively think in terms of religious difference but in simple geographical terms, and this proved she was not a bigot.

At first she was pleased, then she felt condescended to, and next she thought, *What kind of question is that?*

He answered without her asking. "I had a girlfriend in college who was Muslim, but my parents refused to let us marry; they said they were disappointed in my choice. I fought back, but this led to altercations, which she was too delicate to handle. She fell into depression, and we ourselves began to accuse one another. We had no choice but to part company, and I was so distraught in the year that followed, I would run to the mosque, where I prostrated myself in prayer for hours."

Should he not be allowed to marry the girl he loves, why should a Hindu not weep in a mosque, finding a home for his grief, calming his emotions in its geometry of shadows?

Then the mathematician fell deep into the well of his own thought as he and Sonia took the paths of red gravel into the jungly park interior. Red grit in her slippers, yellow-gray evening in her hair, shrieking birds, darkening tombs, Sonia fell into her own depression and thought that this, here, was the end of love, surely. How could new love grow in this sad city forest?

The mathematician attempted to come out of himself and asked, "What is that birdcall, do you know? Is that a quail?"

"A partridge," Sonia answered, thinking of Sunny. Did this mean that Sunny, too, had been distracted by a past love rather than flustered by an attraction to her? Yet again she had wrongly surmised a man's interest.

Ten minutes later, he asked again: "What is that birdcall?"

"A partridge!"

They circled the pond, where a fountain in the shape of a rusty boat sprayed water. Papa rushed by, calling out, "They finally found a way to get rid of the algae. Remember how it used to stink like the billy-o's? We had to walk like buccaneers, hankies about our faces!" Then he was gone, moving practically at a gallop to keep his promise to his daughter to stay out of her affairs. Sonia and the mathematician observed a watchman trying to chase the recalcitrant pond ducks into a cage for the night. "Why are you putting them in a cage?"

"So they aren't eaten."

"Who would eat them? Animals?"

"Two-legged animals."

Would hungry road workers camping in the park consume the park ducks, trap quails and partridge for dinner?

Papa was waiting for Sonia in the Peugeot when she emerged. The mathematician departed on his motorcycle. Sonia killed what was already dead. "It was obvious he was trying to move on by meeting someone new, but he could not leave his tormented past behind."

Papa said happily, "How tragic. That's what the best of us do in today's world, isn't it? Try to make these difficult connections that are already cursed." He'd now defeated three men by his count: Sunny, the lawyer, and the mathematician.

Still, that night he could not eat. There was that metallic taste in his mouth.

*

THE NEXT MORNING WHILE Papa was showering to the music of the Dagar Brothers, Sonia sat at the computer that her father had turned on, slowly warming each part of the apparatus so it might not explode from effort. She logged on to her Hotmail and saw with joy that Sunny had finally sent her a message. She responded hastily because if Papa emerged from the shower and heard the click of keys, he would be unable to bear the thought of a message being sent without him knowing what it contained. *Yes, I can meet you in Goa. Do you know your dates?*

Sunny wrote to say the last week in January.

Sonia returned to the library at the India International Centre and tried to ignore the anguished mathematician who could not free himself by replacing one love with another. She found a volume on the history of Goa. She read about the landscape that aroused such greed in the Portuguese when they arrived from their cramped land to islands, mangroves, ocean, sky; about the eleven python rivers through palm jungle that disembogued into the Arabian Sea; about Our Lady of the Rosary, where Afonso de Albuquerque had given thanks for defeating Adil Shah and where St. Francis Xavier had uttered his first sermon. And the basilica, where the saint now lay embalmed in a casket made of Carrara marble, missing a toe because someone had bitten it off in an attack of passion. She read about the country estates of the Agostinho friars and the Portuguese viceroys on the banks of the Mandovi and the homes of the Brahmins and Chadors, many of whom had converted to Catholicism but retained a link with their Hindu past and were persecuted during the Inquisition. These were families with histories as extravagant as their homes. She looked at photographs of the Palácio Santana da Silva, the Menezes Braganza mansion, and Casa das Conchas, which was owned by the merchant Placido Rumaan Raman Pinto, who was imprisoned when he refused to salute "Hail Salazar."

She proposed to *Kala* magazine a story on Old Portuguese Goa, or Goa Velha. This proposal was accepted. "Ya, ya," said Maya Mithal, "this sounds like an enjoyable story. Try to find some aristocrat mad hatters."

Sonia wrote an email to an authority on the region, Dr. Teotimo Menezes. He replied: *You won't understand Goa by staying in a hotel. Every house here has a story, and every story has a house. Mostly it is a tragic story.* Dr. Menezes put Sonia in touch with the lawyer representing the Borda d'Agua family, who hoped to preserve their Loutolim mansion in the rice fields by turning it into a home museum or a boutique hotel, the same way the palace and fort hotels of Rajasthan had been preserved. The lawyer invited Sonia to spend a few nights. He would inform the caretaker, Clayton.

As Sonia and Sunny sent messages back and forth and continued to make plans to meet in the winter, Ilan's voice—and his face, sometimes that of a child, sometimes that of the devil—sounded in Sonia's ears: *Obey me!* He had betrayed her, not she him, but she felt as if she had betrayed him and was now betraying him even more egregiously. *Happiness is for other people.* She dreamt the walls leaked blood. She dreamt she ate a pie, and when she bit into it, the pie filled with blood. She dreamt she had a hideous baby and it died, and when she cut it open with scissors, it was not a baby at all—it had a child's head but a lizard's skeleton. She dreamt a lascivious hound awaited her. He came with his friends, a scorpion and a snake. It was difficult after such thoughts and dreams to normalize her day. Why did the phantom of Ilan persist? Why was the fear in her still, a chronic condition that may, at any moment, resurrect.

Although she was preoccupied, Sonia noticed that her father's sudden loss of appetite had caused his weight to plummet, his cheeks to cave, his stomach to flatten. "I'm not hungry, it's the strangest thing. I had to use a belt on a pair of pants that was too tight a month ago."

They walked down to Dr. Pamela Lalwani's neighborhood clinic, and she advised a series of routine tests. Within a day they learned Papa had tested positive for H. pylori, a parasite that caused an unbearable vapor to be emitted from the stomach. It may take months to rebuild the intestinal flora after antibiotics had tackled H. pylori, said Dr. Lalwani, but they were relieved it wasn't anything worse. She said to Sonia, "It was very foolish of you to turn down my nephew. He is already engaged to a lovely young lady. Beauty plus brains."

"Good for him," said Sonia.

"If you wait too long, the craze will go," warned Dr. Lalwani.

"What craze?"

"The craze! After some time, it vanishes—and then it will be too late for you!"

White Hound
Ocean

37

....

SUNNY FLEW FROM NEW YORK TO NEW DELHI SEPARATELY
from Satya this time and found Babita standing at the edge of the
crowd outside the arrivals area at Indira Gandhi airport alongside the
driver who was this time holding aloft the *Sunny, Welcome Home!* sign
that had been salvaged from his last visit. As they drove home to Panchsheel Park at five in the winter morning, the streetlamps still on, their
neon merging with the first light of dawn, they encountered several
knackered white wedding horses being ridden home by their owners,
flanks stamped with black shoe marks. They saw an entire wedding
band's red uniforms laid out to dry on a traffic island. The city was at
the height of an auspicious marriage season, and Sunny mentioned this
must have been why Satya's family had been unable to find a proper
venue and decided to hold the wedding in their own home, which
would anyway be more economical and less embarrassing to the bride.
They were paying for the wedding in a reversal of roles to save her
widowed mother and student brother the expense.

Babita said, "I told Vinita to make gnocchi and ravioli for lunch
tomorrow. That chef from New York stayed for a few days and taught
the girls."

"He *actually* came?"

"Yes—and he said our chicken liver pâté was as good as anything
you'd get in France. But then he told me his girlfriend would be joining him. I said, 'Girlfriend was not part of our agreement, Charlie
boy!' He left in a huff and a puff, so the girls have been perfecting the
gnocchi under my direction. I discovered it's better to beat the pota-

toes, then dry them ever so slightly in the oven, then beat the potatoes again—it's that difficult to get the gnocchi fluffy."

Gnocchi *and* ravioli! It was slave labor, Sunny thought, to have to make *both* from scratch while also preparing breakfast, washing dishes, going to the market.

"Isn't that too much?" Italian food always harked back to his misguided fights with Ulla.

"You're only here for the shortest while; you'll be in Goa most of the time."

"Not most."

"Well, before that you'll be preoccupied with Satya's wedding. Perhaps I'll fly to Goa with you—Delhi winters are getting to me. My toes are covered in chilblains."

It was as if Babita had intuited his secret plan to meet Sonia. "What, you want to join in Satya's honeymoon, too?" he asked.

"Tsk, I wouldn't join in the honeymoon. I could visit Vanya. Do you remember her husband, Cecil? More Portuguese than the Portuguese? With the Malacca cane, the goatee, the Cuban cigars? Who insisted the wine in the neck of the bottle be decanted and discarded because it would be of an incorrect temperature?

"I wrote to Vanya when Cecil died, expressing sympathy although privately thinking it was the luckiest occurrence for her to be free of him, and she wrote back saying she couldn't get used to rattling about the great house alone."

Babita noticed Sunny did not say, *Come along, then!*

But Sunny extravagantly praised the ravioli and gnocchi, which was indeed feathery after being thoroughly beaten, slightly dried, beaten again. He didn't want to be a pompous, green-card-approved son returning home saying, *But I eat pasta all the time in New York City!* Nor did he want to be the person whose entire luck had been built on the ill luck of servants, spouting hypocritical ideas of human rights.

Babita said, "Well, Vini-Puni are improving in their Continental cuisine, but Indian dishes they still make a mess of. The other day Vini made a shammi kebab we had to toss to Pasha." Sunny froze. Had his mother divined his plan to meet the woman whom she blamed for the failure of her kebabs?

After lunch Sunny went to the bridegroom's house, where Satya was being fitted with a bridegroom's turban that kept falling off his head and would need alteration. When he could nonchalantly slip it in, Sunny said, "While we are in Goa, I'll take a little time to research an article with Sonia. She's writing about Old Goa, and I thought I might investigate Vasco port." How enviable it was to be two adventurous writers out in the world together.

"Who is this Sonia?" Satya asked.

"I told you, the woman I met in Allahabad."

"You didn't tell me."

"You must have forgotten; you've been busy with your wedding."

"No, I would not have forgotten." When Satya considered this development logically, this was an ideal situation of having some support while also being left alone for a span with his new wife. But his friend's deceit gave Satya an uneasy feeling at odds with the satiated happiness he had anticipated. How to trust anyone—a new wife?—when he couldn't even trust his childhood friend.

"Why are you roaming around with someone you don't know?"

"You're marrying someone you don't know."

"But I'm *marrying* her!"

On the day of his nuptials Satya left his house in jeans. He changed into his silk sherwani at his cousin's and returned in a car crisscrossed with silver strings of roses and tuberoses, as if he were a suitor arriving at his bride's door. Across the street, they had cleared a plot of contested land that had been serving as an unofficial neighborhood garbage dump, and here they had erected the reception tent.

At the ceremony, Sunny was noosed by jet lag. His head fell and fell again. Periodically he jerked awake and saw a crowd of people and a wedding fire burning in a metal pail that resembled a garbage can. Eventually the couple was moved to a raised stage and seated side by side on plywood thrones covered with red satin that matched the table-cloths upon which the buffet was arrayed. Down the road some construction workers were burning plastic bags for heat. The winter fog, damp and granular, sank low, and many people were coughing, their eyes watering as they sought warmth by the angithis burning along the edges of the plot. Here they indulged in every winter's conversation: How many parts of what they were breathing constituted genuine fog and how many parts pollution smog?

In between warming themselves, discussing the fog-smog, and coughing from fog-smog and plastic-bag smoke, they went up to congratulate the newly married couple, but Satya's wife sat with her head bowed. The expression on her face, if you peeked under the brocade, was one of trauma. As the first minutes of being married extended into the first hour and as Satya continued to sit upon his plywood throne, he began to feel exposed. He plucked a splint from the corner and was struck by the terror of no conversation between his wife and himself, a fact highlighted by the quantities of conversation down below. He ached to read any sign she might proffer. They had, after all, been sending shy Hotmail messages to each other.

"Hey hey, Pooja," he said behind his hand, "what are you thinking? Was the ceremony all right for you? Too long?"

She did not lift her head.

He noticed that the videographer he had hired to make a recording they might one day show their children was filming the coerced bride.

"At least smile for the camera," whispered Satya, but she didn't, and because he could hardly be the only one grinning, he had no choice but to look equally unhappy. With knit brows, he ate grumpily from the plate of food that had been brought for him, as if he was unconvinced by the quality of the wedding the bride's family had provided (although, in fact, his family had provided it), the dowry (there was none), and even his new wife, whom he had thought more fatefully destined than what was fated by his horoscope.

The evening progressed long enough that the men became drunk, and jealousies over jewelry made some women trade unconcealed barbs. There was chaos at the buffet—the guests throwing sucked bones and cartilage underfoot, littering the churned dirt with upturned paper plates and napkins. A band played, some uncles jigged a tomfoolery atop the slick cartilage and purply bones, and a woman was heard to say, "Anyone can go up and shake themselves; why do they think they are being so smart?"

"No, they are *not* going to a *hotel* in Goa, they are going to a *resort* in Goa," Satya's aunt loudly proclaimed.

A few stray cows and dogs came by, stitching their way in and out of the crowd, shy but also stubborn, searching for their missing garbage. Some men aimed purposefully missed kicks at the dogs, for they didn't want their shoes to touch a mangy animal, while the mournful cows the color of the missing moon chewed the paper plates and napkins. The women's gold and silver sari hems were wet from the toilets that were being liberally swished by an ayah with plastic mugs of water. Then someone lost an envelope with a gift of cash for the married couple, and everyone began searching for it. They wanted to accuse the staff—the ayah, the bearers, the cooks—but they resisted. Someone said a cow might have eaten it, and whether that was true or not, the envelope of rupees was never seen again.

At this moment Sunny shuddered awake, picked his way over the field of bones, dropped paper plates, napkins, and churned mud. "Congratulations."

Satya looked at him with an expression Sunny had never seen on his face before. It was that of an aggrieved and aggressive man.

"Why are you coming now?"

"I fell asleep."

"Why don't you keep on sleeping? You already missed everything."

*

ONE DAY LATER ON the flight to Panjim, their throats were sandpapery, their heads were clogged, their noses drippy. Satya occupied the cramped middle seat between Sunny and his wife. Her substantial wedding finery spilled over their thighs. There were many brides on this flight—some in saris, some in salwar kameez, some in jeans, but with the same arms laden with red bangles and hands painted with henna.

Sunny had plucked Hemingway's *For Whom the Bell Tolls* from his childhood bookshelf for this journey. War was never noble; it turned

on itself. The book read differently to him now from when he was a
boy, when he had been erotically aroused by the prose—masculine,
heroic, laconic. It would be impossible for an Indian to behave out in
the world in such a manner, and Sunny couldn't think of a single war
hero Indian journalist. While he kept his eyes on the page, Sunny was
curiously noting the silence between Satya and Pooja, although tears
coursed down Pooja's cheeks.

The stewardess helping with Pooja's seat buckle said, "I was the
same when I got married, crying all the time." She offered Pooja the
sweet tray.

Interestingly, Pooja took three sweets, Sunny observed, which made
him wonder if she was perhaps not as sad as she pretended. Perhaps she
was putting on the lugubrious act she thought she was expected to put
on, rendering the occasion—a parting as much as a union—as weighty
as it should be. Maybe she was still more a child than an adult and could
not say no to a toffee even when she was scared. Who was she?

The honeymoon party of three exited from Dabolim airport at
sundown, traveled north, crossing first the Zuari River and passing
Panjim, then crossing the Mandovi, smelling the sharp funk on the opposite shore where the little fishing boats docked. The winter fog-
smog in Sunny's head cleared. His sandpaper throat felt less sandpapery
as they continued along the road that connected the coastal towns and
villages. Night fell, and finally they located a sign for their resort in a
clutter of signs lit by the car headlights. The roadway turned into a dirt
road from which sandy footpaths twisted in every direction into the
palm groves, where there were still starry Christmas lanterns hanging
in the long snakelike verandas of homes.

Sunny lifted his head and inhaled. "I can smell the ocean!" They
arrived at the Susegad Resort strung with fairy lights and got out of
the car. Sunny said, "Can you hear?" There was an enormous curly
sound.

They went, the three of them, down the path to the beach, and
Pooja saw for the first time, ancient and grand, black waves slowly rising and slowly breaking, first into a dull shimmer to the left, then at

their feet, then farther away to the right. They saw the moonlight riding the waves toward them, the far-off lights at Chapora, the pulse over the ocean of a Russian nightclub playing techno music.

Sunny felt an almost desperate desire for the relief he knew he'd find in the spooky water, undoing the strain of the journey, relieving his still undone irritation at his mother making her forsaken widow face over his leaving for Goa without her, relieving his anxiety over meeting Sonia—he hadn't even given it proper thought. He said, "Do you think I could go for a swim?"

"Swim at night in the ocean? You'll drown."

He saw from the look on Satya's face that it would be inappropriate to throw off his clothes in front of the overdressed bride and leap into the sea.

At the beach shacks, an aged clientele—with weathered faces and the expressions of those who have surveyed the world on the sidelines for a long while—stared out, drank beers, ordered Chinese. The waves' thunder mixed with the music, "Lady in Red," then, "You Look Wonderful Tonight," and lantern lights swaying in the sea breeze rocked this scene of German, English, Russian pensioners, of Sunny, Satya, and Pooja. The breeze filled their hair with thick, salty moisture. A man with long, gray hair beside them had a single monster crab in its shell upon his plate, and with strong, ringed knuckles, he was cracking it, then gnashing it with his teeth. His arms were tattooed with gravestones and roses.

When the waiter came over, Satya asked, "What would you like, Pooja?" and Pooja whispered, "Anything." Peeping at the man gnashing his crab, she was imagining herself to be in the presence of the irreligious and foreign—Satan for all she knew. When he saw her peeping, the foreigner winked at her.

Again, Satya felt this was all wrong. Pooja was too old-fashioned and timid to say what she wanted, which wouldn't work in the United States, where women were respected when they were not passive, had defined likes and dislikes. A wife who didn't know her mind would put the burden of responsibility on him. "You have to choose!"

Pooja had been to a proper restaurant only a few times in her life, and if you were going to be in a restaurant only a few times, so much rode on the choice that it was impossible to decide. It was harder yet because of the unstable sand, waves, breeze, and moon.

"You decide," said Pooja. "Whatever you like."

This made Satya feel it did not matter, he did not matter, the expense of coming here was unimportant. "Try something new. If we dictate what you should eat, we won't be nice men, will we, Sunny?"

Sunny said, "I understand, Pooja—how to decide before you taste?" But forced to wait himself, he was cross and ordered a beer. *This was rude,* Satya's eyes said. Pooja didn't drink and neither did Satya.

Sunny sucked his beer down. He fidgeted three straws into three stick insects. The waiter was coming back again.

Satya said, "Would you like the Hong Kong chicken?"

Unexpectedly Pooja now said, "Will that be good?"

"Veg hakka noodles?"

She was silent.

Satya said, "Jumbo prawn chili fry?"

She slightly dipped her head, assenting.

"Okay! Jumbo prawn chili fry!"

As with the incident of the three sweets on the flight, Sunny became interested and wondered if this was a method of getting what you wished for when you came from a place where women were more successful at getting what they wanted by being indirect. Perhaps she felt there was no way she could brazenly say, "I want the jumbo prawns." The prescribed modesty of a bride would never allow this, nor the fact that she would not be paying the bill. If a mother-in-law had been present, the mother-in-law would never forget the prawns for the rest of her life; it would be the defining moment of a doomed relationship. If she said, "Anything," there was a percentage chance Satya might order the prawns, and if she asked a sideways question, "Will that be good?" indicating uncertainty, this, too, might deliver her jumbo prawns with little dent to her reputation.

The prawns were so pink and gold, so oily and magnificent, Sunny felt bad about his bitchy thinking. He ordered another beer. "To cut the grease," he said to moonlit waves. For a moment he thought about Ulla. Where had she taken her pale beauty? How can you leave some-one overnight and never give in to an urge to call that person or to see him ever again?

....

AFTER A NIGHT LYING AWAKE ALONGSIDE POOJA LYING awake, each with their head upon a flattish pillow, not touching, not speaking, Satya got up at dawn and left the resort room. His wife listened until she could no longer hear his footsteps, then she immediately got up and rushed to the bathroom. She'd been too scared to pee next to a strange man, and now she had to pee for what seemed like a half hour.

The evening before, when they had stood as small as wedding tinsel at the hem of the night ocean, she had thought, *Why here exactly? Why am I married to this man exactly?* No particular reason for him over another man, no particular reason for Goa instead of another place. A few chance occurrences had brought them together. Thus Pooja had her first sharp experience of the *why-here-why-not-there* emotion, and it unnerved her. She had, in the past, always been where she was supposed to be without thinking about it.

She reflected that her husband was kind. Only a kind man would have whispered on the wedding stage, "Hey hey, Pooja, what are you thinking?" Only a kind man would have ordered prawns and put the last one on her plate. Only a kind man would have spent the night silently away from her pretending to sleep.

She thought the fact Satya had such a close friend, one who would buy an expensive ticket and come along to smooth over the awkwardness of two people being alone together for the first time, was another sign of a good person who inspired loyalty.

She dressed in a special honeymoon salwar kameez and wondered where Satya was. To cry and be silent had turned false. She no longer wished to be the person she had been the day before. She looked out of the window and saw Sunny down below reading the newspaper. Just as she was wondering if it would be appropriate to go down and ask him if he knew where Satya was, Satya arrived.

Pooja was relieved. She gave him her heart-shaped smile. "Look, there is your friend," she said and pointed out Sunny. Satya was hurt that this was her first proper sentence to him, and he was jealous to find her watching Sunny, who was unaware. Sunny wore shorts, stretched out his bare legs, whistled to himself, tossed a sparrow idli crumbs.

"Why doesn't he dress properly in a resort?" said Satya.

"He must be intelligent," said Pooja.

"Because he is not dressed properly?"

"He's always reading."

"You can be a fool and sit with your nose in a newspaper."

"He must know a lot," she said.

"He's a journalist, so he has to read the news, but ask him in depth, he won't know anything. He couldn't get into medicine if he tried. I had to do all his math homework for him in school."

She thought it odd he would thus dismiss his dearest friend whom she was trying to praise for his sake. "Do you stay with him?" she asked.

"No, he lives in New York, and I live in Rochester."

"Where will we go?"

"I told you, I applied for several jobs, and I am not sure where I will be assigned one."

"Why don't we also go there?"

"Where?"

"To New York City."

"Why?"

"Isn't that where your friend lives?"

"Just because my friend is there, we have to live there? You don't understand the world," he said.

"But wouldn't it be better to go where you know someone?"

*

IN A ROOM DOWN the hall, Sunny had woken just before dawn and, looking past the metal grille in the open window, he had seen the dark, ragged coconut palms against the paling sky, breathed the ocean's brine. When he walked to the window he saw a neat cement house opposite painted a bright yellow with a mint-green balcony. Next door was a house that was entirely orange—balustrade, balcony, steps, pillars, all orange—and in front of it was a tulsi plant in an elaborate urn sculpted in the shape of four cows and four buxom ladies in pink and gold. By the side of this house there was an earthen ruin with a palm thatch; two sticks made its gate, a plastic sheet covered a stack of firewood. Looking out upon this lane—half country, half town—Sunny felt the strangeness of being here. A jauntiness was what he needed to face the days ahead.

He exited the Susegad Resort, where a man yawned at the reception desk that was open both to the scrappy street and the plush interior garden. He felt the pleasure of a morning weighted warm and leisurely even at daybreak. He wore his swim shorts and a T-shirt; his toes squiggled free in chappals. He walked down the road to the beach and through a coconut grove—giraffe trunks all stretching the same direction as they were wont to do—and found a view so wide he could discern the curve of the Earth. He left his slippers and T-shirt high on the sand and went to greet the waves that came rushing to meet him, encasing his ankles in frothy soda water socks: *Zsa zsa zsa. Where have you been? Zsa zsa zsa.*

Sunny said, "I should have come ages ago. You are my childhood ocean."

He swam out to where the water was so gentle, it was as if it were still asleep. He floated on his back, he turned like a seal, dove down, and came popping up, he webbed his fingers and felt the mystery trembling under his palms. He thought the first time you swim after a long while is as close as you'll ever get to happiness.

Heart high now, Sunny returned and showered, scraping himself with the pink tablet of rose-smelling soap that refused to yield any suds, and he went down to the breakfast buffet, where he found toast so weightless it almost flew away and sugar syrup jam—but real idlis, real mint chutney, and real cubed papaya.

He carried all the papers he had managed to find in the hotel—including *The Navhind Times, O Heraldo, The Times of India,* and *Hindustan Times,* encased in sleeves of advertising and celebrity gossip—and found an outdoor table. He thought, *I am happy. Why? I swam, I am warm, my feet are bare, I'm eating papaya and reading newspapers.* The front page of *The Indian Express* showed a goat whose markings the owner claimed read *Allah.* Seeing this as a sign, the owner saved the goat from slaughter, even though he was a Hindu. Sunny laughed.

Then he remembered Satya and Pooja, who may this minute be searching for him; he looked up and saw them both looking down.

"I went swimming," crowed Sunny. Then he saw Satya's face.

Satya couldn't swim, and Satya no longer wanted Sunny in Goa staying at the same resort. He was certain he would not manage to make his wife love him if Sunny were there. Before he knew what he was doing, he knocked on Sunny's door, Sunny having returned to his room, and when Sunny opened it, Satya, shaking with emotion, said, "You should leave."

"Why?"

"All you are doing is showing off."

"Do you want me to at least come back for Pooja's birthday?"

"I don't know."

"You don't want me to?"

"If you don't feel like it, don't come."

When Satya returned to the room, Pooja asked, "Your friend is leaving?"

"He is going to meet his girlfriend."

"But isn't he coming back?"

"I told him not to come back."

She was quiet for a while, and then she asked why.

"He was causing a disturbance."

"How? He didn't even speak much."

"You will not be able to tell, but I've known him for twenty years. Instead of behaving like my friend, he was behaving like my enemy. Why do you keep asking about him?"

Pooja knew without clearly thinking that she was attracted to Sunny more than she was to Satya. Enough to make her fall silent, enough to worry she was going to order the wrong thing from the menu and reveal her ignorance. But she was married to Satya, who was a good man. Anguished at being more drawn to his friend, feeling sympathy for her husband, she now tried to see the situation from Satya's viewpoint. That night she sliced an apple for Satya.

"Is this for me?"

She felt unable to say so because it would be like admitting flirtation, and this made her bashful.

He became confused. "You brought it for yourself? Or for me?"

Silence.

"For both of us, then! From now on we share everything, right?"

When the phone rang, it was Babita, who had tried Sunny's room and was told he had checked out. Satya, desperate to quell his upset for all time, said, "Aunty, he is not staying in the resort any longer. He had arranged to meet a girl in Goa."

"*What girl?* He said he was keeping you and Pooja company!"

"We also thought so, Aunty," said Satya. "He was telling lies to you and telling lies to me." Satya knew, as he was speaking, that he was betraying his friend in such a manner that he would never have the gall to meet Sunny again. "I thought Sunny was coming to help me, Aunty, but he was using me as an excuse." He must kill his friendship to save his marriage.

CHAPTER

39

....

THE TAXI DRIVER SUMMONED BY THE RESORT RECEPTION desk was not convinced by the address in Loutolim Sunny gave him— several hours away in South Goa beyond the Zuari. He turned the paper over to look at the blank side, then back again, and said, "Well, when we get to the general area, we will ask." Then he stopped his minivan abruptly as they left the property. "But wait, sir!" He jumped out to unhook a plastic bag from a bush. He returned and stuffed it under his seat. A short while later, he stopped again and fished several plastic bags from a ditch. "Outsiders come and throw plastic bags, they go home, and we have to live with plastic bags everywhere."

Anand, it turned out, was a one-man army against plastic, and Sunny saw that the drive would be a long one, for there were very many plastic bags strewn about the landscape, which also revealed during the slow journey such sights as a white church perched on a hillock like an egret receiving the sun, a pink temple by a small offshoot of river lined with coconut palms, a shuttered Mushroom Cafe Dance Hall, and a giant, half-built moldering Disney-style castle hotel, which indicated developers had been too hasty anticipating a spread of tourism from the north to the south and inland from the coast.

Sunny's eyes didn't register these sights or the sleepy life of small villages; he looked at his watch and saw it was growing late. "Drive faster, please, Anand." He had sent a message from the hotel internet to Sonia with an anticipated time of arrival, but could she check the internet?

A stubbornness overcame the driver. He looked at Sunny as if Sunny were mad. Sunny looked at him as if he, Anand, were mad.

They were slowed by construction near Verna, and then, when they reached a stretch of countryside where the green of rice paddy fields ignited in their eyes, they became lost. They drove down country paths, looped back, and returned to where they started, lost themselves anew in a spread-out landscape of hamlets and paths that puzzled through the fields and coconut groves, making sense only to those who lived there, unfolding according to the history of the inhabitants.

Somewhere back on the main road they encountered the sudden appearance of a giant mountain of compacted garbage. It appeared to be made entirely of plastic bags and rivaled in size the outcrops of red rock and black rock that showed in the distance. At the top of this pile, way up in the sky, was a broken tractor hauler that had been defeated. Anand stopped, his face showing anguish.

Sunny said in a steady, muted tone, "Drive on, Anand, drive on. There is nothing you can do. This is a municipal problem."

Anand in consternation took a wrong turn and drove almost to Margao, where on the way he found a plastic bag moored in a pond. Sunny didn't have the heart to scold. He got out to help find a stick with which they might reach the bag. They were now so late, he'd become reconciled to the fact that he would not make a good impression upon Sonia. But thinking of Satya, Pooja, and relationships too forcefully forged, he thought this might prove lucky.

They circled back and finally—after asking many passersby, including some policemen idling in a banana grove whose expressions turned diffuse the minute they were asked and whose memories dissipated the more they thought—Sunny and Anand arrived by accident at the mansion surrounded by rice fields. Hidden in a dense thicket of wandering cashew and wild starfruit, Sunny spotted a coat of arms that showed one knight, three boars, two palm trees, and a pomfret. The place looked deserted, but inside in front of a spotty mirror, keeping herself company, muttering and negotiating how she might proceed, Sonia was waiting—and remembering there was no worse waiting than waiting for a man who may or may not arrive, the old fear again of being both the one abandoned and the one accused. She was anxious enough that she, too, like Sunny driving through the extravagant beauty of the landscape, had not been able to see the house in which she would be resident for twelve days. She had not told her father or her mother about this meeting. They believed she had traveled solely to write an article for *Kala*. To mix work and romance, romance and lies, was a bad idea.

She was so relieved when she saw Sunny that she began to shout as if she knew him well; the anger proved helpful because they were able to overcome the situation of their being relative strangers. "You're so late!"

"The driver was lost."

"I sent you instructions." She noticed his shirt in a pattern of waves—it was a carefully chosen shirt. His hands trembled slightly the way they had when Sunny and Sonia first met, contrasting with the sure stance of his nose.

"The instructions didn't match the landscape." As Sunny observed her beauty, it loomed.

"Where are we?" He changed the conversation and looked up into the ribbed ceiling from which descended a decrepit chandelier missing some extremities, like a moldering octopus. A collection of what seemed like hundreds of china plates was tethered high upon the walls. Below the chandelier were several marble-topped rosewood tables, extravagantly carved and crowded with faded family portraits, ghost brides, ghost children, ghost men returned from Europe with ghost diplomas.

"It's extraordinary."

"Yes, but I was so upset waiting for you that I couldn't properly see it. Meanwhile I told the caretaker, Clayton, we were married because Dr. Menezes told me Goan Catholics are conservative and offended by the indecent behavior of tourists. So now Clayton thinks I have such an awful husband that I was worried he might not show up."

Clayton came out of the kitchen dressed in a stained, tan, terrycloth shorts-and-shirt set. He carried a net bag with a blackened hand of tiny bananas. His English and Hindi were poor because he was a Konkani speaker, but he put down the bananas to point at the fleur-delis floor tiles: "Portugal," he said. "Upside-down monkey eating breadfruit." He pointed at the carved legs of a table. "Carrara," at the tabletop. "Belgium," at the chandelier and the mirrors. "Hat and umbrella stand." He pointed out two enormous sea turtle shells: "One hundred and fifty years old."

They stepped through French doors into a long gallery with a central row of more carved tables, these laden with bibelots, statuettes, vases, Manila fans, ashtrays with humorous sayings, a carved coco de mer from the Seychelles, postcards showing Notre-Dame, the Statue of Liberty, Big Ben.

Clayton took them to the pistachio-green Allwyn refrigerator made in Hyderabad that ran on kerosene and a German soda-water machine. "France," he said, pointing at a set of pink china; "Macao," at another set with willows and pagodas. Tureen lids weighed down piles of old magazines that rested upon every spare inch of space. "Portuguese treasure chest." Clayton pointed at the row of chests on carved lion paws set along the walls. Inside them, tablecloths and bed linens embroidered by widows, spinsters, and nuns.

They walked through a bachelor's quarters at the front of the house, where above the lace canopied bed was a stopped clock. Instead of numbers, the hours were marked by letters that, when strung together, read *My Dear Mother,* and in the center, *Ernestina.* They were shown into the chapel, where there was a listing altar, a Mary cradling a Christ blooming with blood roses.

"Germany." Clayton pointed to the rotted piano in the ballroom where the walls were painted to look like marble, and he waltzed a bit to show how it might have been when families of the right sort came to the house from all over Goa—families that were rich in scandal and ambition, who were impoverished after fortunes were frittered away in drink, gambling, and extended sojourns in Europe, which had made them restless and unfit for life isolated in the family mansions overseeing the rice paddy and the coconut harvest.

"Shooting BANG BANG!" shouted Clayton. Sonia and Sunny jumped. He laughed hard and pointed out two holes on the side of the window shutters that were for slotting your gun and aiming at an unwelcome visitor. He showed them the portrait of a dark man in a military outfit and white gloves who had owned the guns. The sons of this family had been educated in Lisbon, and they were proud of the one who had worked in the Salazar administration as a diplomat in Rio de Janeiro, but no matter how far the family traveled or tried to escape, they were brought home to be buried. Out of the window was a white monument in the rice paddy. Said Clayton: "Family bones."

Seeing their reflections mingled with these curios in the mirrors, hearing their footfalls that set the porcelain and the chandeliers chiming and the crystal casting rainbows, they felt some of the wonder of the place seep into them, as if they, too, were part of the curiosities and vanities.

Sonia pinched Sunny, not looking at him, and said, "Argh," with a vehement look to wring free the last of her waiting anxiety.

He said, "Sonia, it is the fault of my trying to be kind to other people. I was worried about Satya. I was sympathetic about the plastic bags—what if a cow ate them or they washed out to sea and smothered a sea creature? Now I realize that one should just look after oneself, for I upset you, and you were the only important part of this."

Sonia sighed. "Well, I am far too kind as well. All my problems have come from sympathizing with people who then ate me alive."

"Who ate you?"

Sonia didn't answer.

At dinner they were seated at either end of the long, narrow table in the long, narrow dining room under three dim chandeliers and sconces set with candles that had sloped in the heat. A pedestal fan cooled Sunny at one end of the table and another cooled Sonia at the other. They were served mackerel cutlets along with a dried shrimp pickle upon Macao china. Their slim acquaintance against the lavishness of their surroundings, the imposing history, the presence of Clayton with ears stretching to listen, made Sunny panic and fear a resurgence of the formality and shyness they had dispelled. How could they be husband and wife as they claimed to be? Where were they going to sleep? How would they overcome the rituals of bed and bath? He was worried, as at their last meeting, that they had nothing to say.

He thought he might ask about Sonia's parents. But wouldn't Sonia follow with a question about Babita? The very invoking of his mother's name would damn them. He thought of asking about the article Sonia said she would be writing, but then she would ask about *The Fingernail Man*. He couldn't ask about previous lives, previous relationships because he didn't want to know as much as he *did* wish to know, and if Sonia asked the same questions back, he'd have to confess Ulla. He considered mentioning the tasty mackerel cutlets—but wouldn't that resurrect the cutlets Babita had brought to Cadell Road upon the occasion of Dadaji's funeral? Sly camouflage for her to steal Khansama by the back door?

Sonia thought of asking about Sunny's life in New York, but then what if he asked her about *her* life in New York? Any mention of Ilan would doom them. She thought of asking about Babita, but what if he asked about Mama's escape to Cloud Cottage? Everyone hoped to find a partner who came from a joyful home and wanted to be with a whole, sane, lighthearted person, not one who lived among betrayals, rifts, and rancor. Then if she asked about his work, she would have to confess her kebab article—what a dangerous topic, as it would lead to Khansama and Babita!

Lizards chased one another out from behind the Macao plates, the photographs of faded brides, and the framed altar cloth embroidered silver and gold by Doña Ernestina, whose son had made the stopped clock that hung in his bachelor's bedroom so time might revolve eternally around *My Dear Mother*. No wonder he had never married. The silence persisted. Clayton stood in a corner of the room with the jug and refilled their glasses at the slightest drop in water level.

The sound of the fan, the cutlery, and their gulps grew louder. "It's true what you said in Allahabad," said Sunny in despair. "You are right about life in the States. The number of things one has to learn to do by oneself! Cooking, cleaning, grocery shopping, washing—"

Said Sonia: "How to assemble furniture, how to change a tire, stop a running toilet, use an electric drill to put up shelves—"

"Find health insurance, call doctors and insurance companies, hunt up test results—"

"Advocate for yourself, volunteer, become a leader—"

"Live your dream, follow your passion, never forget you're special—"

"Computers, televisions, DVD players, CD players, speakers—"

"Jogging, kayaking, mountain biking, skiing—"

"Horseback riding, aerobics, golfing, surfing, tennis—"

"All in different outfits—"

"Bowling, ping-pong, pool, card games, Scrabble—"

"Dance the this and the that—"

"Football, baseball, basketball—"

"And you have no hope in hell, these are complex cultures that take a lifetime."

"The American presidents. I can never keep them straight. Jefferson, Lincoln, Adams, Roosevelt."

"How to learn the wars? Vietnam, Bay of Pigs, Pearl Harbor, Korea, Japan, Guatemala, Cambodia, Cuba, Haiti, Laos, Libya, Tanzania, Argentina, Chile, Kuwait, Guam, the Philippines, Gulf . . ."

"You'd have to be a hundred people in one."

"Meanwhile here you can get by with being one-hundredth of a person—you don't have to do anything."

"Other than give orders to poor people."

"Which is disgusting—"

"There is something so wrong—"

"So wrong—"

When Clayton collected their emptied plates and left the room, Sunny blurted, "I like your dress. The flowers are so large—it's as if I'm seeing you inside a jungle." Sonia wore a dress of enormous lotus blooms.

"What about my ring?" she said, spreading her fingers to show him her beaded lotus flower ring.

He dared: "I prefer the hand."

Sonia tipped her glance. And Sunny's heart began to sing, just as if he'd discovered his natural inheritance: warmth, low lamplight reminiscent of a Tagore painting, a tree frog up high on the wall among the china plates, a slight chill coming off the rice fields, mosquitoes at their ankles despite mosquito coils set into empty soda bottles under the table, wreathing charmed snakes of smoke about a girl whose eyes imparted more light than the low-voltage bulbs.

"Sir, madam, I made up the main bedroom." Clayton smiled too much, as if it were obvious they were not husband and wife. As upon the Allahabad veranda, Sonia's first instinct was to flee. How could she share a bed with Sunny? She wanted to be alone to consider the events of the day, to rue, in fact, that she was not with Sunny, to regret her cowardice, so she would be brave the next day. Sunny, too, didn't want to share a bed just as much as he wished to share a bed. He intuited her ambivalence. He wanted to go for a vigorous jog as was his habit, to rid himself of all he was feeling. He walked the long span of the narrow table to pour port wine into Sonia's goblet to go with the cream serradura. He said, "I think I should sleep in the bachelor's room. That seems appropriate." He dismissed the thought of the stopped clock— through history, men had suffered the same fate.

At which moment Sonia wished he'd said the opposite, and again the memory of Ilan passed over her eyes.

And Sunny remembered Ulla, who was so nonchalant about such matters that it made negotiations around sex as natural as a conversation between children playing in a sandbox.

As they awkwardly went to separate rooms, Clayton watching interestedly, Sunny extended a snail finger that touched Sonia's hand briefly: "Call out if you see a ghost?"

Sonia retired to the vast bedroom assigned to matriarch and patriarch, opening onto an equally vast dressing room and bathroom. She bathed and, parting the starched sheets made up like an envelope, climbed into the high wooden bed carved with the family arms of one knight, two palm trees, three boars, and a pomfret, the canopy above crocheted by *My Dear Mother*.

The stillness of the rice fields outside contrasted with Sunny and Sonia tossing and turning, giving themselves friction burns on either side of the courtyard. Sonia thought how ridiculous it was to worry about what Clayton thought of herself and Sunny. And Sunny was thinking the hourglass had been turned, their time together was limited.

He opened his insect-netting door and felt along the interior courtyard to Sonia's insect-netting door. "Sonia?"

"Yes?"

"Can I come in?"

"Okay." They had complained about the United States, but what a
useful word was "okay"—not giving too much, not taking too much,
neither hot nor cold.

He made his way to the bed, which he remembered was exactly in
the center of the room, under the fan. "Can I climb up?"

"Okay."

He climbed in. It was the pure countryside dark that allowed Sonia
to move her length exactly against his, and after a minute, because
their mouths were virtually together anyway, their breath quickening
and mingling, Sunny brought his lips all the way about Sonia's lips. It
was Sonia who pushed out her tongue.

They recovered the pleasure of being stark naked in pitch-dark, a
feeling of conspiring with another and with the night so one couldn't
tell quite what kind of creature one was, where one began or where
one ended, so entwined one couldn't feel the barrier of skin but instead
a mysterious, cavernous space. Then they slept, and when Sonia woke,
Sunny was not in bed. She called, "Sunny?" and he popped his head
around the door. They were relieved they no longer had to make conversation. Even if the awkwardness returned, they had a way to get
past it now; the nights could undo the embarrassments of the day. And
how sweet it was to call out and receive an answer. Sunny had been
remembering the yoga of his youth on the veranda outside, and while
his sun salutations were comically stiff, the feel of the polished red
floor under his bare feet, the sun slatting through the palms and the
morning haze of humidity, the stray dog sleeping in the pile of swept
dust and leaf debris, were familiar. He wondered if, even after his
mother was gone, India would feel familiar to him, more familiar, in
fact, than he was to himself.

"Just look at that." He opened the door wider so Sonia could see a
pigeon that, when Sunny called to it, "piu roo, piu roo," puffed itself
up, and ruffled its neck feathers flirtatiously: Piu poo, piu coo.

"She thinks I'm doing yoga to impress her," he said, adding, "Why don't we go to breakfast? I hear Clayton."

"Go ahead, and I'll join you."

"I'll wait for you."

"I'm too shy to get dressed with you here."

"Oho, then I'm not going anywhere."

"Then I'm not getting out of bed."

"Okay, I'll just sit here."

"Well, look the other way."

"Okay."

"It's too bright."

"I'll close the shutters."

When Sunny did so, he saw Clayton standing on the brick wall trying to peer in. And when he turned, he saw Sonia reflected naked in the wardrobe mirror.

At breakfast, Clayton was slow. Finally he brought toast, but then it was a long while before the eggs arrived. The tea came last.

The stray dog had climbed out of her bed of leaf debris that was burned every week, and she came to breakfast as well, patched with ashes. She found a piece of last night's mackerel cutlet under the table, which she ate. Then she licked the essence of the cutlet, then she licked the hope of the cutlet, then, losing hope, she became slightly desperate and licked the memory. A lunatic look burgeoned in her eyes. They chased her out.

"What were you doing standing on the wall, looking into the bedroom?" Sunny asked Clayton, following him into the kitchen.

"I was sweeping the wall. Dog sits there and makes it dirty."

"First thing in the morning you were cleaning the wall?"

"Before it gets hot."

....

THEY DROVE OUT WITH ANAND, WHOM THEY HAD KEPT ON
for the duration of their stay out of sympathy for his environmental
passion. He had spent the night in the room adjoining Clayton's in the
servants' quarters meant for a staff of twelve. Hot country-smelling air
blew their hair back, and warm soothing gusts blew slowly up their
sleeves and wobbled them about. Others passed them on mopeds and
scooters, also with their shirts and pants wobbling delicately. The
beauty of the landscape they had not seen earlier when they were jit-
tery about meeting each other was now revealed, and they no longer
minded as Anand stopped and chased plastic bags that took flight, because it made time longer. Sunny and Sonia saw much they had forgotten from their childhood and that no longer existed in their lives, not
in New York, not in New Delhi. Small shops in the crevices of banyan
trees with sparse shelves of candles, pencils, soap, country eggs specked
with chicken droppings. Shopkeeping families who yawned and
rubbed their heads, eyes, and stomachs before reaching slowly out
for what their customers requested. They stopped at a bakery in a family home for cashew, palm-sugar, and coconut pastries—Melting Moments, Angel Wings—kept in a glass case along with the children's
school medals. A priest in a long, white cotton smock (albeit smudged
a little with red earth) blew his horn as he drove his moped hurriedly
past, the tail of a pomfret for his lunch peeping from the bag that hung
from the scooter handles.

Maneuvering skillfully about several pigs slumbering with their
stomachs spread across the road, Anand said abruptly, "My neighbor's
pig was stolen!"

"Is it a big thing, the stealing of pigs?" Sunny asked.

"Oh yes. Kidnapping of pigs, but you have to be careful because they make so much noise. Later you hear someone running around saying, 'Where is Euphania?'"

"The pigs have names?"

Anand gave another inch toward friendliness after this information had been appreciated. "Why have you come?" he asked.

Said Sonia, "I am writing about Old Goa."

"There is an old house." He pointed at a red-tiled roof sprouting with plants.

"It could be our house," said Sunny.

Sonia kept the "our" like a small star.

"That is an old house, that is an old house—all are old houses!"

Sonia noticed several homes that looked abandoned, then spotted a bespectacled whiskery lady in a faded nightie, just like Mina Foi, peeking from a window, a pair of knickers from the past age of knickers on the washing line.

The taxi blooming and crackling with pastel plastics, they arrived at a historic mansion divided by two brothers into two wings, each with a lady awaiting visitors, beckoning from the upper veranda. "No photographs," they warned, but Sunny hadn't brought his camera anyway. Had he not done so because this was a secret meeting? Did leaving his camera behind mean that he trusted a future with Sonia, or that he did not? He was glad in this moment, that this time was not about the falsity of posing.

One lady showed them a Bohemian chandelier, the other showed them a Murano chandelier. One indicated a mausoleum by the side of what looked like a car mechanic's yard, the other a mausoleum moored in traffic. One had a sliver of St. Francis Xavier's fingernail ensconced in the center of the altar in a darkened glass cavity of a case otherwise gold, the other had two medicine jars brought by St. Francis when he sailed to India.

The brother of the east wing had supported the king of Portugal and was rewarded for his work as the consul to Spain with two chairs sent by the king, each carved with the family crest of one knight, two boars, turtle doves, and Christmas stars. The brother of the west wing had supported the liberation and built a library of five thousand volumes. Two ballrooms, two chapels, two brothers, one supporting the king and one the liberation—but what had happened in the end?

"*Liberation?*" said the lady whose ancestor was faithful to the king.

"*Botheration!*" said the lady of the house that had loved the liberation. Their disparate beliefs had conjoined when their land had been confiscated by the Indian government as part of land reform, and when the families had fallen into the exact same poverty. Both ladies pointed to a donation box.

Anand said, "What did they tell you? They said that India has taken away their land and their money? All lies! Their money used to come from high taxes; they would tax all of us without mercy! Now they are angry they cannot!"

They continued to the Santa Monica convent and the Chapel of the Weeping Cross, where a painting that had the stigmata had been found in the basement quarters of a nun who had been a resident in the 1600s. Every now and again the wounds of Christ on the cross bled, but otherwise it was a peaceful picture on wood pecked by termites that were also consuming the altar of chipped gilt that squawked with ecstatic bats. Tepid droppings of pigeons roosting in the roof fell like manna upon the open book of petitions written in English and Konkani: *Dear Jesus, I ask for only one thing. That my family and myself will be happy always.* They went up the hill to Our Lady of the Mount to watch the sun set over the delta. There were many men photographing themselves romantically here. Sunny wished he had brought his camera after all. When they stopped at a backpacker's favorite eating spot on Rue 31 de Janeiro in Panjim and sat on a balcony with a lantern rocking in the sea breeze, Sunny took Sonia's legs between his under the table and said, "Psst!"

"What?"

"*I'm happy with you!*"

Back on the veranda with the stray dog covered in ashes and leaf debris darting by to give another deranged lick to the memory of mackerel cutlet under the dining table, Sonia made notes, Sunny made notes. Sonia said, "How is it we both make notes?"

Sunny said, "I began to keep a diary to train my eye in case what I see differs from the news. I thought if I simply describe situations that are complicated, the sense may be reflected back."

"What about the Vasco port story you said you wanted to write? Nobody knows about our meeting or I could have asked my mother's friend Ferooza about her colleague who set up an AIDS clinic in Vasco."

"I realized it would be hubris to try to write that story in a few days." The story of the Vasco port—the men who traveled the world on ships, the women who were brought from all over India by their madams—wouldn't be a contained subject. It would take a long while to understand the people behind the statistics, the hundreds of different communities, the stories behind the stories. And he could hardly behave like an American with Sonia watching—jet in for an assignment that was more accurately a vacation, return to New York high on adventure to show off to a group gathered in a tapas restaurant in the West Village. Sonia would know how Sunny was making use of the girls being trafficked, of the men who worked desolate years, for whom the ocean was a desert.

"What about you, are you making notes for your magazine article?" he asked.

"I think I'm secretly trying to trick myself into writing fiction again."

"Why did you stop?"

"Because when I was in the States, I wrote what people wanted to read over there. I began to write charming stories that didn't correspond with my life when life took me to a dark place."

"Why didn't you write darker, true stories?"

"The darkness was stronger than I was. If bad things swallow you, you can't see the bad things." By simply inscribing what she saw and heard, would Sonia retrain her eye to rewire her brain?

"What bad things?"

"I'll tell you another day," Sonia said.

At this moment darkness and loneliness were far away. They continued to write. They looked up once in a while, when a coconut detached and crashed down or to see mating butterflies tumble from the sky. When dusk fell they put away their notebooks and reclined their forms back within the large planter's chairs. Sonia said, as if continuing a conversation, "Finally I was so much within myself in New York that I couldn't see myself in the mirror; I looked at myself the way an animal does. I looked at other people from a far distance as if they did not actually exist."

Sunny could see only Sonia's legs and her feet, which she held up and out before her, a frankness of two legs, ten splayed toes. He said, "I can't imagine either of us are simple people. How could we be? We've lived different lives in different places."

Sonia said, "Are you looking for simple?"

Sunny saw both her hands held out now, ten frankly spread-out fingers.

He said, "I am not looking for simple."

"But we are simple here."

"We are simple here."

They went to the beach at Arossim. "The first time you swim after a long while is as close as you'll ever get to happiness," said Sonia.

"But, Sonia, that is so strange. I thought the exact thing my first morning in Goa!"

She wore the turquoise-green bikini she still had from a New York shopping trip with Ilan—ready for Portofino, where the film stars went. It was old-fashioned in the style favored by Ilan's mother, ruched about the bust, tied behind her neck, frilled briefs up to her navel. They swam up the waves, and at the peak, they could see each other splayed in the transparence before they came sailing down into the sizzle of foam. They pretended to be octopi with limbs that ensnared each other. They made fish kisses on their bare bellies underwater. They made seaweed mustaches.

When they were back in the house in the rice fields, Sunny confessed: "You know in the mornings you ask me to look away when you get out of bed? Well, I do, but I happen to see you—"

"Aren't you looking away?"

"I accidentally catch your reflection in the wardrobe mirror—"

"Oh?"

"The sight is worth more than all the chandeliers in Belgium—"

"Oh?"

"All the marble in Carrara, the tiles of Portugal, the tureen lids of Macao, the fingernail of St. Francis Xavier, one-hundred-fifty-year-old sea turtles, Melting Moments and Angel Wings, three rice crops a year, the *botheration of liberation*—"

"Worth the ocean?"

He pretended to think.

That night in the creaking bed: "Even the ocean."

Their lovemaking became more free, more experimental, fanning out. They pleasured themselves, pleasured each other, their voices mingled. "I can't see you at all. What part of you is this?"

"It's my elbow."

"Your elbow? What is it doing all the way there?"

The bed shook and creaked like a tree in a storm. "Should we move to the floor?"

"There's nobody to hear."

Clayton stood outside the window, masturbating in the dark despite the swarms of mosquitoes. Earlier he had watched Sonia take a bath through a hole in the wall that only he knew about. When he was a boy he had watched the curvaceous beauty of Bertha Borda d'Agua that had lured a rabbity Australian and drawn the family away.

The sentence came automatically: "I'm very happy."

"I'm happy, too."

"We had better stick together."

"We had better remain simple."

"Let's remain simple."

It was strange, then, that Sunny woke startled as if by a sound. The measured beat of his heart had vanished, and his chest heaved with fear.

Sonia was invisible, sleeping folded upon him, although he could feel her hair, her arm across him, her soft round breast. The stillness felt portentous. He tried to reach back into his dream to locate a cause but couldn't.

Night thoughts assaulted him. Why was he here? What could it lead to? His life was elsewhere. It was foolishness. He wasn't going to stay in Delhi. How could Sonia come to New York City? It would take two unwavering wills. It would take considerable money. It would take asking her to be his wife. He was too young for a wife.

Was it their happiness that had spooked him? How could they possibly know enough about each other to lie side by side like a long-married couple, playing at being owners of a mansion? He felt a return of the playacting he'd felt with Ulla. It was too soon. Modern life forced one to make a decision upon a vacation, pulled one into intimacy as fast as an arranged marriage. Briefly he remembered Satya and remembered it would be Pooja's birthday tomorrow—but there was a deeper fear that he couldn't name, a panic similar to his panic when Ulla left, and he didn't want to remember that panic because the minute he remembered it, he felt his throat tightening and worried the memory might trigger his inability to eat, swallow, or speak the way he had been unable to in the weeks following her departure.

He turned Sonia carefully over, got up, and went out into the living room, where he switched on a lamp. He noticed the house didn't have the feel of a place sleepy within the past anymore; it felt as if it were lying in wait. The lizards on the walls were watchful, the chairs were splayed in anticipation, the stuffed deer with its slim face and coral antlers had eyes laden with unspilled tears. The ghost brides in their frames and the ghost children, the thousands of objects on the tables and in the cabinets, the plates on the wall, the tureens, were accusing. *What now? Why? When? It isn't fair!*

He opened the glass bookcase holding volumes so disintegrated they looked like wormy driftwood, but it was possible to make out a few titles: Gide, Montaigne, Balzac, Zweig, Machado de Assis, the Encyclopaedia Britannica, the Portuguese Oriental Archives in vellum.

The portrait of the dark man in white gloves and a blue military suit watched Sunny search his books. Why couldn't he remain dead? He was still awaiting summons from the king of Portugal perhaps; the chairs still awaiting the return of the kingdom, maybe; the piano wishing for the waltz; the gun for the revolution. The ghost brides forever anticipating their happiness; the book by Zweig praying for the war to end before the author shot himself in the fairy-tale mountains above Rio de Janeiro. The soup bowls awaiting the banquet, the tureen lids mourning their lost tureens. *My Dear Mother Ernestina* waiting for the hands of the clock to move again, to be alive once more, darling and dear once more to a son who would never betray her and marry—

It was then Sunny became aware that lying in wait within all of this waiting *was his mother's waiting* and his guilt waiting to claim him for his mother's waiting for him to telephone and own up to his lies. Because without him, she was as lonesome as a book nobody has read for three hundred years, as bereft as a Macao lid without a Macao tureen for two hundred years, as grief-stricken as a widowed ghost bride in a mansion in silent rice fields for one hundred years, whose owners have abandoned it for suburban Adelaide.

He remembered that Babita had said she, too, would like to escape to the warmth of Goa and relieve her chilblains. She had suggested she might fly with Sunny to visit her college friend Vanya. He'd made unscrupulous use of his mother. It was she who had suggested Satya honeymoon in Goa. He remembered the kebab cook from Allahabad who had not in the end arrived. Babita would interpret his happiness with Sonia as a betrayal so grave, it would be a death blow.

He went to look at sleeping Sonia. He didn't know she was dreaming of another man. He didn't know that there was an eye watching her that never left her, that one of the ghost brides in this house was, in fact, Sonia, for Ilan had made certain she would never be a bride in real life, he had killed her prematurely. Sure she was dead, Sonia awoke and said, "I've been murdered."

"Surely not!" said Sunny in a rough voice, as if he'd had enough of something.

"You don't believe my nightmare?"

"Maybe someone was murdered here once and you are picking up on that."

She sensed mockery. "No, it wasn't anyone else's murder. I was the one murdered!"

"By whom?"

"Evil," she said. "I think I'm lonely."

"Lonely? After all this lovemaking?"

"Because of all this lovemaking. Because we will be leaving soon and will be parted." They had changed their flights to return to Delhi together.

Maybe to drown out these questions about the future, they decided to swim one last time. Two people, united by the ocean—maybe nothing can undo that, the future cannot undo the past. They drove with Anand to a deserted part of the coast, where they found the ocean rough. But because they'd saved this as their final pleasure, they entered the water, whereupon they found the waves even stronger than they'd appeared from shore, mounting so high they had to plunge almost to the ocean floor to escape being caught in their crashing down. There was little time to fin up and catch their breath before the next wave came racing and they had to dive again, never diving too shallowly, which would have caught them in a dangerous tumble.

Sonia looked for Sunny, and Sunny searched for Sonia's head bobbing. Finally she called, "I'm turning back"; although he couldn't hear, he could see that she was trying to return. It took a long while, turning repeatedly to plunge down, fin up—no time for a proper breath—diving deep again, finning up to scrabble toward land before the powerful draining of the water breaking upon the shore swept them back out once more. When they finally staggered forth, the ocean moved with such force between their legs it left them knee-deep in sand. For a while they lay with their hearts hammering, their eyes closed, still feeling the tug of the waves.

There was a breath on Sonia's foot, and when she opened her eyes she saw a dog that had suddenly appeared—a huge, white, hairless hound with a harlequin face; had he been washed up by the waves as well? He staggered and struggled, slowly recovering. He had a broken chain, deep, septic bite marks in his back, and a torn, bloodied ear. He snarled.

"Are you all right?" asked Sunny. "Let's get out of here." They could quite easily in this moment of being alive be dead. Life was thin and terrifying on the side of *not* having died.

They got up and began to make their way back to the taxi. The hound followed them, sniffing after them, pissing, roaming the beach, owning the beach, loping back, picking up their scent, gaining strength. There was something strange about this pursuit; he came always too close with the big, lipstick-pink of his penis out of a mottled white shaft, his leering jackal face, his pocket ears. Sonia said, "That dog is as cocky as his cock. It's probably learned from lecherous men slavering over women on the beach." His face was like that of a dog wearing the mask of a dog.

Sunny said, "He's taking what you said for flattery and becoming more aggressive."

Did sexual jealousy cross species? Sonia wondered.

The dog began to wag its stump tail, but when Sonia held out her hand, it growled and snapped.

When Sunny threatened the hound with a pretend stone, he bared his teeth and leapt closer. Sunny noticed froth dripping from his mouth. "It might have rabies!" A rabid dog, dying of thirst, hallucinating, would pass on its brain fever to whomever it bit.

They walked faster to get away—not running because you should never run if followed by such a beast. The dog trotted faster as well.

When Sonia's foot painfully cramped as a result of swimming in ocean currents and then hurrying on uneven sand, she was forced to stop. She bent down to press her foot in the opposite direction of the cramp, and the dog lunged. She smelled his dog smell in her face, his hard dictator eyes looked right into hers, his lips were blubbery and his teeth pointy. Sunny took off his slipper and smashed it down on the back of the dog's head. The dog turned to sink its teeth into Sunny but caught his slipper, and Sonia and Sunny ran together now, Sonia hobbling, Sunny turning every now and again to pretend to pitch a stone—

when suddenly the white dog overtook them and, before their eyes, made a turn in to the sand and dissipated like vapor. There was absolutely nothing up ahead but a washed-up log.

"Where did he go?" Sunny examined his slipper with the deep punctures of a ferocious bite going all the way through the rubber.

Anand was asleep in the taxi. He woke with a start and leaned back and over to open the door for them.

"The current was very strong," Sonia said. "We almost could not get out, and a mad dog came after us."

"Why did you swim?" he said, moving his lips about distastefully— in this climate even a short nap grew a coating upon one's teeth. "It's not safe to swim. You can see there is a red flag flying."

They hadn't noticed the fraying scrap of red fabric like a religious pennant. They didn't know they were supposed to notice it. "You never said anything before."

"It's my job to take you wherever you want."

As they drove along silently, he said, "I thought you would only stay in the shallow water, like other people. How was I to know you were going to swim out? Nobody does that."

They continued on, silent and aware of the dark stretch at their backs that was the writhing ocean, furious it hadn't claimed them. Of its emissary, the drowned dog, seething it hadn't sunk its teeth into them. Sunny took Sonia's hand. They had looked for each other to make sure they were safe, it was true, but the fight against the waves had been a private desperation. Each had known that they could only save themselves.

That night Sonia read her *Brothers Karamazov*. It was a murder mystery—who was the murderer? She said, "One of the characters says something interesting: Active love is the only way to dispel fear and disbelief."

Sunny had opened his *Farewell to Arms*. "This is essentially what my book is about as well."

But if you love, you fear, thought Sonia. You fear and believe you will lose love. But if you don't love, you also fear. You feel safe only when you are alone and cannot be betrayed, yet you feel unsafe being alone.

Sonia caught herself before she said the sentence that was never a good idea: *What if you leave me?*

She turned to face away from Sunny, and he felt compelled to utter the line Sonia had forced herself not to say. "Let's not leave each other."

She replied, "If you don't leave me, either. Because that's how life is. It's always the person who begs you not to leave who then leaves." She remembered Ilan: *Don't ever leave me! Take me seriously! Darling, you are my dear!* If a person is assured of loyalty, he might then experiment with other options while being certain of someone waiting should he fail.

"I'm scared that you're scared you will be hurt, and so you'll be the one to hurt me by leaving. Do you really think I would risk you so foolishly?" Sunny said.

Sonia remembered Ilan had uttered the exact same sentiment: *Do you think I would throw you away so cheaply? I love all of you, even your strange fingers, even your crooked little toe. I even love your temper.* "I know enough to know that anything can happen," she said.

Sunny thought: *Something is bound to go wrong.* He remembered the foreboding of the night before. "Let's make sure nothing will happen. Look, I will make a vow: *Nothing is going to happen here!*" he called out of the window into the rice paddy. If they ever mislaid their happiness, the rice paddy, the belching frogs, the stars, and even the ocean that had tried to kill them, would remember and preserve it.

They continued to lie side by side, looking at each other solemnly and silently. Sunny shut his eyes, then opened them anew, looking directly into Sonia's.

After a span of surveying each other and understanding they were stranger to each other and more unpredictable than they may have expected, Sunny said, "Let me see your hand."

She gave it to him. "Can you read palms?"

"Yes. You bite your nails and your fingers are dirty."

"They are not!"

He put a finger in his mouth. "And your nails taste salty."

"They must still be salty from the sea."

"I wonder if your ear is salty, too?"

He put her earlobe in his mouth and tickled it with his tongue so first she laughed, then she was aroused.

The last morning in Goa, Sonia and Sunny bathed together under the shower that was like a silted watering can dispensing erratic plops of warm water. They soaped each other carefully—front, back, between the legs, breasts, buttocks, balls. They made love one last time in the slow warmth, and after poi toast and mango jam, they left the house in the rice paddy.

Who was the most heartbroken? Not Sunny nor Sonia; not Clayton nor Anand—each of whom had been awarded the over-the-top tip that is given by two people in love—but the creature nobody had given a thought to: the little leftover-rice-once-upon-a-time-a-mackerel-cutlet-no-name stray dog who never barked but only squeaked with love. They saw her at the edge of the property watching them; then before Anand started the car she had turned her back to slink away. Sonia closed her eyes. They had left her to the mercy of the ghost hound.

On the flight, Sunny said nothing, neither did Sonia. Other passengers sat so close about them, practically in their laps, it would be impossible to speak soft words. They stepped out into Delhi, where everyone was coughing. Coughing, Balbir Singh was awaiting Sonia. Coughing, Bahadur was awaiting Sunny. They were forced to pretend they did not know each other. All that Sunny could proffer was a hasty, "I'll come and see you before leaving for New York?"

Their desperate, raw faces reflected in each other's eyes as they turned and walked away.

*

"MA?" SAID SUNNY WHEN he arrived home. It was teatime. His mother sat with the tea tray and a travel magazine.

"Ma?" he said. Because he had fallen in love and felt tenderly, Sunny was full of amends.

"Ma!" he said.

Babita was slow to look up, but when she did, she took it witheringly in: his waterlogged expression, eyes and mouth mealy—Babita could not stand to see her son drowned by love. She said through snake lips, "I never imagined I'd have a son who tells lies."

There wasn't any point in saying "What lies?" so Sunny said, "If I were to tell you the truth, you'd be furious. That only leaves lies."

"So you *did* go meet *that girl*?" She found she could not bring herself to spit out Sonia's name.

How did she know? Sunny would never have suspected loyal Satya of betrayal, no matter their silly squabble.

"Am I required to report every detail of my life to you? I might have, or I may not have, it isn't any of your business."

"Might and may? Speak straight like you were brought up to do."

Ten minutes of antagonistic silence.

"Well, actually, I could think seriously of Sonia."

"Think what of her seriously?"

Twenty minutes of antagonistic silence.

Babita said: "Believe me, she had to come back from America because of a mental disturbance. Like her mother who went up the mountain and never came down."

Another ten minutes of antagonistic silence.

Babita added: "Once, I saw her at the Taj Hotel café with a baldy— I felt sorry for her."

Incredulous, Sunny said, "You felt sorry for her because she was with a bald person?"

"You know, feeling sorry for someone is not a reason to marry them," she said.

Five minutes later: "Chaloo—a lot of stupid people have a primitive slyness. I hope you didn't tell her about your green-card application?"

One minute later: "It's despicable to obtain a green card through marriage. Is it you the woman wants—you'd have to wonder—or what you can procure for her?"

Sunny went to his bedroom and shut his door, while Babita poured herself another rum beyond her usual two. Thirty minutes later, Sunny heard loud footsteps and a despairing alcohol-laden sigh by the keyhole. "Oh, Lord, protect me!" moaned Babita, which was ludicrous for someone who was an atheist. "You know that girl's grandfather in Allahabad blackmailed your nana—that is why he was forced to forward the marriage proposal."

At this Sunny leapt to his door. *"What are you talking about?"*

"Nana suggested Sonia's grandfather invest in a military blanket business. The business failed, they lost money, and so you are the compensation—"

"What do you mean?" hollered Sunny.

"I mean what I say. No might and no may. You've fallen into their trap. Expensive American education didn't save you."

"You're drunk!" he slayed her.

At 10:30 P.M., hearing no more irate thumping, Sunny crept past his mother's door and sneaked out of his mother's gate, lighting his way with the torch that always stood on his bedside table in case of a power outage. He turned in to Uncle Ravi's gate and rang the bell. Because Uncle Ravi's asthma always worsened in fog-smog, he never left the house during the cold months. He shut all the doors and windows tightly and played pirated movies from a video rental in the Panchsheel market at the end of their street. He was watching Hitchcock's *Key Largo,* sipping jasmine tea.

"What's up, kiddo?" said Uncle Ravi mirthfully.

Sunny sat down. "I don't know what to do. I just don't know what to do." He hung his head and cracked his knuckles, reminding Uncle Ravi of his poor, dead brother. His shadow on the wall, too, exactly resembled the profile of Sunny's father, sunk in despair.

"She keeps me on a short leash, she forbids me to meet you. Last year when I was here, I could only wave at you, remember? She is terrified I will meet a woman and marry. She notices if I went to the bathroom and turned on the light at night. I never leave her gaze— I feel it on me even on the other side of the world. She has refused to make a life for herself, so I cannot make my own life because I am her entire life. Ever since Daddy died, it has been a nightmare."

"No!" Uncle Ravi lifted his cup and breathed in the jasmine steam. "Mistake number one: This has nothing to do with your father dying. First she was in love with *my* father, which made my mother crazy with hate. Then she fell in love with *you*. Husband was the disappointment—he was far too gentle for her to appreciate him. She purposefully created a relationship with you that shut him out. She brought you to sleep in the bed next to hers and turfed your father to the guest room. Your father died of a broken heart.

"If you marry," he went on, sagaciously, "it will be a fake marriage. If you have a child, you will be masquerading as a father; your child will be a fake child. You will be a fake husband. Only she knows and possesses the real you. Only as her son will you be allowed to be a true person."

"How do you have such insight?"

"Because my mother was the same! Why do you think I'm a bachelor?"

"A psychologist would have a field day," remarked Sunny gloomily.

"Western psychology is no match for an Indian family. We are too slippery, we change shape, we don't distinguish truth from lies. Lies are truth and truth are lies—you can't pin us down."

When Sunny got up to leave, Uncle Ravi said, "Live your life. And think of us—we also need to escape. Please encourage your mother to sell this house."

Sunny sighed. "She won't listen to me. But now that I've broken the law by visiting you, I may as well pay my respects to Uncle Rana. Or is it too late at night?"

"He's awake past midnight. Don't be surprised if his girlfriend is with him—she is what you in the States would call a 'hot cookie,' a coat-check girl from the Oberoi. Goes by Ruby."

Uncle Ravi restarted his movie. "I myself prefer the company of Katharine Hepburn."

"That old dame!" exclaimed Uncle Rana. "How she goes on and on about Minnie's will, the egg cups, and the losing investments that have, in fact, kept her quite adequately provided for. Ruby knows all about it," he said when a woman entered the room, "don't you, Ruby? Please, Sunny, beg your mother to sell so Ruby and I can bhago to New Zealand. Freedom!"

Ruby wore white high heels, white jeans, and a clinging, low-cut, white T-shirt with a sparkly gold Valentine heart. Her salon hair was streaked blondish. Her mouth and nails were vampire red.

"Naughty man," said Ruby, sitting on the arm of the sofa by Uncle Rana. "Making me such promises always—but yet to deliver!" She winked at Sunny.

"Ruby talks only nonsense," said Uncle Rana.

"Sunny," she said, "tell your uncle to stop being mean to me. He's a meanie." He pinched her behind, and she began to giggle and tussle.

Babita had always contended that while Uncle Rana's girlfriends were supremely silly on the surface, their vapidity was nothing but strategic. They were hardheaded women, plotting to claw a fortune the only way they could. Some of them were call girls from an escort service, Mr. Habib had informed her. How did he know?

"I told Rana your mother must be wanting more money, no? What else?" Ruby said. "But don't go listening to me, Miss Big Fat Foot in My Mouth. When you rang the bell, Rana said, 'Don't say a word to Sunny—he's a mama's boy!'" She winked at Sunny again, leaving him perplexed as to her meaning.

*

"WHY DON'T YOU THINK of selling and be done with the battle?" blurted Sunny to Babita the next morning.

"Oh? And are you going to buy me an apartment in New York?"

She spoke in a sprightly manner on the phone to Sara so she would be heard. "I can tell you one thing, Sara, what we succeeded at was bringing up perfect foreigners. They call themselves global citizens. Bah! Global bastards, more like!"

After two more days of suffering his mother's abandoned-widow face, with the hour of his departure growing nearer, Sunny could not stand another moment. He'd felt acutely lonely and uncertain in this act of turning away. He had betrayed the woman who had never betrayed him. He had visited his uncles, Ravi and Rana, determined to make a stand against his mother, seeking reassurance that he was in the right. His uncles had reassured him, but they wanted something from him, too. What they wanted would render his mother home-less.

"I think I might swing by the clinic," said Sunny, giving in. "My eye was bothering me in Goa, and the irritation hasn't gone away. It might be an infection from the ocean."

"Your eye? Why didn't you go to a doctor immediately? Vanya told me the ocean is filthy. Doesn't that girl know that one must prioritize an eye over absolutely everything?"

Off they went to the clinic for eye drops. Later, Sunny said, "Do you have any Disprin? Sonia took mine."

She looked at him silently for a spell, long enough to grant this statement proper import, then slowly brought out the medicine box.

"Why did she take your Disprin?" asked Babita, giving another quarter inch.

"She had a headache from the afternoon heat."

"Why would that girl drag you about in the sun? Goa is always too hot, Vanya says. Just stay quietly here, peace and calm, nobody to bother you."

And so, Sunny began to betray Sonia to cure his mother's grief, and his new love became a complaint to lull her. Could he secretly love Sonia behind a false refrain? The woman with whom for the first time in his entire life he had been his natural self?

Babita rewarded him. She called for the Shropshire Blue that was being stored in the freezer—to keep the cheese going as long as possible—to be defrosted and ceremoniously served at cocktail hour. She divulged the servant gossip. It seemed Vinita and the Habibs' D-R-I-V-E-R were having a R-O-M-A-N-C-E. She sent Punita to fetch her homework. Punita's English had improved beyond the stage of *Miss Cat and Miss Mouse*. She had written *My Summer Holiday* and *My Birthday Party*. Slum children would feel badly about what they had missed once they were taught to hanker after it.

Sunny, looking up from his chair in the garden, happened to see Vinita brushing her hair on the rooftop, her neck moving right then left as she bent her head to the tug of the brush. She disengaged the caught hairs from the bristles and let them float away, like wishes blown into the universe. Vinita caught him watching her, and when Sunny was next in the kitchen getting a glass of water, Vinita said, "The cooks of your uncles told me you went to visit your uncles."

"So?"

"Your mother doesn't let us talk to them. She gets angry if we do."

He felt a dislike for Vinita. It was as if this statement were prelude to blackmail. "Well, then don't tell her, or she'll be angry at me as well."

"She cuts my salary each month."

"Who does?"

"Aunty."

"My mother?"

"Yes. She says she is keeping it in a bank account so the money will grow, but she keeps the passbook. I want to keep the money I earn myself."

Sunny questioned his mother.

"I give them an allowance each month to teach them about banking. I explained to them how the money will earn interest and eventually they can use it for their dowry or for college."

But this was a sly way to keep a servant bound to you, thought Sunny.

Babita suggested, "Now that you are being sponsored for your green card, perhaps you could also contribute to their accounts."

"I am not going to pay into a dowry fund!" exclaimed Sunny.

"They don't have the luxury of thinking that way; they belong to a social class, and they have to abide by its rules. The rich of this country make their fortunes on the backs of the poor. The least we can do is help their children achieve a different life."

Sunny thought how absurd it would be for him to clean and scrub in Jackson Heights, strive to the subway in all kinds of weather, and labor all night to maintain his meager existence, while contributing to dowries for his mother's servant girls. But it was true that his Indian life and his American life were in some way owed to Vini-Puni.

"Look, I am promising before my son," a triumphant Babita declared to the girls' mother, Gunja, the next morning, "your children are the responsibility of this family, so never worry about anything.

We will take care of you—understood? If I am not around, my son will fulfill this vow. Vini-Puni are also my daughters. They are his sisters."

And when Sunny was next in the kitchen getting a glass of water, Vinita said, "Sunny Bhaiya, take me to America!"

"I can barely afford to buy a plane ticket for myself."

"But take me one day!"

*

IT WAS ONLY DURING afternoon siesta on his last day, with his mother asleep and Bahadur the spy asleep, that Sunny dared escape in a scooter rickshaw to meet Sonia as he had promised to do before he returned to New York. He took with him a copy of instructions on how to swim out of a riptide, which he had researched and printed out. In case Sonia ever found herself in such a lethal predicament again.

Papa was at his office dictating to his secretary a formal proposal for investigating the singing toilets of Japan. And so worried was Chandu that Sonia might attempt to bake a cake and squander his supplies—as she had upon one single occasion when she was eleven years old and had followed *The Landour Cookbook* to make a Wacky Crazy Cake— that he had taken his flour, sugar, and margarine up to his rooftop quarter and placed them under his bed while he took his nap. Because he had his larder with him, Chandu was sleeping deeply. He didn't hear the doorbell.

When Sunny was smuggled into her bedroom, Sonia couldn't help herself; she turned to hide her tears. Sunny saw her beauty, felt joy at her tears upon his cheeks, and was ashamed. "Come to New York!"

They had under an hour. They didn't waste more time speaking.

Dark Place
Mountain

41

....

OU WOULD THINK MRS. SHARMA FROM NEXT DOOR IN HAUZ Khas would consider herself lucky—as lucky as Clayton had considered himself standing on the wall outside the window in Loutolim—when she climbed to her roof to check the water supply and received an unexpected view of two beautiful people engaged in the intense sad sex of parting without knowing when they would next meet, if ever, or whether one of them might betray the other. But Mrs. Sharma didn't consider herself lucky. She almost toppled down the stairs in her haste to telephone her husband at his workplace and inform him that the America-returned girl next door was in bed with a boy, stark naked both of them, while the cook was asleep, her father at work.

That evening, Papa settled deep into his Laphroaig and qawwali music, the volume turned up to overcome the fierce sound of Chandu frying masala, when the bell rang.

Mr. Sharma declined to enter when he saw Sonia demure upon the sofa. His face was swollen. "This is a decent neighborhood. My wife was on the roof and what should she see?"

"Hold on, what did she see?"

"Why don't you ask your daughter?"

Papa became nervous. "I will speak to Sonia."

"Speak to her? Attack her!"

"Look," said Papa to Sonia when the door had been closed on Mr. Sharma and she had confessed Sunny's afternoon visit. "Tell Sunny to come over right now. If anyone wants to see my daughter, I expect him to come to the front door while I am home and ring the doorbell. I cannot abide a sneak." He didn't ask what Mrs. Sharma had seen.

"He is leaving for New York tonight." Sonia had told her father she'd happened to run into Sunny in Goa, but she hadn't told him that they'd stayed together in the crumbly Loutolim mansion.

"After causing this mess?"

"He didn't know."

"He's up and run!"

"We're going to meet in the States."

"Hold on—is he going to foot the bill? He's taken you for a ride."

"He doesn't have money."

"Lives in Panchsheel, has no money? Tell him to change his ticket."

"He has to get back to work."

"What about *your* work? Don't make out that you're passing time waiting for a man."

Papa's warning seemed prescient. At the visa window of the white-and-gold U.S. embassy, Sonia's answers to the very first questions doomed her, as always: "Are you married? Do you have children? A job?"

The embassy clerk did not have to give an explanation, but he did. He was cordial because he was from Vermont and upon questioning Sonia had learned that she had studied at Hewitt College. He said she could not convince him that she would not stay on in America, for she was young, single, and childless, with an American education and no proper occupation. By returning to India after her internship with Lala, Sonia had ensured she might never go back, not until she made a life in India strong enough to convince a visa officer that a visit to the United States would be merely a vacation. The Vermont connection had been a trap, her reply revealing she was primed to become one more unwanted immigrant. She had said, yes, she had some dear friends there, such as Marie, Armando, and Audrey. She had said it was so ethereal in winter you could scarcely believe you existed on earth.

This misfortune of being denied dazed her. She had been mistaken in her certainty that she'd be desirable over the other applicants camped outside, with her perfect English, her Westernized manners. But others who spoke little English and were not Westernized in their manners but had degrees in engineering, medicine, computers, and chemical science were getting their visas processed. America needed them; it had no use for Sonia, who had only been given employment because of Ilan. Within the emotion of shame, the memory of Ilan inevitably returned. *Don't you have any shame, you shameless person?*

Driving back, Balbir Singh commiserated, "Oof ho!" Was he the handsome navy-turbaned driver of a rich family who should feel a sense of security? Or was he not? "Oof ho." He wondered. He had thought perhaps one day the family might send his son to America the way they had sent Sonia. Now he wasn't sure.

Sonia snapped: "Don't keep saying, 'Oof ho.'"

Was she the daughter of the family who lived by the principle of always being polite to those less fortunate? A child came begging at a streetlight and Sonia automatically rolled up her window. The little boy added his own hostile agreement to her denial of mutual humanity: He squashed his face right against the glass, let his eyes roll back and a line of spittle dribble down against the glass.

"Are you an animal?" Balbir Singh shouted at him.

Sonia rewrote her email to Sunny several times. She hadn't been truthful to him. She hadn't told him who she really was. Now the lies were becoming apparent. She was giving Sunny too much bad news, like a Third World relative whom your only choice is to ditch before their problems disrupt your First World life. Earlier she had written: *Mrs. Sharma saw us having sex and told Mr. Sharma. Mr. Sharma came and told my father, then he told the whole neighborhood, so the neighbors spit and mutter "dirty girl" when I walk by.* Now she wrote in falsely blithe fashion: *It seems I am an unwanted alien.*

Sunny wrote back: *Bastards. Let me think. Editing a story on the firebombing of Tokyo. Meanwhile, a blizzard is blowing outside. The skyscrapers have vanished in the storm.*

I miss you, Sonia replied. *I'm unhappy being back with my father. If I'm not with you, I want to be alone to think of you. I'm impatient with everyone.*

She remembered the intimacy of two people alone together when it snowed. She remembered the pure white upon the hemlocks, the black walnuts, the maples, the winged wahoo, the dark shadows of the white trees on the white snow. She remembered morning revealing

the footprints of many creatures: tiny, light claws, deep four-leaf clo-
ver prints, the whoosh of a tail. Who had been here? Skunks or rac-
coons, deer or groundhogs, mice, squirrels, rabbits, bears, foxes? A
wolverine or a catamount? A ghost snow hound?

Where was Badal Baba now?

....

SUNNY WAS AT HIS DESK EDITING AN ANNIVERSARY STORY
on the World War II firebombing of Tokyo—which included Yoko
Ono's memories of living through the bombing when she was a girl—
and he felt shaken by the black hole in his knowledge. He had never
heard about this event. He thought, *Wait, but after 100,000 civilians were
killed on the ninth of March in 1945*—after *such a tally, the United States dropped
the atomic bombs on Hiroshima and Nagasaki on August sixth and ninth?*

He remembered the presence of Dan, the veteran who had chosen
to be permanently on the night shift at the sports desk. He went over.
"I never knew about the firebombing of Tokyo. Is it less known, or is
it because I grew up in India that I didn't properly learn about it?"

Dan didn't reply, but his expression showed how inconsiderate this
question was. Sunny went back to his desk and carried on working until
Dan said—bringing down his fist all of a sudden, as if in judgment upon
himself—"*We shot them so hard! They kept coming, and we shot them so hard!*"

Now it was Sunny's turn to wonder how to respond. He thought a
man who had killed once could surely kill again. He wanted to say that
Dan was right to be tormented. He wanted to tell him that it was not
his fault. He thought that if you kill innocent people, it is always your
fault. He wished his colleague would not reveal his demons.

Then came Sonia's message. Sunny had been mortified that Mrs.
Sharma had watched them engaged in sex, nor did he want to know
about Sonia's experience at the U.S. embassy. It made him feel as if he
must take on her visa problems before he'd properly solved his own.
Save her before he'd adequately saved himself. Would his green-card
application be approved? But alone on Saturday night in Jackson

Heights, facing a Saturday-night depression, he missed Sonia and wrote: *We wanted our story to be simple.*

Returning to New York City he was once again in a place where he felt almost entirely subtracted. Back to editing and sending news stories out on the wire, back to living vicariously by reading the papers and listening to the radio, back to going to movies on his own. Back to finding his ideas of privacy altering to where, like Ulla, he began to take off his clothes without being concerned that his neighbors may see him. Back to thinking of himself not as a man particularly, or as an Indian particularly, or as someone on his way to being a full-fledged Indian American, but as a creature rapidly shedding definition, beginning to mingle what he had previously thought were poles apart: maleness-femaleness, memories–present life, night-day.

Yet there was an innocence and ease to life in New York City when you were alone and kept it small—and if you could see all parts of a small life, you could trust it. Sunny remembered Albana the bartender's scolding: This simplicity was, in fact, the unimaginable luxury of a lucky man in a country of plenty. Of a man who has newly arrived, unshadowed by the history of the place he has arrived in, so long as he doesn't try to learn it.

Sunny asked to follow a story that had come via a phone call to the news desk about a homeless black man named Eugene who was sleeping on the subway grate outside the Ottoline hotel on the Upper East Side. The Ottoline had taken to opening a window to pour a pail of dirty water on Eugene's head to dissuade him from this spot on the pavement, which he had chosen because of the warmth and relative peace. He could lay his head down between two ornamental plants and imagine being in another place. Eugene had left the homeless shelter because it was too rowdy to get any sleep. He telephoned the AP himself and asked for a reporter. A week later Sunny's story went out on the wire, and he was prouder of this story than of "The Fingernail Man," but it was a tiny story on the precipice of a history he didn't know and was scared of trespassing upon and getting wrong.

Sunny filed another local story on a night in the twenty-four-hour laundromat in Jackson Heights. Who did laundry in the middle of the

night? Recent immigrants who were subway workers, hospital cleaners, parking garage attendants, waiters, nannies, taxi drivers, caregivers
for the dying and the newly born. People who worked throughout the
day, who worked throughout the night and the day. Sunny felt his lack
of Spanish. He may have studied it in college, but without purpose,
and because he had learned it without purpose, it had fled his brain,
seemingly without a trace. He restarted classes at an extension program at the New School, beginning once again at the beginning.

¿Qué tal? ¿Cómo te llamas? ¿Quién eres? ¿Cuál es tu nombre?

Soy Sunny. Mi nombre es Sunny. Me llamo Sunny.

The very first words of a new language made one reexamine who
one was. ¿Quién eres? or ¿Cómo estás? Ser or estar? Was his state per-
manent or nonpermanent? ¿Dónde vives? ¿Cómo está la noche?

Me gustan las enchiladas y la Coca-Cola y el Cha Cha Cha. Nor did
you speak the truth when you learned a language; you said whatever you
could with the words you had, and you spent a long while in kindergar-
ten simplicity, in the sunshine of the perpetual present tense, the way the
Buddhists prescribed. Wasn't this contradictory to a good journalist?

Sunny's Spanish instructor came from Puerto Natales. He showed
the class where it was on a map of the serpent-shaped country of Chile,
its serpent tail in the Atacama, its mouth in the ice floes of the Antarc-
tic. He said that when the CIA had observed that the Pinochet junta
was as ruthless as the gestapo, it was because they were, in fact, sometimes the gestapo; men who had emigrated when Hitler fell, who had
been recruited to work for the military dictatorship along with the
collusion of the CIA. When his father disappeared, the family, sponsored by an uncle in the Bronx, immigrated to the States. Sunny's instructor played them a film of the military coup, of Allende's last
speech before he killed himself.

*

UPON ANOTHER SATURDAY, FACING a Saturday depression, Sunny
went to Film Forum to watch a documentary about Hemingway that
divulged the startling news that Hemingway hadn't been a hero on the
front lines after all but had been injured delivering candy to the troops.

He learned that his cowboy style had its origins in his reporter's train-ing at *The Kansas City Star,* that journalism fed his novels—or was it that his novels fed his journalism? He learned about his overbearing mother, his weak father, how Hemingway was a womanizer, a closet gay, a cross-dresser, an insatiable killer of animals, and a paranoid alco-holic. The more famous he became, the harder it was for the man to uphold and survive the ballooning image he himself had created, what it was to be an American war reporter or a white big-game hunter in Africa. His suicide was inevitable. If only he could have gone straight to the mystics and overcome his contradictions. Sunny reflected on So-nia's papa's refrain and was moved to write an essay, "Reading Heming-way in Allahabad, Reading Hemingway in Jackson Heights," about his cynicism of the big press of a big country. If a country was big and a press was big, it needed to eat. If it was voracious, it wanted to hoover up a war. He wrote humorously about hoping to become an immi-grant journalist in the shadow of gonzo journalism and hypothesized that the secret mission of journalism in the United States was to project an idea of what it was to be American out in the world, rather than about reporting on the rest of the world. Would this destroy the nation that created these stories too big to uphold, as it had Hemingway, along with the rest of the world that could not afford the cost of pro-viding Americans with this extravagant idea of themselves? Because once the press began the excited drumbeat of big war and made big war inevitable, then came millions of small migrating men, women, and children. They came to Jackson Heights with a dream for the United States, an abiding hate for the United States. How could they in turn overcome such contradictions?

Then if Sunny was a journalist for the Western press, wouldn't he be writing news from the perspective opposite to himself? There was per-haps a fundamental flaw in a brown person going to the brown world to tell the white world about the brown world, as if he were a white person believing in the centrality of the white world—and because of the cen-tral power of Western news outlets, also telling the brown world about itself (upside down) from this location. The brown world scrambled to gain access to this news (being assured the news was accurate because of

Western standards of quality control and fact-checking), and if they knew English they may understand how they were being contained (which they learned upside down, wrong side up). So a journalist like Sunny, performing this acrobatic service, would in the end have no idea who he was, and his readers would have no idea who they were.

He dared submit this essay to a competition held by the writers' organization PEN. A writer under thirty-five who showed an aptitude in conveying a global perspective would be awarded a travel grant and be assigned to a magazine for publication. It was at this time—after he'd performed what felt like an act of disloyalty to the country that had taken him in and to the AP, which had sponsored his residency—that the approval for Sunny's green card arrived upon one ordinary afternoon, pushed half in and half out of his mailbox in the lobby of his building. It had fallen upon the scuffed linoleum and lay there along with a sheaf of Que Rico Taco! menus until Mario the janitor scooped it up, almost tossed it out, but didn't. He spotted it just in time and stuck it back into Sunny's mailbox. Sunny, returning from Patel Brothers with a heavy sack of basmati rice, almost forgot to check his mailbox, but he did, and then he forgot his basmati sack as he rushed the envelope upstairs. He sat for a long time by his one window holding the miraculous piece of paper, experiencing the seismic shift to his fate from heaviness to lightness, weighing this lightness of being against the gravity of what had occurred, mulling, as if at an occasion where one simply does not know what to feel, what to think, how to behave—as at a circumcision, a loss of virginity, a rite of passage that is a wake and a celebration at the same time. He anticipated that no struggle would feel as important or real as this one. The green card would proceed staidly to citizenship, he'd live at an even farther, safer distance from true life, and life would never be quite real again. He thought the blasphemous thought that even his mother's death would now not be so terrible as it would occur at a remove. His good-luck citizenship would exist between himself and her death. Was this how well-off Americans felt without perhaps knowing they felt this way? That death was not death to them the way it was to others because their lives were so dreamlike and luxurious?

Sunny, lighter than air with his green-card approval, could do anything he pleased. So what was he to do? He went to Central Park, where he sat on a bench next to a man who introduced himself as a visitor from Cape Town and a representative of a garbage workers collective. He was staying with a friend while attending a United Nations conference on waste reclaim. To test out his emotions on a stranger, Sunny mentioned that he had just received news his green card would be processed. The man said, "You're a journalist, did you say? If you change your citizenship, you will lose your understanding of the majority of humanity, the side you need to advocate for."

A fresh, green bud fell on Sunny's head. Sunny got up and walked on. He stopped for a hot dog—this may be a way to celebrate becoming American—and decided not to immediately tell Babita, as it was *her* triumph, this green card. It had been her idea in the first place from before he was born. But she would disguise her colossal triumph and plan to relocate to the United States with the pretense of duress: *How can I leave my country? But I must for the sake of my son.* Just as Sunny himself would have retained his dignity by using Ulla as an excuse, if there was still an Ulla. *I would never have left India had I not met Ulla. Now here, despite myself, I find myself.*

He didn't tell Sonia, either. He kept the news to himself, for himself. The door had only just creaked open; if joined by others—Vini-Puni-Babita-Sonia—wouldn't it slam shut? *Don't be two Indians, don't be three Indians, don't be four, ten, fifty, a million, a billion.* He didn't tell his neighbors, who might be undocumented and waiting without an end to their waiting. Nor did he tell USA-born Americans that he was now one of them, for fear they would be justifiably disappointed. *We are all immigrants, unless we were forcibly brought here, unless native,* they would remember to say, but how could they not feel dread at uncontrollable numbers?

Sonia wrote from the internet center: *Sunny, we have to move fast—I think everyone will do everything they can to make sure we are not together. That is what happens. The whole world becomes alarmed that two people might be happy, so they attack at the first sign of joy. They try to destroy the love before it is too late for them to do so.*

Sunny recognized the truth of this statement. People want the friend to remain the same friend they always were, the son to be the same son he always was. They feared that love meant undoing one thing to remake it into another. They counted on the loveless to buoy their own existence, make their own loneliness less lonely, their own love brighter, their own luck luckier.

Please tell me, wrote Sonia, *if this love is going to be bad for me, I don't want to turn into a pestering harridan.*

Sunny replied, upon his next Saturday-night depression: *It won't be bad for you. If you cannot get a visa to the States, let's meet somewhere else.*

Portofino? wrote Sonia flippantly, sensing his ambivalence, intuiting the feathery ease of someone with fewer visa problems.

Why Portofino?

Where the film stars go.

He felt her sarcasm. *I don't want to go where the film stars go. Venice? It may also be touristy,* he wrote to Sonia, *but I want to see what other tourists want to see.*

Reading Hemingway, he had become interested in Americans abroad the way a previous generation of Indians had studied the British abroad. He had embarked upon Henry James. Earnest Americans were seduced by Europe and cheated out of their innocence by an older civilization. The cynical Old World was amused and beguiled by the fresh New World. While Europeans loved cowboys, Americans were besotted by aristocrats. The romance continued, venturesome enough to save them from having to seek scary adventure in the Third World. How would this story include immigrants like Sunny? Soon, with a U.S. passport, he would be free to attain Europe as well as the United States. Would he, too, play mirror to Europe's desire? Would he make the life in Europe he never could as an Indian but could as an Indian American?

Sunny locked up his magic paper in a suitcase and was somber so as not to rile other seekers of fortune. He gave Mario, the janitor who he knew was illegally in the United States, and who helped with his Spanish homework, a big tip for no reason.

....

THE PROMISE OF ITALY WAS A PLUMMY TREAT THAT GREW riper, too much good fortune to show off about, safer to be circumspect about. Sonia decided to visit her mother and finish her *Kala* article on Goa in the grounding discomfort of Cloud Cottage. It was raining in the mountains—wind gusted, opening channels through the forest trees, the leaves and branches flowering forth from within—and then came a torrential downpour. The deodars turned raven, and it smelled of snails and wild chives. The snows were obliterated, and so many clouds blew through the house that it was tragic and hilarious to see the ones captured within Siegfried Barbier's frames—the efforts of a holy fool. The electricity failed, the tin roof boomed, and because the gutters had rusted through, the rain fell in sheets closely about the house. Millions of leeches waved their bloodthirsty stumps when Mama and Sonia ventured outside, and the grasses twisted to the movement of snakes. Forced indoors, Mama gave Sonia the notebook that contained her most recent translations. "I made a discovery that I've been waiting to show you."

> *The boardinghouse is full of nincompoops. I flee from Miss Moffatt,*
> *who yesterday tried to teach me how to paint—she had the insolence to*
> *come to my studio. I don't understand perspective and she will instruct*
> *me how to see correctly. I told her to bhago. Anjolie said to her, "Don't*
> *mind my husband. He should have been born a bear." I refuted,*
> *"I should have been born a cloud."*

> *I will never return to Germany, although I am under no illusion that*
> *there is any difference between the two countries when it comes to capac-*

*ity for cruelty, violence, or deceit. In Germany, it is simply harder to be-
come a cloud.*

*It has been raining for a month, days barely distinguishable from the
nights. Leeches feast on me. The monks will not kill the bloodsuckers;
they carry them outdoors on a leaf after they have finished gorging.*

*Watercolor, agent of lightness and transformation, is the medium I prefer
now because it is close to the climate and my spirit—it forces an unadulterated, internal vision upon the page.*

*Years and years. I broke down and wept. I am tired. The effort is too
long. Instead of improving, I regress. I felt, suddenly, today, as if I had
never held a brush before.*

*I continued. I continue. My stubbornness surprises me. It has its own
existence, which is separate from mine. It feeds on nothing. It pays me
no attention.*

HERE!
    2am Little Cloud Monsoon 1958—
    *When my studio swam with fog, and it was pelting outside, and I
could scarcely see the paper. I couldn't see myself. I sat sunk in gloom,
when my frozen hand was moved by a spirit beyond my will. I felt its
grasp. I felt it move my brush. After all these years of wondering if—
within repeating, moving, echoing images, images moving beyond the
frame of my life—there would be, could be, a moment of culmination,
my patience has been rewarded. I reached beyond my consciousness, and
something reached back from beyond the illusion of this existence.*
    *I looked down—a shadow delineated in jewels. When I held my
paper to the lamp, I saw the imp had no face! Its visage was black breaking to white, white breaking to black. I laughed. I saw that whatever it
was, it was laughing at me; the mystery was answered by confirmation
of the mystery. I have been given a companion.*
    I went outside, briefly the rain stopped and the clouds parted, I

bowed to the moon. For a moment, the clouds over the moon made my imp's face. I shall call it Badal Baba, Hermit of the Clouds. I have housed my unpredictable prankster in my gau case from Tibet, which has traveled for several centuries, which knows the weather and the secret mountain passes.

The leopard came from the mountaintop to look into the window. Green eyes veined with red. She looked through me. She had come to see Badal Baba, who can take any shape including that of a leopard. I address my companion by many names: My Lord of the Clouds, Keeper of the Mountain, King of the Wastelands, Companion of the Accursed, Bagheera Baba, Bhoot Bibi. While Badal Baba might take the form of a mendicant, he is vain and enjoys being flattered by superlatives, just like any deity worthy of being one.

"But what does this *mean*?" Sonia felt panic. The rain increased its drumming on the tin roof.

Mama said, "I learned that it was your *grandfather* who painted Badal Baba."

"I thought a lama had given the amulet to him on his travels."

"That is the story my mother told us. My father never contradicted it. Maybe he had been given an empty amulet case. Maybe the monk predicted the arrival of Badal Baba, cast a spell. In any case, those old seekers were vague on purpose. Even when there was a perfectly ordinary explanation, they contrived mystery. And when something was inexplicable, they presented it as self-evident. It would annoy Meher and myself."

Sonia hadn't yet confessed the amulet's loss. She had lied. She would have to go back to New York to retrieve it. But how could she when she couldn't get a visa? She was on her way to Italy instead. In her need to confess to *something*, Sonia told her mother she would be meeting Sunny in Venice. She pretended ordinariness. Mama contemplated her daughter. "Who is Sunny?"

"The grandson of the Allahabad colonel with whom Dadaji used to play chess. I met him at the time of Dadaji's funeral. Then when I was in Goa, he happened to be there with his friend."

Mama winced. She said, "You can make a wrong choice when you are young and haven't decided on the life and career you want. You might unwittingly put yourself in a small place—imagine being trapped in the culture of Allahabad."

"But what about a lonelier place?" she challenged her mother.

"There are worse things than loneliness." Loneliness could mean abiding peace. It could mean understanding your happiness backward, when you happened to exclaim out loud, surprising yourself when there was no apparent reason, *I'm happy!*

"I am already trapped in a small place," added Sonia. "I can't sit with Papa forever."

Mama softened. She said, "Well, it's true that you should travel when you are young, when travel can change your life. You will see marvels."

"Didn't you ever want to go to Germany?" Sonia dared ask.

"No. My father was adamant we think of ourselves as Indian. It would have felt like a betrayal to go."

"He never spoke of it?"

"Almost never. After he died we found an unopened letter in his bedside table drawer. It was from a distant cousin. He must have known what it said. His mother had perished of natural causes. His father was already dead and he had no brothers, but his male cousins and uncles had been drafted into the army."

Mama salted a leech that was inching toward them and remembered her father hiking in Garhwal and Kumaon hoping to see a snow leopard—with a snow leopard's satisfaction in not being able to prove itself apart from the landscape, or maybe even itself to itself, unless it caught sight of its blackberry nose—and for that wild leopard to look through the mountaineer and turn him into nothing.

CHAPTER

44

....

SONIA SAT AT HER GRANDFATHER'S MASSIVE TEAK DESK surrounded by the esoteric presence of his paintings of the remote Himalayas, portals to a world where human concern has no purchase. People may love the high snow mountains, but the mountains did not love people. If love were an insignificant matter to the mountains, well, so were hate and fear. To be neither loved nor hated, to learn one's unimportance, to make oneself beside the point, was surely a relief. A man might rebalance himself against the massive indifference.

There was a gravity to the piece on Goa that Sonia wrote—about an old order changing for new.

She wrote about women bravely maintaining their pasts. She recorded Anand, the enemy of plastic bags, saying how much an ordinary man had been taxed until land reform. And she referred to the brutal inquisition in Goa and also to the high rate of suicide in the state. She described the path gashed through the mangroves down which the trucks never stopped coming from the mines, tipping red mountains into the moored barges that, day and night, ferried ore to ships waiting to set sail to China. Oil spilled on the surface of the wetlands, choked its peeping life, but occasionally a smell of melons still wafted from the water and a person experienced it as a recollection from the past.

An opposite emotion overcame her while she was describing the fretted coconut palm light and the juxtaposition of pompous portraits of bearded viceroys in black pantaloons and doublets against the splendor of pink pom-pom-flowered rain trees hundreds of years old. She felt love of a place so great that the same tingling overcame her as when she read a book she loved too much to bear, bringing her to the verge—

the verge of what? She was aware of trying to paint a picture with words. She felt her memories—the rose gold, marine blue-green, wedding pink—as a reverberation.

Sonia looked up from the desk, and when her eyes rested on the photograph that hung above it of her mother and Aunt Meher at tea with the Rosenthal teapot, for the first time she saw in the dark of the deodars an animal shape she had never noticed before—hunched like a hyena, skinny, camouflaged black against black, eyes glinting from the shadow like fireflies in the jungle.

When she called Mama to look, her mother said, "Strange, I've never noticed it, either. A creature must have been hiding in the woods. My father used to say he felt as if he was being followed, that he never trekked alone on those monthlong expeditions. While he was stalking the elusive snow leopard, the snow leopard was stalking him. When villagers told him the yeti had come down from the higher passes for the winter and he went looking for it, the Monkey Man was following him."

The eyes in the photograph looked familiar, in fact. Maybe they were those of an ancestor of the wild bagarbilla, Babayaga's half brother who came caterwauling, though one never knew when—that was part of his menace, to show them who owned this household of two women and one rachitic Moolchand. When Babayaga heard him, she, the unrepentant killer of mice, birds, and snakes, crouched down low.

Or maybe the eyes belonged to one of the ancestors of the stocky hill mastiffs that followed women when they were menstruating, leaky penises out, joker silly grins, trying to hump the women's legs, then switching from grinning to mauling each other. The same ones that followed Sonia when she returned from the market with a chicken, growled, and came closer. Mama, who knew of the dangers, filled Sonia's market bag with stones so she might threaten the dogs. By the time she arrived home to Cloud Cottage, she'd spent her ammunition.

And Sonia remembered the ghost dog on the Goan sands that had targeted her, snarling, wagging, seeing her without seeing her, not as if she were Sonia but as if she were prey. He had vanished into the sand—and that couldn't be true, either. The dog couldn't possibly have transported himself here to Cloud Cottage. She remembered this was Ilan's trick—the sane person dismissed what was actually true.

When Sonia went to the attic and rummaged about, she found Mama's grandparents' wedding picture in the album kept wrapped in her grandfather's fox fur. It showed a long-faced Tante Lily and a sloshed Onkel Fritz, stout Oma, willowy young Mutter, and terrifying Vater covered in military medals.

She thought those were the eyes in the deodar dark, the eyes of ghosts that had followed them across the world. The journey was long; they had just arrived.

The Itch

....

WHILE HIS DAUGHTER WAS AWAY VISITING HER MOTHER, Papa felt oppressed. He wished to play a more gratifying role in his daughter's life, to insert himself indelibly so she could never move beyond his control and leave him the way his wife had. He itched. His work didn't soothe him. He had proposed hiring a team of experts to create a Hindi word-processing program, but the recruits, with their training, were recruited in turn by Silicon Valley, and they departed so fast it was like a bloodletting.

The itch carried over, and Papa fought with a grandson of the Gupta family by the name of Atul, who had made a reverse journey and returned after his degree from Rutgers Business School because he believed his fortune lay in India with the family business. He informed his elders that it was essential, if they expected to survive modernity, that they realign themselves according to international standards of management. Doing global business meant adopting a different vocabulary from that of an extended Indian household that accommodated each member's eccentricities, pilgrimages, tantrums, digestion. The various endeavors of the Gupta clan needed to be analyzed and streamlined, and those that were unprofitable must be jettisoned. Atul Gupta had identified Papa as an impediment—a promoter of peculiar, disparate schemes construed toward the purpose of holiday travel. Atul Gupta circulated a memo ridiculing Papa's proposal for a business trip to Tokyo to ascertain whether the singing toilets of Japan might find a market in India.

But this was not the sole reason for the grandson's hostility toward Papa. Along with expansive ideas of international business, Atul Gupta had returned to India with a narrow vision of his native land, a vision that had been propagated by a professor whose appointment to a newly declared India studies chair had been sponsored by a group of New Jersey Indian American professionals. In the United States, this group believed in minority rights and a secular nation that would tolerate people like themselves, but in India they drove the engine for a Hindu nation because—ha ha—there their families were in the majority! Aren't Indians just so smart? When Atul Gupta learned from a tattling employee that on December sixth of 1992, Papa had thrown out the sweets with which the staff was celebrating the destruction of the Babri mosque—shouting, "*The British have won!*"—Atul burst into Papa's office without knocking and accosted Papa: "Can't you put some Indian art on your wall? You should have some pride for who you are."

Said Papa, "I have put up Indian art. Can't you see?"

Papa had decorated his office with prints of Mughal miniatures depicting hermits and seekers of no particular religion and one of Emperor Akbar worshiping the sun. Why, after all, shouldn't a Muslim king find the sun holy and stand to receive it in his manicured garden in the same manner as a sadhu on the ghats in Benaras or an elderly, white-chinned cat waiting at the top of a clammy mountain after a chilly night in a deodar forest?

The next day, Papa's managing director plaque was missing and the prints had vanished from the office wall; in their place was a poster of the Hindu pantheon in flamboyant, clashing colors. When Papa went to inform his boss of the thefts, the gentle, vague man—who had joyfully clapped his hands upon hearing about the toilets of Japan that warbled like springtime thrushes—looked downcast.

He said, "This young generation is of a different mindset. My advice is to begin looking for employment elsewhere before—"

"Before?"

"How much longer I can protect you, I do not know."

An anonymous caller telephoned Papa and threatened, "Go to Pakistan or your wife will find your body."

Papa replied, "Do you know how overjoyed my wife would be?" But he did not know whether to laugh or cry—

Or scratch his itch some more.

At home he turned the volume high to play Nusrat Fateh Ali Khan, the invocation to Allah that carried on long and ecstatic—this music only claims you at full sound—and even though he congratulated himself on there being no wife around to tell him to turn the sound down to save the neighbor's dog's ears, he itched some more.

He worked his jaw, ground his teeth, and remembered Sunny sneaking into Papa's house without paying his respects to the head of the household, without formally requesting the pleasure of Sonia's acquaintance, without succumbing further to Papa's musings: *You see, Sunny, beauty is the motivating force of the universe, said Ibn Arabi.* Beauty led to jealousy. Was jealousy the stronger force? Papa still didn't know *what* Mrs. Sharma had seen from her rooftop—he itched and itched. He telephoned Babita Bhatia and said, "Look here, Sonia has been suffering the consequences of your son's misbehavior—*he misbehaved with my daughter!*—and now he is roaming around scot-free."

"What do you mean?" And Babita, with her evening rum and nimbu, listening to a cricket fiddle its leg in the Chinese orange tree, learned that her reconciliation with Sunny, his criticisms of Sonia made to achieve this reconciliation—*Sonia had taken his Disprin! Risked his eye to ocean fungus!*—was yet another insidious duplicity. The truth was that Sonia had, in fact, usurped her place in Sunny's heart. He had slipped out to see Sonia during the siesta hour. Mrs. Sharma had gone innocently up to the roof—thank goodness she had not taken her little daughter—and had seen . . . *what?*

*

THE TABLE WAS LAID in the formal dining room, and Chandu served a chilled creme vichyssoise from *Mrs. Beeton's Book of Household Management,* calm and pale greenish, to cure the itch.

"Your son, Mr. Sunny Bhatia, had better make up his mind. Look at the consequences for Sonia. The neighbors spit upon her."

"Sonia is equally to blame."

"A man always has the advantage in our country. With advantage comes responsibility. He's living in New York. For him it is a vacation, for Sonia it is her life."

"What is this? Raita?"

"Soup."

Chandu served a second course of idli and sambhar.

"Another soup?"

"It's sambhar."

"It's more soup."

"It's sambhar. I'm not going to let Sonia hang about waiting."

"She shouldn't hang about waiting any more than Sunny should be forced to make a decision. I'm not a fussy eater—give me cheese toast and salad—but I can't have soup after soup!"

"When they meet in Italy he had better make up his mind, one way or another."

Italy? She made a heroic effort to control herself and pretend she knew already. She examined a fork as if it had been inadequately washed. "I'm not going to deliver an ultimatum."

Papa had imparted his itch to Babita. Sonia was back on her brain. Sonia and Sunny in Italy was now on her brain. Europe was on her brain. The Western world was on her brain. All over again. She remembered Buckingham Palace and the bus driver: *Stolen, stolen! Chori, chori!* Something had been taken from her and she wanted it back. Something that was unfair to her, she wished it—whatever it was—to be fair to her now.

She took out her bank papers and studied the dwindling returns from the portfolio of investments. She could not travel to New York again. Why had she recklessly gone the year before? It would be more crucial to intervene in Sunny's life now. She cursed Uncles Ravi-Rana, her husband, Ratty: *I would NOT have loved you after all!*

She made herself sick with bitter rage.

And now she opened *Kala* magazine and saw—*Sonia!* Writing so tenderly about Goa, where she had holidayed with Sunny. Writing about women, fragile as Macao teacups, still speaking a formal Portuguese, living on in mansions with sala doors opening to river deltas. She read about the nunnery in the palm jungle that had been abandoned during the black plague. Once, more than a hundred nuns lived there, well-born women who came from all over the Portuguese colonies with their slaves. The afternoons were so long, boredom that much longer, they had nurtured the patience needed to invent bebinca. She had never tasted a layered bebinca cake.

Didn't jealousy create the plot of one's life? If Sunny and Sonia had enjoyed themselves in Goa—*Goa had been her suggestion in the first place*—why shouldn't she go, too? She itched and itched. She must allay it. She called her friend Vanya.

"Come," said Vanya. "I could do with company. I miss the man."

"What man?"

"Cecil, my husband—the one who died."

There was no reason to delay. Babita gave instructions to Vini-Puni, who would be left alone, although their mother would be coming to clean as usual.

Babita had recently overheard them fighting, shouts emitting from the kitchen. "What is going on?" she had confronted them.

Punita had blurted, "Vinita is washing the Habibs' driver's shirt with our washing soap, drying it on our washing line, and ironing it with our iron."

"You mean the Allahabad driver?"

"Vinita keeps his extra shirt."

It turned out the driver had asked Vinita to keep a second shirt because he was sometimes so soaked in sweat, even by early morning, he needed to change. Vinita washed and ironed this sweaty shirt; she hung it on a hanger behind the door of their servants' quarters so it would not get a crease.

Punita had observed that her sister's day had turned into an itch of waiting for the driver and being tense and silent until she saw him and exchanged a word. Subsequently, she talked too much, laughed too much, was uncharacteristically kind. Puni had observed that when the driver said, "Blue color suits you," Vini kept on wearing blue. When he said patterns didn't look good on her, she stopped wearing patterns. Bit by bit, everything in her life was being turned on its head and becoming the opposite of what it had been. Punita had asked, "Can't the driver keep his own shirt? Or why can't the Habibs' maid wash it and keep it?"

"He doesn't get along with the maid."

"What if Aunty finds out? He is married!" When Punita had threatened to snitch on Vinita, Vinita threatened this would be the end of Punita's fancy education. They would both be returned to Begumpur. Vini's itch, her hope—and her fear that her hope would be dashed—were transferred to Punita.

Babita looked at their itchy faces, and she said to Vinita, "While I am away in Goa, you are not to make eyes at the Habibs' driver or to wash and keep his shirt. Full stop. Do you understand? There will be no romances in this household!"

46

....

IN THE SPIRIT OF REVENGE—A MOTHER IN LOVE WITH HER
son is quite capable of taking revenge on her beloved—Babita traveled
to Goa, where Vanya's driver, Falcon, was waiting at the airport holding a sign written out by Vanya: *Welcome, Mrs. Babita Bhatia!*

"Here is the River Zuari," said Falcon, indicating as they drove
along. "There by the side of the road, they are selling feni—feni is very
good for health. And now here we are coming to the Mandovi River.
Look there, a man planted that avocado tree, and in season he sells avo-
cados. Foreigners eat them."

Babita began to shake off her Delhi malaise by the time they had
arrived at the Ribandar ferry stop, where the riverbank burbled and
popped with mudskippers and crabs. As she watched the sky-blue ferry
strung festively with orange life rings move slowly across the sleepy,
brown spread of river muddling the saltwater, she was struck by how
accurately Sonia had described this landscape—as uncomplicated and
there for the gobbling as when the Portuguese first arrived. It took an
age to labor across as unhurriedly as they may have a hundred years
ago. She couldn't quite tell if they were going forward or backward,
and when they arrived on Divar, she felt she had been meditating without even trying.

Falcon pointed out a mango tree. "Not very many of that kind in
the village anymore, only two Mankurad. By March is cashew fruit
time; by April, May is mango; by early monsoon, jackfruit. There is a
chikoo—bats eat them and then they do their droppings onto every
veranda. In jamun season they do purple droppings."

They drove up a hillock and sailed down the other side, where there was a pond of exulting frogs and Vanya on her balcão in a checkered lungi, smoking a cigarette, tapping the ashes into a Chinese cherry-blossom-patterned portable ashtray that flipped open. At middle age, silver-threaded hair cut short, fingers laden with rings of coral and mother-of-pearl, Vanya was sexy. Babita said, "It took us a long while because your driver stopped and showed me every fruit tree along the way. I've never seen a man more charmingly obsessed."

"Falcon follows the fortunes of every fruit tree on the island." She showed Babita around while there was still light. The late evening upon the red earth was copper gold. Vanya had buried her husband, Cecil, behind the papayas.

"Whatever were you thinking, Vanya?" Babita spoke in the frank tones of a longtime widow to a short-time widow. "Now you can never leave, and nobody will ever buy this property. I imagine people are as superstitious about ghosts here as anywhere."

"Far more."

"Then?"

"I don't plan to leave. After I die whatever happens, happens."

With the shadows of fruit trees and palms drifting upon the walls, the swoop and chirp of bats beyond—little flowery ones first and then the flying foxes—and the moon climbing over the gable, they dined on prawn croquettes under lamps of thin and ancient wiring, the metal corroded by sea air, the bulbs loosened by the sea breeze, flickering gently on and off. Warm peace billowed at them. "Just look at this divine peace," Babita said accusingly, because she was jealous of this peace, even though she knew that to be jealous of peace destroys the peace.

"Sometimes it is boredom, sometimes it is loneliness, but sometimes it is peace," said Vanya.

When Babita was in her appointed bedroom, brushing her hair before the dressing-table mirror in which she could only dimly see herself—the mirror overwhelmed by the reflection of deep-red tiles and dark furniture—she heard Vanya say quite clearly although her door was shut: "So what did you think of the prawn croquettes?"

This made Babita leap. The sound was right over her nose. She

looked up and saw a latticed false ceiling for the afternoon heat to ex-
hale via the far roof tiles and for the cool air of evening to be drawn in.
This meant it was possible to hear everything that went on in every
room, and the house—no matter how grand—had as much privacy as
a tenement.

"Delicious," called Babita. "I don't know how they were so crunchy
outside and so velvety inside."

Crossing the Mandovi again one Sunday, driving almost to
Quepem, they visited Vanya's friend Umberto at Casa das Conchas,
named for the two enormous conches molded at the entrance and for
its magnificent oyster shell shutters. Casa das Conchas, Babita remembered, had figured in Sonia's Goa article in *Kala*.

Umberto was Italian and gay. To be his friend made the widows of
Goa feel automatically cosmopolitan. If he accompanied one widow to
an event at the cultural center on Altinho hill, another was envious and
phoned for his recipe for tiramisu; then another was jealous and asked
his advice on which neighborhood her niece should stay in while in
Rome—this side of the Tiber or that? Dressed in a starched kurta—
woven in the red of coconut husk, the khaki under a banyan, the purple of sea monsters drawn from the depths by monsoon tides and cast
upon the beach—Umberto handed Babita a Campari soda. "You see,"
he said, "when I was fifty-six, I had a stroke; it affected my sexual life
and—the last thing I expected—this turned out to be a gift. It freed
me. I traveled all over the world. I saw *Madama Butterfly* performed at
the Great Wall. I took the Trans-Siberian Railway, and a mail boat
through the Norwegian fjords. I drove from Iran to Afghanistan to
India. I came here and fell in love—this landscape, these people! I
bought Casa das Conchas from the last descendant of a merchant
whose vessels the *Husnara,* the *Paloma,* and the *Nagini* traded between
Goa and Zanzibar. It was in a dilapidated state; bit by bit, I restored it."
An Arab via Zanzibar influence could be discerned in the star-pattern
woodwork.

"Umberto must be independently wealthy," Babita gossiped on
their way home.

"He's the sole descendant of wealth. While he might have been living a wild life, when he went home, everything was sober and Catholic, a mother in a palazzo in Milan, a maid in an apron, maintaining order. Umberto says he might one day have to leave Goa to be with his bedridden mother."

"How is it," reproached Babita, "that all of you are having such a fine time? Why is it that I'm not living in a grand mansion in Goa, too?"

That night, through the fretwork ceiling, Babita heard Vanya muttering, "Even if Babita Bhatia gobbled the whole world, she would still be hungry."

Babita was annoyed. She picked up a magazine from her bedside table, and it was the same *Kala* magazine with Sonia's Goa article! Even in Goa, Babita longed for Goa.

....

HER FOOLISH SON! THE POSTCARD WAS WAITING FOR
Babita when she returned to Delhi, mailed by Sunny before embarking
on his Italian holiday, admitting he would be ten days in Venice but
making no mention of Sonia. How could Sunny imagine Babita didn't
know?

Unhappy back in Lodhi Gardens, making her usual circle about the
tombs into which she never ventured for fear of encountering drug
addicts, bats, or masturbating boys as one may expect—she thought
how she must bide her time, wait to use useful information most
usefully—when the familiar figure of Mr. Khanna, her husband's former boss, moving at a clip ahead of her, made her reflect: How many
of her class were forced to be fraudulent to allow their children to remain innocent abroad, allow them to be vociferous and self-righteous
on the subject of corruption? Financial honesty in children was a cost
that had to be paid for by parents. During stressful times it was inevitable that you began to think your child was an idiot who would be
able to handle nothing—until you were drawn in the other direction
by pride in their naïve honorableness, a desire to share in their shadow-
free lives in rich countries where it was normal to criticize Third World
corruption, ignoring the massive corruption of the First World, before
which we are all ants trying to get an impossible view of an elephant.

Babita couldn't count on Sunny as she aged. The moment your
children achieved their American citizenship was the moment they
made it clear their parents should not expect to be taken care of in the
old-fashioned Indian way. Why? Those backward days were over.
Your children couldn't be expected to compromise their lives and min-

ister to doddery mothers and fathers. And who had encouraged them to believe such ideas? Who had sent them abroad where they grew cruel and hypocritical?

Their parents! Their parents who agreed with their children out loud, yet secretly did not.

Babita stopped at the Pigpo store on her way home, and next door, as if to taunt her, she saw a giant volume of *Beautiful Italy* in the window of the Bookworm. She went in, wrestled with the book until she found the chapter on Venice, and came upon images of fabrics designed by Fortuny. She imagined herself in the photograph of the Accademia Bridge over the Grand Canal, looking to the lagoon in her azure-drowning-in-turquoise silk ikat that replicated the patterns of water. How Venetians would appreciate her sari collection!

She remembered her trip to Scandinavia when she had received several compliments on her sartorial style. When she had returned to Delhi, she had reported no racism from white people, only from brown people, because she had followed her secret motto: If you reported or noticed racism from white people, you lowered yourself; if you said you were loved and welcomed, you raised yourself. To be happy in Europe, to admire Europe, to feel at home in Europe, to make a friend in Europe, was a deliberate act of freeing oneself.

She boasted to the observing bookseller, Mr. Singh, "My son is in Italy right now."

"Why did he not take you with him, then?" questioned Mr. Singh.

"He asked me, but young people should enjoy themselves without their mothers in tow." Her armpits itched. Without having ever been to Italy, Babita wished to reside in Italy. She wished to be a woman renewing her life, taking the more adventurous path. She set *Beautiful Italy* aside. It was too expensive to buy and would have obviously been a silly purchase.

The next early morning she powdered her face, lined her eyes, and dressed in aubergine grading to umber. She exited her section of the divided house and entered the adjoining gate to Uncle Ravi's, and when he opened it, she said in a graveyard tone: "*All right! All right!*" A drastic change was necessary if she were to remain undiminished. If

Babita were to forgo her court case and accept a third of the proceeds of the house, and the egg cups, she would lose her home, but she might buy a house in a location more salubrious. If she joined Sunny in the United States, she would have money awaiting her. But why tell Sunny any of this now? She would wait until the sale went through—

Uncle Ravi rushed to telephone Uncle Rana. "*News! News!*"

Uncle Rana exited his gate. "*Well, well,*" he said in the triumphant voice of someone who has brought something about. Babita wondered if all of it, the long-ago turd outside the kitchen, the delayed court case, the withheld egg cups, was part of an orchestrated scheme.

"*Well, well! The queen surrenders!*" Uncle Rana stuck his fingernail between his teeth trying to excavate a bit of food, indicating to Babita that he was being as rude as possible in the moment of her defeat. "Well, well." He flicked last night's goat meat into the air.

Babita restrained herself from slapping him and wondered where he had been the evening before. He had the look of a man who prowled and was carnally satisfied. It showed in his sprawl, in the hot flare of his nostrils, the puffiness of his lips, the rubicund boils on his face, the tufts of chest hair that sprouted from the collar of his sweatshirt.

"*Well! Well!*" Time was running out for Uncle Rana. "May I pay you the compliment, Babi Bhabhi, as someone who has long been your adversary"—he smirked—"of saying I know you are a savvy operator and that unless we sell for one-third, some two-thirds will come in black. Nobody has enough clean money. We'll get the official value, not the true value. We cannot be foolish."

Babita had no intention of being foolish. "Give me practical information," she said. "I can't be hiding suitcases of cash and gold under my bed."

"The legally recorded sum will be paid with a check. The rest of your share will pop up in Sunny's bank account in the States."

"How?"

"The hawala system, a network that operates out of Dubai."

"*How* does it operate?"

"It is impossible to know. Nobody can know."

"Then what if it doesn't show up?"

"It's more reliable than a bank. One default and the entire system based on trust, a handshake, goes kaput. How do you think I send money to Chiki-Chika in Auckland?"

Countries that allowed immigration if you were rich enough that you could buy it were receiving criminals from all around the world. Which raised the question: Why should New Zealand or Canada be considered squeaky-clean, while poverty-stricken police, clerks, and thugs of the countries left behind—India, China, Brazil—were considered dirty for taking bribes to forget they had seen what they had seen, heard what they had heard, smelled what they had smelled?

Babita asked, "And if the fact that I took black money comes popping up years later and causes me trouble?"

"There isn't a sale in Delhi that's not a black-money sale," assured Uncle Ravi. While he didn't have threatening debtors, time was running out for him, too. He had asthma. He wished to live in a place where he could breathe. "Anyway, don't you know how we Indians think? We think: Oh, she is so smart, she accumulated a treasure chest! Let's make her prime minister!"

As she left Uncle Ravi's garden, Babita noticed his gardener crouched low weeding the flower beds. Probably he would now tell the rest of the servants about the conversation he had overheard, including Vini-Puni, who would start squawking: "What will happen to us?"

What *would* happen to them?

Is Italy True?

....

THE PLANE DIPPED OVER THE LAGOON, AND FOR A SPAN
Sonia was immersed in transparent turquoise spotted with outcrops of
burgundy seaweed and bearded rushes like marsh birds' nests. She took
the Alilaguna line—furrowing water mingling with the furrowing
water from other boats—and saw the chimney pots of Venice drawing
closer. Then she saw a scene simultaneously before her and at a distance, for it was too fantastical to feel close even when it was at her
nose. She tried not to observe the domes of the east or the campaniles
of the west. She saved the sight to view with Sunny, who was arriving
on a flight several hours later. She got off at the Ca' Rezzonico stop by
the Hotel Bauer, followed a narrow lane just wide enough to wheel a
suitcase, turned left, and then was lost for a long while as the guidebook assured her she would be. She found herself at a place with a sign
saying *Stazione Marittima,* where naval vessels made the aching call of
migrating geese, and finally made her way to Campo Santa Margherita
and the bed-and-breakfast where Sunny had made a booking to present at the Italian consulate in New York as part of the process of applying for a visa.

The bed-and-breakfast was atop a pizzeria called Al Canton, the
check-in was at the cash register, and their assigned room was in the
garret—small as a closet, smelling exactly as overpowering as the sewage used to water the municipal parks in Delhi.

Unlike her experience at the U.S. embassy, Sonia hadn't had any
trouble getting an Italian visa because Ferooza was a friend of the Italian ambassador's wife. Giovanna had asked the ambasciatore to send a
message to the visa department and also sent Sonia the details of Vene-

tian friends, an academic couple—Indophiles, like herself—who received travelers from India with as much hospitality as they'd received from strangers in Calcutta.

*

FIVE HOURS LATER, Sunny's flight arrived, and he, too, took the Alilaguna line from the airport; he, too, got off at the Ca' Rezzonico stop and followed the narrow lane; but instead of turning left, he turned right through the Campiello dei Squelini. He didn't stop at a shop with glass that looked like the lagoon in different moods, and he didn't look toward the Grand Canal to catch a glimpse of sea grotto palaces—he saved these sights to see with Sonia. He crossed a bridge by the university Ca' Foscari and arrived at an area with many small tourist kiosks. At one of them he decided to try the Jackson Heights Spanish he'd practiced with Mario the janitor, the Dominicans at the hardware store, and at the Colombian photo place where you paid to restore the faded pictures of family in your home country, bringing them close and dear to you again. Italian and Spanish were related: "Buenas tardes, señoritas. ¿Dónde está el zócalo?"

The shopgirls burst into laughter.

Ironically, it was Sunny who'd had trouble getting an Italian visa, despite applying from New York City. He had finally admitted his green-card approval to Sonia, but only to underscore that his fortunes remained essentially unaltered.

He'd joined a wet-rat line of non-Westerners standing in the wet-rat rain outside the Italian consulate on Park Avenue. The door set into the wall buzzed open briefly to let a few petitioners squeeze through. Inside, Ms. Bassani, visa officer, was an expert. She raised her voice for everyone to hear when a newlywed Cambodian woman approached the window. Her American husband didn't need a visa, and they were going to Florence on their honeymoon. The young woman had the confidence Sunny had possessed when he had lived with Ulla.

"Collect your visa in three weeks."

"But I'm flying in two weeks."

"You should have made an appointment at least two months before."

"I tried, but you didn't give me one."

"Step away from the window."

"But we've already paid thousands of dollars for our tickets and hotels! Please!" She broke down. "*Please,*" she cried. "*Please, please—*"

"Step AWAY from the window NOW!"

Everyone in the waiting room went rigid. They had it wrong. Italy was serious business. Italy was for other people. Happiness was for other people.

A man from Haiti seated next to Sunny began to agitate. "Why am I here?" he asked Sunny. "I'm never going to get a visa, and I don't care, man. I want to go to the Caribbean. But my girlfriend, she wants to go to Italy, so here I am. I don't know." He kept looking down and shaking his head. "I don't know, I don't know why I'm here."

"Only the illegals and terrorists are going to get into Italy now," one of the denied comforted another denied. "They make it impossible for the honest, so only the cheats will populate their country!"

An Indian couple in business suits had not looked at Sunny, had sat so strenuously not looking at him for hour upon hour it must have hurt the sides of their faces to not acknowledge him. *One Indian alone is luckier than two Indians together.* They felt this in their gut. Sunny could tell from having felt the same way once. *Two Indians in business suits with irreproachable bank accounts are luckier than three Indians in business suits with irreproachable bank accounts. Two Indians in business suits with irreproachable bank accounts are infinitely luckier than three Indians, if the third Indian has a bank account like a bucket with a hole in it and is dressed in a mustard-colored handloom kurta, no matter how crisply he has ironed the kurta before setting forth in the morning.* The couple hoped they wouldn't encounter any other Indians on their vacation. The wife had already dyed her hair a toffee color to occupy a more-elevated sphere of existence. Her skin was pale, of this she was proud, although her husband was dark. This was because as a paler woman, you could marry a man far wealthier if he was far darker than yourself. These were not bargains they had ever mentioned to each other, or to anyone, because it was part of their mutual secret pact: *We won! We won!*

By the time Sunny boarded his flight—having provided a letter from the Associated Press on an official letterhead to say they guaranteed he was employed; a booking from Al Canton faxed directly from Al Canton to the consulate; health insurance for $100,000; and bank papers dating from no more than forty-eight hours prior—he was aggravated enough to spite the idea of Italy. But then, as this way of thinking and behaving only hurt himself, Sunny decided to rise above his resentment: He would love Italy even more than those who didn't have to labor so hard to achieve it, claim his entire shame's worth of a good vacation.

To whet his appetite, he read E. M. Forster's *Where Angels Fear to Tread,* and it occurred to him that Italy was the Englishman's first India, their first scorching sun, swarthy skin, their first garlic and hot temper, their first people whom they viewed alternately as children and as savages, charming and suddenly cruel—ultimately baffling. Perhaps Italy had allowed them to attempt India. This would suggest Italian charm had some truth to it, or else the English would have returned to their sunless, un-garlicky island and saved the world the ruinous empire.

*

FROM THE ATTIC CASEMENT, Sonia looked out onto the Campo Santa Margherita where in a scene made distant by November light, a group of fish sellers looked medieval. But she watched from a distance not only because the scene looked pale and far, but because she was waiting for Sunny and felt enclosed by the familiar emotion of being abandoned by a romantic partner.

She read her guidebook's list of the top twenty-five attractions in Venice. Twenty-five made too long a list—she grew muddled. It was two P.M. before she heard a knock at the door. When Sunny walked in, she was so relieved she began to accuse: *"Where were you? I had to wait again. I always have to wait!"*

"I was lost. I went all the way to the railway station." He was taking off his gray coat of restrained elegance and he was unwinding his Kullu scarf.

"I thought we wouldn't find each other."

"How can one not find someone who has been introduced to you by your nana-nani?" He was shedding the khadi handloom shirt the Delhi tailor had stitched. Sonia was wriggling from Aunt Meher's Bavarian trousers. She was removing her glasses; her eyes were black and gold.

"Remember Goa where I also had to wait—"

"That was Anand's fault. Anand and his plastic bags—"

"Next time I'm going to arrive second so you can—"

"I can what?"

"Know what it's like—"

"Okay," he said, jumping into the measly bedstead made of metal tubing and holding out his arms. "It'll be worth waiting—all the way to the end of time."

"Don't curse us."

Using their disagreement to drown the shyness that had built up in the months of each other's absence, they spent a long time in that bed—until they were reacquainted, until they had recognized their familiar scents beneath the veneer of Air India and Delta, until they heard church bells chiming and noticed the light had altered to that of dusk. They forced themselves not to fall asleep.

They tried to shower together the way they had bathed together in Goa, although they could barely fit into the brittle shower stall in the corner of the room. The water blew hot and cold, the trough filled and spilled.

"Do you think they gave us the worst room because we're Indians?" asked Sunny, mopping the floorboards with their bath towels.

"The owner was friendly," said Sonia, drying herself with the hand towel.

"Ah, but is he using friendliness to distract from having put us in the worst room?"

They dressed, Sunny admiring Sonia's long-haired lilac coat, her mauve suede boots, her garnet brooch. "Where did you get such frippery?"

"Once upon a time I was fashionable," she said, remembering when Lala had clothed her in vintage Gucci, in a Versace gown for an art opening. She may have loved the clothes were they not so expensive that wearing them made her feel as if there were a cobra in the room—the presence of evil, which was unfamiliar wealth.

They stepped out into the city of water light and plash, their vision focused now that they had found each other again, and they saw a city of creatures—half human, half beast, dragged from the depths of a dream, mermaids and mermen loitering at sea-sprayed corners. They saw three tuberous faces at a window of a gloomy palazzo—possibly, according to Sunny's pursuit of literature, a comte, a principe, a baron, watching cormorants through binoculars. They may have passed a red-bearded ship's captain and his sister in a fox fur tippet, the vixen's dead face snuggled under her chin. There was a glassblower, a woman crafting a chalice swirled in gold seaweed. Over there may be an American heiress of a Pyrex, Tupperware, or photocopy-machine fortune, searching for a husband with a title, and that may be a Malayali student of Machiavelli. They saw a hundred tourists from Beijing in a parade of boats. They saw a cruise ship higher than the tiled rooftops with a thousand people making a carnival on the Carnival cruise. They stood on a bridge and saw a gas tank barge worked by men in green overalls, a fireman's boat, a garbage boat followed by gulls, a boat laden with mandarins. Sonia was trying to hold herself still, but she wanted to wring her hands and run about declaring, declaiming, celebrating, and despairing at the same time, to render heightened emotion, surprise, envy, desire, distress, joy, and anguish. She looked at Sunny, rueful, accusing: "Sunny—*Italy is true!*" She pinched him.

The tourist dinner hour was in full swing and cherished outdoor tables under heat lamps were occupied, but finally they found a place to eat on Campo dei Frari, where the waiter was a foreigner like themselves. He wiped down the plastic-clad menu and handed it to them. "Where are you from?"

"India."

"Yes, I recognized you were from India. You don't eat beef?"

"We do eat beef," said Sunny shortly, although, in fact, Sonia did not.

"Why do India people not eat cow?" the waiter persisted.

"Well, some people don't eat pigs."

"Because pig is dirty. India people don't eat cow because they think cow is God!"

They understood the waiter was trying to tell them that while he may be their waiter, he was superior to them because they came from a people who ate pigs but not cows.

Sunny tried to deflect him, saying jocularly in a cartoon Indian accent, "Well, in India, God is so far away that we have to worship cows instead."

Why did he say something so dumb? thought Sonia.

Sunny saw her face. "Cows are not God, they are respected *like* God; there is a crucial philosophical difference," he said, retreating to an ordinary Indian accent. "Or *like* Mother. Or maybe *exactly* as Mother. Cow is Mother." He sounded deranged.

"Should we go and see the basilica first?" Sonia asked.

Sunny was thinking: *But then equivalently, God would be respected* like *a cow. Mother would be like God. Or if* exactly *a cow, then Mother was God.* He said, "Or should we do the opposite of what tourists do and slowly work our way to the center to see the basilica and the Doge's Palace our last day?"

The waiter returned. "I met an India guy and the guy he tell me he pray to a donkey."

"A cow!" yelled Sonia. "What is your problem?"

"Enough! Let's go," said Sunny. He got up and took Sonia's hand.

"Why are you leaving? You can't leave," the waiter said. "I already brought your wine."

"My God," said Sonia, "why are we having a Hindu-Muslim fight?"

But she was mollified by the way Sunny took her hand, as if they belonged together.

They walked until they saw another outdoor restaurant with a vacant table, and when he and Sonia sat down, the couple next to them moved.

"I'm going to ask them why," said Sunny.

Said Sonia, "It's the cigarette smoke from the man who was smoking on the other side of them. I saw the woman frown and blow it away with her hand." She recalled that to be American was to test each situation for racism, as Sunny was doing.

"Anyway," Sonia said to Sunny, "even if someone moved tables because they didn't want to sit next to us, it may not be racism. People can dislike us for other reasons."

This struck him as reassuring. "Yes!" He laughed and raised his Aperol spritz. "*People can dislike us for other reasons.*"

"Will you still talk to me if I order the rabbit?" she asked.

"If you talk to me when I eat the boar."

"And if I get the squid?"

"I might get the octopus. Psst—"

"What?"

"I'm happy with you!" he said from behind his hand.

CHAPTER

49

....

ON A CLOUDY DAY THE LAGOON DID NOT TURN DARKER AS
you'd expect but a more milky turquoise—the color of his mother's
favorite silk ikat—and Sunny began to see her, Babita, out of the corner of his eye. There was Babita in the vaporetto traveling the length
of the Grand Canal. Babita at the Guggenheim finding her own spirit
reflected in the spirit of Peggy Guggenheim—both women with style
and chutzpah, with oversize sunglasses and dogs. She would say, "Let's
go to Caffè Florian and Caffè Quadri even if it's expensive; it's once in
a lifetime," and she would adore the waiters in black jackets, capes, and
scarlet bow ties, gray hair combed back, clapping hands and chasing
pigeons too fat to fly from her Indian Wedding Tramezzino, feeling
especially welcomed by a sandwich named for Indian vegetarian extravagance. She would remark that the basilica looked like something
made by one of the mad maharajas who had all of the money and none
of the taste. She would call to the waiter, "Look here, chump, there are
only five peaky clams in my spaghetti with clams!" She would spot a
sardarji in a crimson turban across the fondamenta and say, "Indian
men are all ugly except for the sardars, thank goodness for them." She
would pause on the bridge over the Rio de Ca' Foscari, delighting in
the glamour of a funeral boat with a coffin covered in black and gold
velvet, a Teatro La Fenice boat with black and silver chests containing
theater props. She would sing back to a gondolier, *O mio babbino caro*.
She would go to the Rialto fish market, test the fish for springiness,
and advise the fishmonger with a carbuncled face, *You see, the secret is
you must marinate the fillet in ground mustard and lime before you batter and
fry—that magically brings out the flavor!*

She would enjoy herself madly.

Sunny heard Babita's voice inside his ear saying, *Why don't you look around, Sunny, and see if you can find a reasonable place where I might stay?* From inside his heart he felt her yearning—if you were a parent, it didn't mean you wouldn't long for the same transformative vacations that you, with such sacrifice, had granted your child.

To dissuade his mother's spirit from following them and to stand up for the Third World—who else was going to?—Sunny continued to do Italy the favor of treating it with skepticism, of suspecting his susceptibility to Italian charm. He put forward the hypothesis that Italian charm was a fake construction by and for foreigners but so desirable a story that Italians themselves bought it, believed it, and therefore made it at least somewhat true.

"A train that is late and breaks down in a charming way is Italian. A train that breaks down in a not-charming way is Indian.

"Laziness in India is infuriating and equals animosity. In Italy it indicates an enjoyment of life's pleasures.

"Candlelight in a trattoria is romance. In India it equals power failure and a testing of romance.

"Then when you look at tourists numerous enough to sustain a myth for the sake of their own vacation tales, how would one know, anyway, if the place is real or not? You said, 'Italy is true!' but if tourists—ourselves included—number more than natives, doesn't that fact automatically make the place untrue?"

Sonia said, "No, it is still a true country."

"Why?"

She pointed at the laundry blowing from windows, flapping amongst the ruins and the churches. She said, "Look at those underpants. They say, 'To hell with you tourists. Here are my bucket panties, my stained pillowcases, my shabby nightgown of ghost roses just like Mina Foi's in Allahabad.'"

"Why did Mina Foi live such a sad life?"

Sonia told Sunny that Mina Foi was divorced from the already-married Belgian, that when her true love Ernest had returned to *chirrur-chirrur* like an owl from the rain gutter, Dadaji had been determined nobody would lure his daughter away because she was now required to look after him in his old age.

They saw a gull murder a pigeon. "Are the gulls hungry because there are not enough fish in the lagoon?" they asked a glassblower, who had just crafted a sea urchin. She replied, "They are hungry by nature."

They saw fishermen at the San Zaccaria ferry stop bringing up their nets. They tossed back a seahorse, its eye shocked, its nostrils *pffffooooting* alarm. But they kept a little squid holding tight with its tentacles to the net. They unclasped it, its heart poured out its ink upon the rimed marble, and it died.

Sunny had brought his camera this time. How can you *not* photograph Italy—what if they never came again? He took photographs of the murdered pigeon and the dying squid. He took a picture of Sonia against a plain brown wall with some undecipherable but obviously rude graffiti. It was best not to attract the evil eye by taking a glamorous picture that would, anyway, be stereotypical.

Then one morning the kind proprietor—who was kind either because he was kind or because he'd put the brown people in the worst room—told them they'd be advised to be leisurely over their croissants and emerge later because neo-Nazis were holding an anti-immigrant rally. Sunny became excited. He was definitely going to see something true. "I'll go out with my camera."

"Sunny, you are such a strange man."

"Does that mean you don't like me?"

"It means the opposite."

The next morning he was there before the neo-Nazis, ready with his camera as they came down the street, shaved heads and leather jackets, other Italians standing with counter signs, and a few bedraggled African handbag sellers holding up pieces of cardboard that read *Geneva Convention! Human Rights for All!*

Later they saw some of these handbag sellers suddenly gather up their bags and run swiftly, followed by stout police chasing them like dogcatchers despite being impeded by their weight, stiff uniforms, and paraphernalia. Tourists from countries that need no visas to enter Italy stopped in their tour-group lines, some to chuckle, some to decry the problem of migrants. The bag sellers dispersed, slipping through the crowds like water, yet the police nabbed two men. The minute they were trapped, life exited their bodies—they stood wooden and stared past. They didn't appear to hear the laughter, nor did they recruit sympathy. They made the whole scene nothing. Perhaps they had come on one of those boats in the news, 465 on a boat meant for one hundred, a mix of people from Afghanistan, Senegal, Nigeria, Yemen, Indonesia. Not all would have made it.

Sunny took photographs, and he decided to stand exactly *there*—as they advised citizen activists in the United States—in case there would be subsequent need for a witness to police brutality. "What about Ethiopia? What about Somalia?" he reminded Sonia but spoke loudly so everyone around would hear. "And while they keep on talking about everyone who was in the resistance, where was the first ghetto?"

Sonia was deeply ashamed to be with a man hectoring the tour groups, for surely neither destitute African migrants nor European Jews would tolerate being defended by the likes of Sunny.

"Where in Bangladesh are you from?" Sunny asked a Bangladeshi magic-wand seller by the Bridge of Sighs. "Sylhet," the man answered shortly. "There were terrible floods in Bangladesh last year. Indians are cutting down all the trees and so Bangladesh is flooding."

The Sri Lankan waiter in the restaurant in front of the Arsenale had traveled through India, Uzbekistan, Georgia, Turkey, and Greece to arrive at the osteria. He proffered a risotto.

"Here it costs a fortune, but in our part of the world, this is the food of poverty," said Sunny. "Isn't it? Mushy rice with a few vegetables."

The waiter didn't answer. He went back to speaking in Italian with his fellow waiters and made sure he kept his gaze away from Sunny's promiscuous one. His focus was on Italy, on white people. He didn't want Sunny's condescending ten-minute friendship. *Don't be three South Asians. Don't be two South Asians, one in a kurta, no matter its beguiling shade of mustard. Don't be one poor fucker going over to hug another poor fucker.*

With the man keeping his gaze away for the remainder of their meal, Sunny—again speaking loudly in the hopes of being overheard—said to Sonia, "Why don't they have any Sri Lankan restaurants here—

why not a prawn pilau?" For only one cuisine to be on offer in any city, let alone a cosmopolitan seafaring town, was fascistic, was it not?

Said Sonia, "But I *want* to eat Italian food in Italy." When they stopped at the vegetable boat in Campo San Barnaba, they saw different kinds of radicchio: pink, red, round, thin, speckled, stripy, curly. "This one from Chioggia," said the seller, "and that one from Treviso."

Briefly she remembered Papa, whose appetite had vanished. Had he overcome the H. pylori infection?

"Do you know which country takes in the most refugees?"

Sonia lost her temper. "Sunny, don't you see there is a disconnect between our enjoyment and your lament?" She thought his bluster was so as not to focus on her, so as not to have to love her enough to present her with a glass ring that moment when the light was pure upon the Zattere. If the world was to maintain its optimism—its generosity and warmth—on the fact of Italy existing, then it was important that Italy remain intact and uncomplicated. If you believed in its beauty, it would save you. Maybe if there was ever a crisis in Italy, this belief held by others would save Italy, too, for we're all better when we are loved, when we believe we know who we are, and when people tell us they know who we are and their vision is gentle.

"You are being condescending," said Sonia.

"How?"

"By playing the role of savior, you're sending a signal that you think you are on a higher plane. Anyway, in African countries, or in Bangladesh, they don't think Indians are nice people. They think Indians are imperialists."

"The point isn't comparison."

"You weren't fighting racism in India while we were traveling in Goa," she said. "In India, too, everyone favors Europeans, Americans. The tour guides say horrible things about Nigerians and Israelis."

Sunny looked moodily off, and for a span they did not speak. Sunny thought Sonia was right, but when he stopped his bluster, he felt nervous. Perhaps his personal failure at being unable to accept the extravagant allure of Italy had made Sunny concentrate on the handbag men. Then they happened to be drinking a Piona wine from the Italian lake region after walking about and viewing a row of smiling, non-ferocious stone lions with girlish curls. One dated to the fourth century BC and came from Athens. The papal throne alongside was composed of a gravestone with Arabic lettering, stolen in the Crusades. Sunny was experiencing two strands of history—one bloody and one beautiful. The mushroom risotto he had complained about was as simple as perfect.

"You're right, Sonia," he acceded. His legs stretched out under the table and entangled Sonia's legs. "You see the story behind the story. I feel comforted by your intelligence. I feel safe in your intelligence."

But when Sunny kissed her in the room over the pizzeria, Sonia half kissed him in return, uncertain as to which way her mood was slanting, allowing his mouth upon hers but showing him a vehement eye a few millimeters away from his own that said, *Now you're happy, but I'm still stuck in the unhappiness you created!* When he reached for her in bed, she decided she was still on the raft of anger and turned away.

"Shouldn't we immediately have sex to get over our upset?"

She wouldn't turn to him, pliable, flip like a fish for him to sample first one side of her and then the other. She wouldn't ambush him and attach a wet mouth upon his neck suddenly in a surprise, as if she were a squid. Or place long monkey arms about him and clamber over to his front. "No," she said. "I might kick you."

"A small kick might be all right."

"It wouldn't be a small kick. Let me calm down a little."

In a bit she said, "No. I just can't. I'm not going to have sex. My mind is full of refugees, brutalized continents, the Holocaust, Mussolini—and my own anger that we're leaving without having been happy in this extraordinary place. For just a few days I wanted to forget I'm a Third-Worlder who must worry about other Third-Worlders."

"I can never be with a woman who says that!" said Sunny.

"Go then!"

This statement, or perhaps the fury at being denied sex, propelled Sunny. He got up and left the room on top of the pizzeria in his Lucknow pajamas, absurdly slight for the cold weather, but they had been so light to pack! He threw on his coat. He smelled of Sonia's neem toothpaste as he ran down the stairs.

Sonia thought, *Good.*

He ran across the Campo Santa Margherita. He went over the white marble bridge at Campo San Barnaba like a shivering Lucknow ghost, the reflections of the lights of homes and lampposts in the night canal making the water look full of ghosts as well. At the top of the bridge he saw a man standing, looking out. The moon was waxing full and the water was high, sloshing under the long wooden doors ragged at the bottom from water rot. Sunny stood brooding on whether to turn back or stay out until Sonia became worried and felt sorry.

The man on the bridge turned and said, "It is pretty, no?"

"Yes."

He wore jeans, a woolen cap, a jacket, brown leather shoes. He looked as if he was from the same part of the world as Sunny.

"Where are you from?"

"India, but I live in New York."

"I could tell from your pajamas where you are from." He switched to Hindi: "I am from Baramulla in Kashmir. Now I live on Bodensee, at the border between Germany and Switzerland. I have a shop, a grocery."

This, despite his spoiled mood, made Sunny curious, and it beguiled him once more unto the cause of migrants. How odd to meet a Kashmiri at midnight on a bridge of carved marble as if they were actors upon a Shakespearean stage. "It must be nice living on Bodensee?"

"It is nice. Here there are more Africans. I traveled just to see this place. I have an uncle in Bologna, but my luggage was lost. I called the lost-luggage office, and they said my suitcase is in Naples."

"Naples!"

"And my flight is tomorrow. I don't know what to do, I have nothing with me."

"What a problem!"

"If you have something extra you can give to help me?"

Sunny was surprised by this turn—from admiring the view with a Kashmiri and thinking Sonia was wrong, to thinking Sonia was right, although in what way was she right? No, she wasn't right. For him to be tricked by a migrant didn't make her right at all.

"Anything, if you have, anything, even money for a bus ticket."

"I don't."

"Just some liras—"

"I have nothing on me. I am in my pajamas as you can see."

"For a phone card then, a few dollars—"

"I don't have any money on me. I left my wallet in my hotel."

"Please help me, please, brother—I'll wait for you. *Please go see if you have something. Please, please, please, brother, please, brother . . .*" The voice wailed after him, soft but insistent, an illegal migrant on a bridge who had perhaps escaped the brutality of the Indian army or recruitment pressure from militants or simple poverty. "*Please, please, please, brother. I am waiting right here for you. Brother, brother . . . help me.*" He kept his voice low so no natives might be disturbed, lean out, and see two brown people up to no good. But the low voice cut deeper than a loud voice and held insistent—like a shehnai note, or a mosquito, or a sentence uttered by a mother.

At three A.M., Sonia woke and found Sunny was not there. She worried she had made a misstep. If she had allowed him to simply get away with his bad behavior, this might have incited a feeling of grateful love—you love the person who is nice to you even when you behave badly.

Sunny, in his distress, had rushed all the way over the Accademia Bridge and entered a maze that brought him each time to the same discount luggage store. He went right and left, each time finding the same tangerine suitcase, handbag, and wallet display. It was four in the morning before he returned to the room, whereupon he and Sonia clasped each other like fierce squid that do not wish to die.

"I love you so much! Why are we fighting?"

"Maybe that is why we are fighting."

They had fought perhaps to make themselves of primary importance to each other and to keep other problems away—mothers and fathers, work and visas, secret pasts and former loves. If the other elements took center stage, their love wouldn't stand a chance.

They were in sober moods the next afternoon when they went to visit the friends of Ferooza's friend, the ambassador's wife. Paola and

Matteo Fabi, in quilted block-print waistcoats, were scholars of India—in particular of the communist movement in Bengal. Sonia and Sunny were awed by their apartment, which was modern in its design within an edifice several centuries old. A wall of bright bindu serigraphs by the artist Raza went seamlessly with a Calder-like mobile and the colorful spines of thousands of books.

As they sipped espressos and sampled from a box of Sicilian almond sweets, Sonia and Sunny were discomfited to find that the couple knew India better than they did—and they could not converse upon the topics brought forth because they were not familiar with the places being discussed, nor the history of their country, nor the political parties of various states. They had not heard of Charu Mazumdar, who had so inspired this couple, let alone how he connected to Gramsci, whom they were also unaware of. Looking across at the abstractions by Raza, Sunny had a sense of having misunderstood the country of his birth, of having considered it primitive for the purpose of leaving it, and misunderstanding Italy as well, misusing it to solve his personal anxieties and shames. He'd spent so long focused upon the West, he knew less about himself than many Westerners did, and how could he not be doomed to get everything wrong, the East and the West, the First World and the developing world, himself and Sonia?

Sonia was thinking that she should, in fact, move out of the Hauz Khas flat. How would she ever become a woman with an adult life and a sparkling cosmopolitan intellect similar to this couple if she continued with Papa and Chandu or with Mama and Moolchand?

Before Sunny and Sonia left, Paola and Matteo suggested they visit the nearby Fortuny Museum, a more obscure museum that was probably not on the Top Twenty-Five Attractions list. It had an unusual show about migration from colonial days to the present. Paola said, "There is a Balthusian quality to them. They are beautiful in the old way of paintings; at first you are seduced, then they unsettle you. You wake in the middle of the night. My favorite is of a Sri Lankan cook. It is called *The Tagliatelle Cannot Wait*. The Tamil lady is making tagliatelle in a villa outside Florence. The Italian family are in modern clothes but have the same Florentine faces as the paintings on the wall; the dogs have the same faces as the dogs in the paintings. You can tell everyone is in their ancestral home except for the staff. Just see the expressions on each face. Who will accuse whom? It is beyond dissection."

Feeling abashed by the elegant company provided them, they took leave of their hosts, became lost down wormhole passages, turned cat-piss corners, until, as if by accident, they bumped right into the Fortuny Museum. They entered a dark interior and were immersed in disorienting, darting light. At the far edge of their vision, a woman in a ruffled, turquoise-green bikini jumped from a jetty into a lake, *boom, splash!*

She turned. She waved. Elated, laughing—

"*Mummy!*" cried Sonia.

Nobody heard her because her cry merged with the cry of a piratical gull, the slap of lake water, distant boat traffic, and Mummy herself calling, "*Come! The water is perfect!*" Then Mummy swam, serene as a swan, all the way out. But there was no horizon; the film of the lake looped back like the trap of memory. Again Mummy jumped, dark-haired, vivacious as a movie star in a Fellini film. *Boom, splash!*

Ilan de Toorjen Foss. The artist's name in yellow unrolled like a type-writer typing across the screen. Then in brighter yellow: *Does the Lake Remember?* Yellow as Sonia's first winter coat, as yellow as Ilan's car, as yellow as Ilan's velvet divan. Sonia smelled the sulfur of betrayal. The writing went on to inform her that de Toorjen Foss's artistic, erotic, and spiritual awakening had come when he had been seduced by the sight of his mother swimming. He had captured it himself on the film he had made with his father's camera when he was a teenager.

Sunny was considering that black-and-white films capture movement and light so much better than films made in color. He was experiencing the trembling leaves of olive trees glinting like a lake, the trembling of a lake glinting like olive leaves, the water movement of lizards and shy water snakes. Undulating gulls rocked the sky like water, the sky became lake. He did not notice as Sonia rushed to the next room. She was looking—what was she looking for?

A canvas with Ilan's wife larger than life. She was exhausted from illness, yet an even worse fate had overcome her gaze. Distempered photographs and objects in vitrines in a display alongside, related to her previous existence in Essaouira, Alexandria, and Paris. There was a photograph of Ilan and his young wife on a cruise up the Nile to the Valley of Kings. Egyptian museums were museums full of the eyes of the past, and tens of thousands of eyes interrogated the couple from heaps of dusty figures in glass cases, the eyes of kings and queens, jackal-headed gods and sacred cats, crocodiles and ibises, slaves and priests. They examined the history, history accused them.

Ilan's wife accused Sonia. How intimate was betrayal: She reclined upon the same bed Sonia had once slept on; Sonia recognized the coverlet and Ilan's watch by the bedside, exactly as she had seen it placed. Even the water glass. Sonia had played a part she did not know she was playing. She had encouraged and flattered Ilan, provided him with the solace that had allowed him not only to paint, but to hold out in his mistreatment of others, that they might be mercilessly defeated, that he might win. Was it this woman's eye that had locked onto Sonia's when she had climbed to look through a gap in the window of Ilan's locked studio in Vermont? She couldn't remember the color of the pupil, but the eye menaced her still.

Sonia didn't stop. She ran up another flight of stairs—

Three ladies of the manor taking tea in the grounds of their Scottish estate. Cliffs in the distance, a glimpse of brown sea. The ladies were in hijabs, and they made totemic shapes with crossed-out eyes. They could see you, but you couldn't see them.

A young African woman in a miniskirt on a scooter in the European countryside. Had she delivered hashish to the people in holiday villas who were smoking, who were swimming in a pool in the midst of vineyards? Behind this scene were medieval villages perched on hilltops as in the medieval paintings. She held a baby. The baby looked like Ilan. Was it the young mother's eye she had seen?

Sonia didn't stop. She went upstairs—

She walked into her own eyes. Was it herself that she had seen through the gap in Ilan's studio window? Was she the woman like a Gauguin woman, however, not in her native land but in a bath in Vermont? The snow light and magnifying water could not have revealed her more purely, but her expression was enigmatic. Sonia's gaze dissolved into her own gaze, the painting opened a wound in her heart. There was something hindered and interior, something grief-stricken and beseeching, something selfish and incensed, also something absolving. Was it she who had inspired the painting, or was it the artist who had created the emotions with which she looked from the canvas—was he invisible between them? The image knew Sonia better than she knew herself. She wanted to understand herself backward, but she might never discern her components and their meaning. Her hair, eyebrows, and pubic hair were painted as if in barbaric contrast to New England pilgrim austerity. In her hand, she held Badal Baba. Your gods are impotent when you don't save them. When you don't save them, they cannot save you. If you lose them, how can you know yourself?

She turned to the same lilac coat she was wearing now. The lilac coat hung over a familiar yellow divan. Sonia was on this divan, stomach down, naked. On top of her was naked Ilan. The expression had slid off his face in the sexual act. A clementine skin lay curled on the windowsill. The woman was complicit; she had eaten the fruit. Sonia stared—and stared—and projecting from the white space of the canvas, enclosing her, transfixing her, she saw a ghost hound in a harlequin hound mask of shadow and light. The hound from the deserted beach in Goa. The hound from the Cloud Cottage forest dark. The hound that could dissolve into the space between the trees, into sand, into snow. This was the trick: The devil wears the devil's mask. *What if one night you have a dream of a dog? This dog is both victim and perpetrator. In the moment of its attack, you fight back, you try to kill the dog, but your face becomes its face.* Where did Sonia remember this from?

She fled, but she was immediately pinned by the eyes of a patroness of the arts at the Metropolitan Museum of Art. The woman sat by windows that looked out upon the obelisk from Egypt. The waiters behind her made their smiles a little too broad, because if you can't afford to be angry, you smile too much—

What was that totem about her wrinkly neck, set into an oriental necklace? A demon-goblin-prankster with a cracked-open void. *Badal Baba, Lord of the Clouds, Demon of the Wastelands.* You need a god who can understand you.

Sonia's legs began to quake.

One clear thought projected through her consternation: She must prevent Sunny from seeing these paintings! Sunny was still in the first room of the exhibition. At what cost to others had Ilan's family savored their colonial life? How could the disaster not overcome them as well?

Sonia came rushing at Sunny, her braid flying. "Let's go!"

"Why?" He was writing *The colonizer is as trapped as the colonized* in his notebook with a violet ink brush pen that he had mistakenly bought and made it hard to write. It was meant to capture an island in last light—an island where two people might escape together. *Why are we fighting?*

"We got no sleep last night. Let's return to Al Canton."

"You go back and nap. I want to hear the artist."

"The artist?"

"In a few minutes. Didn't you see the notice at the entrance?"

"Ilan?" choked Sonia.

He looked at her. Sweat beaded upon Sonia's face. "What happened to you?"

"We have to leave. *Something bad is going to happen!*"

"Why?"

"This is a very dangerous person!"

"Who?"

"Ilan!"

"Why do you keep calling the artist by his first name?" This casual familiarity is what irritated Sunny—

"Because I know him," hissed Sonia.

"Who?"

"Ilan."

"How?"

"I had a relationship with him."

"When?"

"In New York."

She had said she was lonely in New York. *She had lied.*

"I told you something bad is about to happen!" she said. She took him by

the sleeve; then when this didn't work, she took him by his elbow. As he pulled back, she took him by the hair. Sunny pushed her violently away. There is no greater humiliation than to be pulled by the hair. But then, as Sonia took off, he was forced to chase after her, nevertheless.

She took the narrowest streets and darkest alleys, because to walk across the Accademia Bridge—impossible! Ilan would be roving. He would be walking by Al Canton to the plaque stating Ruskin had stayed on the Zattere; he had copied Ruskin's democratic ideals. He would be going to the Frari church to study the Bellini Madonna, domestic yet hallowed like the moon Sonia and Sunny had watched rise over Loutolim. He would be visiting the tombs of Monteverdi, Titian, and Canova's heart and be plotting to live into perpetuity himself. He would be crossing the bridge this very moment on his way to give his lecture. He would be high on his conquest. He would be shining: *I won! I won! I did it! You lost! I won!*

They arrived at a dead end, where black water sucked against a wall encrusted with seaweed and mussel colonies. Sonia reversed, raced over a little bridge and then over another tiny bridge, Sunny chasing after her. They arrived at the same dead end of distilled marine rot, crustaceous lagoon silt, and iodine, where you'd imagine a victim of murder being shipped out. They set off again, to a neighborhood that was poor and deserted, a row of stone heads that looked as if they had been decapitated, and returned to the same creepy, dim dead end of nefarious water slopping and glugging.

"Stop, Sonia, stop a minute." Sunny caught up with her. She was shaking and stinking now of sweat and foreboding. He put his arms around her and felt her falling through. He did not know that the person who terrified her and from whom she was running was the same person that she was drawn to still, to whom she longed to be close to still so she would no longer be scared. The fear resided in the distance, in the consciousness of danger that remained because she had not been entirely swallowed. The fear would leave only if she were completely destroyed.

She wriggled free.

"We're thoroughly lost," he said.

There was nobody on the street. Night had fallen. They could see a light through red curtains. Sunny knocked on the glass, the window opened, and a man with a centaur's goatee, dressed in a golden Fortuny silk bathrobe, looked out from an interior wallpapered in red velvet. Opera played at crescendo from behind him. He looked at them as if they were in a play, and they looked at him as if he were in a play.

Sonia, again chased by Sunny, took off, slipping down the seaweed-slick passageway that the man in the golden silk bathrobe indicated, and finally they found a deserted vaporetto stop with a vaporetto moving toward them, its lights on the lagoon giving the impression of a sea centipede with glowing legs moving seriously and comically on the black water.

*

"YOU'VE CLEARLY GONE MAD! I thought the plan was to stop fighting. You physically attacked me," exclaimed Sunny when they were safely inside their garret with the door and shutters shut.

"I did not attack you."

"You humiliated us! In public! You made a spectacle! You pulled me by the hair!" Nothing worse for brown people than to make a primitive melodrama. "You know, I almost hit you. This terrifies me. I only just managed to restrain myself."

"I was scared."

"But *why*?"

Why? Sunny had neglected to propose to Sonia, that was why. They had been followed by a hound that was the darkness manifest, that was why. Ilan had painted the dog before it had followed them on the beach; now they were caught in Ilan's plot. Sonia had tried to forget Ilan, but in the same way a murderer keeps returning to the scene of a murder, the victim, too, cannot leave her own death alone. She has to repeat the occasion of her murder over and over.

She said, "Do you remember in Goa when I woke up and said I had been killed?"

"No," said Sunny.

"Remember the time we were followed by that strange dog that came out of the ocean?"

"Yes." Sunny did remember the dog.

"In the museum was a painting of myself with the exact same hound that attacked us and then vanished into the sand. I am not free in my new life."

"That can't be true."

"Yes, it can't be true, but it is! That's the trick."

"But you said you were alone in New York!"

"I said I was *lonely*. Ilan displaced me."

"With *what*?"

"With himself. He didn't leave a chink. His demands displaced me, his rage displaced me, his happiness displaced me, his love displaced me, his madness displaced me, his nonstop talking about himself, his cruelty and violence—it all removed me. I became a ghost. There is nothing lonelier than being a ghost."

"Did you ever see him after New York?" Sunny only asked because the Venetian night was so black, not a traffic light, not a sound but the mournful, digestive rumbles of restive gulls.

"No. But the darkness hasn't left me. It follows me. It watches me. It waits for me. It thinks I belong to it. It wants to complete the story."

They were lying side by side, but Sunny didn't put his arms around her again. Sonia continued: "That same dog that came after us on the beach also appeared in a photograph in Cloud Cottage, where we'd never noticed it before. The same eyes are still in the forest outside my mother's home."

"Sonia, it doesn't make sense."

She knew it didn't make sense, but Sunny was naïve and unable to grasp the way in which darkness followed a person, across centuries, across geographies. It never made sense, and because everyone thought you were mad, it gained in power.

"I lent Ilan my grandfather's demon amulet," Sonia confessed, "when Ilan said he was scared that he was being followed by evil. He has harnessed its power to learn the devil's purpose."

"Don't be silly!"

"I am not silly. There are artists who make an exchange with the devil, who gravitate to darkness because they know that their knowledge of darkness, the plot and plan of darkness, will make them famous. Without my demon, I will be killed, although I already died."

"A painting can't conjure a murder or prevent a murder, let alone the murder of someone who is already dead!" He understood again: Sonia was mad.

"It can. Without my painting, I feel I've lost my own face—which is an irony because the creature has no face."

A long silence passed.

Then Sonia said: "Maybe we should just get married. If you are married, you have to be on the same side in life—it sends a message to the world: 'Hey, it's us against all of you.' Bad things slink away." Sending this sentence out into the air, she was testing its truth, its falsity. *Maybe we should just get married.* She felt its truth.

Sunny remained silent. Then he said, "You know it doesn't work that way."

Yet in the middle of this night without a glimmer to reveal or embarrass them, they reached for each other, and Sonia let her sadness wash over Sunny. She really cried; she cried a Ganga. There was no reason to hold anything back at the abrupt end of love. She wept into Sunny's hair, into his neck, into his mouth. She held on to him and howled for her past that would most certainly doom the future. The sound she made was a hoarse, gasping, harrowing sound of a phantom that wails all night long in a country place where there is nobody to call and nobody to help. Sunny gulped her tears, and she said, into his mouth, "Can you at least retrieve my demon amulet for me? That's all I ask, because we were happy for a moment, weren't we?"

When she fell into exhausted, parched sleep, Sunny crept out of the bed-and-breakfast with a catalog from the exhibition he had put into his satchel before Sonia had come racing. He stood in the swirl of vapor under a streetlamp and saw a photograph of Ilan de Toorjen Foss. The artist with a lean, distinguished face stood looking out past winged, warted cacti and ancient magueys tall as trees to a landscape of spare distance. He was dressed in a gray, linen kimono and wore a mask of his face alongside his face. Jealousy flooded Sunny. He turned the page. He saw Sonia naked in service to Ilan. And as he looked, he saw—but did he?—rising from the page, then retreating back into it, the hound that had followed them out of the ocean, that had attacked them and melted into the sand, like an omen. Sunny had thought he was living one life, but he'd been living another.

He walked to throw the catalog into the canal and saw sitting upon a bench his mother's living ghost. She said nothing, but he knew all he needed to know from her look, a look older than civilization.

*

THE NEXT DAY, SONIA stayed in bed, shutters closed. To be certain she would not be drawn by magic power to circle back to the Fortuny Museum to find her face. To be certain she would not run into Ilan, who would be seizing this city of treasures like the spoils of war: *I won! You lost! You go around crying—wah, wah, wah—and end up dead. Life kicks me down, I survive!*

Alone Sunny went to the basilica—like a glittering dream of a mad maharaja—and the Doge's Palace, apricot and light as a parfait outside, sinister with courts and prisons and a history of terror inside. But he couldn't see the raja's glittering basilica. He couldn't see the Doge's apricot parfait. He was thinking: *But she lied!*

More closely linked and more irrevocably apart, they took the vaporetto to the airport, speaking in a subdued, rational manner—of their flight connections, their times of arrival, a wintry mix in New York, fog-smog in New Delhi. They did not look right or left in case they passed Ilan. They did not look at the families traveling cozily together or saying goodbye, certain their love would knit the rent of their absence. They hugged briefly and found they could not kiss—not even lightly, fearful any ambivalence may show itself.

Sonia turned right to her departure gate. Sunny turned left to his. Briefly he turned and saw Sonia's long braid down her lilac coat. She turned as well, but by then, he was far away and she could no longer distinguish his gray coat from all the others.

Indians Cannot
Be Cool

....

FROM JFK, SUNNY TOOK THE BUS TO SEVENTY-FOURTH AND Roosevelt. He stopped at Little Yak for momos to steady himself, adding his bag to the pile of luggage belonging to other travelers under a message board alerting patrons to a Tibetan girls' soccer match and a lecture by a visiting rinpoche. Tibetan refugees congregated here, as did Indian immigrants who came to recollect their student days in India when they had frequented similar Tibetan dhabas. Radiant afternoon light filtered through the chili noodle steam, and Sunny coughed. As his head cleared, he sipped butter tea and overheard a conversation between two friends and the daughter of one of the friends. "Who are the cool Indians, do you think?" asked the teenager.

"Indians cannot be cool," said the coolest of them, sporting large aviator frames and mandala tattoos, his hair in a greased ponytail. "They can be smart, they can be funny, Indians can be many things, but not cool."

"Why not, Vijay Uncle?"

"Think about what 'cool' means. The root of the idea of cool is not caring what other people think, following your own path, riffing to your own rhythm, but Indians can never be free of what Mummy-Papa, Nana-Nani, Uncle-Aunty think."

Indians may not be cool, but this scene was. Sunny, registering the coincidence of Vijay Uncle's genius observations, could feel the tug of Babita's waiting to speak to him, while all around was the bustle of Jackson Heights and the cool, the swagger of working, moving people, of a thousand rough experiences, of never belonging, of knowing an intensity of life that the comfortable could never guess at. This cool was greater than Italy's cool, he decided. Immigrant New York would restore him and lend him its jazz after the injuries to his ego suffered on his first trip to Europe. He walked to La Fruta Donna for a pomegranate, to Key Food for milk and a can of Café Bustelo, to La Gran Uruguaya for empanadas—pausing to watch a goal being scored in a soccer match in Montevideo—to the hardware store for roach motels. "Amigo!" he called to Hugo.

"Good, you're back," Hugo said and went on with his business. Home is where life continues and doesn't abruptly come to an end; where they don't care where you've been, because if they ask, or if you tell, it makes the first pinprick hole that begins a reckless unraveling. Home is where they fill you in on local news instead: The kebab place had become a fancy cheese shop! Gentrified Brooklyn was arriving; the gentrifiers would proclaim it was for love of community, but they would immediately close their doors and set about destroying community because they had too much wealth for it to make sense to share.

When he was back in his studio, the phone rang, and Sunny knew it would be his ma. Like Hugo at the hardware store, Babita didn't ask about Venice, and she didn't mention the postcard she had received. She certainly didn't mention Sonia. Instead, she had something to tell him.

Babita informed Sunny that she had acquiesced to Uncles Ravi-Rana's plan to sell the Delhi house. In the aftermath of this decision she had begun to wonder where she might settle, and during the dawn hours of widow phone calling, she had consulted friends and acquaintances who had already left the cities to find quieter retirement locations. Several had made impractical, romantic, and illegal choices. Saloni and Vivan had bribed to build in designated forest-grazing land. Alva and Benjamin had built out near Corbett National Park, where the milky, green Ramganga River almost leapt into their windows. Others had moved to Dehradun, Nagpur, and Mahabaleshwar. They came to the phone at a fast hobble, galumphing gummy knees, clearing throats eagerly. "Why not Panchgani?" Someone sent her a brochure of a development in a litchi orchard showing glass from floor to ceiling, an "Italian modular" kitchen, and a meditation hall. The developers hoped Indians from the States might return in their old age for an inexhaustible supply of inexpensive servants. This "retirement estate" had been conveniently built opposite a brand-new luxury hospital linked to a credit card specifically for non-resident Indians that would offer a 15 percent discount toward medical expenses.

Babita had no intention of moving to the wilderness or living amongst foolish nonresident Indians building glass houses in a blistering climate and being fleeced by hospitals built for the express purpose of fleecing them. She told Sunny that she had been conferring with Vanya over her predicament, when Vanya had exclaimed, "Well, you are in luck—you always land on your feet, don't you?" Umberto had informed her that he was indeed required back in Milan; his mother had suffered a stroke. He would be selling Casa das Conchas. The edge in Vanya's voice—"You always land on your feet, don't you?"—indicated to Babita that Vanya was resentful of Babita's prospective good fortune. She became cognizant of the need to move quickly. "The house will be virtually impossible to maintain," said Vanya. "I wish I could move to a convenient flat in Panjim, but Cecil is buried here, so here I'm stuck."

Babita recalled the arcade of temple trees and the operatic front steps leading to Casa das Conchas painted white with a shade-blue trim. The rooms, she recalled, were tall and serious with hexagonal oxblood tiles. The oyster shutters at the long windows filtered the light so you felt as if you were inside a cool shell. She had liked the wide teak cupboards on splayed lion paws and the austere beds planked high to catch the breeze, with canopies crocheted by widows, spinsters, and nuns in the Catholic old-age home in Chandor. She had liked the brilliance of palm and banana; green at every window and door, a green that continued to sparkle through cracks and keyholes when the doors and windows were shuttered. She had liked the lamps of clear blown glass, as simple as the simplest sea organism, and the fans dangling like spiders on long, slender stems from the far latticed ceiling carved with a geometry of stars. In the kitchen, she had liked the patina of the hearth burnt by coconut husk fires over hundreds of years and the open porthole gaps in the roof tiles above that were angled to prevent monsoon torrents from falling in but allowed the light to shimmer through. The bathrooms opened upon an interior courtyard where you might hang your underpants to discreetly dry. The balcão had a fan so you could comfortably watch the world going by and gossip about neighbors while concealed by the gracefully curving shadows of the molded conch shells. To the side, there was a preserved altar room, and Babita may be irreligious, but she appreciated the sobriety of religion, the aura of a house where the architecture suggested the residents be respectful of tradition, solicitous of grandparents and servants, with food and care apportioned according to hierarchy from a lavish table to leftover rice for beggars and stray dogs at the back door. She felt this calm regality may be conducive to creating a calm regality within herself.

"Sunny," she said regally, "you and I will soon be the owners of Casa das Conchas, a mansion more than three hundred years old, the seat of the traders who sailed the *Husnara,* the *Paloma,* and the *Nagini* between Goa and Zanzibar, and more recently the residence of Signor Umberto. You know that foreigners have a knack for restoring homes, preserving the history while putting in comfortable bathrooms and kitchens, which we Indians—let's face it—can never in a million years figure out."

"*What say you?*" Sunny yelped into the receiver.

"I am selling my share of Panchsheel Park, as you advised me."

"I did? But why move to Goa? You're a city person!"

"When your brother-in-law has wagered your safety on deals with the underworld," said Babita, "when the city is so polluted your eyes burn and your throat aches as if with sorrow, and when each time you venture out there is an altercation, it's best to concede. As you said yourself, Goa has the feel of India of the past. I want to find a quiet corner, wind down, and watch the sun set into the Arabian Sea during this second half of my life."

This did not at all sound like his mother. Had Babita bought the house to avenge his gentle vacation with Sonia? If so, it was to no purpose. Sonia and Sunny would never go there again to be innocent and free because they were innocent and free no longer. *We were happy for a moment.* He heard Sonia's admonishment in his head. *Maybe we should just get married.*

"Remember," said Babita, "your cousins hired thugs to evict the property adjoining the nightclub bar Olive, a man was killed, and all hell broke loose, which may be why Uncle Rana hasn't summoned his goons against me—he's worried about a repeat—but there is no guarantee he won't if I refuse to sell."

"You don't know anyone in Goa but Vanya," Sunny said to Babita. "How will you occupy yourself?"

"So many Dilliwalas are moving there, to concrete blocks in the rice fields that exactly resemble Delhi flats. The Punjas, for example— poor things, they really are a dumb family. Then there is a Cross Currents film, dance, and music festival. They are trying to start a literary festival." She knew this would entice Sunny.

Vini-Puni lingered within earshot, listening to Babita on the phone, and when she came out of her bedroom from where she had made the call—so as to be sure they didn't overhear—she saw them on the staircase.

"These days you don't stop hovering like flies."

"Aunty, are you selling our home?"

"I haven't yet sold, have I? These things mostly fall apart."

"What will happen with my school?" said Punita.

Was it Babita's duty to send Punita to this luxurious school? She said, "I will do what I can, but in the end, your parents have to take responsibility for you."

Vinita's and Punita's faces took on the slow, dubious look that Babita associated with the servant class. "But we have to stay together," said Vinita. "Or it won't be safe for us. It isn't safe for girls alone."

The next day Babita mentioned her predicament to Sara. Sara said, "Vinita is the worst cook, and Punita behaves above her station. She treats my husband as an equal. You've spoiled them, and nobody in their right minds would take on the responsibility of two young women." The day after that, however, Sara called to say that a friend, a single lady who taught economics, needed help. Maybe she could be persuaded to take them together, if one cooked while the other cleaned. The charity school, though, would be too far for Punita to attend.

*

THE SALE OF THE house in Panchsheel Park proceeded in an orderly, swift fashion as only a black-market deal could. The buyer, based in Dubai under the mysterious name Sheherzade Investments Ltd., owned several properties in Delhi where he was represented by a cousin via power of attorney. Uncles Ravi-Rana and Babita drove to the municipal office—a pleasant bungalow where sales were registered—the uncles in one car, Babita following in her own vehicle driven by Bahadur. They had their photographs taken, signed numerous forms, attested signatures, had them notarized, and eventually, after a long day of waiting, were each given a bank draft for the clean money part of the transaction that Babita could use to buy Casa das Conchas. Then, incredibly, it was done. The feud that had swallowed decades of their existence evaporated with such suddenness that they felt a little shy.

The gentleman who had represented his Dubai cousin returned to the house along with the three of them, and taking a small soapstone Ganesh from a plastic bag, he placed before it flowers and a stick of incense. He opened a box of sweets and passed it around.

Babita contacted the lady professor of economics, who told Babita she ate only Continental food and asked to meet Vini-Puni in person. When they arrived at the flat in R. K. Puram, Babita showed off about Vinita's ability to make ravioli and gnocchi, while the girls stood with their heads hanging as if they were being punished. When she asked where the girls might sleep, the professor said that the only place would be in the kitchen; the latrine they could share with the servants of the other flats. It was on the roof.

On the way home, Vinita said, "But we would have to sleep with our heads between the gas tank and the garbage pail."

Babita felt ashamed of herself when she retorted, "If she lives by herself and eats only Continental, how hard will that be for you?"

"What about my school?" asked Punita.

In the evening, Babita saw Vinita and the Habibs' driver leaning against the Habibs' sedan. Vini briefly rested her head on his shoulder, and as she was turning to go, he held on to her hand. She laughed; her laugh was joy. Babita waited until the girls had left for the night before she called Sunny to say in as nonchalant a manner as she could summon, "You will see a cash deposit in your account soon. The check I received will go toward purchasing Casa das Conchas. The rest of the proceeds will be transferred to you—"

"Why to me?"

"I'd like to invest it in the States—it will eventually be yours, and it's easier to send it to you now."

"But how will the money be sent?"

"Your uncles are arranging it."

"Ma, this must be illegal—"

"Prim and proper? You know how we paid for your master's degree!"

Sunny remembered what he had forgotten. When his scholarship had not been renewed, there had been a crisis. Sunny's grandmother Minnie had said, "Look, I can send you the money, but on one condition: You don't ask where it came from."

And desperate Sunny, in full knowledge that the money was black money, had said, "Thank you, I will accept."

Babita had comforted Sunny: "First they admit you with a scholarship to hook you—the plan is not to renew it, so what are you going to do? You pay up somehow or the other. It is a business strategy. Don't think they are so squeaky-clean in America."

He had never told anyone. Not Ulla. Not Satya. Not Sonia. He had buried it.

Babita moved in for the kill: "When I come to America, I won't be a burden on you."

What did she mean about coming to America? Permanently? He did not tell her that awaiting him in his mailbox when he returned from Italy, along with another sheaf of Que Rico Taco! menus, had been his green card.

....

SUNNY STOPPED AT HIS BANK ON ROOSEVELT AVENUE UNDER the subway track, passing Mister Cangrejo, Bueno y Barato, immigration law offices specializing in battling deportation, the skimpily dressed Chinese and Hispanic women soliciting outside massage parlors. The bank was crowded with destitute immigrants. How on earth could he check to see if half a million dollars had arrived in his bank account when most people there were concerned about fifty? With relief he saw that no money had been transferred to his account, and nobody passing by, looking over his shoulder, would be startled or offended. He held the door for a diminutive couple in Peruvian bowler hats and shawls. They thanked him in the high fluting of birds.

In a moment of anguished candor, Sunny confessed to Darko, the colleague who sat at the neighboring desk in the AP office: "My mother is involving me in corruption."

Darko sympathized. "You won't believe what *my* mother did. She put my name on her vacation time-share in Atlantic City, supposedly as my birthday gift, then defaulted on the payments and ruined my credit rating. Now I can't get a loan, and I don't know how I'll make it through to the end of the year."

In a few minutes Darko said, "By any chance, do you have a couple of bucks I can borrow to get a bagel?"

"Sure, can you get me one, too? Sesame or poppy seed."

A few bites in, Sunny felt his throat constrict. He put his bagel down.

"Aren't you hungry?"

"I can't eat." A clenched fist.

And so Darko ate Sunny's bagel as well as his own. This irritated Sunny. Then Sunny's irritation irritated Sunny.

Jackson Heights may be cooler than Italy, but how long could Sunny continue his scant existence, just enough in his wallet for a bagel or two, just enough for a secondhand Isaac Bashevis Singer book about a rabbi's wife and a shrieking dead goose. Was he keeping his life stunted—shuffled amidst moving people—to escape his mother, who would otherwise perch alongside? But if you remained inconsequential, your fate would be wrested from you. He hadn't been able to save Sonia from her past, had he? He wouldn't be able to save Babita from her future, would he? He couldn't save himself. He'd felt the lack in his thinking when he'd been in Europe—a lack of freedom, a lack of lightness. He must release himself from the trap of India–United States–United States–India in the same way the past generation had felt trapped by India-Britain-Britain-India. He needed a third way, a sideways gesture, a kind of jazz, a riff on a raga.

On his days off, Sunny began researching and was surprised to learn that an entire world he hadn't suspected—and that his colleagues had apparently kept secret—not only existed but was open to him now that he had achieved his U.S. residency. He learned how Darko had spent a winter in Recife on a travel grant for young journalists, how another drudge like himself was at a newspaper in Phnom Penh. He uncovered exchange fellowships from Berlin to Tokyo, from Prague to Oaxaca. There were freedom-of-the-press conferences in Geneva and Brussels, internships in Cartagena and Oslo, summer institutes for deepening your craft in Helsinki. All you had to do was relentlessly apply, and he knew from living with Ulla and his days at university that no nationality excelled at applying more than Americans. They treated applying as a career in itself: They asked for recommendations from people for whom they had written recommendations specifically so they could one day ask for recommendations in turn; wrote essays about their commitment to women's rights, gay rights, minority rights, international human rights, quashing the meager unprofessional applications of the minorities themselves with vitamin-fueled, gym-healthy, life-coach-coached persistence; printed crisp résumés on heirloom-grade paper, on latest-model printers, after they had been checked for grammatical errors and tweaked by professionals trained in the secret language of persuading others.

And out of Americans, New Yorkers were the ones who excelled the most. "We can't have nine people out of twelve from New York City!" the organizations may feebly protest, but they wouldn't be able to keep New Yorkers from endlessly excelling at applying the globe over, for their ambition never lay down to rest in this city that never slept. And soon they would have not only too many New Yorkers, but also an overwhelming number of Indian New Yorkers from the same class as Sunny, who had even more advantages than white New Yorkers in the process of applying because they could convincingly play the minority card—but how to claim you are a minority if you come from a people that number over a billion?

Sunny composed a project proposal that would require him to travel from country to country interviewing the Roma, who were early Indian migrants. He completed an application for an internship at an English-language newspaper in Santiago. To one in Morocco, one in Costa Rica, one in Denmark. He came up with reasons why he should be awarded a Soros grant, a fellowship at a castle in Tuscany, a lighthouse in the Hebrides, a cargo ship. He applied for a scholarship to attend a brainstorming on the subject of borders being held in Tepoztlán, famous for being the birthplace of Quetzalcoatl, the plumed serpent that conjoined the underworld and the heavens. He filled out required forms that asked him to demonstrate his commitment to racial and gender diversity and how he planned to contribute to the well-being of the planet.

Babita telephoned—had the money arrived?—and exhorted him to check again. She herself rechecked the account and routing numbers she had given Uncle Rana: "They are cheating me, your uncles are cheating me!"

Sunny went again. He went again. His throat clenched, and he panicked and worried he would not be able to unclench his jaw and speak when he needed to speak.

"Something is off!" One week, Babita called him every single morning at her bedtime hour.

On the sixth day, Sunny told his mother that the money had still not arrived and that on the seventh day, he would rest. "I am not going to check on Sunday. I am so stressed out, I can't sleep, I can't swallow."

"It's because of me you have a life in New York, anyone would agree, and now it is too much to walk over to the bank?"

Sunny jogged down Northern Boulevard and beyond. He jogged, ignoring his stiffening knees, to where flights landing at LaGuardia almost sheared the top of his head. It occurred to him that he may not be attempting to flee and coax his life bigger to help others but to escape to where he could help nobody, to where he may simply begin anew and even more anonymously. Remaining thus unsure of his motives, he continued to be certain it was necessary to make a change. He thought of Satya. If they were still friends, he might have called him. He thought of Sonia. If they had stayed in each other's company, would their rift have turned out differently?

Once more Babita telephoned to inquire about her lost rupees-to-dollars.

....

"I TOOK A TURN FOR THE WORSE." PAPA'S SMILE ARRIVED from afar. Even in the short time Sonia had been away, Papa appeared to have grown thinner, the pallor of his skin stained as if by shadow. And although it wasn't so cold in Delhi, he was wearing his woolen Kashmiri dressing gown, and though he was indoors, he was wearing a Kullu hat, gloves, and scarf. Sonia noticed he had tied the tasseled dressing-gown cord around himself twice.

He didn't ask any questions about Venice. Instead he said: "What about Sunny's friend, can't he help us?"

"Sunny's friend?"

"Didn't you say his best friend is a doctor in America?"

"He had a fight with him."

"Hah?" Papa said and lifted up the earflap of his hat, looking hard at her as if trying to understand a crazy person. Was it intelligent to fight with a doctor friend?

Sonia retired to her room and stood under the whooping shower, dried herself with the threadbare towel, opened her cupboard that held the funny, flat smell of centuries to extract faded pajamas. Rummaging in her carry-on case, she found a thick Venetian paper envelope tucked into one of the compartments. It held crisp dollar notes, enough to cover her air ticket to Italy that Papa had helped her with. Who could have put it there but Sunny? Sonia's first thought was that this signified that Sunny was telling her in a surreptitious manner what she already knew—that he had decided to exit their romance while he easily could and that he was paying her off to assuage his guilt. Remembering she had suggested they marry, she was consumed by cataclysmic hate and shame and wanted to immediately call and accuse him of treating her like a prostitute. But the painting of Ilan humping her like a stray dog entered her mind. She had proffered herself for sale in return for a rich man's home. She could not ask anyone to love her now. She would not write to Sunny or telephone him unless he reached out first.

*

IN THE WEEKS THAT followed, Sonia accompanied Papa to a pranic healing practitioner who held sessions within the Sri Aurobindo Ashram compound. He sat Papa on a chair before a basin filled with water and stood before him with his hands raised—first as if he were judging an invisible jelly mass, then as if he were tugging something almost impossible to dislodge; he struggled valiantly and wrung the invisible goop into the basin. Next, Sonia and Papa went to a homeopath in South Extension and came away with hundreds of miniature paper packages filled with miniature white pellets. They went to Tibet House to consult the resident doctor-monk in a yellow-and-maroon-painted clinic redolent of herbs, returned with hard, dark balls to grind in a mortar and pestle, boil into a foul brew. Ferooza was friends with the uncle of the mullah of Jama Masjid who was rumored to be clairvoyant, and when Sonia took Papa along for an audience in a residence behind the mosque, the mullah's uncle, fingering jade prayer beads, said Papa need not worry, he had a curable malaise. When the padre in Allahabad sent word through Mina Foi about a healer named Michael Faith renowned for his miraculous touch, they lined up along with other petitioners at a location in Friends Colony, where a man in a tracksuit and long hair looking like Jesus—if Jesus were an athlete— laid his hand upon Papa's head and said he would certainly recover. The reading and thinking Papa had done in the past few years allowed him to treat the diagnosis made by Michael Faith and the pranic practitioner with the same seriousness he treated Dr. Pamela Lalwani's. And illness, he was discovering, was yet another life change that bestowed gravitas upon a clownish, deserted man.

However, despite bitter brews, a healing touch, and sugary pellets, despite the bustle and consultations that turned the atmosphere of the flat pleasantly into one of a clinic-workshop, Papa's health did not improve. When Mina Foi sent—with Sister Teresa, who had taken the overnight train—a murgh musallam cooked whole in a clay pot by Khansama, whom she had roused out of retirement for the task, Papa could not taste the royal bird of his childhood.

On Christmas morning, Sonia woke at five A.M., saw a sharp knife of light under her bedroom door, and found Papa awake, trying to rise, although his trembling limbs made him sink down. Chandu was packing a travel case, and because Balbir Singh was away in his village attending his father's funeral, Chandu telephoned the taxi rank by the decomposing garbage dump, where the drivers slept on cots outside and ran their taxi operation from a tent with a telephone and a locked, steel cash box.

By 6:30 A.M., having driven slowly through the fog-smog with the sun still sunk in the murk, they were at a diagnostic hospital and nursing home that was set peacefully away from the city in Mehrauli. Papa was claimed by a team of nurses chattering unceasingly to him in English transformed by the rhythm of Malayalam. "*Aiyo-aiyo, ande vande mande?*" replied Papa, making a nonsense doggerel, weakly trying to poke fun. The nurses fell silent. They admitted him to a private room and put him on a drip.

Later that morning after Sonia called the health insurance number on the card in Papa's wallet, a clerk arrived in the hospital room with a folder of papers that included a feedback form. Papa, one of the first businessmen to usher in modern global business concepts—no matter the disdain young Atul Gupta had for the secular version he proposed— tried feebly to educate him: "*First* you provide the service; only *then* you ask if the customer was satisfied. You *see?* The feedback form comes *after* the service."

The man became belligerent. "But I have to return this form to my boss."

"Explain to your boss!"

"He is not the kind of man to listen."

Papa scribbled, *Service not yet provided.*

"Why have you written *this*? You *called* and I *came*. In two hours max, I was here. Now my boss will be angry with me."

After visiting hours were over, Sonia waited in the lobby where they had put Christmas lights on the Ganesh statue at the entrance, so his elephant ears, trunk, and tummy winked red and green. She hoped Papa would be discharged, but a trainee doctor came by to say that they had decided to keep Papa for a few days to run a series of tests. At ten P.M. she ordered another taxi, the vehicle emerging out of the fog-smog, the driver muffled against pollution, his meter also discreetly swaddled under a cloth, a picture of Guru Gobind Singh atop the wheel and kirpan stickers on his mirror. They drove back through the dark city, past sleeping road workers on the pavement and an encampment of cardboard *basti* homes closed against the night as adamantly as it is possible for cardboard, plywood, and rags to be closed. At home, Sonia drew the curtains tightly because looking at the big night sky isn't exhilarating when you are by yourself facing a trauma.

She felt hysteria rise inside her. She felt like blaming somebody, but who? Then she thought there were two people to blame: her mother, who had left her to this, and her father, who had remained alone. They'd each stubbornly made no life other than one that would leave her accompanying them all by herself to a hospital. Now it had come to it.

She telephoned her mother, who sounded unsure Papa was ill. "He always made an enormous fuss, even over a common cold, seeking attention."

"This is not a cold," snapped Sonia.

She telephoned Mina Foi. "I have lost my appetite as well," said Mina Foi. "If the food is lukewarm, I find it hard to eat, but Mother Superior spoils me, she makes sure I have piping hot chapatis. Somehow, though, ice cream goes down without a problem."

Sonia put down the phone.

There was yet another person to blame. She blamed Sunny now, who had not saved her. They had each fatally revealed too much of themselves to the other. She repeated her vow to herself: If he called, she would speak to him; if he did not, she would not.

She found herself with the phone in her hand. Perhaps she had misunderstood the money in her bag, misread what had passed?

She called, hung up, called, hung up. She put the phone back in its cradle and went to bed.

She got out of bed, into the cold, called again. She hung up. Wouldn't Sunny guess that it was her and call her back?

And then she did it to herself. She pulled out, from where she had buried it deep in her cupboard, the catalog to Ilan's show that she had secreted in her bag. *De Toorjen Foss undoes the orientalist gaze, but he does not exclude the surreal, although all labels fall away when confronted by his personal sensibility. The paintings are morally ambivalent. In this world nobody is a victim. Every individual has absorbed the qualities of their antagonist.*

The introduction was written by the same effusive art historian and curator who had composed the *Le Monde* article. She wrote that Ilan's was an enigmatic and complex portrayal of women, unusual for a male painter. One couldn't deny that these were women whose lives were defined by men, yet the paintings undid assumptions. These were women vulnerable yet strong, damaged and willful, spoiled and coquettish, domineering, provocative, seductive, deceitful. The lack of an obvious feminist lens proved far closer to feminism than feminism.

I learned from women all my life, the writer quoted Ilan. *My grandmothers, my mother, my aunties, and my former wife, to whom I remain grateful. I do not want you to pity the young woman in bed with the grisly man. She has something to gain, and she seeks it fiercely. She is as manipulative as the man is pathetic, as pathetic as the man is manipulative. I respect her.*

When you painted something, some of its life force surely seeped into you. Did Badal Baba now belong to Ilan? Did *she*? But wouldn't the painter then also belong to the subject?

When Sonia slept, she was back up the snow path into the snow mountains of Hewitt. An invisible beast was following her. She turned again and again. She was scared of the beast, its footfall soundless. She was scared of the man in the house on the hill. What was she searching for? In the window glass, she saw the man's night face, suffering from a crisis of shame and nonexistence that could only be avenged by fame. Fame was a creature of darkness best stoked past midnight. Fame took talent, it took being aggrieved, it took study, it took persistence. Fame was always hungry, and fame was smart. It was higher up the food chain. It fed upon others for sustenance. There was an urgency to Ilan's pacing; he must make a fame so enormous and so quickly that anyone coming forth to discount it would be discounted. He would become real, the truth would become false, anyone who encountered him would turn into a ghost—

Thwack! Her fright woke her. The morning paper was thrown up into the front balcony by the newspaper man. It was collected by Chandu and brought to Sonia along with the tea tray. Sonia unfurled it. Sunny's family name was blazoned across the front page: *The Bhatias of Panchsheel Park.*

She dropped the newspaper into her bag, put on a pair of sunglasses as if she needed a disguise—she *did* need a disguise—and hurried to the nursing home. As she strode up the steps, she saw—could she be sure?—Babita Bhatia being carried in on a stretcher. *"Babita Aunty?"* escaped Sonia, but the woman was also wearing sunglasses. She didn't reply, even though one of her perfectly plucked eyebrows shot up.

"Look!" Sonia handed Papa the newspaper.

"The Bhatias of Panchsheel Park! Sunny's family?"

"Yes. I just saw Babita Bhatia go by on a stretcher."

"Aha! Escaping questioning by the police!"

If the Mosquitoes Knew, They Did Not Tell

CHAPTER

53

....

ON A SUNDAY, BABITA HAD TELEPHONED UNCLE RANA. "The money has still not arrived in Sunny's bank account."

"Be patient," he had advised. "Sheherzade Investments planned to sell some investments to pay us, but the investments lost their value—you know all about how that can happen—so they have to find an alternative."

She said, "Well, I'm not leaving for Goa until the money has been paid into Sunny's account. Inform whoever needs to be informed."

She walked out upon her terrace after the phone call, taking deep breaths, feeling consoled by, yet penitent before, her magnificent bougainvillea—which had shielded her from so many ugly things with hundreds of thousands of magenta blossoms year after year—and she happened to see the cousin of the buyer in Dubai who had signed the sale agreement via power of attorney drive up and lug out two large suitcases, which he wheeled to Uncle Ravi's home. This time he wore a baseball cap. Then he jumped back into his car and drove off.

Babita immediately clopped to Uncle Ravi's part of the house: "Hey, hey, what did I just see?"

"What did you just see?" Uncle Ravi's glance hovered like a fruit fly, darted away.

"What were those two suitcases? Did you receive a payment of cash or gold that I was not privy to?"

"What suitcases?" A look of guilt passed obviously over his face.

"I happened to be looking out, Ravi."

"You must be imagining things—and you would be right to be paranoid. We are being watched this very minute."

"By whom?"

"Rana is being watched to make sure he pays his debts, and if Rana is being watched, we are being watched. Would I be so foolish as to keep bars of gold or cash in the house right after we sold our property? Like keeping diamonds unsecured on the eve of a wedding!"

She conceded that it would be of extreme stupidity, and while she had little respect for her brother-in-law, surely he would not be as stupid as this. *But then again, knowing Ravi, he certainly may be!*

She began to suddenly push past him using clawing toes, and taken unawares by such a weird ambush, he began to push back and exclaim, *"Don't you dare! Don't you dare!"* Then he gave in. "Look, I'll tell you. A friend received a tip his house would be raided by tax inspectors, and he asked if he could leave some suitcases with me. I think they are full of foreign black market goods."

"Liar!" She began to claw again.

"Don't you dare! Don't you dare!" shouted Uncle Ravi again.

Uncle Rana popped out of his window above—he must have been watching—and called: *"Ravi Bhaiya! Babi Bhabhi!"*

"What?" called Uncle Ravi, relieved by this diversion.

"Don't let the babalog come back to India. The kids must stay away, or the underworld will get them."

"Why would the underworld get them?" asked Babita, releasing her toehold on Uncle Ravi.

"We sold the house, and they'll want their share." Then Uncle Rana shut his window and wouldn't answer when Babita clopped across, rang his bell, hammered on his door.

Babita returned to her section of the house, and when Vini-Puni came home after spending Sunday with their parents—no doubt the suitcases had been deliberately delivered on the servants' day off—Babita said, "They are cheating me, the pair of them! Someone just wheeled bursting suitcases to Ravi Uncle's door, and Rana Uncle was watching from his window. When do their cooks return home on Sunday night?"

"Sometimes only near morning," said Vinita. "They stay drinking with their friends and come back drunk."

"Punita, can you climb over the back wall into Ravi Uncle's property and tell me if you see anything?" Nimble Punita, slender from childhood malnutrition, could surely manage that. "Take the ladder."

"Aunty, what if I am caught? Then I can't jump from the wall to the ground on the other side."

"Maybe you can exit out of my upstairs window and edge yourself along on the parapet."

"Aunty, I will fall."

"Go on the Habibs' roof with my binoculars." Then she remembered Mr. Habib pulling Punita onto his lap. *Say I'm your only boyfriend!* "Vinita, you go."

Vinita returned. "The curtains are drawn."

Babita said, "Will the Habibs' driver be willing to break in? I'll pay him."

Vinita stared. "Aunty, what if Uncle calls the police?"

"I get no help even from those I watch over like my own children," said Babita. "Meanwhile you refuse this job, you refuse that job—so you will have no job when I leave for Goa, and I won't have any money to give you, either."

That night someone called and hung up, called and hung up, called and hung up, called. "*Sunny?*" she said. "*Sunny?*"

"No, it's me," said a male voice she did not recognize.

"Who?"

"Who are *you*?"

"You're the one who's calling. You have to say who *you* are first."

"*You? Kaun?*"

"*Who?*"

"*Kaun?*"

"*You?*"

"*Whooo?*"

She put down the phone. The phone rang again. She heard deliberate breathing. "Are you trying to threaten me? No point. I don't have what you're looking for. I am not the one with suitcases of cash, with bars of gold. You can check next door at my brothers-in-law!"

That night, for the first time, a menopausal hot flash overcame Babita, although she didn't diagnose it as such—she was certain it was her mental torment that caused a sensation as if burning coals had been placed into her. She threw off all her nightclothes and lay naked. *Ratty, you left me to this.* And then she fell into a stupor.

Next door, Uncle Ravi had ordered out for gustaba from the exiled Kashmiri Pandit couple who ran a home catering business. As he ate, he rewatched *Casablanca.* He had no love to whom he could say, "Here's looking at you, kid," so he spoke the line to himself, looking in the mirror and raising a special martini glass in self-congratulation. He would soon leave for Dehradun. A coral and an amaltas tree grew in the garden of the house he had rented there and the sky overhead was still blue. Every day a band of rogue monkeys came by, made naughty faces, and opened the garden tap to drink.

Two doors down, Uncle Rana drew the heavy, cigar-smelling drapes in his bedroom, then went to his Romeo y Julieta cigar box, which held a key that opened a cupboard of jackets, and from the inner pocket of a sporting vest, he removed another key that opened the walk-in closet, where, under a sheet of newspaper lining a shelf, he found the key to the black, tin trunk that had once contained his grandmother's trousseau, which led in turn to the suede pouch that held the key to the steel Godrej almirah. From here he accessed the safe with a key hidden in the tear of the lining of a briefcase on the top shelf, and he extracted his passport and ticket for the next morning. His money, he had learned, had been wired to New Zealand. Soon he'd creep out, treading softly on his soft-soled shoes, and be on his way, debts left behind. Like his brother, he, too, went to the mirror and surveyed his face. He thought he was an especially ugly man. His face had made him unsatisfied and ambitious. He had striven more, he had enjoyed life more. He felt sentimental about leaving in this moment of triumph. He already missed the thrall of illicit deals, of illegal hunts of black buck, of putting your feet up on the restaurant table, twiddling your pedicured toes amidst the post-lunch mangoes while talking bombastically, nobody making fun of you for doing so. He felt nostalgia for the discos and the racecourse, for his escort service girls, Patty, Jahanara, and Ruby. New Zealand would not be to his natural taste—the people there did not respect ostentation and oversize fun, so his sons had told him. It would be emasculating.

Uncle Rana chuckled to think of how furious Ruby would be to learn of his Houdini escape—never again would he undo her temper with quack-a-duck kisses. He clipped the hair that sprang from his ears, his nostrils, the wart on his cheek, and looked forward to the welcome Chiki-Chika would give him. To be a rich daddy was to inspire loyalty and love. They had already prepared a strawberry cream cake and a banner: *Welcome Down Under, Dad!*

*

SO MUCH WAS LEARNED from the evidence: Uncle Ravi's empty martini glass in his kitchen sink. Uncle Rana's ear, nose, and wart trimmings in his bathroom sink.

More than that, not much was discovered the next morning when Uncle Ravi and Uncle Rana were found by their staff with their skulls bludgeoned beyond recognition by a heavy object. Who had bludgeoned their skulls? If the lizards on the wall knew, they did not tell. If the mosquitoes knew, they gorged on blood and did not tell. If the mirror knew, it refused to regurgitate the image. If the drivers knew, they said they had been fast asleep in Shahpur Jat—oh, but it was discovered now that driver Bahadur had not come to work. If the cooks knew why, they said it was their night off and they had spent it with other servants from the same village who met each Sunday—oh, but where were Vini-Puni? Babita hoisted herself up the outside spiral staircase to their servants' quarters—and tumbled down. Vini-Puni were missing. Sara Habib came to report that the Allahabad driver, too, had not shown up at his 7:30 A.M. reporting hour.

The police came swarming. They secured the crime scene. They searched everywhere and found no forced entry and no murder weapon, but footprints, fingerprints, a chloroformed rag. Had Vini-Puni, Bahadur, and the Allahabad driver run in fear that they would be accused? Or were they the murderers? Had they been recruited by the underworld, had they killed for a pittance? Or had Vini-Puni been chloroformed and kidnapped? Kidnapped? Why? To be smuggled into prostitution, it was suggested. This had happened to a little girl in Begumpur, where Vini-Puni's parents lived. When the police went to Begumpur to inform Gunja and her husband—that seller of bones—of their daughters' vanishing, their quarters had been emptied and tethered with a padlock. When tragedy strikes poverty-stricken children, their powerless parents must disappear so they are not blamed. They must try to escape the second, third, and fourth tragedies that will inevitably follow the first. Nobody could remember the name of the village they came from; the neighbors refused to speak. They grew more and more unsure. They knew nothing about nothing.

The phone rang at Babita's. The same male voice, slow and low. "Leave immediately. *Or you will be transferred very, very far . . . Very far . . .*"

"*Who are you?*"

"*Very, very far . . . Leave now . . . or . . .*"

"*Who are you?*"

Said the caller, "*You?*"

"*Who?*"

"*You?*" Babita saw the investigating officer watching her through the window. He lifted his chin, winked, and laughed. He came in, sat cross-legged on the sofa, and ordered her to bring him a glass of water, "*Behenji, pani pilau.*"

Babita fainted. When she came out of the faint, she whimpered, moaned, and shook. "Ploiwwww," she said. "Bbbb aaam ooo." She could not formulate words. Her heart whirred, pounded, and lurched. She was certain she was suffering a heart attack.

Later, Mr. Habib came into her bedroom and, bending down, whispered softly, although there was nobody now to overhear: "Admit yourself to a hospital for psychological trauma. Say nothing to anyone. The police are in on this, it's obvious—they are interrogating and torturing the servants up and down the street."

Babita's father, the Colonel, telephoned. "This is serious, daughter. The underworld got them. Say nothing about anything to anyone."

"You don't think it was a case of robbery gone wrong?"

"Unlikely, and if you find out how they were killed, you may be killed. Don't push for an investigation. The less you know, the better. Cut your losses and leave."

"Mr. Habib suggested I go to the hospital."

"Do that, it'll be safer!"

She noticed her father was not inviting her to Allahabad. Did he distrust her? Did he wonder why she wasn't a suspect, why she was the only one with knowledge of suitcases of gold? Or did he love his daughter only as long as she was not being pursued by the underworld? Who was she?

Mr. Habib drove her out to the nursing home set peacefully away from the city in Mehrauli. A woman's voice called, "*Babita Aunty?*" as she was rolled in on a stretcher. The voice was familiar—or was it? She kept her eyes shut behind the sunglasses she had bought in New York City, even if one of her eyebrows shot up.

She swallowed the pills they brought her. There was something upon the surface that was dangerous—there was something under the surface that was far more treacherous. *Ratty, ask your father what I should do! He would know! He was a brilliant crook, unlike his three stupid sons. Only the mafia can counter the mafia. Only a bigger crook can defeat a crook. Tell him to tell me what to do! Tell me if I am in danger! Am I in danger? You are my husband. You have to tell me!*

She heard the ghost of her husband replying in his meticulous fashion: *What has happened, Babi Bibi, was bound to happen. Corruption begets corruption, corruption begets murder, corruption begets suicide, suicide begets suicide, murder begets murder, suicide begets murder, murder begets suicide, murder begets corruption . . .*

She remembered the last thing Uncle Rana had said to Babita and Uncle Ravi as Babita was trying to push past Uncle Ravi to enter his house and examine the two suitcases:

Don't let the babalog come back to India. The kids must stay away, or the underworld will get them.

Uncle Ravi had no children. This would mean Uncle Rana's own children in Auckland, who weren't planning on ever returning. And it would mean Sunny. *Sunny! Sunny?*

*

SUNNY COULDN'T RECOGNIZE HIS mother's voice because it was slurred by sedation. "I can't believe it," said Sunny because what else was there to say? "*I can't believe it!*"

"*I can't believe it, I can't believe it, I can't believe it.*"

"There was blood everywhere," said Babita, slowly articulating. "It trickled out of the doors. You must not come back! 'Don't let the babalog come back to India, or the underworld will get them'—those were Uncle Rana's last words to me. He must have known this could happen."

"*They might have murdered you!*"

Babita dropped her voice. "Can you check one more time if the money showed up in your bank account?" she said meekly.

"*Your greed has ended in murder, Mummy!*" escaped him now. "*And you're asking me if the money came?*"

Sunny fled the phone, and he began to jog. He jogged into the path of a blizzard spiraling down from Canada. He did not swerve for passersby; he jogged right through the middle of a small procession that also strove against the whistling storm. It was led by a brass band: *Parumpara! Parumpara! Boom! Boom!* Women in black lace mantillas carried banners, and under an umbrella was an image of the Virgin of Guadalupe embroidered in blue, silver, and gold threads. "Save me!" he prayed to her as she went by, the mother who would never ask her son to perform a corruption. "Save me!" And he jogged on, all the way to the massage and dim sum parlors in Flushing. "Massage? Massage?" the women called.

....

SWEETZ N NUTZ—THE PARTY PLACE, MR. BILLIKEN'S CHAPATI Restaurant & Mess, Peter England, the Honest Shirt. Every morning Sonia noted the same signs on her way to the nursing home, hoping to catch the doctors at their morning rounds. Every afternoon Papa suffered a low fever, which made the doctors suspect malaria, so they prescribed malaria pills, also medicine for tuberculosis, just in case. Then they put him on antibiotics, in case. Experts of kidney, heart, diabetes, pancreas, liver, bone, visited him. At first they debated, but as the days passed, they looked uncomfortable and began evading Sonia. "Where is Mummy?" they asked.

Sonia rang and rang the bell when Papa couldn't get to the bathroom without being unhooked from his IV, and when nobody came, she ran out into the corridor, where on a small two-seat sofa, a heap of young Nepali boys slept, all on top of one another like puppies. They were teenagers. They did not wake until she hauled them up and shook them, but it was too late, Papa's pajamas were soaked with pee. Sonia screamed at the sleepy boys, then she stopped—where did they come from, these destitute children looking after the ill through hospital days and nights? Who were their parents and where were they? The children desperately wanted to get back to dreaming. They were asleep even as they changed the sheets.

She went outside to drink tea in the nursing home garden, crows and kites wheeling like ash in the sky above as if the hospital were a crematorium. She watched family groups endlessly arriving, younger members touching the feet of the elders, proffering boxes of sweets to celebrate babies being born, and the parade of babies being born felt an

affront. It was rude and irresponsible the way people were going on
having babies and celebrating babies.

Sonia chased the doctors down the hallway and waited around corners. When she pounced they tried to rid themselves of her as fast as
they could. They spoke as if it was her fault: "The tests are not showing results." They began to send Papa to other hospitals for more tests.
They went to Batra Hospital for an MRI and to Ganga Ram for a bi-
opsy, where the doctor had an electric heater, an armchair, and a tin of
fancy, assorted butter biscuits. He offered Sonia the armchair and
opened the tin for her to choose. "But where is Mummy?" he asked.
Papa was taken away for a bone aspiration. Sonia shut her eyes and
winced imagining the pain her father must be experiencing, but Papa
was stoic. After the procedure they waited a long while in the waiting
room for a laboratory worker to deliver in a little, flat plastic case the
slides of a lymph aspiration of the right axillary lymph node and blocks
and slides of bone marrow tests from the hip. Before Sonia and Papa
left, the wheelchair assistant, who looked about eighty years old and
was wearing a kurta-pajama that was white in front but black behind—
he'd obviously sat somewhere dirty—lavishly patted Papa, his hands
flowering sideways like anemones after each pat, indicating he took
from good luck and he took from bad luck, from survival and death,
indiscriminately. Collecting his tip, he assured them everything depended on God, and he stood salaaming when they drove away.

By evening of the next day the doctors had diagnosed Papa with
cancer of the lymphatic system. The situation was urgent, they said; he
must immediately be transferred to a larger hospital with a cancer wing.
They bundled him out as if they were worried he would die on their
hands. Sonia packed his pajamas, his toilet case, his new mobile phone,
his mothy poncho from Dadaji and Ba's world tour that he liked to
wear for a certain je ne sais quoi, his slippers, his volume of Faiz.

In the hand of time is not the rolling of my fate
In the hand of time roll just the days, that is all

Siren going, heart monitor thrumming, they rode in an ambulance,
crashing through potholes, ruts, and bumps. Motorists blew their
horns.

"Can you believe this?" said Sonia. "Instead of getting out of the way of an ambulance, the cars are trying to overtake it!"

"Damn Punjabi city!" Papa said, his eyes closed. "Terrible what we did with my father," he added. "We dumped his ashes in dirty water, muck all around. Whatever you do, just don't put me there."

They drove up to the massive complex of Athena Hospital, where the doorman was almost seven feet tall and had a mustache that curled upward, an imposing stomach wrapped in a wide, purple cummerbund matching the trim and tail of his pleated turban, and an achkan done up with a double row of polished brass buttons. He belonged in a child's fairy tale. This sight was misleading. Papa and Sonia passed into a world that was far from a quiet nursing home where babies were born and where wealthy women escaped police questioning after their relatives were murdered. Sonia focused upon Papa in his wheelchair and maneuvered through crowds. A trail of women in burkas stepped out of a dazzling vehicle and were met by translators, then went swiftly up to the private deluxe rooms as staff unloaded a multitude of suitcases. Nigerian women in turbans walked by, as did men in Pathan suits and a girl in tall, black boots and cutoff pants, hair dyed blond, everyone turning to stare as she complained to her father with a silver mane and an ivory walking stick: "But it doesn't *look* like an affluent-type hospital!"

In the intensive care unit there was a submerged feeling—the patients lying on torturous beds, covered by masks, heaving and strapped, each with their own collection of plastic bags on hooks that contained liquids being delivered or drained. Papa beckoned Sonia to whisper, "Go for a walk, Sonu—don't hang around."

She went out. There was a temple at the entrance to the parking lot, and to the other side, a dry fountain in which families had spread out sheets upon which they settled. Farther beyond the fountain, there was a hangar shed where families of patients could live for weeks or months, if necessary. On a muffled system in this hangar shed, they made announcements when someone was needed: "Attendant Mrs. Mirza, bed 1105. Attendant Mr. Pal, bed 219." The windows were open, but the air inside did not budge, and the look and smell of unwashed clothes, bedding, food, sweat, and urine resembled the smell and look of a refugee camp. People disappeared into the flooded toilets and came out combed crisp and clean as if for a job interview, hoping they looked like somebody so their sick relative would be treated like somebody, not dismissed as an anonymous member of the anonymous, dismissible poor.

Sonia left the hospital and walked into the adjoining grounds where the administration planned to make a park. A few quick-growing ashokas had been planted, the saplings hadn't caught. She continued into what felt like encroaching desert, and upon this wasteland she came upon a man selling eggs and tea. He had a board balanced on top of a few bricks, upon which he had placed some packets of rusks. He had a kettle on a burner and a pot of potatoes cooking that you could eat with bread. A rough, trodden path led to him. Farther along, a man sat on a plastic chair reading the newspaper while getting a shave. About him scattered litter, wrappings. Why this spot? For some people, it was a particular place, it was their home, it was where they relaxed, although there were not the usual signs that marked a place of repose: no tree, no edifice, no shelter. Outside a building site with a sign reading "The Forum" large enough to be seen by travelers on the highway, a tanker had parked, and its driver was standing by a barrel of water meant for construction work, bathing and brushing his teeth. In somebody's bicycle cart that had been parked to the side, a wandering sadhu was taking a nap, covering his face from the sun with a portion of his orange rags.

When Sonia walked by, the watchman of The Forum said, "Ram Ram," in a low voice. By this "Ram Ram," the words and the fraternal tone like a password, she understood he identified her as a Hindu and was making a trusted connection that extended protection to Sonia walking alone. What if she said "Ram Ram" back to the watchman, while her father was ill, while her boyfriend was no longer her boyfriend? Would the softness of dusk feel holy, would the little lights coming on above the tea seller resemble temple diyas? Would she, the watchman, the encampment of road workers living in the sewer pipes—until they laid them into the ground and rendered themselves homeless—all be part of the same pastoral of evening peace, despite the desolation? But in this protection wasn't there the threat of its opposite? Would the "Ram Ram" condemn a Muslim like Ferooza to something beyond this broken scene? Sonia thought she would like to jot these thoughts down, but how to do so when there was nowhere to place a pen and paper?

Papa, feeling a little stronger now, rasped, "You've been sitting in the dry fountain or walking about aimlessly? Speak to the hospital director. Say, 'I am alone here, and I am a decent girl from a decent family, so I would like somewhere decent to sit. May I sit in your office?'"

....

Sonia wanted to be the woman who said, "I *hate* scenes! I *hate* melodrama!"

She made a scene. She made a melodrama. She screamed, "You need to come now! How can you leave me to deal with this alone?"

Mama packed her smallest case and left Cloud Cottage when the morning mist lay thick and the clawed shapes of the bunioned oak, the shaggy conifers, showed dramatically through the gloom. She felt a sinking feeling as she descended into the valley, thinking it unethical to stay in the home of the husband she had left, to reenter his debt. She took her overnight case into the guest room, a situation that everyone pretended not to notice. At least the problem was back in the family.

In the morning Mama went along with Sonia to the hospital, and when she arrived in Papa's room, Papa perked up. He opened one eye, nodding wisely. "We have a lot to talk about," he said, as if his wife was back for good. Then he sank back into his illness, but in a state of joy.

Later he said, "You can't imagine the performances they put on here at night. The nurses turn into temple dancers and the whole place becomes a lamplit grove." Was he hallucinating because of the steroids he was taking? Or had the cancer addled his brain?

Mama went alone to see Papa's doctor. When she came out of his office, her eyes were wet. "Nothing," she said. "Dr. Mohan is trying. That is all."

Yet Mama was glad to be reunited with her library, and in the evenings when she and Sonia sat reading together, Mama following the lines on a page calmed everything around as if she were centering a chaotic world into the rhythm of pages turning, of breathing. Sonia read Nabokov and found rising in her—like mountains and ocean without end—the unbearable longing for a book that could only be cured by writing. She picked it up and dropped it, picked it up and dropped it.

Mama read Tagore's diaries. She had found a photograph of Tagore pasted into the pages of her father's notebooks, corroborating the story he had told her about meeting him in Berlin. Tagore stood like a prophet in his robes, and to the far right was her father draped in a shawl, and her uncle Bibhu, who had on a bow tie. Underneath it read, *Schokolade and I, 1926*. Had Siegfried given the nickname "Schokolade" to Bibhu? Had Siegfried borrowed Bibhu's pashmina? Had Bibhu borrowed Siegfried's bow tie?

Upon the next page of her father's diary was a photograph of a dignified bronze bust. It must have been around this time that Siegfried had introduced Bibhu to the sculptor Kolbe, who also cast a respectful bronze of a young African, the noble head of a Chinese, figures of young Aryan women that found favor with the Reich, a bust of Franco that was a gift to Hitler. And what had become of the replication of Bibhu that Siegfried had transported to the ancestral home in the riverine countryside some days away by boat from Dhaka? Nobody knew because this uncle that Mama had never met, who had become prominent in the freedom movement against the British, had died of pneumonia contracted in prison. In 1926, walking arm in arm in the Tiergarten, they could not have imagined what would unfold.

*

"WHERE IS BADAL BABA?" Mama suddenly asked.

Badal Baba! Sonia had still not confessed the amulet's loss! "I left the amulet in New York with a friend," she half lied.

"Sonia, that is an unforgivable mistake." Mama drew her breath sharply. "Which friend?"

Sonia said, "My studio was not secure; I left it with Lala. Then when I returned to India, Lala was away on a trip." What if Mama saw Ilan's painting of Badal Baba replicated? It could pop up in the foreign periodicals in the India International Centre reading room, for example, upsetting the sleepy news of the past. Or what if Ilan returned to India to paint and gave a hundred and one interviews? She felt faint.

"I'll go back and get it."

"But you couldn't get a visa to the States." Mama could tell her daughter was lying. Sonia had returned to looking like a wastrel. Why hadn't she mentioned her time in Italy? "Where is that boy, Sunny?"

Sonia told her mother that she and Sunny had ended their insignificant romance. "He comes from a family of crooks. Did you see the news about the Panchsheel Park murders? His uncles were murdered, and two little servant girls were kidnapped." Sunny's abandoning Sonia was a sort of murderous crookery, wasn't it?

"What if Sunny had been in Delhi and you had been with him— *you* could have been killed!" exclaimed Mama.

"Yes," said Sonia. Why did it feel as if she had been part of the plot? Bad things were happening because she had lost their protective deity. If she did not recover Badal Baba, how would Sonia ever reconcile her internal darkness with the light? There was no rational path.

Would Mama have pressed Sonia more if she were not feeling guilty herself? She got up and looked out at the mosque. Dr. Mohan, the lymphoma specialist, was a sad-looking, large man of amorphous shape. He had said, "I know your husband wants to live. We will try to grant him time, but the prognosis is not promising."

"How much longer does he have?"

"We discovered the cancer when it was already at stage four. I do not think he will last the year."

"How much longer does he have?"

"Three to nine months."

Mama now said to Sonia, "Your father will be out of the ICU tomorrow. He should be home before long, and then it will be several

more cycles of chemo and radiation with resting periods in between. I
need to get back to the hills."

Maybe Sonia, Papa, and Chandu had hoped that the pitch of emotion surrounding Papa's illness would render a Bollywood-style reconciliation, a reawakening of love, a gushing. They had thirsted for it. It
was leading up to it. It had not occurred. Chandu suddenly broke into
loud wailing.

"What is it?" Mama was alarmed and lifted him from where he had
flung himself at her feet. He blubbered like a child. He felt Mama did
not value him or his food. Meanwhile he'd never forgotten the time he
had been sick with gastritis and she had nursed him, bringing warm
milk up to his quarters as the doctor had prescribed. A husband and
wife must compromise, must reconcile, because civilization rests upon
the ability of a husband and wife to be harmonious. Or it left people
like Chandu at risk. He could hardly depend on the government.

"The *government*? Am I to make up for the shortcomings of the *government*?*"

Sonia didn't say anything. She recognized the tiredness and disappointment she felt was the tiredness and disappointment of inevitability. The truth was that it was not Mama's duty to look after a husband
she had left. Papa would never have granted her a divorce, but she was
still not his wife. Sonia knew also that after you've lost respect for a
person, you have to walk away. She knew you can scream and demand
that the love be resurrected, but it is of no use; you can't resurrect love
by screaming and demanding. Mama had already stayed long enough
in her marriage to lose her love so thoroughly that there wasn't a crumb
left behind to make her reconsider.

Mother and daughter embraced before Mama climbed into the car
hired from the taxi service by the garbage dump. "Come to Landour
when you need a break," she said to her daughter, making this an ordinary and temporary parting. Sonia, holding on to her mother with an
emptiness of heart, suddenly wanted to bite into her mother's neck.
She drew back and watched as the car turned the corner and continued
on to Cloud Cottage. Up and down the street, the neighbors watched

as well: the Sharmas openly from their balcony, the servants from their rooftops, Mrs. Joshi, who prided herself on her discretion, from behind her curtain.

*

EVEN A HOSPITAL BECOMES a home. Papa was moved out of the ICU into his own room, and they became familiar with nurses Princy, Rency, Rani, Sonam, Gracy Philip, Gracy Matthew, Jessy Matthew. When each nurse separately asked, shocked, "Your Mrs. didn't stay?" Papa bravely responded, "Is she my servant? She has her life, and I have mine. That's the way I like it."

He said to Sonia, "My God, she looked like a Pahari witch! Gave me a bloody fright to see her!"

He asked Dr. Mohan, "Doctor, are you a kebabi-sherabi?"

The doctor looked down at himself wistfully. "No longer a kebabi."

"Well, come to my house and you will change your mind—I have the best kebab cook in the whole damn world. The galawati, the kakori, the shikampuri served with a tawa ki roti aanch pe—you cook it on an upside-down tawa, a bit of ghee in the dough, then finish it on the fire like a joker topi; you know, the smoke comes out of the tip of the triangle hat."

He told Nurse Rency that he felt like a cognac. He summoned the dietician. "I want ham. Can I have ham?"

"No, Uncle," she said with a waggling finger. "No, Uncle, in this hospital you will never get ham!"

"But I can give you chocolate pudding," interjected Nurse Jessy.

Nurse Jessy became Papa's favorite nurse. "Where are you from, Jessy? Kottayam? All the nurses are leaving for America. You must go. How much money do you earn?" He looked gray, but his glance hooked all the more vitally upon her.

Jessy turned the question around in embarrassment: "How much do you get in America?"

"A lot, but you also have to pay for everything—here, hostel is there, food is there."

"Yes."

"But my future son-in-law lives in New York—"

"Who?" said Sonia.

"Sunny Bhatia," said Papa. "And one day my daughter will join him. In fact, my future son-in-law's best friend is a doctor—"

"*Who?*"

"What is his friend's name? So why don't you go to work for him in the hospital, and then when she needs you, you can look after her— she is growing ancient!"

"*Who?*" said Sonia. "*Me?*"

"*No! My wife.* I have an ancient wife. You saw her? So then she can go to America, and you can go and help her—okay?"

"Send Jessy to America," he said to Sonia.

"But they have nurses already."

"Forget those big lumps. Take one of these girls."

There was a slight crack in Jessy's watertight manner; she looked anxious for a moment.

After Jessy left the room, Sonia said, "But, Papa, don't you remember that I am no longer with Sunny?"

"You're not?"

"I told you. We ended the relationship."

He felt sorry to see his daughter's face. "But didn't you go all the way to Italy to meet him? Wasn't he going to propose? If he didn't, why didn't you? Girls can take the initiative these days."

"His corrupt uncles were murdered. Don't you remember—it was on the front page of the newspaper."

He thought a moment. "That was Sunny? I remember now. Your own reputation will suffer—stay away. He dressed like an Edwardian cad—sneaky fellow. Ran off, did he?"

"He didn't run off!" Her pride!

"Where is he, then?"

"Probably having a nervous breakdown somewhere."

"I'll tell you, Sonu, it's a way of running off, a nervous breakdown," he said, nodding wisely. "You just say, 'I'm feeling damn peculiar, and I need to be alone.'"

*

IT WAS SIX WEEKS since the day he had been admitted that Papa was finally discharged from the hospital. He requested he may receive the head of catering to say goodbye. "A restaurant couldn't do better— Chinese, Continental, South Indian, North Indian, snacks! Five different menus in a hospital!"

He patted Jessy's hand. "Jessy, you are my favorite girlfriend. Did you give your information to my daughter?" That Sonia might give it to Sunny, that Sunny might give it to Satya, that Jessy might go to America and nurse his ancient wife, who happened to be in Landour but never mind that.

"Donkey, idiot!" he yelled at the hired driver. "I can drive better. Stop the car!"

"You cannot drive; you just got out of chemo," admonished Sonia.

"Don't tell me what *not* to do. Driver, get out and make your own way home. Take the bus."

And hurtling up the wrong side of streets, blowing the horn, swearing out of the window at anyone who swore at him—"*Sala, bhenchoot, shoot the jingbang lot!*"—Sonia and Papa arrived home triumphant, as a few drops scattered from within a dust storm. The smell of wet dust is a sharp pleasure, strong and sweet, like barnyard and roses. Invigorated, inhaling the perfume of his freedom, Papa was king of his domain once more. He put his legs up and called for his kahwa tea, which Chandu brought on a tray, trembly with the relief of having Papa home, the security it gave Chandu, therefore.

What Solace
Is That?

CHAPTER

56

....

THE COFFEE-TABLE BOOKS WERE ON THE COFFEE TABLE, the Daniell lithographs of slumbering ruins hung on the wall, and when Babita woke in the early morning hours in Casa das Conchas, it was to passionate birdsong, to the sight of paradise flycatchers, sunbirds, a woodpecker, a Malabar whistling thrush, a kingfisher that lived in a hole in the mudbank of the dry creek bed but hunted midges from up on the telephone wire.

Now what?

The fruit on the sideboard had been gnawed. The soap in the bathroom had vanished.

"Good morning, madam!" sang out Olinda. Babita had inherited Umberto's maid, Olinda, and his driver, Naresh, who lived in the neighboring hamlet and could amble over to Casa das Conchas.

"Rat is coming in night, madam," Olinda assured her.

"Why would a rat eat the soap?"

"Rat is dirty, maybe rat wants to take bath." Olinda laughed.

Later, Olinda showed Babita that she had discovered the bar of Lux in the garden covered with crunchy red earth. Olinda wore dresses, gold earrings, and a nose ring. She had gold-rimmed glasses and fresh jasmine in her hair. Babita was always relieved to see her, but after Vini-Puni, Babita knew she shouldn't relax into trusting Olinda. By afternoon, Olinda left; by five P.M., Naresh did, too, and Babita was stranded and unprepared for the enormity of village dark. It was not safe to wander down rutted country paths alone, and it was a long drive, a ponderous ferry ride, between villages and hamlets where you might visit a friend. When she suggested Naresh come occasionally at night for overtime pay, he claimed he had poor night vision. He scowled as if it was a comedown to work for an Indian instead of an Italian. Babita's life had taught her that rudeness was not a sign that someone was *not* out to cheat you. She shouldn't trust him.

She wandered from cavernous gloom to cavernous gloom, followed by timorous Pasha, who jumped at the baby lizards darting at his paws because the baby lizards hadn't yet learned the difference between floor and ceiling. They were trailed by the mosquitoes that drifted in at dusk and that Babita found in the mornings bobbing at mirrors and window glass, seeking a way out, unable to get past their own reflections, jigging in self-puja, nasal self-wooing.

They also had the company, if you could call it company, of the unfriendly ancient who lived in the ruin invaded by banyan roots at the foot of the driveway. And the company of the flea-tormented dogs that skulked in the lane waiting for leftover rice. In the rainy season, she was told, when the snake holes were flooded, poisonous snakes would invade. Then many dogs died of snakebite.

Babita had an attack of panic. The dead white Christ nailed to his cross—several hundred years old in the altar room—suddenly scared her. Wasn't it macabre to have God tortured and dripping blood into your home? The bleeding Christ, the dark timber, the oxblood floor, the voltage barely ticking, the mosquitoes feasting on her, brought back the killing of Ravi and Rana. Somebody would be murdered in this house, too, and the culprit would never be found. She screamed out loud, "*I can't see! I can't see!*" She had been besmirched by the deaths of her brothers-in-law, as if she were guilty of them. Even strangers meeting her would think she was complicit—or why had she survived when two others in the same residence, even if a divided residence, had been killed? And where were the girls? Vini-Puni might be suffering a fate worse than death. She had all the time in the world to dwell on this now.

"Why didn't you bark?" She transferred a portion of her guilt to Pasha. Pasha brought his toy cat in case it was the right answer, but from his shy wag, it was clear even he knew it was a hopeless reply. Babita telephoned Sara Habib ostensibly to share her new number but really to find out if Sara had any news, but she could barely understand what Sara was telling her in a torrent that did not have to do with Ravi-Rana but another, tangential story—or was it?

Sara said it was the ironing man who had first divulged to her that the Allahabad driver—along with the staff of the staid guesthouse at the end of their street that was owned by a pharmaceutical company for visiting management—had been operating an informal brothel in the neighborhood, using the empty rooms whenever management executives were not resident. And one of the men who worked in an illegal basement tax office a few houses down said that the ironing man—along with the drivers, scooter-rickshaw men, taxi drivers, and storekeepers—were pimps. A maidservant admitted that she along with other neighborhood maids and some girls from the beauty salon were voluntarily prostituting themselves—how else could they make enough money to survive on their sparse salaries? Among the maids selling sex, they agreed, was regrettably an underage girl. And this girl was Vinita.

"What are you saying?" whimpered Babita. She wound the telephone wire around and around her hand, choking it. She wanted to wind it about her neck.

The girl who came from the salon to wax Sara's brows and upper lip said that Vinita had confided in her that the Allahabad driver had told Vinita that they would have to elope to Dubai if they wished to be together because he was already married. And if she wished to elope with him, she must help earn the money for them to do so. Vinita had been doing her part—they almost had enough—but her sister had become increasingly envious. She had surely run away with the driver, seducing him.

"But what about that chloroformed rag?"

"It must all be part and parcel—how, we don't know. It's not a simple story."

Had the drivers vanished because they'd been running a brothel or because they had killed Ravi-Rana? Had the Allahabad driver and Vinita stolen suitcases of gold? Had both the girls been abducted? Or had Vinita and the driver conspired to sell Punita into a brothel—no, no, of course not. She remembered Vinita: *We have to stay together, or it won't be safe for us. It isn't safe for girls alone.*

Coincidentally, she realized, Dubai was twice involved—the buyer of their home was in Dubai, and the Allahabad driver had said he planned to leave for Dubai. Mr. Habib had advised her to flee Delhi immediately and not say a word. She wondered if Mr. Habib was linked to the buyers. She remembered him hugging Punita's sparrow shoulders. "Don't be afraid, little darling."

"Did you tell the police about this brothel?" she asked Sara.

"Of course not. We are Muslims, we can't tangle with the police." At their summer home in Ranikhet, Sara said, neighbors had set cows free to munch their lilies. They dare not say anything about that, either, and lived in terror that a cow might fall ill or die and that they would be accused of poisoning it.

Babita thought of how Hindus in her circle often muttered that a Muslim's loyalty was inevitably located outside India—how could it not be after waves of sectarian violence? Wouldn't you be an idiot to be patriotic? She turned on all the lights, so many switches hidden behind curtains and shutters, at floor level and high on the wall. She was always confused as to which switch turned on which light—some twenty of them together created an eerie glow. *Everyone is corrupt, Ratty, so why isn't everyone murdered? Why us? It's because you thought we would be murdered that your brothers were murdered. If you behave in a guilty manner, if you believe in retribution, crime finds you. Sure as a bloodhound.*

Ratty, don't leave me! Don't leave me alone! I will love you—after all!

Babita drank Old Monk, stamped her foot to scatter the brainless baby lizards, and read *The Navhind Times* and *O Heraldo,* which reported that an eighty-three-year-old woman had been killed in Saligao—why and by whom? Nobody knew. And that a young woman, recently divorced and embarking upon a new life, choosing Goa for its apparent cosmopolitanism, had been raped and strangled in a gated condominium complex in Sangolda by the watchman, whom she had accused of stealing her umbrella, in consequence of which he had lost his job. This particular murder was sensational: The young woman was a former model, and the press galloped to Goa. She had been photographed for

British Vogue in the mangroves with a giant crab and a baby python; in the Hotel Mandovi, ruffled skirt, sultry look of an old-style singer of Konkani jazz; at the Basilica of Bom Jesus, murmuring prayers under a mantilla as priests in vocational training peeped from behind the ornamental palms in the seminary garden. These pictures were replicated everywhere. The only image they had to show of the old lady was a blurry, unsmiling ration card ID.

Babita thought of her own umbrella from London, which she had purchased at the V&A Museum gift shop. It sported a William Morris design, and she would be tremendously upset if it was stolen. She remembered her visit to London: Chori, chori. That is what the Indian bus driver had said driving by Buckingham Palace: Chori, chori. Britain's treasures had been procured via outrageous robbery and murder. The diamond in the crown: Chori, chori, chori. All of India was chasing its lost jewels.

She got into bed before she was sleepy. *It was ingenious,* she thought. The company guesthouse was the last house on the street, and it was across from the Panchsheel Park market with its small businesses and offices. A restless man might telephone the guesthouse, and the staff could call for a neighborhood maid—*Vinita!*—who wished for an hour's afternoon employment while her mistress—*Babita!*—was taking a siesta. A maid might make a devil's exchange simply to experience an air-conditioned room with an attached bathroom. On the surface it would look normal—innocent staff members on innocent neighborhood errands.

Night was a ten-hour purgatory of blended nightmares and wakefulness, of lightning hot flashes and torrid night sweats. Over and over Babita repeated to herself the stories of Ravi-Rana-Vini-Puni. A murderess returns to the scene of her crime to make sure she did not leave a clue—she must be guilty! But why, when everywhere one saw powerful individuals enjoying themselves, although they were physically distorted as if they'd gobbled all they'd stolen, chomped all those they'd destroyed. They dressed in glitzy Bollywood outfits, threw Bollywood-style weddings for their children attended by Bollywood stars, serenaded by American pop legends flown in on private jets and compensated in millions of dollars. So why did she, Babita Bhatia, feel this way? Because she was *not* guilty. It was the innocent who felt shame to see the guilty. It was her shame on behalf of *others* that made her feel guilty!

Each time she told the story to herself, she tweaked it. *I told Rana and Ravi that I am not taking black money! It has to be clean, or I won't sell.*

Would I dishonor the memory of my son's father, all of whose problems came from being honest? That is what caused his heart attack—his honesty!

If you are a talented raconteur, all the bits need not exactly add up; nobody notices a chink. Only Sunny would notice—*Sunny! Sunny?*

He was absconding as if *he* were guilty—

What happened to our son, Ratty? Send your children away too young, they become strangers. There is no longer any feeling that one should strive for family, for community, for nation, or any entity larger than oneself.

The United States had stolen her sweet son and transformed him into a foreigner trumpeting the American mantra of individuality and self-sufficiency in order to disguise his selfishness. By attacking the United States, she excused her Sunny. *Ratty, I made a mistake sending him abroad.*

Could she exonerate herself by telling the story of her innocence to someone? A story unheard may as well be a story untrue. Should she invite Vanya to join her on a sunset walk upon the beach? The waves would impart a sense of ageless truth. The intimacy of falling dusk might increase her listener's sympathy. By telling and retelling her tweaked and re-tweaked story to the ocean's regurgitation, Babita's innocence might one day be rendered as ageless and indisputable a truth as the ocean.

Vanya arrived in a bad mood. It was too cumbersome a journey from Divar, and Babita had miscalculated the time; the sun flamed upon their faces. Vanya donned giant sunglasses, shielded her head with her dupatta.

"Do you, did you, ever suffer from menopausal hot flashes?" asked Babita, suddenly overcome as if by an electric shock. She wished to jump out of her skin and into the water.

"No, I never did, I never do," responded Vanya.

Why was it women refused to admit to menopause? What was this shame? What was this lie?

"Let's go somewhere air-conditioned," said Vanya, and Babita's other confession, the one of innocence, remained unconfessed.

BY MAY, THE AIR WAS TOO FAT TO BREATHE. BABITA DREW a swampy breath and inquired: "Olinda, why are there so many robberies and murders here?"

"Sometimes there is a robbery." Olinda was trying to dust the starry Arabian rafters with a bamboo pole topped with a feather duster, although when she looked up, dust fell upon her spectacles.

"I am nervous at night," said Babita.

Olinda had been born in the neighboring vaddo and had a husband, Vincent, who'd lived in this very vaddo all his life. She bent down to wipe the lenses with the hem of her dress and then looked at Babita as if Babita were out of touch with a deeper understanding. Olinda said: "It is only in your mind, madam."

"How is it only in my mind when someone has been killed?"

Olinda half nodded, still looking skeptical. "Everywhere something happens," she said. "In Delhi also."

What solace was that? Babita phoned Vanya and heard the greater isolation of the river island expanding on the line. "I'm sleeping badly," she confessed. "And it isn't only because I am menopausal in this infernal climate. I'm nervous with all the windows open and only flimsy bolts on the doors. The rats come in and steal my soap; they are too big for traps."

Vanya said, "That is because they're not rats. They are bandicoots, stealthy country rodents with country habits and a tribal sensibility. They operate in family groups, scale coconut trees, climb drainpipes."

"What solace is that? Is it just my unfamiliarity with the countryside? Or do you ever get a creepy feeling?"

"I had a creepy feeling the other night," Vanya admitted, "but then it went away. It comes and goes." The silence made galaxies of pulsating aloneness.

"We are fifty-three. You'd think we'd be too old for creepy feelings—have you ever been robbed?"

"Three times, each time when I fell into an unusually deep sleep. Once they took my mobile from right under the pillow next to me. But here they rarely kill like they do in the big cities unless you surprise them."

"What solace is that? Wasn't a woman in Mapusa attacked by someone with a knife?"

"That was a mad person."

"What solace is that? Then there was a robbery in Baga."

"That was drug-related."

"What solace is that? Then there was a murder of a grandmother in Saligao."

"That was because her house was isolated on a dry creek bed."

"I'm also isolated. What solace is that?"

"They are mainly outsiders who come and rob."

"What solace is that?"

"You have to change your psychology. Think that it is your home and you cannot be scared in your own home." This didn't make sense to Babita. Why hadn't Vanya warned her of the danger before she bought this house? Why hadn't Umberto said, "But it won't be safe for a single lady of caliber."

"Do you want to come and spend the night?" asked Vanya.

"Naresh has left."

"Can't you call him back?"

"He says he has bad night vision. Even during the day he's proving impossible. He gets hungry and flies into a fury. He refuses to eat outside food, and he refuses to bring his lunch—he wants to go home to his vaddo for prawn curry rice and a nap. If I keep him waiting, he speeds and curses at other drivers. Yet I'm nervous of firing him; he might be vengeful. You heard about the woman who complained the security guard stole her umbrella, and when he was fired, he raped and throttled her?"

"But that was a crime of vengeance and sexual obsession."

"What solace is that? Meanwhile, I confess," said Babita, "that I'm drinking too much rum stuck here alone."

Babita accepted Vanya's invitation to a French film that was being shown at an outdoor screening in the garden of the cultural center on Altinho hill, cajoling Naresh by offering him not only overtime pay but dinner money to eat in Panjim with Vanya's driver, Falcon. *Jean de Florette* was screened in partnership with the French consulate, and it was introduced by a Frenchwoman in high heels, a white linen dress, a mauve agate on a long chain, and matching, complicated mauve and blue eye makeup. Babita examined her closely as she spoke about how *Jean de Florette* was a universal film—the story of an outsider, a city dweller with romantic notions of village life. The audience included fellow widows, some scruffy, long-haired youths trailing cigarette smoke—the kind who attend French films everywhere—and some retirees and foreign residents she may like to know. She watched for a sign they recognized her as *that woman of the Panchsheel Park murders*. Was she behaving normally, or was she muttering aloud her diseased thoughts?

After a bit, Babita stopped noticing the audience or herself. *Jean de Florette* was a powerful story, and it scared her. She watched as the hunchback gentleman farmer who moved from Paris seeking a salubrious life was deceived by the locals, cheated of his land and his water spring. Dusk fell and soon mosquitoes and bats were thick in the sky overhead.

They dined at Saudade by Ourem Creek, the road outside quiet at the night hour, the crowds having ceased crossing to the bus station at the end of the workday, the women selling fish spread upon the bus-stop bridge having gone home. Babita said to Vanya, "But this is what will happen to me, what happened to *Jean de Florette*. The villagers are unfriendly. It may end in *my* murder."

"*Your* murder?" asked Vanya. "Because your brothers-in-law were murdered, it doesn't mean you will be murdered."

And then, despite herself, it came falling out like water. Babita told Vanya the pent-up story of her innocence, starting with her mother-in-law Minnie's will that left her out, save for dwindling investments and rabbit-design Spode egg cups, which were now missing. This Vanya enjoyed, but when Babita began to tell Vanya about Ravi-Rana and the underworld, Vanya snapped. "Either you have gone along with corruption, or you have not. Ever since you married, you've relished the money. You've lived your entire adult life upon it, that's the truth!"

Babita lost her temper and responded, "But it's common knowledge what a crook Cecil was."

Vanya said, "Nobody was ever murdered, my dear."

"How would I know?" responded Babita. "I don't know. The dead don't speak."

The owner brought out freshly fried clam fritters. He'd been a member of the French Foreign Legion and had participated in ambushes and atrocities of the kind no government admitted to, of the kind no reporter had ever written about, in countries few in India had heard of, that he himself had never heard of until he was there.

"Are you still drinking too much at night?" asked Vanya, trying to make up their spat as they paid their check. *Better two widows having a spat than one widow with nobody to spat with. Better three widows going to the movies. Better four widows braving widowhood.* "The rum might be giving you nightmares. What I do is sip a cup of hot water at the end of the day to relax before sleep."

Naresh cursed, swerving almost off the road when lorries came toward them beaming their lights. When they were back in their own hamlet and Naresh had switched off the engine, the loamy dark was so dark, Babita peered for a speck of light and, other than a star, found none. She comforted Pasha, who was hiding under the bed. When he came out, he suffered fits of trembling, his back legs giving way. She put on the kettle, poured out a cup, took a few sips, happened to look down, and found a young lizard in the boiled water. "*Ratty,*" she wept. "*Ratty, I have grown old before my happiness!*"

WAITING IN THE SHADOWS WERE VINI-PUNI: *SUNNY Bhaiya, take us to America!*

And Uncle Rana came to Sunny in his dreams: *But where is my head? My head has gone.*

Uncle Ravi joined Uncle Rana, still in his paisley dressing gown: *Where are my hands? My hands have gone.*

The fact that they followed him, bloody as Shakespearean ghouls, made Sunny suspect he himself was responsible for their murders. It must be so. Every component in a scene has a role, even the weather. He had sneakily visited his uncles, and Uncle Ravi had said, "Think of us— we also need to escape." Uncle Rana had said, "Please, Sunny, beg your mother to sell." Sunny had urged his mother, "Why don't you think of selling the house and be done with the battle?" He had not become rich, which made his mother fret about her future. He had holidayed in Loutolim with Sonia, which had made his mother so livid, she had impulsively purchased Casa das Conchas. Vini-Puni's vanishing was linked to the Allahabad driver, who was in Delhi because Sunny had refused to allow superlative kebab Khansama to be stolen.

It was easy to become convinced of an argument pinning you as the guilty one, to become what others accused you of, and it was even easier when you constructed this argument yourself. The certitude and conviction it took to overturn guilt when something terrible had happened within one's purview—only the guilty had the impetus to summon. It was they who fanned an uproar of indignation enough to terrify the truth and make it slink away. Sunny then wondered if he felt guilty of abetting murder precisely because he was *not* guilty.

The ghost of his father said to Sunny: *Sunny, if you are corrupt, you are doomed—and if you are* not *corrupt, you are also doomed!*

"Don't notice," he said to himself at his folding kitchen table, fists on each side of his plate.

His gut refused to listen and told him he was a liar, a false son, a false lover, a false reporter—a fake eater! He was becoming intolerant of spice: His digestive system was inflamed, he suffered hemorrhoids, his intestines contracted in cramps, his jaw locked so tight he couldn't open his mouth to chew. He tried again, and again he couldn't.

"Did they find Vini-Puni?" Sunny croaked through this meager mouth when he answered Babita's call. "Don't the police have a lead?"

"I am not in touch with the police, and the police are not in touch with me. They have been paid off by the underworld, and because of your uncles we ourselves are implicated. If we make trouble, the underworld will retaliate." Her voice despaired. "Anyway, the police won't make an effort for anyone who is poor, nor will the parents want Vini-Puni to be found. Nobody will marry them now. I remember the day their mother came begging me to take them in, two little slum birds. . . . Well," she said, "no good deed goes unpunished. One's own country keeps on breaking one's heart.

"The murderers may come for me," she said when Sunny remained mute, his jaw more intractably tightening, his ear inflaming. Over the next days, the inflammation and pain in Sunny's jaw and ear traveled and made a large, red hump at the back of his neck. The hump on the back of his neck began to throb. The swelling flared and traveled down his spine. He could not move without pain. He couldn't think. His mind was not straight because the world was not straight. The world was upside down, so he was upside down.

He wondered if any of the several applications he had daringly submitted had come through. The one to a Tuscan castle? Or to the expat English-language paper in Santiago? He might disappear into Patagonia like Bonnie and Clyde.

"Save me, save me, save me," he prayed to an invisible God. "Save me."

Save me.

And then the miracle came through. When fresh mustard greens and Ataulfo mangoes were being sold on the springtime streets of Jackson Heights again, Sunny received an email informing him that his submission to the PEN competition, "Reading Hemingway in Allahabad, Reading Hemingway in Jackson Heights"—written in the aftermath of Ulla leaving him—had won the annual essay prize. Along with a travel grant, he would be published in an issue of *Granta,* the magazine Sunny held in holy esteem. Writing about *not* making it as a journalist, Sunny's name would appear alongside the legendary names Martha Gellhorn, Joan Didion, Carolyn Forché—and Sunny's hero, Ryszard Kapuściński. The citation lauded not only his Hemingway piece, but also "The Fingernail Man," which indicated that the committee could not distinguish between the falsity of one attempt, the truth of the other.

Hobbling with a walking stick and wearing his mustard kurta to receive the award at the PEN gala held at the American Museum of Natural History, Sunny walked in to find—under the suspended whale skeleton, by the dinosaur bones—the fashionable, mixed-race, brownstone-owning Brooklyn authors he had so envied and despised. He said to someone at the cocktail bar, "Writers are the new dinosaurs, I see," and the person replied, "Ah yes, that's the joke Orfeu Cantu made, isn't it?" by which Sunny understood a famous writer had made the same joke as Sunny and now Sunny was being called a copycat.

The famous writers were seated at the front tables, with their velvet suits, dreadlocks in ponytails, vintage dresses, librarian glasses. The less-famous writers were seated at the back of the room. Some of the ones in front had once been seated in the back, others had migrated from the front to the back. Sunny was seated at the last table by the perpetually swinging kitchen door at a table of bored men from a real estate firm that had felt obliged to sponsor a table because it did business with a publishing company. They soon glanced at the time and snuck out, and Sunny was alone watching the self-congratulatory speeches about imprisoned writers who had been saved from Cuba and Iran. The white savior complex was being showcased and shored up by the persons of color. You could be destroyed and saved by America at the same time. Was Sunny being saved, was he playing the game of saving others?

The famous authors in the audience, suave and schmoozy, talked over the librarian who had fought a lonely battle against book bans in Nebraska, but they fell into reverent silence when Orfeu Cantu got up to speak about himself.

Male authors, until they migrated to the front seats at the gala, often looked as if they'd crawled out of a garbage can, the head of the prize committee reflected as Sunny slunk onto the stage, yet time and time again she had been surprised: The author may look unkempt or be deceitful, smarmy, and a dreadful human being, but they would nevertheless incite a fervent following of attractive female fans. By this time next year, Sunny might be the Cucaracha Kafka of Jackson Heights, at the table by center stage.

As he accepted the check, Sunny was glad Ulla wasn't around to witness his hypocrisy. Then he thought he should write about his hypocrisy. But if he did so, he wouldn't win any more prizes. He fretted his grant wouldn't last long enough for him to get over Ravi-Rana's murders and find something to write about to fulfill the suggested goal of his travel grant.

"Why not go to Mexico?" advised Darko. "It's a country where something extraordinary is always happening, and you can go with your green card, live cheaply for six months."

Sunny wrote to the AP reporter in Mexico City, who said that when he was writing his book about the mothers of the vanished young women in Juárez, collating the news reports he had been filing, he had retreated to a fishing village in the state of Colima, south of Puerto Vallarta. The Pacific was a rough ocean, and the waves were sometimes ancient waves that had gathered strength traveling a vast span of the globe, but the village was secreted in a deep gullet bay, where the momentum of the waves was considerably reduced. He could work all day, swim to look back at the world resettled by his distance from it, and then go to a beach shack for a beer and a snapper á la Veracruzana.

One voice in Sunny's head told him he should use his grant money to return to India and help his mother—what could you say about a grown man who hadn't returned when his uncles were murdered, who had deliberately made himself inconsequential and was planning to sneak across the border like a fugitive while other people trudged a heroic path the other way. Another voice said he'd never get anywhere unless he made a complete break. *Don't be two people accused of being accomplice to murder. Don't be two terrified people plus a terrified dog. Don't be several gouged souls.* He needed to find his riff on a raga. Might he go to Mexico with an excuse of studying Spanish? *¿Cómo es la noche oscura del alma?* You could slip your skin through language if you had failed to do so through romantic love. Sunny applied for a leave of absence from the Associated Press, and the alacrity with which it was granted made him wonder if they wouldn't use his absence as an excuse to let him gently go.

He tried for days to reach Babita, and when he finally got through, it was as if there was a deluge inside their phone call. She told him that the monsoon had arrived in Goa with a dhar bhoom that snapped the telephone and electric wires and a black gale that had taken the kitchen door off its hinges. A carnival of objects had flown by Babita's window and come clattering up the street: a motley collection of tin, branches, a woman's ribbon, a bumping bucket, and fleets of ardent plastic bags. The palms had turned emerald, thrashed their stars upside down, inside out. The Arabian Sea had turned seasick, rising high as the Himalayas, vomiting from its depths upon the sand bottles and cement sacks, coconuts and jellyfish, ballpoint pens and sanitary pads.

"I may be leaving for Mexico."

"What?"

"I am going to Mexico."

"*Mexico?* Why Mexico? When everyone else is heading the other direction!"

"To study Spanish."

"You gave me hell telling me I had prevented you from learning Hindi properly, that you wish to be fluent in *Hindi!*"

"Look, Ma, I need to get out of New York. I don't believe my life will ever change here, and I can never return to India because you yourself told me to stay away or the underworld will find me."

59

....

ONIA WENT TO MEET MAYA MITHAL OF *KALA* MAGAZINE at her farmhouse on the city outskirts to discuss a new venture Maya had suggested. Maya's baby was in a dinosaur float in the swimming pool and Sonia felt envious—how long was it since she had been swimming? She was distracted by the baby splashing while Maya recounted a speech her husband had made at an international tourism conference in Bali about how tourism was a crucial tool in cultural preservation. Faltering history that could not survive the onslaught of modernity on its own merit could be saved by "high-end" tourism. At the conference, the term "high-end" was used sincerely, and by coincidence, many other attendees presented the same argument tailored to their own respective nations. Maya and her husband were conjuring a scheme to restore heritage homes and transform them into boutique hotels to add to her husband's hospitality empire. Could this boutique hotel venture work in tandem with *Kala* to offer tours to "high-end" tourists? The hotel business and the altruistic magazine might combine forces.

Maya said, "You have no idea how lucky you are, Sonia, to wander freely. I burst into tears when I first left my baby to attend a meeting, and yet I know I must continue to work to counter expectations. It's expected by everyone—family, society, nation—that I sacrifice myself for my husband and children. Meanwhile, mothering is not respected as a career choice, and it *is* work! Why shouldn't we be compensated?"

Did people have children for their own happiness, or did they think of it as a job or a social service? Was it contributing to society to assiduously add to an overpopulated country? Who should pay Maya?

Her husband? The government? Sonia? Sonia knew enough to know that her thinking was politically incorrect.

Maya noticed Sonia looking sullen. She must be unhappy to see Maya's happiness no matter how Maya allowed herself to be chagrined.

Maya said, "You are alone? Such a beautiful woman—no boyfriend?"

Said Sonia, "I don't think it has to do with looks."

Whereupon Maya was certain Sonia was jealous and said sympathetically that she herself had suffered heartbreak with a landscape gardener from Massachusetts before her marriage. "It was impossible to overcome race *and* class. It will work out for you one day," she assured Sonia.

Sonia said she was simply exhausted from days at the hospital.

Maya said, "You must take self-care breaks. I have a proposition."

Could Sonia make a trip to a hunting lodge owned by the Maharaja of Jodhpur at Sardar Samand? It might be a stop on a *Kala* tour from Bikaner to the fortress of Kumbhalgarh to Udaipur. Sonia would need to ascertain how long the drive was and to check whether there was any prospect of comfort to be had in matters of bed, bath, and meals for an international group of textile designers whom Maya would be hosting. Now that she had made the offer to Sonia, Maya regretted she had done so, but she forced her better self higher. If women like herself did not support other women, even women more attractive than themselves, one day she would not be able to look her daughter in the eye. "How tall are you?" she asked. "Some tall women look gangly, but it suits you."

She gave Sonia *A Princess Remembers* by Maharani Gayatri Devi to read; the book was an account of glamour wrung from wretched poverty. Gayatri Devi's mother, the Rani of Cooch Behar, had traveled to the casinos of Monte Carlo with a jewel-studded tortoise as a lucky talisman. What spin could *Kala* put on palace and fort tours for a modern tourist interested in culture, accustomed to luxury, harboring the latest ideas on equality and human rights? They should comprehend the atrocity, but of course they must continue to enjoy the luxury. This was Sonia's job—to seamlessly marry two incompatible things in the article she was contracted to write.

Sonia did not wish to take on this assignment—she longed to escape back to a time before she had walked into the Fortuny Museum with Sunny and experience once again the solace of love that feels like freedom—but she traveled to Bikaner because a woman should not refuse to travel to the forts of Rajasthan just because she is by herself. And when she arrives at her destination is it not fair for a woman on her own to partake in a glass of wine after she has toured the palace museum listening to an audio guide by the current maharaja relating the history of his kingdom in an Oxbridge accent? Sonia settled into a quiet alcove of the hotel bar in the Laxmi Niwas Palace designed by Sir Swinton Jacob in 1902. She made notes. Why was it that perspective in art was considered a Western sophistication, when a goal on a hill through a crescent-topped casement looked as much without perspective in real life as it did in a miniature painting? And how interesting it was to observe that the royals were persuaded by every carpet salesman, every tchotchke bearer. How dissonant it was to journey six, eight, twelve hours through the desert and view jeweled scabbards, crowns, evening bags, and cigarette cases; stuffed Bavarian hogs, civet cats, and jackals; the skin of a long-nosed alligator and a snub-nosed crocodile; menu cards written in French: *Filetes de Bectis à la Mornay, Plat de Bikaner, Bombe Pistache;* a letter from the archives to ask when might they expect payment for the open-topped Ford for the maharani.

How Ilan would love these crazy fort museums; he shared the rajas' itch to aggrandize. He had been to Rajasthan, she remembered; he had perhaps learned from them, just as from the pharaohs in Egypt. He had been everywhere, so everywhere she went he would have been. She was angry she had thought of him. *Happiness is for other people.*

She carried her glass outside. This was a good idea because she could now watch langurs loping from afar to sit, shoulders relaxed against the ramparts at sunset. They preferred what was man-made to sitting in trees; they appreciated a vista to the horizon. It made the monkeys philosophical. They looked outside and inside themselves at the same time.

She took a deep breath, stretched her legs, and tried not to hold her spine so tightly—to be more like the contemplating monkeys.

In the morning a man named Madan who ran a small tour operation met Sonia in the lobby to take her to the hunting lodge between
Bikaner and Udaipur. She was pleased to see someone her age, in jeans,
sunglasses.

"Ready?" he asked.

"Yes. Is there a pool at the hunting lodge, by any chance? I brought
my swimming costume hoping I could swim in one of the hotels."

He said, "Of course you can swim! Not at the lodge, but there is a
new resort on the way that has a pool. In fact, I have one or two matters
to take care of, so we can stop, you can swim, then I'll collect you, and
we should still be at the lodge before dark."

On the way, the driver, who was from Pokhran, told Madan and
Sonia about the day in 1998 when India successfully tested a nuclear
bomb: Operation Shakti, following Operation Smiling Buddha, aka
Operation Happy Krishna in 1974. "Afterward the scientists threw salt,
potatoes, and onions into the pit to absorb the radiation, and for weeks
there was an onion shortage, but we were celebrating so much we did
not care!"

"Hmm," said Sonia, "what were you celebrating?" She was thinking how cynical it was to call a bomb after the Buddha, after Krishna.
She was thinking that the skyrocketing cost of onions was usually an
occurrence that brought down a government. Was it worth expensive
onions to stick it to Pakistan for a millisecond before Pakistan exploded
its own nuclear bomb? But Madan took the driver's side: "Now nobody can tell us to bow to them!" But now how could they bow before
the Buddha? Before Krishna? Surely nuclear annihilation would go beyond Krishna's teaching of duty upon the battlefield?

They stopped at a resort in faux raja style at the outskirts of Bikaner. India was becoming rich enough to become a faux version of
itself, Sonia thought, and one of the advantages of this was a sunshiny
pool big enough to circle in. A family—women and men in T-shirts
and shorts—stood in the water and talked about how abusively women
were treated in Saudi Arabia, not even allowed to drive.

In an instant Sonia's body remembered happiness. She floated on
her back, she splashed like Maya's baby, swam until her fingers and toes

were wrinkly. Eventually she got out and ordered a club sandwich. When Madan arrived, she offered to share her chips.

He dipped each one carefully, exactly halfway in ketchup. "So you travel alone? I admire you."

"What is there to admire?"

"Most women say, 'My husband won't let me.'"

"I don't have a husband."

"Then your family?"

"My father wanted me to take a break from looking after him because he is ill with cancer. My mother thinks it is more intelligent for women to be without men. But what about your wife, doesn't she object?"

"I don't have a wife."

"That's unusual. How often do you get two Indians our age who are unmarried?"

"True!"

Sonia felt reckless. "I had one bad boyfriend who was abusive, then I had a nice one who was controlled by a corrupt family. Neither worked out. What about you? Didn't your family find you someone?"

"I have a more unusual situation. I'll tell you about it later. We should drive out now or we'll reach the lodge in darkness."

The evening sun was red as a bindi, the grass at the roadside was yellow, the desert had eaten into the snake-black tar and whittled it to barely the width of their vehicle. They drove for a long while on this road, which at first glance took them through uninhabited land without electric poles or tube wells, but Sonia saw that thorny bushes had been collected in piles of kindling—twenty, thirty equidistant piles across the emptiness they traversed. So there must be people who lived here who had no electricity, no running water.

They arrived at a spindly metal gate that was locked, but there was no fence or barricade on either side of the gateposts, so they simply drove around and proceeded up the weedy gravel to a collection of art deco cubes high on a rock that was pink in hue, flat atop, and pleated below. The guesthouse was to the side of the main hunting lodge, and both residences faced a vista of empty plain stretching away from a marshy lake with a long, extended arm of water. Resting on this arm of water were three pelicans. Shouldn't they long ago have flown north at winter's end?

An elderly man in a white turban came out to meet them. Madan questioned him. Who owned this hunting lodge, how many tourists came here, how much did it cost?

There were lights on at the main building, but there was nobody there.

"Why are the lights on?"

"They are always on, and the table is always set exactly the way it was when George V came to stay."

The rooms opened onto verandas, and each bedroom had a private dressing room and bathroom in art deco style, large enough to wander about in, remote enough that you could believe the modern world did not exist.

"This is the best place for a bachelor party," Madan said to Sonia, which struck her as a peculiar observation.

At nightfall the space turned vast, the land shed its heat, and the breeze blew dry and strong and smelled of grasses. The hunting lodge was high enough on the rock that there were stars pulsing not only above but also below. The few lights on earth were dim in comparison, with a far saltish glow. A thousand lizards lived here, maybe a hundred thousand, and they settled upon the insect screens. So many stars, so many insects, so many lizards—the rest an austerity.

The caretaker brought them dinner outside on the terrace. He had cooked a chicken in a clay pot, and he had made dal and roti. He brought a bottle of warm beer.

"I have been declared dead," said Madan. "You asked why I was not married. That is why."

"Are you really one of those?" Sonia exclaimed. There had recently been a series of articles and reports on the numerous people registered dead so their assets might be grabbed by unscrupulous family.

"I was registered dead by my own brother. When I was working in Malaysia, my brother's wife encouraged him to pay for a forged death certificate, and then immediately they built a house on our ancestral land using the entire compound."

"How could your own brother be so evil?"

"He had an irrational jealousy that went back to our childhood, and he's spent his entire life finding excuses to rationalize it. For example, he said I did not help look after our mother, although I was the one working and sending money to her from abroad. I know from experience that the hate between two brothers is deeper than any other hate. You cannot overcome it."

"Aren't you going to court?"

"The case will either never come up or be decided against me. I cannot bribe anyone, you see, while they can bribe whomever they please because they stole my property. And when my mother died, my brother also took all the money I had sent her, because according to the law, I was dead. There has been problem after problem—it's hard to prove you are alive when everyone tells you that you are dead—but once it affected me in a manner I could not forgive, and this was when I had a girlfriend. She was a tourist from Oslo."

"Oh," said Sonia. "What happened? I'm an expert in sad love stories. I can give you advice."

"I was her tour guide when she was traveling through Rajasthan, then she became my girlfriend. But when I revealed my life—I am an honest person, I cannot help but tell the truth—she became nervous. She began asking questions as if she was trying to catch me out, and she began pulling away. 'Oh, but how can I trust you?' I protested, 'But I'm not really dead, as you can see. It isn't my fault.'

"But if I didn't exist on paper, she said, I could be anyone. Her family could not accept me. I could cause her harm and be untraceable. In fact, she was the one who was unreliable. She left me overnight without saying she was leaving or giving me any way to find her. I tried to telephone her home in Oslo and found she had given me a false number. I found the real number. A man, maybe her father, said to me, 'If you phone again we will call the India police.'" Madan snorted.

"No girl is willing to stay with me. They eventually say, 'Where is your family? Why doesn't your family meet me?' Then their parents begin to say, 'Who is this person you are with who has no family? How do you know he is who he says he is?' So I am alone."

They sat in silence. Sonia looked out upon the night sky glowing deep and black, and it was as if they were floating upon a small lamp-lit island. She looked back and found his eyes on her. He said, "You know, I told you the most private thing, I don't know why. I never trust anyone enough to tell them this story immediately."

She caught his veering into flirtation—their voices communing in a way she did not want—and stopped it. "It's travel," Sonia said. "Strangers who meet while traveling always tell each other their most private secrets. You can share anything without repercussion because soon you'll be on your way and never meet again."

"That is not always true."

She looked down at her plate. When she looked up, again she saw his eyes fixed upon her with an unmistakable, puffy, feverish look. "There is almost nobody for me to talk to over here."

"Why is that?" she said.

"Different mindset. This place is too conservative. I am thinking of leaving for Goa."

He was eating with his fingers. She picked up a knife and fork. He switched to a fork and spoon.

Sonia caught sight of a shooting star but didn't mention it for fear of encouraging another soft confession.

"I'm tired," said Sonia. "I need to sleep. Where will you stay? Will you drive back to town?" As with the knife and fork, she was invoking a class difference and informing him she knew that nobody would be paying for him to stay lavishly in the maharaja's hunting lodge, that while they both wore jeans and sunglasses, there remained a significant gulf.

He started to say something, then stopped. "I have somewhere to stay," he said, and he left awkwardly and abruptly, saying another driver would collect her the next day to take her to Kumbhalgarh and Udaipur. She was glad to have him gone. She had been careless and talked too much. She had tried to create a small holiday from her life via a small flirtation.

She sat out for a bit longer. She could hear intimate sounds carried in the silence, the sound of the waterfowl scratching, adjusting themselves, hiccups that may have been frogs, two men invisible on the far side talking in low voices as they walked home to an invisible village.

She showered in the art deco bathroom with its mirrors that multiplied her infinitely, smaller and smaller until her smallest image was projected all the way to space and she could no longer see this minuscule self. She thought she had reentered the world of Ilan and Lala, which was the world of extreme privilege, which was the world of fantasy. She remembered that beauty and strangeness were two qualities she had desired together. Her room was decorated with hunting trophies from Africa, with watercolors by Snaffles. Could the notes she wrote for this magazine article be toward writing a book? When you became a real artist, all roads led to your art: the people, the landscape, the news, the gossip, the suppressed shame, the dream, the flutter in the night of a pelican who should have flown north. A writer itched and itched to put everything into a book, or it became unbearable, the tingling. She thought it was almost too late to reclaim all she experienced before it vanished into oblivion.

Madan had said this was a good place for a bachelor party. In fact, this was a good setting for a murder mystery where a portrait of a woman who had been murdered might begin to speak and beseech a traveler to avenge her death. But why should the portrait trust a stranger? Why should the traveler trust a portrait perhaps painted by the subject's murderer? A painter cannot help but include himself in the canvas; the murderer's identity would surely be reflected in the woman's eye. Sonia thought that her anger and sadness over Ilan were not dissolving with time because in the years following, no door had opened; instead doors had kept closing into smaller spaces. Then came the inevitable curse of a sweeter memory. She remembered Ilan had given her a kitschy figurine of two dogs from the Chelsea Flea Market. *I won't let any harm come to you. If anyone dares to attack you, I will* woof woof *and drive them off.* Kitsch means true love. That is why kitsch exists, to show you love someone so much that you are willing to be sentimental. Therefore kitsch has power. Sonia had believed what Ilan said must be true because the figurine couldn't care less about the barriers of poor taste and embarrassment. Again, this was the trick: You believed what was not true. The terrifying master protects and betrays, assures and cheats, gives and takes, all at the same time.

It was only 9:30 P.M., but she got into bed, enjoying the luxury of being exhausted under clean sheets starched and ironed to parchment. A little tiger-striped moth whirred about Sonia's lamp, and she made a mental note to remember not to drink from her water glass in the dark, in case the same moth would soon be drowning in it.

It was now that she heard a knock at the door to her room, which was on a veranda extending from the guesthouse living room.

"Who is it?"

"It is Madan. You forgot something in the car."

She opened the door, and he was in her room.

"What did I forget?"

He gripped her wrists hard to pull her toward him and clasped her awkwardly in a painful embrace. He was violently shaking, pleading and desperate. "I like you," he said. "I like you very, very much."

"I'm just about to go to sleep. I'm very tired." She struggled to get out of his grasp.

"You cannot say no to me." He was grimacing, threatening, smiling in a twisted, miserable way, cringing yet demanding. "I love you very, very much."

"I need to sleep."

"Weren't you telling me how you are lonely by yourself?" His teeth gritted. "Now you cannot say no to me. I drove all the way back from town."

She said, "I will report you. You leave right this minute."

He became angry. "Who are you going to report to? What are you going to report—you were swimming and eating with me, drinking beer and joking."

"I did not invite you to stay for dinner, you stayed on your own. I did not know how to ask you to leave politely."

He was insulted. He pushed her hard, unsteady but forceful, collapsing her under himself upon the bed. He licked her face like a starving dog licks a plate. She noticed his fingernails were dyed yellow from turmeric. He stuck his bitter, sour fingers into her mouth and pushed his tongue so forcefully in her ear that she felt she was drowning. She smelled the stench of liquor, sweat, food, fear, and aggression. She could feel something uncoil and press against her and she knew it was his penis within his jeans. Then she couldn't say anything; he held her throat and she could not breathe. She was conscious of fighting for her breath while he writhed on top of her, fumbled at his groin, trying to unzip his zipper. Before he did, he fell limply and heavily upon her, then he pushed her away. He spat on her face, he upturned the lamp, which went dark, he threw the water pitcher, which shattered—and he was gone, leaving a bounty of lizards and stars, the rest an austerity, empty spans of sleeping land.

When Sonia got up she was trembling in a way that made it almost impossible to walk, but she managed to bolt the door. She sat on the floor and wondered whom to telephone. There was no phone in this guesthouse room. She couldn't remember any number. The mobile Papa had lent her received no signal. She could hardly leave to clamber up the pink rock or to some prince's cenotaph, searching after a stray phone signal. Then she could not think any further. She was not linked to her thoughts, they did not carry through, she and herself were not linked. She turned on the tap and stood under the shower until she had emptied the tank and the water ran out.

*

IN HER OWN BEDROOM two days later, after having driven on to Udaipur with a different guide and flying back to Delhi without stopping to visit the mirage of the Lake Palace, Sonia screamed one terrible shriek, the shriek she had been unable to scream to alert help when she was attacked. Not that there had been anyone to hear.

Papa didn't hear her crazed shriek either. He didn't notice his daughter's expression. Even though she had been gone only four days, he had important news. He'd been for a checkup.

"Sonia, sweetheart," Papa said, "this cancer is a cussed thing! They did a test. They found a new lump."

They'd had barely a month's reprieve. She was sure her father would soon die by the law of misfortune that stated those who had been harmed would be further harmed.

She confessed: "I had a terrible journey. A man attacked me." She didn't know if it was fair to say this to her father now that he was sick again, but, well, she'd gone and said it.

"Who?" He looked at her with a bewildered face, but he was thinking about his cancer.

"The tour guide."

"What did he do?"

"He pushed himself into the room and threw himself on top of me." She saw from Papa's expression that he did not wish to hear this. She needed to walk the drama back. She could not bear to use the words "almost raped," "sort of raped," "sexual assault." They felt like humiliating words, these words that were not part of any comfortable vocabulary between fathers and daughters. They would embarrass and hurt her father, who now should not be hurt.

She opened her mouth and shut it. She opened her mouth again and said, "Then luckily he jumped up and vanished."

"Did you say anything to the hotel manager?" Papa asked.

"There was no manager, only an elderly caretaker who had gone home. Do you think I should go to the police?"

"What proof would you have? How could you bring a case? You had better stay away from the police in this country—they'll insinuate you are to blame. Sonu, the best thing is to put it out of your mind."

Was this what a father was supposed to say? Surely not. Was he right? Was he wrong? How to put it out of her mind?

"Always look ahead, never look back. What has happened, has happened. Just take it as a warning. Never put yourself in that position again."

How, as a woman alone, would she manage not to put herself in such a position again? Her entire life as a woman alone would mean putting herself in such a position again.

"Should I tell Mama?"

"What is the point of upsetting her? She can't do anything about it."

Again, was he right? Was he wrong? Her parents belonged to the past age of parents, unassailable as religion. They found themselves right. They admitted no shortcoming—and the confidence of their child, their servant, their cat, and their bird depended on their certainty that they were right. There wasn't any point in telling them they'd misread the world as their parents had misjudged it before them. Sonia, now an adult, had to protect them from what they had brought about. And if Sonia informed her father and mother they were wrong, she would lose whatever stability she had, which still rested on their being right. She would only harm herself.

Papa said, "Can you find the folder with the previous X-rays and test results?"

She went to fetch the medical files. At night she examined the purple and yellow bruises on her neck that she had covered with a scarf.

Madan didn't know her, but he hated her. He was a stranger, but his anger was familiar. She recognized it, it was ubiquitous, it was in the air, it was in every man she'd ever met, that resentment. It was in her father, in the dinner-party uncles, in Ilan, in Sunny. If she had a brother, it would be in her brother. He would be brought up to express his resentment differently, being of a certain social class, but the hate would have some component of the hate of a man who might throw acid upon her face. It was the anger of being countered, refused, surpassed, denied, not adored enough—or simply ignored, because hell hath no fury like a man who is not the center of attention.

Madan had tried to transform his hate into an intimate dinner conversation, but it had flipped to hate again. He had said he'd been declared dead—had he been telling her that he couldn't commit a crime? Probably his name was not Madan.

In Light
of Mexico

60

....

"THE MURDERER WILL GET ME," SAID BABITA ON THE telephone to Sunny, "and you'll be free of your mother."

Where to take refuge? Sunny burst out of the Mexico City airport larga distancia booth. Feeling a desperate longing for the cleansing ocean, its high waves and its independence from any human concern—guilt, but especially love—he directly boarded a bus he was told was heading toward the Pacific. At least he hoped he understood the Spanish correctly. When he had rid himself of brain fever, he would return to Mexico City to see the great flag with the Aztec eagle, serpent, and cactus flying over the presidential palace, the courts, la Catedral Metropolitana de la Asunción de la Santísima Virgen María a los Cielos; the Indigenous drummers drumming on one side of the zocalo, the aerobics instructor prancing on the other; protesters protesting against NAFTA, placards on behalf of Zapatistas and teachers; a Harmonipan organ grinder with a pocked face saying "mi amor" to a sad street sweeper, giving her pesos from his collection hat before returning to his churlish music; a Native dancer in a feathered headdress as magnificent as Moctezuma's pausing to ponder the writhing serpents of the empire of Tenochtitlán being excavated beside the cathedral. He would forgo these glories because even if he was present, he wouldn't see them. He wouldn't have the heart to raise a margarita to the snowcapped Popocatépetl and Iztaccihuatl, even if he had caught sight of the volcanoes that were briefly visible after rain, like certain rare flowers.

The murderer will get me, and you'll be free of your mother.

Sunny disembarked at Guadalajara and took another bus to Manzanillo. Then another to Barra de Navidad, where a clown jumped on and tormented the passengers in the voice of a parrot until they paid him to hop off. From Barra de Navidad, Sunny took a country rattle-trap that labored among the fishing villages of the Costalegre, stopping where country paths emerged and country people stood waiting by the roadside with their heavy sacks and containers. When they arrived at the outskirts of a village on a bay surrounded by low jungle hills, Sunny got off. He tottered to the center and found it was deserted, holding only the enormous sun.

The murderer will get me, and you'll be free of your mother.

Where to take refuge? The door to a festooned church on one side of the zocalo creaked open. Sunny knelt down before the merciful Virgin, who occupied an alcove to the right of the martyred Christ, and burst into heaving tears, whether from the strain of the journey or from knowing his mother's death by murder would never free him. The church smelled medicinal and heavenly. He noticed in the dark another on his knees, then several more immobile on the benches. Sunny was a mere speck of pain in an ocean of human pain, upon a planet of striving souls. The people praying alongside him didn't notice Sunny's weeping, their own problems so absorbing. It was not very strange in this country, a man who weeps before the Virgin of Guadalupe.

Sunny was as minuscule as an ant stepping back out of the church, slugging water from a giant bottle to keep from fainting, when he felt a breath on his neck. He jumped—who could be so close? He turned—

"What are you doing here, Ma?" His crying had summoned Babita! The Virgin had misunderstood his tears, thought he needed his mother, and conjured her! But he did *not* need his mother. He had fled his mother. But then he was without her, so why else would he be crying and praying in a far land before the Mother of God, who, like Babita, had lost both her husband and her son? The Virgin had naturally sided with the Mother. As any Indian goddess would have done.

Sunny envisioned Babita so clearly he wondered how she had managed to manifest herself so precisely—her hair neatly coiffed with a single silver streak to herald her years, a matching silver sari with two slim stripes at the hem, one of amethyst and one of carnelian, small

pearl clusters in her ears—repeating her mantra of being an ambassador for her nation when she traveled abroad. Not that India was worth
her effort, but still, what could one do but do what one could? Even
here, in a little village washed up on the bay, before jungle hills that
traveled in waves up to a volcano blowing smoke rings. Why hadn't
Sunny stayed in Mexico City? They might have seen it together!

*But there's no point in sulking. I'm not one to hold a grudge. That's one
thing I can say for myself.*

Don't follow me, Mother! I came so far to get away!

*You are alone and I am alone—we have only each other. It's natural we
should travel together.*

Sunny felt Babita's longing like a yoke upon him: *Life! Son! Adventure! Brave new world!*

Afternoon progressed to evening, the shade extended, shutters
were raised, people emerged, waiters began setting up tables. A man
with a stoat on a rope walked by. Someone appeared to be selling an
ointment made from iguanas out of a pickup truck. By dusk came a
band lugging giant, polished instruments. They wore jackets and bole-
ros embroidered with gold flames; their trousers had gold flames siz-
zling down the seams. A little boy practiced a bullfighting move with a
red flag. A lady complained that her son was with *una mujer sucia.* A
mime performed heartbreak. The Virgin was giving Sunny reasons to
find his courage—how could he not feel exalted? From the little band-
stand with a decorative cupola, the musicians began to *oompah-pah*
under the moon that expanded upward like a fire balloon. This brave
new world may subtract his personal pain, it may fill him with beauty
now that he'd emptied himself of his tears. *Don't hang your eyes on me,
Mother! Your eyes are committing suicide on my eyes!*

People danced with restraint and nobility, and without a flicker of
expression. Among them a young couple, controlled and serious, an
occasional glimmer of humor in their movements, an impulsive, loosening gesture before a return to curtailed formality. When this couple,
dressed all in white, passed by, Sunny saw that while the girl's beehive
hairstyle and clothes were those of someone older, her face revealed
her to be perhaps sixteen or seventeen, and the boy was equally young.

In between dances, they greeted their elders respectfully, not realizing the strength their elders received from watching them. Nor, as they danced in and out of the pools of light from the lamps, did they consider they might have returned a scourged traveler to his memories—that he might experience the contradiction of having seen a joyful sight that made a long journey worthwhile and the melancholy of having squandered his own true love in his own true life. Feeling his mother's thwarted love instead. *Don't follow me, Mother!* The phantom of Babita shimmied her shoulders and tossed her head.

The village danced until a pickup truck arrived. The band members stopped their playing, staggered their instruments into the vehicle, climbed in, and drove off down a road that ended in jungle and hidden farm plots, buzzing with myriad insects, as if they reverberated from within one's blood.

Sunny slept at a beachside campsite near a graveyard for fisherfolk, which offered hammocks under a palapa thatch. Here he fell more gravely sick: fever, nausea, a burning head, frozen feet, Montezuma's revenge—even against an Indian, albeit an Indian American. He suffered mixed-up nightmares of iguanas and scorpions that may have been real-life occurrences at the camp, and now the ghosts of his uncles and of Vini-Puni joined the phantom of his mother: *Where are our feet? Our feet have gone! Where are our eyes? Our eyes have gone.* Oh, why had he settled near a graveyard? He heaved, he jabbered, he clawed at his heart in anguish like a man driven to pluck out his own torment. *Where are our hands? Our hands have gone. Where are our heads? Our heads have gone.*

After these hallucinatory episodes—when the sun rose and the light extended over the dry hills on the opposite side of the bay before slowly traveling across the water toward Sunny—he lay still in his hammock and observed nothing more than the heat stealing the moisture from under his eyelids. A vulture with a prospecting eye tested him for further signs of lifelessness. They spent a long, patient time looking at each other, eye into eye. Who would give up first?

When he managed to drag himself back to the village center, the pharmacist at the farmacia diagnosed him simply with the gripa. Beckoning him to the side of the counter where she sat surrounded by long-haired daughters and their babies, she pulled down his loose pants and injected him straight into the behind with antibiotics.

He crawled to the shops for supplies and stopped at a delicatessen that advertised a chicken curry pie. The owner was Irish Canadian, one in the small community of year-round gringos, friendly to Sunny because if you unraveled connections back to their grandparents' time, they had a mutual history of being abused by the English. He said that perhaps the red tide invasion of ocean algae had infected Sunny— every now and again it washed into the bay, rusty red, with an overpowering mineral stink. Or maybe it was that the dog turds in the streets had dried and the dog-turd dust blowing on the wind had affected him.

"Try my curry pie, it'll cure you."

"My stomach can't take spice!"

"An Indian who cannot take spice?"

Rejection of spice is like rejection of Mother!

A cheerful chef of pre-Hispanic foods—who worked at a treehouse restaurant favored by snowbird gringos who wintered in Mexico— came to the campsite bearing gifts. He'd heard from the pieman about Sunny and wanted to know this weird visitor. No doubt Indians from India were related to the Indigenous of Mexico? His brother, a shaman, had uncovered similarities in the spiritual realm, in which the shadows of all things become the other if you pursue them long enough. When he told Sunny the ingredients in what he'd brought— perhaps he had been influenced by the Hallmark vocabulary transported by gringos—he always added at the end: *y amor!*

"Huauzontles—*y amor!* Frijoles, epazote—*y amor!* Tomatillo, serrano—*y amor!*"

Ulla would say, "The love is in the sauce," which had always irritated Sunny. He wanted only sauce in his sauce. Or, if anything, a touch of irony in his sauce, or the devil in his sauce, or sauciness in his sauce.

"Please leave amor out! I'm allergic to it," begged Sunny. "I need to stay away from amor—it's what has made me so ill in the first place."

The pre-Hispanic-cuisine chef had learned to cook a curry in Monterey. He said some Indian road workers had taught him so it was the real thing, as opposed to the fake curry baked in a pie sold by the Irishman with a Canadian passport.

Road workers in Mexico could be Indians from India? Who knew?

"I can make it for you—your ears will sweat."

"No!" Sunny's stomach squelched. "No *chilies*! No *amor*!"

What a contrarian! Whatever had happened to *Namaste! I bow to the divine in you, which is reflected in the divine in me*? Sunny wasn't using his culture to any advantage. If he were savvy he might team up with his shaman brother to make a tremendous business with the gringos, moving suavely from a Hallmark vocabulary to satsang, then to Indigenous drumming and chanting: *Be the light! Be the love! I am the light! I am the love! You are the light! You are the love!*

Sunny thought he was in an upside-down mirror of his life. That Mexico presented the United States in an upside-down mirror, he may have predicted, but that it could also present India upside down was a revelation. When the pre-Hispanic chef left, Sunny, without light, without love, clutched his stomach and closed his eyes. Lime and gray, pink and puce, played on his lids as he remembered how Satya would go to the card shop in Defence Colony market just to browse because he loved cards and the language of cards. He had once surprised Sunny with a card of two bears sitting side by side fishing. It was a supersize card—because the more you love someone, the bigger the card you choose:

> *You were my pal when I was sad*
> *You stuck by me when things were bad*
> *Now that I am on the mend*
> *I want to shout out, Thank you, dear friend!*

Sunny wished he could speak to Satya about his mother's terror lassoing him on the other side of the world. He crawled to the zocalo phone carrying the long-distance phone card with a toucan on it that he'd purchased at the airport. Flesh-and-blood Babita said, "Sunny, I made a decision—I'll be joining you in Mexico!"

"How can you come? You lost your fortune!"

"I'll sell a piece of jewelry. It's silly to stash it in a bank safe—waiting for what, your future wife? These days girls don't wear heavy pieces."

First thing the next morning, Sunny returned to the phone. "I think it may be too dangerous for you to come. This country has a strain of violence. They recently found heads on stakes in Guadalajara, and decapitated heads were rolled onto a disco floor in Michoacán. A group of lefty students were tortured and killed and their bodies dissolved in acid. Entire towns and states are shut down by the cartels. Wealthy people are being kidnapped. Journalists are being killed like canaries in a coal mine."

"Danger? Danger is *here*! Danger was your uncles being murdered on the other side of the wall! I am too scared to stay through the monsoon."

"What does the monsoon have to do with it?"

"Because the police sleep through the monsoon—not that one can trust them in other seasons!"

"I only just arrived. I can't plan a vacation now."

"Don't then. Vanya said she'd be delighted to come with me."

"Vanya! How will she take a flight? You said she cannot stop smoking."

"She can manage if she takes a sleeping pill. She said to me, 'If Sunny won't go with you, I'll come.'"

Sunny sat on a bench and put his head in his hands. Mexico may have ancient troubles, but its mornings were fresh and young. The day at its dawning smelled of oranges being squeezed by the juice seller. It smelled of the last bit of night escaping as people opened their doors. It smelled of the pomade and cologne of the man who ran the internet center. It smelled of morning suds from the stones being scrubbed outside the village bakery, which also smelled of sweet, glazed rolls. Marmalade-colored wasps flew into the bakery honey. A little boy skipped to school, shining like the sun, or an orange, or a honey-glazed roll, that is how much his mamita loved him, scrubbed him, anointed him with brilliantine. The fountain outside the church turned on, and he shouted, "*Arriba! Arriba!*"

61

....

IT WAS A WEEK BEFORE SUNNY FELT BETTER AND BEGAN TO explore. One day he spotted a sign outside a one-room home that said *Renta o Venta*. The house was a single-story, coral-like layer of white-washed brick and mortar, but it had the aspect of something more special because it was surrounded by a garden of organ pipe cacti tall as trees, and also thorned bearded cacti, and swollen blue-green succulents towering high. A ladder led to the roof, where he may sit under a shady palapa thatch and watch the pelicans clumsily fishing, the dolphins dexterously cornering shoals into the bay, a cloud of startled tiddlers jumping. A rusty bicycle was propped against the wall. Sunny went to the bank in Melaque for the pesos to pay the owner, who was also the caretaker of the graveyard, and then he settled alone in a country where nobody else appeared to be alone—without love in a country famous for being in love with romantic love and without music in a place where it was unthinkable to live without music, maintaining it a matter of principle not to dance in a place where everyone danced. While people may have looked curiously at the gaunt stranger with tomcat eyebrows hobbling by in an Indian fisherman's gamcha lungi, and while they were kind because they were naturally kind to strangers, their own happiness and sadness were all-consuming, requiring so much chattering, so much gathering, so many funerals, weddings, baptisms, quinceañeras, religious holidays and saints' days, civic processions, and death and birth anniversaries of revolutionaries and martyrs. There was so much life in this country that Sunny needn't bother to create one. His life could be simply looking upon life.

In the afternoons it rained—it had turned to rainy season here, too—and Sunny read in his hammock a heavy volume of Latin American history from the secondhand charity bookstore that sold mostly beach reads donated by gringos to raise money for children's scholarships. He read about colonists and dictators, coups and revolutions, gold, silver, oil, bananas, and cocaine. He thought that just as you should live in India to know the British the way you never would from living in England, you should live in Mexico to know the Spanish and the United States, to gain insight into what made the United States shine, *I won, I won! I'm winning! I will win! I'm the most powerful! I am the greatest! I love myself! So much!*

He read Frida Kahlo's diary in Spanish. The words were simple and strange because they came straight from the soul. He examined his fingers instinctively to make sure they hadn't been bloodied by her bloody paintings of hearts, wombs, and accidents.

One day Sunny arrived at the charity bookstore just as a bundle of *Artes de México* was brought in. An expat had died, and his fanciful villa was being emptied for sale. *Artes de México* was the inspiration for *Kala* magazine, for which Sonia had written, Sunny recalled, and he bought them all. There was an issue on the architect Luis Barragán with an introduction by poet Octavio Paz, who had written *In Light of India,* to suggest that Barragán's modernism had its roots in ancient Mexico. There was one on huipils; one on insects in Mexican art; one on retablos—the Virgin had protected so many from flood and from fire, from border crossings, but she hadn't saved Sunny from Babita; instead she had saved Babita from her son's abandonment.

Sunny picked up the volume on foreign artists who had worked in Mexico. Some were muralists, some photographers, many of them were interested in the surreal. Pablo O'Higgins and Edward Weston, Tina Modotti and Leonora Carrington, Carlos Mérida and Cartier-Bresson, Remedios Varo and Kati Horna. The last profiled painter in this grand company was Ilan de Toorjen Foss. Sunny sat there in his little jungle shack and stared at Ilan, whose distinguished face looked away toward his collection of clay creatures from pre-Hispanic funerary shafts. Some of these graves were from the same Pacific coast where Sunny was living now and their contents had washed up on Tenacatita

Bay. Some had been excavated by archeologists, some by farmers plowing their fields. He saw clay coatis that seemed alive, that would always be alive as long as the clay did not crumble. He saw sleeping potbellied dogs, a cicada, a stingray coasting, moray eels, hummingbirds—a lost world of nature.

And he found himself trembling. Why? It didn't have to do with de Toorjen Foss. He was experiencing the beauty of these creatures and the lost bounty of the planet. Imagine a time when humans lived a life cut to size, simply one of many creatures, outnumbered. These animals were made by artists who wished for the opposite of fame. They didn't want to be known; they didn't sign their names at the bottom of their creations. They simply wished for what they loved to live forever.

How could a hound have come out of the ocean, attacked Sonia and himself, and melted into the sand when it had previously been in Ilan's painting? Sunny remembered Sonia's quaking fear. The fear indicated a crime. He was angry at himself, but he greedily turned the page to a canvas Ilan had been working on. It depicted a woman with an eye reflected in a many-paneled mirror, projected to eternity. One hoped she might escape into the myriad reflections of her own eyes, for it was obvious there was nowhere else for her to go but through the looking glass.

Was it Sonia's eye? It was. No, it wasn't—or was it? Sunny had a flash of insight: The eyes in the portraits by Ilan were all Ilan's eyes—everyone he painted became trapped in his gaze, everyone he painted turned into him.

Ilan de Toorjen Foss had apparently told Sonia's story. But there was a story behind that story. A story that lived behind a story that had been told was often a story that could not be told because the person who could tell it had been destroyed.

*

A LARGE SHELL WANDERED into Sunny's home at midnight; the creature inside peeped out, ran clackety-clack on the tiles under the wardrobe, peeped out, withdrew, and clackety-clacked under the fridge, going the wrong direction from freedom always, drawn by instinct toward the worst option. Why should Sunny trust in what he was thinking? The creature put out a sad eye and a beak; it cried a salt tear. It closed itself in when Sunny caught it in his bucket and released it back onto the beach. Shells skittered sideways across the sand. It felt like watching magic, but of course it was just creatures under the moon, running about the way they were supposed to run about in the moonlight.

Sunny called Babita from the pay phone in the zocalo with his toucan phone card. He looked around to make sure nobody overheard, by chance, the words "murder" or "black money."

Babita said the voltage stabilizer had burnt out in a puff of smoke, and the lightbulbs had exploded. She was without light.

"Didn't you ask Olinda to change the lightbulbs?"

"She doesn't have it in her; she isn't so bright."

"Not bright enough to change a lightbulb? What about Naresh?"

"Naresh? He's too smart!"

"Too smart to change a lightbulb? Then how will you manage? I can't fly from Mexico to India to change a lightbulb."

"Sunny Bhatia! I've been managing by myself all my life, haven't I?"

She said the bandicoots were stealing the fruit and the soap.

She told him the lizard that lived behind the toilet tank and ran out in terror when she sat on the potty had dropped its tail.

She told him she'd seen a snake slithering along the high rafters. The snake catchers told her it was an iridescent serpent, so they recognized it was a deity and respectfully bowed and set it free. Babita had scolded them. "What superstitious rubbish! No wonder this nation will never succeed."

She said the poi wallah bicycled too fast to be an effective bread seller. He poop-pooed his horn from the street to the right, and by the time you got there, he was at the street to the left. He excited the stray dogs, who created a ruckus gamboling after him. She had to enter the melee to purchase her morning bread as it whizzed by, and she had fallen, spraining her ankle, so she was hobbling in pain.

"Who will buy your morning poi for you now that you can't chase after the poi wallah?"

"Nobody."

Lightheaded, Sunny went to Palapa Bob's, a beach shack by the rocky cliffs. He took his notebook along so he might return to his previous habit of inscribing everything down. One day it might settle into sense. On the television playing behind the bar, there was news of a drug boss in Manzanillo who had escaped the police through the city sewer system. What if he popped up here? Rumor had it that he planned to build a five-star resort at the tip of Tenacatita Bay and was already paying off the gobernador. Sunny ordered a beer.

"Man, your Spanish sounds like you're speaking Hindu," said Bob, the owner of Palapa Bob's, a gringo from Wyoming whose own Spanish was extended by such an elastic twang that people giggled when he spoke. Bob went by "El Camarón" because he had turned as pink as shrimp when he moved under the Mexican sun to stretch what little he had after a third divorce. He lived on a jungle plot that had a resident toad—large and warty, the kind you could lick for hallucinogenic effects—and for six hundred dollars a month, he told Sunny, he could live here easy. Sunny must try Raj, the excellent Indian restaurant in Puerto Vallarta owned by an Englishman named Billy from Leeds. "You can get a curry for like two dollars." Listening in, a gringo sitting on a barstool made from a tree stump said resentfully, "When I was in India, I could eat two idlis for fifteen cents."

That gringo refrain: "*So cheap!*" Sunny heard it spilling triumphantly from Palapa Bob's and Bar Bambu, from the zocalo benches, from the taxis ferrying gringos from the Manzanillo airport to their fantasy jungle and oceanside homes:

One peso for two dinner rolls!

Dental work in Barra de Navidad, forty-five dollars? In the States it would be a thousand!

A gardener, only sixty pesos an hour?

Thirty-five pesos per square meter! I don't believe it!

The bar may be owned by El Camarón, but it was manned by a local boy named Ulises. Ulises did not know what to do with his dilemma of hating the "*It's so cheap!*" expats, snowbirds, tourists—upon whose money he also depended. Well, that was most of the world's problem.

When there were no white people around Ulises told Sunny that in all of the six years he'd spent in the United States, only three fucking white people had ever been nice to him. He pulled at his angel curls. "They all fucking come here and buy all the best fucking houses on the beach. Then when we go there, they treat us so fucking badly. When we come back here, to our own village, we have to work for the same fuckers. If they go back to their country, they sell the house they bought from us for nothing to another gringo for a million!"

He liked Sunny because despite his green card and desi Spanish accent, he was not a gringo. Sunny tried to persuade him this was not a good reason. "If you met ten Indians, you wouldn't like me, either."

Sunny mentioned he'd passed a crocodile while swimming in the ocean. When he scurried from the water, he saw three of them coasting the waves with their jaws open, swimming toward Boca de Iguanas. Shouldn't he be worried?

Ulises said the crocodiles swam between the mangrove swamps in search of love, or else to follow the fish shoals. In the old days, before a fence was built and an ecological park established, the crocodiles would promenade down the main street—but the crocodiles of this particular village never attacked people.

"Why?"

"We feed them."

"With what?"

"Dead dogs. Whenever a dog dies we throw it over."

*

ONE MORNING, PASSING BY Palapa Bob's on his way to the internet center, Sunny stopped to greet Ulises: "Buenos días." Ulises, who slept in a plywood cabin on the fetid creek behind, was sleepily cleaning up the slop of the night before, raking the sand clean. He had turned on the television, as he always did as soon as he entered. It was the anniversary of the military coup in Chile. A grainy clip played of Hawker Hunter jets bombing the presidential palace in 1973, followed by Allende's last speech at La Moneda before he shot himself and the junta took over—the same footage Sunny's Spanish teacher had showed his class. Sunny stopped to watch, when suddenly the story on the television switched—

In New York City, upon a perfect blue-sky morning—a plane had flown into the World Trade Center.

"Fuck!" said Ulises. Bob came racing his scooter from where he lived in a jungle hamlet. The shaman had shouted the news into his window as if he had known in advance. Standing side by side, the three of them watched the planes flying into the twin towers, people jumping from the skyscrapers, a plane crashing into the Pentagon in Arlington, and then the news that a flight heading to the White House or U.S. Capitol had crashed, killing everyone on board.

The foreigners arrived: a Dutch couple who had bicycled through Asia; a Frenchman who had spoken to Sunny about the shock of seeing dead people, cows, and dogs floating together in the Ganga; an elderly Texan and her young Mexican horse trainer with whom she was having an affair; a yoga instructor from Mount Shasta who planned to team up with the shaman to organize an Equinox for Peace; the sports fishermen. They watched President George W. Bush being given the news of the attack while attending a classroom reading of *The Pet Goat,* and some of the expats stood outside with their mobile phones trying to reach friends in New York City, though it was impossible to get through. Afternoon turned into evening, evening to past midnight. They continued watching, beer and tequila flaming down their throats. "Cowards!" yelled Bob. "They are *fucking cowards*!" He got up, gave a finger to the stars. "*Cowards!*"

The creek where a young crocodile had become separated from the other crocodiles in the mangroves smelled putrid as it glided about and stirred the miasma, and a cloud of mosquitoes came swarming. "Well, they are not cowards," Sunny spoke up, "whatever else they are. It takes guts to fly a plane into the World Trade Center, to attack the U.S. government, to kill yourself and others. They are obviously trying to start a war."

Bob shouted, "They are *fucking cowards,* do you understand?" And he pointed at Sunny, as if with a pistol. "You kill innocent people, you are a *coward,* that is what you are!"

Sunny understood this was not the time to initiate a tally of innocent civilians killed by American bombs and gunfire. Still, his restraint, his silence, his behaving as if he was mature and Bob was immature, demonstrated he had not been properly affected by the disaster but remained at a distance from it, as he was apparently at a distance from all things.

Infuriated, Bob wanted to kill Sunny's immigrant-enemy-distance. He realized that Sunny had always annoyed him, creeping creepily about the village, suspiciously alone, behaving as if he was a cut above the expats, sitting silently at a table with his watchful expression and diving, judgmental eyebrows, making notes—to what purpose? Why was he here? He might be a fugitive; he behaved as if he was guilty.

"You immigrated to the States," he said. "It was your dream that the U.S. handed you on a platter, so why are you siding with the attackers? *Why aren't you grateful?*"

Sunny recalled the day his green card arrived. It was true he hadn't felt gratefulness; he had felt overwhelming relief. If he had felt grateful, it was gratefulness he was saved from Babita, from India, from his natural fate.

Perhaps because of Bob's hostility—besides the honest truth—Sunny pushed back. He answered, "The U.S. is built on the labor of immigrants. The United States should be grateful to Mexicans!"

Said Bob, "It's because of the U.S. that you're here in Mexico. It's because of the U.S. that I'm here leading this good life. If I were Mexican, I'd be trying to get to the U.S." Sunny's face showed he could not understand the logic of Bob's patriotism. "Who gave you an education?" asked Bob. "Who gave you a job? How are you here? Why don't you head back to India?"

"Calm down, guys," said the Dutch couple.

"Hey, hey," said the Frenchman.

The yoga teacher said, "The problem everywhere is out-of-control, aggressive male energy." She wore a T-shirt with *LOVE* written in rainbow colors across the front.

Bob got even angrier, and as Sunny got up to leave, he aimed a tequila bottle at Sunny's head. Sunny ducked. The bottle narrowly missed him and shattered upon the wall. Glass flew about and cracked the television. Tequila splashed across Sunny's face and his mustard kurta.

He heard someone mutter, "He may be Moslim?"

Ulises squeezed Sunny's shoulder as Sunny pressed by him on his way out and whispered, "In the end someone does it back to you."

When Sunny was at home in *Renta o Venta,* his heart still palpitating, a stray triangle of glass fell out of a crease in his bag without his noticing. When he took his slipper off, he stepped on it, and it deeply pierced his foot. When he pulled out the glass, blood gushed forth. He left bloody footprints as he searched for a dishcloth to bind his foot because he didn't have a bandage.

Despite the humiliation and fright of having had a tequila bottle launched at his skull, Sunny thought that Bob was right to have thrown it. He must have intuited the truth. The truth—and Sunny would have admitted it to nobody—was that while he felt incredulous horror, secreted within the horror, in the crosshatches and shadings of incredulity that anybody would dare such a thing, when the World Trade Center towers fell with the same ruthless lack of care for human life as Americans expressed when they went abroad on war or business, he had thought, in the deepest recesses of his mind: *Let them see what it is like!*

But he himself had no clue what it was like! He himself was far removed from an experience of American bombs falling upon him. He knew, meanwhile, that the men who flew those planes would kill him, Sunny, without mercy. He shared nothing of their beliefs, their way of life. He was on the exact opposite side—irreligious, Westernized—so why did he feel this way? He realized also that while he felt so sorry for the waiters who had died, he felt less sorry for the bankers; he thought that the death of poor people mattered more than the death of rich people, although he himself—heir to the three-hundred-year-old Casa das Conchas—counted as a very rich person. He realized that he had never noticed the World Trade Center towers because he was not fond of tall skyscrapers and had never sought the landmark out; he had an innate cynicism for what it represented. Just as he had never been to the grand shops, not Bergdorf Goodman, not Tiffany, scandalizing Babita. Later, when he saw the photographs of the altered skyline, he couldn't tell that two buildings were missing. And despite having been given every break by the United States and its citizens—even if it had been paid for with his family's black money—instead of being thankful, he began to suspect that he was camouflage, a story that hid the truer story, the clown show to detract from sinister goings-on, part of the problem, not the solution.

Gamcha lungi hitched high, Sunny bicycled past the crocodiles in the mangrove ecological park to the village internet center every day to jealously read the articles he might have been assigned to write were he still working his way up the ladder at the Associated Press. On the streets of New York, Sikhs were being attacked because they wore turbans and beards and might as well be Osama bin Laden. Dominicans and Puerto Ricans were being attacked because they might as well be Arabs. A Bangladeshi man was arrested for driving from Jackson Heights to Canada with pressure cookers for his relatives, which he might have been planning to refurbish with explosives. A Jewish man had been attacked because he had a beard and was driving a nondescript white van about the airport. In fact, he was a performance artist making an oblique statement via an art project sponsored by a liberal-arts collective operating out of Tel Aviv. The Sikh academic who had run for his life as men chased him across the Brooklyn Bridge had been compelled to remove his turban and cut his hair, the same way his father in Delhi had been compelled to do after the violence that followed the assassination of Indira Gandhi by her Sikh bodyguards.

Along with such articles, the American news agencies began to publish the obituaries of those who had died. While obituaries printed in the national press are usually about men and women of note—those who are born famous or have magnificently attained their potential— the obituaries of the victims of September 11 were accounts of ordinary people, and sometimes it was as heartbreaking to read about their living as it was about their dying. Some had only acquaintances to make impersonal observations:

Lenny was private and reserved. He had a poodle, Tomboy. He kept a photograph of Tomboy on his desk.

Julio came from Venezuela. Nobody really knew him. He was divorced, and he lived alone. His family was somewhere in Venezuela.

Voahirana loved shoes, and on her lunch break, she went to shoe sales. On Saturdays she took the train to visit her elderly mother, who lives in a nursing home for Alzheimer's patients in Poughkeepsie.

Sunny thought the dead would be humiliated to read their obituaries and, again, as with his innermost thoughts on the attacks, he thought he should keep these illicit notions to himself. It was not fair to opine that someone who had a quiet life, a darling dog, a love for shoes, a mother to visit (one whose mind would hopefully not retain the news of her daughter's demise), might not have had a life quite as meaningful as a life brimful.

Had Sunny been killed, his co-workers would have had to rack their brains to think of something to say to the journalist who was perhaps reporting the story from a desk in their own newsroom. Had they contacted Ulla, she might have identified him with the emotions that had led the terrorists to attack a symbol of capitalist pride, but Sunny trusted she wouldn't divulge this to the press—Ulla was never vengeful. What would his neighbors in Jackson Heights say? They would say he most definitely had a mother: *When will Mummy come? Mummy must come! Everyone should live together!*

It was now he received an email from Satya: *Are you all right?* Satya was the one person in the world other than Babita who would have plenty to tell an obituary writer. Sunny immediately wrote back: *Yes, I'm not in New York City. I am living in a village on the Mexican coast. Are you all right?* He ventured: *Where are you?*

Bob happened to walk in. When he saw Sunny, he went back out, plucked a bird-of-paradise flower from the bush outside, reentered, walked up, and presented it to Sunny with a bow. He said, "I apologize. If we fight we are giving the terrorists what they want." They should be bonding in the face of evil, not tearing themselves apart. Bob, El Camarón, was a Mexican resident and a Polish American, but he was an American first. He tried to explain himself to Sunny. His parents were immigrants. "They were so proud. We always had a flag flying outside our home. It seems like nobody cares anymore. And when you look at the rest of the world, and then you look at the States, you think, well, it's not so bad. Why is everyone constantly attacking it when it's where everyone wants to be?"

It was at this moment, Sunny felt gratefulness. He felt grateful to Bob for using his sentimental emotion resulting from the atrocity to reconcile. Should he write to Sonia? *Look, just come! We will get over it— whatever it was. Everyone should live together.* This calamitous event might be a way to overcome the shame that had taken root between them. But what would Sonia rightfully say? *Why tell me to come now? Do you need an act of terrorism to desire my presence? Had the towers not blown up— what then?*

He hoped Satya would reply to him. He went back several times to check, but there was nothing, and Sunny continued to read the avalanche of news stories and opinion pieces from all around the world. One by a pundit in *The Santiago Times,* the newspaper to which Sunny had once applied for an internship, reported that it felt to them in Chile as if the United States had stolen the Chilean day of disaster—which was, after all, instigated by the United States—and had now made it their *own* day of disaster. He wrote that he couldn't rid himself of the suspicion that the two September 11s were twinned—Chile and the United States, part of the same story in ways not obviously apparent. When the dead were tallied, the number of victims was spookily similar, as if there were a kabbalah-like spell in motion. Then Sunny read and contemplated the fact that members of the bin Laden family were business associates of the Bush family and had been airlifted to safety after the terrorist attack plotted by Osama bin Laden, a member of their sprawling clan.

How would the dead be memorialized in addition to their obituaries? Would the city of New York rebuild the World Trade Center even taller? With an ensconced memorial? Would tourists flock to the site of a memorial museum with enshrined objects from the rubble? If so, afterward, they would surely need to eat? They might go shopping to balance out the trauma, because you could only take so much misery when you were on holiday. Next to the site of death, would there be use for a luxury shopping mall? Informing the enemy they hadn't dented the American way of life? Where tourists could browse handbags, dresses, and shoes made in the sweatshops of Dhaka or Guangzhou? Perhaps these wealthy shoppers would include the relatives of the very same man responsible for the terrorist attack? In some countries, as in India, Saudi Arabia, and the United States, money was concentrated in a few dynasties.

The Man Who
Gets You
Will Be Really Lucky

....

MAYA MITHAL HAD WRITTEN TO ASK WHERE THE ARTICLE on Rajasthan was, with the travel logistics she had requested, and why had she been sent a bill for a broken pitcher? Sonia reached for her notes: Could she fashion something for *Kala*? Instead of journalistic notes, she found the sketch for fiction she had been inspired to write just before Madan blustered in and placed his hands about her throat. *I love you very, very much.* Out of the small earnings from her previous articles, she mailed Maya a check for the broken pitcher and her hotel stays in Bikaner and Sardar Samand. She wrote that while she hadn't managed to complete this assignment due to the recurrence of her father's cancer, she would propose another article when she was able to leave her father's side—perhaps about her grandfather's paintings and the artists who traveled to India for inspiration. What had they been escaping? What had they been looking for?

Papa was also fretting about bills. He rummaged about his papers in the manner of Dadaji and Dari, finding and losing figures on a fickle solar-powered calculator. He called his stockbroker: Should he divest his stocks to pay his hospital bills? But he was loath to sell his stocks. He felt the panic of his father's ghost—*Never sell the principal!*—and felt compelled to heed this advice, even though he'd learned his father was a sham investor whose divisions served only to disguise the zero. It occurred to him that he might visit his bank locker to check if there was anything within that was worth selling.

Just like Mina Foi in Allahabad, Sonia scaled a rickety metal ladder to the safe in the Hauz Khas market bank branch, watched by a guard— thin as a bean, with an un-ferocious rifle that looked as if it dated to the

1800s, but with a very ferocious mustache. She unlocked the safe and handed down bundled plastic bags, boxes formerly used to present Diwali dried fruit and nuts, and the Pan Am and Aeroflot toilet cases that contained Mama's share of Ba's jewelry, given to her when she married Papa, including her mangalsutra, which a married woman is never supposed to remove. There was a single gold coin from Germany; bent medallions of dull gold alloyed with other metals; ladles and cream jugs bearing the initials of people whom nobody could remember.

She and Papa went to one of the many jewelry stores in South Extension for an assessment of the value. The shop was dimmed, the cases lit as if in a museum. The salesgirls were groomed like airline stewardesses, dressed in official silk saris, made up with flawless creamy faces and dewy, pink lips. One of these salesgirls cut the threads from the necklaces. She put the medals, chains, and bangles for babies in one pile. Papa threw in the cuff links Mama's family had given him. They had belonged to her father.

"Ha, your mother came with nothing to my house," he said, his jaw working in his cheek. "Where is that German coin? Get rid of it once and for all."

"It doesn't belong to you, it belongs to Mama. It may be worth more than the value of the gold. It could have come from Bismarck, who knows!"

He became violently emphatic—why had Sonia never condemned her mother to her father as she should have?—and he threw the gold coin into the mix with cruel rage, just as he used to throw Mama the household money each morning.

Sonia tried to control herself from responding to him, reminding herself that her father was ill.

Splotched yellow and purple, Papa tottered about looking into the display cases while he waited for the gold to be melted down to separate it from the other metal, for the exact carat to be ascertained. They would offer a separate price for the heavy necklaces, the head and foot ornaments, the nose rings from Gujarat.

Sonia ignored her father and watched a couple choosing a ring as if viewing a version of what her life might have been had she wedded an affluent businessman and escaped into the safety of money, the way all the rest of the *haha hoho* dinner-party daughters had done.

Papa's eye settled on an abstract design of diamonds fitted as sleekly together as serpent's scales. A man with an interest in art will naturally be interested in women's adornments. He asked to see the necklace. He held it up. His mood switched from his former fit of vengeance. He said, "How unusual. Sonu, I am going to buy this for you."

Sonia whispered, "I can't take that. You have to pay your hospital bills." The jewelry stewardesses didn't step aside as father and daughter disagreed but stared and listened openly, as if to shame them into a purchase.

"I have plenty of money."

"But you don't. That is why we are here."

"Tell your mother to send me all the money she owes me! Half that house in which she lives, by right of marriage, is mine. At least a crore's worth. She still owes me money for Chandu's wife's hospital bills! I told her to repay me—and *damn all!*"

"Papa, you're not to buy that necklace. I'm leaving the shop now."

"Get out, then. Scram."

She left her crudely speaking father and took a scooter rickshaw home. All along she muttered: "*I am angry, I am angry, I hate my father, I hate him, I hope he dies.*" The drama of his dying often felt false in the same way Dadaji's dying had seemed false to Mina Foi. This, and Papa's cruelty, helped keep Sonia going, for his cruelty allowed her to hate her father, which prevented her in turn from collapsing in grief.

And yet he was trying to give her a gift. Maybe he remembered what she told him had occurred in the hunting lodge at Sardar Samand and felt he had failed. A father of a previous generation would have made sure his daughter was married to a protector before he found himself dying. Now at least his daughter could possess a piece of jewelry—one she might adorn herself with if fortune smiled on her or that she could sell when fate doled her misfortune. The pain of it. The confusion.

To avoid speaking to each other that night, they put the news on extra loud. They looked down at their shepherd's pie, then they looked up in unison. It was a blue-sky morning in New York City, and a plane had flown into the World Trade Center. Then it flew into the World Trade Center again. Then again. The scene played over and over, and they kept watching as if in paralysis. Chandu came out of the kitchen to join them. Americans had been attacked. America would certainly go to war. But with whom would America urgently go to war?

Ilan! Was he in New York? thought Sonia. *Sunny! Was he in New York?* thought Sonia. Then she felt dread. Her first thought had revealed that Ilan still claimed her mind most powerfully, and wouldn't that mean she loved him more? Call it love, call it fear, call it her duty to run toward disaster to save Ilan, to put out the fire, or she wouldn't be safe from the conflagration herself.

But Sunny or no Sunny, Ilan or no Ilan, Sonia, who had once been a New Yorker, felt as if a dire, consummate event pertinent to herself had occurred. Once a New Yorker, always a New Yorker, no matter if one's experience there could be likened to a bucket with a hole. She experienced fascinated horror, and somewhere secreted within this horror, she felt a click-click of alignment. And within the crosshatches and shadings of this alignment was a secret comfort she would have admitted to no one: While her life felt like an emergency, the world outside was actually exploding. Her internal drama and this external drama were twinned. She felt, nether and dark, a small fanning out of the relief of a parallel disaster, a major world disaster to go with her own personal disaster. It was company to her, this bad news: Her father, herself, two men who did not love her, and the world, all going to damnation together.

"My God!" said Papa, watching in thrall. Sonia saw that his wide-open gaze glued upon the television had shaded into excitement: This event may be taking place far away, but here in Hauz Khas, too, some people like himself were frightened they would soon be departing for their final destination and believed that death was abnormal, although everyone had been telling them otherwise. He wasn't isolated, but part of a larger pattern of stolen lives and destinies.

Papa loved to attempt a Yankee accent. And before he had transformed into a Hindustani, he had listened to Frank Sinatra on Sunday mornings and Ella Fitzgerald on Friday nights. He'd sent his daughter to study in the States and been disappointed when she returned, although he had stepped up to the challenge: "India is your home! In case your green card did not come through, I told everyone you were not interested in becoming a second-class citizen elsewhere—so you don't have to feel ashamed now that you are back."

That night, she found the preposterous serpent necklace of diamonds on her pillow.

There was nothing to say but, "Thank you, Papa."

He said, "We've had some wonderful times together, Sonu. One day you'll have wonderful times with someone else. The man who gets you will be really lucky."

CHAPTER

63

....

THROUGH JUNE, JULY, AND AUGUST IT HAD RAINED. BABITA'S life continued to dwindle while the world about her brimmed and multiplied. Shadows slithered out of the drains, a salamander from the water filter. There were lizard droppings upon the dining table and rodent gashes in the soap. Babita might cut open her poi and find it teeming with minute red ants that also crowded upon the pineapple and excavated the cashews. Without her glasses on, she munched the ants.

She got up, she sat down, she stood by the window. She could see nothing before her eyes but the interminable rain, and at night, not even that. *Hellooo? Who? Kaun?* She couldn't see herself. Was she out there? She listened to the rain drip into buckets under leaks, emptied the buckets when they filled, out into the rain, the rain into rain, upon rain. She poured another rum. She had given up on hot water.

If the sound of the downpour lessened, her hopscotching thoughts were interrupted by the mournful glug of Pasha drinking from the toilet, which was a jungly habit he'd taken up. He had the stubbornness of age now—as well as the innate stubbornness he used to display sitting in the Lodhi Gardens sewage pond—and he could not be persuaded into returning to his water bowl. With his weak hind legs, he was unable to turn around in the narrow space the toilet occupied; he would get stuck and keep, like a mechanical toy gone wrong, trying to turn about and exit. Babita would lift him around and—blanketed in his hair and the gloom of his decline—sometimes sit distractedly on the toilet seat strewn with saliva and toilet water. Irate, she would roll up the O Heraldo and smack him on his snout and rear.

She would watch the television news when the electricity switched on, when a crow wasn't sitting on the antenna making the picture go wobbly. While in the past the newsreaders would speak in calm voices conveying reassurance and balanced consideration, now they spoke in shrill tones that created panic in a viewer's heart. They created the disaster before it occurred. They had reported on the Panchsheel Park murders in just such tones.

Babita switched the television off and opened a box of DVDs. She used to love an Agatha Christie film—now she was too scared to watch a murder mystery on her own. She started an episode of *To the Manor Born,* but it made her long too much for England. *Chori, chori, chori.* England had been stolen from her. By whom? *Kaun?*

When there was a break in the rain, to put off the expectancy that Sunny would telephone in the morning since he hadn't called the night before, Babita wiped the mold off her leather jootis and handbag and left for the Ocean of Stories bookshop at the Altinho cultural center in Panjim. They had invited her to join their reading group, but not only was it too far, it would also be pathetic to claim she loved to read simply to have company—like becoming a Buddhist because you were lonely. She was there for a specific reason, she informed them. Could they procure a travel guide for a distinguished traveler to Mexico? Because she would be visiting her son just as soon as he was properly settled in a larger town and properly enrolled in a Spanish program. Sunny may not want her to join him, but she didn't pay that pesky matter any attention; she would simply outlast his fussing until he felt guilty about the mean things he'd said.

The bookstore promised they would have one couriered from Mumbai, and Babita went to lunch at the Hotel Mandovi, where the atmosphere was like being in a museum of the past except for the size of the pomfret recheado. She summoned the waiter. He brought her complimentary prawn curry rice. She summoned him back. A gentleman seated at the neighboring table informed her that the minuscule prawns were the ones with flavor; Babita misunderstood the concept of the dish. It wasn't about a chunk of seafood with a tablespoon of sauce, it was about the flavorful gravy you needed to drench your rice. It was about the rice. He introduced himself as Gerson, the manager at the Pousada Fontainhas. His eyes were green and he carried a starched handkerchief embroidered with the crest of the family that had once owned the home that was now the pousada.

Babita felt a flutter in her lower abdomen. When you are lonely and need to make friends fast, you want to lure a promising stranger with your most compelling story. Babita longed to tell him about the Spode egg cups and the Panchsheel Park house, but she remembered her spurned confession to Vanya, her spurned conversations with Sara.

This man was unknown to her, and light eyes were suspicious when they lived in a dark face, she thought. Then she deliberated that this made no sense. And light eyes also made her feel as if the gentleman were apart from society—and a person apart from society was someone she could more freely tell her story to. But a person apart from society was more untrustworthy. But then again, to a stranger, you could tell falsehood after falsehood, looloo after looloo.

She said: "Can you imagine, less than a year ago I was supervising a staff of five, traveling the world with my son."

"You moved here alone?" he asked. "That's brave."

"My son won a travel grant," she said, feeling proud, "and moved to Mexico. He gets his gypsy genes from me."

"Aren't you the new owner of Casa das Conchas?"

"However did you know?"

"This is Goa, word gets around. Are you settling in?"

"I confess I am not. I won't tell a lie; all my life I've been an honest person and paid the consequence. The bandicoots steal my soap—they are too big for rat traps."

Gerson said they were plagued by bandicoots, hulking and silent, at the Pousada Fontainhas as well. He'd designed special traps, which he had forged at an ironworks. "I can bring them over for you."

Babita returned home, her heart like a dog on a leash, rushing, straining, hoping Olinda would say the phone had rung.

"No, madam, phone did not ring."

*

GERSON CAME BY WITH his men to set the bandicoot traps and back again the following day to check the traps. He reported they had killed a tribe of seven—babies and elders. Babita must not look, it was bloody genocide, but he showed Babita the gnawing in the wire netting in her bedroom that she hadn't noticed. The bandicoots had been trooping nose-to-tail soundlessly past her bed, past Pasha's bed, branching out to the kitchen for fruit, poi, and cashews, then to the bathroom to steal the soap.

He accepted a rum and nimbu, and again Babita imagined the quenching relief of telling a stranger about her innocence in murder. Gerson would have no reason to doubt her but she had every reason to doubt *him*! A man who killed animals could more easily kill people.

She admonished herself to continue to keep her silence.

The very time you planned to hold your silence was exactly when your tale came pouring out as if challenged by your vow of discretion. . . .

She must remain doubly alert. When you were doubly alert, you were twice as likely to betray yourself. . . .

She must be triply careful. . . .

But now she thought she caught something in Gerson's criminal eyes as well, and again she felt a flutter in her lower abdomen. It was a revelation—one she could hardly admit to herself with boundaries loosening away from Delhi society—that an older woman is quite as capable as an older man of being sexually aroused by a more youthful companion. Gerson must be at least a decade younger.

"Stay to dinner?" she invited. "My Olinda made stuffed crab."

"No, I must get going."

"One for the road?"

"I've had one for the road."

"One for the ditch?" She dangled the bottle.

He jumped up. "No!"

As she saw him out, she moved awkwardly to hug him, to thank him for his help—she longed for a strong embrace from someone, anyone.

Then, oh buzz of rum and rummy moon, she placed her mouth on his cheek. She had forgotten the feel of a man's hay stubble. She froze with her wet mouth on his face. She felt Gerson stiffen, recoil. He thrust her away and ran down the steps. The light went on in his jeep, and she saw him rinse his face out of the window with a plastic bottle of water before off he went, vroom-vrooming into the fruity night.

Babita continued to sit in the too-big planter's chair, alone with the lizards, the mosquitoes, the stray dogs with their lantern eyes of hunger skulking in the lane outside, the tree frogs exuberant in the bathroom, the fruit bats hanging upside down in the veranda doing upside-down colorful droppings down the wall. But *not* the bandicoots tonight. And nobody to *not* tell the story of her innocence upon a night of murder.

It was still raining when Babita collected *Mexico Past and Present* from the Ocean of Stories bookstore. She set two twisty candles into two twisty, silver candlesticks when the electricity failed, sipped her rum, and underlined pertinent information. Mexico had won its independence in 1821. What was the matter with the Spanish? The British had managed to stick on in India until 1947. The Portuguese stayed in Goa until they were bombed by the Indian air force in 1961, the last troops drunk on feni crawling out of the taverna.

And what was *Mexico Past and Present* saying about the pillage and barbaric enslavement of Spanish rule? It was hard to accept. Why? Because what you find beautiful, you also find good. She underlined that Porfirio Díaz had modeled Mexico City on Paris. She thought the dictatorship of Porfirio Díaz was obviously a lucky interlude for Mexico.

She opened her wardrobe and began putting aside the saris she might take with her—this crinkled pink in the gulab of India, surely sister to the rosa of Mexico? Would she be considered an elegant ambassadress? Or were Mexicans like Indians, happiest when white people visited their country, believing other brown, and browner, people to be lower than themselves?

In any case, how could she afford to go? But she needed to. This was the truth, therefore nothing else could be allowed to be true.

Thus Babita was conspiring with herself when, one day after the rains were over, she opened her door to a lady under five feet tall holding her umbrella against the sun. She had a bun; a neat, flowered cotton frock; a neck brace; and plastic sandals. Her name, she said, was Edelweiss. She owned, she said, the corner of the property that was occupied by the well.

"What do you mean by that?" asked Babita.

She said there was a well at the back of the property, and it was her well. Along with sisters Ida and Clotildes, she owned the well, the water in the well, the driveway, and that corner where they had buried Daddy.

"What do you mean, 'Daddy'?"

"Daddy was a crooner on the ships," said Edelweiss. "He traveled the seven seas, then he came home to rest."

"Here?"

Sure enough, buried deep in the thicket to the side of the property was a wrinkly gravestone Babita had never noticed.

"We learned the property was sold," said Edelweiss. "We never gave our permission. Permission needs to be collected from sixty-three direct descendants. We span the globe. We would like to build a house, us three sisters."

"But there isn't any room to build."

"We'll build right here, by the well and Daddy's grave."

"But then how will I access the water?" asked Babita.

Another resident of the vaddo by the name of Adolf came by when Edelweiss left to say that Edelweiss's ancestors had been employed by the family of the big house and that they had claimed a plot of land legally through squatters' rights—then life had taken them elsewhere. But Goan property was now valuable, so they had returned.

What solace was that?

The bent woman who lived in the perilous ruin near the bottom of the driveway came over, her tortoise head at the level of her waist. She told Babita that she was, in fact, the owner of the driveway and also the love apple tree—her ancestors had been residents the longest, and it was only due to her generosity that Babita could access her home from the road, although she would now prefer to be compensated.

Harsh life had made her neighbor harsh, thought Babita, *but then what solace was that?*

She telephoned the number she had for Umberto. He sounded frustrated and said in a tone that implied it was Babita's fault that he didn't enjoy Milan, it wasn't an empathetic city, it wasn't a *conducive* city. He preferred Rome, but it was impossible to make a change. He'd never heard of Edelweiss. The deed to the house was clear, he'd been told, although foreigners couldn't buy in India, and he had purchased the property through a young Goan. Babita would recall the owner had been listed as a "Selwyn" in the mess of power-of-attorney documents and various other papers. In Goa the paperwork was a thousand times more complicated than anywhere else. "I think, Babita, they may be asking to be paid off. Every new owner presents a new opportunity to make money."

"Would Selwyn know anything about Edelweiss? Can you ask him?" Babita pressed.

Selwyn had left for Kuwait with the money Umberto had given him. "I thought there was some genuine feeling. But once he knew he wouldn't be getting any more cash from me, he vanished."

"That's how it is," concurred Babita. Despite her fury, her sympathy was still situated on the same side as the white person in distress. "I had thought my maids had some grateful regard and honest affection for me—but I was someone to be made use of, that was all." If she rode the tide, the universe would gradually shift her gently to the other side of blame.

"Don't let anyone scare you," said Umberto. "It's the Goan way of life, you'll see. Someone in the village will wander into your garden for the hoe, someone will send around a section of coconut cake—it's neighborly. Yet every house will have a quarrel of some kind. Always a little property will be stolen here, occupied there, a boundary wall slyly moved. Goans have emigrated all over the world and properties are often untended—you must have seen all these oddly shaped bits of land? There are so many cases making their way slowly through the courts that grandsons inherit the lawsuits taken on by their grandfathers. For that reason alone, don't worry. Even if they take you to court, nothing will be resolved until long after your time on earth has passed. This is what Selwyn assured me."

Babita had not spoken to Vanya since Vanya's suggestion of sipping boiled water had delivered her a boiled lizard, but she was compelled to phone. And Vanya was compelled to answer, even though Babita had said, "But it's common knowledge what a crook Cecil was." Because this was friendship in their social class: Your friends were corrupt, so what were you going to do, have no friends? *Better two corrupt widows who might rat on each other than one corrupt widow. Better three corrupt widows who might tittle-tattle than nobody to tittle-tattle to.* Puffing on her cigarette, cradling the phone at her chin while she flipped open her portable cherry-blossom ashtray, Vanya said, "There were reports of jealous brawls. Selwyn was blackmailing Umberto." Once, as she was approaching Casa das Conchas, Vanya had overheard him shouting at Umberto, "*You want me to throw crap at you? You want me to throw crap at you?*" which was such a vulgar and bizarre combination of words. Where did they come from? Where did *he* come from?

"You have to be careful," Vanya had said to Umberto. "You can't go picking up boys on Baga Beach."

Umberto had become suddenly crude in a way that Vanya thought cruel. "That's how it happens, Vanya: You meet a boy on the beach, you fuck, he moves in—what did you think?"

"Didn't he say his sexual life was over?" Babita asked.

"Still, he did some fiddly nonsense and fell in love with every chokra who then made use of him," Vanya told Babita. "But in any case, I told you to go to a lawyer and make sure the deed to the house was clear."

"*You did not!*"

"Everyone knows you have to do that."

She suggested a lawyer in São Tomé.

*

ALOYSIUS DE NORONHA SAT at an ancestral desk of almost black teak carved with the sun and its rays. A fan stirred the air exactly right, like a spoon in thick vindaloo, enough for a current but not enough for important papers to take wing and plonk into Ourem Creek. His office was in the front room of his home, and from the interior wafted the smell of lunch already at eleven in the morning. This smell made a man automatically good-tempered and optimistic.

The documents for the sale of Casa das Conchas were couched in negatives; it took a lawyerly mind able to think backward to see the story behind the story. After an hour of reading, Aloysius de Noronha burped and declared: "Dear lady—alas!—you have fallen victim to the most ubiquitous of Goan bamboozlement: powers of attorney and addendums couched in a density of dastardly clauses. Anyone can read what the document says, but only a prescient lawyer—so you should never squabble over a few rupees—will uncover for you what it does *not* say. I advise you never to leave your property, not even for a single night."

"I was planning to visit my son in Mexico!"

"If sisters Edelweiss, Ida, and Clotildes move in, you will find it very difficult to dislodge them legally—only by thuggery could you do so. Thuggery has a way of going haywire."

"Tell me about it," said Babita. She fanned herself with a manila folder as she was ambushed by a menopausal hot flash.

"They are poised to claim your home with no recourse to you whatsoever. The sale of the house to you, and of the well and the driveway, is, in fact, illegal." She noticed Aloysius de Noronha's viceroy's profile and felt a flutter in her lower abdomen. She put it aside, remembering her humiliation by the bandicoot trapper. Anyway, how could she accommodate a gentleman in her life under a canopy crocheted by spinsters, widows, and nuns; when her home was in jeopardy; when she was burning up? A woman might need to fight her most challenging battles in her fifties—and how to do this when she is going down in flames? *Ratty, I have grown old before my happiness!*

Aloysius de Noronha instructed his clerk to make out a bill that she dared not look at but promised to pay, and she hurried home. The phone rang: *Sunny?*

It was Vanya. "*Turn on the television, turn on the television! You won't believe what terrible thing has happened!*"

"I've had enough shocks."

"A terrorist attack has blown up Manhattan! They almost blew up the White House! They tried to kill the American president!"

Babita rushed to watch, openmouthed, as a plane flew into the World Trade Center. She, too, was almost a New Yorker. She had stayed in a doorman building on the Upper West Side. How much untimely death was unfolding upon a single day? She clasped her hands, trembled like a leaf in a storm as a way of paying tribute, and felt, somewhere in the crosshatches of tribute, the satisfaction—she could not deny it—that others, too, even white people in a lucky country, had found themselves brushing against inexplicable darkness. They, too, had to wonder why they were so hated—hated enough for people to wish them dead. She, too, was part of a murder mystery that was part of a larger murder mystery.

Could there be a better excuse to reach out to her son? They might use the disaster to reconcile. They might have a passionate conversation, converting their troubled but immeasurable love into mutual outrage. But she couldn't phone him because he had no phone. Wait: She had the number of an Irish Canadian pieman whom Sunny said she could call in case of emergency. This was an emergency. Maybe for other people—not herself or Sunny. But still.

The gentleman took Babita's message and walked over to *Renta o Venta* to inform Sunny that he must immediately call his mum.

Off Sunny bicycled, gamcha lungi hitched high.

"Sunny, thank goodness you weren't in New York!"

"I'll have to stay in Mexico as long as I can."

She felt upset now. "What is the reaction there?"

"They think eventually someone does it back to you."

Babita's spiteful side felt redeemed.

Later Babita thought that while her son appeared to have no luck, say, in comparison to Sara's San Francisco son or Mohini Fuchs, who never failed to excel, Sunny did have the extraordinary luck of avoiding disaster—the murders of his uncles in Delhi, the terrorist attack in New York. Perhaps if you kept yourself small, kept moving, kept as distant from your own life and fate as it was possible to be, the odds would be in your favor in this regard. Just as your luck would fail to find you, so would your tragedy.

Her tragedy had found her because she had stayed on in India to wrestle her fate. She returned to thinking about the wrenching sight of people leaping to their deaths in New York.

Then the phone rang. The familiar voice from Delhi said, very low, very sweet, *"Where is Minnie's will? Where are the egg cups? Where is the gold? You cannot escape."*

"I don't have anything!" she screamed and hung up. They had tracked her down. Was this their idea of a prank? She listened for a murderer amidst the din of hoarse night owls, crickets, bats, frogs, barking dogs, the feline opera of lovelorn cats. But murderers and thieves are silent as bandicoots, everyone knows.

She retreated to the only room that had the safety of having no window, which was the altar room, and she collapsed upon the listing confessional chair. She felt guilty—but she was not! The screen of the confessional chair was woven of airy rattan so that the priest would certainly know who was giving him her confession, which he would doubtless discern anyhow from the voice that would have earlier suggested chilled cashew juice in a Bohemian goblet.

But if the priest can see you, you can see the priest, too. If God can see you, you can see God, too. If you are to confess to God, God should confess to you, too. She said to Christ upon the cross, *"But I am not guilty. Why can't you help me?"* But because he had died for her sins without her asking him to, she was made to feel beholden. Catholicism was about guilt and absolution. Hinduism was about retribution. It was about your karma being balanced out beyond your consciousness over millennia, so why even bother thinking about it? But that meant those who suffered tragedy either deserved it or must behoove themselves to forgive those who caused it.

Ratty, it's your fault. You were weak. You died. You left me alone. I would have loved you.

Ratty, don't die. If you don't die, I promise I will love you—after all!

But you should not marry someone you don't love, and you cannot promise to love him had he survived, when he is dead because of your lack of love.

....

The River of Love
Runs in
Strange Directions

....

....

OWN THE FAMILIAR ROAD TO ATHENA HOSPITAL, WITH
a "Namaste" to the giant doorman in the purple cummerbund and
fanned peacock turban. Once more Papa needed to be stabilized before
the next round of chemo and radiation; his leukocytes had dangerously fallen. He checked in to a shared room because he had bought
Sonia a necklace instead of using the money from the sale of the bank-
locker contents for his medical bills. His neighbor was settling in, accompanied by a worshipful retinue.

"He's a Haryanvi Jat, some sort of headman," Papa whispered to
Sonia. "Every Jat in the hospital is coming by to pay his respects."

The group turned on the television loudly and tuned in to a religious program that showed Krishna with his mouth being smeared
with curd and butter. Papa began to agitate. "Where is the remote?
They've taken my remote." There was one TV but two remotes.

"But if you change the channel, they will get angry."

"Let them!" Papa wanted to watch the stock market numbers. He
agitatedly summoned the nurses: "Jessy! Rency! Gracy?"

"Good girl," he said with relief when Jessy came in.

She patted his hand. "How are you, Uncle?"

"Happy to see you, Jessy," he said, patting her hand back. "I could
even give you a kiss. You must go to America. All the girls want to go.
But last time I had chemo, the nurse you sent dropped half the chemo
into my bathroom slippers. And what they sent, you cannot call it vegetable crepe. It has another name, maybe, but that name is not crepe. If
man doesn't eat, man dies. That is point number one."

Jessy negotiated that the television be switched to a news channel and sent the dietitian so Papa may grumble to his heart's content.

The dietitian was dressed in sneakers and a long, white laboratory coat. She held a clipboard. "Banana! Banana, banana!" said Papa. "If I were a young father, I would insist and teach my child—cheap, hygienic, all the vitamins and minerals!"

"Okay, Uncle, I will send a banana with every meal."

Irate, he said, "But I hate bananas. That is the problem."

"All right, Uncle, so *no* bananas?"

"Yes, *no* bananas!"

The eyes of the dietitian grew bigger and gales of giggles mounted. Outside the door, the giggles exploded.

"That's an American song," said Sonia. *"Yes! We have no bananas today!"*

"Bloody strange song."

Sonia thought: *This is my real life. This is where my luck lies, my tragedy lies, this is where my love lies—and a certain happiness.* She couldn't imagine ever finding any love as big as this one here. You had to love someone for a long while to put up with them and feel this way.

In the span of quiet that followed these negotiations, Papa lay on his side looking fondly and approvingly at Sonia, the gleam in his eyes revived after battles fought and instructions given.

"How elegant you look, Sonu, my darling daughter. That green dress suits you—it's what they call style! What nice, slender legs you have. Not even your Ma has legs like yours. Tell me, did you ever take up the foxtrot?"

The Jat headman left a few days later. He put his head around the curtain to say goodbye and good luck. He and Papa had come to the same conclusion: Television is useless rubbish! Papa, however, was not allowed to return home. Dr. Mohan looked unhappy and said he would like Papa to consult a lymphoma expert who had flown from Mumbai to see patients. They took the elevator down to the netherworld of the basement oncology department. Why was it in the basement? It felt sinister because farther along from it there were two arrows pointing down the same subterranean corridor; one read *Morgue,* the other read *Parking Garage.* Death was the inevitable final parking spot.

Sonia turned her emotions inside out. She shouted at the receptionist, "Why can't the doctor come on time?"

Many doctors considered themselves to be half gurus; they expected patients and their families to show up and wait endlessly for darshan. Waiting was a sign of respect, a form of praying, and if you waited long enough, you took admission to the doctor's presence as an omen, which made you trust divine grace would follow.

Finally Sonia accosted the receptionist. *"Don't you have any brains?* Why can't you just have a normal system of appointments instead of everyone having to wait six hours? My father's leukocytes have fallen dangerously; this waiting could kill him."

"Have patience; doctor is also a human being," she said, whereupon Sonia began to scream in lunatic fury, *"Then why is he behaving like a god?"*

What was her anger against? It poured from one thing to another so easily. Fear was like this, too, she remembered. And, sadly, love was like this, so if you had love, it lent its shine and tenderness to all things, and if you did not have love, the lack dulled every quarter of your existence.

The receptionist looked back unconcerned, just like a cow, a pilgrim cow. "Getting angry won't help."

Sonia was disrespectful. She was modern, impatient, brash. Something ancient was going to teach her a lesson. Only it already had.

This cancer doctor was in a wheelchair, which made Sonia contrite. He said Papa would get better. "Seventy to eighty percent chance." Was he being optimistic to encourage a miracle for himself? Did he believe that if a patient believed, that was half the battle?

Papa grew sicker. The sicker he grew, the worse he behaved. The worse he behaved, the worse Sonia behaved. Any criticism made her scream, any contradiction made her attack. She fought in the parking lot. She yelled in the nurses' station and in the blood bank when they told her she was too anemic to donate blood. A rough band of men who looked like highway dacoits with mufflers around their faces were there to give blood for their fellow dacoit. They watched Sonia and began to laugh. As did a crowd of soldiers lined up to give blood for their fellow soldier. So many reasons to join a robber gang, to join the army.

She phoned everyone in her parents' address book and asked: "Can you show up tomorrow to give blood?" Someone was too sick, another out of town.

She went to the kitchen and told Chandu to round up the servants on the street and drag them to the blood bank, although it turned out they were superstitious and thought this would fatally weaken them. "Force them," she told Chandu.

Those who knew Sonia less well began to stay away from her and whispered, "Her poor parents. Sent her to America, allowed her every freedom, and take a look at her! She ran her extraordinary opportunity into the dust."

Those who had known her well, Ferooza and Chandu, attributed the harsh change in her personality to fear and grief. When Ferooza came to donate blood and Sonia said, "How does Papa never think about what will happen to me?" she said, "Sonu, it's fear more than selfishness. He is as scared as you are."

*

"SHALL I COME DOWN again?" asked Mama wearily.

"No! Of what use would you be?" Whatever her mother did would be wrong because she had not saved Sonia.

"What do you want from me, then?"

"Become a useful mother!" Sonia assailed her.

Mama would not be assailed. She was made of a substance that Sonia could not comprehend. It appeared stony, but whenever Sonia had sat by her mother's side, she was filled with freeing peace. The quiet her mother had anchored took patient work. It was her achievement. A monk would be called selfish by the family of the monk, yet if many dedicated themselves to creating such peace, the world would be quieted. If Sonia destroyed her mother's hard-won calm, she herself would not be sustained by the rooted quiet. And what would she do without it when Papa was gone?

Papa was far angrier than Sonia. Steroids fueled his rage and made his crude speech cruder.

"Donkey, idiot," he said to Nurse Rency. "Go that way around the bed, not this way around the bed."

"Don't cross me," he shouted at Nurse Gracy. "I'm paying you, and if you cross me, I'll fire you. I'll get you thrown out, you low-class girl from the gali."

"Doctor, you see that I pity you—but is this a proper way to run a hospital? Shame on you lot."

"Papa, don't speak like that."

"Don't tell me what *not* to say. Go, get out, Sonia, you, too! Make your own way home."

When he was taken in a wheelchair from one test to another, he pretended to be a terrorist. "Bang! Bang!" He shot at the crowds to get them out of the way. "Bang! Bang! *Shoot the jingbang lot!*"

He was concentrating on prolonging his life at least long enough to exact final revenge on his wife. He telephoned everyone he knew, keeping his investments unmentioned, insinuating Mama had wickedly stolen from him and wouldn't extend help now that he needed to pay his bills.

"Tell her, 'Papa says he needs his money by the end of the week,'" he said to Sonia. "And don't you dare give your mother anything when I'm gone! She came to my house with nothing but one rutputty suitcase. Tell her I'm cleaning out the house before I die. Her books are mucking it up; I'm going to chuck them."

But it was his wife's books that had granted him the poetry of Faiz and Ghalib, that had in turn shown him a way to escape the prison of a man whose wife had left him. *There are other sorrows in this world besides love. . . .*

"You know," he said, "the only one who really loves me is Chandu."

"Chandu?"

"He can't say so, but he loves me the most . . . Sonia, you don't care for me—the only one who has ever cared is Mina Foi."

"Mina Foi?"

All of a sudden he began to shout, "They both dumped me! They both dumped me!"

"Who?"

"Your mother dumped me, and you dumped me."

"But here I am! No matter what hell it is—and it *is* such hell!" yelped Sonia.

"You have a guilty conscience, that's why."

"Why would I have a guilty conscience?"

He didn't say, but she knew she had not become a grown-up daughter, a daughter a father wouldn't have to worry about, who succored him instead. A daughter with an important husband, a fashionable address, one son, one daughter, and innumerable servants to cater to the insanities of the elderly.

∗

"HOW ARE YOU FEELING?" Dr. Mohan asked Papa.

"Doctor, I am mad. And I am going to die soon, so I'm mad and I'm terrible."

Dr. Mohan suggested he bring in a neurologist.

"If you bring him, I'll chuck him out of the window!"

"Doctor," he said later, "just don't go by what I *do* or *say*."

They whispered outside: "Mix in the antipsychotic medication."

"Corruption," he thundered. "I'll expose it! There is corruption here in this hospital; you are selling blood!"

"We are *not* selling blood."

"Then why whisper?"

∗

"LOOK, SONIA, I HAD to hide everything." Tucked under his blue and purple shrunken arm was his watch. "Yesterday Rency stole my fruit juice."

"No, Papa, you drank it. I saw you."

"I did not. Gracy took my Coca-Cola."

*

"SONIA, DARLING, I'M DEPRESSED."

"Why?"

"Because I haven't got the prize."

"What prize?"

"I don't have the prize, my poor little . . ."

"What? Your poor little what?"

"My poor little . . . my poor little . . ."

"What, Papa?"

*

A WEEK LATER, HE was admitted to the ICU for an infection that didn't respond to antibiotics or antifungal medications. The doctor said, "The organs are shutting down: the lungs, kidneys, liver. We are trying, but we are losing him."

"My poor little, my poor little . . . It is a dead body," he said. "I can tell, my body is dead. My poor little . . ."

"Hang on, Papa."

He said, "What?"

"Are you in pain?"

"I can't hear you."

"Papa?"

"You'll have to try later, my sweetheart."

He was already on the other side.

*

HE HAD SAID, "The best thing I did in my life was to have you, Sonu."

He had said, "Go fend for yourself. What are you doing still living with your father at your age?"

He had said, "Don't give anything to your mother!"

He had said, "Jessy, you go look after my ancient wife."

He had said, "The British have won. India is dead."

He had said, "India is your home. Without family one is nothing."

He had said, "You dumped me!"

He had said, "The man who gets you will be really lucky."

He had said, "My poor little . . . My poor little . . ."

"What, Papa?"

He'd forgotten what. He had run out of time. This was the only occasion in Sonia's life when her father had let her down. Never once before had he not been there to answer her call. Larger than life, larger than the nation, he had been all things. Without him, this father who was all things, what would "life" do? Life would now have to roam the wilderness and howl at the winds' crossroads like a country ghoul in a desolate place.

When he had been taken down the hallway, following the subterranean arrows pointing to the morgue and the parking garage, Sonia was joined by Ferooza. They kept vigil with his poetry book, his poncho, his stiff toilet case that held a simple comb, razor, and toothbrush. How little Papa had been protected from death by his possessions. She told Ferooza the story of Papa, the dietitian, and the no bananas.

She phoned Mina Foi, who was doing a Bible quiz. "You'll be sad to hear—"

"Yes," she said, unusually alert. "It is sad for me, but it is sadder for you. After all, he was your paa-paa." She made the word a child's word.

It was worth believing in an impossible story of God, so when death occurred and the impossible happened, you already believed that anything could be true, and if you believed in heaven, you would be so much less sad. So many reasons to be religious.

The neighbors came now. And the dinner-party friends Papa was too ashamed to see when Mama left for Cloud Cottage. Uncles Dilip, Jehangir, and Neil. Aunties Khushi, Margo, and Daljit. Sonia told them each the story of the no bananas. By night, Mama arrived. Sonia fell into her mother's arms and wept. Mama grasped Sonia sturdily. She was a strong, wild spirit of the mountain.

Ferooza stayed on after the other mourners had departed, and the three of them slept in Sonia's room, pushing the twin beds together. She was so relieved to have their company, she didn't care about occupying the crack between the mattresses. And briefly she experienced the feeling that sometimes comes with death that she also remembered from Dadaji's dying, of a picnic amidst the ruins. A picnic with no bananas.

In the morning before she opened her eyes, she heard her father's voice articulate, *Don't come to the cremation, Sonia, sweetheart. When the soul is gone, the body is nothing, forget it.*

Mama said, "You've done enough and seen enough."

Sonia stayed home when Mama and Ferooza left for the crematorium off Lodhi Road that Sonia had passed countless times without noticing, perhaps deliberately, on the way to Humayun's Tomb. Mina Foi did not go to the cremation, either. She had been leaving for the train station with doddery Khansama for company—he had also wished to pay his last salaams—when she stumbled on the steps and fractured her tailbone. The nuns would look after her. So many reasons to join a convent.

Sonia swallowed the numbing pill Dr. Pamela Lalwani had slipped her, wandered to Papa's bedroom, and looked at the empty pallet of Papa's single bed—a flat pillow and drab bedcover, as meager as Gandhi's bed. She cried for her father being reduced to ashes. She cried for Mama having to face the jackals who blamed her for absolutely everything—when all she had done was walk away when there was not a crumb of love left to stay for. She cried for herself because her parents had not been happy forever after, because you can't have children if you're not going to always be happy or if you're not going to live forever—how could you be so careless and heartless? The hundred contradictory ways she felt about her parents would make her an insane person, a divided person, a person who would never be calm or whole.

By the side of Papa's computer was a photograph of the aged mystic Sai Baba. He leaned against a devotee, his eyes wavering upward like a blind dog. He didn't have the imperturbable contented smile of most gurus on the market; he looked bewildered. There was a yearning in his expression and an incomprehension of the soul's engagement with the body. On the other side was a photograph of Sonia's mother with the soft, unguarded expression on her face that Papa had loved and that he himself had been responsible for destroying.

After they held the memorial and a vocalist Ferooza contracted sang Papa's favorite Khusrau poem—*The one who loves, drowns, and the one who drowns, gets across*—Papa's death was declared over and finished with, and any accompanying sympathy for Mama and Sonia vaporized.

"He died lonely," said the neighbors. "He was so brave, poor man. We knew his wife had abandoned him, but we never said a word. We didn't wish to hurt his feelings."

They grimaced little smiles at Sonia. "We knew you had contacts in America, and everyone must be asking why you didn't take him to Sloan Kettering. . . . Who knows, they may have saved him. May not have, also, but . . ."

They hoped Sonia would overhear as they remarked to each other, "While her father was dying of cancer, the daughter flew off to holiday in Italy with her boyfriend." The fact that it was Italy made it monumentally more sinful.

"So where is the boyfriend?"

"Nowhere to be seen," they said with satisfaction. Fate was playing out the way it should. "Do you remember the Panchsheel Park murders? *That* was the family of the boy." They hoped Sonia would be repaid by having to remain alone forever. It would make their lives a little brighter.

They spoke to Mama not at all but said extra loudly as she passed by, "Here comes the vulture. Now that he is dead, she's turned up for the money."

Fairy Moon

....

ALREADY BY OCTOBER THE FIRST U.S. PLANES HAD BOMBED Afghanistan, although it was impossible to get a clear view of an enemy who melted across borders, vanished into caves, popped up to study engineering in Amsterdam or work baggage claim in Toronto. An enemy who interchanged seamlessly with the innocent and unlucky—someone who happened to be named Mohammed, who happened to have taken a wrong turn and spent the night in a place other than his destination.

Sunny swimming laps in the ocean—keeping a wary lookout for crocodiles—recalled a United Nations conference on Press Freedom Day that he had attended as a volunteer usher. During lunch, a gentleman from the State Department who was writing about his experience in the Iran hostage crisis sat down across from Sunny and told him about his father, who had grown up on a dairy farm in Michigan and had woken before dawn every day, often in blizzard weather, to milk the cows before going on to school still in his denim overalls. All the rest of his life his father refused to wear jeans because they reminded him of his harsh upbringing. Later, this father had been recruited to the army and had been one of the men trained to release Little Boy or Fat Man on Hiroshima or Nagasaki. The mission had been assigned to a different group of men, but had one of them taken ill, he would have been the one to take his place. This man, leaning toward Sunny, jolly and pink, said, "My father passed a year ago, and one of the questions I wished I'd asked him was, 'Dad, were you ever regretful that you were not chosen for the mission—the bomb that ended the war?'"

Sunny felt a disconnect: Did the family feel sorry that Dad hadn't been given the chance to drop an atomic bomb? Yet Sunny had experienced the gentleman's confiding tone as a kindness. It granted Sunny fellow status even though Sunny was a foreign student at that time. He spoke as if they were certain to be in agreement, an agreement based on American decency, transparency, a belief in international human rights that this conference at the U.N. was espousing.

These confusing experiences—the unsettling merging of the harrowing cost of war with the sentimental exaltation of it—were what inspired Sunny to write "Reading Hemingway in Allahabad, Reading Hemingway in Jackson Heights." Now once again it would be wartime—the press allowed just enough doubt for a false narrative to run amok and for the drumbeat that made war inevitable to beat louder—so how could Sunny return? *So how could Sunny not return?* He was supposed to mature into a proper journalist, and how to miss the story that might launch his career? An unmarried, indebted, immigrant journalist would surely be given the cannon-fodder shift? And while a migrant might become a citizen by volunteering for the army, it was a devil's gambit: You might gain a passport and simultaneously lose your life.

Sunny breathed in, and he breathed out. He matched his breathing to the ocean. He would need to return to the United States to apply for U.S. citizenship, because with a U.S. passport he could live outside the United States, yet if anyone (such as the United States) bombed to smithereens the country in which he was living, he'd have the right passport to hook him out of the war zone. The ship would be at the port, the helicopter at the landing pad. There would be an authorized pause in the shelling that he might dash to safety. Under this logic, all of those most wary and fearful of the U.S. would be compelled to immigrate to the U.S.

He breathed in, he breathed out. Routine and simplicity, simplicity and routine. Living alone in nature, it was possible to find one's natural habits, and they were surprisingly regular and reassuring; like the creatures around him, he had fallen into a rhythm. He got up at the same time almost to the minute, drew the curtains he had sewn himself, and stood at his door brushing his teeth and surveying the morning that traveled across the bay toward him. The opossum walked along his wall at the same hour of early night and early day. The hummingbird came by at midday, as did the flock of chachalacas. The whales were wintering in the bay just as they always did. The resident iguana sat on one of two favored branches upon the same pepper tree. If Sunny watched too long, as if he were blushing the iguana's stripes would come forth. He was a gold-and-green-scaled dragon with talon claws, eyes of shattered gold like Venetian treasures. It made Sunny remember Venice and how he and Sonia might have swerved from their divergent paths to a natural common fate—he might have offered to marry her with a Murano glass ring like an iguana's eye—how naïve they were! As innocent as him and Ulla investing in the same Grimm's fairy-tale loaf, the same organic greens as everyone else at the Brooklyn farmers market, imagining that this was what it took to slip their skins, their past lives.

*

HE WAS WALKING TO the internet center when the pieman hailed him: "A man from India is looking for you!"

The yoga instructor, putting in a volunteer shift in her *LOVE* T-shirt, came to the door of the charity bookstore: "A man is searching for you. He was trying to speak to the fishermen in the fishermen's cooperative, but he didn't know a word of Spanish."

A fisherman tossing the innards of gutted fish into the sky, calling out *yip yip*—the gulls and pelicans returning the *yip yip* and swooping to eat—stopped to say: "A man who looks to be from your country is walking about in circles."

The local shaman and his brother, passing a joint back and forth on the beach, shouted out that they had seen another "El Hindu" in town.

Sunny panicked. Probably one of those annoying new entrepreneur Indians who had suddenly made a computer fortune and retired at forty to live out their dream of traveling the world, snorkeling, bungee jumping, motorcycling. "I don't want to meet another Hindu. I came here to escape from a billion Hindus."

Ulises said, "Fuck, but I already told him where you live!"

Sunny walked to where there was a small waterfall and pool in the jungle. He ventured home when it was almost dark and the fishermen were setting out to catch marlin and dorado, their small boats bumping down hard in the waves until they reached the calm ocean. He was grateful to see his casita glowing like a beached coral, when he suddenly detected a hulking shape stuffed into an equipale chair. The shape saw him and leapt up, and before Sunny had a proper glimpse of it, the shape embraced Sunny, moist and close, closer than Sunny had been to anyone for a long time, and the shape burst into hot tears.

"It's me!"

"Satya!"

"Sunny," he said, struggling to speak. "You must forgive me. I was wrong. I cut you off. It is my fault."

Satya began to heave with crying, then tried to wave his sobs away and downgrade his emotion by pointing to some mosquitoes he had killed and laid out in a row. "The mosquitoes here are very slow and don't bite." He blew his nose into a cactus.

"They bite only toward dawn. How did you find me?"

"I remembered Sara Aunty. Through her I found Babita Aunty's phone number in Goa. She told me the name of this place. You know what is so sad? Just a month ago, Pooja and I came to get our H-1 visas in Juárez. I didn't know you were so close!" As planned, Satya had accepted an appointment as a general practitioner under the Appalachian scheme whereby foreign doctors were contracted to work in underserved rural America in exchange for their immigration documents.

Again he waved his hand before his eyes to dispel being overemotional. "We were told it's very dangerous, stay at the Ramada Inn, eat at McDonald's, cross back to the States as soon as you can. We were so scared, we didn't look right, left, behind—and now I see there is nothing scary! It is just like India, except there are fewer people and it is so much cleaner! I said to the customs official, 'Where is your famous pollution? Come to India and see pollution!'"

And he'd had a charming conversation with the man seated next to him on the bus from Mexico City: "You have tortillas, we have makki ki roti. We have curry, you have mole. We have rice, you have rice. You have chilies, we have chilies. We have beans, you have beans. You have cilantro, we have cilantro. You have tamarind? We have tamarind! The Mayas had zero? We had zero! When white people had less than zero and lived in filth, we donned gold and knew astronomy. You were robbed by the Spanish, we were robbed by the British. You are cursed, we are cursed. You are big family people, we are big family people. Indian women with long, black hair can be mistaken for Mexican women with long, black hair. In fact, you are 'Indians' and we are Indians, or we are 'Mexicans' and you are Mexicans! Columbus was a fool, but who could blame him? He had the wrong continent, but too many things were same-ish. If you dig a tunnel here, you will burrow out in India—more or less.

"'Ah, ha ha, but who has the hottest chili?' said the man.

"'He-he, that may be a point upon which we cannot agree!'

"That man got off the bus to make sure I had the right village. So I said, 'Okay, señor, you have the hottest chilies!' Then I walked into the village and asked everyone I met—it was simple to find you!"

Satya wore wide shorts, white knee socks, psychedelic-colored gym shoes, a baseball cap, and a big digital watch clocking every second in the thicket of his arm hair.

"You've become an American!"

"Yes," he said, looking delighted. His money and passport were zipped into a belt pouch concealed by the swell of his tummy.

They climbed up to sit under the palapa thatch over Sunny's roof, and Satya proceeded to talk. He'd been saving it up since the day they'd parted in Goa, but several things had prevented him from seeking out Sunny sooner. Principal among them was this, he would be frank: "If you marry the way I did, you cannot be sure the person you have married will love you. I was so sure Pooja would not love me that I attacked you!" Satya paused. Was he betraying his wife? But nothing is betrayal if you tell a friend the truth. He looked at the moon, which was a fairy moon with a ring around it, and took a draw of the coconut water Sunny had brought for him. "I could not believe our marriage would *not* fail. Pooja was unable to adjust to life in the States."

They had been bashful with each other again after the interlude between their honeymoon and their reunion in Laurie, Kentucky, when Pooja received her accompanying spouse visa. It was almost as if she wished to flee his presence. Yet she spent all day waiting for him to return from the clinic to take her grocery shopping in the second-hand Toyota he had learned hesitantly to drive, despite the accompanying blast of horns and curses. What had she done while she waited? The phone had flickered with a message. "You were home, why didn't you pick up?"

Pooja didn't pick up because Pooja was terrified of speaking to foreigners. She hid inside and swept the house with a broom, eschewing the bucking, thundering vacuum cleaner because she needed each task to be as slow as possible to fill the slow hours that could never be filled because her husband was a doctor and away most of the time. And because there wasn't enough dust in this country, for dust that needed to be swept each morning, for it to be dusted away twice a day, for it to fly back by night.

Satya suggested they buy Pooja a pair of pants so she would feel less a stranger.

"Pants!"

"Or a dress."

"I feel bad to even show my upper arms, let alone my legs!" Pooja said she understood women who were so used to covering up they would regard their own noses and toes as too peculiar to parade down the street.

"If you wear a sari or salwar kameez here," Satya pleaded, "people will think twice about approaching you. You won't be able to walk through snow; you'll die of cold."

He pointed out that Dr. Puri's wife had bobbed her hair, wore jeans and sneakers, and had contributed a five-bean salad to the clinic pot-luck held on the picnic grounds that adjoined the nuclear power plant on the outskirts of Laurie. Dr. Puri owned the clinic that had employed Satya, although he himself lived two hours away in the rolling hills outside Lexington in a six-bedroom brick mansion.

Pooja said, "Mrs. Puri is trying to be too smart."

"She's only trying to belong."

"I was alone managing everything," Satya told Sunny. "New job! New visas! New house! New work! New car! I would beg, 'Come sit with me, Pooja. Explain to me how I can help you settle.'"

Satya did not tell Sunny that what had kept him trying was the memory of their Goan honeymoon after Sunny departed and their honeymoon became a honeymoon. They had joined other lovebirds on the beach, posed for photographs alongside the tourist attraction of bikini-clad Siberians. On Pooja's twenty-second birthday, they had embarked on a sunset river cruise—the band playing "Just the Way You Are"—and Pooja had sighed: "I never saw anything so beautiful."

"Just *please* make *one* friend," Satya now begged Pooja. People in Laurie must have thought they were witnessing a barbaric culture of arranged marriages and unequal women being kept locked indoors. "You must learn English properly. You must learn to drive."

"What if I have an accident and kill someone?"

This was a valid fear, and while they compromised on driving lessons in the cemetery—where it wouldn't be so bad to lose control and drive over the already-dead—watching out anxiously for her, Pooja was not the companion Satya had hoped for. He hated to admit he was ashamed of her. Maybe she was ashamed of him, too, because he also felt ashamed of himself. The nurse practitioner and the office administrator opened the windows no matter the weather when he unpacked his lunch. They claimed they could not pronounce his name. They called him Dr. Sat. They would *not* understand his accent. It slowed everything down. The slowing down made him feel inept also in his medical diagnoses. The person who could least understand him was Dr. Puri's wife. "Vhaaat? Vhaaat ya say?" she said in a fake American accent. Satya was forced to make cartoon Indian American sounds, just like hers, so she with her false accent could understand his false accent.

Meanwhile, he had to believe his patients were honestly bewildered because he was often equally bewildered by them. "I have a charley horse," said one. Nana, an eighty-two-year-old woman, whispered, "Doc, it's my howzy doozy." Nana was dressed in a housecoat and smelled of cigarettes, television, air-conditioning, and carpeting. She clutched tightly at Satya's hand with her mottled one. He had to ask the nurse practitioner what a charley horse was, what a howzy doozy may be.

There were other matters Satya also found puzzling, such as the notice they received in their mailbox saying that in case of a leak from the nuclear plant, which was situated in the park where they held their annual office picnic, they should lie in a bathtub submerged in water with a straw out of their mouths to breathe. And that a van would be stationed outside the Allstate Farm Insurance bureau to distribute iodine pills to be taken in case of radiation exposure. Was this normal? Was this abnormal? He wished he could talk to his friend Sunny since he could not speak to his wife. Was Pooja downgrading herself to unequal-servant level by endlessly sweeping, by rushing hot rotis to the table instead of sitting down to eat with her husband, so as not to feel guilty about her lack of love? Satya began to brood. Had he married the wrong person? Should he have married the girl the astrologer had recommended? Someone his parents had found? Was he being paid back for the hubris of attempting to forge his own fate, veering from an arranged marriage to a love marriage? A failed love marriage was so much more painful than a failed arranged marriage, where you might blame the planets as well as your family. Here, with Pooja, he was the one to blame.

Satya exited their marital bed at the first light of dawn. On a Tuesday morning, before driving to the clinic, he had stopped by Nana's cabin deep in a humid copse to make sure she understood the prescription he had written out for her. He intuited she would not have confessed her embarrassing vaginal inflammation to anyone other than an immigrant outsider. Cards of the Virgin Mary were pasted to Nana's front window. The cabin was tilting. Her son emerged—he seemed bigger and sturdier than his mother's house. He said, "Something just happened."

At that exact time, September 11 had happened. Like the rest of the nation Satya and Pooja had turned on their television set and watched the jets crashing into the World Trade Center towers in New York City, towers that Satya had failed to notice before, just like his friend Sunny, because New York City hadn't been important when he had visited. Sunny was important. Telling Sunny about himself was important. He used the clinic computer to send Sunny a message: *Are you all right?* Sunny might have been at the World Trade Center on a work assignment or nearby at the immigration office, he might have joined the ash-covered exodus over the Brooklyn Bridge.

Satya bought an enormous flag like other scared immigrants who had not yet learned the American habit of patriotic display and attached it to their front porch. Pooja succumbed to wearing jeans. She jigged about saying, "I can't sit, I can't sit. Why do they make clothes so tight and stiff?"

Satya might have collapsed into laughter were he not terrified that someone might attack his wife. "Did anyone *say* anything to you? Did anyone *do* anything?" he asked. Someone had said something to him when he had driven to Lexington to stock up on rice and dal, ready for a siege. A homeless man had appeared out of nowhere and shouted, "*Get out of my country!*"

It had come as a dreadful shock to learn that someone so badly treated by his country sided with it against Satya. Satya's American accent grew even more pronounced and fake. He was a cartoon buffoon.

While Satya, the cartoon buffoon, and Pooja, the scaredy ghost, were stockpiling rice and dal—despite feeling extra worried the smell of their cooking would upset the neighbors; *don't use too many spices!*—Satya was certain his neighbors were not only carrying thousands of bottles of water and cans from Costco, Walmart, Best Buy, and Sam's Club into their homes but were also hoarding firearms. What if they saw a shadow and decided to take aim?

This was when he received Sunny's return email: *I'm not in New York City. I am living in a village on the Mexican coast.* Satya felt all over again that his friend was escaping his karma, was being unfaithful to his dharma, wasn't holding true to his loyalties and keeping the center at the center. He wasn't putting their story in his story. Sunny should have written: *When can we meet? Let us spend Thanksgiving together.* That would have been correct, would have provided solace in an exploding world.

"We had no friends, save for one disabled neighbor who never spoke to us but waved if she saw us from her window. I fell into a depression. I thought Pooja must realize she had married a man who could not take care of her. I began to stay away from Pooja. Finally I understood her—just like I didn't want her near me because I felt so bad about myself, she had a secret of feeling deficient, too, so she would keep trying to stay in another room. One day, an elderly patient who was dying said to me, 'I want a white gentleman doctor.' I said, 'You can take me, or wait some hours.' She said, 'I will wait'—and while waiting, she died."

The moon rode the water toward them just as when Sunny and Satya were last together in Goa on Satya's honeymoon. They heard the waves crash down and then the chatter of pebbles in the maw of the retreating tide.

"I am sorry, my friend," said Sunny.

My friend! It made Satya emotional. "I wanted to run away from my problems—*like you,*" said Satya, at this moment seeing a parallel.

Said Sunny, "In movement and solitude are safety. But also a lack of safety—a solitary wanderer, even a poor one, might be murdered for just his shoes."

Satya said, "One day, I got into such a mental state that I called in sick, and then I got into my car and drove away."

Satya had finally pulled up at a mall where there was a Barnes & Noble, in which he could spend time like many homeless people did. In the evening there had been a reading by a psychic who claimed to have solved the Son of Sam murders, attended by an unusual group of people. A lady in a large hat wreathed in feathers put up her hand and said in a strong voice as if declaiming in court: "I! Too! Have! Been! Psychic! Witness! To a Murder!" For some reason this had given Satya a moment of relief. An immigrant story is also a ghost story and a murder story. You become a ghost, the people left behind become ghostly, sometimes you kill them by the heartlessness of leaving, sometimes you psychically kill yourself. Another audience member, whose skin looked as if it had never been touched by sun, said he listened to an alien broadcast at two A.M. Again Satya felt better. An immigrant story is a story about becoming an alien, to others and to yourself. At night Satya slept in his car; in the morning he went to Barnes & Noble again.

Three days passed before he telephoned Pooja from the pay phone outside the restroom. She picked up within a single ring. "Where are you?"

Six hours later she was in the Barnes & Noble.

"How did you come?"

"I drove."

"On the highway?"

"You think you're the only person who can drive on a highway?" Unbelievably, she had borrowed a car from the neighbor who sometimes waved at them from the window and driven in this unfamiliar car down a road she had never driven on before. And by this courageous act she had miraculously found her courage. At this time when Satya collapsed, Pooja's personality switched.

"She would say, 'Do we have a roof over our heads?'

"I would say, 'Yes.'

" 'Do we have food on the table?'

" 'Yes.'

" 'We are healthy?'

" 'Yes.'

" 'Then?'

"Once Pooja had this experience of being the stronger person, our marriage changed. With her strength, I am looking for another job." Satya had interviewed for a new position in an Appalachian mountain town. They hoped to move soon because in three months Pooja was going to have a child.

Again Satya grew teary. He recovered his balance with a joke. Their daughter—he hoped with all hope the baby would be a girl because there were enough boys in the world—would surely have a Southern American drawl, one so strong that Pooja would have to keep asking Satya, "Hey, what did *your* daughter say?" And Satya would have to keep asking Pooja, "Hey, what did *your* daughter say?" They had already decided on a name. They would name her Karuna because karuna meant compassion.

"How could I not have come to tell you in person? I knew you would never forgive me." It was obvious to Satya now that he had been the lucky one, while Sunny, whom he had envied all through their youth, was the unlucky bastard.

The Unlucky Bastard accepted the insult peaceably. He lay on his back and surveyed the stars.

Satya said, "Sunny, what happened to that girl?"

"We lost touch." Sunny continued to look up, while Satya turned intimately toward him, curling himself about his stomach.

"She was a nice person," Satya said, although he'd never met Sonia.

"She was complicated."

"In the end we are all simple."

"She believed she was being chased by darkness," Sunny said, surprising himself with this sentence. "That something evil believed she belonged to it and wouldn't leave her alone."

"Evil?" Satya was fascinated.

"It took the form of an injured ghost hound. Once, I saw her go mad."

"Oh no," said Satya. "Oh no, not mad. She must be right. You cannot make up such stories."

"You believe this?"

"Of course I do. Things happen beyond our sight."

"You're a doctor?"

"That is how I know there is a limit to science. My grandfather once saw a sorcerer casting a spell upon a fire. He gathered the fire into a serpent and led that fire serpent to the door of the man who had raped a little girl in a remote village after which that man had torn out the little girl's eyes and tongue."

"And then what happened?"

"The man lost his mind. Who cursed Sonia?"

"A painter she had a relationship with. In fact, Satya, there was something inexplicable occurring. There was a likeness of Sonia painted by this man in a museum in Italy, including the exact same dog—like a shadow of a dog—that attacked us *after* the painting had been painted. I couldn't understand how this could be true. It was as if the dog came out of the ocean and vanished into the sand. I almost wouldn't have believed it but for the bite mark into my chappal, although of course I began to wonder if sea glass had pierced my slipper and I had imagined it all."

"What did you do to help her?"

"What could I do other than try to fend off the dog?"

"You didn't help her?" Satya was incredulous. "Why did you not go and confront the bad person? You should go now!"

"The time has passed," said Sunny.

"Not so much time. You're still alive. She is still alive. If the painter is still alive, you at least need to go and say something."

"What good will that do?"

"That is not the point. If you do one small thing, a bigger thing may happen—it will reverberate out into the universe."

"Strangely, he has an estate in Mexico in the former silver mines of Guanajuato."

"Strangely? Fatalistic life, my friend!"

A fisherman who had set out at dusk returned at dawn. They watched him and his boat in a contemplative, peaceful moment, engine turned off, letting the tide rock him in. A pelican rested on the edge of the boat. His dog, waiting all night on the shore, swam out to meet him, and they returned together, drifting into the bay: man, dog, bird. "How brave that man is," marveled Satya. "How can he go out into the ocean at night on such a small boat?"

He turned to examine his friend in the morning pearlescence. "There are so many animals here, you yourself seem to have turned into a half animal. You yourself look a little scary." He thought Sunny looked unsettlingly like a stick insect.

When Satya left—waving out of the bus for the airport—alongside the restful silence of being alone, Sunny felt a loneliness of a kind he hadn't felt in a long while. He had not had a friend in his home in years, and it had wounded him, this sweetness from his past. He thought that only with perspective granted by age did you understand where in life you had been lucky. He had been lucky for having Satya, for his friendship, which seemed old-fashioned—old-fashioned because while it included the possibility of betrayal or loss, it never included the notion that human connection itself might become impossible for some people. Satya had no need for newspapers and news, he had no need for art—he had life!

Sunny picked up the airline magazine Satya had left behind. It was a glossy object at odds with his casita. It smelled of money, of a "high-end lifestyle" folded into a perfume sample that Satya had tested on his wrist. But before Sunny threw it away, he leafed through—he could never let words go without at least running his eyes over them—and there:

Ilan de Toorjen Foss

How could it be? But how could it *not* be? Not for fatalistic reasons, but when a person becomes famous, you simply cannot escape them. There they are, in the Sunday supplement, the style magazine, the travel article; for their clothes, their stylish spouse, beautiful home, favorite destination; for their dinner party with a recipe to indicate they are a down-to-earth, nice person despite their fame. You encounter the famous person in the airport and on television, in articles about what to look forward to at the beginning of the year and in end-of-year roundups, quoted in free-floating inspirational lines that surprise you on a tote bag. They are name-dropped at dinner parties; traded and sold by hacks, social climbers, corporations; bartered so much there is surely nothing left of them but fame and the desire for fame. Protesting they crave solitude, they dispense an interview a week.

A short notice read that the artist was painting a chapel on his Mexican property with a version of his signature work, *Mother Swimming,* as if to create a jewel watering hole in the landscape of dry hills, caverns, and underground rivers. De Toorjen Foss believed art shouldn't be sequestered in museums. It was important to undo the center of power, travel to see the work in a landscape that held meaning and inspiration for the art and the artist, and to recover the intimacy and emotion of pilgrimage, the lure of adventure, even the exhaustion and discomfort of travel. The place, the pilgrimage, the art, all in synthesis, created that sublime tingling we all yearn for whether it be in art, in religion, in love, or in nature. De Toorjen Foss wished to create a whole universe for his art to live in, to protect the art by making also the world that sustained it.

The name Ilan de Toorjen Foss, thought Sunny, *was probably made up.* He looked carefully at the accompanying photograph, and, as with the one Sunny had seen in the catalog in Venice and the one in *Artes de México,* it was compelling. Fame requires a good photograph against the right backdrop. Ilan held up a mask carved out of a tortilla and mischievously looked out of the primitive cutout eyes and mouth. About him was his collection of masks from around the world and of naguals that were creatures half human and half animal, bat men and scorpion women. Masks were a way to communicate with spirits from other times and places. You could speak a hidden truth—or else the worst falsehood. When a man wore a mask, nobody knew who he was, not even the man himself.

In the middle of the night, Sunny woke and recalled Sonia pleading, crying into his mouth: *Can you at least retrieve my demon amulet for me? That's all I ask, because we were happy for a moment, weren't we?*

He remembered swallowing her sobs. He remembered Sonia in the catalog he had opened under a streetlamp in Venice. Sonia vanished into the painting of herself and Ilan. The painting was real, the real woman untrustworthy. He remembered holding on to Sonia and feeling her falling through his arms. He remembered diving deep into the black of the dangerous ocean to escape the crashing of waves. They might have wanted to save each other, but they could only save themselves.

....

I See You,
Demon of the
Clouds

....

....

"TERRIBLE WHAT WE DID WITH MY FATHER. WE DUMPED his ashes in dirty water, muck all around. Whatever you do, just don't put me there." Mama and Sonia had saved Papa's ashes from being driven out to Garh Mukteshwar and sunk into the polluted river after being held ransom by greedy priests and boatmen for a little more money, a lot more money. Instead, they decided to immerse Papa's ashes at a place beyond Uttarkashi where Mama recalled the Ganga, slate green, rushed in her mountain incarnation and the air was resinous with pine. They hired a car, and when they arrived in the Uttarkashi valley, they looked out of the window to their right where the Ganga should have been—and they saw that the river was missing. It lay in pieces stranded in a plain of boulders, where bulldozers were at work trying to piece the water together again, trying to clear the roads that were beset by landslides. It was obvious that the cleared landslides would be immediately replaced by others because the denuded mountains were falling out of themselves. Despite the broken river and mountains, pilgrim minivans and buses in caravans flying orange flags went rollicking dangerously over the unmade earth, overtaking each other aggressively, blaring devotional music through loudspeakers mounted on their roofs as they made a circular pilgrimage of Kedarnath, Badrinath, Gangotri, Yamunotri.

"What happened here?" Mama asked the driver.

The driver was thumping the steering wheel to the music as they stalled behind the cavalcade. He said mildly, "There was a flood last year. Houses were swept away, some people died. It will take time to fix the damage." The floods had carried boulders down from the high Himalayas, breaking the natural river course.

"Why isn't this in the news?"

"At the time it happened, it must have been in the news."

Where had Mama and Sonia been when this had been in the news? Had they forgotten in the river of bad news, this small bad news that was now revealed to be cataclysmic?

Sonia thought it was surely a test of faith to conjure God within this scene. How would people continue to go on pilgrimage and set souls free into the Ganga if they couldn't trust in pure water flowing from the pristine snows into the Bay of Bengal? If ice lingams melted in holy caves, if caves caved, if mountains fell, if rivers lay shattered? What was religion but trust in a divine order on earth?

Perhaps it didn't have to do with what the seekers could see before their eyes, though. What did the truth matter if you believed? Maybe the more effort it took to envision a divine order, the more it proved a pilgrim's devotion. But the travel-sick pilgrims she saw through the windows of their vomit-streaked vehicles looked as if they'd passed into another degree of not caring—and perhaps this was religion as well. It could bestow upon you a degree of not caring that was essential for many people if they were to survive their lives.

Her father had cared too much, that had always been the problem. Cared too much about his daughter, cared too much about his wife—*who was still his wife,* God or no.

Papa's ashes sat on the seat between Mama and Sonia, in a plastic container from the crematorium.

They drove beyond the town to where there was a rustic cabin used by mountaineering expeditions, where a section of the Assi Ganga was being worked on by people who sat breaking the mythical boulders with tiny hammers. The sun was more direct here than in the city where it was softened by pollution, but only a few of them had the luxury of a black cloth umbrella to shield themselves. By the side of the avalanche of rubble was their encampment of tents, where some women were washing clothes and babies in a pooled section of the water. The thunderous sound of the rocks being broken and loaded into trucks ricocheted down the valley. Sonia noticed a spot between the broken river and the broken hillside where a cloud of violet butterflies had found salt.

If they walked higher and farther to a still-living mountain stream to release Papa's ashes, Papa would yet be stranded in the desert plain below. Sonia and Mama decided it would be a better idea to wait until the river was flowing again or to find another body of free water. They stopped at the mountaineering cabin for the night, and in the diamond, silver, gold frost morning, they found a hill man with a face like a wrinkled walnut and teeth like a rotten corncob, squatting alongside the steaming bucket of water that he had carried for them to wash. He cleared his throat and expelled tobacco phlegm. "He would camp higher up where we graze cattle in the summer."

"Who?"

"I remember your father."

"*My father?*" choked Mama.

"Yes. I brought eggs to the kitchen and the manager told me you were here. I waited to see you. I recognize you by your face. You resemble him. You have the discolored complexion of foreigners—your daughter looks more normal."

"You spoke to him—you knew him?"

"Yes, we would talk to him even though it was hard to understand his Hindustani. He was fluent, but his accent took some time to get used to. He would buy potatoes, milk, and eggs from us."

"What did he do camping here?"

"He would write in his notebook and make paintings, he would open the amulet about his neck, hold it in his hand, and speak to the figure inside: *O Badal Baba, O Bagheera Badal, O Bhoot Bibi, O Chirya Nath!* He had many names. The figure inside would speak back."

"Surely not!"

"Yes, yes, we heard it."

"What did it say?"

"Depending on how he named it, it would answer. It made the sound of rain, or birds, or leopards, or the ocean, or wind—which is the same thing as the voice of a ghost. All these sounds are related."

"Are you sure?"

"Oh yes. We asked him, 'How do you understand?' He said you understand from your senses what is beyond words, but it is something like, 'Waking up we are parted, but in the dream world we are the same.'

"We asked, 'Does your Badal Baba protect you when you walk alone in the mountains?'

"He laughed and said, 'Oh no. My Badal Baba is not a chota pota phaltu baba. Protection against evil energies, chasing ghouls, is a small-time game. My Badal Baba is a powerful sorcerer. Badal Baba doesn't believe in protection; Badal Baba believes in transformation! Even taking the form of a ghoul, if necessary. Or becoming a cloud, if necessary.' We assumed the foreigner was mad. He said his dream was to climb Bandarpunch. He said he had tried three times before and each time the weather was against him and he turned back. That year the monsoon came early—he must have caught its tail. We never saw him again."

Mama pinched her lips with her fingers, although she wasn't speaking. On the way back to their vehicle through a stern pine forest, she dropped the container of Papa's ashes and some spilled out. They scraped them back in, mixed with a little earth and pine needles. When they arrived back in Cloud Cottage, the green-black deodars opened their wings to let them in, closed behind them. Within minutes Mama regained her balance and strength, her hearing, her eyesight. She picked up a mouse that was clawing up the back of the sofa and tossed it out of the window by its tail, leaving her city daughter awestruck.

Moolchand had been sleeping in Aunt Meher's bed to keep the house safe from local goons. He retreated to his hut, leaving behind the smell of woodsmoke, soil, and onions. Babayaga trotted to greet them. Why hadn't she kept the mice away? She lay on her back among the sour cushions and showed them her crooked crocodile smile. At dusk, they saw a line of cherry-tobacco smoke rising from the bench at the corner of the lawn. "Grandfather Siegfried is here again," said Sonia. Had he come searching for his lost-face demon? Was he returning over and over to tell Sonia to retrieve Badal Baba?

But if Badal Baba was the deity of transformation, not of protection, then her grandfather's painting wasn't meant to keep them safe, as they had thought. Rather, it was a message to displace their vanity, a human self, a male self, a female self. *Even taking the form of a ghoul, if necessary.* How could they have misjudged? Sonia, taking a bath, stood in her rubber chappals in case of a wayward electric current and poured the bucket of steaming water warmed by the immersion heater over her head. In the moment of the water rushing over her, she became a river. The bathroom's window looked into the drenched, mossy world, and she watched the steam trickle and vanish through the trees. She thought of Tanizaki writing about shadowy old bathrooms being gateways to the past. She thought that you have to honor your parents, who reside irrevocably in the past, so you must forever revere the past. But you couldn't actually live in a beautiful, dignified past when it was being uprooted and disgraced each day, her mother's home the last toadstool in the last forest.

It was snug in her brass bed with a hot-water bottle, even if her nose smarted with peppermint cold. An owl's call traveled down the chimney and sounded startlingly close, right at her ear. Maybe it had swooped to gobble the mouse Mama had tossed out. Sonia remembered the faraway love story of Mina Foi and Ernest. At least Mina Foi knew that Ernest had loved her; he'd returned and waited in the rain gutter outside her window: *chirrur*? Maybe all you needed was to be loved once. It was too much to ask to be loved all the way through life, and you could return to the memory for sustenance. Being loved all the time might be a curtailment, a redundancy. It was wild and restful to think without attachment.

As the colder months of winter settled in, Mama and Sonia fed the woodstove and huddled close enough to singe their shawls, and there was something now in Sonia of her father's death, of the stern forest, of the broken river. She felt herself turn into her mother's jailor. Her mother was all she had. She watched and pounced. She didn't allow Mama to indulge in treats—a run of cream, a macaroon baked by the missionary teachers who lived in Middle Cloud—without warning Mama to stay healthy. Had Sonia become someone with the life and love of an adult woman, maybe she would be kind, but if Mama failed before Sonia grew up properly, now that her father was dead, well, it was not to be allowed.

She threatened, "You can't live up in the mountains on your own forever."

Mama stirred her tea and kept on stirring.

Sonia snatched the spoon away.

Her mother fingered the tablecloth while thinking over some thought that wouldn't let her go.

Mama didn't like the fact that her solitude was interrupted, that she could no longer yawn loud enough to cause a bird to call back perplexed, that she could no longer speak out to the ghosts of her parents, that she could no longer talk to herself.

"Mama, look at what you've done."

"What have I done?" Meals took too long with another person.

"Look at how you are living!"

"What is wrong with how I am living?" There was a value to living in a past world when you have no love. The present was for those who were proud of the abundance of love they possessed. It was they who would inherit the future. She read through in silence, with the stubbornness she had mastered over many traumas in her life—until Sonia pulled the Chekhov out of her hands. "Don't you understand? We have become characters in your book, a mother and daughter living together in the jungle, speaking to nobody. We have to think of a new plan."

"I don't want a new plan. You must live your life."

"I have no life." Indignant, she threw the Chekhov into the stove, and it went up in phoenix flames. Sonia, who had wanted to be a writer, had burned a book like a savage, like a fanatic. No worse sacrilege in this house.

Mama got up, went into her bedroom, and shut the door. A woman must stay alone for a long while until the hate men have for women has left her, and even longer until the jealousy women have for other women has left her, and longer still until the anger her children have for her has left her—until she is no longer a woman altered by the resentment of men, women, and children, no longer what others have forced her to be, but empty as a skull or a shell, filled only by whatever she pleases, forest air perhaps.

Sonia wanted to immediately return to her mother's love, but she could not. She walked outside. She watched the smoke from the book spill from the chimney, and there, from the deodar forest, she saw—collecting evidence, totting things up—the familiar eye. She blinked. The eye remained burning. Vagrant wisps drifting over the moon made Badal Baba's broken face.

She crossed the foggy forest, hoping the last hungry leopard wasn't prowling, and took refuge in Little Cloud. The roof sprouted ferns; the walls were covered in lichen rosettes. Snails and slugs had crisscrossed the floor and walls, leaving silver trails. It smelled of turpentine, paint, resin, damp. It was cluttered with easels, palettes, cabinets stocked with brushes, pastels, charcoal sticks, oil paints sealed with Vaseline.

Sonia put her face close to the photograph of her grandfather that hung on the wall. He was on a mule in the mountains, holding his amulet as if on his way to Baba's mountain holdout. Sonia needed Badal Baba to save herself before she could save Badal Baba. How else could she meet a challenge as great as defeating Ilan's curse, which was a closed maze with a monster prowling. It would take a mystic's feat. Wishing to be close to Baba's wild spirit, Sonia scratched with an obstinate piece of charcoal upon a sketchbook:

Grandfather without a face
   Owl's chirrur! Leopard's eye looks
  through me I see you
    Demon of the Clouds

She felt an almost unbearable tingling enter her nostrils—a sublime vapor too rarefied to breathe. She looked into the deep, thick deodars, the splotches of slug gray and yellow. She thought she glimpsed an unformed figure that gestured at her from the other side. *The void of the East is not the void of the West.*

If you had no face, was it the path to no nationality, no gender, no religion, no race? Was this not a relief—to have no attributes? Or was it only the powerful who could indulge in such romantic notions? How could one suggest such a solution to the dispossessed?

....

WHEN FEROOZA RANG, SHE SAID, "RIOTS HAVE BROKEN out in Ahmedabad." Then she struggled to speak.

"Ferooza?"

"Turn on the news and see for yourself."

There was no television in Cloud Cottage. Mama and Sonia, relieved to find a reason to broker an unspoken return to comradeship, walked to Middle Cloud on Tehri Road, where the missionary teachers were watching TV while knitting long johns made of leftover bits of yarn. Hindus who were in Ayodhya to advocate for a temple to be built on the grounds of the destroyed Babri Masjid mosque had crowded onto a train. The train had caught fire. Muslims had been blamed for setting the fire. Or had the pilgrims been cooking on the train? Mobs were going from house to house in Muslim neighborhoods in Ahmedabad. They were parading people naked and cutting off genitals. They were spearing unborn babies through their mothers' wombs. They were butchering, blinding, raping, dousing in kerosene and burning. The six women stared at the screen in the same way they had when the planes flew into the World Trade Center towers. They watched housewives gathering stones into kitchen utensils to more efficiently stone their neighbors to death. Mama said, "We lived through this at Partition. It must be that a country is forever trapped in the story of its birth. It is fated to circle back for eternity."

Mama and Sonia returned home and telephoned Ferooza. There was worry the violence would spread to Delhi. Wouldn't it be better for Ferooza to stay safely with Dilip and Khushi? Ferooza did not want to leave her cat, but when she climbed the stairs, carrying food to last a while, she had passed her landlord and landlady, who stood and watched her, who did not return her greeting. Her landlady said into Ferooza's face, "We always had Muslim problem, now Muslim problem is worldwide problem! It will cause us trouble to have this woman under our roof."

Ferooza said to Mama, "When a mob comes, there is nothing you can do. It's a tsunami you can't fight against; even a gun would not help." She said, "I had the chance to remain in Paris once. I should have taken it."

*

AT NIGHT IT WAS as if a coating of snow lay upon Sonia's red satin quilt with a green chinar-leaf pattern. Sonia wondered whether becoming a cloud like her grandfather was not only a way to escape but to grow one's intelligence and make it whole. A cloud might move and encompass, travel faster, see from up high, dissipate before it was captured. If a woman had been made into a ghost, was she not on her way to becoming a cloud? A cloud became a river, a river became an ocean. If she returned to the coast, could she let go of the stern thinking that imprisoned herself, that was imprisoning her mother? But Goa, where she had been happy, was also where the ghost hound had come out of the water, where she and Sunny had almost drowned. Some places, some people, are portals to an artist's work. Sonia said to Mama, "I felt free in Goa the way I have never felt elsewhere in India. I might go there for a bit, try to return to writing fiction."

Mama said, "You had so much talent, but you gave it up. I never understood why."

Said Sonia, "It's not so simple. You have to live enough life for a story to unfold."

"Do you think you have one?"

"I catch a glimpse in the forest. I felt it beneath me in the ocean when I swam."

They could rent out the flat in Hauz Khas for Sonia to receive an income. Mama telephoned Ferooza, who telephoned her colleague who had organized AIDS clinics for sex workers in Goa.

She confirmed that Goa was a place where an educated young person might build an independent life. She'd met several women on their own who were relocating to Goa for the same reason as Sonia. The state retained the appealing cosmopolitan air of a port. It lacked the misogynistic constraints of the northern Indian states. A woman may go out by herself wearing shorts. Off the top of her head she could think of a lawyer who had given up lawyering to open a bookshop in Panjim, a young woman from Assam who made jewelry in Siolim, a PhD student from Harvard who worked at a mental health clinic, a certain widow fleeing the pursuit of the underworld in Delhi. And who was this widow? Through the India International Centre coffee gossip, Ferooza learned that Babita Bhatia had purchased a mansion in a remote corner of south Goa built by a merchant whose three vessels, the *Paloma,* the *Nagini,* and the *Husnara,* had sailed between Goa and Zanzibar and whose descendant's refusal to salute "Hail Salazar!" had lit the flame for independence from the Portuguese.

"So Babita made enough money for that!" exclaimed Mama.

"What if she'd married into that family?" said Ferooza. "The corruption would have devoured her."

"But isn't it shocking that Babita Bhatia never searched for her little servant girls?"

"They are all right," said Ferooza. "They were certain the police and the underworld would pin the blame on them and had the presence of mind to flee. The younger girl contacted our office for a microloan. They are in a small town in a different state, living under assumed names. Keep it to yourself—although you may wish to quietly tell Sonia, who must be traumatized by her connection to this sordid tale."

....

TRAVELING ONCE MORE WITH PAPA'S ASHES IN THE KITCHEN storage container, Mama and Ferooza flew down to Goa with Sonia to Maria-by-the-Sea, a gated complex of holiday cottages with twenty-four-hour security that Ferooza's colleague had recommended. Maria-by-the-Sea possessed the air of a run-down holiday place in offseason. On one side was the River Sal, and on the other, a short way down the coastal highway, a path shuffled to the ocean. From a distance Sonia's appointed cottage imitated in miniature the Portuguese bungalows of the past. It had a small veranda with two squat pillars and a red-tiled roof. Closer up you could see it was a modern concrete cube with criss-cross grilles in the windows. When Mama lit the gas burner, it skittered across the countertop. When Ferooza stirred the pot, the flighty pot flitted away. The plastic spatula melted; the particleboard beds fell off the bricks they were propped on. The sheets were synthetic and crackled with hot sparks; the stiff, brown curtains did not draw; and the yellow-and-pink Mickey Mouse towel did not absorb water. Not even the refrigerator or the stove had the weight of real objects. Only by the telephone was an enormous, leather beanbag properly a leather beanbag, and upon it Ferooza got stuck. The climate was sticky, and she was sticky. Chuckling, Sonia and Mama had to peel her off—making a peeling-off sound—and hoist her up.

They hired a fisherman's boat when the palm jungle was growing woolly and indistinct, rowed to where the water was calm, and at the moment the sun's belly rested on the horizon, they emptied the plastic container of Papa's ashes into the sherbet pink and orange ripples. As his ashes floated away and sank, his voice was resurrected and sang into Sonia's ear: *Always look ahead, never look back. What has happened, has happened. As for the rest, don't even bother to try to think it through. Go straight to the mystics!* When a pod of dolphins appeared—leaps, huffs, and snorts—Ferooza said, "Take that as a good omen! They are saying bon voyage."

They all had wet eyes, even Mama, although with her it may have been relief. It was a deeply happy time, for they were together by the sea, it filled their ears and their eyes. They sat together and rested. Then a week later, Mama and Ferooza departed and left Sonia on her own. "What will you write?" Ferooza asked her.

"I don't know yet."

"What I love most are cozy stories of women living peacefully by themselves. Small, simple things: a toothache, a boiled egg, a neighborhood quarrel, a lost cat that you find in the end, before it grows skinny."

*

SONIA WOKE AT 5:30 A.M. on her first day by herself and walked to the complex swimming pool, the first light spinning into the humidity that hung like cobwebs in the palms. Two thickset, middle-aged Russian men stood at the shallow end, drinking beers and smoking, the tepid water ringing their tummies. They spoke slowly and urgently and quietly and didn't look at Sonia as she glided by, nudging aside the big, brown leaves that spanned the surface. They left, and later she got out as well, when three mangy dogs jumped into the mustard-colored water to relieve themselves of fleas and a crow dropped some unidentifiable garbage in to soften it up. A gardener came by and chased the dogs out. He told Sonia the pool hadn't been cleaned since the tourist season. She should swim in the ocean, which naturally cleansed itself.

The kettle was silent in the moment before it came to boil. When it began to whistle, a watchman popped up suddenly at the window. Sonia wondered if he'd been hiding behind a bush.

He asked, "You came six days ago?"

"Yes."

"Our night watchman told me. Your family went where?"

"Delhi."

"You are married?"

"Yes."

"Where is your husband, then?"

"My husband is a rocket scientist," said Sonia. "He works for NASA in USA. Where are you from?"

He said he was from a village in Nepal, an eight-hour walk from the nearest bus stop. At fifteen he'd been recruited by the Maoists, not as a fighter but to carry supplies. Then he worked in road construction across the border in Darjeeling district, then at a honeybee farm in Kumaon, and now he was a security guard in Goa.

Sonia thought it had been stupid to say her husband worked for NASA; she would be worth robbing, and one should never trust a watchman who was likely to be a brother to the thief. She put on a light cotton dress, greeted Perpetua, the maid who worked in the complex, and ventured out. Goa was a different place when you were away from the protection of village life and in the broken land of tourism—without Sunny, Clayton, and Anand. There were eyes on her: guards, gardeners, cleaners, taxi drivers.

A shopping complex made a semicircle around Maria-by-the-Sea, and there were more gem and handicraft shops on the road that ran between the coastal towns. In the window of one was a pair of nine-gemstone earrings. An inner voice repeated the mantra of female empowerment available in every women's magazine she'd ever read during her days in America, during her days sitting in the defunct fountain at Athena Hospital: *Pamper yourself. Don't wait for anyone else to do so. Love yourself first, or nobody will love you. Spend without guilt. Buy yourself something beautiful.*

A man was reclining on a pile of carpets. He hopped up. It smelled of men's sleep. He laid out an earring and began: "Where are you from? You cannot be on a holiday by yourself? Is your family here? I saw you walking alone."

"Where are *you* from?" Sonia asked.

Very hastily he answered, "Kashmir," kicking the question aside, annoyed at being distracted from his roll-call of questions. "What does your husband do? Your father?"

She saw he was scrutinizing her with a hard look—not a sexual look, but a look of trying to uncover what kind of use she may be. There was the sound of water running, and another man emerged from a bathroom behind the pile of carpets, tying his pajama string and resettling his testicles. She realized that the tourist shops were half shops, half bachelor dormitories, full of young men who slept upon the carpets and sat outside during the day, bored but with eyes alert for some useful idiot to come sauntering.

The shopkeeper quoted a high price for the earrings. Seeing her expression, he said, "But jewelry is an investment. It is your wealth, your savings, your *daulat,* your worth."

Adornment is the other side of nonexistence. Beguiling gems are illusion, are divine play, are pleasure. Pleasure is adornment is illusion is beauty that attracts love, moving briefly into the orb of the sun. Beauty is the motivating force of the universe. The earrings were too expensive.

As Sonia walked on, other shopkeepers noted her approach, stared with minute appraisal, called out: "Hello, hi, how are you? Are you NRI? Where are you from? India? England? USA? Come and see my shop. Just look, good price just for you. Hello, nice day. Good morning. I said good morning—did you hear me? Hello, madam. You want to go to turtle beach, madam? Hello? Namaste? Why you not speak? Cannot hear? Bonjour. Buongiorno. No English? No Hindi? Parlez-vous français? No language?"

Sonia wondered if her dress let the sunlight in.

When Sonia discarded her dress, her ruffled, turquoise-green bikini made the beach-shack boys hysterical. "Where you come from? Delhi? South Delhi? I can tell from your accent. Where is your family? You are married? Why you came alone?"

"My husband is a doctor, a surgeon, he is busy all the time, I had to come without him."

She walked farther out to where the beach was empty of men, launched herself into the octopus arms of the sea, which caught her, raised her. She put the ocean between herself and her life. She tried to give her human self to the water. She felt as if her swimming was a kind of prayer to the ocean. She swam and cried a little at the same time, dropping tears into the water, which nulled them as they fell, lesser saltwater into the greater. For a little while after her swim, before her human self claimed her again, she felt unburdened.

She remembered that one always remembers happiness in the water. *Sunny, despite everything, I still think of us swimming high up the waves and sailing down into the fizz and pop.*

She spoke to her dead father: *Papa, the sea calms me. It is the only thing large enough to soothe my sadness.* Often her father joined her in the ocean of her tears: *Sonu, never look back, move on.*

She defied Ilan all this time later: *You don't know what the sea is, no matter how much you say you love it. You're a bad person. Only those with clear hearts can love the sea the way a sea creature does.*

How he would laugh at her child's curse.

She spoke to herself: *I no longer want any human love. I want to be free and not scared.* She thought this was perhaps also a way in which to consider death—a way to be free, safe, without the trap of being female.

The beach shacks were named Dom's, Bay Watch, Betty's, Pickin's. If Sonia got a foot cramp walking on uneven sand, or if the currents were strong, she stopped at Betty's until it released. Betty's had a billiard table and a shelf of humidity-warped, ketchup, curry, and chili-sauce-stained magazines, thrillers, and romances left by tourists. Sonia leafed through *Hello!* magazine, perusing the obituaries that eulogized lives akin to advertising. She found she couldn't feel anything about the demise of such people because she was so impressed by the photographs of their vacations in Saint-Tropez and Portofino, by champagne with club sandwiches at the Grand-Hôtel du Cap-Ferrat, by Malibu sun and Malibu air.

These stories confirmed to Sonia that all deaths were not the same, although others proclaimed there was no competition in the field of loss. The death of a Third World man is different from a First World man, a rich man's different from a poor man's. In the poorer world, most men died before they'd arrived, before they'd achieved their destinies, even a man who was well-off like Papa. And it made these men who would die before they arrived very bitter; it made them plot and scheme, scam and yell; and it stifled their children with sadness, just as it ruined the lives of their wives, their cooks, their dogs, their cats, their mynah birds, if they had any. Death as Sonia had experienced it was not as dignified as it was in elegant magazine obituaries. It was ugly, desperate, vengeful. She had screamed at her dying father and everyone else, including those far less fortunate than herself. Snot had streamed from her nose, animal sounds from her mouth, donkey sounds, baboon sounds, pig sounds.

Sonia had watched for, wished for, and hoped never to see the obituaries of Sunny and Ilan. When it was obvious they had not died on September 11, why did it feel as if they had remained lucky as surely as she was unlucky, the hole in her bucket of fortune linked to their overflowing source?

She thought of Sunny, who would by now have a green card, who had escaped living a harsh life battling the Indian problems that were his birthright. Maybe one day his life would consist of nothing but fancy sandwiches in fancy locations. He would live a life that was not a life, die a death that was not a death. She remembered how they had to dive so deep into the black when the waves rose as high as the Himalayas before they came crashing down.

On her toy veranda, she opened her notebook. The second story she had written, the one her dear professor Conti had praised, was the story of Mina Foi and Ernest. Could she write all the love stories she knew? Grandfather Siegfried and Grandmother Anjolie, that was a love in contradiction to the events playing out on the world stage, a love that undid the historical narrative simply by the way he had caught her glance, how she had caught his. Ba and Dadaji would never bother with the word "love"—they were rooted somewhere deeper, more reliable, more elemental. Armando and Lazlo, one tugged bigger, one shrank smaller. Marie and Cole, who never knew what the other was thinking, but who never, ever fought. Papa's itch and torment, her mother's fleeing into the past. Sonia having turned into a ghostly ghoul. Would these stories intersect and make a book? How would they hold together? How to trust herself to do her part to sustain what existed beyond her vision? What if she stepped back to survey what she had wrought and saw that it lay in incoherent pieces?

If she waited long enough, observed long enough, worked deeply, would everything conjoin—if she respected and preserved the shadows? She went to the ocean and jumped into the babbling script that held the stories and secrets of centuries—of mermaids and sea beasts, colonists and spies, merchants and soldiers, fishermen and charlatans. What united these wayward stories? The ocean. When she swam, she felt swimming beneath her in the depths a chimera. She couldn't see its form, but it was still an intimacy.

CHAPTER

69

....

SLIGHT TEENAGE BOYS WAITED AT THE SHORE FOR SONIA
to emerge; they beckoned and hopped, they smiled, their patience was
long. When she came out of the water, they glommed on to her. She
couldn't rid herself of them, yet it was unclear what they wanted. If
they met her gaze, they smiled and stuck.

"Those boys won't stop following me," she said to a foreigner sun-
ning himself on the neighboring chair at Betty's.

The man opened one eye to look, shut his eye, composed himself,
and said, "They are little-boy prostitutes who think you are a solo
woman tourist in need of company."

"Really?"

He chuckled. "Can't you tell?"

"No, but I don't know how I wouldn't know—it isn't as if I have
any innocence left."

He laughed some more, carefully, not moving as if not to mar his
tanning.

"Where are you from?" asked Sonia, desperate for conversation with
someone who would not attack her or cheat her—therefore someone
who was initially disinterested in her.

He said he was German.

Sonia told him that her grandfather was German, what a coincidence. The man rolled over to face her. He said actually he'd been born
in Tehran. Now he was an actor in the theater. He was working on a
play about a young migrant and an aging film star forging an unlikely
friendship. One was anonymous, one famous—and it turned out this
was more or less the same thing.

Darius said he had left Iran because it was impossible to be openly gay. His parents were resolute in their belief that he didn't have a wife because he was bohemian.

Sonia said, "It can't be simple to be a Muslim immigrant in Germany?"

"I went from one set of problems to another set of problems," he said, laughing.

She laughed, too. "And it's illegal to be gay here—you must always take the difficult fork in the road, like myself."

How easy it is, after all, to make a kind, little joke and be happy. Wasn't Darius lonely traveling alone? No, he had arranged trysts on the internet with men all along his travel route. Observing her curiosity, he relished the telling. He said he had sex with a boy in a rickshaw in Delhi, parked in a deserted area, and the rickshaw driver merely stared ahead as they went at it like demonic rabbits. He said most of the men seemed impoverished, most he guessed were also married, some were students. One, a Zoroastrian, was a novelty: He was obviously well-educated and wealthy; they met in a hotel near India Gate called the Godfrey, and fucked quickly, furtively.

"Do you ever have a conversation with these men?" Sonia felt naïve, but she wanted to know the conversation in case she could put it in a story. What on earth would they say, two people from such different worlds? Could her stories include unusual bedfellows, people who would never normally meet, happening to share a pillow?

"It's just sex," said Darius. But he told Sonia he held to the strict principle of never paying for it.

She couldn't quite make out the morality of this, so she primly asked, "Isn't it dangerous? They may plant drugs on you, then call the police—the police may blackmail you."

"Yes." He sat up and lit a cigarette and looked out at where the little fishing boats looked like ragtag pirate vessels on the curve of the horizon: fishing nets, cooking pots, slippers and buckets, plastic sheets attached to sticks for shade. He turned and looked at her with a sheepish comic expression.

Sonia relaxed into the delightful freedom of nonthreatening male company. She felt it almost ecstatically, undoing the hunched way she'd been holding herself, stretching out and looking at her long, bare arms and legs sanded with silver, feeling her soft hair at her shoulders. "Look at you," said Darius admiringly. For a few days before he traveled on, Darius stayed with Sonia to save money, and side by side in bed they talked more frankly than lovers. Sonia told Darius about Ilan, how she still felt trapped, and he said he, too, had once been entranced by a violent madman. He had been oppressed also by the wealth, so it felt; the schloss outside Munich was so big that by the time he made a cup of tea in the winter kitchen and carried it across the halls and upstairs to his lover, it was cold. With his last flint of strength and self-awareness, he had escaped by pretending he was only going out to buy the pitted black olives his lover had been screaming that Darius had dared to replace with unpitted green olives. He left his belongings behind, save for his passport, and never returned.

"Did anyone help you?"

"Nobody." The lover had most unfortunately been a renowned film director, and when their mutual friends consequently saw Darius, a look of fear came into their eyes; they ran to the other side of the room and pretended not to see or know because Darius now embodied an inconvenient truth. Others who had also been misused by this man, meanwhile, didn't want to be Darius's friend, either. Why? Because it was too painful to the ego to admit a famous man has humiliated you. People blame the spouse for surely encouraging the humiliation, but, in fact, Darius had tried and failed to protect these people. *Don't be two humiliated people together, don't be three ashamed people. . . .* There was no winning. He had exited the poisonous scene and now lived peacefully with his spotless cat, Latife.

"I cannot find peace," said Sonia. "The bad thing is still following me."

"Psychologically?"

"Not only. Once, it took the form of a ghost hound that came out of the ocean. I later saw it in Ilan's painting, one he had painted when I was with him."

"A real ghost hound?"

"Yes. At first I wondered if I was mistaken. It vanished into the sand—but I saw the bite mark in Sunny's slipper; it gouged the slipper when he tried to hit it."

"You are very lucky," said Darius, listening keenly. "How many people are stalked by a ghost hound? That's like meeting the actual Serpent in the Garden. The theater helped me. I thought, I will use *everything* I learned from this person and put it *all* in a play. I realized it wasn't that my partner was famous and I was anonymous; it was that I was anonymous so he could be famous. In the end, the hell weirdly felt worth it. But I had to create that ruthlessness—and that ruthlessness I learned from him!"

"I am trying to write a book, in fact," said Sonia, "but I feel I am circling the story. I see a glimpse here and there, like a fin, a ripple, but I can't see the whole beast. I can't put the center in the center. I wonder if I will have to write all my stories to reveal it."

"That's a long journey?"

"Yes. It feels too daunting to even begin."

"Why don't you put yourself and Ilan in the center?"

"I still hear him saying 'obey me' and feel as if I am betraying, trespassing, stealing."

"It's good to steal from a thief—steal from thieves!"

"I would also have to write about myself. How to write about myself during the time I was missing? My thoughts were Ilan's thoughts. Then if a woman has become a mirror, if art is a mirror, how can a mirror create a mirror?"

"Go through the mirror!" said Darius. "But didn't you ever meet anyone else? I can't believe you wouldn't have."

"You can't meet someone, or love anyone, if you don't exist!"

*

SONIA WAS SORRY TO say goodbye when Darius left on a train to Hospet, on his way to a rave of post-army-service Israeli kids at the ruins of Hampi. She went with him to the station, and they embraced. "Travel safely, darling Darius. Will our paths ever cross again?"

"If you visit me in Berlin, I'll take you to the best nightclubs!"

He was such a handsome, curly-haired, brown-eyed man, waving out of the window dressed in a white kurta, that people turned to stare at the two of them making a romantic Bollywood-style scene of good-bye. As the train pulled out of the station, Darius leaned out farther—and would have fallen from the train had he not been held back by fellow passengers moved by his beauty, by his plight. He shouted, "Sonia! *The ghost hound! Follow the ghost hound! That may be your answer!*" He blew her a final kiss.

*

TO CHEER HERSELF UP now that she was alone again, Sonia went to the River Cafe on the Sal, which adjoined Maria-by-the-Sea. The river had a dark smell—salty, like mussels. Sometimes it flowed in one direction, sometimes in the other, according to the tides. Quite often, the very same potato-chip bag that had floated downriver past Maria-by-the-Sea in the morning, the same persistent plastic slipper, proceeded upriver past her table at the River Cafe in the evening, measured and sedate. From here she could also watch egrets returning at dusk to roost, making a pattern of waves, individual birds parting from the group to make swift, adamant turns in to the trees as if they called a precise twig home.

Had Ilan deliberately lived the life he needed in order to make the art he wanted to make? If you painted entrapment, wouldn't you have to learn the harrowing intimacy of what it is to tell a woman to get down on her knees and swear to obey you? Will she, won't she? Will the spark of hate be lit in her eyes? Will you yourself be threatened? Or will her sense of self be extinguished? Where will her hands go? Where will her eyes? But wasn't Darius right, that the story had simultaneously been given to Sonia? If, when it comes to writing novels, the worst thing that happens to you is the luckiest, then Sonia was lucky. If you had to achieve tragedy before you might ever hope to begin, she had achieved it. Why else would a woman forgo a real life, sequester herself, and execute what would take a lifetime of striving to achieve—

what would sometimes take destroying her work so nobody would even know it existed, what would take driving herself to God and the devil until she couldn't tell the difference between them?

Yet if Sonia managed to write the story of herself and Ilan, it would fall into a tedious stereotype of older, monster male artist and younger, aspiring female artist. A story that kept occurring, kept on being repeated ad nauseam. Wasn't it inevitable that it kept on being relived after it kept on being repeated? Wouldn't a reader determine that at this point of redundancy, it was the victim's fault? Or that the truth was the other way around—the famous man being relentlessly pursued by women of feebler talent? Were Sonia to consign herself to this mediocre vocabulary, she herself would make unforgivably ordinary what had exiled her—in shame, in primitive fear—from ordinary existence to the same nightmares and real-life nightmares that had afflicted her prehistoric ancestors. How to combine the real and supernatural the way they had so implausibly entwined in her own life? To write realistically about the hallucinatory fear of a woman who believes she has made acquaintance with the devil? Darius had called, "*The ghost hound!*" How to follow the aggressor? Live to tell the tale of being stalked by a ghost bloodhound in the dark?

Perhaps a writer must hunt what was hunting herself, her eye searching for the creature that held her within its gaze. But if you followed a creature, while a creature followed you, wouldn't you begin to grow into each other? Stopping when it stopped, moving when it moved, looking to see what it saw? If she followed a rabid ghost hound, wouldn't she become one?

Just don't write magic realism nonsense, she heard Ilan's voice from inside herself. *Just don't write phony pseudo-psychology. Just don't write orientalist rubbish. Just don't write about arranged marriages. Just don't write about painters; everyone gets it wrong.*

*

BEHIND THE SPIT OF the opposite bank where the egrets slept was the open ocean. Casino boats and party boats came by on weekends, playing music loud enough to shake, rattle, roll your organs. The noise increased at nine P.M., when somewhere in the network of paths, an establishment called Barry's Pub played amplified music past midnight, as did the River Cafe, as did Bito's nightclub. An electronic pulse, *boom-shick, boom-shick,* sounded from the Fisherman's Fiesta, shaped like the prow of a ship in the entrance to the hotel behind the River Cafe. Beyond this fanciful entrance, the hotel consisted of several barracks that were occupied in season by European pensioners and large groups from Siberia. The meeting point for these battling sounds was in Sonia. She felt the thumping throughout her body, *boom-shick, boom-shick.* The *boom-shick, boom-shick* destroyed her ability to be alert, to think enough to save herself. The racket would drown out the sound of an intruder. It made Sonia feel unsafe.

She went to the hotel to complain. The slender boy working there may have been sixteen or seventeen. He said, "If there is a wedding party, they will not turn the music down, no matter how much we keep telling them. But I will try, I promise."

"Thank you, you're sweet to try."

He said, smiling, "Madam, *you* are sweet."

She said, "No, I'm not sweet, I'm angry."

"No, madam, you are *sweet*. I see you going on the road every day. I looked you up in the resident list."

"How do you know my name?"

"I asked the watchman. He said you had a boyfriend, a foreigner, now you are alone." He smiled, and his smile stuck. "Madam, if you want my number, I can give it to you."

"Why would I want your number?"

"You can call me for anything you need."

Boom-shick, boom-shick, boom-shick, boom-shick, boom-shick. He poofed, puffed, and moved his shoulders to the music.

That night her phone rang; she picked it up but didn't speak, and nobody answered. She could hear *boom-shick, boom-shick* and a male voice in the background presumably speaking to the person making the call saying "danger" in English. It came crashing in as if it were a

tidal wave that had been gathering strength: a paralyzing fear. She put
the melamine dinner plates against the bathroom window, which did
not have a grille, and pushed the pasteboard dresser against her fake-
wood bedroom door.

Sonia called her mother. "I am scared."

"What are you scared of?"

"There are eyes on me all the time." Madan's eyes had been Ilan's
eyes; Ilan's eyes had been the ghost hound's eyes; and everywhere she
went she saw the same eyes on her, whether they looked out of a dog,
a man, a snake, a pig, a crow, or a lizard on the wall. All these eyes were
in her eyes.

"Do you want to come back here?" asked Mama. Wariness in her
voice. How many times could a daughter run to her mother for help?
Sonia must leave her mother's home as her mother had left her husband's home, as her grandparents had left their landscapes, exiling
themselves, saying goodbye to what they knew, saving themselves
from one fate and another, until there was no fate to give Sonia. All
they had to give her was herself. When she looked in the mirror, she
had no face.

"Take it practically," said Mama. "Don't read anything into anything; that's when you go mad. Get a broom, get a shovel, cover the
gaps through which any creature might crawl, come in by sunset, lock
your door, turn on the lamps, turn on the television." And now Mama
gave in to her fear. "I didn't mention it before, but Ferooza heard that
despicable woman Babita Bhatia lives not so far from you."

"Babita Bhatia?"

"She bought a Portuguese mansion called Casa das Conchas. In case
of an emergency, you could ask her for help."

"I mentioned that house in my *Kala* article!" Sonia couldn't help
but think there was a link.

And, no, Sonia wouldn't be calling Babita Bhatia. She would rather
battle on alone. *Go through the mirror,* Darius had encouraged. *Use your
fear,* she commanded herself. *Use it.*

She wrote another paean to Badal Baba, whom she desperately
needed now:

You who care for the faceless
I who have lost my face
Bat grazes the moon

At night she woke. There was a bat in her room. She ran outside, where the moon confronted her, harsh as an interrogation lamp.

In the morning, Sonia went to Margao and bought a whistle. She told the maid, Perpetua, to retreat down the path to test if she could hear it, then around the corner. This made Perpetua laugh: "Madam, there is no danger."

"How can there be no danger? A woman was raped and murdered by a watchman in Sangolda not long ago." A woman like Sonia, young and making a new life as a single woman. It had been all over the news because she was a fashion model.

"Everywhere something happens," said Perpetua.

After the watchman had raped his victim, he left her tied up and took a shower. He dressed in her brother's Superman T-shirt. He fried himself eggs. After he had eaten the fried eggs, he asked her where she kept the key to the almirah. After she told him where to find the key that led to the key to the key to the key, he robbed her of her valuables. After which he strangled her. For three days, before he was captured, he had enjoyed the life of someone from the lucky classes. He went to the casino boats, to the red-light district in Vasco port. His justifiable anger at the wealthy was at the heart of his unjustifiable crime. The class difference meant he didn't see his victim as human.

A thought came to Sonia that startled her. It was a simple and obvious thought. That the way she thought about Ilan was similar in some crucial aspects to the way Khansama, Chandu, Moolchand must think about her. If women were necessary yet despised, the poor must also stay poor so the rich can be rich. Her ideas were splintering, proliferating—how to include them all in what she may one day write?

Sonia left the house while Perpetua cleaned. She saw two golden-skinned, golden-haired, dozy Russian beauties in skimpy bikinis sunbathing on the balcony of the barracks hotel when she walked by the back of the property, past the funky garbage heap fermenting in tropical heat. The women smiled and waved. They had no language in common with Sonia, but they saw themselves reflected in one another—the first generation of ordinary women in the history of women with the ability to travel without men. She felt a smidgen of pride in herself and in them. She remembered two African American women on holiday in Venice sitting at a table adjoining Sunny and herself. They were lawyers from D.C. The waiter was flirting with them; light from the pink glass lamps in the piazza fell pink and gold on the canal; the water picked this light up and tossed it in a careless spaghetti upon the walls.

Sonia had felt a camaraderie with the women, and she was simultaneously smug that she was with a man, even a man like Sunny. She and Sunny were the first generation of young Indians—boyfriend and girlfriend, unmarried—who could go on holiday in Italy. Now she felt she was being paid back for that brief feeling of being as lucky as others, luckier than others.

To be a brown woman alone traveling, to be two white women traveling, to be a brown man and a brown woman traveling, to be a brown woman and a white man traveling—all of these things equaled startlingly different experiences. Sonia examined her attraction to Ilan. Had she thought he was more Westernized, and superior? Had he thought so? Why else had he been so free to show her his worst side, his most insecure side, his cruel and naked ambition? She was certain Ilan would never have revealed himself to a white woman in a similar manner. Nor would he tell a Frenchwoman not to eat her smelly French cheese. Would he spit on her face?

Once she made it past her pride, she knew that Ilan's affection (when he was not spitting on her) had been the affection you have for your young, dark maid whom you are fucking and expect will forgive you—no matter your having revealed your horrible personality—for the favors you throw her way. And if she betrays you, what would it matter?

The beautiful people of Europe and the United States who were applauding Ilan's fame, the fame they had granted him, were really admiring themselves. Believing in Ilan meant believing in themselves.

In the moral ambiguity of his canvases, they could absolve one another. They wouldn't plan on believing in Sonia, the mouse from Hauz Khas. But in anonymity was also freedom.

Use your fear, she told herself again. *Use it!* Follow the ghost hound. How much of what she wrote was remembering? How much was making up what was already true?

"Don't move!" Ilan admonished—he had been sketching Sonia. "Or you will ruin my painting, and nobody should ruin my painting, do you understand?" He sighed. "Okay, I'll tell you a story about yourself—maybe you'll be interested and behave better." And she had listened because we all carefully listen to stories about ourselves:

"What if one night you have a dream about a dog. Not a normal dog, an enormous hound. Its ears are torn, its back shows deep wounds, it drags a broken chain. It is dead-white except for a harlequin face, as if it's a dog wearing the mask of a dog. It is apparently friendly and comes up to you appearing out of nowhere, and it follows you, bowlegged, dogged, as if it's identified you as being alone, too, and maybe you both could do with a companion. Dogs by instinct search for a person to belong to, to walk with. Maybe you are sympathetic. Maybe it reminds you of yourself. It is lonely. It is wounded and a stray. You feel sorry for and threatened by it. It is both victim and perpetrator. It wags, but when you put out your hand, it shows its teeth and growls. Yet it keeps following you. When you go into your home, you think you've lost it, but then in the morning, there it is, waiting. And when you throw a stone to get rid of it, it doesn't run away. The opposite—it attacks, frothing at the mouth. So what choice do you have? Accept an aggressive and dangerous enemy into your home or try to drive it away eliciting a violent response? You let time pass. Again you throw a stone, and it flies across at you. In the moment of attack, you become the dog. You fight back. You try to kill the dog while it tries to kill you. Your face becomes its face. Your eyes become its eyes.

"One day after this nightmare, you happen to go for a swim and see a red-and-black, diamond-patterned sea serpent. You know it is poison-

*ous, so you swim fast toward the shore. And on the beach, you see wait-
ing for you in real life, the same dog, the harlequin-faced one from your
dream. Did you conjure it, or did you intuit it?"*

The following morning Sonia walked out, and in the ornamental
bush right outside the front door, draped as if an offering or an omen,
was a snakeskin several feet long. The serpent's mouth was perfectly
formed with a crisscross pattern on the translucence, like Venetian
glass. She called the watchman. "But the snake will be long gone," he
laughed. "It was using the bush to slough off its skin." She walked to
the beach to swim, and a wave tossed a sea snake onto the sand before
her as she entered the ocean. It writhed, trying to scramble back into
the retreating water. Three times the waves brought it back to shore
before it vanished.

There was a family just a little way down. "Did you see that poisonous sea snake?" she asked.

"No," they said, "we were looking right there. There was no
snake."

She telephoned Mina Foi, who was doing Bible puzzles. "Mina Foi,
evil is chasing me." Mina Foi believed in Satan, in the eternal battle
between good and evil, but she couldn't hear Sonia—she was getting as
deaf as Ba—so she said whatever she felt like saying, whenever she felt
like saying it. She said, "Naughty girl, always *khee-khee-khee*!" Then
she said, "I think I'd better go now. Someone is at my front door."

Sonia knew that she had no front door.

"Mina Foi, how can I run away from it?" she bellowed.

"From what?"

"EVIL!"

"If it's evil, there's no point in running. I can tell you that much."

Snakes know rats know dogs know men know women on their own.

A shadow moved, and Sonia screamed.

Perpetua had just walked in, and she said, "But it is only me, madam.
I brought you red spinach, madam, from the farm near my house."

Sonia said to Perpetua, "I dreamt about a snake, I wrote about a
snake, and now real snakes leap out at me."

She said, "Madam, if you were in Mumbai, you might write or dream of a snake, but a real snake could not jump out at you. These things are not connected." Then she glanced at her watch and dropped the spinach. "My son's ship is passing in ten minutes. When it goes by he calls me on his mobile while I watch from the beach. He is heading to the Suez."

Her son worked on a merchant ship. Because of him, Perpetua kept an eye on storms, hurricanes, typhoons, tsunami warnings, all over the world. His name was Frankie Francis Francisco Fernandes, in honor of St. Francis Xavier. They hoped this would keep him safe and to remind the saint, they slept all night outside the basilica before his feast day to celebrate in the morning.

"You need to have faith," she called to Sonia as she ran out.

But the other side of faith was doubt!

"Why didn't you leave before you were killed?" the ghost of the woman killed asked the portrait of the woman who had become a ghost.

"I was living in a world that possessed an intensity that ordinary life did not have. For a span of time, it felt like a fair bargain."

"Why did you stay so long?"

"I couldn't belong normally to India anymore. I couldn't belong normally to the States. To do something strange was possible, to do something normal was impossible."

"Why did you let yourself be mistreated?"

"Ilan mixed life and art, and I confused him with his malevolent art. I was loyal to the art."

"Why did you persist?"

"I forgave this madness because I thought he was ill, and I forgave a turn of the hourglass too long. There is, in the end, just a scintilla of time during which you can save yourself: You don't before, and you cannot after."

"Why did you wait until he spat out your bones?"

"I wanted to be a writer of beautiful and strange novels, and I thought a writer must believe anything can be true. But because I couldn't believe what I was experiencing was true, I kept watching and

*saying: 'Can this possibly be true?' The less I was a person, the less I
had the ability to tell what was true and what was not. I no longer believed a glass of water was a glass of water. And then I couldn't write. I
couldn't trust anything, including what I might write. How could I believe in a ghost hound?"*

There was an illness to writing without seeing that gave a person an
internal vertigo. Sonia went down to the ocean. After the ocean goes
pink and orange, before it goes indigo and the dusk turns to dark, the
ocean turns very pale and very still. Its movement becomes absorbed in
this shade of milk; it levitates, otherworldly. Sonia floated on her
back—it was like being rocked in a cradle. She wasn't sure how long
she stayed this way. When she finally opened her eyes and looked
around, she found herself so far from shore that she couldn't see it, and
so lulled was she by the heavenly hush, swarming, brimming, that her
intuition flipped. Instead of calling out alarmed, telling her to turn
back, it suggested she float on deeper into the murmuration, farther to
where it was even more ethereal, no determinate shade or color. To
where she would be safe from the nightmares that persisted on land.

It was now she sensed her father soundlessly urging her back. Papa,
too, was in this ocean, wasn't he? He did not wish his daughter to die.
And just as much as he wished to avenge himself on his wife, he did not
want his wife to be bereft of her daughter. Or maybe it was Sonia's
own conscience that made her turn back, loyal to her dead father, loyal
to her mother, although she was so far from earth, heaven was the
closer destination. Although she was so tired. *Rest, rest, let go, let go,* the
murmur agreed, the hush hushed. Once more, she felt herself succumb; the return was too daunting, she would tire before she could
make it. *Let go, let go.* Again, she felt her father's love, stronger this
time. She turned with the kind of superhuman effort it takes sometimes to retrieve oneself from a weighted, deathly slumber. And when
she did, within a moment, the ocean's temperament changed. Denied
its will, it revealed its murderous intent. She had been almost seduced,
almost tricked beyond being able to save herself. It had almost claimed
her. She began to strive back in earnest—

When from out of the ocean shards came lunging at her the harlequin hound. She kicked. It drew closer. She swam away. It followed. Sonia's panic would exhaust her, endanger her. Again and again, the ghost dog, opaque of eye, met her and drove her farther out. Sonia turned to swim horizontally to land, remembering that this was the trick to escaping a riptide. The beast disappeared; it might be under her, it might be up ahead.

It was a long while before she reached the sand. She crawled out on her belly, lay in the grave made by the ocean's draining. And there, waiting for her in the sepulchral twilight, was the phosphor of the hound.

"Go away, you bastard," she hissed, too tired to run. "Go away—"

And it did. It climbed inside her and vanished.

·······························

BABITA TURNED OFF THE TELEVISION NEWS AND SUMMONED
Naresh to drive her to her bank locker in Panjim. Should she finally
succumb and sell a portion of her wedding jewelry to purchase a plane
ticket to Mexico? She couldn't leave Casa das Conchas empty: Edelweiss, Ida, and Clotildes would move in. They had come at Christmas,
when star lanterns had been lit in the verandas and in the boughs of the
trees, in chapels that one might come upon unexpectedly, shining
sweetly in sandy coconut palm groves. "No festivities here," she had
told Sunny when he remarked Christmas in Goa was surely festive.
"Nobody came by."

Sisters Edelweiss, Ida, and Clotildes had brought a Christmas pudding. They said, "We are God-fearing people." For a mere sixty lakhs
they would withdraw their claim to the well and that crooked patch of
land. "Only twice a year, on Daddy's birth and death anniversary, we
will lay flowers on Daddy's grave."

Babita hadn't dared. "This isn't Christmas pudding! This is simple
fruitcake!" Yet here she was, up on an unsteady ladder at her bank
locker, following her life's battlecry: *Despite! In spite! Despite everyone
and everything!* She examined the necklace and earrings her mother had
given her on her wedding day, star and crescent cloudy gems, rubies
and emeralds, gold and knobby pearls, meant to be passed on to a
daughter, or a daughter-in-law, in turn.

With the jewels heavy upon her sweaty lap, she rode back and forth
between the bank and Shamrock Jewelers in Dona Paula, where, according to Vanya, they gave an honest assessment, though with a friend
like Vanya, one didn't need an enemy. At lunchtime Naresh reliably

lost his temper, and when Babita suggested they return to the bank one last time, he refused. "You cannot make up your mind whether to sell or not to sell. Think it over while I eat." And he drove like a maniac toward prawn curry rice and a siesta.

Back in Casa das Conchas was Babita, although it was foolhardy to keep rubies and emeralds in one's house when the driver knew they were there. Was Naresh part of the plot to defraud her of Casa das Conchas? Naresh, Edelweiss, Ida, and Clotildes had all grown up in this very same vaddo, so why wouldn't they conspire to oust the outsider? Just as in *Jean de Florette.*

She locked the balding, royal-purple velvet box in the almirah and the key to that in the linen chest on lion paws, the key to that in the liquor cabinet carved with monkeys eating breadfruit, and the key to that she hid behind the bleeding Christ. She picked up *Mexico Past and Present,* which made her feel as if she were accompanying Sunny on his travels. Just as in Hinduism, the Aztec and Mayan gods came in aspects terrifying and benign, and their view of the world rested upon dualities: sun-moon, war-rain. She examined the photographs of Moctezuma's iridescent feathered headdress, like a peacock's rainy-season dancing feathers, and the mask of the bat god Piquete Ziña, which had adorned a skeleton in a sacrificial tomb in Monte Albán. She read about the practice of human sacrifice, hearts pried out by temple priests on sacrificial altars—again, the subject of murder!

She poured her first rum by five P.M. She planned not to carry on drinking through the evening but to stop at a point that would create a low buzz that would buzz her gently on till bedtime.

Three and a half hours later she was speaking out loud to herself— "You know you promised to keep it at two rums, and you've already had two and a quarter. Be honest, there is nobody else at the tribunal—" when someone rang the brass bell polished to a shine by Olinda.

The murderer the murderous thief the thieving murderer coming down the avenue of temple trees, climbing the operatic front steps, seeking a pair of cloudy gem earrings transported from a dingy bank locker in Allahabad to one in Delhi to one in Panjim, the kind of thief who politely knocks and when you politely answer bludgeons you with a steel rod or a concrete block.

Babita ran to the altar room, Pasha following to stuff himself under the confessional chair with the airy rattan screen, which would reveal priest to confessor, and confessor and her dog to priest.

After a while Babita reemerged into silence, save for the starry-flowery, thrumming Milky Way of insects. But the bell shrilled again, then, "Babita Aunty?" A woman's voice. "Babita Aunty?"

Babita tiptoed to the door and said in an unwelcoming, suspicious manner, "*Whooo?*"

"Sonia—Lawyer Shah's granddaughter from Allahabad."

When Babita unlatched one half of the tall, thin door, just a crack, at first glimpse she thought a wild animal was at her door, or a jungle demoness with salty hair and no recognizable face. An emotion more primal than a human one had claimed it—it was a face of cracked-open fear. Moths thick about the entrance lamp broke the light that fell upon this apparition.

"What on earth are you doing here?"

"I don't know."

"Are you ill?"

"I was being attacked."

"By whom?"

Sonia didn't reply. She stood arms wrapped around herself, but this didn't stop her from violently quivering. Babita let her in—what else could she do? When they were seated, Babita leaned back against the sofa cushions and stared. They continued to sit without speaking, the two nemeses. The sound of insects surged, subsided.

Sonia had made a mistake in coming. What should she say? In desperation, she almost blurted, *I was sorry to hear about Uncles Ravi-Rana.* But that would expose the fact that she knew about their deaths and hadn't bothered to proffer her condolences earlier. Because of the contagion of corruption? Because Sunny had forsaken her?

She twisted her legs about each other. She opened her mouth to say that she must get going, but she found herself unable to speak the words because she realized she did not want to be alone at Maria-by-the-Sea, more than she did not wish to be here. She was grateful to sit in a house imbued with the dignity of the past, and in the company of an aged, gentleman dog and another woman—even *this* woman. She didn't want to exit back into the puzzle of country-night lanes to find a taxi.

But what to say? They listened to Pasha glugging mournfully from the toilet. He began to *choo choo,* unable to turn around. Babita went and turned him around. She kicked *Mexico Past and Present* under the sofa before she went so as not to carelessly reveal her doomed plan: the flight ticket being plotted, Goa–Dubai–Frankfurt–Mexico City. *Despite! By hook or by crook! By gemstones meant for a daughter-in-law!*

But what to say?

Should she tell Sonia she must gather her courage and go home—what was she scared of? Should Babita claim that she herself was unwell and couldn't entertain a visitor? But just as she resolved to do so, she realized that she was eager, in fact, for company. And here was her enemy vanquished at her feet, so to speak. She realized she was glad that Sonia was a woman on her own like herself, not a safe, pampered woman.

She switched her thinking. If you treat the defeated person kindly, it is as if you had never conspired against her. The more magnanimous Babita was now, the more she would undo the harm she had perpetrated, the more margin there would be for her innocence to take root and flower. Then the proof of Babita's innocence was there for Sonia to see. There was no kebab cook, there was no Sunny.

But what to *say*?

She almost proffered, *I was sorry to hear about your father's death,* but she hadn't felt anything at all, she was too full of her own tragedy. Most men, it was a good thing when they were dead; you could resurrect them as Ideal Father or Ideal Husband. She thought of saying, *I read your kebab article,* but that would invoke the kebab cook and her attempt to steal him. She almost admitted, *I read your piece on Goa,* but that would lead to the halcyon days of Sonia and Sunny in Loutolim, which, in a roundabout way, was why she was stranded in Casa das Conchas.

Her stomach growled and all of a sudden she found herself blurt-ing, "Did you eat? Olinda leaves my dinner. She won't stay to serve it, no matter how much I offer to pay. She wants to be with her own fam-ily. Goan servants are different from servants elsewhere. Olinda drinks from my glasses and sits on my toilet—in Delhi it would be a scandal, but I realize I prefer it this way." In fact, Olinda's assumption of equal-ity had shocked her; she blamed Umberto for it and surreptitiously rewashed glasses and disinfected the toilet. But what sense did this make? It was all right for Olinda to swab the toilet but not sit upon it? All right to touch the glasses with her hands but not her lips? Anyway, lying to Sonia made her feel like a better person, so what she said was in some way true. She turned on the toaster oven and clattered the dish out when it was hot, a lady comically unused to kitchen work. "Olinda makes a seafood lasagna nice and cheesy." She dropped the dish towel from up high, carried plates to the table, and then thought it would be just as uncomfortable to eat silently together as it was to sit together without conversation in the living room.

Babita suggested they watch one of the DVDs she had hesitated to enjoy on her own. She hesitated again for a moment, but murder in the rich world is not murder in the poor world; in an Agatha Christie film, murder is secondary to the pleasure of observing the country homes of aristocrats, the travels and foibles of the wealthy. And if she and Sonia watched it together, she wouldn't be scared. Sonia assented because a murder mystery was less intimidating than no conversation between herself and Babita. They watched *Murder on the Orient Ex-press,* plates held aloft, linen napkins embroidered with conch shells on their laps.

The travelers boarded a train in the chaos of Stamboul station. In-side there was civility and hushed wealth, but the train itself was an overheated beast, heaving, panting coal black through the snow-white Alps. Finding the murderer came down to reading the suspects cor-rectly, and everyone behaved delightfully according to their ascribed national traits: pukka British colonel, blabbermouth American momma, finicky Frenchman, sharp English nanny.

Out of the corner of her eye, Babita observed Sonia's beauty, albeit reduced from the travails of the past months. But with nobody else around, Babita found she could appreciate the long limbs, the eyes and skin and teeth that flashed, the face planed like a panther, the down-turned mouth of noble reproach. It was a weird beauty—in fact, what would have been called ugly just ten years ago, but now ideas were transforming. Sonia delicately wielded her fork. Her slender bare feet, sparkling with sand, were folded over each other.

By the end of the film, the women were fatigued, and Pasha, at the door leading out of the living room, raised his head and howled.

"Did the film scare him?"

"It's past his bedtime. He likes to go to bed early, but he's scared to go alone and wants me to retire with him. At nine-thirty he moves to the door and sits watching me with pathetic eyes. At ten he begins inching down the corridor. If I don't follow, he returns to the living room and begins to wail. He waited longer today because we have company."

It's the little things one wants to share. Babita drew a breath and told herself she did not wish to be alone with jewels in the house after watching a murder mystery, it would be tempting fate to repeat itself. "It's past eleven. I would never be able to rouse Naresh, and no taxi would venture this far now. Why don't you take a shower—you look like you need one? The guest-room bed is made up." *In case Sunny unexpectedly rings the bell the way you did instead.*

"I'm embarrassed to have stayed so late," said Sonia.

No, you're not embarrassed, Babita thought in a return to sense. What if Sonia stole the earrings? But no, Sonia would surely not go rummaging behind a bleeding Christ to find a key to a key to a key to what might have, in another life, been destined for her.

"Thank you," said Sonia.

At least there were scant manners. In any case, save for bandicoots, ghosts, and thieving murderers, Babita could detect the slightest sound anywhere in the house.

"Did you find the light switch?" she called when Sonia went into the guest bathroom with one of Babita's flowered caftans. Sonia jumped. Where was the voice coming from? She looked up and realized the ornamental ceiling of geometric Arabian stars was fretted and you could speak between rooms.

"Is there soap?" Babita's voice projected overhead. "The bandicoots steal it. I had them trapped, but a new tribe invaded."

"There is soap."

"Watch out for the tree frogs," Babita warned as Sonia stood under the random plops of water, balmy night air passing through the insect netting that opened onto the leafy interior courtyard. "They think my caftans are blossoming gardens and hide in the folds."

Tiny frogs whizzed from wall to ceiling all over the bathroom, joyous in the wet. Sonia soaped the sticky ocean from her body.

"Did you find the carafe of water?" called Babita from her four-poster bed under a canopy crocheted by a nun.

"I did," Sonia replied from the guest-room bed under a canopy crocheted by a widow. She had wrung out her hair and spread the damp mass over a towel laid upon the pillow.

"Good night, then."

"Good night."

"Are there any mosquitoes?"

"There is always one."

An hour later Babita woke when her body ignited itself. Along with lightning flashes came intimations of evil. A viscous sweat stagnated under her armpits, and a wetter perspiration drenched and steamed her bed of coals, her heart of coals. She considered *Murder on the Orient Express:* How many individuals may hate a person and have reason to take revenge? In a society as riven as India, you could not solve a murder even if you found the murderer; the class difference was so great, one couldn't read what the other person was doing, thinking, or why. There would be a story behind the story; justice would fall between the two. Shouldn't she tell Sonia about her innocence upon the night of— *Don't say, Babita. Don't go condemning yourself.*

Sonia woke. She switched on the light to find her water glass and make sure no moth was scrabbling upon the surface or trolling the depths. She felt the ocean's tug on her, and the ghost hound reentered her mind. Was it really inside her? Were its eyes in her eyes?

"Can't you sleep?" She heard the voice of Babita. What on earth was she doing in the house of the mother of her betrayer? The mother who had emotionally blackmailed her betrayer to betray her? Could she put Babita between herself and the monster? "Insomnia," answered Sonia.

"It could be the murder mystery," said Babita.

"Afterward one can't stop thinking."

"Night thoughts are diseased."

How freeing it would be, thought Sonia, *for a group of people who had each been harmed by a brute to kill the brute, to murder the murderer.* If twelve people plunge a knife, it wouldn't be possible to tell which dagger blow caused the death; it would absolve everyone of the crime. And because it would right a wrong, it would absolve everyone twice over. "In the day things happen to make night thoughts diseased—"

"There is something in the air—"

"And in the water. Even the ocean that I love so much is turning against me. Snakes come jumping out of the waves but nobody else sees them."

"Why does nobody else see them?"

"I fell into a world beyond this world."

"Is that what made you scared?"

"A phantom—"

"A phantom?"

Din of insects, squeak of bats, strangled screech of screech owl, tut of frog, opera of lovelorn cats, bark of stray dog pretending it has a house to guard.

"A ghost hound," admitted Sonia. "A ghost hound came after me."

"A ghost hound?"

"Friend of the sea serpent and a man who was declared dead and assaulted me in the maharaja's hunting lodge at Sardar Samand."

Silence from Babita.

"Bad things keep happening to a person who has been harmed. Evil sniffs out the wound. The witness must be destroyed."

Silence from Babita.

"I sound as if I have a screw loose."

Babita did not think Sonia had a screw loose. She thought that Sonia had, like Babita, caught hold of the tail of an invisible beast. What the beast looked like exactly, they did not know, but it peeked up here, then it peeked up there, a nose, a tail, a threat, a sign—they were following and being followed by a dangerous enemy. It sent its emissaries.

"My mother said be practical, turn on lights and lock doors—"

"How can you be practical against a phantom? The animals sense danger. Pasha follows me from room to room and we sleep barricaded inside. Sometimes I get out of bed at midnight and wander around in my nightie, checking locks, thinking, *Wasn't I brought up to belong to society? Why have I been cast out?* I don't even know who I am anymore."

"When I look in the mirror I can't see my face," said Sonia.

Pasha went to drink from the toilet and cried out, *choo choo.* Babita switched on the light, turned him around, returned to bed, switched off the light.

"Sonia?"

"Yes?"

"I am also followed by phantoms—and threatening phone calls."

"Threatening calls?"

The curse of a single woman! Who to tell things to? Wasn't it normal that a woman alone divulges to another woman alone what should otherwise remain within a family? The affection and help that one should get from a son one must seek from a former enemy.

"*Murderers!*"

"Murderers?"

"The murderers of my brothers-in-law."

"What do they want?"

"The fact I don't know is their power. They threaten me with what I don't know. A voice says, 'Where is Minnie's will? Where are the egg cups? Where is the gold?' They are telling me they know my private details. But I don't know if they think I actually have any gold, or if it's a reminder to be silent, or if it's their way of making a joke—the underworld has a peculiar sense of humor. 'Who are you?' I scream into the phone.

" 'You? Kaun?' "

" 'Who?' "

" 'Kaun?' "

" 'You' "

" 'Whooo?' "

"The line goes dead. I feel certain I am going to be murdered for a crime I didn't commit."

"It must be scary to be here on your own."

"It's scary to age alone."

"It's scary to be young alone."

"We are all ultimately alone."

"That isn't so."

"Yes, why are we told that? Some of us are, and some of us are not."

"There are those who have never known loneliness."

Two lonely people who had assured each other they were not crazy, Babita and Sonia drifted into sleep, and while Babita dreamt not at all, Sonia dreamt, once again, that she returned to Ilan's estate to retrieve her amulet. In this dream, Ilan wanted to kill her. But she was a ghost hound. "So come and kill me, what difference will it make now?"

*

BABITA HAD TRIUMPHANTLY CHASED after the poi wallah on his bicycle for their morning bread. Over tea and toasted poi, she asked Sonia, "So why are you in Goa?"

"I came to write a book."

"What is it about?"

"I don't know yet. It's all in pieces." Sonia was spreading ambrosial pineapple jam.

"I'm not a novel reader, so what do I know, but whatever you write, be careful. When you wrote about kebabs, I wanted kebabs. When you wrote about Goa, I bought a house in Goa. You have a witchy talent."

A week later an envelope, smudged a little with red earth, was delivered to Casa das Conchas. Babita sliced it open with her silver inlay letter opener. The envelope enclosed a thank-you note for Babita's hospitality and two sheets of paper upon which Sonia had written out the recipes for galawati and kakori kebabs—from the days she had re-searched kebabs and copied household recipes from Chandu's exercise book, which he kept under the tin can with the checkered orange-and-blue waxed-paper sticks he rolled from the bread wrapping in order to light the stove.

71

························

S UNNY BICYCLED PAST THE CROCODILES IN THE MANGROVE
ecological park into the village. The snowbird gringos had flown north
at winter's end, and the zocalo was empty save for the sun. He telephoned Babita for her flight details, Goa–Dubai–Frankfurt–Mexico
City. He would meet her at Benito Juárez airport. They would go to
the zocalo, see the giant flag being ceremoniously lowered to the call
of a bugle, soldiers rolling it into a python—their movements switching between soldierly and housewifely—all that fabric!—and marching it to its sleeping quarters by the presidential palace. Babita and
Sunny would join the crowds washing into the soot-and-gold Catedral
Metropolitana de la Asunción de la Santísima Virgen María a los Cielos
and perform darshan before the merciful Virgin, who would be pleased
to see she had brought about their miraculous reunion. They would
spend the night in the Gran Hotel Ciudad de México, ignoring the
evangelical with a microphone remonstrating, "Señor, señor, centavo
por centavo, peso por peso," wanting the rich to hear the eternal cry of
poverty, to tap and tap at their eternally closed hearts—because it was
worth it to splurge just once. They would travel to San Miguel de Allende, which Babita's guidebook had informed her was like Europe—
a historic town full of white people.

Babita squeezed her eyes shut and forced herself to say what she
could hardly bear to say but managed: "Sunny, I will not be able to
come to Mexico."

She squeezed her eyes tighter: "Umberto turned out to be a scoun-
drel. Casa das Conchas was illegal for him to sell."

"Why did you trust him? After the disaster in Delhi?"

"Umberto himself had been cheated and felt justified in passing the cheating along to someone else—anyhow it doesn't matter because court cases are decided after everyone is dead." She didn't say she had trusted Umberto because she couldn't be cheated by an Italian. *Italy is true. Italy is not true? No, no, Italians are true! Or we all go down!*

"I checked with a lawyer. I wasn't some foolish woman being charmed by a foreigner."

Sunny was flooded with anger—after all she had put him through! And relief—Babita might have lost yet another home! Babita would *not* be joining him in Mexico!

Babita squeezed her eyes tighter yet, so there was nothing before her eyes. She stepped through:

"That girl was here."

"Which girl?"

"The one from Allahabad."

"Sonia?"

"She turned up suddenly at night."

"Why?"

"She said she was being attacked."

"Who was attacking her?"

"She said a ghost hound—honestly, it made sense in middle-of-the-night ramblings, but in the morning I was not sure what she meant. Maybe it was a metaphor of some sort. She said she was trying to write a book but she can't put the center in the center because the center is occupied by a ghoul that has the same eyes as a dead man who assaulted her in Sardar Samand.

"It sounded completely crazy, but who am I to call anyone crazy? I am also being pursued by phantoms, and everyone tells me I am mad—and who wouldn't be mad after what I have experienced?"

"Don't you know how fucked-up you are?" blurted Sunny to his mother.

An Indian boy saying this to his Indian mother!

"Where did you learn to speak like this?"

"From you. How else to speak to you?"

"I fed her Olinda's lasagna. We watched *Murder on the Orient Express*. I practically tucked her into bed." What had she done wrong in this instance?

Sunny was the one to blame. He hadn't been in India to help his mother. Sonia had been attacked, and she had not turned to Sunny because he had given her no reason to think she could. He knew Babita would be the last person in the world Sonia would approach unless— *unless*? Sunny recalled the painting in *Artes de México*, the many-paneled mirror reflecting a woman watched by her own myriad eyes. Where could she go but through the looking glass? What Ilan painted had once again come true. He had opened Sonia to the darkness of his world. It had cursed her, it had reincarnated, it was maturing to its fullest potential. It would never leave because the darkness believed she belonged to it. Sunny bit down on the side of his cheek and tasted his blood.

It felt as if Satya had been correct in his admonishment. Could it be that this was what had secretly drawn Sunny to Mexico? He had thought he was hunting a life story, but a life story had been hunting him, calling upon him to play his part. He rummaged in the heap of junk behind his casita, which he would have thrown out were it not for the fact that he felt guilty throwing precious recyclables into the garbage. Anand's anguish had remained in him, and no matter how much the gringos complained about the insufficiencies of the developing world, they had failed to establish a recycling system—and their failure they also blamed on the insufficiencies of the developing world. Sunny's tower of recyclables that could not be recycled was growing taller—bottles, cans, plastic bags, and paper. He unearthed the airline magazine Satya had left behind and the *Artes de México* he didn't want to keep inside his home because of the article on Ilan. He went to Melaque to purchase a magnifying glass at the papeleria. With it, he searched the magazine photographs: the walls, the cabinets. He saw wooden masks of demons, cane mermaids and pigs, tin Madonnas, talismans of palm and corn husk, skeletons made of papier-mâché, Christ woven upon a cross in the guise of a cob upon a stalk, clay creatures from plundered funerary shafts. But, no, he didn't see a silver case carved with Tibetan clouds and dragons, one that might have traveled centuries, escaping persecution across a Himalayan mountain pass where only a cloud would have found a way.

Ilan's eye bloomed up at him through the magnifying glass. He dropped the magazine—the eye was the same eye as the ghost hound on the deserted stretch of beach near Loutolim. Sunny's thinking went to a quagmire. It was only by action that a way forward might be revealed.

72

....

FROM THE ROAD THAT MEANDERED ALONG THE COAST, SUNNY caught the country bus that farted gently up and down the low hills to Barra de Navidad, where the parrot-voiced clown boarded and tormented passengers until they paid for him to jump off at the traffic light. From Barra de Navidad, he caught the bus to Guadalajara, and in Guadalajara, the bus got stuck in a parade with a cavalry of horses, a marching band, schoolchildren, three beauty queens, and a float upon which sat a giant papier-mâché Osama bin Laden waving a gun. Men dressed as American marines shot at the Osama bin Laden. Then came a lewd band of rapscallion devils and skeletons. Everyone laughed hard. Sunny, watching from the window, thought he was in a country linked by the devil to Los Estados Unidos. While Sunny did not believe in God, he *did* believe in the devil—therein may lie his life's problem.

From Guadalajara, he boarded a bus to Querétaro, and by a further circuitous bus route, he arrived upon his third day of travel at a hamlet by the deserted Angustias mine ruins, where at the front desk of the only posada in these parts, engrossed in a Spanish version of *The Big Book of Alcoholics Anonymous,* sat a formal man with an immense, drooping mustache. He was, he said, bowing, a descendant of the owner of the former Casa de Moneda. The mines had been raided during the revolution, after which they had flooded, after which the town had become a ghost town. The family had fallen on hard times, and he had left to live in San Luis de la Paz. But because he had also fallen on hard times in San Luis de la Paz, he had returned and restored the ruined structure into an inn.

"Why are you here?" the proprietor asked.

"To meet the artist de Toorjen Foss."

"That is the only reason anyone comes. Not so long ago a boy was here to see him, and before that, another. They looked like the artist and said they were his sons. They were foreigners. I never saw them again. Before that a young woman came, and I never saw her again. After that another woman came. She, too, disappeared. Then another. She also vanished. Journalists often come, thank goodness—they are the only ones who return happy—and with them we make a few pesos. They always write well about the artist because he is famous. That brings more journalists."

A wind rattled the black skeletons of dead prickly pear in the square outside, clanged the corrugated metal and plywood of boarded-up windows and doors. Bats flew into the night from the curtains of the room Sunny occupied, and when he opened *Pedro Paramo,* a book he was trying to read in Spanish, a scorpion crawled over the page. He threw the book into a corner and turned out the lamp. Loveless men may be the driving force of ruthless history. And was Sunny, too, like the traveler in the book, entering the world of the living dead? How many people had been killed in these mines? How could their souls not make a rushing? The wind blew unceasingly. If only he had company under the thin blanket-rug he had lifted off the floor to cover himself. He lay rigid in the cold, his spine and limbs refusing to unclench, and remembered how luxurious it was to sleep with someone whose embrace provided comfort for the next day, an embrace one could soften into as if into a buttery pastry knot, into Melting Moments from a country bakery in the jungle palms. Why had he come here for Sonia's sake when they would never sleep entangled again the way they had? What if life together had accrued? What if there had been so many nights entangled and so many mornings of Sonia calling out, of Sunny *coo-roo*ing like a silly pigeon in reply? What if there had been so many weeks, months, and years of swimming out over and under the waves; so many pages of reading on the veranda; so many mackerel cutlets and friendships with stray dogs; so many plastic bags saved; even so many arguments— coasting up, cresting, coasting down into the fizz and pop? In the end, a person simply needs to sleep. So many times resting then, because even if one's tongue argued with another, one's limbs remembered peace and kept their loyalty. What would it be like if the smell and feel of each other remained comforting, and just as one or the other was on the verge of saying, *Look, we can't go on like this,* a wave of familiar, basking scent might come wafting. They might reach over without thinking to wave away a fly near the other's face. Or yawn in tandem. Sunny might lift Sonia's bag to the overhead rack in a bus, she might automatically hand him a napkin when a tureen lid dripped with steam from the caldinha. They might find they scratched the other in bed feeling an itch themselves, because they wouldn't know whose arm was whose—and each time, such familiarities might dissuade them from parting. Would such habits over time mount into an ocean that nothing could overcome? After a while of looking so much at another's face, wouldn't that face become more familiar than your own face? How could one make a decision never to see it again?

Nothing is going to happen here, Sunny had vowed out into the paddy, the stars, the exchange of sea breezes in Goa, so they would remember in case Sunny and Sonia forgot.

Sunny got up when what sounded like a forest of doves began to call and a pure apricot light broke over land that was the color of agave. There was no sign of the proprietor or any other guest. He packed his satchel with his reporter's notebook, gulped lukewarm cafe de olla from a thermos that had been left on the counter, downed a stale, sweetish roll. He unlocked two padlocks with two large, iron keys he had been given and slid the metal bar they held in place. He walked uphill on the street of El Águila, where he found a single store open among the ruins; the shelves were empty save for a few packets of crisps and bottles of water. A man sitting at the counter looked like a skeleton, with eyes that were not entirely of the living. He had no teeth. In front of him was a heap of round stones formed by volcanic lava. He spoke an antiquated Spanish, lifted a small stone, and asked: "Veinte centavos?" Sunny bought a bottle of water and one stone. He asked for directions. "Take a right, señor, then take a left and another left."

The sun was now hot, but the wind still blew chilly. Sunny walked past the ruins of the tannery, the aqueduct, the rail tracks, and a swath

of hillside cordoned off with signs placed at regular intervals advertising a future luxury development. There were several distinct ranges of
mountains, some sharp, others in gentle lines. Through the dips in the
ranges, falcons angling above, Sunny could glimpse the land falling to
plains and further ranges of the Sierra Gorda, so he knew he was higher
than he may have imagined. The silver route from Querétaro to Ber-
nal, meeting with El Camino Real, had once passed this way; the landscape was webbed with white paths that vanished around bends.

He passed a goat herder who lived in a hut under a flowering pepper
tree, dense with the buzzing of bees. The herder brought out a clutch
of faded photographs in plastic sleeves of life on the mines, miners
descending to underground tunnels before a chapel. He held out his
palm for a few pesos.

Sunny walked on, burrs gathering about the legs of his trousers,
which were also covered in white dust, until, in the bowl of a valley
below, he saw a collection of ruins in a stand of magueys, presided over
by the chapel with a belfry he had seen in the goat herder's photograph
and whose interior—he had learned from Satya's airline magazine—
Ilan was painting.

A plume of ocote smoke waving like a handkerchief from a chimney revealed someone was resident, but when Sunny descended, he
was confronted by an impenetrable fence of organ pipe cacti, high and
locked tightly into each other. The door to an entrance set into this
bold cactus fence was as massive as the door to a castle, weathered timber held together by iron tacks, seldom opened, the bolts rusted. There
was a smaller door set into this massive one, the bronze door knocker
in the edifice modeled like a child's hand holding a little ball. Sunny
took the child's hand into his own, knocked, and waited. He knocked
again and continued to wait.

Still not a sound from the interior, Sunny wrote out a note on a
page torn from his notebook: *Maestro Ilanji, I fell in love with Mother
Swimming. Like walking through the desert to see a painting of the Madonna,
the pilgrimage is sufficient even when the chapel is closed. The painting manifests
in the heart.*

He made a sketch of a pair of eyes at a pair of feet. A gift of the eyes, a veneration, darshan.

He slid the note under the door. "*Mother Swimming!*" Sunny called into the jagged termite-eaten keyhole. "*Mother Swimming, Mother Swimming, Mother Swimming, Mother Swimming,*" he yodeled like a madman in love with a painting. *The blessing and the curse! The hallowed and the damned!* Why is a child born but to create an ocean for his mother to splash in? For him to be curtailed that his mother may swim free? For her to be reflected in the mirror of his eye, in the ocean's eye, the universal mirror? *I was a hidden treasure. I wanted to be known.*

Then Sunny heard steps approaching, the rustle of the paper being lifted. After a moment, the door wheezed open a crack, and the face that Sunny had studied in photograph after photograph sidled out.

"Who are you calling *Mother Swimming*?" Transparent eyes that could not be interrogated looked through Sunny. Nor could Sunny place the accent.

"I am in love with *Mother Swimming*."

"Why?"

"One can't stop looking at it, that's all."

The door wheezed open an inch more. "And where did you see *Mother Swimming*?"

"At the Fortuny Museum in Venice."

Ilan de Toorjen Foss flung the door open. Sunny walked into a tomb-like entryway that opened onto a brilliant courtyard, and they crossed into the rooms Sunny had studied with a magnifying glass. He may have seen them in a magazine, yet their actual magnificence awed him. He saw a thousand gleaming, beaded Huichol skulls, a stone conch from the Mayan ruins in Yucatán, an enormous painted spider. Ilan wore thick cochineal robes of intricate and minute geometric design, as if woven by insects. He had a modern green coffeepot and a packet of orange chewing gum. His eyes were bright and mischievous. He chewed wildly, *chup chup chup*. The incongruity caught Sunny and charmed him. There was something aristocratic here and something Bugs Bunny.

"May I ask for an interview—I write for the Associated Press."

"Aha, that was clever of you to get in with *Mother Swimming*—okay, okay, but if you write only good things! And I won't show you my studio or my paintings, that we agree on?"

"May I catch a glimpse of the chapel you are painting?"

"The chapel least of all. Nobody can see my work in progress." He wagged his finger in front of Sunny's nose. "It's locked and only I keep the key." Was this the person Sonia had loved? Sunny felt small.

Ilan was tall. He sat down to drink his coffee on top of a giant, gold-and-green lacquered fly. Above him, suspended from the ceiling, were skeletons of wood and papier-mâché Judas figures.

"Would you agree that a famous person is less known and more misunderstood than anyone?" Sunny asked, taking out his notebook.

"Yes," said Ilan eagerly. "You are like me—I make note of everything, I photograph everything. The more famous I become, the less I belong to myself, I grow even further from myself, I lose even more of myself. But I long ago transferred my life into my art, which is to say I am whatever I am working on; besides that, I don't exist. I displaced myself long before fame displaced me. Fame simply made me ever more distant from my already-distant self."

Ilan got up to lift a photo from a pile of photographs on a large table. He showed Sunny a woman as lush as a Fellini movie star swinging a child over the waves, laughing wildly. "This is the day Mummy loves me!"

Sunny was moved. He said, "If Mummy loves you every single moment of every hour of every day, it is a far worse fate than if she loves you for only one day of the year."

"Ah, aha, I like you!" said Ilan. "I sense you know something."

Sunny was being drawn in. He understood the visitors, the journalists, their wish to be counted as Ilan's friend. He had an erratic, disruptive energy. Knowing him might change their ordinary lives; maybe they could tell the tale of their deepening friendship with the brilliant, eccentric artist—drop his name here, there, supposedly discreetly everywhere.

Sunny was scanning the walls: the fearsome collection of naguals, of demon and animal masks, of woven-cane creatures and retablos. He was looking for Badal Baba. Was there a glint inside a leopard's mouth? In his native mountains Badal Baba's hermitage would have been a leopard's lair, his consort a snow leopard, his pelt a leopard's fur.

"You're interested in my collection?" Ilan took Sunny to the cabinets of clay creatures from the funerary shafts, the priestly praying mantis, the stingray in flight. He showed Sunny an inescapable maze by Josef Albers painted after his visits to Monte Albán, orange on orange on pink on orange like an Allahabad afternoon when heat built on heat and one dreamt of happiness that was not for other people, but for oneself. He revealed a Tina Modotti photograph of a peasant's rope sandals. A small Frida Kahlo painting of her monkey. Ilan said, "Her genius was her mustache, do you see? It allowed her to escape the constraints of being a woman, to become closer to her beloved Fulang-Chang and to Diego. Her physical and emotional pain transformed her into a mystic."

Diego . . . mirror of the night. . . . Your word travels the entirety of space and reaches my cells which are my stars then goes to yours which are my light. Sunny remembered Kahlo's diary. In her lunatic passion, despite the torments and humiliations, lay her strength. *Her* art became more vital than *his* art.

"Heh?" said Ilan, as if he detected Sunny's thinking. "She was very sly; without him she'd have been nobody, and she knew that. I bought this painting from a frame maker who confessed he had stolen it from the Blue House in the last month of her life."

To tell a stranger such a secret—an illicit purchase—Sunny felt flattered. He forced himself: "Where is that little demon figure that is in your painting of a young woman in the Vermont snow, and also in the portrait of an oil magnate's wife in the Metropolitan Museum?"

"Cloud Baba?" Ilan's unreadable eyes grew more diffuse.

"I recognize it's from India, and I'm from India, so of course I'm interested in how it relates to your work."

"Aha, again I sense you know something. You won't see him. Only occasionally when a gale blows and merges with the wailing of coyotes he may show himself. Or sometimes, if I whistle:

"*O Badal Baba, black diamond light*
"*What won't be linked by day will be linked by night*
"*Gift me darkness, grant me strength*
"*All the jewels of my cavern are for you meant!*

"He may have no face, but he is vain. He longs to be garlanded with jewels and painted; that is how I can tempt him."

Sunny summoned the entire strength of his austere existence. "All your life has been intense art," he said. "This leads me to surmise that while your work is about sad themes, and it could not have been easy, you must be a happy man."

He said: "A contradiction, yes! There is a line by Mandelstam—you know?—about 'bees that once turned honey into sun.' That is what I did. I became a bee. I turned honey into sun. Now they say, 'Oh, you are famous!' Do they even think of the humiliation, the loneliness, the slaving, the struggle? Well, all that unhappiness is what made me happy—explain that! And it is what made me rich—explain that to a banker!"

Sunny had focused on one line and was thinking, *You are happy! You are happy at Sonia's expense! Rich and happy!*

"Have there been casualties to your happiness?"

"What do you mean?"

"Was your happiness at the expense of other people who, unlike you, have not had the privilege of displacing themselves into art?"

Ilan lost his temper promptly—in a flash, and frighteningly. A new person broke through the face he'd worn before. "*Huh?* What's the matter with you? Which people? Do you see any people? *Am I responsible for other people's happiness? Only a weak person would ask such a question.*

"Simplifying idiots like yourself wrote about Picasso, Balthus, and the others—now we all have to suffer. If you are a genius, which Balthus and Picasso were not, by the way—they were phonies—then the jackals gather. Little people like you attack. Why did you come? What did you ever do with your life?"

Sunny's startled silence encouraged Ilan. "This is what happens when you become famous—people come and stare as if you are an ape. They don't think of you as a human; they feel free to insult you to your face: 'What do I care about fame? I told him exactly what I think of him!'" And then encouraged by his own outrage, he ignited to greater fury. He said, "Fuck out of my house this minute. *Fuck out, fuck out, fuck OUT.* Take every trace of you and your curry stink with you."

Sunny said, "I can no longer tolerate spice."

Ilan said, "I know your type. First you lick my ass—'Maestro Ilan*ji*'—because it comes naturally to flatter power. You genuflect with flowery language, then you stab. What I have learned is that the most vicious enemy is the same person as your greatest admirer: The man who writes the wrecking review is the same person who is desperate to be your friend, who becomes obsessed with you, who comes to drink your wine, who asks you for help in his own art project—expecting that you will, so as not to garner further attack. Or that you will admire him so much, it will overcome his canards. Or that you will be too noble to remember his sniveling cringing nastiness. You cannot rid yourself of this obsequious attacker." He sighed. "I understand this psychology. It is of ashamed people."

"Isn't your anger out of proportion?" said Sunny.

"*Aren't you embarrassed you are still sitting here when I told you to fuck out?*" shouted Ilan. "You tricked me and entered my home." He pulled the notebook out of Sunny's hands and tossed it from the window into the cactus jungle. There was quiet, and in the quiet, the sound of a spoon dropping in the kitchen across the courtyard. Who was there?

Then Ilan stared down at his dusty shoes and said, despairing, low and soft, "I hate my shoes." He looked as if he was about to weep. Sunny was startled to find he felt sorry for Ilan. He noticed the shoes beneath the robe. A man with shabby, clumsy shoes is defeated. A defeated man is poor and ashamed. A man with clownish shoes, whose mummy doesn't love him, comes from so far away he will never arrive. "I hate my nose," said Ilan.

"You have a nice nose." Sunny couldn't help himself.

"You shat in my work. You made me feel badly. I have to recover my strength now. I will go for a walk against the wind to cleanse myself." He picked up a hat and said, "You see this hat with a bullet hole through it?"

"Why does it have a bullet hole through it?"

"Because someone sent me a message to be alert always, to tell me I have enemies who want to kill me, and I forgot for one single moment because you tricked me and tempted me with *Mother Swimming*. You knew the secret password. Leave now! I will watch you disappear before I venture out myself."

A brilliant man brought low by an inferior person, a lion attacked by a jackal, Ilan opened the door, and Sunny exited. He walked out and down the long, white road. He climbed the hill, and when he reached the crest, he sat down in the shade of a giant maguey, feeling a hollowness. What Ilan had said of him was true. He had, in fact, come to trick Ilan. What had he done in his life in comparison? He *had* stared at Ilan as if Ilan were a monkey. In addition, it was accurate to say he had combined a diarrhea of flattery with insolence. He continued to sit in the shade of the maguey with marine limbs on that hillside of big, paddled nopales nibbled by goats, untidy palm de vegas, cacti with yellow flowers. Bees had come to these flowers, as they had to the flowers of the pepper tree, and their buzz filled the air. Galleons of clouds grazed the hills, swift white ones above, heavier black cumulus below.

The purpose for which Sunny had come had remained unfulfilled. He was debating how to proceed when he saw the figure of Ilan emerge, not out the front door but as if out of a rabbit hole farther down the valley. He saw him walk swiftly up the opposite swell of mountainside. When the clouds moved on, Ilan had vanished. He must have walked over a crest that Sunny could not discern amidst the pale and dark striations of the terrain.

Sunny crept back down the hill to the place where Ilan had emerged and found there was a crude entrance guarded by briars that must be a tunnel to the mines. He remembered the photograph shown to him by the goat herder of the mine shaft that emerged before the chapel. He lowered himself into the stone entrance and found himself in a low, narrow passageway for the transport of silver. He knew the landscape was treacherous. He knew the ground opened into crevices with open shafts that had collapsed into the underground rivers, and you could, in a second, plunge to your death. Who would know if he *did* plunge to his death? Only the bats, scorpions, and snakes—and the ghosts of the miners who had died. It would be sheer luck to emerge on the side of the living.

Emerge he did, where he surmised he would, and he was rushing toward the chapel when he heard the sound of sobs. He ran on. He turned back. He looked into the window from which he'd heard the sobbing drowning into more sobbing. There was a young woman with her head down on a kitchen table.

"Psst," said Sunny. "What's the matter?"

"*What! You are still here? How did you get in?*" In fear we are all the same. Her face was Sonia's face! But a younger version of Sonia.

"I came to retrieve my notebook."

"He'll kill me if he finds you here."

"Is that why you are crying?"

"It was my job to mind the door and make sure nobody gets in. He screamed at me, 'Why didn't you stop me from opening the door?'"

"But it wasn't your fault that I shouted, '*Mother Swimming.*'"

"I let him allow in a stranger who will be spying and prying, trying to find a way to ruin him. He said, 'The visitor starts yelling "*Mother Swimming,*" so of course I stupidly open the door. Why didn't you prevent me? You live off me, eat off me, you make use of me—I ask you to just please mind the door, and you don't even do this small thing!'"

"Are you the artist's daughter? You have his eyes."

"All his paintings have his eyes."

"But you aren't his painting."

"When I became his painting, I received his eyes."

"Your name?"

"It does not signify."

She was falling apart, the same falling apart as Sonia. She made gestures with her hands as if they were wounded birds. "What if you write this? Promise me you won't write this."

"But what is the matter? Just that you let Ilan open the door?"

"He dreamt an enemy is coming for him. He dreamt a demon leopard would come for him. He dreamt a demon serpent would come for him. He dreamt a demon spider would come for him. He dreamt the demon's mate would come for it, the way the mate of a snake will come searching for its mate if you kill a snake. He dreamt a faceless demon would come searching for its face. He made an offering to his demon god. He said he would paint him as if in a retablo, but he leaves the painting unfinished so the imp will stay until he completes it. Badal Baba may have no face, but he is vain and longs to have the face that completes his destiny."

She clapped her hand over her mouth. "Oh, why did I tell you this? Ilan told me not to speak to anyone, not to say anything. The trouble is that I'm alone all the time, and so when I speak to anyone I have no ability to distinguish what I should say and what I should not say. I say everything. I cannot tell a lie. I don't know how *not* to reply. Ilan can't take me anywhere. *Don't tell him I told you. Don't say anything!* Get your notebook and leave. If he sees you with me, he'll kill me!" Her eyes were on him—yet when he searched for the person behind the pupils, she was not there.

"Leave, if he is scaring you so much."

"I can't leave."

"Why not?"

"I'm too scared."

"Too scared to leave?"

"Yes."

"Too scared to stay?"

She covered her face.

"That demon talisman belongs to my friend Sonia. It's her grandfather's talisman."

"No, Ilan was traveling in the forests of the Himalayas where a monk gave it to him. The monk said it was a deity for those who have no face. Ilan always keeps it by his side when he is painting to inspire him."

"Sonia worried the same way as you."

"I never heard of her. What happened to her?"

Sunny could not say that bad things continued to happen but that it was still better than staying, when even worse would occur. He said, "Can you see the future?"

She said, "I cannot imagine the future." A falcon passed over the sun—the world was for a moment in penumbra—and then the sun blazed forth again.

Sunny said, "That is because the future is already here. There is nothing else up ahead. You know that, don't you?"

She looked out of the window, scanning the hills. "*He will be back soon. Go and find your notebook quickly and leave—or he will kill me.*"

A lock hung on the chapel door. And when Sunny stooped to look through the keyhole, an eye locked onto his, as if there was a living person trapped in there. Where was the key to the key that led to the key to the key to the treasure? He didn't have time to search—it was probably around Ilan's neck.

Months of swimming several times a day against the ocean waves had made Sunny lean and strong. He broke the latch with his stone of volcanic lava and tumbled into eyes, clouds, and jewels. He followed them from the vestry into the interior of the chapel, which was painted across the walls and ceiling with *Mother Swimming*. There she was, coming into view, receding, Mother and her reflections, refractions, splashing in the light and the dark, in the lake, in the ocean, in the heavens. What is religion but the beauty of a woman swimming over the edge of the horizon?

In the alcove to the right, Sunny detected the likeness of a young woman crying into the ocean. Was she weeping tears of sorrow or tears of compassion? Or even a sort of happiness, of the release of lesser saltwater subtracted by the greater?

He turned to the alcove grotto to the left, and here, veering high, blackened by votive smoke, was a dramatic shadow puppet. It was Badal Baba delineated in jewels. And before the painting, facing it, lay the open amulet case of clouds. Wouldn't Badal Baba be in thrall to his reflection? Smaller to the greater?

Sunny, whose father brought him up never to steal, grabbed the gau box, turning it to face his own face, and he started back as if he'd innocently put his head into a sadhu's cave and, instead of seeing one, had encountered a leopard-black, blood-red tantric figure. A dark heart, a crooked pelvis, missing digits, a single leg whittled like a sadhu's staff, maimed and triumphant, ornamented with pearls, rubies, and gold. Sunny put it about his neck. He got to the door. He paused. He turned back around. He chose a thick, soft brush from the hundreds of brushes lined by size. From neatly arranged rows of bottles mixed with different gradations of black—ivory black, violet black, deodar black, graveyard black, bat-cave black—he dipped into the blackest, richest black. He filled the eyes of the crying woman with the black of a teeming Goan night, birthing galaxies and insects, apparitions and figments, terror and also a certain happiness.

The young woman called, "*He's coming, he's in the tunnel—did you find your notebook?*"

"Not yet—"

"*You have to leave anyway, or he will kill me! Leave! Run! Now! You don't have another minute.*"

Sunny collected his notebook and raced across the courtyard and through the door that she held open for him. It occurred to him that she was in grave danger now that he had stolen Badal Baba, her situation far more dire than she imagined. He called back as he ran, "If you come to the posada tonight, I can help you escape—I won't tell anyone."

"Why wouldn't you? You said you're a journalist—wouldn't this be a good story?"

"Because of my friend, the woman who makes the ocean of tears. If I betrayed you, I would be betraying her." His voice got lost in the wind, as did her reply, if she'd made one.

It grew colder the moment the sun dipped. His heart hurting in his ears, his legs, his throat, Sunny rushed, not straying from the white path in the gray dusk. He thought he heard a chapel bell ring at the end of the miners' workday, but there was no bell in the belfry. He thought he heard a train, but there was no train. He smelled nopales cooking, but there was nobody cooking. He heard mules, but there were no mules.

The proprietor with the tragic mustache looked up in the greenish posada light, from a portion of goat stew and *The Big Book of Alcoholics Anonymous*. Outside a skeletal dog gnawed on the skull of a goat. "It's dangerous to wander around here in the dark. You are crazy to do so."

Sunny asked: "Who is the woman who lives with the artist?"

"The artist lives alone."

Sunny shut himself into his room, barred the door with the heavy iron bolt. The bats flew from the curtains. He barred the window. He ignored the scorpions crawling out of the holes in the volcanic stone. He opened the amulet case again. This creature had no face. A god or demon, human or beast—he could not tell. Inspiration or menacing terror—he could not say.

Sunny said: "I am a thief! I stole a stolen treasure. I destroyed a painting. I may have caused that young woman grave harm." He stayed awake—listening to the wind rattling the boarded-up windows and doors of the disused homes of the town and merging with the keening of coyotes—when past midnight, there was a knock. It may have been the wind, but the wind would have knocked louder.

"Whooo?"

There was no answer. He stooped to look through the keyhole. An eye at the keyhole looked back at him. The trembling young woman with wounded birds for hands did not speak when Sunny let her in. She indicated she wanted to hide inside the cupboard in case Ilan came looking for her. Only when she was in the cupboard did she say, "I had better go back."

"You can't."

"I have to. He will be alone, and he cannot be alone. If he is alone, he doesn't exist. He suffers a crisis. I will be taught a lesson."

Sunny sat outside his room, the amulet as freezing as the highland night upon his chest, in case the young woman wished to come out of the cupboard and sleep in the bed, but the young woman stayed inside in case Ilan came searching. Ilan had eyes on the back of his head, Sonia had told Sunny. Because a bad person is a paranoid person who expects retribution, they develop excellent intuition. You then believe that the person is the devil because they *know*.

At dawn Sunny heard what sounded like a forest full of doves and saw the approach of a van full of participants from the San Miguel de Allende Biblioteca tour to raise money for Libros Para Todos. It was on its way to the former haciendas Cinco Señores and Santa Brigida. Even at this early hour, they were rollicking:

"Jacob got his hair cut for thirty-five pesos; a little old lady cut his hair!"

"Laser treatment for age spots, forty-five dollars!"

"Three tacos for a dollar twenty-five!"

They stopped at the posada for coffee. "Doves love the sun," said the proprietor, serving steaming cafe de olla, scattering seed for the birds.

"I thought doves love the shade!"

"Oh no, doves are most contented in the sun."

"Twenty cents for a cup of coffee!"

Sunny's heart welled with affection. They were innocent American tourists, buoyed by their currency, trusting in their luck, safe anywhere in the world—the ambassador would personally take up their case should they encounter any misfortune. Sunny was virtually a citizen of the United States, and they said, sure, they'd give him and his friend a ride back to town, there were extra seats at the back, if they were willing to sit through the tour.

Sunny rushed to the cupboard to tell the young woman she was safe, that she could come out, but when he opened the cupboard, it was empty. He ran outside to where the proprietor sat. "Did you see a woman leave my room?"

"I saw no one."

He went back. It smelled of Sonia's fear.

"Didn't you see her come in last night, a few hours after me?"

"Nobody came in after you. I locked the door with the metal bar and two padlocks before I retired. It's impossible to climb over the walls."

"You look like you just saw a ghost," joked a man from the biblioteca tour. "Where's your lady friend?" Sunny must have suffered a lovers' quarrel. "Jump on," they called, "she'll follow, or else it isn't meant to be."

He jumped on. Babal Baba burned upon his chest like a brand heated by the fire of the highland sun. He couldn't linger—off they went.

"Tamales from the lady at the bus stop outside the Oratorio—one dollar!"

"Jackie says you can get a maid here for nothing!"

....

The One
Who Drowns,
Gets Across

....

....

*T*HE KAKORI AND *THE GALAWATI*. BABITA WAS IRKED BY FEEL-
ing two contradictory ways: joy at having yearned-for recipes in her
hands at long last, gobbling them straightaway with her eyes, and embarrassment because this revealed that Sonia had remembered that
Babita had attempted to steal Khansama, an occasion carefully left
unmentioned during their night under the same roof. "What nonsense
is this?" Mina Foi had said to Babita all that long time ago. "You try to
steal our cook the minute Daddy dies?"

"You are unhinged," Babita had retorted. But Mina Foi hadn't been
unhinged, it was that everyone kept telling her she was, to allow for
their own misdeeds.

Babita indulged in joyous pretend confusion, reading the recipes
aloud to Olinda, balancing the delicate act of being an expert on cook-
ery and a snooty lady who did not cook, while Olinda enjoyed herself
with exaggerated bewilderment at the peculiar customs and cuisines
of the north. When, after the prescribed marination, roasting, slicing,
grinding, and browning, Babita experienced the harmonious thrum of
a kakori upon her tongue, she took another bite. She considered. She
retested. She reconsidered. She perambulated from cavernous gloom
to cavernous gloom. She stood before the figure of Christ, enveloped
by a blur of sweeter spices, of cinnamon, cloves, cardamom. The one
missing ingredient—that one quantity that a woman graciously giving
away a recipe should always jig to preserve the family treasure, that sly
alteration—had not been made. She took another bite. Her heart
wordlessly told her: Sonia's honesty was outrageous. Her honesty was

folly. And honest Sonia was a perfect match for her honest son. Had she welcomed Sonia all that time ago, would Sunny have run away?

It had been unexpectedly simple to have Sonia in the house. What more did one want from life, after all, but to eat dinner with someone, to watch a murder mystery that you'd be too scared to watch alone? One's perspective normalized. When one's perspective was askew, one behaved in a manner that was askew. She remembered the unrequited kiss with the bandicoot trapper. She had placed her lips upon his cheek and her lips had stuck. Stuck, because she had longed through that wrong kiss for a right kiss.

Now Sonia had come up the pathway of temple trees, up the operatic front steps. Shouldn't Babita welcome luck into her life, if luck rang her polished brass doorbell, even if it wasn't the luck she pined for?

Upon a widow-colored hour of dawn, before the sun rose, everything set by then in stone, Babita picked up the phone and said to Sonia, in a practical, no-nonsense voice: "Look, there isn't any point in sitting about by oneself—it leads to maudlin thinking. If you're alone and I'm alone on a Sunday, why don't you come and give me your opinion of Olinda's galawati? The kakori was a success."

Sonia was awake, reading and trying to make sense of what she had written late the night before. A fable about a woman who becomes a black cloud, an ability that is her inheritance from her grandfather, an occult artist who could transform himself into whatever he painted. The fantastical felt right because it was only by fantasy that most people overcame their reality. If she continued to write multiple narratives until the truth of something she wrote became apparent—whatever those narratives may be labeled by others: surrealist, realist, orientalist, occidentalist, fable, legend, nightmare, daydream, myth, satire, kitsch, tragedy, comedy—wouldn't every story become equivalent to every other story? If the center did not hold, maybe it should not hold. Maybe when reality shifted shape, a writer should let it shift. If Sonia scattered her being into an ocean of stories, could they, like waves, bring her to another shore?

Once again, Sonia walked down the red lane overgrown with

weeds, climbed the balcão stairs to the giant shells that flanked the entrance, and rang the polished brass bell. Babita, one half of her mouth twisted up, one half twisted down, opened her door to the woman she had harmed for no reason other than jealousy and ushered Sonia into the dense smell of a royal kitchen of Lucknow. She warmed the kebabs on the lowest heat. "The trick, you see, to how it is textured so smooth, is to use no egg or any kind of binding agent, and then one must always be personally present for the turning of the kebab." Then seeing Sonia's expression, it occurred to her she was explaining Sonia's own family recipe to Sonia, in Sonia's own words. "Not bad for a Goan cook?" was all she ventured when they sat down to eat the kebabs redolent with memories of their fraught past. They conjured the lost world of Allahabad, the gracious exchange of kebabs, cutlets, soups, and puddings being promenaded down scritchy-scratchy back lanes, delivered in Ambassador cars, on plates wrapped in napkins tied in rabbit ears, in tiffin carriers, thermos flasks, festival boxes covered in gold paper. Upon scalloped silver platters, from a household of a lawyer to that of a colonel. *Today I am raising a delicate matter. My granddaughter is feeling lonely in America, and she has entrusted us with the task of finding her a life companion from a family in which we place the highest trust.*

Again so as not to venture into sensitive topics, they watched a film they wouldn't have ventured to watch had they been alone. *The Hound of the Baskervilles* gave them a pleasurable, shivery chill in the mounting pre-monsoon heat, the air too fat to breathe, the fan twirling floral and useless.

At nine P.M., Pasha began to wail.

"Is it his bedtime?" asked Sonia.

"He's upset we scared him with a ghost story before sleep." Babita didn't mention that *The Hound of the Baskervilles* was one of Sunny's favorite books, by a favorite author he always read on the night train to Allahabad, and that he had been reading this book when he had first seen Sonia, which was an alignment of no use to observe, yet an alignment nonetheless. She said, "It's too late to call for a taxi, and I can't rouse Naresh with his bad night vision. Why don't you sleep in the guest room the way you did before?"

*

"IS THERE SOAP?" BABITA'S voice projected overhead.

"There is soap."

"The bandicoots haven't gashed at it?"

"No."

"Watch for tree frogs."

Again Sonia finished bathing in the random plops of water, the frogs ping-ponging about, and again she donned the same caftan she had worn the last time she stayed the night at Casa das Conchas, which was still hanging on the bathroom hook.

"Good night, then," called Babita when she was in her four-poster bed under a canopy crocheted by a nun.

"Good night," Sonia replied from her guest-room bed under a canopy crocheted by a widow.

Better two single ladies in the dark, stewing in the heat and in their dinner spices, under a ceiling fretted for the exchange of coastal breezes. Better two single ladies and a gentleman dog (even one with a jungly habit of drinking from the toilet) in the dark, stewing in the heat and in their dinner spices, under a ceiling fretted for the exchange of coastal breezes.

Only there weren't any breezes. Din of insects, squeak of bats, strangled screech of screech owl, tut of frog, opera of lovelorn cats, bark of stray dog—but where the thief, where the murderer, where the demon and the ghost, where the ghost hound?

"It's very stuffy."

"Goa is always too hot." *Try a hot flash in stupendous heat.*

"It could be the murder mystery?"

"But it was also a lot of fun."

"But afterward one can't stop thinking." Sonia was considering that the murderer in *The Hound of the Baskervilles* was revealed by a painting.

"Sonia?"

"Yes?"

"Let's go back to sleep.

". . . Sonia, I think I was—"

"What?"

"Oh, nothing.

". . . Sonia, I think I was—"

"What?"

Don't say, don't say . . . try a hot flash, air too fat to breathe, and a blood-thirsty mosquito. "Sonia, I was not quite right—"

"About what?"

Don't say, Babita—don't go circumscribing yourself.

"I was sorry to hear of your father's passing." She skidded in the banana-peel dark.

"He was larger than life—life now feels so small."

"We had a silly argument—soup after soup."

"Soup after soup?"

"It blew up into something else. He was a difficult man, as much as I am a difficult woman, but I've always had respect for a man who is particular about his food—and we were of the same generation. That alone counts for something."

"You were born near the time of Partition."

"Nobody else can understand. Our parents had lived their lives in British India. The turmoil of the freedom movement, independence, and Partition was still about us—our parents were not normal. They were masquerading as normal. My father—"

"The Colonel?"

"He got onto the train with his family in Lahore, and when they got off in Delhi, the women of the family were all missing—just as was true of trains going in the other direction." In the exchange of trains, two different stories emerged on either side of the divide. *The emptiness is full, the fullness is empty.*

"That is not a tragedy a family can overcome."

"My father never spoke of it, and he never felt settled or at home—which is perhaps why he never bought a house in Allahabad, like your grandfather. He could not put down roots or feel safe."

"Like we can't feel at home."

"You are right."

They tried to sleep again. *Don't say anything about anything, Babi, nobody will ever know.* Pasha dragged his hind legs to the toilet.

"Sonia?"

"Yes?"

"I quite enjoyed—"

"Pardon?"

"Your article."

"Which article?"

Never praise, Babi, never give your power away. "On kebabs."

"It wasn't disjointed?"

"It's a huge subject; you can't keep a huge subject neat."

"It was as if I had to write a history of India. The kebab story is a Hindu-Muslim romance."

"That's hardly simple.

". . . Sonia, I think I was—"

"What?"

"Nothing. . . . I was not quite right." *Don't apologize, never give up your advantage.*

"*Khansama.*" It burst out.

"Did you say Khansama?"

"I should not have tried to steal Mina Foi's cook!"

"Neither should Mina Foi have forced him to keep cooking at his age, just from greed."

"But right after the funeral!"

"He's in retirement. His son sends him money."

"Son?"

His son? The son? Vini's lover? The thief? The murderer? The pimp? Where did the son get that money to send his father? Gold from a stolen suitcase? From two young girls betrayed?

Cried Babita, piercingly, before she could stifle herself, "*Vini-Puni!*"

"Vini-Puni?"

"Khansama's son, the driver, ran away with my little Vini-Puni after Ravi-Rana's murder and sold them into prostitution."

"No! They are perfectly fine," blurted Sonia, and then remembered she wasn't supposed to tell. "I wasn't supposed to say—"

"You must!"

"Take it as something I muttered in my sleep."

"It may as well be a dream."

"The little one telephoned my mother's friend's nonprofit for a microloan. They are in a different state; they have assumed different names. They had the presence of mind to flee."

In one swoop, Babita felt her spirit unburden. She lay there trying to absorb this news. *If you die, so will I. Ratty, don't die. If you live, I will love you—after all! Dear God, just let him live and I promise I will love him and believe in you.* Was this the first time the fateful divine she did not believe in had done something for her? "Thank you, God," she said out loud in penance, to make sure her luck would hold—when she was stricken by another purgatorial hot flash. She squashed several mosquitoes in her thrashing, which bloodied her sweat-sodden sheets. She threw off her clothes, dipped a small towel into the water on her bedside table, and mopped her face and neck, her back, wrung it out between her breasts.

It was all very well for an atheist to believe in God in retrospect, when her false prayers have been answered. There was still an imbalance in matters between herself and the universe, between herself and herself and the God she did not believe in. What was her residual guilt?

It wasn't Vini-Puni, they were no longer her fault. It wasn't the killings of Ravi-Rana—never her fault. Not her fault the missing cash, egg cups, and gold. Nor kebab Khansama any longer. Nothing to do with her, Bahadur, Umberto, Sara, Vanya . . . She counted all her not-faults like cloudy sheep to lull herself to sleep. But she circled back—

Oh, but keep this petty guilt to yourself, Babita, keep this puny aberration. She had meant to tell Sonia the tale of her innocence, not of her guilt.

But this residual guilt was the stubbornest of all, and without the rest of her guilt to create a blather of indignation enough to make the truth slink away, as the first bird of dawn was beginning to call from within its dreams—

"*Sunny,*" Babita breathed. The whisper carried, magnified, as does a whisper that reveals a crime. Even a deaf person who may not hear a normal tone picks up this rustle. It winged its way to Sonia's pillow.

Sonia woke. "*Sunny?*"

"I drove him away."

"Why?"

"You."

"*Me?*"

"I worried Sunny would love you more."

"He didn't—"

"He would have—"

"He couldn't have—"

"Why not?"

"The ghost hound."

"The same hound?"

"It asserted itself between us."

"Was I the ghost hound?"

"The universe tries everything it can to prevent love. If one thing doesn't work to keep two people apart, then it tries another. Darkness follows darkness, across geographies, across centuries. It has its own life, unspooling."

"By that logic, so light should follow light."

"Darkness is aggressive. Darkness has intent."

"It would be better if we put our brains together."

"Let alone our hearts."

"Why do we try to solve other problems? There is only one that is necessary to solve."

"Loneliness?"

"The other problems would melt away in importance."

And two people at peace with each other, at least for the time being, Babita and Sonia drifted into sleep, and while Babita dreamt not at all, Sonia dreamt once again that she returned to Ilan's estate to retrieve her amulet. She asked herself, *Are you scared?* She was not. She should be. She was not. Someone was sleeping next door with a fretted ceiling overhead. What you lose in privacy, you gain in solace. She knew the way because Ilan had shown her the photograph. She traveled over the dry white hills, and she was swift covering the distance. She went past a herd of goats that began to bleat and huddle. She was a stranger—was that why?

Her nose began to twitch. She swore she could smell a rabbit. She could see into the distance to the circling of falcons. She could hear the drone of wasps in a mine shaft, the squeak of a baby bat covered in pale pink fuzz in the mine glinting with gold and silver. When she arrived at the ruin painted earth-red, she saw Ilan in a haze of hashish. Through this haze burnt a plot. An artist must plot his death so that he may be assigned eternal fame and live forever. How does one plot one's death? He was writing his own obituary. When Ilan saw her he began to scream. He got down on his knees and dragged himself around on the floor: "Who are you? Why are you here? Why are you chasing me?"

She said, "I only came to get what is mine."

"What is yours?"

"My brain and my face, my heart, my liver, my past and my future— you ate them, and you now must give them back. *You give them back!*"

"Who are you? I am scared, I am scared, I am scared!"

"Didn't you say that people would come for you? We are *coming for you!*"

Ilan howled and wept and made a big noise to distract her.

Sonia was not to be distracted. "I want my grandfather's talisman." Sonia crossed the mirror. She wasn't a human shape; she was a shadow slung with lost gemstones. She feared it, but it was herself.

She woke into passionate birdsong, the sun already high, Olinda sweeping the veranda with her twig broom.

"What a noise you were making," called Babita when she heard Sonia getting out of bed.

"I was dreaming of my book again." Could she re-create and re-store Badal Baba in another form? Would Badal Baba deign to manifest himself through her?

The shadow cast by oyster shell shutters made it easier for Babita. After tea and toasted poi, Babita brought out the key from behind the bleeding Christ that led to the key in the liquor cabinet carved with monkeys eating breadfruit, that led in turn to the key in the linen chest on lion paws, that unlocked the almirah that held the balding, royal-purple velvet box. "Forget my nighttime ramblings; when one lives alone one drinks too much and talks out loud. Look—I have been waiting for someone to give these baubles to. I am too old for such ornaments."

Sonia opened the box to shining gemstones. "I can't take them; they are too valuable!"

"Try them on." The stones picked up the morning even in the darkened room and shone amber, garnet, cerulean, moss, pink.

"I think," said Babita, looking critically and turning Sonia this way and that, the way Lala had done so many years ago, "that they have found their home."

....

Would Ilan trace Sunny to *Renta o Venta* and abduct the stolen amulet, albeit one he himself had stolen? Would he send the police after Sunny? Sunny hid the amulet in a plastic Tupperware container in the palapa thatch—which would be all right, he surmised, until the rains came—and stayed very quiet, very still, waiting for the sky to fall.

The sky did not fall—not the next day, nor the next week, nor the week after. Yet Sunny experienced an imbalance. He waited for whatever was askew to come to maturity and reveal itself. But it persisted, the missing component. Whatever could it be? The sky was the usual sky over the slumbering hills. Under the hammock, the shadow was the shadow of the hammock. He looked behind himself; he didn't see anything. He hopped up and down without encumbrance. He swam out without feeling the impetus to dive deep and struggle against the waves, to exchange the heaviness of his guilt for an unbearable lightness of being. The sun's eye looked down, the ocean's eye looked up, the vulture prospected him, the iguana watched him. And then it came to him—there was one gaze that was missing.

Sunny had lost his mother's gaze! He looked in the mirror. He saw his reflection without seeing himself through his mother's eyes. They weren't on his back, not inside his heart. He was terrified she had died, but when he telephoned, Olinda picked up the phone and said, "Mummy has gone to D'Mello's to return the prawn patties; she says no prawns in the prawn patty."

Still, he tiptoed, and he knew he must not pay this lack of her attention too much attention, in case the paying attention to her lack of attention drew *her* attention back. Yet without her attention upon him, a tiny aperture of a passage back to India opened in his mind, his heart. He did not pay this attention, either. He let it mature and grow. He breathed in, and he breathed out. Routine and simplicity, simplicity and routine. He made his bed. He washed his dishes. He mopped his floor with fabulous-smelling Fabuloso. He boiled his water. He rinsed his fruits and vegetables in Microdyn. He washed his clothes in the outdoor sink and hung them on his washing line strung between the cacti, taking care to straighten them so they would dry with as few creases as possible. In the internet center, he read the news of unfolding war. He went to Melaque for the newspapers, his Spanish strong enough now to muddle through. And one day, ironically on the AP wire sent out by his Mexico City colleague whose news reports he had once edited, he read with less surprise than he would have expected a news item reporting that the reclusive artist Ilan de Toorjen Foss had vanished from his Mexican estate. When they searched for him, they found no trace. The police were considering all options. He lived alone and might have met with an accident. The property where he lived was a former mine, and the countryside where he walked each evening was full of unmarked shafts. Maybe someone had shoved him. But who? He might have fallen afoul of businessmen who wished to develop the hills and build condominiums along with a club de golf. He might have crossed purposes with the cartels, or the state government, which were the same thing. He might harbor a secret that nobody wished to come to light. He might have a hidden treasure and someone had killed him to steal it.

The goat herder was the artist's only neighbor. He told the police and the journalists that animal forms of sorcerers regularly roamed at the hour of dusk. The artist was one of them. At night he transformed into a great dog, larger even than a coyote. That is why the artist had chosen to live here, where it was possible to have such a predilection. He said around the time of the artist's vanishing, there had been an extraordinary visitation, one he had never seen before, by a shadow beast. The beast climbed out and vanished into a black cloud. It was a strong omen. What it meant he wouldn't know.

The art critic who took credit for discovering his genius—and who had written the seminal, rapturous article for *Artes de México* on de Toorjen Foss—conjectured that he had fulfilled his own work in a consummate creative act: Not so long ago, he had written his own obituary. The obituary had said precisely this—that he would vanish, and it would not be known whether he'd been murdered or whether he had vanished into the world of his own creation. Nothing had been stolen from his home, which was filled with a valuable collection of art that she herself had cataloged for a future museum—save for one object of indeterminate value: a talisman of a demonic figure, its face a cracked void. The artist believed it kept him safe from harm and gave him creative powers. He had been working on a retablo of thanks to this figure, which remained the only incomplete portion of his great life's work: the painting of a chapel with *Mother Swimming*. Before de Toorjen Foss had vanished, he had painted in the eyes of an eternally weeping woman, counterpoint to *Mother Swimming,* in the shade of blackest black, as if it were the void to the universe. He was surely putting himself up for a challenge. He would no longer be reflected in a woman's eyes.

Sunny took down the amulet from the thatch that night, and Badal Baba sprang triumphantly forth, poised like a scorpion raising its sting. *I brought this about,* he seemed to be saying. In the intimacy of looking at the painting Sunny held in his hand, he had an inkling of Sonia's attachment to this goblin, and of Ilan's covetousness. Badal Baba was Sonia's story to tell. He needed to take Badal Baba home.

But there was another vow, too, that he had made, he recalled—another story that had been placed in his trust, one he had inherited. "Look, I am promising before my son," Babita had said, "your children are the responsibility of this family, so never worry about anything. We will take care of you—understood? If I am not around, my son will fulfill this vow. Vini-Puni are also my daughters. They are his sisters."

Vinita had said: "Sunny Bhaiya, take me to America!" It was because of Vini-Puni he had his American life, his Indian life, and by extension, his Mexican life. His life had expanded, theirs had contracted—contracted to *what*?

Wasn't it a story that made a journalist, not a journalist who made a story? Wouldn't a good journalist be able to efface himself, to have no face? What had been the point of telling his mother that he belonged neither to India nor to the United States, stuck in the in-between place where the news disconcertingly morphed from one thing into another? This was a fortunate place to work from—but while a man might travel the world and chase all of its shifting stories, when something dire happened in the landscape of his childhood, wouldn't that man circle back to fight for what his parents had fought for, his grandparents, if it were in peril again? Sunny thought of his own father, Ratan, who had wished to bequeath his son his innocence. Not his wealth— his innocence. Sunny's face bathed in tears.

*

THREE ROOSTERS THAT HAD escaped the hatchet and flown into the jungle began to crow. They woke a donkey corralled in a jungle field because they were riding on his back ready to feed on the grubs that hatched plentifully in donkey dung. The donkey put his head up and down, making a circus sound. The donkey and the roosters woke Sunny, and on waking, his first thought was: *I will miss this place.*

The mosquitoes that always attacked before dawn began to attack. Sunny went out to where white-bearded and winged cacti were tall as trees in the moonlight. He walked to the cemetery by the ocean, and in front of it, he did his yoga sun salutations and prayed without religion but a concentration of intent and desire. He asked the demon god to keep the ocean and moon safe. He asked the ocean and moon to keep the demon amulet safe, so the demon amulet could keep him safe, so he could keep the amulet safe. He asked that the quiet of this place as it was at this moment always stay with him. The full moon touched the ocean, the sun came over the hill, the moon instantly faded. Sunny swam far out and watched the sun extend over the dry hills opposite the village that was still mostly asleep. He asked the demon god to keep the sun safe and the sun to bless his journey. He knew the light would travel slowly across the water and the pelicans sleeping in the curve of the bay would be the last creatures to wake when the sun blazed upon them, for they fished as late as they could and slept as late as they could in the green shadow of the jungle hills upon the water. When the sun touched the tree, the iguana would crawl up and sit on one of two branches. The hummingbird would visit at midday.

He had measured and left exactly enough coffee for the last morning. The coffee was Coatepec coffee from Veracruz; it scented the single room he lived in. He made it weak and milky to suit his stomach. He scrambled the last two eggs and ate them with black beans and a strip—oily and fat—of Oaxaca cheese and sweet-smelling tortillas. A Mexican breakfast can set you up for the life beyond this one. His little case was already packed. He took nothing but his notebooks.

Later that day, Ulises went to the door of the shack in the cactus garden, where El Hindu lived, and called, "Hola, Sunny!" There was no answer.

When he went in, it was neat with everything in place, the bicycle against the wall. He went down the path and surveyed the ocean, wondered if El Hindu had been eaten by a crocodile when he swam far out where nobody else ventured.

"Did you see El Hindu?" he asked. But the ocean, so ancient and so grand, did not reply. It harbored the secrets of millennia, and a speck of one more secret, or one less secret, was beside its concern.

CHAPTER

75

....

THE LUXURIOUSNESS OF THE AIRPORT BOUTIQUES SELLING
supple leathers, panama hats, and mezcal decanted into flasks like rare
elixirs; the restaurants and bars with screens broadcasting sports games;
and the bright lights and whooshing automatic taps in the bathrooms—
made Sunny understand how roughly he had been living. He looked at
himself in the mirror. He was a brown man who might have been of
several nationalities, or in-between nationalities, or no nationality. An
anonymous brown man of no importance. He looked like a stick insect, as Satya had observed, but he also had the composure of a stick
insect—nothing would rush him or rattle him.

"Why did you overstay your visa, señor?" he was asked by a stern
immigration official whose mouth emanated a potent fanged chili
salsa.

"Amor," Sunny answered with dignity.

The immigration official asked him to repeat himself, and then he
began to chuckle. "Amor? Better luck next time. I hear Indian women
are just as beautiful as Mexican women." He sent Sunny to another
window to pay a nominal fine, and Sunny was now properly on his
way. He was not stopped in Frankfurt, nor in Dubai, where he boarded
along with a planeload of laborers returning home—anonymous brown
men of no importance, who kept entire nations afloat, the countries
they labored in and their homelands. He stepped out into the crowd
gathered outside Dabolim airport in Goa, took a bus traveling south,
and felt the exhilaration and fear of hundreds of thousands of stories
crossing paths with his, the fear and relief of being only one of a multitude of stories amidst which he was about to make his own singular

one. He got off at a countryside crossroad and became lost for a long while in a maze of country paths. As he walked, carrying his little case, he heard a conversation of love in the trees at the edge of someone's garden that startled him, a young woman's voice, honey-sweet, deep, and laughing. She spoke in Konkani but said one line in English: "You cannot say 'no' to me. I already know it."

It was quite dark by the time he made his way down the rutted path and arrived at the address he had for Casa das Conchas. He saw the lights of the home glimmering in the palms and bananas. He sniffed and sniffed again, raising his head, snuffling like a stray dog. If his nose did not deceive him, he smelled a distinctive aroma— Surely not?

He stood there for a while. The shutters made of oyster shells were open. He saw shadows behind the white curtains. Two shadows. He made a call like an owl's *chirrur-chirrur.*

Babita said to Sonia, "Is that an owl? The owls here make a different call."

And Sonia knew. When she threw open the two wings of the long, prayerful doors, Sonia and Sunny were too scrawny and crooked to fit into each other's arms. They saw, with a pang, that they were not quite so beautiful or quite so young. Sunny was angular, his face thinner— but his eyebrows still dove about quizzically. Sonia, too, was gaunt, her shoulders hunched as if they had curved to protect her heart, and her eyes were wary. She was dressed in a caftan too big for her form, and dangling from her ears were cloudy gem earrings of the kind unearthed from a dusty bank locker, destined once upon a time for a daughter, or else a daughter-in-law.

Sonia said, "But are you real, is this really you?" She rummaged about his embrace and searched his gaze.

"I was beginning to wonder myself," he said.

"If I am real, or if you are real?"

"Both."

She saw about his neck a battered, tarnished case carved with clouds swirling into dragons—an amulet that must have escaped from supernatural and real disasters through the high Himalayan passes. She reached for it.

*

IF YOU DON'T HAVE love, you don't properly exist. If you don't properly exist, you don't have love. One morning, after the rains had passed, Sunny woke into a memory of being half asleep just the way he was now, of waking into the bloom of affection greater than himself. It was greater because it no longer existed inside himself and Sonia—they were encased within it, the countryside was colored by it, the news was shaded by it, maybe one day even their deaths would be small matters within it. He turned to tell Sonia this, but she was not by his side, nor was she at her desk. He walked down the path that shuffled to the ocean and searched for her amidst the waves. The waves subtracted his thinking. He launched himself into the water and swam straight out to her in the manner of a seabird joining another seabird.

ACKNOWLEDGMENTS

....

*M*Y GRATITUDE

To my patient and astute editors, Robin Desser and David Ebershoff. To Anita Desai, Simon Prosser, Manasi Subramanium, and Luke Epplin.

To the Santa Maddalena Foundation, Yaddo, Hedgebrook, the Bellagio Center, and the Marie Residency Program. Also, to the Guggenheim Foundation and the American Academy in Berlin.

To everyone at the Wylie Agency, especially Andrew Wylie and James Pullen.

And to maestro Francesco Clemente for the precious gift of Badal Baba.